# BRIDE OF BRUTAL HEARTS

A BLOODBORNE COURT NOVEL

USA TODAY BESTSELLING AUTHOR
KATE STEVENS

3AM PRESS

Title: Bride of Brutal Hearts | Kate Stevens

Description: First edition | 3AM Press

Identifiers: 978-1-990551-12-3 (e-book) | 978-1-990551-13-0 (paperback) | 978-1-990551-14-7 (hardcover)

Subjects: BISAC FICTION / Romance / Fantasy

Cover art and jacket design by Silvermist Cover Designs

Map of the Azarasian Impire by Melissa Nash

Character portraits by @madirune

Red Queen Revelry illustration by @mangomangoj

To the readers who always wanted the "or" in love triangles to be an "and."

Stefan *and* Damon.

Angel *and* Spike.

Bill *and* Eric.

Why have one gorgeous, homicidal vampire boyfriend when you can have two?

# CONTENT NOTE

*Bride of Brutal Hearts* contains explicit content, graphic violence, and themes some may find disturbing. You can find a detailed content list on my website at www.katestevensbooks.com or through the QR code below.

TROST
Thaddeian Ocean
Mabon Farm
Ignaius Strait
Montaurère
Alvareu Republic
Surrosa Isles
Tenebra de Mar
Azarasian Sea
N
W
E
S

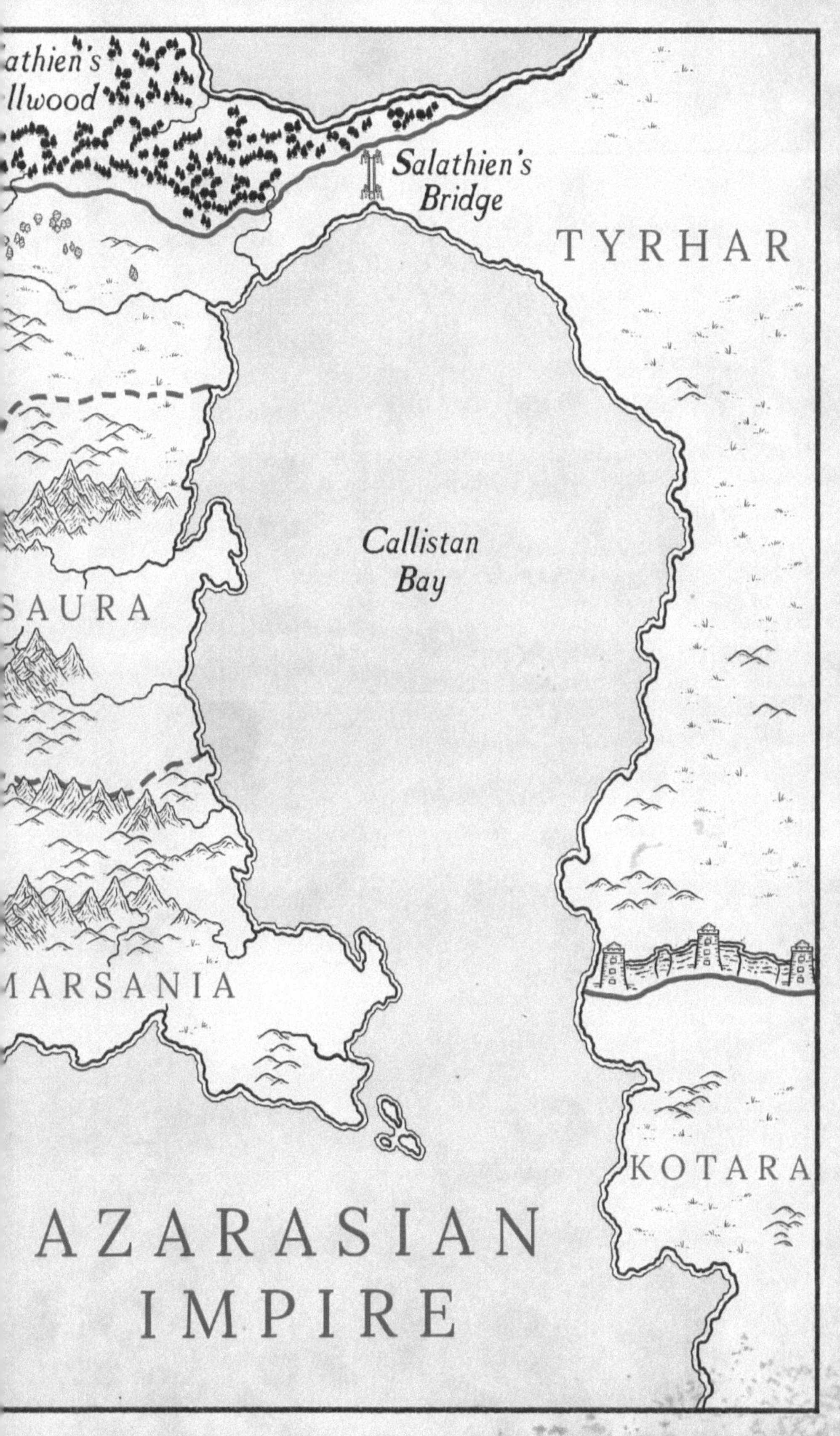
athien's
llwood
Salathien's
Bridge
TYRHAR
Callistan
Bay
SAURA
MARSANIA
KOTARA
AZARASIAN
IMPIRE

# DEAR READER

I'd say welcome to the Azarasian Impire, but humans find this place anything but welcoming.

I do, however, hope *you* find this book welcoming. Nessa isn't one of the sword-wielding badass heroines we all love in our romantasy books. Have you tried picking one of those things up? They're heavy! Nessa lifts books, not weapons—like me and you, I assume. Why should young, beautiful, battle-trained princesses get to go on all the adventures? Why can't a quiet, brave bookworm nearing thirty meet two tall, dark, and dangerous vampires and not die instantly?

But no matter how "welcoming" I wish the book to be, *Bride of Brutal Hearts* is still a **dark** fantasy villain romance. The main relationship occurs between two morally black vampire kings and their wallflower bride. They live in a world where humans are livestock, used for their blood and bodies.

On top of all that, Nessa also has a boatload of issues: anxiety, chronic illness, unhealthy body standards, and trauma from childhood abuse, oppressive religion and purity culture. She'll *slowly* regain hope and learn self-compassion in the most depraved of places.

If any of this sounds upsetting, this might not be the series for you. If you're not sure, you can find a detailed content list on my website at www.katestevensbooks.com. I know, opening up a webpage is annoying. Blame the bots. There's a QR code on the Content Note page that will take you right there. What I can say is: ***Bride of Brutal Hearts* contains explicit content, graphic violence, and themes some may find disturbing**.

**She's their *captive* bride. There's *two* kings. This book is *spicy*. You do the math.**

Two more points before you go (nooo, don't turn the page): 1) there's a glossary at the end for all my worldbuilding nerds, and 2) if you like the book, don't forget to check out the steamy bonus content in my newsletter (click the link *after* you've finished, unless you're a chaos gremlin and like spoilers).

Happy reading!

XOXO,
Kate
(circa May 2025)

P.S. If you don't like LGBTQIA+ relationships, my books aren't for you.

P.P.S. The word "fuck" appears 500+ times, so ditto if you don't like swearing.

P.P.P.S. This is the start of a series, so while some storylines will conclude, others will remain open-ended until the final book. I promise there will be a HEA for the three main characters! We just have to wade through a lil' bit of trauma, death, and groveling first.

P.P.P.P.S. (I know, I'm sorry) There will NOT be a pregnancy, despite all the talk of infertility, babies, and breeding.

Okay, I'm actually done now. You can turn the page...

# 1

*"I HATE YOU."*

A bell jingled as the shop door opened, but I ignored it to turn the tattered page of my book, even though I knew the next sentence by heart. I knew every paragraph in this book. Neither that nor the potential customer was a good enough reason to hunt down a ribbon.

In three months, none of this would matter anyway.

*"Hate me all you want, Karra. It doesn't make you any less mine." Azaras released my chin, trailing his hands down my throat past my collarbones—*

"Nessa!"

I yelped and dropped the book. My tabby cat, Beans, hissed as the leather-bound hardcover nearly smacked into her. In a flash of brown-black stripes, she disappeared between the shelves. The book skittered across worn wood and bumped against the cerulean skirts of a petite woman with plaited red hair. Her hand rested over the curve of her rounded belly.

I stared. My brain reluctantly pulled itself out of *The Soulborne Queen* and took in my pregnant sister.

Aislin raised her eyebrows at me expectantly.

It took me a second, but I figured it out.

"Shit." I pushed from the chair and nearly tripped over the blanket I'd thrown over my legs for warmth. "What time is it?"

"Time to go." Aislin tried her best to appear stern with me, but a grin cracked her heart-shaped face. "When you didn't show up for breakfast, I knew I'd find you lost in a book. Thank the godstars I convinced Donal to come check on you."

"I would've remembered."

"The harvest starts in ten minutes."

"Well... yes." My hands went straight to my head. My hair was in a simple braid instead of a neat plait, but I didn't have time to change it. "I might have been late."

I lowered my hands. It would do. Patriarch Meallán might be aghast, but he already kissed the star on his pendant every time we crossed paths. I couldn't compete with Aislin anyway, not in piety and certainly not in beauty. Being four months pregnant had somehow only enhanced her glow.

"We're *definitely* going to be late if we don't leave now."

I grabbed my shawl off the peg by the door leading upstairs to my tiny loft. "Yes, ma'am."

On the counter, a days-old loaf of half-eaten bread and a block of nearly molding cheese lay wrapped in an old cloth. It would have to last until my next stipend in two days. Some weeks, I had enough. Others, I stretched what little I had, trading meats and cheeses for porridge and stale crusts. I only ever had enough to feel full. Not that it made a difference. My body clung to every ounce, a cruel joke played by flesh that reveled in betrayal.

I tucked the bundled food into one deep pocket of my shawl, my book into the other. The coarse wool scratched at my neck as I pulled it over my shoulders. My hand drifted down the fabric, fingers snagging on a rip near the hem. My throat tightened. I prodded the tear's frayed edges. Another hole. Another patch to sew. As if the thing wasn't already more stitches than cloth.

Aislin looked away, her thumb rubbing the taffeta cloak that brushed her shoulders like a cloud. My stepmother had always stitched a jewel into each of her children's cloaks, as all the richer Maboni did with harvest clothes. Since marrying into the Milligan merchant family, my sister probably carried a year's earnings in her linings alone.

Mine carried old cheese.

Before pushing into the outside air, I twisted and cooed into the shop, toward a pair of slitted, yellow eyes peeking between a shelf. "Bye-bye, Beanie."

"Goodbye, Beans," Aislin called, waving at my cat. The glow of her eyes disappeared. My sister snorted. "She's never forgiven me for leaving."

*I've never forgiven you for leaving.* But I forced a laugh and linked arms with my sister as I stepped through the doorway.

Sunlight flared into my eyes. I blinked and squinted. Red-bricked row houses with shops on the ground floor and lofts above twisted to my left and right, a maze of streets in the town's center. Everything had a slight white tinge to it as my vision adjusted. Godstars, it was bright today. I hadn't noticed from inside our—no, *my*—shop. A narrow sliver served as the only window, but I still hadn't bothered lighting the hearth or the lamps this morning. There was no reason to waste wood or oil on a day no one shopped.

It helped that I had grown used to the chilling gloom years ago. My stepmother used to warn me I'd be as blind as my father if I spent too much time reading in dim rooms, but she'd stopped chastising me the day I moved out of her house. Just like she stopped commenting on my weight, my quiet personality, or my nonexistent marriage prospects.

We didn't really speak much at all anymore, truth be told.

"We're going to be late, Aislin," Donal said the instant we stepped outside. My sister's husband returned his pocket watch into the blue of his waistcoat, his handsome face twisted into the usual grimace he wore in my presence. I bet the man had noted the time to the second when my sister ventured inside *Books & Bows* to find me.

"How are you, Donal?" I asked, trying to smile pleasantly at him.

*Trying* being the operative word.

Donal's family was wealthier than most, but he walked around with the pride of a prince. I had disliked him instantly and grown to hate him more during his short courtship with my sister.

When they were newly engaged, Aislin had invited him to see her latest creation. The elaborate wedding gown had a gossamer chiffon train, just as the mayor's daughter requested. His only reply was that she'd wear something far nicer at their own wedding.

Aislin hadn't sewed or embroidered anything since then.

She didn't need the income, but the sister I remembered always had a needle in hand. It was why I had turned the bookshop into a hybrid dressmaking boutique for her fifteenth birthday. The joy in her smile at the realization was seared into my mind.

I missed *that* sister sometimes.

"Not well, Nessa." Donal stepped closer and wrapped his arm around my sister, tugging her from my grasp. Aislin went with her eyes downcast. "We risk joining the harvest if we're late."

I stared down my nose at my brother-in-law, but tried my damnedest not to make it a glare. He already hated that I was two inches taller than him.

I failed miserably.

With a sharp look, Donal set a brisk pace toward town hall, practically pulling my sister along with him. "Unlike you, some of us care about the purity of our bodies and our souls."

I flinched. I couldn't help it. I hadn't looked directly at my shop's front window, but with Donal's words, my gaze drifted back. While I had inherited the shop from my mother's aunt, my father managed the property as I had no husband. He had placed the 'For Sale' sign in the window a week ago without word or warning.

I had closed up early that day and lost myself in a book. Anything to push the dread from my mind of the path I'd chosen.

Not that anyone *chose* to become an Azarasian blood thrall.

But I hadn't tried to avoid it.

Even if I had, I wouldn't have succeeded.

As if summoned by the thought, a spike of agony flared through my core. I had grown used to the dull throb of my ailing body over the last decade, but stress always made it worse. Sweat beaded on my brow instantly, my skin going clammy in response. I clenched my fist, but kept pace at my sister's side as we weaved through the shop-lined streets to town hall.

If I ignored the pain, I could *almost* forget it was there.

"How are you feeling?" I asked my sister, my voice perfectly level.

"Well enough. My feet and my back ache, but every time she kicks, it makes it all worth it." Aislin rubbed a hand over her belly, a soft joy in her eyes. "I can't wait to meet her."

"I'm sure she'll be perfect." I squeezed her hand. I'd never meet my nephew or niece. Aislin wouldn't deliver for at least four months and I turned thirty before the next harvest in three.

"We don't have time to chat," Donal snapped.

"Even if we arrive on time, Donal, we could still end up in the harvest," I said. "Your cousin was never late."

Donal shot me a glare with his beady eyes. "Don't talk about my cousin."

I repressed a scoff. Since his cousin was selected for the harvest last year, Donal acted like he was the only one who had ever lost a family member. Every human in Mabon was haunted by a loved one who was neither dead nor alive, their fate forever unknown. According to rumors, some of the harvested survived decades, but a vast majority did not.

Half didn't survive the first week.

I shuddered. It was easier not to think of it. I'd spent too many nights wondering if my mother lived. Two decades after she was harvested and sometimes I still found myself asking the question.

Thankfully, the stout brick building that was Corraidin Town Hall came into view at the next intersection. I did *not* want to continue this conversation. I counted down the seconds until I could return to my shop. There wouldn't be any customers even after the harvest. Everyone would either be at home celebrating or at church mourning. It was one of the few afternoons I allowed myself to curl up in my chair and dive into a good book without guilt.

I had read *The Soulborne Queen* countless times before, but I would devour it again today. Once I became a thrall, I doubted I would read another book again.

The town hall's clock tower struck twelve.

I stiffened. Each strike of the clock kicked my heartbeat up a notch. A cold sweat drenched my neck. My lower belly flared in pain. I'd attended dozens of harvests, one a quarter since long before I could remember, but I'd never overcome the fear. No one in their right mind could.

"Come on, Nessa," Aislin said, grabbing my hand and dragging me into the crowd before the stairs leading to town hall's front square.

Donal strutted through the space like he owned it, leaving Aislin and me to scurry behind in his wake. I peered over the heads around me—the only benefit to being taller than most human men. I didn't know where Donal was heading, but I searched for the red of my stepmother's hair. She was likely near the middle. Any closer to the back and we'd be jostled by runners. Any closer to the front and we'd have too good a view into the harvested's terrified expressions.

But when I spotted the flash of her elaborate red plaits, it was near the front.

Of course. A too good view into the harvested's terrified expressions was exactly what my stepmother wanted. She wouldn't look away from confirmation that her precious godstars loved her more than our neighbors. If They didn't, surely she or a loved one would have had their name called by now.

Patriarch Meallán always picked a spot close to the front for the same reason.

Sure enough, the next family we wove around revealed the patriarch. The yellow thread in his white satin robes was a poor imitation of gold in the sunlight. It was much more convincing when the sky was its normal dreary shade. His hair had thinned from the last time I saw him, his beard more white than brown, but he wore both neat and trimmed. He spoke lowly with his eldest son while his wife listlessly bounced a toddler on her hip. She was heavily pregnant, dark circles under her lowered eyes.

Eileen. Or was it Eireen? I never remembered.

I never *wanted* to remember.

Familiar nausea twisted my belly at the sight of them. I couldn't even blame it on my illness. Patriarch Meallán's first wife of thirty-five years was selected for a harvest a couple of months before I turned nineteen. By then, my fertility results had long been public.

My stepmother framed it as if the patriarch would be doing the godstars' good work by marrying me. He had already met the birth quota six times over and had only recently lost his wife, after all. *It's his godly duty to save your soul, Nessa,* she'd claimed. *The godstars will bless Their loyal servant's union like They did mine with your father. If you pray, perhaps They'll grant you a fourth or fifth child with the Patriarch by your thirtieth birthday. Wouldn't that be wonderful?*

To this day, whenever he looked at me, I heard an echo of her words and had to resist hurling.

If I hadn't adamantly refused the match, would that be me at his side instead of Eileen? Would my eyes be that dull and lifeless? Would I be nothing but a vessel for the patriarch's children, the quota fulfilled but my fate just as miserable?

"Oh, Aislin, thank the godstars you arrived on time."

Spine stiffening, I stopped when Donal and Aislin did, turning away from the patriarch and his wife.

My stepmother rushed forward and pulled her daughter into her arms. Deidre Halloran never went outside without looking her best, and the harvest was no exception.

If my sister and Donal were one matching set, then my stepmother, my father, and their four younger children were the other. With her slight frame and bright eyes, Deidre looked like a doll in her yellow skirts. The matching doublets my father and teenage brother, Orrin, wore were a hideous mustard color that didn't complement the reddish-brown hair the three of us shared. Saraid, Finola, and Urrick were in a brighter shade like their mother, though Urrick's tunic was already mud-speckled.

I was the obvious outsider. In my patched shawl, deep green kirtle bodice, and off-white skirts, I looked more like their maid than they did my family. It didn't feel right to call them *my* family, but there was no other word for them. They were mine and they weren't. My stepmother hadn't tried to hide the fact since I chose my doomed path and moved into the bookshop's poorly insulated loft.

I quickly kicked the thought back into the crevices of my mind before it could settle and ruin this already-terrible day.

"*Books & Bows* isn't that far from town hall, Mother," Aislin said.

"You know that doesn't matter to the Azarasians." My stepmother eyed me disdainfully. I loomed over her, wider in every way, from my shoulders and breasts to my hips and thighs. I was never more aware of my size than when I stood beside Deidre. "How selfish of you to risk your sister's life, Nessa. Is that truly what you want your last act to be?"

Aislin flinched. "She's not dying, Mother."

"She might as well be," my stepmother said. "Thralls will never see the godstars' light, as marred as they are."

"Mother."

"It's alright, Aislin," I said. "Deidre speaks the truth."

My stepmother flinched at my use of her first name, but she didn't reprimand me. She likely counted down the days until she never had to see me again.

I was doing the same.

"I might meet my end on an Azarasian's fangs in three months. I might live for decades, trapped within their castle's walls. Either way, I'll be *thoroughly* defiled." A decade of anger rose in me, but I didn't bother holding it back. Not anymore. "But there's one benefit to dying a blood whore, stepmother, and it's that I won't have to spend my afterlife with you."

Deidre clasped at the chain around her neck, the rising star representing her gods in polished brass. "You ungrateful—"

"Citizens of Corraidin," a female voice rang out across the square. Each word was clear and resonant, effortlessly silencing the crowd.

I smirked. Maybe I did have a pinch of luck. My stepmother frowned, but she swallowed her comments. Talking while Lady Delphine or Lord Raul addressed the crowd was another great way to find yourself in a wagon to the Azarasian Impire.

The magistrates stood at the top of the steps leading to the town hall. Lady Delphine's toned skin peeked out between flowing layers of silk, her gown the maroon of the Court of Dawn. Her dark hair cascaded unbound down her back. The heavy gold jewelry around her neck mirrored the color of her eyes. Her soulbound, Lord Raul, stood beside her, representing the Court of Dusk in a deep navy vest. His ebony skin and hair made the molten silver of his gaze shine even brighter.

We rarely saw the Azarasians, but when we did, they always seemed *more* than us, their otherworldly beauty and glowing eyes remnants of the godstars their demon ancestors had once been.

"It's with great pleasure that we gather here for the second harvest of the year 10,533 after the Fall," Lady Delphine continued, her sweet voice laced with an edge that sent shivers through the crowd. "But let us not forget—the harvest is a transaction, not a celebration. We provide for you, and in return, you provide for us. It's a simple arrangement, one that has stood for centuries."

"If Mayor Kavanagh calls your name, you're to report directly to the stables," Lord Raul said. "We do *not* tolerate disobedience. If you think to hide, your entire family will be harvested as thralls, as will any who attempt to interfere. There is no escaping your duty."

"And there is no escaping us." Lady Delphine smiled sharply before snapping her fingers. "Mayor Kavanagh, if you will."

From behind Corraidin's true leaders, Mayor Kavanagh jumped forward. His overly embroidered doublet looked tacky beside the magistrates' opulent wealth. He dropped the town's spelled ledger into the carved divot of the balustrade with a heavy thunk. The vampires lurked behind him as he took his place at the forefront of the crowd, forcing a tight smile to his lips.

"We thank our generous lords and masters for allowing us to live on their lands in freedom, bliss, and harmony." A black rune twisted on his neck, the same one the magistrates wore to project their voice. *Amplify*, some part of my brain whispered. "In return, per the accords signed three hundred and fifty years after the surrender of King Turlough the Last, we tithe a portion of all we own and have to the Azarasian Impire, the Imperium, and their Courts of Dusk and Dawn..."

I stopped listening. Every harvest, the magistrates and the mayor had the same script. If I ever suffered a head injury, I bet that would be the one thing I retained. Blah blah, praise to our benevolent overlords, blah blah, they allowed us mere humans to live in relative freedom and we owed them everything, blah blah.

The entire thing was a work of fiction.

The Impire's brutal rulers, the Imperium, had given King Turlough two choices: sign the accords or die. They had already killed half his family and claimed his wife as their blood thrall. It wasn't really a choice, not for a human king. It just made for a good story.

Not that Turlough's short-lived kingdom was even a footnote in the books the Azarasians approved and provided. To the vampires, we had never really ceased being Mabon *Farm*. If not for their centuries-long war on the mainland, Turlough's rule never would have happened. A human governing any nation thousands of years after the First Godsfall was nothing more than a temporary miracle.

After a minute, I concentrated on the speech, just in time for the only variation in this entire terrible event. The mayor finished his spiel and cleared his throat.

Shit. My stomach rolled. That wasn't a good sign.

"This harvest, our generous lords and masters require twenty new thralls from Corraidin."

Gasps and light grumbles echoed through the crowd. Most harvests, the vampires took around ten Maboni per town. In all the harvests I'd attended, they had never wanted over thirteen. I shuddered to think why they needed more this time around.

Behind the mayor, Lord Raul laid a hand on the hilt of his sword. Everyone fell silent instantly. The magistrates had once thrown a woman into the transport wagon for coughing too loud. They wouldn't think twice at the whiff of dissent.

"Nineteen of those new thralls will be selected by the ledger at random, but the twentieth was selected by the law," the mayor continued. "Fergus Sullivan, for failing the birth quota."

I stiffened in the suddenly tense silence. The crowds shuffled as a dark-haired man crossed the square with a lowered head. Fergus celebrated his birthday a mere two months before mine. We had attended school together, though I had rarely seen him since. Last I remembered, he had married around the same time I left home.

The godstars clearly hadn't favored his union.

A bitter laugh nearly bubbled out of me. Fergus's fertility score had been low, though not as low as mine. No one's was as low as mine. It was deluded of Deidre to think the patriarch could've sired a child on me, much less the three the quota demanded by our thirtieth birthdays. I'd just be a body to warm his bed.

After Fergus disappeared down the path toward the stables, the mayor pulled a thin blade from his belt. Holding his hand above the ledger, he sliced across his fingertip. Blood welled from his pale skin. It dropped to the ledger's case and sunk into the groves of the runespell carved on the cover. Shadows flared as the magic activated, absorbing his blood.

He quickly wrapped his finger and then cracked open the book. I had never seen the ledger up close, but I imagined the names appearing one by one in neat, red script.

Aislin and I gripped each other's hands, as we had always done since my first harvest at sixteen.

"Bridie Gallagher."

Somewhere behind me, a woman cried out.

The mayor called another name, then another. With each one, I flinched. Both with relief and pity, as some poor soul shouted or screamed or cried or dropped into a horrible silence.

I'd happily never listen to another harvest again. And after the next one, I wouldn't have to. Pain twisted harder through my core. I didn't regret my choice, but the closer I got to that deadline, my looming thirtieth birthday, the more my body thrashed and rebelled.

"Una Cavey."

My jaw dropped. Through the crowd, a blond-haired woman stared blankly at the mayor. Had it only been a week ago that Una had passed me in the streets and sneered at me for choosing damnation? I couldn't remember. That might have been the time before. My former childhood friend hadn't said a nice word to me since my fertility results were announced.

Unlike me, Una had done everything right. Married at eighteen. Three children by thirty. She had fulfilled her quota to avoid the life I walked toward, only to end up fated for it anyway.

"Oh, not Una," my stepmother said, her hand pressed to her star pendant. "I always said the godstars wouldn't look kindly on the arrogant pride she had in her beauty. I always said that, didn't I, Padraic?"

"Of course, Dee," my father said absently, agreeing by default with my stepmother as he was oft to do as of late.

"Mama?" Two little girls tugged at Una's skirts. Her husband held their toddler, his lips moving in soft words as tears streamed down his wife's face. Her children were all younger than I was when my mother was harvested. Would her eldest even remember her?

"Aislin Milligan."

Everything within me went cold.

My sister's hand clenched in mine until pain shot through my arm, a faint mirror to the stab jolting through my core.

No.

Not this.

Not my sister.

My little sister.

My *pregnant* sister.

But there were no exceptions to the harvests. The vampires didn't care if Aislin was pregnant. To our immortal overlords, a pregnant human was a bargain. If she survived the harvest and the birth, her child would grow up as a thrall, too.

For a moment, no one moved, all of us frozen in shock. Then my stepmother wailed, a pitiful, dying noise. She shoved my father and brother-in-law out of the way to pull Aislin's stiff body into her arms. My sister released my hand.

"No, he must be wrong. The godstars wouldn't let them choose you. Not *my* daughter."

"The godstars must have a reason, Mother," Aislin said automatically, patting her mother's back. "I'll accept the path They have chosen for me."

"You will not." Deidre spun, her green gaze fixing on my father. "Fix this, Padraic."

He flinched. My father had stood by and done nothing when my mother was selected. Would he do the same for his favorite daughter?

His eyes dropped.

The bastard.

Donal wouldn't be any help either. He was already backing away.

Tendrils of dread clawed through my stomach. There was really only one choice, wasn't there? One I could live with, that was.

Though Aislin and I rarely talked about it, she knew how hard it was for me without my mother. Her own mother conspired to make it worse, treating me like a stranger who lived in her house and ate her food. I wouldn't wish my childhood on my worst enemy.

And if Aislin was harvested today, the fate awaiting my nephew or niece would be a thousand times worse.

I steeled my spine. The final three names had been called, but none of them mattered to me. I wasn't selected. Only Aislin. It was a simple fix.

I opened my mouth but nothing came out. I'd spent most of my life with my head in a book. Talking wasn't my strongest skill. Neither was courage. Already, people drifted from the square. I wanted nothing more than to run through them back to my shop and hide within crinkled pages.

But I'd forever be haunted if I didn't say the words.

"I'll go."

As soon as the sentence escaped my mouth, I wanted to swallow it back. Stars, I was going to puke. I didn't want to die. I didn't want to be a thrall. But life had never cared what I wanted. Why start now?

Every member of my family went still again. But it was far shorter than a pause this time. Deidre's shoulder slumped instantly in relief. Donal, my father, and Orrin stared at me with wide eyes like I had said something insane.

I didn't disagree.

After a second, my sister rushed to me and dug her fingers into my arms. "Nessa, no."

I gripped my sister's hand and squeezed it. "I have to, Aislin. You can't go. You and your child don't deserve to be harvested as thralls. This is my path either way."

"Nessa..."

I pulled her into a hug and squeezed her tight. The harvested never returned to Mabon. They couldn't send letters. They were as good as dead, even those that managed to survive. I'd never see Aislin again. Never meet the child I volunteered to save.

A small part of me whimpered and screamed, but I shoved her down. My eyes remained dry. There would be a thousand more reasons to cry today.

I met Donal's gaze over Aislin's shoulder. He looked... relieved. I wanted to blame him, but could I? If someone offered to take my place right now, I'd feel the exact same way.

I simply stared. He would protect my sister. He would love her and cherish her until the end, whether that came by death or harvest. He would be the best father Corraidin had ever witnessed, or I would haunt his ass for the rest of eternity.

He straightened under my glare, swallowing audibly.

I released my sister and pulled back to study her. My mother's face was a blur in my mind. Had her eyes been hazel brown like mine or a lighter gray? Did she have my straight nose or a rounded tip like Great-Aunt Cloda? Had she smiled at the antics of her young daughter or frowned like Deidre always had? I didn't know. I wouldn't ever know.

I'd hold on to every memory of Aislin for as long as I was able. "I'm volunteering. You can't stop me."

"Nessa—"

"You don't know how wonderful it is to hear those words," a deep, melodic voice said behind me.

My nausea disappeared, wiped away by a wave of pure fear. It prickled across my skin, *under* my skin, an uncontrollable compulsion to flee or fawn.

The innate sense of prey in the presence of a predator.

I turned slowly, knowing what I'd find. Half the people shuffling from the square around me had peered over at the entrancing sound, but now stared straight ahead with stiff backs. Proximity made the air tense with fear, even though an Azarasian could easily kill a human from three feet or three *hundred* feet away.

A cloaked vampire in the Court of Dawn's red stood at my side. I stared for a second, dumbfounded. Where had he come from? I knew vampires were stronger and faster than humans, but I'd never witnessed any of their superior abilities outside of stories. The magistrates paraded around like they had all the time in the world. But this vampire wasn't one of the magistrates.

That couldn't be right. The magistrates lived here, along with a handful of warriors and a rotating roster of healers. But no other vampire had ever attended the harvests.

From within the depth of the cloak, luminous golden eyes ensnared me. "May I?"

My mouth went oddly dry. I dropped my gaze, from the white-blond hair brushing his sculpted shoulders to the black, hardened leather that fit him like a second skin. I finally settled on the hand he held extended. Gold rings bejeweled with rubies and pearls decorated the ivory of his knuckles.

I stared at that pale, glittering hand for a thousand years. The vampire had phrased it as a question, but I didn't really have a choice in the matter.

Without shaking, I placed my hand in his palm. The magic in his veins made him a few degrees warmer than a human, but his skin felt normal otherwise, soft, flawless, and unscarred. He raised it to his mouth like he meant to kiss my knuckles.

An inch from my skin, he stopped.

Then he inhaled.

I almost wet myself. Honestly, I was impressed I stayed standing. I couldn't see his eyes from this angle, but his lips twitched into a small smile, flashing perfectly normal teeth. I had never seen a vampires' fangs before, though I had learned about them in school. The Azarasians taught us everything we'd need to know to be a good thrall.

"Lovely," he all but purred.

Heat flooded me. Whether it was fear or something I refused to name, I wasn't sure. No one had ever called me lovely. Especially no one who sounded like that.

Then again, he was talking about my blood.

I tugged my hand back without thinking. The vampire let go of me. His smile grew into a dazzling grin. Great. Glad I could be entertaining. I backed up—

And bumped into a chest that felt like solid steel.

I stiffened. Fuck. Shit. Fuck. I couldn't do this. I wasn't meant for life beyond my bookshop. I especially wasn't meant to be a vampire's afternoon meal. *Two* vampires' afternoon meal. Azarasians always traveled in pairs and shared everything with their soulbound.

"Who's this?" The second vampire's voice rumbled through him, vibrating lightly across my back. I had wider shoulders than most, and even my sides barely brushed the inner part of his massive arms. I might have been short next to the Dawn vampire, but I was tiny compared to his Dusk counterpart.

"A volunteer," the Dawn vampire said, sounding absolutely delighted. "It only took a month."

"Hmm." A huff of breath brushed my ear. Was the vampire leaning... closer? I didn't dare turn. I didn't think I could.

"I haven't volunteered yet." I don't know why I said it, but the words escaped my lips before I could stop them. The breath tickling my ear stopped. My heart nearly seized. "Sir," I added quickly, like addressing him properly would make him forget I had spoken without permission.

After an eternal moment, the solid heat left my back as the second vampire circled me.

A figure in a dark blue cloak entered my line of sight. He towered over me, the top of my head in line with his broad shoulders. The black, curved blade of a daemium axe wafted faint shadows from the holster on his back. I glimpsed bronze skin, a strong jawline, and silver eyes before ducking my head down.

"Haven't you?" he asked. "Shall we take your... sister, was it?"

Aislin paled as the Dusk vampire focused on her.

"No," I nearly shouted the word. "Fine. I volunteer in the place of Aislin Milligan."

The Dawn vampire clapped. "Excellent! Glad we could come to an agreement."

I started to glare, but stopped myself mid-expression and ducked my head. *You idiot. Never make eye contact with a vampire.* The few texts I had on vampire biology and culture were heavily redacted, but I didn't need a book to know that. It was one of the first things every Maboni child learned. To hold a vampire's gaze was to issue a challenge—one they always answered.

But the blonde didn't react beyond the curl of his lips. Thankfully I had found a vampire amused by my idiotic slip-ups or I'd be very dead right now.

"Come with us." The Dusk vampire crooked his fingers once, silver rings circling each digit except his thumb. He turned firmly on his heels and started through the crowd, forcing humans to scurry from his path. He didn't wait to see if I obeyed. Even if his soulbound wasn't beside me, I had a feeling he wouldn't have waited. His tone was absolute, following his command the only option.

I faced my sister, who watched me with terrified eyes. Poor Aislin. I wasn't leaving much behind, but I would miss her. The only person in my life who had ever cared. I took her hand and searched for something to say, but no words felt right.

How did one say goodbye to someone forever?

I thought I'd have more time to figure that out.

"Take care of yourself, Ais." I gave her hand a final squeeze. "I'll miss you."

My sister released a small sob before slapping a hand over her mouth. She nodded and backed away, like if she stood any closer, she'd try to grab me and hold me back. Deidre stepped up to her daughter's side. At her touch, Aislin spun and dropped her head against her mother's shoulder.

"May the godstars shine upon you, Nessa."

Though my stepmother's voice was soft, it didn't reach the bitch's eyes. I almost slapped her. It was now or never, after all.

I settled for a cathartic, "Fuck off, Deidre."

The Dawn vampire cackled and dropped an arm around my shoulder. I stiffened at the touch. "You're hilarious. I like you already."

# 3

Agony burned through my core and radiated into my thighs, like someone twisted a knife deep in my gut. I huddled on the transport wagon's bench, holding myself together with pure will. The stress of the harvest always triggered my symptoms.

The stress of *joining* the harvest apparently doused my symptoms with oil and then tossed a match.

The wagon went over a rough bump. It jolted through me, rattling my clenched teeth. My nausea spiked, rejoining the party to destroy me from the inside out. The roads outside Corraidin were rough and twisting, urging me to puke my meager breakfast on the older man to my left or the teenage girl to my right.

Maybe both for good measure.

I focused on the thin, moss-covered trees above the heads of the Maboni across from me. One tree. Two trees. Three trees. Counting didn't make the pain or nausea stop, but it kept my mind busy—

The wagon buckled. I jolted, my body falling forward. My elbows dug into flesh. We must have hit a hole or something as half of the wagon's occupants were on the floor.

"Watch it," the man to my left snapped at me, like he hadn't *also* fallen from his seat.

I grabbed the edge of the bench and crawled back to my seat, ignoring him. His words barely even registered, not when my own body was trying to kill me. The bloating in my stomach. The tremor in my bones. The stabbing in my core.

But even if I wasn't in pain, there was no point in making friends. No one knew for sure what happened once the harvested reached the vampire's fortress near Mabon's south coast and boarded the ships to the mainland.

What we did know was all vampires across the Impire required blood to survive and they preferred it from humans.

"Where do you think we'll end up?" a small voice asked.

I twisted toward the teenage girl beside me. Fuck. I had tried not to focus on her and my illness had happily obliged. But now I couldn't help it, taking in her pale face, wide blue eyes, and dark swash of hair.

She probably wasn't that much older than Orrin, making her... sixteen? Seventeen? Had that been her first harvest? My nausea flared again. I didn't want to imagine my fate, much less hers.

I swallowed and tried to come up with an answer that wouldn't terrify her. "I only know the names of two cities in the Impire. There's Tenebra de Mar to the south, on the edge of the Thaddeian Ocean. Then they have a northern mountain stronghold, Montaurère. Or had a northern mountain stronghold. My information might be really out of date."

She blinked blankly at me, but now that I was talking, I couldn't stop. "I think we're closer to Montaurère, so maybe there? But I really don't know. In the book I read, there was only one court and one king. Now the Courts of Dusk and Dawn each have a king. Who knows what else the Imperium changed?"

She nodded. I thought that was the end of our conversation when she whispered, "Are the Imperium really named the Conqueror and the Butcher?"

"I assume they have another name." The current kings were soulbound and had ruled the Impire for over four hundred years, ever since the regents Azaras the Beast appointed when he left for his hell realm died. I hadn't pieced together much more than that from my readings. "They just haven't bothered to tell us."

"They don't sound very nice."

I laughed, a sudden, harsh bark I couldn't hold back. Everyone in the wagon twisted to glare at me. I stiffened and murmured, "I doubt they are."

The girl sunk into silence.

I didn't pull her out of it. Crossing my arms, I curled into myself and closed my eyes. I couldn't save her anymore than I could save myself. Neither of us would ever see our homes again.

My sister, her baby.

My shelves of books.

My grumpy cat.

The rare visits from my father, stepmother, and younger siblings, usually at Aislin's urging.

I shook my head. It was better not to think of the life I left behind, even the few good parts. But my nausea pushed forward into the space left by my thoughts of home and brought stabbing cramps with it. My only choices were pain, emotional or physical.

Just my luck.

Deidre had called my illness a curse, a punishment from the godstars, and the word had never felt more right.

The light changed, flickering against my eyelids. Had we reached the fortress already? I knew we were one of the closest towns to the coast, but the few maps I had access to didn't have any details on distances, that information redacted by the Impire.

I glanced toward the front of our wagon, where our two horses followed behind the one ahead. Runes flared on their rumps. *Follow.* The rune's meaning wasn't hard to infer, but my whisper of a sense had always seemed like more than that. All demonblood read Demonic instinctively. Many humans had distant demon ancestry, the blood diluted over centuries, but I had never admitted the ability aloud. I had watched Patriarch Meallán perform too many exorcisms to risk saying anything.

With a shudder, I tore my eyes from the rune and took in the sights beyond the wagons.

The forest opened onto a field of green grass stretched across a hill, the winding path leading to a fortress atop a cliff of white stone. The building rose higher than any I had ever seen, a beautiful monstrosity of soaring walls and pointed towers. Below, the shoreline curved slightly, showing an expanse of sand.

Over the edge of the cliff, blue waters stretched as far as the eye could see. *Further* than the eye could see, the sky and sea blending into one in the far distance.

My jaw dropped. Was that the ocean? I had read about it in textbooks and stories, but none of the descriptions or illustrations did it justice.

Three ships—galleons technically as they had four masts with square-rigged sails—were tied to the end of a long dock off the beach. Each flew the Azarasian flag, red on the top and blue on the bottom with an eight-pointed star on the horizon between them. Whether it was showing dusk or dawn was up to the eye of the beholder.

I traced my eyes across the lines of the ships, taking in every detail. I would never return home, but before I became someone's midday meal, I'd see more than I had in my first twenty-nine years of life.

A chill tickled across my skin. I pulled my shawl tighter around my shoulders but that didn't stop the sensation.

When had the people on the opposite side of the wagon stiffened, dropping their gazes? I hadn't noticed, too enamored with the sights around me.

I turned slowly, already knowing what I'd find. The second of our town's surprise vampires, the imposing figure in a navy blue cloak, rode a gigantic horse in pace with my wagon. *Hellsteed,* I mentally corrected. A hellsteed had about as much in common with a horse as a vampire or witch did with a human. Namely, that we shared a common ancestor and were roughly the same shape.

In the last three or four hours since we left Corraidin, a dozen other vampire warriors had joined our convoy with their own collection of wagons carrying hundreds of Maboni. Only the two vampires from my town rode hellsteeds. I tried not to look, but I couldn't stop my curiosity.

Demon blood made everything bigger and meaner. The hellsteed had to be nearly eight feet tall, with a deep black coat over rippling, strong muscle. In *The Soulborne Queen,* Azaras's hellsteed had run twice the speed of a normal horse and tore through enemies in battle. Seeing this hellsteed, I could believe it.

I met its shadowy gaze. The intellect in those eyes chilled my blood.

I pulled my attention away, but the only other thing to look at was the vampire. Strong thighs, a broad chest under hardened leather with far too many clasps and buckles, a strong chin of smooth bronze skin. He hadn't lowered his hood—none of the vampires had—but through the shadows, bright silver eyes ensnared mine.

Fuck, not again.

I dropped my gaze to his chest. I could see just enough of his face, unfocused in my peripheral. His nostrils flared. Everything within me stiffened. I had forgotten my pain at the sight of the ocean and hellsteed, but it flared within me at my spike of anxiety. It never stayed in the background for long.

I twisted back around, trying to ignore his icy gaze on the back of my head. I couldn't check, but sometimes I spotted when my pain was this bad. Could he smell my blood?

That was a stupid question. Of course a vampire could smell blood.

I closed my eyes and breathed through the pain. I couldn't stop myself from bleeding. I couldn't stop my body from cramping and twisting. I couldn't stop the Dusk vampire behind me from murdering me for meeting his gaze *again.*

My fate was in the godstars' hands now.

I let myself drift until the sound of wheels on dirt softened. I sighed as the wagon's jolting settled but kept my eyes closed, not needing to see—

A short scream cut off my thoughts. My eyes flashed open. We rolled onto the beach at the end of two rows of wagons on the soft sand. Vampire warriors instructed people to unload one wagon at a time and join the line leading to the dock. I couldn't see what happened at the front, but the sounds told me enough.

The scream turned into a muffled wailing that chilled my blood. My heart stuttered, my fear flaring to life. I flinched as a sharp stab flashed through me.

Our wagon pulled to a stop in the second row. No one moved. There was nothing else to do. We outnumbered the Azarasians ten to one, but it wouldn't have mattered if we outnumbered them a hundred to one. An army of humans was no match for a vampire.

"What do we do?" the girl beside me whispered, her voice somehow even lighter than it had been as we traveled through the forest.

"Wait, I guess."

We didn't wait long. The Dusk vampire hadn't strayed far from our wagon. In the corner of my vision, he dismounted his hellsteed. He said something to the beast, too low for me to hear, before it turned to wander off toward the dock.

Shit, did it understand us? The book I had on hellbeasts was rather introductory and didn't get into that.

Then the Dusk vampire turned toward our wagon, pushed back his hood, and the questions fled my mind.

I had noticed his chiseled jaw and bronzed brown skin earlier, but now I looked into a perfect, masculine face carved by an expert hand. His every feature was strong and regal, from the slash of his dark brows to the sharp edge of his cheekbones. The only feature at odds was the softness of his lips. His short, tousled black hair had an almost blue sheen to it in the light, like the color of the midnight sky. One loose curl brushed his forehead. My fingers itched with the urge to grab that silky strand and run through his hair.

I flinched at the thought. What was wrong with me? He was gorgeous, yes. Inhumanly so. But so were all vampires.

Those cold silver eyes found me instantly. My heart stopped at the sight. This time I couldn't look away, entranced by him. His gaze stabbed into me as sharply as my illness, but it was the black rim around his irises that nearly made me faint. All demonblooded creatures had a shadow rim in their eyes, but his was pronounced and visible even at this distance.

He was a *demonborn* vampire. He had to be. Even if *The Soulborne Queen* was an entirely fictional work, what little it told me of demons, vampires, and magic seemed to match what the textbooks said. Karra had avoided vampires with thick shadow rims, knowing one of their parents or grandparents was a demon. They were the strongest and most dangerous of their kind.

I had never thought I'd see one in person.

The Dusk vampire—the *Lord* of Dusk, if he was demonborn and the customs from Karra's time still applies—walked to the end of our wagon. The girl beside me shied into my side, the entire bench seeming to scoot over an inch at his approach.

I stayed still, caught in those eyes. A part of my brain screamed at me to *look away, dumbass,* but I couldn't. I was caught in the predator's trance and I did not give a shit.

"Nessa Halloran, was it?"

I shuddered as his deep, silken voice washed over me. No one else in my wagon moved, leaving me alone to face the vampire. Not that anyone here could do anything to help me.

"Yes?" My voice didn't shake.

He waved me forward with a smooth movement. "Come with me."

I BIT DOWN THE *Why?* that climbed up my throat. I doubt he'd answer. I also doubted I really wanted to know.

I didn't move at first and the Lord of Dusk didn't climb in to pull me out either. Odd. The other vampire warriors in Corraidin had no qualms forcing people into the transport wagons, but this Lord of Dusk and his cheerful Dawn companion had surrounded me like an honor guard and left me to enter of my own volition.

Now it seems I was to exit on my own, as well.

I started forward, ignoring the roar of blood in my ears and the cramps in my belly. While they didn't force me, it wasn't like I had a choice. No human in the Azarasian Impire did.

The Lord of Dusk raised a hand for me. Like a gentleman. Could that be all this was? But no, vampires didn't think of humans that way. We were livestock.

There was something else going on here. *A volunteer. It only took a month.* What did the Dawn vampire mean by that? Why did the Azarasians need a volunteer?

Another question I was sure I wouldn't like the answer to.

Teeth clenched, I took the Lord of Dusk's hand. The warmth of his skin clashed with the chill of his four silver rune-carved rings. A spark shot through my arm, but I ignored it. If the vampire felt it, he ignored it as well.

I jumped from the cart and landed on the sand. I nearly pitched forward as my legs went weak from the pain, but the Lord of Dusk's grip on me tightened, righting my balance. My other hand went to that wide chest of its own volition, using him like a wall to hold me up. A warm, solid wall of flesh, toned to perfection from centuries of wielding that massive axe on his back.

He cleared his throat. I jerked away from him, gaze flickering to him and then down again. The edge of his lip twitched ever so slightly.

"I would normally remove the hand of someone who touched me without permission. Especially if they'd made eye contact multiple times in the hours before." He brushed his knuckles along my jaw and tilted my head until I met that unyielding silver gaze again. I shuddered at the touch. "But staring isn't always a challenge. It can be an invitation. Which is yours, Miss Halloran?"

My mouth went dry. Fuck. "Neither?"

"Is that so?"

I don't know why I did it, but I raised my chin ever so slightly. Obstinately. Everything in me screamed to back down, but I didn't hear it through the exhaustion and pain. "It was neither."

The twitch of his lip grew into a half-smirk. "A challenge and an invitation? Intriguing."

"It—no, that's not—"

Another scream split the air, then cut off just as quickly. I straightened. The Lord of Dusk didn't react, but a callous chill overtook his expression at the sound. He turned on his heels. "Come, Miss Halloran."

I glanced around. Two unfamiliar vampire warriors straightened from where they leaned against the side of the empty wagon next to mine. Had they been there this entire time? I hadn't even noticed them.

Their luminous gazes traced down my body like I was nothing more than a walking meal. Every instinct in me screamed. I scurried after the Lord of Dusk to the pounding drumbeat of my heart.

We weaved between the rows of wagons. Most of the Maboni had been unloaded and ushered toward the dock but some remained in their seats. They watched and frowned as I passed, the only human moving freely. I ducked my head, examining the glittering sand like it was a great work of art.

When gilded, black boots entered my vision, I halted a second before I crashed into a hard body. My gaze ricocheted past a red cloak and a familiar wicked smile into bright golden eyes noticeably lined with shadows.

Fucker. Two demonborn vampires? The Lord of Dawn's black rim was almost imperceptibly thinner than his soulbound's but it was still there.

Like all the vampires on the beach, the Lord of Dawn had lowered his hood. Pale blond hair brushed his shoulders, a slight wave to the artfully messy strands. His skin was a smooth, flawless ivory. He had a strong jawline and cheekbones sharp enough to cut, but there was something softer to his face compared to his soulbound. He'd fit perfectly with the godstars in the murals adorning the Church walls. Everything about him screamed gentle divinity—except for those eyes.

The playful, mischievous spark was that of a predator, like a cat toying with its food.

I stepped back instantly.

The beautiful lord circled to my side, the rubies of his earrings and rings twinkling in the sunlight. His cloak differed from the standard army issue his counterpart wore, the faintest hint of gold thread weaved into the fabric. *Real* gold unlike the patriarch's.

His thumbs looped around the gilded hilts of his daggers at his hips. "Enjoy the ride?"

"Uh..." When I licked my lips, those glowing eyes followed the movement. "I guess?"

The Lord of Dawn barked out a laugh. "You guess?"

I gaped for a minute before shrugging. I'd had a terrible time, but it didn't seem wise to tell my new masters that. Make that new master. The Lord of Dusk had continued on toward the dock near the line of Maboni.

"You're going to love this, then." The Lord of Dawn offered out his arm, like he was escorting me to a dance and not my death.

"I doubt that," I murmured under my breath, but looped my arm around his.

"You got me there."

My heart stuttered. I couldn't tell from what—his nefarious reply, his gorgeous grin, or his rock-solid arm under hardened leather.

We crossed the beach toward the Lord of Dusk. My anxiety and pain spiked the closer we got to the water's edge. I tried not to flinch, but I couldn't stop my reaction in time.

The Lord of Dawn halted and twisted to look down at me. "You're in pain."

It wasn't a question, but I answered anyway. "It's nothing for you to concern yourself with, my lord."

"Jules."

"What?"

"That's my name."

I stared, trying not to gape. "Why?"

His smile widened. "Why is my name Jules? I believe my father named me, may he suffer for all eternity."

"No, I mean... why are you telling me your name?"

He paused for a moment, almost like he wasn't sure, but then shrugged. "I felt like it. Just like I feel like doing this."

The Lord of Dawn—Jules—raised his hand. Shadows wafted from his fingers, flickering between solid and incorporeal. With a quick flick in the air, he drew a small pattern in the air above my chest. The rune flared into life, into my soul. *Soothe.* A warm heat spread through me.

I straightened slowly. The pain was... gone. Completely. My nausea and exhaustion still lingered, but without the agony, I could manage.

I pressed a hand to my belly. How long had it been since I hadn't hurt nearly every other day? Months, at least. Within a blink, a vampire had eliminated the ache that plagued me for over a decade.

Emotion welled up within me, but I shoved it down. "Thank you, my lord."

"Anything for our volunteer."

There it was again, dangled in front of me. Volunteer. What exactly had I gotten myself into?

More importantly, did I really want to know?

"How long will the rune last?"

"A couple hours."

So it wasn't a permanent fix. But a couple of hours without pain was better than nothing. I tried to stop my expression from falling, but I obviously wasn't successful.

Jules arched an eyebrow. "Are you expecting the pain to return?"

"It always returns." And I didn't want to talk about it, not with my vampire captor. "What exactly did I volunteer for?"

Jules didn't respond for a moment, but his frown quickly became a smile. "The harvest. It only happened a couple of hours ago, lovely."

I narrowed my eyes, but quickly washed away the expression. If I wasn't murdered in the next couple of days, I'd need to learn to control that. There was clearly something wrong with these vampire lords if they were letting me talk and stare.

There was clearly something wrong with me since I continued to do so. "I didn't forget. What *else* did I volunteer—?"

Another scream ripped through the air, this time much closer. My head twisted toward the sound. The Lord of Dusk waited a couple feet away, but a quick glance to my left revealed the front of the line.

A Maboni man bent over a waist-high stone, his arms splayed, his trembling hands pressed against the rough, bloodstained surface. At his side, a vampire warrior blocked part of my view. The man's scream had stopped quickly like all the others, but not because his pain had stopped. His face was turned toward me, his skin flushed and sweating. He thrashed weakly, but neither of his feet left the ground nor did his hands raise from the stone. A rune held him still, I was sure of it. But what were they—

The warrior shuffled to the side, and I had my answer.

With sharpened black claws, the warrior *carved* a runespell *into* his skin. The brand every Maboni received at birth was gone from the back of his neck, shadows slicing into smooth flesh. I spun away, my nausea flaring and not because of my illness, but the Lords of Dusk and Dawn stood to my right, watching my every reaction.

For the first time today, I couldn't bear to meet their eyes.

Reluctantly, I twisted back toward the man and the line of Maboni behind him. The man's mouth was open, his eyes bulged in a silent scream. Blood gushed down his neck, most of it devoured by the vampire's runespell and shadows, but stray droplets escaped. They spattered against the stone, deepening the red stain across its surface.

At the sight of all that blood, a man split from the line and made a beeline for the water. He couldn't outrun or out-swim a vampire, but his terror didn't care.

No one moved to chase him. The warriors milling across the beach followed him with their gazes and nothing more. Why didn't they—?

His foot touched the water. At his neck, his brand flared, the black lines becoming twisting shadows that pulsed through his spine. *Brand. Track. Boundary. Retribute.* The final rune burned brighter than the rest.

His entire body seized like a shot of lightning coursed through his veins.

He flopped down into the water and didn't move again.

Corpses tended to do that.

I stared. Stared. Stared. Gentle waves brushed against his body.

His *dead* body.

Stars, I was going to hurl and scream. Maybe at the same time. I resisted the urge to claw at my nape. The brand at the base of my spine marked me for exactly what I was—one of the Azarasian herd.

I hadn't known it could *kill* me.

I'd assumed *Retribute* meant pain, not death.

I swallowed hard. "I thought the brand just stopped you from leaving."

"It did stop him from leaving," the Lord of Dusk said simply.

I stared, jaw agape.

A pair of warriors headed for the corpse, but the vampire near the runestone stepped away, drawing my attention. The runespell on the human's neck flared suddenly. The shadows drank up the blood as the magic activated. I tried to peek, but I didn't have the right angle to read the runes.

"Stand," the warrior commanded.

The man pushed from the stone. There was a bit of resistance as the shadowy rune on the rock's surface held tight. *Anchor*. When the rune dimmed, he finally broke free.

"Walk to the end of the dock and wait for further instruction," the warrior said in a bored voice, already turning to the front of the line and his next victim.

Without hesitation, the Maboni man marched for the dock. His eyes flickered around, a wild panic in his gaze, but it didn't show in the way he moved—

Oh. Oh, no.

"What does the new runespell do?" I asked softly, suddenly afraid of what I suspected was true.

"Beyond extending your range to the entire Azarasian Impire?" Jules ran a hand through his blond hair. "It's for obedience, mostly."

My insides went cold. The thrall runespell. Karra hadn't worn it as a witch, but humans in service to the vampires and demons of Azaras's court had. The Azarasians called their servants thralls, but I hadn't known for certain if they were magically bound.

I'd naively hoped we wouldn't be.

The obedience wasn't even the worst part of the spell. Through a loyalty rune, it made thralls *want* to please their masters. And if it was sealed at the end, it couldn't be removed as long as the spell remained powered.

And the Azarasian Impire had power to spare.

"You won't be receiving a thrall runespell," the Lord of Dusk said.

I jolted, turning to him with wide eyes. "Why not?"

"You're our volunteer," he said. "We'll need to remove your brand runespell instead."

That didn't answer my question. My stomach dropped.

Jules wiggled his ruby-ringed finger toward me. "Move your hair."

Hesitantly, I pulled the long braid over my left shoulder, baring my brand runespell... and the side of my neck.

Both vampires' eyes dropped to that pale expanse of flesh over my pulse. Everything within me stiffened. I didn't even jump when the next of the Maboni screamed. I had frozen, my heart racing in the blind terror of prey caught in the predator's jaw.

Jules didn't touch me, but I felt the warmth of his skin as he waved his shadowed finger in some pattern over my brand. The heat of magic brushed my nape a moment later.

"There." Jules pulled back. "Now you're one of the few humans in all the Impire unmarked by a brand or thrall runespell."

I ran my fingertips up my spine. The runes hadn't even left a mark, the skin smooth like the brand had never existed. "Lucky me."

Jules flashed me a bright grin before turning toward his soulbound. "I don't think they need supervision, Luc. They've only done this quarterly for nearly four hundred years."

The Lord of Dusk—Luc, I assumed—turned toward me. "Tristan?"

Tristan? Who was—

A gold-eyed vampire with chestnut-brown hair flashed into existence beside me. I almost shrieked. Almost. This warrior wore the standard dark leathers, his cloak the red of Dawn, but a gold insignia in the center of his chest showed the Azarasian eight-pointed star. Perhaps he was a higher rank than the others on the beach.

The vampire dropped into a quick bow, ignoring me. "Yes, Imperator?"

Imperator? I hadn't heard that title before, but something about the word was strong and imposing. Maybe these vampires weren't only lords.

The Azarasians didn't provide any books on their government or military formation—or any government of military formation. I knew nothing about titles and hierarchy beyond what I'd witnessed from the vampires stationed in Mabon or inferred from *The Soulborne Queen*.

"Get another mage down here. I want to leave within the hour."

"Yes, Imperator." The vampire flashed out of sight, moving at a speed too quick for my eyes.

An hour.

A single hour.

In one hour, I'd never see my homeland again.

MABON'S GREEN HILLS AND pale cliffs became a blur over the horizon as the galleon sailed toward the Impire's mainland. I watched long past when it disappeared from sight. If I turned, perhaps new land had already come into view, the continent I had read about for years.

I didn't want to look. My life in Corraidin had been far from perfect, but it had been mine.

I huffed out a long breath. It was time to face my future.

I twisted on the hard wooden bench near the rear cabin. There was no land in sight, sky and sea bleeding together into a seamless haze in every direction. White sails snapped overhead as the warriors-turned-crew moved in synchronized precision. Their steps never faltered even when the ship swayed. All of them ignored me, the only human left on deck. The vampires had led the rest of the Maboni below—alongside the lords' hellsteeds, if the frightened shouts echoing up the stairwell were any indicator.

What was worse? Trapped on deck with two dozen vampires or trapped in the hold with two demon horses and a hundred strangers.

The ship lurched beneath me. My stomach swayed with it. Fuck. There was my answer. I dreaded losing sight of land on the horizon for a second reason. Pushing to my feet, I scurried to the side of the ship. The hairs on my arm rose, a dozen vampire eyes flickering toward me as I moved, but no one tried to stop me.

Lucky for them.

I grabbed the carved wooden rail with one hand, the tail of my braid with the other, and hurled over the edge of the ship.

I focused on the ripples of the water far below as I heaved. One ripple. Two. Three. I lost count after that, far too many forming as the water slapped against the ship's hull.

A spark of twisting shadows caught my eye. There was a line of runes near the waterline. I wiped my mouth and leaned closer, releasing my braid and placing both hands on the rail. My stomach was empty, aching, but I didn't care, too enthralled by the runespell.

What did this one mean? My brain tried to parse it out, but I couldn't read runes upside down. The lines of it were sharp compared to the edges of the soothing rune Jules had drawn. It reminded me of a... shield? Not in shape but there was something—

"Are you planning on throwing yourself overboard?"

The deep voice of the Lord of Dusk vibrated through me. I jolted at the shock of it. In the same second, the ship rocked, dipping to the side. I slid forward, losing my balance.

Oh, fuck. I tried to scramble back. But gravity had grabbed my shoulders and pulled me down—

A solid, leather-clad arm circled by waist and tugged.

Luc deposited me on the ship's deck. I landed shakily on my feet as he released me right away. "Shit. I am really not made for travel."

"I can see that." That silver gaze assessed me with eerie detachment, like I was something to study. "What were you doing?"

"Puking?"

"You stopped puking minutes ago."

I quickly pushed away the thought of the vampire lord silently watching me hurl overboard. "Why is there a runespell on the bottom of the ship?"

One dark eyebrow raised ever so slightly, a crack to the chilling exterior. "The strait may not be part of the Thaddeian Ocean, but it's within Thaddeus's territory."

"The runes are there to protect us from a demon *sea monster*?" The Impire was marked at the edge of our country's map, but our overlords had deemed even the name of the ocean bordering our western and southern coasts too dangerous for us to know. I had read stories about Thaddeus, though. How the ancient demon's godcurse blunted his ability to feel anything at all. How he dragged sailors down to his Trove to spend the rest of their lives in his service. How he killed anyone who escaped his underwater city, the location a well-kept secret.

Maybe it was best I hadn't known what swam off Mabon's coasts.

"Thaddeus hasn't terrorized these waters in his kraken form in centuries." Luc paused and cocked his head to one side, the blue sheen in his black hair catching the light. "Most Maboni don't know the names of any demons besides Azaras. How do you?"

Shit, had the kraken tidbit only been in *The Soulborne Queen*? I couldn't remember. "I, uh, owned a bookshop. It's not restricted knowledge."

"Most humans still don't know it. Your people prefer scripture to history and culture."

"I didn't say I had many customers." I forced an unconvincing laugh. "If the school didn't order all their textbooks through me and the Impire didn't pay a stipend, I would've had to find another job. Most Maboni don't read much."

The corner of his lip curled slightly. "Your Church always hated reading. Humans find it easier to control other humans if they're uneducated."

"And you don't?"

"No," he said without hesitation.

"Oh." My heart stuttered at the surety in that one word. Everyone knew vampires didn't consider humans a threat, but I thought we'd at least count as a mild irritation. "Why bother then?"

Luc considered me for a second. Perhaps he wouldn't answer. Perhaps I had finally asked too many questions. Perhaps I'd have my head torn off in a blink.

"It makes for better workers and conversation."

My eyes widened. The Azarasians educated us to *talk* to us? The better workers part wasn't much of a surprise, but I had never witnessed a human conversing with a vampire. Grovel, sure. Not talk.

Excluding me right now, of course.

I tore my gaze from the Lord of Dusk's imposing figure. "So if Thaddeus isn't a threat, why the runes?"

"I didn't say he wasn't a threat. I have no interest in visiting his Trove."

"Can you call it visiting if he kills everyone who escapes?" I asked. "I know your Butcher King made it out alive, but he's the only one who ever has."

"He was the second, actually. Thaddeus's soulbound was first."

Oh. I didn't even know Thaddeus had a soulbound. If casting the runespell on the Beast King to bind his life to Karra's was considered insanity, what did you call whoever used it on the Demon in the Deep?

Dead, likely.

The ship rocked noticeably beneath me as we hit another wave. My stomach rolled with it. Fuck. Not again. My stomach was empty now. This wouldn't be pleasant. I stepped closer to the rail, the nausea building to a peak—

Warm fingers pressed against my throat and traced a small symbol. My seasickness stopped just as suddenly as my pain had. I straightened, twisting toward Luc. He pulled his hand back, the shadows weaving between his fingers fading. My eyes met cold silver.

For a second, I thought I spotted confusion there—like the Lord of Dusk didn't know why he had helped me any more than his soulbound did. But it was gone the next second.

The hatch to the lower deck thudded open.

I spun around. A warrior climbed up the ladder, a line of Maboni exiting one by one behind her. I frowned. They had just spent an hour herding everyone into the hold. Why bring some up halfway into the voyage across the strait?

Whatever the reason, the Lord of Dusk's attention was no longer on me. "Tristan?" The vampire from earlier crossed the deck in a blink. "Ensure our volunteer doesn't fall overboard."

"Of course, Imperator."

There that title was again, this time accompanied by a bow. I narrowed my eyes at the Lord of Dusk ever so slightly. Not that it helped me figure out who he was in any way.

But Luc was already on the move, crossing the galleon's deck with confident strides. Excluding Tristan, all the vampires headed for the two dozen humans who had exited the hatch. Jules nearly skipped down the stairs from the upper deck over the quarter gallery, a gleeful smile on his face. It made my stomach twist. There was a slight chance that was just the seasickness, but there was something unnerving about the vampire's excitement.

About *all* of their excitement.

"A good harvest?" Luc asked the vampire warrior who accompanied the other humans.

"Yes, Imperator," she replied. "All of them are fine quality Maboni, but these are the best of this quarter's harvest aboard this ship."

Fine quality Maboni. Fuck. The vampires weren't excited.

They were hungry.

"Excellent." The Lord of Dusk crossed his hands behind his back, nearly touching the haft of his axe. "Line up. If you're selected, step forward."

The Maboni obeyed instantly, without hesitation. Whenever Lady Delphine and Lord Raul had given a command, the people of Corraidin had listened, but never this quickly. There was no dragging of feet, no pause—just instant obedience. Our magistrates' short temper made sense suddenly. This was the compliance they expected.

Jules joined his soulbound before the line. "Half now, the other half on the road? Like a little present to our future selves."

Luc continued surveying the humans before him, but he nodded ever so slightly to his counterpart. He walked the line like a commander before his troops.

"Him," Luc suddenly said, those shadow-rimmed silver eyes fixed on an older man in the fine clothing of a merchant.

The man's eyes widened, but he didn't cry out or object. He only stepped forward as ordered. None of the Maboni made a sound. They must have been commanded into silence in the hold.

"Her." The Lord of Dusk selected another human.

I dug my nails into my palms. I didn't want to watch this. My dreams had turned to nightmares of starving vampires tearing into my throat months ago. I didn't want them to become my reality.

I scanned through the crowd of Maboni, examining every face, strange and familiar. My terror echoed theirs. But I stood apart, no thrall runespell marring my skin. For some reason, I was spared from this fate. Whatever awaited me couldn't be good, but the other humans didn't know that. More than one person glared. I skipped over those faces, going to the next—

I met Una's hateful blue eyes. I flinched at the unspoken words. Sinner. Betrayer. Whore.

The Lord of Dusk raised his hand, pointing at... Una. "Her."

I opened my mouth, but snapped it closed just as quickly. Speaking to the lords alone was different from shouting out across the ship for everyone to hear. That wouldn't be tolerated. I didn't even need to ask.

And even if I spoke out, what could I do to save Una? I was just another human. This was our life now. This had always been our life. We just hadn't known it.

When Luc was done, a dozen of the Maboni stood in a second line in front of the first. I couldn't tell what set one apart from the other. They were a mixture of young and old, heavy and thin, with hair and skin in all shades.

The female warrior pulled open the hatch and instructed the back line to return to the hold. One by one, they disappeared into the dark, relief on some faces. Their fate was delayed another day.

If they were lucky.

Luc twisted on the heels of his dark boots, turning from the Maboni to the vampires watching behind him. "You must all be parched from the journey."

The warriors cheered.

"Starving, Imperator," one shouted, drawing a couple chuckles from the crowd.

"The army takes its harvest first and you are the representatives of the army onboard, are you not?"

A resounding cry of "Yes, Imperator."

Jules hooked an arm across Luc's back, slapping his hand down against the man's shoulder. "Lucero's curated quite a collection for you today. What do you say?"

"Thank you, Imperator."

Luc let out a soft sigh before giving his soulbound a gentle nudge toward the door leading into the quarter gallery. "Let them eat already."

"Fine, fine." With a flourish, Jules started toward the door. "Drink well, my friends."

"Tristan," Luc said without turning our way.

The vampire warrior raised his arm toward the quarter gallery. "This way."

Thank the stars. I sped-walked across the deck. I was eventually going to see a vampire feed, but like the Maboni who returned to the hold, today I was spared such a fate. Jules disappeared through the doorway into the quarter gallery. By the time Luc reached the entrance and turned, I was a step behind him. He backed out of my way, holding it open for me. I barely paused.

A narrow hallway led to more doors, the furthest opening into a spacious cabin. A grand mahogany table dominated the room, surrounded by eight chairs and shelves filled with books and maps. The far wall was mostly window, with another door set into the glass leading to a narrow balcony at the ship's stern.

I had never imagined ships having this many doors. In my books, characters always walked straight into the captain's quarters. How many rooms could a boat possibly need?

Jules crossed the cabin to the table and dropped into a chair. He kicked back in his seat with a long exhale and propped his legs on the tabletop.

My eyes must have widened ever so slightly, since he smirked and said, "You Maboni and your manners."

"It's unsanitary."

"I didn't plan to eat anything off the table."

I stiffened. The door clicked shut behind me as Luc entered the space. Tristan had disappeared, perhaps joining the other vampires on the deck. It was me and the lords.

Alone.

It occurred to me that just because they had led me inside didn't mean I was safe from witnessing a vampire feed today.

I might get a firsthand account.

My heart skipped a beat and my palms started to sweat. Fuck, fuck, *fuck*—

The Lord of Dawn's smile grew. "Neither did I plan to eat you, lovely."

That didn't calm me down one bit. "Today."

"Yes," he agreed. "Today."

Luc circled me, heading for his soulbound. "You're going to give our volunteer a heart seizure."

"Pah!" Jules waved a hand in my direction. "She's fine. You're fine, aren't you?"

"I—"

A scream pierced the air. I jumped halfway out of my skin. The scream twisted at the end, turning from pain and terror to a deep moan—

I stumbled away from the door, further into the room. I had known what was going to happen outside. The harvests were for one purpose—we were food.

And vampires, beasts that they were, loved nothing more than to fuck as they fed.

The Azarasians didn't tell us much about their kind, but every Maboni learned about vampire venom before their first harvest at sixteen. Once it hit your system, bloodlust took over, flooding prey and predator alike with intense desire. Whether our overlords intended to scare us, mock us, or simply inform us, it was well-known that becoming a thrall meant you were hours away from fucking a vampire—and enjoying it immensely.

Even if it killed you.

VOICE AFTER VOICE FILLED the air, pitched first in fear before the venom hit their bloodstream. Then the tones changed, dropping into moans and pants and whines. Fabric tore and flesh slammed together.

The warriors were having an *orgy* on the deck.

Blood rushed to my cheeks and spread throughout my face. I didn't wear a star pendant, but if I did, I'd be clutching it hard. Patriarch Meallán's favorite sermon decried all demonblood and their sinful ways. I had known this was my fate as a thrall. I thought I'd come to terms with it. Venom had pain-numbing properties, at least.

But even Karra, a witch and therefore half-demon, her body unbroken and therefore experienced, had been shocked by the hedonism of the Beast King's court of immortals.

I was *not* prepared for this at all.

"Sit, Miss Halloran," Luc said, standing before a bar cart in the corner. When I perched on the edge of a chair next to Jules, he asked, "Brandy?"

Jules didn't answer, instead staring directly at me.

I glanced between them. Waiting. My eyes widened. "You're asking *me*?"

"I already know Jules's answer." Luc filled a glass with dark amber liquid and handed it to his soulbound. "What's yours?"

That was a great question. "We don't drink in Mabon."

"Some of you do. I've seen the import ledgers."

Another pitched cry sounded through the two layers of doors. Alcohol was a sinner's drink, but I was on a sinner's ship, sitting before two incarnates of sin itself. Karra had taken a shot before entering Azaras's lair to bait the Beast. Liquid courage, she had called it. I could use a bit of courage.

Before I doubted myself, I nodded. Luc filled two more glasses. He handed one to Jules, who passed it over, and lowered the other to the table before the seat beside his soulbound. I stared into my brandy, but didn't take a sip as the Lord of Dusk unclasped his axe's holster. He lowered the daemium head to the floor until only the silver knob at the end remained visible, leaning against the table.

As he sat and raised his glass, the cabin dropped into silence. Well, mostly into silence. Everyone on the ship could likely hear the dinner party outside.

"So, uh… who's steering this thing?" My gaze flickered up to the lords. "Unless vampires are skilled multi-taskers?"

They stared. Oh, stars. Why had I said that? I shouldn't have said anything. I dropped my eyes back to the glass, the blush spreading to my ears.

Jules burst out laughing. "I like you. So many humans get quiet when they're scared. It's refreshing to speak to someone so… bold."

"It's just delirium," I muttered into the glass before raising it to my lips—

I nearly choked. Stars, that was strong. The rich taste had a slightly sweet undertone, some flavor I couldn't identify. Delicacies from the Impire were imported for the magistrates and what little surplus remained cost far more than even my father and stepmother could afford. Aislin might have been able to identify it.

I pushed the thought of my sister from my mind with another swig of brandy.

A half-smirk returned to Luc's expression. "Nearly everything on this ship uses magic," he said, answering my earlier question. "It's steering itself."

"That's not dangerous? Aren't there pirates?" Vampires from an archipelago had loved to raid the coast of the Impire in Karra's time. If we were on the Thaddeian Ocean, then these were the waters they terrorized. Assuming three thousand years and two new kings hadn't changed that.

"The Alvarese wouldn't dare come this close to our shores," Luc said. "And even if they tried, the Imperial Navy would stop them before they got this far."

"What if your navy failed?"

Jules snorted. "Then we get to murder some pirates."

He sounded delighted by the concept. Of course he was. He was a vampire. Who I was casually chatting with while drinking brandy on a ship bound for the Impire.

"But our navy won't fail," Luc said. "So it's a moot point."

Jules pouted at his soulbound. "Pity, isn't it? When's the last time you killed a pirate?"

"Decades ago." The Lord of Dusk rested an elbow on his chair's arm, leaning back into the seat. "Perhaps longer."

"That's no fun."

I shuddered. Murder wasn't meant to be fun. But that was a mindset I'd have to get used to. No one had died on a vampire's fangs or claws yet, but we'd only left Mabon a few hours ago. Outside the window behind the Lord of Dusk, the sun drifted toward the horizon. A full day hadn't even passed.

I shuddered again and pulled my shawl tighter around my shoulders. It wasn't cold in the cabin yet, though the nights were chilly, even this late in spring. If I'd known this morning would be my last in Corraidin, I would've worn an extra layer.

"You'll catch your death in that patched shawl."

My gaze ricocheted back from the window at Luc's words. "What?"

The Lord of Dusk set down his drink and rose to his feet. I followed him up, up, up. Fuck, he was tall. My heart raced as the vampire circled the table. But he didn't approach me, instead heading for cabinets embedded into the wall. From within, he pulled out a navy blue cloak like all the Dusk vampires wore over their black leathers. "We can't risk you freezing overnight."

Jules lowered his feet from the table and leaned forward. "We don't have a better color?"

The Lord of Dusk shot his soulbound a look.

Jules smirked. "What? I think she'd look good in red."

"And she wouldn't in blue?"

"Not as good." Tilting toward me, Jules planted his elbow on the table and rested his chin on his hand. "Luc is much better at giving orders than picking outfits."

My instincts screamed as that inhumanly beautiful face drew closer, but I kept my voice steady. "And outfits are your specialty?"

Jules clutched his chest, feigning offense. "What are you saying? Do you see these rings?" He wiggled his fingers dramatically before me, then stood, his cloak sweeping around him. "This intricate stitching in my cloak?" The light glinted off the gold thread as he flung the fabric back to reveal his gilded daggers at his hips. "My hand-crafted daggers?"

Luc let out a heavy sigh, exasperation clear in his breath. But beneath it, there was a flicker of affection, a warmer emotion I hadn't known he possessed.

"Are those ruby-eyed cats?" I'd noticed the gold hilts of the daggers earlier, but now I could clearly make out their shape. The bodies formed the handle, while the heads were decorative tips with snarling jaws and flattened ears.

"They're hellynxes, I'll have you know," he said, that cheeky grin I was learning to hate spreading across his face.

"Is that a, uh... sensible choice?"

In a blink, Jules had the curved blade unsheathed. The black daemium leaked shadows as he spun it with practiced ease. The ridiculous hilt shape didn't hinder him at all. "I didn't need sensible weapons. I needed a statement piece."

"They certainly make a statement." I slapped my hand over my mouth. Why the fuck did I just say that? What was wrong with me? The fear and exhaustion must have been messing with my head.

Jules sheathed the blade and pinched his thumbs at the top, as if covering the lynx's ears. "Shh, don't listen to her, Thérèse. You're beautiful just the way you are."

"You named your *dagger* Thérèse?"

Jules pulled out the second dagger, the blade wide with a sharp tip. "Don't forget her sister, Adé."

Were all vampires psychotic, or was I just unlucky? "I have nothing to say to that."

Luc pinched his brow. "Jules."

The Lord of Dawn blew out a breath and flopped back into his seat. "You ruin all the fun, Lucey."

"Are all soulbound like this?"

Jules raised his brows at me. "Who told you we were soulbound?"

"Oh, I, uh, guessed." Shit. I needed to be careful. The Azarasians shared some details about their society, but never the full truth. The magistrates hadn't mentioned their soulbond before, though everyone knew they were connected. "You seem to move around in pairs. Don't soulbound usually travel together?"

Luc returned to the table with a navy cloak. Jules pouted at his choice, but the Lord of Dusk ignored him as he placed it beside me. The heat of his sudden proximity was like a summer breeze against my skin. "Something you read in your unsellable books?"

I swallowed. Azaras and Karra were the first soulbound pair, their connection forged in the early pages of *The Soulborne Queen*. I knew more than most, more than I should have. Every vampire born in the Impire over the past three thousand years had a soulbond, though the runespell had originally been created to kill demons. Demons were nearly indestructible, but vampires, witches, and humans weren't. By binding Azaras to a weaker creature, they made Karra his one vulnerability.

But no sanctioned source had ever explained soulbonds beyond a passing mention.

"It was probably in a textbook," I said vaguely.

"Egh, textbooks." Jules curled his lip. "Why are you reading textbooks?"

"...to learn?"

Jules cackled. "You're hilarious."

"That wasn't a joke."

"Of course not," Jules said. "You read *textbooks*. Luckily, you'll never run out of those since Luc's a bit of a book hoarder."

Luc crossed his arms. "Book collector, Julien."

His grin widened. "I've seen the Duskfell library. Hoarder is more accurate."

Duskfell? That was Azaras's palace in Tenebra de Mar. Why did Luc have access to the palace's library? And why would I have access to any of his books in the long term?

Were they... keeping me?

My flush had faded throughout the conversation, the moans and grunts from outside sinking into background noise. But it suddenly raged back to life and spread through my entire body.

My cheeks burned.

My chest heated.

My core throbbed.

I clenched my thighs together. Not now. Jules's soothing rune still kept the worst of the pain at bay, but I didn't need to add desire on top of the stress. Both were equally aggravating to my illness.

Jules inhaled and hummed. "Why the flush, lovely girl?"

If I could've turned more red, I would've. Azaras could smell Karra's desire and vampire noses were as good as demon noses. I pushed to my feet and pulled off my patched shawl, ignoring the Lord of Dawn's smug grin and the Lord of Dusk's looming presence. It dropped to the tabletop with a muffled clunk. My bundle of food. My book.

I reached into the pocket—

Jules plucked my shawl from my hands. At least, I assumed he did. One second it was in my grip and the next it was in his. "What's this?" He pulled out the bundle of food, reached inside, and yanked out the molding cheese—then immediately dropped it. "Eww."

Luc reached in next, retrieving the bread. One dark brow raised. "Did you intend to eat this or use it as a weapon?"

He said it so dryly, I didn't know if he was joking or not. "It's not *that* stale."

"Incinerate it with the shawl," Luc said, dropping the bread back into the cloth.

The Lord of Dawn grabbed the mass of wool and food, but he paused, likely feeling the book's weight. "What—"

I grabbed my shawl and tugged with all my strength. Which, admittedly, wasn't much. But Jules must not have been holding on tightly since I somehow ended up with the whole mass of fabric in my hands again.

Triumph flared through me—for a split second.

Jules stared at his empty hand before his golden gaze slid to me. His pupils had expanded slightly, darkness overtaking the bright gold.

Luc arched a brow at his soulbound. "Did she just steal that back from you?"

"It's not like I was trying to keep hold of it."

Luc's second eyebrow raised to join the first.

"I didn't think she'd grab it back." Jules frowned at me. "You are aware I'm a vampire, yes? Do you want to die?"

My heart jumped into my throat. "What?"

"Is that why you volunteered?"

Fuck, had I finally crossed the line? I quickly glanced between Jules in his seat and Luc standing at my side. "You—you wanted my pregnant sister."

"Yes." Jules paused, waiting. "And?"

I crossed my arms, clutching the shawl—and my book—to my chest. "I couldn't just let you take her. She's my sister. And she's pregnant."

"So?" Jules didn't look any less confused. "She wouldn't be the first pregnant human in a harvest."

"She wouldn't be the first in *this* harvest," Luc said.

"Well, I... Does it matter?"

The Lord of Dusk cocked his head to the side. "Yes."

"I... I don't want to die. Especially not at a vampire's hands. But my life was forfeit either way. I'm only a couple months away from my thirtieth birthday."

"And why is that?" Luc circled around my chair. The hairs on my neck rose. "It's an odd choice for a human to make."

"How do you know it was a choice?" I snapped.

Luc stopped between Jules's seat and mine. The hints of warmth I'd witnessed from him over the last hour had vanished. Only a callous vampire remained behind.

I hadn't only crossed the line. I had *run* past it. *Idiot.*

I dropped my gaze, my legs starting to tremble. I didn't want to die. I was too young to die. I had barely lived. I swallowed. "It's not the shawl I want, my lord."

When neither vampire replied, I plunged my hand into the bundle of fabric. It settled on the book's spine. I yanked the book out with one hand and tossed the shawl down to the table with my other.

Did the cloak have a big enough pocket for a full book? I hoped so. I wasn't sure I could carry it all the way to wherever we were going. Assuming I wasn't murdered—

A silver-ringed hand plucked the book from my grip.

Oh, stars. "Wait—"

"*The Soulborne Queen: Volume I* by Katalina Estevez," Luc said, examining the worn hardcover. "I didn't realize this was in circulation in Mabon."

I was red-hot again. Not that my blush had faded this time. Luc had joked about my heart seizing, but I didn't think it was a joke anymore. "It's not. I think someone accidentally added it to a shipment. I never got another copy or the sequel."

"So you read textbooks and vampire erotica?" Jules asked, a purr to his words. It did weird things to my insides. I ignored it. The lords had all but threatened to kill me a minute ago.

"It's demon-witch erotica," I muttered.

"Oh, my apologies," Jules said. "Demon-witch erotica."

I ignored him to risk a glance at Luc. "Can I have it back?"

The Lord of Dusk considered me. After the longest ten seconds of my life, he continued around Jules's chair and returned to his seat. He placed the book on the table between us. "What will you give me for it?"

"I have nothing to trade."

Luc raised his glass and sipped at his brandy, not in a rush to reply. "That's not true. You have yourself."

I sunk down into my seat, a controlled fall. I don't know why those words impacted me more than the death threats had. "I've been harvested. You can do whatever you want with me. Honestly, you could've before the harvest, too."

The edge of a smirk returned to Luc's lips, the utter cold of him fading slightly. "We can do whatever we want with you. But we can't force you to do what we *need* you to do."

That was nefarious. "What do you need me to do?"

"We need you to volunteer once more for us."

I TRACED MY FINGERTIPS along the veins of my arm as the wagon lurched beneath me. Three days had passed since we landed on the mainland, and I'd run out of things to stare at as we traveled through dense woodland. The trees here looked the same as they had yesterday, the day before, and even back home. I had read about the famed architecture of the demons and their offspring, but I had yet to see anything beyond a fortress near where the galleons docked.

I had prepared for terror and pain but not for boredom.

The weight of *The Soulborne Queen* bumped against my back, stored in a small leather satchel that looked army issue. I didn't dare pull my book out, though. The rest of the Maboni in my cart already shot me enough unfriendly looks.

I didn't try to dissuade them of whatever betrayal they thought I had committed. Let them think what they wanted. Their distance meant extra space, a small mercy when my hips and legs ached from sitting for so long. Their disdain didn't matter.

Nothing they thought about me did. All our fates were in the Azarasians' hands now. Mine more than most.

My life for a book. Well, that, and as many soothing runes as I wanted. Neither was difficult for the vampires to give me. The trade seemed almost silly, but it wasn't really a trade at all. My blood, my body, my life—they were theirs either way. I might as well claim what I could to make myself happy through the terrible things to come.

They still hadn't told me why they needed a willing volunteer, but it couldn't be worse than the alternative.

The sound of hooves on stone echoed behind me. Two vampires rode past on giant hellsteeds. Back in Mabon, only Luc and Jules had ridden them, but here, every vampire had one.

The red-cloaked warrior pulled a bundle from one of the straps dangling from her hellsteed's saddle and tossed it into the center of our wagon.

For a second, no one moved, though we had more than grown used to our overlords' routine.

Vampires didn't need rest or sustenance as often as we did. Neither did their hellsteeds. We hadn't stopped for over twenty minutes at a time since reaching the mainland. The vampires tossed bundles of food and water onto the wagons twice a day and stopped a couple of hours later to shuffle us off to relieve ourselves.

Despite the hunger gnawing at my stomach, I didn't grab for the food. No one did, except for the woman closest to the bundle. She pulled a hardtack biscuit, dried sausage, and small block of cheese from the bag, then passed it to the person beside her.

No one spoke. No one fought. A vampire had ordered them not to during the first meal. We were to distribute the food calmly, and there was no way to disobey, not with the thrall runespell carved into everyone's necks.

The runespell remained flat like black ink most of the time. Fergus sat beside me today, the markings flaring a couple of times, making him grit his teeth or clench his fist. *Submit. Obey. Loyalty. Track. Boundary. Seal.* Maybe he wanted to leap from the wagon and make a run into the forest. They'd ordered all of us to stay with the convoy before we left the coast.

I glanced up into the forest, staring between tree trunks into the creeping darkness. The sun was setting. I pulled the navy blue cloak tighter around my shoulders. Now would be a terrible time to escape, even if I wanted to jump from a moving wagon. I was the only human who could do it.

But just because I could didn't mean I would. I wouldn't escape the vampires, and even if I did by some miracle, I'd probably be eaten by the wolves we heard baying at the moons last night. I thought I'd spotted one in the dark, a massive black creature nearly as tall as me with eyes of pure shadow.

I had stared at the woods outside Corraidin for years but had never ventured into the forest. Vampires and witches weren't the only demonblooded creatures that walked this world—hellbeasts wandered the wilds. A couple of years before I was born, a hellbear had ventured into town and killed nearly fifty people before the magistrates dispatched it.

Escape wasn't worth the hassle, just to trade what killed me.

The bundle of food reached me... and was empty. Each wagon held a different number of Maboni, and the vampires weren't about to count every time. At yesterday's dinner, we had two extra meals to go around. I glanced at the three people to my right. An older, sleeping man, a woman my age, and a teenage boy. Better two extra than four too few.

I sighed. "Great."

"Better you than me," Fergus muttered, biting into his biscuit. "Ask your vampire lords for more."

Fergus and I hadn't spoken since school a decade ago, but everyone at risk of failing the birth quota remembered each other. He had married and tried. I hadn't. I heard the judgment in his tone.

"They aren't *my* vampire lords."

He eyed me, his lip slightly curled but his gaze considering. "Is that why you didn't marry? Did you want to fuck a vampire that badly?"

I flinched. "I didn't—" I swallowed my words. Arguing would only make me sound guiltier. Either way, I lost.

"Then what did you give them to stay out of the ship's hold? You have nothing else a vampire wants."

I remained silent. If I didn't respond, he'd stop. Eventually.

"Here." Fergus held out his half-eaten biscuit. "I'll trade you for it."

I blinked at him. "What?"

"Give me whatever you gave the Azarasians, and you can have my remaining food. Your mouth and cunt must be divine to persuade two vampires."

An older woman across the cart spoke. "The vampires said—"

"They said we couldn't fight," he sneered. The woman stiffened. It was rude to speak to an elder like that. "They didn't say we couldn't fuck. The blood whores haven't stopped since we left the ship."

I shuddered. The dozen humans chosen onboard had been placed in a wagon together. At the rest stops, some vampires ordered a thrall from their cart and fed from them right there in the open. The moaning made peeing rather difficult, but I'd managed.

Vampire venom didn't just create desire in the short term. There was a burst of lust during the biting, sure, but it also increased libido over time.

Those thralls had experienced multiple bites now. Their wagon had turned into a full-on orgy yesterday afternoon.

We were a couple of wagons in front of them, but if I focused, I could hear someone panting.

I tried my best not to focus on it. Una was on that wagon. We hadn't been friends in years—maybe not ever, given how easily she abandoned me—but watching her become an eager, glassy-eyed thrall felt wrong.

The older woman lifted her chin. "The godstars will punish you all for your wickedness."

I flinched. What did I do? She sneered at me as much as she did at Fergus and the bitten thralls. Like the suggestion I fucked a vampire was as unholy as him asking me to suck his cock for a biscuit.

"The godstars abandoned us ten thousand years ago when They littered this world with demons." Fergus twisted back to me. "What's it going to be, Nessa? Consider it practice for your new masters."

I bristled. "Fuck off, Fergus."

His eyes darkened. "You don't get to speak to me that way."

"Why not?" I leaned forward, closing the space between us. I was tired. I was hungry. The soothing rune Jules had drawn this morning was fading.

Fuck this day.

Fuck this week.

"We're the same," I hissed. "I'm not the only one who'll be a vampire's whore soon."

"You bitch."

Fergus lunged at me. Eyes widening, I jerked back, but I wasn't fast enough. I spent the last decade reading books. Fighting wasn't exactly my forte. But Fergus had clearly worked on his feet, his body strong and built.

He wrapped his hands around my throat.

I clawed at his grip. My lungs demanded air. My vision wavered. In my periphery, the last bit of sunlight disappeared through the canopy of branches.

"Fuck..." I choked out the words. "...you."

He squeezed. "Vampire whore."

My nails sunk into Fergus's flesh, drawing blood. His grip didn't loosen. Darkness crept in. Not just from the sky, but from my vision. I wanted to laugh. I'd feared dying at a vampire's hands, but I'd never even make it to my new home.

A stupid fucking human would kill me.

As I faded, something twinkled in the shadowed edges of my vision.

Long fingers, decorated in jeweled gold rings, curled around Fergus's shoulder.

In a blink, the human was gone. I collapsed off the bench onto the wagon's floor and gasped in air.

Above, through the branches, stars twinkled down at me from the dark sky. I huffed and huffed, my heartbeat slowing. Tears burned down my cheeks.

I had almost *died.*

Fergus had almost *killed* me.

If the vampires didn't need me alive, I'd be *dead.*

I pushed onto my elbow, every breath painful. The other Maboni cowered, heads lowered. No one had said a word in my defense. With a glare, I hauled myself back onto the bench.

Jules leaned a hip against the side of the wagon, casually flipping his curved dagger. Fergus had landed in a bush off the road, uninjured. So far, at least. He rose to his feet with his fists clenched, but he didn't face Jules alone. Luc and four other vampires, including Tristan and the dark-haired woman I assumed was his soulbound, watched stoically from the back of their hellsteeds.

Fergus paled but didn't move.

Jules smirked at him before his gaze flashed over to me. His attention quickly dropped to my neck. With every breath, fire flared through my throat. The bruise must have been stark against my pink skin. Jules's luminous eyes hardened into a flat gold, the shadow of his pupils expanding.

His smile didn't fade.

If anything, it sharpened.

I couldn't stop my shudder. I didn't know which was worse—Luc's callous stare or his soulbound's vicious glee.

Jules stopped twisting his blade and pointed the black tip toward Fergus. "You tried to kill our volunteer."

His mouth twisted into a nasty scowl. "Fuck you."

Jules's grin widened. "You're a feisty one, aren't you?"

"And you're a pompous asshole," Fergus spat.

"Big words, my friend. Don't waste all your brain cells on insults, you'll need them in a minute."

"Not that it will make a difference," Luc said, his voice as cold as death.

Fergus shied back. "Just kill me already, you fucker."

"Where's the fun in that?" Jules flipped his dagger around, pommel toward the man. "Here."

"What?"

"Take it."

"You're giving me a weapon?"

"A daemium-hilted blade. You could cut through bone with this." Jules glanced over at the mounted vampires watching from the sidelines. "Get our challenger some light. I don't want him to stab a wagon."

Behind Luc, two of the silver-eyed warriors lifted clawed hands, tracing a rune in the air. *Light.* Shadows coiled before flaring into a burning ball. Runelights. The vampires thrust them upward, where they hovered over the grass beside the road.

Fergus's narrowed gaze flickered between the Dusk vampires, the lights, and the smiling Lord of Dawn. "Is this a trick?"

"No trick," Jules said, his tone almost too friendly. "Take the blade. You get the first strike."

Fergus stared at the hellynx-carved hilt. He had no other option and he knew it. He took three hesitant steps toward Jules and snatched the blade away like the Lord of Dawn set a trap.

I tensed, waiting for the strike, too. But Jules just pushed off the wagon, straightened and raised his arms at his side, hands empty. "I'll even stand still, make it easier."

It was still a trap, but Fergus charged. Fergus wasn't short, standing around my height, but the Lord of Dawn had seven inches and fifty pounds of lean, sculpted muscle on the man. More importantly, he was a vampire.

This wasn't a fight.

It was a beast prowling around its cornered prey, stretching out the moment before the kill.

Fergus drove the blade deep, straight into Jules's shoulder. It cut through leather, flesh, and muscle. Jules didn't flinch. Neither did his soulbound. Pain was one of the first sensations Karra had felt through her bond. The Lord of Dusk must have felt the wound as clearly as the Lord of Dawn, but neither of them showed it.

The blade punched clean through, its tip bursting from Jules's back. I clamped a hand over my mouth as bright red blood bloomed along the metal. In a blink, the daemium drank it down.

It looked so... human. So normal. Not at all what I expected vampire blood to look like.

Fergus stumbled back, but he didn't pull the blade free with him. He gaped at Jules. Daemium was one of the few materials that could injure a vampire. If placed right, it could even kill a weaker one. But Jules wasn't a weak vampire. I didn't know how strong he was, but he and Luc were clearly the leaders of our convoy. Demonblood hierarchy was always strength-based.

Still. It was *daemium*.

"Doesn't that hurt?" I whispered.

"I've had worse." Jules pulled the blade out. Blood gushed from the open wound. It didn't close up instantly. Jules might have been powerful, but no daemium wound healed without magic.

From his hellsteed, Luc drew a quick rune with his shadowed claws, his attention entirely on his soulbound. *Heal.* The injury closed near instantly. *Mend.* With the second rune, Jules's leathers and cloak stitched back together, too.

Fascinating.

Jules rolled his shoulder, then blew a kiss toward his soulbound. "Thanks, Lucey."

Luc shook his head gently. "Stop letting people stab you with your own daemium blade. One day, someone will hit something vital, and then I'll owe you for stealing your kill."

"You've been saying that for five hundred years. Most barely stab me." Jules twisted toward Fergus. "You really committed, though. It wasn't even that terrible attempt. But if you wanted to do damage, you should've aimed for my heart." Jules tapped his chest with the tip of the dagger as he stepped forward. "Still wouldn't have killed me, but it might have made me twitch."

Terror rose in Fergus's gaze. "Godstars, forgive my sins—"

Fergus's prayer cut off as Jules suddenly stood before him, a hand wrapped around his throat. "The godstars didn't forgive their own brethren their sins. Why would they absolve you?"

He didn't wait for an answer. The Lord of Dawn struck, a smooth, efficient move that worked perfectly with the curve of the blade.

His weapon wasn't meant for stabbing. It was a blade for cutting and slashing.

It was designed to bleed an enemy dry, cut by cut.

Jules didn't have patience for that. He sliced Fergus from navel to neck.

Blood burst from the man's gut and splattered to the dirt, followed quickly by a slick mass of pink that might have been intestines.

He screamed.

I screamed.

The Maboni awake in the wagon screamed, which woke the sleeping man, who then also screamed.

Beside me, someone vomited.

Inspired, my stomach joined the revolt. My throat burned with my heaves.

With a laugh, Jules wrenched the man's head back and buried his fangs in his throat. Fergus's shriek somehow pitched higher, despite his internal organs already slipping to the ground.

A vampire's dry bite was agonizing, but I hadn't known it was worse than dying with your guts in the dirt.

How was he not dead yet?

Then the Lord of Dawn pulled back harshly, taking Fergus's windpipe with him.

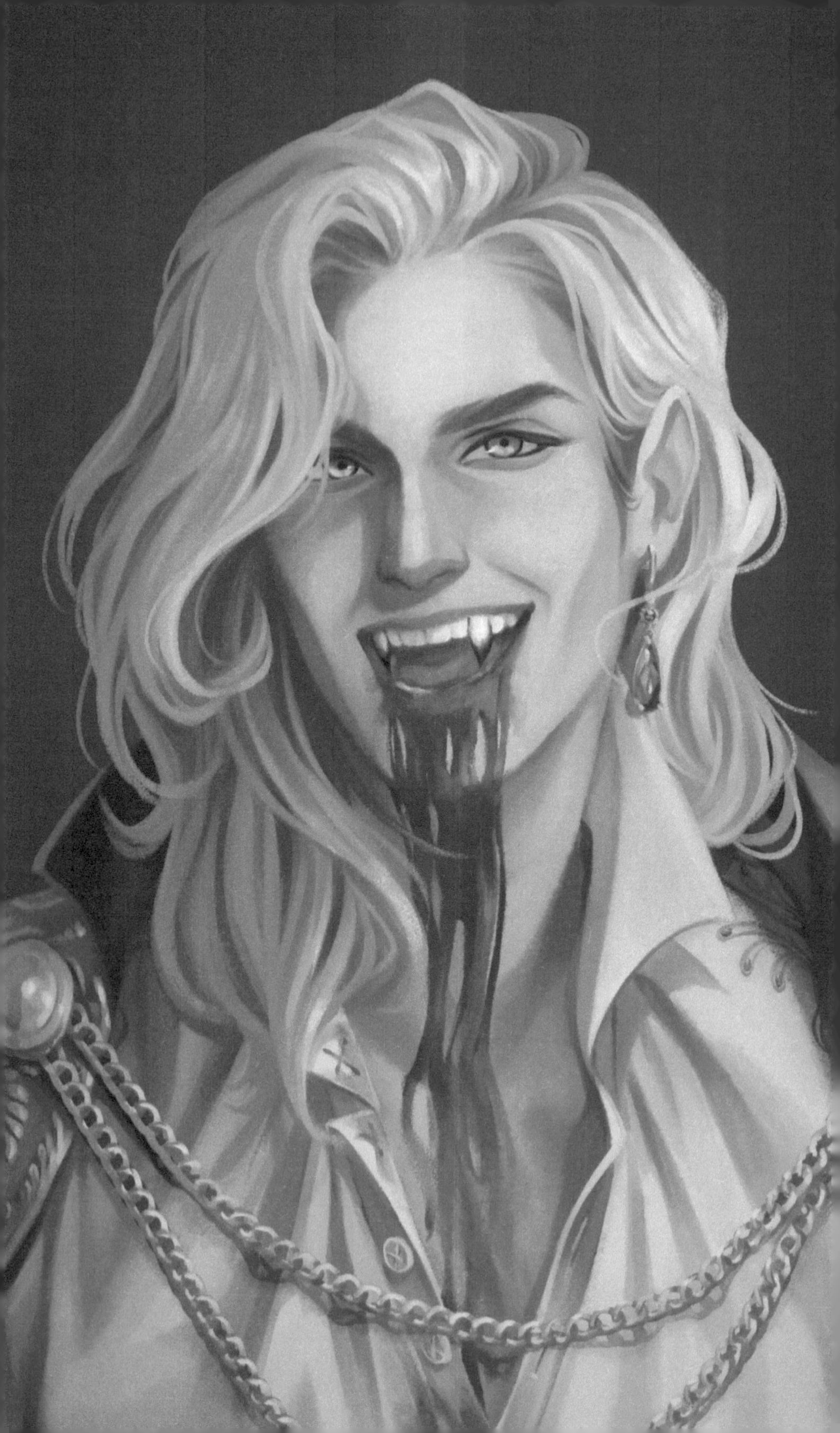

# 8

BLOOD SPEWED FROM THE gaping hole in Fergus's neck, splattering across the Lord of Dawn's face. Jules released the dying man, who crumpled to the earth, and spat out a glob of—

I glanced away, my nausea flaring again. There wasn't anything in my stomach but that didn't matter when I was staring at a shredded trachea.

"Egh." Blood drenched Jules's lips and chin, dripping down to the collar of his black leathers. He frowned, not at the blood and literal guts, but at the puking humans around me. "Now it's going to stink."

"And it wasn't before?" I asked, my tone nearly shrill.

"I'm a vampire, lovely. Blood and guts don't bother me."

My gaze flickered between my eviscerating savior and my eviscerated assailant. Fergus twitched in the dirt, a gruesome sight. Jules wasn't much better. "But you draw the line at vomit?"

"No one likes vomit."

"You—" I coughed. Pain surged through my throat. My eyes watered. The bruised feeling wasn't worse than the stabbing jolts and cramps of my illness, but I hadn't grown used to it. I was familiar with pain, but not this pain.

I hadn't realized that mattered. Probably because I'd never been strangled before.

When the flare under my skin passed and my vision cleared, Jules was standing a foot away, a godstar dressed in blood. I flinched back, my heart climbing my throat. Thankfully, I didn't scream. My throat couldn't handle that.

If the Lord of Dawn noticed my fear, he didn't show it. "Let's get that healed. Luc?"

The Lord of Dusk dropped from his hellsteed. I frowned at Jules. He hadn't used magic to create a light or heal himself. "Why don't you heal it now?"

"It's after dusk, and we're in the wilds."

I glanced at the night sky above, like it held my answer. "I know?"

"You don't, actually." Luc crossed the space to his soulbound in three long strides. "But that doesn't matter now. May I?"

May he? I didn't think he'd ask. The vampire healers in Corraidin never did when assuring the health of the Impire's herd.

I nodded.

Luc gently tilted my head, studying my throat. For the bruises, I told myself. Not because he was hungry. But it was hard to remember that with a vampire touching me. My heartbeat stuttered.

The lord's nostrils flared, but his touch remained light. "You must have truly angered him."

"He called me a whore and a bitch, but apparently me saying it back was crossing a line."

"Hmm." Luc traced a rune against my neck with shadowed fingers. First, the familiar brush of the soothing rune, followed by a second, less familiar rune. Probably one for healing like I'd witnessed earlier, but I couldn't tell from the lines against my prickling skin. "Small men like him can be overly sensitive."

A wave of warmth flashed through me and dragged away the pain. Luc lowered his hand, his claws fading into smoke. I rubbed my throat. When I closed my eyes, I could still imagine the pressure of Fergus's grip, but the injury was gone like it had never happened. "Thank you."

The Lord of Dusk nodded.

"Where's my thank you?" Jules asked. "If he gets one for healing you, I should get one for saving your life."

I shot him a dry look before I even realized it. I was in the middle of reeling it back since he was a *starsdamned vampire, idiot,* when he grinned back. Less than a week ago, I would've passed out if a vampire with blood staining his chin smiled at me.

Now it was almost comforting.

Almost.

"Um, thank you..." I met those intense golden eyes for a moment before dipping my gaze. Behind Jules, Fergus's body had stilled, but blood slowly pooled in the dirt. I dropped my attention to the edge of the wagon. "For saving my life."

"I can't seem to hear you. You'll have to come closer."

My spine stiffened. "What?"

"That's a great idea, actually," Jules said to himself, wiping his blade across his leathers. It absorbed the blood. I almost hopped off the wagon just to search for the rune in the fabric. "Come with us. We're better company and we don't stink."

I inhaled and then scrunched my nose. He wasn't wrong there. I glanced around at the other Maboni in my wagon. Most had their heads lowered, hiding tears and terror. The few who met my eyes glared like it was my fault the vampires had stopped the wagon and killed Fergus.

In their minds, the ideal scenario was the one where I died. No one had cared when Fergus was strangling a traitorous blood whore.

I stood and walked to the end of the wagon. Fuck them. At least the vampires didn't want me dead. They couldn't bite me if I was dead.

When I reached the end of the wagon, Luc appeared in the blink of an eye and raised a hand. I placed my palm in his with far less hesitance this time and climbed from the wagon. "Thank you."

"Don't thank him again," Jules whined. "What did he do to deserve a head start?"

My brow crinkled. "A head start?"

"You'll find my soulbound and I can be rather competitive," Luc said, still holding my hand.

I tugged away. "Over thanks?"

"Over everything," Jules said with a wink.

I didn't ask what everything included. I didn't want to know. Steeling my spine, I approached the blood-streaked vampire. Luc followed behind me, a giant shadow at my back. Something in my chest tightened, coiling like a snared animal. Trapped on both sides. Nowhere to run. Some ancient part of my brain didn't like that, even if the logical part knew that running would be a terrible idea.

I stopped a few feet away from the Lord of Dawn. "Thank you for saving my life again."

"You're very welcome," he purred.

I tried to stop my blush, but I failed miserably. Stars save me, this wouldn't end well. A drop of kindness and a couple of smiles were all it took to lure me into the monsters' trap.

Jules smirked, then spun on the heels of his boots to face the hellsteeds alongside Luc and me. With the lords on either side of me, I kept my attention on the terrifying beasts. Better that than eyeing Luc's broad, muscular form or Jules's lithe, toned build.

I cleared my throat. "Which wagon am I riding in?"

"None of them," Jules said. "When I said near us, I meant near us."

My gaze flickered to Luc in confusion.

"You're riding with Jules," he stated plainly.

My jaw dropped. "On a *hellsteed*?"

"Well, I'm certainly not getting in a wagon or walking," Jules said.

"But... but... you're covered in blood."

"This is hardly covered in blood." Jules swiped his thumb through the crimson on his chin. "Lightly splattered, more like."

I grimaced.

Jules sighed dramatically at the expression. "Fine, fine."

He slid closer to Luc and brushed his thumb against his soulbound's bottom lip, smearing blood across his bronze skin. Luc arched one brow, but his eyes darkened, pupils expanding to swallow the bright edge of silver.

Then Jules wrapped an arm around the Lord of Dusk's shoulders and kissed him.

Their lips brushed, a soft movement so at odds with the blood now staining both their faces. My eyes widened. My pulse dropped from my throat to my lower belly.

Stars, they were beautiful.

Vampires and demons hadn't cared much about gender in Karra's time. Neither did soulbonds. Patriarch Meallán considered it another deviancy from the godstars' path, another entry on the Church's long list of sins. Love was love, so I didn't see why it mattered.

Jules pulled back a second later. "Clean me up, will you?"

Luc smirked and licked the stain of blood from his lips. "You're more than capable."

The Lord of Dawn dropped his arms and pouted. "It's so much more effort at nighttime. What if we're attacked by hellwolves? I'll be defenseless and you'll have to save me again."

"Julien."

"Lucey."

The Lord of Dusk merely stared back.

Jules sighed. A second later, blood peeled off of his skin and leathers to float into the air as droplets. My mouth dropped open. I'd witnessed plenty of magic over the past three days, but Jules hadn't drawn a rune this time. This was a vampire's innate control over blood. They didn't need runes to channel this power, just like how their demon ancestors didn't need runes to rip out and devour someone's soul.

Before I realized, I had reached out to one of the blood bubbles, like I could cup it in my hand. They just hovered there—

The vampire lords stared at me, unblinking. They were right there in my line of vision, but I hadn't processed their reactions, not when there was something new and otherworldly in front of me.

*Focus, Nessa.* I dropped my hand and ducked my head. My heart raced in my ears. "Sorry."

"Don't apologize for curiosity," Luc said.

I opened my mouth, but snapped it shut when another "sorry" tried to escape.

We reached the massive hellsteeds, which saved me from having to reply. Luc's was a pure black while Jules's was a sable brown dappled with white spots. They each wore wide saddles, the seat long enough to fit two comfortably.

I had never thanked the godstars for littering this world with Their spawn before, but for once, I praised Them for creating demonblooded horses. Not only would a regular horse have trouble carrying both our weights, but sitting astride one would essentially mean sitting in Jules's lap.

This wouldn't be much further away, but it was enough.

Jules hooked a thumb toward his hellsteed. "Up you go."

I nearly laughed. "How?"

"Imagine she's a horse. Just bigger." The hellsteed snorted, blowing out a mass of shadows. Jules waved his hands through the smoke. "Stop it, Cala, I know you're not just a large horse. You're a terrifying beast and all who see you fear you."

"I certainly do."

"See?" Jules stroked the hellsteed's snout. "You haven't lost your touch, my girl."

"This is the closest I've ever stood to a... horse." I wrung my hands together, trailing my gaze across the beast's hulking form. "I always watched from outside the riding ring during my sister's lessons."

For some reason, my words made both lords turn back to me. "Your sister received lessons and you didn't?" Luc asked.

"My parents could only afford lessons for one of us?"

"Why was that a question?"

I bit my lip. I hadn't meant to phrase it that way, but Luc had heard it anyway. While I hadn't received lessons, Orrin had years after me and my twelve-year-old sister, Saraid, had started a few weeks back.

I had always known my father preferred his children with Deidre. When I had turned down Patriarch Meallán's offer and told her I wouldn't ever marry, Deidre had said no future blood whores would live under her roof. My father hadn't said a word against it. I left their home a couple of months before my nineteenth birthday, but on my own, I could barely afford food, let alone the lessons my siblings had received for free. If my great-aunt hadn't left me her bookshop, I don't know where I'd have gone.

"Even if you were an experienced rider, I wouldn't expect you to mount a hellsteed on the first try," Luc said, breaking the silence. "It's a rather difficult task for humans. You're all so little."

I straightened. "I'm nowhere near little."

The lords glanced at each other, communicating with a single look. Without a word, Luc turned and wrapped massive hands around my waist. I went stiff. Luc lifted me. Up. Up. Up. Higher still. His arms didn't even flex, like my weight posed no strain at all.

He dropped me on Cala's back without so much as a harsh breath. "I'd have to disagree."

Something fluttered in my chest. "To you, I guess."

Luc glanced over at Jules. "Must I lift you on as well?"

The Lord of Dawn batted his eyelashes. "Will you?"

Luc only shot his soulbound a look.

"You're so mean." Jules mounted his hellsteed with ease, settling behind me. His thick, solid thighs pressed against my own softer ones. My back grazed his chest. The unnatural heat of him radiated into me. I straightened, but that only bumped my ass into his groin.

I tried to wriggle forward. His leathers protected him, but I felt him beneath the fabric, long and male and hardening—

Jules's hands shot out and gripped my waist. "Relax, lovely. I won't touch you, as long as you stop grinding that luscious ass of yours against me."

Luscious? Heat flared in my cheeks. My face was surely as red as his cloak. "I wasn't grinding. I was trying to give you space."

"The only thing you've given me is an erection."

The flush spread down my neck.

Luc mounted his hellsteed at our side. "Does our volunteer need to ride with me?"

"No," Jules huffed. "Like you'd be any better. "

Luc glanced back at his soulbound, those silver eyes briefly flicking to me. What did Jules mean? Luc had given me a few brief, half-smirks, but the man was otherwise as stoic and cold as ever.

Without a response, Luc twisted back and kicked his steed into a trot.

Jules must have done the same since we started moving forward, the convoy following behind us. I gripped the pommel at the foreign movement. I would not fall off this horse. Embarrassment aside, it was at least a six-foot fall to the ground and that would hurt.

Unfortunately, my grip didn't stop me from sliding back against the Lord of Dawn's hard, perfect body—

Jules rolled his shoulders back and let out a deep sigh. His erection disappeared as quickly as it came on. Instead of relaxing, my spine stiffened further. I hadn't touched many men—make that any—but I'd read a lot of books, fiction and nonfiction. It didn't seem normal that he... softened almost right away.

But of course he had. I had moved against him, and his body had reacted, but I was just the human volunteer. If Jules ever drank my blood, we'd have sex—but only because of the bloodlust flooding both of us. Vampires were all gorgeous, and plenty of humans were attractive enough by comparison. I wasn't one of them.

What was there to desire about me?

My perfectly ordinary features?

My broad shoulders?

My soft stomach, ass, and thighs?

I resisted the urge to dig my nails into my palms and forced myself out of those toxic thoughts without the help of pain. It didn't matter what I looked like. To the vampires, I was just flesh and blood. But I had a mind. I had thoughts. I was more than my body.

Not to them.

But to me.

And my opinion was the only one that should matter.

Jules rescued me from my inner spiral. "Controlling blood can come in handy."

"What?" I processed his words, and heat flooded to my cheeks. "Oh."

Huh. I never considered that. Azaras had perfect control over his body, but he was a demon. He could literally change shape. Vampires could make fangs and claws out of shadow, but they couldn't shift their whole body.

That apparently didn't mean they couldn't control their own blood.

Jules's grin widened, his chin in the corner of my vision. It had only been three days, and I could count on one hand the number of conversations we'd had, but I knew he was going to say something that would make me want to throw myself off his hellsteed.

I seized the first question that came to mind. "What's it like? Having a soulbond?"

For a second, I thought he wouldn't answer me. That was honestly one of the better options. Who was I to speak to an Azarasian? I had no idea when I had suddenly become so bold—or insane.

"I've never known life without Luc, so I don't know if I could describe it properly." He glanced over at Luc beside us. The Lord of Dusk didn't turn, but he was close enough that even a human could have heard. "What's it like not having a soulbond?"

"Lonely." The word came unbidden to my lips. I had never voiced that aloud. "It can be nice sometimes to sit with your own thoughts, though."

"We sit with our own thoughts all the time," Jules replied.

"You can't read each other's minds?" Karra didn't slip into Azaras's head often, but she'd always seemed to know what he was thinking.

"Soulbound companions can't."

"Companions?"

"Ah, right, you only know about Azaras and Karra's soulbond. Lecturing is more Luc's style, but I suppose I can play the teacher." Jules cleared his throat, his tone shifting into something almost authoritative. "Those of us born with soulbonds can be companions, beloveds, or heartmates. Companions share the weakest bond, while heartmates like Azaras and Karra have the strongest."

I glanced at Luc, but he showed no reaction to Jules's mockery. "And you two are?"

Luc didn't even blink.

"Companions," Jules answered for both of them, his usual tone returning.

"So you can't sense each other's thoughts or talk in your dreams?"

"I have an intuition about Luc," Jules said. "I always know where he is and what he's feeling. If I were to guess at his thoughts, I'd probably be correct, but I never slip into his head. We do usually dream together, though sometimes it's hazy."

"Oh." I fell silent, rewriting my favorite book in my memory. There was only so much I could infer from Karra's story and heavily redacted textbooks. There were a thousand follow-up questions I wanted to ask, but I didn't want to seem too desperate for the scraps of information they threw at me.

The moonlight brightened overhead, pulling me from my thoughts. I looked up as we left the woods, the canopy of branches giving way to an open sky. Stars shimmered above, scattered across the clear night. On the horizon, half of the Blood Star's Guard emerged, the constellation creeping higher as summer neared. In a few nights, the telltale red glow would appear.

Would the Azarasians host a revelry? They hadn't celebrated celestial events in Karra's time since Azaras's godcurse activated between dusk and dawn. Hard to have a nighttime party if your sovereign was a vicious, winged Beast hunting loyal citizens from the sky.

But that had seemed to change after Azaras and Karra left for his hell, at least from what I'd read. The vampires had returned to their roots, celebrating the stars once more.

The road ahead took us through a wide, open meadow cloaked in somber silver. Tall grass swayed gently in the soft breeze as far as my eye could see—

Until it didn't.

Dark, glowing rock scarred the earth in a wide circle of impacted ground. The pit stretched across the entire meadow, its edges like claws gouging the land. Shadows wafted from the otherworldly stone, daemium in its purest form. It almost seemed to absorb the light of the bright moons. The darkness was nearly transparent at the edges of the pit, but it rose like a plume of smoke at the center.

At the impact site.

"Is that a starcrater?" I asked into the sudden silence, the Maboni in the wagons behind us falling quiet at the sight.

"It is."

I licked my lips. Fuck. A real-life starcrater. "Whose?"

Jules snorted. "I don't have the faintest idea."

"Gadeth," Luc replied. "He's a minor demon in Azaras's court."

"Minor as in weak?"

Luc nodded. "For a demon, yes."

"So this is a small starcrater?"

"In this region," Luc said. "Azaras and Isaura were banished with half their courts in the Second Godsfall. There are almost two thousand impact sites across the Impire alone."

"So we'll see more?"

The corner of his lip curled at my eager tone. "Certainly."

I tried to snap my jaw shut. I would see multiple starcraters. My books were coming to life before me, both fiction and fact. I could almost forget why I was here and who I was with.

A man had died in front of me less than an hour ago. More would in the days to come. But the world was wide, and I had seen so little of it, so a single peek made me forget all reason, all rationale.

I would never see it all. Once we reached our destination, who knew if I'd ever leave? I might spend the rest of my life in an Azarasian city—whether that life lasted a dozen hours or a dozen years.

So for this moment, I watched shadows rise like steam from a starcrater in the moonlight with two gorgeous vampires.

A part of me never wanted this adventure to end.

But this wasn't a story.

There would be no happy ending.

"Pass the stone posts at your own peril."

The warrior's words barely penetrated my mind, not when my gaze fixed on the bundle at my feet.

Soap.

The vampires had dumped bundles of *soap* at our feet.

My eyes flickered to the beach of pale pebbles before a clear blue lake. Twenty feet from the water's edge, wooden posts jutted from the lakebed. A runespell flickered on each one, a faded swirl of shadows. Around a dozen dotted this side of the lake, the furthest one visible beyond a rocky outcrop overtaken by spindly trees.

I swallowed. They wanted us to bathe. Together. All three hundred of us, men and women, standing and sweating in the afternoon sun.

I tried to sniff myself discreetly. We'd spent the past three days crammed in wagons, but time and stress had taken its toll. Especially those harvested from the western reaches of Mabon, who'd endured an extra week of travel to get to the east coast. The vampires still looked perfect and pristine. Their harvest, not so much.

Perhaps that was why I fell asleep in Jules's arms, only to wake in an empty wagon. Someone had laid a deep blue cloak on the floor and wrapped another red cloak around me as a blanket. And by someone, I meant the Lords of Dusk and Dawn. The thick scent of Luc's dark spice beneath me and Jules's rich, smoked honey above me melded into an intoxicating combination I wanted to sink into forever.

In four days, I had somehow memorized the lords' scents.

I'd thought that would be my most horrifying revelation of the day. Then I'd been ushered from my wagon and told I needed to strip down and bathe in a lake with three hundred other people while a bunch of vampires watched from the shore.

"You have twenty minutes." The vampire warrior's tone left no room for argument. Not that anyone but me could argue.

The Maboni started undressing. Some quickly, others slowly, but all with a sense of quiet resignation. They couldn't disobey the command, but they controlled the pace of their obedience. The vampire warrior hadn't specified, so it was up to interpretation.

"While you don't have to obey, you also only have twenty minutes, Miss Halloran."

I didn't spin around. It took everything in me to stand still as I gained two shadows at my back. The lords had stayed near my wagon all day, chatting and laughing. I heard them, but the words never seemed to land, slipping away before I could grasp them. Now, their words were clear. But this was the first time they'd addressed me directly since last night. When I overstepped so many times and yet somehow kept my head.

Why stop now? "You're just going to watch, aren't you?"

"There's nothing wrong with watching."

There was something else in Jules's tone, a joke I didn't understand. I twisted, frowning. Jules only grinned.

"You could drown," Luc said. "Or swim away."

"I'd have better luck running."

Jules snorted. "That's saying something. If you made it to the treeline, it'd only be because we let you." He paused, then added wistfully, "I do love a good chase."

I stabbed my nails into my arms. The flare of pain stopped my shudder at the Lord of Dawn's words. The idea was equal parts terrifying and thrilling. When Azaras chased Karra through his hell, I hadn't understood how she could want to fuck the demon while utterly petrified of him.

Now I had more firsthand experience I never asked for.

Public bathing didn't need to join the list.

"Can't swim?" Luc asked. His tone made it clear he already knew the answer.

"No," I grumbled.

"Let me guess," he said. "Only your siblings received lessons."

I twisted around and almost glared at the Lord of Dusk. But when I saw the edge of his shoulder, I flipped straight back. I needed to get out of the habit of glaring. And honestly, I deserved this one. Why had I shared something personal with vampires? Idiot. Heat flooded my face and chest.

Fuck it.

I grabbed the laces at the front of my chemise and started pulling. If I didn't open my eyes, I didn't have to see anyone looking at me. They already were, whispering about me even more since I was swept onto a hellsteed by monsters with the faces of godstars.

Being naked wouldn't change that.

The final lace went slack in my hands. The neckline of my chemise gaped open. A breeze grazed my chest, tickling along the tops of my breasts—

Nope. Fuck that. I swallowed back a wave of nausea. I couldn't do this.

"And if I don't want to bathe?"

The lords looked at each other over my head. The thralls couldn't disobey. I doubted any former volunteers had either. Did they even know what to do with a disobedient human?

I was sure they could figure it out, but even that wasn't enough to get me in the lake.

Luc took a step and waved me forward. "Come with us."

I swallowed. "Why?"

Jules dropped one arm over my shoulder. I instantly stiffened, but he ignored it. He pointed past the other Maboni to the rock outcropping. "If we go through the trees there, there's a small inlet on the other side. No one standing here will be able to see you."

"Oh." What a... considerate offer. I didn't like it one bit. "Why?"

"You should know the answer by now."

"Because I'm your volunteer." They still hadn't told me what I'd volunteered for, but it was the only explanation.

"Exactly."

"Take the offer, Miss Halloran," Luc said, waiting for me to decide. "It can't hurt you."

"You'd be surprised." This was definitely going to hurt me. Maybe not physically. Maybe not today. But soon.

The kindness of *vampires* was winning me over.

I even knew it was fake, but that didn't matter. There had to be something in the food or water they gave us, some parasite that addled the brain. Either that, or I had grown far more lonely than I thought in my bookshop.

When I became nothing more than a snack, my fanciful heart would break.

Served it right.

But that didn't mean I wouldn't take the offer. "Very well."

Luc led the way, heading straight toward where Jules had pointed. The Maboni in his path scrambled out of his way. An older man tripped on his half-removed trousers and landed on his face, his bare ass pale in the sun.

I glanced away. I was the only one—because I'd been the only one watching. Every other human was too focused on their own embarrassment, and the vampires didn't give a shit about nudity.

When we reached the trees, Luc pushed into the brush. The greenery parted to reveal a narrow beach before the forest took over completely. It was a secluded inlet, exactly like the Lord of Dawn had said. I heard the other Maboni, catching glimpses of their bodies through the trees. But if I wanted to bathe—and I really wanted to bathe—this was the smallest audience I was going to get.

Jules twisted at my side, dropping his arm from my shoulder and gesturing to the beach with a flourish like a showman. "After you."

I barely managed to nod in reply. The Lord of Dawn's bright golden eyes twinkled mischievously. Back straight, I crossed the pebbles toward the shoreline. Pushing off my shoes, I dipped a toe into the water. It wasn't the warmest, but I'd bathed in colder.

And yet, I remained clothed. The lords stood behind me, their attention on my back like a physical caress. I shivered.

Perhaps a small audience was actually a worse way to bathe.

Too late to change my mind.

I looked out over the water. Trees lined the far side, a patchwork of green and brown rising into the foothills of nearby mountains. At the far end, the lake curved left, disappearing beyond the treeline. If I swam out into the depths, ignoring the fact that I'd drown instantly, how far could I see over the open water? Would it be like the ocean, stretching into a seamless blue horizon?

Did it matter? I couldn't swim, so I'd never know. And even if I could, it'd mean passing the posts.

I focused on the one marking this small section of beach. It stood in line with the others, ending with a post on the shore to my right. Each wooden post speared five or six feet out of the water, the flickering runespell the only indication of its purpose. *Protect. Shield. Barrier.* The border stones around Corraidin had the shielding and barrier rune, but I'd never seen the protection rune before.

"What are the posts protecting us from?" I asked. "We're inland, so it can't be Thaddeus you're concerned about. Does Azaras have a habit of pulling people into his hell realm through the water?"

The lords didn't answer for a long moment. I twisted slightly. They were communicating with a look again. They couldn't read each other's minds, but they certainly didn't need words.

"Occasionally," Luc replied, his voice unusually stoic.

"He's a real fucker," Jules added.

"Have you met?"

Jules glanced at Luc. "Unfortunately."

I frowned. "I didn't think a normal Azarasian lord would know one of the most powerful demons on the planet."

"A normal Azarasian lord wouldn't," Luc said.

"And?"

"And I think you're trying to procrastinate bathing."

Heat rushed to my cheeks. "I am not."

Luc arched a dark brow, his lips curving slightly. "I didn't know the Maboni bathed fully dressed and without water."

"There's lots you don't know about us." I crossed my arms. "For instance, we prefer to bathe without two strangers watching."

Jules grinned, all sharp amusement. "So one is acceptable?" His voice turned low, teased. "Which one?"

I stiffened. "What? No, I didn't say that."

"Pity." Jules sighed in faux disappointment. "I wanted to win."

"Would you win?" Luc asked, calm and unruffled.

"You're terrifying, Lucey, so of course I'd win."

Luc's silver eyes fixed on me, his head tilting ever so slightly. "Are you terrified of me, Miss Halloran?"

My heart nearly stopped. "I didn't say that." My gaze dropped to my clothes, my thumb rubbing absently against the fabric. "If you must know, you both terrify me equally."

A moment passed in silence, only the breeze and distant voices breaking the quiet.

"Can't have that." Jules moved in my periphery, his arms lifting as fabric shuffled—

My head snapped up.

He was taking off his shirt.

*Had* taken off his shirt.

Jules dropped the leathers to the pebbled beach. The muscles in his arm flexed as he reached up to run his fingers through his tousled hair. The white-blond tips brushed against the sculpted expanse of his shoulders. He wasn't as broad as Luc, but his body was still a masterpiece of masculine strength. My gaze drifted, unbidden, tracing the defined muscles of his smooth, pale chest. The carved ridges of his abdomen tapered into a sharp V that disappeared into the dark waistband of his pants.

Disappointment almost curled my lip. I held it back, along with my flush. I needed to look away, but my eyes wouldn't leave his body. Why was my mouth suddenly dry? "What are you doing?"

"Taking my clothes off."

"I can see that. Why?"

"You said you didn't want us to watch. It's not watching if we're bathing, too."

Fucking excuse me? My stomach plummeted. "You don't need a bath. You smell fantastic."

Jules stepped closer, slow and deliberate, the heat of him bleeding into the air between us. "Were you sniffing me, Nessa?"

My breath hitched. The lazy way he said my name coiled through me. "What? No. I didn't say that. You were on the same hellsteed, like right behind me—"

"And you fell asleep in my lap, soft and innocent and oh so delectable." His golden gaze gleamed with amusement. "If we're judging who needs a bath based on how badly we want to lick each other, then I'm afraid neither of us gets to bathe."

My lips parted, then snapped shut. "Why—you—I—Fuck."

I spun, facing the water. Godstars, my skin was probably flushed as red as my sister's hair—and nowhere near as flattering. I huffed out a long breath. The faster I got this over with, the faster I could put my clothes back on.

I could do this. I *had* to do this. I was nearly thirty years old. Eventually, someone would see me naked. Neither of the lords was my husband, but the Church's rules no longer applied.

With unsteady fingers, I slipped off the borrowed cloak and set aside the satchel holding *The Soulborne Queen*. I hadn't bothered retying the laces of my chemise, so I focused on working my way down my kirtle instead.

Behind me, buckles clattered and fabric rustled. I stared so intently at the nearest post that my brain started to ache.

I would *not* turn.

I would *not* look.

Jules might not have meant for this, but I almost didn't care that I'd be naked if they were, too.

I pulled the garment open and slipped out of it. My chemise billowed, a shapeless drape of white cloth. Once-white cloth, more like. It was now mostly dirt and sweat, but I didn't remove it right away.

Once it was gone, my drawers would be the only layer left between their eyes and me. Almost every inch of my soft curves, the faint silver lines on my breasts and hips, the dimples in my thighs...

They'd see *everything*.

I loosened the chemise's collar and let the dress slide down my body. I untied the strings of my drawers just as quickly. If I thought too hard, I would panic. I just needed to do it.

But I couldn't contain everything. Emotion flared hot and sharp in my chest as the triangle of dark curls between my legs met the daylight. I stomped it down. It surged again at the sight of faint red spots on my drawers. My bleedings had never been regular, so I hadn't packed spare cloth. Stress always left me cramping and spotting, even if the pain was dulled now. I shouldn't have been surprised. Of course, there was blood.

I exhaled slowly. It was natural. All of this—me—was natural.

Too natural.

I knew how the lords would see me. I knew my flaws. I had lived with them since the day my stepmother moved in and looked down her dainty nose at me. Since the day Aislin was born a little bundle of perfection.

But my time was up.

Two bodies moved behind me, their heat like a breeze against my skin. I didn't need to turn to sense the predators at my back.

If I didn't get in the lake, I had a feeling I'd be thrown in.

I still couldn't see them. Not entirely. But they were there, two shapes in my periphery. I stared straight ahead as if turning my gaze might kill me. Maybe it would. The rippling muscles of Jules's chest had nearly made my heart explode. How was I supposed to handle the sight of two naked vampires?

My gaze drifted to my right, along the sharp planes of Luc's bare shoulders—

I grabbed my soap and marched straight into the lake.

Then scrambled back out. "Fuck, that's cold."

"And here I was, hot," Jules murmured, voice thick with delight... and something darker, something that curled low in my stomach.

"How could you possibly—?" I turned. I don't know why I turned. It was the natural thing to do when speaking to someone, right?

Right.

It was a terrible idea if that someone and his devastatingly handsome soulbound weren't wearing anything.

MY GAZE DIDN'T KNOW where to start first.

Whichever godstar had carved Jules had also sculpted Luc, but with a heavier, more merciless hand. Where Jules was all sleek, effortless beauty, Luc was sheer power, his broad chest gleaming like burnished bronze in the light. Strength coiled in the deep ridges of his chest, the thick lines of his arms. Every inch of him was carved for war, for dominance, for destruction. And unlike Jules, who wore his allure like a weapon, Luc seemed utterly indifferent to the effect he had.

It was simply a fact.

Both lords were relatively hairless, their skin smooth and unmarred, but Luc had a finely manicured line of dark hair that started just below his navel. It was a perfect, deliberate path, one that seemed designed to draw the eye lower. My gaze followed it helplessly, leading down, down, down...

Holy fuck.

I gaped. Just gaped. My brain had finally seen enough. Murder and guts hadn't done it, but a massive vampire cock was my limit.

Make that *two* massive vampire cocks. My gaze flickered between the lords. Neither of them were hard thanks to their control over blood—or lack of attraction to me. I honestly didn't even have it in me to feel insecure at this second. My mind couldn't comprehend the sight.

How would they fit?

I had fingered myself once, an experience that had resulted in a flash of pain shooting through my lower belly. The pain my pleasure had caused wasn't worth the trade, so I had never tried again. And now, standing here, staring at these two monsters, I couldn't imagine how I'd go from nothing to *that* without splitting in two. Even with the help of their venom.

Were they going to feed from me? I hadn't witnessed either of the lords with a thrall. Maybe they had dragged some unsuspecting human into a secluded area of the woods.

Like where we were right now.

"Lovely?"

My head jerked up.

Both lords smirked, but Jules's lips stretched into a full grin the moment our gazes met. "I thought humans found it impolite to stare."

My flush deepened. "I'm... uh, shit, sorry."

"We're not human. Stare all you like." Jules let his gaze drop. "I certainly plan to."

Every part of me locked up as both the lords perused me. Their pupils had expanded, swallowing all color until nothing but black remained. A whisper from the past curled through my mind, a lesson from school buried deep in my subconscious.

Beware the black-eyed vampire.

There was no surer sign you were being hunted.

"We lucked out this time," Luc murmured, his deep voice almost a rumble.

"That we did."

My pulse kicked up, sharp and jittery, like a bird trapped in my chest. It was just the blood in my veins they wanted. They couldn't possibly desire me. But I couldn't calm my heart, not with their black eyes roaming me at their leisure. Heat pooled between my legs.

I lifted my chin like I wasn't petrified and aroused all at once, twisted, and stomped into the lake. This time, I didn't turn back as water crawled along my calves and thighs. I wouldn't freeze to death, not with my ass.

I would, however, die if I had to keep staring at two naked gods made flesh.

When the water reached my waist, I dropped into the chill. My nipples peaked, my exposed shoulders tingling.

Ah, shit. Where was my soap? I stared down at my hands as if the bar might magically reappear. I must have dropped it in shock.

I didn't turn. I would rather float out here until I drowned than turn back to shore and face the vampire lords standing there—

Water splashed. A large shape moved just beneath the surface to my right. A few feet in front of me, before the posts, Luc emerged from the lake. His bronze skin glistened. Droplets traced down the hard planes of his torso. He swept his inky black hair from his face, the motion rippling through him. Those silver eyes flicked up, locking onto mine.

I gaped. Just gaped.

A ruby-ringed finger tapped the bottom of my jaw and nudged it shut.

I startled, tingles prickling up my spine as Jules glided around me, moving through the water with more grace than I could ever hope for on land.

"Seems you lost your soap."

I tried to frown, but my lips just twitched, as confused as I was. "Guess I'll stay dirty then."

"It's another three days to Montaurère." Luc swam around my other side, just as predatory and graceful. "This is your only chance before we reach the Capital of Dawn."

I caught the end of my braid, twisting it between my fingers. If I didn't keep my hands busy, I was afraid they'd betray me. "Well, none of us have any soap, so I couldn't get clean even if I wanted to."

Luc drifted closer. "That's not entirely true. Do you want to be clean, Miss Halloran?"

I swallowed. The water rippled between us, heat licking at my skin like the sunlight on the back of my neck. It took everything in me to keep my voice steady, but I couldn't stop the rasp. "That would be preferable."

"Then let's get you clean."

Luc reached out and brushed a finger along my shoulder. My nipples peaked at the touch. I sank further into the water like that would somehow hide my reaction, but the water was clear and my breasts weren't small. The chill wasn't doing anything to help, either.

Luc arched a brow at me as Jules grinned. The Lord of Dusk's finger remained on my shoulder, twisting and looping...

Wait. He was drawing a rune.

I figured it out a second before the magic flashed against my skin. The rune didn't burn as intently as his healing rune had last night. Jules had mentioned something about his magic being weaker and harder to use after dusk. I didn't fully understand Azarasian soulbonds and how they impacted magic, but since it was daytime now, did that meant Luc was now the weaker one? He didn't seem strained, but he was a master at hiding his emotions. I had watched him strip all emotion from his face in an instant before his warriors.

The magic washed over my body. The change was subtle but instantaneous, just like the soothing rune. I felt... clean. The water had rinsed away some of the dirt and sweat, but this? This was different. The grime from travel and stickiness from stress were simply gone.

So that was why the warriors didn't bathe. They kept themselves clean with magic.

My gaze snapped between them. "Are you serious? If you have cleaning runes, why are we bathing in a lake? Why do you even have soap if you have runes that work instantly?"

Jules treaded backward into the deeper water. "Just because we have a cleaning rune doesn't mean we don't bathe. No rune can compete with a nice bathtub or shower."

What was a shower? I tucked the word away for later investigation.

"The rune doesn't take much magic, but there are three hundred of you," Luc said. "Providing soap is simply more efficient."

"So we got in the freezing water for no reason."

"There was a reason," the Lord of Dawn said, floating onto his back—

I snapped my attention back to Luc. Better to look at him from the chest up than risk seeing the long stretch of Jules's perfect body. "What reason?"

Luc didn't hesitate. "Jules wanted to see you naked."

"*What?*" I squeaked, the word shooting out embarrassingly high.

Luc's half-smirk grew, slow and effortless. It turned the cool, sculpted perfection of his face into something radiant. "I enjoyed the sight as well."

My thighs clenched together. I closed my eyes and breathed in slowly, burying my attraction. My broken body had fought harder and harder the closer I got to my thirtieth birthday. The new stress in my life wouldn't help. Neither would my errant desire. The lords' runespells helped my pain and nausea, but nothing so far had banished the draining fatigue I battled on and off this entire trip.

I couldn't risk it.

A shout sounded from the other side of the rock formation, followed by frantic splashes. My eyes jolted open. A blond human, barely a few years younger than me, had plunged past the posts and was now kicking wildly into the lake.

Jules snorted, his hair a pale gold halo around his face as he floated past me. "Looks like we've got a runner." He paused, brow furrowing. "Swimmer?"

But how...? *Pass the stone posts at your own peril.* The words echoed in my head. "You only *suggested* they not pass the posts. Why?"

"You'll have your answer in a second," Luc said, watching the man paddle further into the blue.

"What—"

The lake erupted. A massive, azure-scaled snake burst from the water, its body cutting through the surface like a blade. A maw of gleaming fangs opened wide. The blond man barely had time to scream before the serpent's jaws clamped around him, piercing clean through his torso. His wail reverberated across the lake—

Then cut off as the snake dove back into the depths, taking its snack with it.

I thought I had moved fast getting into the water. I was halfway to the shore before my brain even finished processing the instinct in me shrieking to run.

Jules's melodic laugh bubbled behind me. I didn't turn until my feet touched the shore. I spun, panting, willing my breath to stay steady. "If you want to bathe with a *giant fucking lake monster*, be my guest."

"The runespell on the posts keep the hellserpents away from the shores," Luc said.

"Oh." I looked back out over the now-quiet lake. All that remained of the hellserpent and the man was a ripple in the water, tingled with blood. "You should've said that."

Jules laughed again. "And missed the sight of you running for the shores? I don't think so."

"Or this delightful view right now?" Luc held my gaze for a second before his eyes slowly dropped.

Oh, yeah. I was still naked. I froze. My heartbeat stuttered as blood rushed to my face, staining my cheeks.

Jules leered at me just as shamelessly as his soulbound. "Look at that blush. You're beautiful, Nessa."

Beautiful? That snapped me out of the trance. Luc was carved from bronze, his silver eyes sharp beneath the tumble of black curls. Jules burned like a simmering flame, all wicked smiles framed by the face of a godstar.

And me? I was the least beautiful thing in eyesight.

I yanked my chemise up from the ground, clutching it like a flimsy shield. Now that I was clean, I really didn't want to put my dirty clothes back on. But I wanted to be naked even less.

Jules pouted. "Pity."

"You're going to get your gown wet," Luc said.

"I'm not standing around naked until I dry."

"No need." Luc approached, unhurried, stepping from the lake like he had all the time in the world. Technically, he did, being immortal and all. The sunlight traced more and more of his brown skin with every passing second. My eyes drifted down—

*Don't look at his cock again, idiot.*

My neck craned as Luc stopped before me, my chemise the only thing keeping our naked bodies apart. Fuck. This whole thing had been a terrible idea. They had tricked me into getting undressed—sort of—but I should have seen the trap.

Everything was a trap with vampires.

Without a word, Luc drew two small runes in the air before him. *Clean. Dry.* I kept my gaze on his face like my life depended on it. That full, arrogant smirk of his nearly knocked the air from my lungs again.

Stars, he was gorgeous. There was something magnetic about his presence. I had felt it with the Lady Delphine and Lord Raul, but they hadn't focused on me the way Luc did. The way both lords did. Their attention made it all the harder to break away.

"Miss Halloran?"

"Yes?"

"You can get dressed now," Luc said, his voice almost amused, like he was suppressing a laugh. "You're dry and your gown is clean."

"What?" My gaze dropped. Shit. He was right. The puddle beneath my feet was the only sign I'd been drenched moments ago.

I spun around and tossed on my chemise, then dropped to grab my drawers and kirtle. Both were freshly cleaned, my drawers free of bloodstains. I didn't think too hard about Luc cleaning my undergarments with magic and shoved everything on as fast as possible.

The lords had no such urgency. Jules twirled through the water, completely at ease, while Luc remained where he was, watching his soulbound. I kept my eyes on the trees, keeping their outlines in my periphery.

Somewhere beyond the outcropping, faint crying reached my ears. My stomach twisted. Had the blond thrall left behind friends or family among the harvest? Or was it simply the raw horror of watching someone get devoured by a hellserpent?

I spoke into the silence. "Did you intentionally make the command vague to see if anyone tried to escape?"

"Some of your countrymen doubted the wilds were filled with hellbeasts," Luc said.

They obviously hadn't seen the giant hellwolves. "You ordered them not to run from the wagon. Even if they believed the forest was safe, why does it matter?"

"The thrall runespell demands obedience, but vague commands allow for interpretation," Luc said, as measured as ever. "If not, that man wouldn't have been able to swim away."

My stomach dropped. "But as he wasn't *running*, the earlier order didn't apply."

"Precisely."

A sharp twist of anger curled through my chest. How callous. It wasn't even cruelty—it was cold practicality, a decision made and measured, already in the past.

"He didn't need to die to prove a point."

Luc's silver gaze remained steady, unreadable. "That's not how this world works, Miss Halloran."

He didn't say the words harshly, but the surprising gentleness stung more than cruelty ever could. I could have argued against sharp words, raged at something brutal. But this? This was just a fact.

Unshakable.

Unchangeable.

I had known the brutal truth for years, but I had never accepted it.

I crossed my arms, a tight grasp around my chest. Like the pressure was the last thing holding me upright. "It should be."

For a moment, I thought Luc might say something else, something more. The moment passed. He moved, stepping toward his folded leathers and discarded axe. A chill prickled down my spine at the awareness of the vampire at my back, but turning meant facing Jules.

When Luc next spoke, all softness had vanished, leaving only the commander. "Our twenty minutes are up, Julien."

Jules sighed. "Yes, Dad."

Luc shot him a pointed look.

Jules grinned but didn't push it. He reached the shallows and climbed to his feet, water rushing down his—

Nope.

I forced my gaze to my hands, anxiously rubbing my fingers. "When will we stop again?"

"We're setting up camp here for the night," Luc said.

I frowned. "We're stopping for a full night?"

"Even vampires need to sleep eventually."

# 11

A SCREECH RIPPED THROUGH the silent night, tearing through my dreams. I jolted awake into utter darkness. My breath caught in my chest. I pulled the cloak that had become my blanket tighter around my shoulders. It smelled less and less like the Lords of Dusk and Dawn, but when I closed my eyes and breathed in, the lingering traces of spice and smoke still clung to it.

Whatever was out there in the darkness, whatever hellbeast, wasn't the real threat. We had traveled *alongside* that for days.

I couldn't see any of the vampires. Couldn't see much of anything beyond the twinkle of stars above. Vampires didn't need warmth or light, so they didn't bother with fires. A dozen warriors could stand at the end of my wagon, staring right back into my unseeing eyes, and I wouldn't know.

I didn't think anyone was there. I couldn't hear breathing or footsteps, but they could hide that. Still, I didn't sense anything. Maybe it was instinct, the same one that sent a prickle across my skin whenever someone watched me.

The hairs on the back of my neck stood.

Like *that.*

I swallowed, my heart kicking into a pounding rhythm. I clenched my fists. I would *not* panic. Hysteria was never the right answer when a predator watched. That only excited them. I had no interest in seeing the Lord of Dusk and Dawn's black-eyed gazes again.

Light flared before me, a small rune of shadows that ruptured the air before bursting into flame. Two sets of eyes caught the glow. Luc stood at the end of my wagon, the runelight hovering above his raised hand. Behind him, Jules lounged with his back against a log, watching.

Both their gazes fixed on me, silver and gold irises reduced to thin rings around blackened pupils.

"Good morning, Miss Halloran," Luc drawled. "Sleep well?"

Thankfully, fear had locked my muscles too tight to shudder at his dulcet tones. "Well enough. Good morning." Shit. Wrong order. It was too early to form a sentence. "Is it morning? Seems a bit dark for a morning."

Luc's lip twitched at my babbling. I think. His smirks were hard enough to catch in daylight, much less in the dark. "The sun will rise in less than an hour. This is close enough to count."

"Will we be—" I swallowed and tried to wet my lips, but my mouth was too dry. "Are we leaving?"

"Soon." Luc's gaze dropped to my bobbing throat. He didn't glance back up. His eyes had been black before because of the low light, but now a different sort of hunger stared back at me.

Jules propped one elbow on the log. "Join us for breakfast."

Every part of me tensed, equal parts fear and anticipation. I swallowed again. Stars, I needed some water. "For breakfast or *for* breakfast?"

"The first," Luc said, extending a hand. "Unfortunately."

My stomach flipped. *Unfortunately*. Fuck, what an answer.

I steeled my spine, ran a hand over my messy braid, and shuffled to the end of the wagon. Luc stepped back as I swung my legs over the edge and fixed my skirts. I could easily hop down to the ground. I wasn't short, except to a vampire. But the Lord of Dusk's hand was there. I hadn't turned it down before and it seemed rude to start now, even knowing he wanted to eat me.

I placed my hand in his and hopped down. I flinched when I hit the dirt, the ache in my thighs from hours on a hellsteed. Luc's thumb traced lightly across my skin. *Soothe*. All the pain waking in my body faded back into slumber.

"Thank you," I murmured, heat creeping into my cheeks.

He only nodded in reply. Without releasing me, we walked toward his soulbound, the runelight floating close beside us.

When we reached the two logs, Luc looped a finger through the rune and tossed it down. It slammed into a pit in the dirt near Jules's boots and burst into a roaring fire. The lords' eyes flared again, and beyond them, the bright flames caught a dozen others. The glowing disappeared as soon as the fire settled.

I had known we weren't alone, but now it was impossible to forget.

Jules patted the log beside him. "Sit."

Luc released my hand and sank onto the log across from Jules, stretching his legs out. I sat. What else was there to do? Jules looped an arm over the log, resting it behind me. His warmth radiated against my hips, close enough to touch.

Luc pulled a canteen from the saddlebag beside him and passed it over, alongside a hardtack biscuit. A crumb-covered cloth sat in a crumpled ball beside Jules. Blood only replenished a vampire's magic, so they needed ordinary food to survive, too. In *The Soulborne Queen*, the Beast King's vampires had nightly feasts filled with dishes I had never heard of and couldn't imagine, the flavors exploding on Karra's tongue. Nothing I'd eaten so far compared.

I bit into the hard biscuit. "I thought you'd have better food than us."

"There's only so much you can prepare on horseback," Luc said.

"You could stop to cook something better."

Jules snorted. "We'd never get anywhere at that pace."

Gold flashed in the dark. A moment later, Tristan appeared, the silver-eyed woman with black hair and brown skin at his side. His soulbound, Estrella. Jules had told me they were heartmates, the closest of soulbonds. Maybe that was why they rarely exchanged words or glances, yet moved in perfect step as if thoughts and actions were one. Azaras and Karra hadn't moved like that, but their bond was still fresh in my book, not centuries carved into stone.

Both soulbound warriors bore an insignia with the Impire's star. While the lords wore no visible mark of status, the four vampires stood apart. It wasn't something they did, exactly. It was in the way the other vampires watched them—or rather, didn't, eyes always averted, always respectful.

My pondering cut off when another shape resolved at Tristan's side. A pretty Maboni woman with long black hair. One of the blood thralls. I didn't know her name, but I knew her face.

Fuck.

I wasn't about to feed a vampire. But apparently I was about to watch. Heat rushed to my cheeks. I didn't know if it was terror, embarrassment... or some darker curiosity I refused to name.

The real breakfast had arrived.

"Imperator." Tristan bowed deeply, fist pressed to his chest. Without another word, he and his soulbound melted back into the dark, their task complete.

Before I recovered from my shock, the blood thrall hurried to Luc and kneeled at his feet.

Nausea swirled in my gut. I tucked the biscuit into my pocket, no longer hungry. The thralls chosen to feed the warriors had been terrified on that first day aboard the ship. Now they almost seemed disappointed when they weren't selected.

The textbooks the Azarasians provided us hadn't lied then. Vampire venom was addictive.

And I'd have that poison in my veins any day now.

Luc's gaze flicked to Jules. "Are you hungry?"

"I ate yesterday."

Luc hummed, then turned his attention to me. His silver eyes held mine for a second before dropping to my pulse. My heartbeat stuttered. He gave a small shake, rolling his massive shoulders back. Then he looked down at the thrall all but squirming at his feet.

"Agony or ecstasy?"

A shudder rippled through me. I had read those words but never heard them aloud. The vampires in *The Soulborne Queen* had asked it of their thralls, giving them the choice between the agony of a dry bite and the orgasmic pleasure of their venom.

"Ecstasy, my lord," she blurted, almost before he'd finished speaking.

I tried not to curl my lip. She didn't deserve my judgment. If I were lucky, I'd never hear a sermon about the sin of lust again, and that tiny voice within me would wither away. "You actually let your thralls choose?"

"It doesn't harm us either way," Luc said, his gaze fixed on the thrall. She tilted toward him, mesmerized by his presence the same way I was every time we interacted. Her shoulders relaxed, tension melting from her limbs.

Jules dropped his head against the log, glancing up at me. "It's only our prey that doesn't have a good time during a dry bite."

Fergus's scream of unimaginable agony echoed in my ears. The evisceration hadn't helped, but his cry had changed the second Jules sunk his fangs in and swallowed down a gulp of blood.

How terrible was the bite of agony if it hurt more than being sliced open?

I repressed my shudder. If I were lucky, I'd never know.

Luc tapped his knee, snapping me out of my thoughts. The woman scrambled up, hiked her skirt, and perched her *bare* ass on Luc's clothed leg. Maboni women wore thigh-length drawers. Always. But vampire venom had a way of unraveling modesty.

My eyes widened, but I didn't make a noise. If you didn't count my heart pounding, a drumming beat to both vampires' ears. The thrall's gaze flickered to mine, something wild in it. Shame crossed her face, but not enough to climb off Luc's lap.

I should have looked away.

But then Luc cupped her jaw, fingers curling beneath her chin. He tilted her head back, exposing the long, vulnerable line of her throat.

She jerked in his lap, her gasp audible. Or had I gasped? I couldn't tell. My flush spread from my cheeks, down into my chest, past my breasts and stomach, and settled between my legs.

Jules inhaled deeply. "You're enjoying this as much as I am, aren't you?"

I stiffened. My thighs pressed together. Shit. I needed psychological help. I shouldn't have been this intrigued. But I always had been by vampires. If their venom numbed the pain of the bite, could it dull the pain of my illness? Could I finally feel pleasure instead of cramping agony?

Or would even venom fail to dull the ache?

Jules didn't wait for my answer. Not even an immortal had that kind of time. "Want me to narrate?"

I blinked at him. "Narrate... what?"

Jules's smile widened. Luc snorted.

Narrate *what*?

Before I asked again—or Jules let loose another quip—shadows flashed in Luc's mouth. They twisted, solidified, and latched onto the tips of his canines.

In a blink, the shadows stretched into hard, black-tipped *fangs*.

My skin pebbled. A chill stopped my heart. I drank in every detail. I hadn't seen Jules's fangs when he tore out Fergus's throat, and what I'd imagined before the harvest hadn't been quite right. They were longer. Sharper. The ends tapered into wicked, needle-thin points.

Then Luc plunged them into the thrall's neck.

She screamed... but not in pain. She had chosen ecstasy, and Luc delivered. Bloodlust hit her fast and hard. She immediately plunged a hand between her legs, craving friction.

Luc released her throat, his fingers trailing downward. But not to touch. One hand wrenched her legs apart, the other unlacing his trousers.

My mouth went dry.

"Bloodlust is nearly impossible to resist." I jerked as Jules's whisper ghosted against my ear. He had slithered onto the log beside me while I was too distracted to notice. "For the prey, certainly, but also for the predator. Look at Luc's cock again, lovely."

I couldn't stop myself. My eyes had already dropped, following Luc's hands. The woman ground herself back against something large and thick and... pierced with silver studs? I hadn't noticed those earlier, but the Lord of Dusk hadn't gotten hard during our swim. With every gulp of her blood, Luc's cock stiffened more.

When those black eyes opened and met mine, there was a wildness to them that wasn't there a moment ago.

The hunger of a vampire for blood and sex.

When the blood thrall next flung herself back, Luc lifted her hips and impaled her on his cock.

I gasped. Heat flared in my core. My entire body tightened at the sight before me.

"Luc plunged into a soft, warm cunt, wishing it belonged to the woman sitting across from him," Jules said.

A shiver wracked through my body. Oh, stars, why did the bastard choose to narrate *this*?

His fangs embedded in her neck, Luc started bouncing the thrall up and down his length. She gripped his knees for leverage and let out a shameless moan. The wild abandon of the venom had taken all her sense, making her just as desperate as the Lord of Dusk.

But his black-eyed gaze didn't leave me.

"Luc lapped his tongue against her pulse again, devouring that delicious blood. Her cunt clenched on his thick cock as he spiraled higher. Lost to the pleasure of the bite."

My cunt clenched, sadly around nothing. I tried to settle my breathing, but it was too hot in my cheeks, in my chest, *under* my skin. Luc wasn't fucking me.

I wished he was.

I wished he wasn't.

And the lords saw all of it, drinking in my every expression. There were four of us around the fire, but to the vampires, it might as well have been three. Through the turmoil of my clashing emotions, I could almost hear my stepmother's judgment, her voice whispering, *Wicked, sinful girl.*

"Luc pulled her off his length," Jules continued as his soulbound's glistening cock flashed in the firelight, the hint of a silver stud twinkling, "before thrusting her back down."

The thrall suddenly thrashed. Her body arched as she screamed. She sounded like she was dying. She *looked* like she was dying. And in that moment, bliss-drunk and shaking, I wasn't sure she'd care if she did.

Jules arched one brow at the display. "And she came instantly. Good for you, Luc."

The thrall shuddered, but Luc just fucked her harder and faster. The muscles in his arm flexed, the same arms that had lifted me easily onto a hellsteed. He moved her like she weighed nothing, the thrall slack in his arms, utterly trapped.

*Perfectly* trapped.

"Luc chased his own pleasure as warm heat squeezed around him," Jules murmured. "Not the cunt he wanted, but he couldn't have that one, not yet."

"Yet?" I asked, the word breathless.

Jules chuckled, a soft brush against the side of my face. "Yet."

I swallowed audibly. The Lord of Dusk followed the movement of my throat. He hadn't torn his gaze away from me once.

I *couldn't* tear my gaze away from him.

"His hands tightened on her hips, his entire body tensing as he tipped into—"

With a quick swipe of his tongue over the puncture wound, Luc pulled back and groaned, a deep rumble like distant thunder. The sound had Jules and me gasping together. The Lord of Dusk's head dropped, eyes slipping shut. Even without them, I remained in his trance. The frown line between his brow smoothed as his lips parted.

Luc *orgasmed.*

The beauty of it stole my breath—and set my aching cunt on fire. I had read a great many things, but never about watching others fuck and enjoying it. Maybe my stepmother was right. I was an odd child and a stranger woman. There was something wrong with me. The other unbitten Maboni prayed to the godstars, begging not to be next.

I prayed to the godstars that I wasn't soaking through my drawers and staining the back of my gown.

"And as he came," Jules said, the word for my ears alone, "he imagined *her* in his arms."

My harsh breaths fought with the thrall's for dominance. The tip of Jules's nose brushed the rim of my ear, eliciting a full body shudder from me. I bit down on the inside of my mouth to stop any embarrassing noises from escaping me. Both lords knew their depravity intrigued me. I wouldn't give them the satisfaction of making me moan with a single, light touch.

Jules grinned anyway. "We're going to have so much fun together, Nessa. I can already tell."

I summoned a glare for Jules, but it just made him chuckle as he leaned back on the log.

"Be nice, Julien." Luc lifted the thrall off him and lowered her to the ground. She melted into a mewling, blissed-out heap at his feet. His fingers traced a quick pattern. *Clean.* Once the sweat and sheen faded, he readjusted his leathers nonchalantly. Like he hadn't just fucked someone in front of me.

To him, it was akin to eating breakfast. Literally.

"We wouldn't want to scare our volunteer so close to Montaurère," Luc said, barely sparing the thrall a glance. He flicked his fingers, a cold dismissal. She swayed, head bowed, and stumbled from the fire's glow into the dark. Forgotten in a second.

"You didn't frighten me." I wished they had. I should be afraid. I was in the harvest, a volunteer for some unknown cause. My fate might have been slightly better than the thrall's, but it would end writhing on a vampire's fangs.

My situation hadn't changed. But in the last two days, my fear had ebbed. Not disappeared. Never that. I didn't think it ever would. But Luc and Jules spoke to me like companions on a journey through the Azarasian countryside.

Not like captors and captive.

Luc's lips curved slightly. "Not yet."

*Not yet.* I flinched. Jules had said those only moments ago, but in a wildly different context. Both were reminders of the truth. This one was far grimmer.

"Not yet," I whispered, almost in agreement. Maybe acknowledgement? The lords didn't hide what they were. They didn't hide that they were luring me in, easing me into false security.

There was no reason for me to hide that I knew. I had nowhere else to go. I wouldn't last a night in the wilds without them.

"Well, that was a depressing end to breakfast." Jules hopped to his feet. "What happened to not frightening the—?"

His words cut off. His gaze snapped toward the trees. Luc was beside him instantly, hand settling on the handle of his axe. Since we met, he hadn't reached for it once unless it was taking it off.

Until now.

That couldn't be good.

A high-pitched wail ripped through the air. A sorrowful, terrible sound no mortal creature could make. It was echoed by another. Then another. All the voices were distinct and yet so eerily the same.

My insides flipped. The hairs on my arm rose. Some instinct screamed at me to flee.

Right. Fucking. Now.

"WHAT KIND OF HELLBEAST is that?" I asked, my voice barely a whisper. Even as I said the words, I knew they weren't right.

"Those aren't hellbeasts," Luc said grimly.

Before he could elaborate, Estrella and Tristan appeared, cutting him off. If he even planned to explain at all. The shadowy forms of other warriors closed in around our fire, half the vampires summoned by the noise. Every eye flashed silver in the flickering light except Tristan and Jules's.

"Your orders, Imperator?" Estrella broke the silence.

The lords didn't glance at each other.

"Set a perimeter to guard the harvest," Luc said with quiet authority. "There may be more, so keep an eye on the forest. We'll handle this."

She bowed. "As you wish, Imperator."

Just as suddenly as they appeared, the vampires disappeared.

I rose to my feet. I couldn't stay still, not when whatever was out there concerned two dozen Azarasians. "What's happening?"

The lords both ignored me as if I hadn't spoken.

"Had to show up just before dawn," Jules muttered. "I swear those fuckers time this."

"Perhaps for your benefit." Luc pulled his axe from his holster. The handle was nearly as tall as me, the daemium head the size of my... well, head. Shadows wafted off it, thick and restless, visible even in the dark. Tiny runes covered the entire weapon, but they were too small to read from a distance.

"How? Are you going to leave me some?"

Luc's lips twisted into a chilling smirk. "No."

"C'mon, Lucey, please. Just one?"

"Focus on our volunteer."

Jules twisted toward me, like he'd forgotten I existed. Those golden eyes pinned me in place. "Hmm, you're right. That is preferable."

"What the fuck is happening?"

Jules suddenly stood in front of me, so close that all I could see was his grinning, perfect mouth. I started to step back, but he dropped his bejeweled hands on my shoulder.

"Is that any way to speak to friends, lovely?"

I forced my eyes to meet his, all the gold nearly swallowed by darkness. The thin line shone brightly between pupil and rim. "You aren't my friend."

"Oh, you wound me." With one hand still on my skin, Jules circled me slowly and came to stand at my side. "Is that any way to speak to casual acquaintances you want to fuck?"

My mouth dried.

A single beat of silence.

Then another.

But the bastard was waiting for a reply. "Yes, actually, I think so."

Jules leaned closer, his breath ghosting against my ear. "Then I look forward to making you curse so hard your stepmother would faint."

I hated the way my breath caught. If only I could pretend Jules meant cursing in anger. I scowled, looking anywhere but at him. This was ridiculous. Some nightmare thing was about to crawl shrieking out of the dark, and I was standing here flirting with a vampire.

Or being flirted with.

No. Being *toyed* with.

"Focus, Julien." Luc had stepped forward, stopping near the edge of the treeline.

"Why? Is one of them going to get past you?"

Luc sent his soulbound a glare. "Of course not—"

Something shot out of the forest. It was human-sized and crawling on all fours, but I couldn't see much more because it was *made* of shadow. Not like the dark mist that seeped from daemium and starcraters.

This was thicker, clinging, suffocating.

Wrong.

It leaped for the Lord of Dusk with an unholy shriek—

Luc chopped it in half with a single swing.

The two pieces of monster flopped in different directions.

I exhaled. That wasn't so bad? Luc had killed it in one strike. Whatever it was hardly seemed worth a dozen vampires.

Then the top half of the creature twitched. Jerked upright. Split its entire face into a gaping, jagged maw.

And wailed directly at me.

I screamed.

The not-dead monster scrambled forward on its arms, terrifyingly quick.

I tried to scurry away. Jules's hand on my shoulder tightened, his arm pressing across my back. Holding me in place beside him. The monster closed the distance—

Luc stomped its head in.

Shadow splashed across the ground like blood, splattering the log between me and the corpse.

No, not a corpse. It hasn't stopped twitching.

But Luc hasn't stopped stomping.

His boot came down again. And again. The wet crunch of breaking bone and ruptured flesh filled the air. He pulverized its back, moving down its spine until it was the texture of rotting fruit. Mush leaked into the grass.

I swallowed hard. What the fuck kind of creature could still move after being hacked in half? And why did a vampire as powerful as Luc feel the need to grind it into pulp?

Just to be sure it stayed dead?

A putrid stench hit me a second later. I clasped a hand over my mouth and tried not to gag. I had never smelled a days-old dead body left to rot in the sun, but I imagined it smelled something like that.

My stomach rolled. Acid burned the back of my tongue as my meager breakfast crawled my throat.

"No puking." Jules traced a finger across my arm. *Settle*. My nausea vanished. "If I have to hold your hair back, I might miss a wraith trying to eat our faces."

"What the fuck is a wraith?"

Jules pointed. "That."

Luc held the mush-wraith down with a flaring rune of twisting, intricate lines. *Burn.* Smoke rose from the creature as it curled in on itself under the heat of his magic. Once the last line of his next rune was complete, he flicked his hand.

*Erupt.*

The wraith exploded.

Bits of it rained down in shredded pieces. It took nearly thirty seconds for them to stop twitching.

Fuck me. The Azarasians' response made a lot more sense now.

I'd thought hellbeasts were the worst thing out here. I was wrong.

"Yeah, but *what* are they?"

Before Jules answered, more wails echoed from the forest, rising in a chorus of hunger. Two more wraiths ran out from the dark, slowly taking shape—

Luc threw his axe. It split through one wraith, slamming it back to the treeline with enough force to pin the creature to a trunk. Daemium sank into bark. The foliage instantly withered, but the wraith only screamed in annoyance, writhing against the blade.

"Witches."

I frowned over at Jules. Witches? What did he—

"That's a *witch?*" I gaped as the second wraith skittered forward, closing the distance to the Lord of Dusk.

"That *was* a witch."

"How?"

The wraith lunged at Luc. In a blink, his fingers extended into wickedly sharp claws of shadow. It wasn't just his nails this time. The black curled up to his knuckles, almost like armored scales. He buried his new talons into the wraith and *ripped* it in half.

Stars save me.

"It's quite a long story," Jules said, completely unbothered by the attack. "But in short, witches can't consume lifeforce, so they have to use their own to fuel their magic. It makes them mortal and they hate that. The everlife runespell is their latest attempt at immortality."

The bisected wraith twitched. It clawed at Luc's arm, blackened fingers reaching to sink into his flesh. Runes flared from within his leathers. *Shield.* The creature's attack bounced off the glowing symbol, repelled like oil hitting water.

Luc didn't give it another chance. *Erupt.* With the flash of a rune, the halves exploded in opposite directions.

Egh. "I don't think their runespell worked."

"It technically did, if you ignore how terribly it back-fired," Jules continued. "They can't be killed unless you throw a lot of magic at them. But they're also ravenous monsters that need to feast on the living to maintain their life."

"Don't vampires and demons feast on the living to maintain their life?"

Jules curled his lip. "Well... yes." He waved a hand, as if that wasn't the point. "But we feed on lifeforce through blood and soul, both of which regenerate with time and rest. Wraiths eat flesh. There's no way to make that pleasant, and the damage is rather permanent. Even for a vampire."

A chill crawled down my spine. "Even for a *vampire*?"

Jules nodded. "Bastards move faster than most of our kind can heal and always go straight for the heart. Consume that, and a vampire's dead."

"So you're letting your soulbound fight them *alone*?"

Jules shrugged. "It's not dawn yet."

Not dawn yet.

I gaped at Jules, maddeningly unfazed, then snapped my attention back to his counterpart. The axe-skewered wraith had wiggled halfway free of Luc's blade, widening the wound in its gut to escape. Its body twisted unnaturally, desperate, like a trapped insect gnawing off its own limb.

Luc grabbed the handle of his weapon and tore it free.

The wraith didn't even need a second to recover. But the Lord of Dusk had known that. Another rune flared hot in his other hand. *Annihilate.* Magic ripped the shadow from its bones in a single pulse.

The wraith collapsed in an instant, the unnatural force holding it together obliterated. The monster was nothing but a black-stained skeleton now. Humanoid but monstrous. Its gaping jaw was locked in a final, warped scream.

Shit. It really had once been a person.

A crack split the clearing. The tree behind the wraith hadn't fared much better. Luc's spell had destroyed a full chunk of the trunk, leaving behind a decaying husk. It splintered under the pressure of its heavy branches.

Fuck. Gravity gripped the tree and tore it down, the foliage right over my head. I braced—

The hit never came. I peeked through squished eyelids.

Luc held the remaining trunk up at an angle. Like it was nothing. Like it was weightless. His spare hand drew a shape. *Incinerate.* In a blink of shadows, the tree turned to ash.

It fell down on Jules and I like black snow. Above, the night sky had lightened, inky black softening to deep blue.

Jules grinned suddenly. He twisted his hair back into a loose knot, a few strands of silken gold brushing against his bare shoulders. "One minute to dawn, Lucey."

The Lord of Dusk didn't react. Between Luc's last attack, the falling tree, and the brightening sky, four more wraiths had emerged from the trees.

"What happens at dawn?"

An unholy gleam entered his golden eyes. "It's my turn."

The Lord of Dusk trapped two wraiths within a swirl of dark magic, holding them still and out of the way. *Imprison*. Their forms twisted violently, writhing inside the rune as they fought to break free.

He poured the rest of his concentration into one struggling, shrieking bundle of deformed shadows at his feet. But the fourth wraith moved freely. It dashed from out of the treeline toward Luc's exposed back.

Luc thrust back an elbow. As he moved, shadows surged from his skin, coalescing into a spike that burst from his bone. The same way fangs slid onto a vampire's canines. My jaw dropped. I thought only demons could do that.

The spike speared through the wraith's skull, impaling it mid-lunge.

The creature jerked violently, clawed at his back, but it couldn't pierce Azarasian leathers any better than its predecessors.

Luc pulsed one last blast into the wraith at his feet. Then he spun, the shadow spike dissipating in an instant. His axe swung in a wide, effortless arc.

The wraith split clean in half under the force of that strike.

Light streaked across the sky.

I don't know what I expected, but I expected *something* to happen. If it did, I didn't see it. But Luc bit out a curse, Jules grinned like it was his birthday, and the swirling magic around the two trapped wraiths flickered.

...was that it?

"Aww, you left me three, Lucey," Jules said, strolling forward. "You do care."

He tossed a rune carelessly at the wraith still twitching near Luc's boots. *Rend.* The strands of magic latched onto the wraith like wire sinking into flesh. A sharp pull in every direction—

The wraith burst into little pieces.

Luc glared at his soulbound. "That one was mine."

"But it's after dawn, so it was actually mine."

"We're both capable of killing a wraith at any time." Luc sounded halfway to grumbling, but he holstered his axe all the same.

"But can you kill one wraith while holding two others still?" Jules raised his hands toward the two trapped wraiths and slowly curled his fingers into fists. The imprisonment rune tightened, squeezing down until the creatures twisted violently. Their shrieks warped into something almost human. "Probably, but you're not, because these kills are *mine*."

"It's still four to three—"

Another wraith lurched into the clearing and screamed.

Luc narrowed his eyes at the creature. "Fuck."

Jules clapped. "I always knew the godstars loved me."

I flinched at the words.

The wraith dashed toward the vampire lords. Jules picked his pace up into a damned *skip*. He cut the creature off before it reached Luc.

The wraith lunged. Jules lunged faster.

With shadow-clawed hands, Jules shoved *into* the wraith's gaping mouth. He grasped its top and bottom jaw. The creature clawed at his leathers, desperate to tear into his chest.

Jules *twisted* in opposite directions.

He tore the creature's skull in two with a snap.

And then he laughed.

I just gaped. Luc had been lethal and efficient, a force too strong for the wraiths to resist.

Jules was just fucking insane.

Luc strode across the clearing to my side. I glanced up at the towering vampire. The tousle in his black curls was a bit wilder than normal, but he otherwise looked the same. He hadn't even broken a sweat.

He gave a slight shake of his head at my disbelieving stare. "You're only encouraging him."

"What do you mean?"

"Jules fights for an audience." Luc drew a small rune against his own skin. *Clean*. The splatters of wraith blood faded from his skin and leathers. "Sometimes that audience is the person he's killing, but wraiths are mindless beasts. He doesn't bother for them."

Jules chose that moment to rip off the wraith's arms and toss them away. Was he *humming*? I couldn't hear it over the inhuman wailing, but his lips were pressed together as he bobbed his head to a tune only he heard. It merged with the wet cracks of bone, creating a gruesome symphony.

I looked away, focusing on the broad stretch of Luc's shoulders. Better that than Jules's dissection.

If this performance was for me, I wanted out of the theater. But I couldn't leave. I had to watch Jules dive into its rib cage next, snapping the bones one at a time. Stars, why wouldn't it die?

"That's not worth any amount of immortality."

Luc linked his hands behind his back and watched Jules root through the wraith's torso. "Most witches would agree."

"Then why use the runespell?"

"A fourth of Isaura's population cast it on themselves before they understood the consequences." His expression darkened, silver eyes hardening to steel. "And once they did, their Exalted Mother used it as a weapon, using a harvest she gifted to us. As she made it bloodborne, the spell activated the moment we fed. It was a massacre."

A chill slid down my spine. I couldn't even imagine a massacre of vampires. But the thought unsettled me less than the implication buried beneath Luc's words. The witches sent a harvest? In Karra's time, Isaura was a neighboring nation of witches, ruled by a demon with the same name. While the Azarasians hadn't been friendly with them, the Isaurans were demonblooded, too. More human than demon, but still.

In the centuries since, they hadn't just fallen in one of the Conqueror's campaigns—they'd been degraded to meal.

But that didn't matter now.

"You didn't seem to have that hard a time killing them." I peeked at Jules. He had finally reached the wraith's hips. With a hand on each hip bone, he tore. The wraith crumpled at his feet. He frowned down at it, clearly disappointed. "Jules, either."

"A single wraith is no threat to a powerful vampire, but most of our citizens can't fight one without help."

I nodded. None of this had been in any textbook I'd read on the Impire. Why redact this information? It wasn't like we could use it. Humans couldn't cast runes.

Were they that concerned about us knowing something could kill them?

Jules tossed a rune down at the last wraith. *Annihilate.* The twitching pieces shattered into ever smaller bits. He glanced around the clearing, but every other monster was dead.

"We're tied, four for four," Jules muttered with a pout. "That won't do."

Without another word, the Lord of Dawn spun on his heels and strutted into the forest.

Luc sighed. When my brow furrowed, he said, "Jules likes to win."

"Win what?"

Luc's gaze slid to me. "We haven't decided yet."

My skin tingled under the intensity of his gaze. Flushing, I faced the trees, the Lord of Dusk in my periphery. "So, uh... is the Imperium's solution to your wraith problem why your magic is stronger at night and Jules's during the day?"

"It is."

I waited. Nothing. "Is it a secret or something? Will the Conqueror have your head for telling me?"

The corner of Luc's lip twitched, gone in a second. "You're quite the little curiosity, aren't you?"

I flushed. Nosy, my stepmother had called it. "So it is a secret."

"It's not. But it is advanced magic."

"Ah." I ducked my head. Of course. I had spent the last decade reading my pain away, but the Impire held back so much information. I probably knew a fraction of what Luc did. The Lord of Dusk might speak to me, but I wasn't his intellectual equal. "So I'm not smart enough to understand."

Luc's gaze traced across my skin, leaving tingles in its path. Considering me. Studying me. Judging me.

"Very well," he said after a moment. "Heartmates share magic through their bond. That shared strength made even the weakest among us able to kill a wraith. But companions and beloveds don't have the ability and account for most of our population. Out of our entire convoy, Estrella and Tristan are the only heartmates."

I nodded, following along so far. So that was why Tristan was the only Dawn vampire to report to our fire earlier. He was the only one strong enough to fight a wraith after dusk. Jules might've been able to as well, if he and Luc hadn't been competing for the kills.

"While we couldn't mimic a heartmate's open connection, we managed to transfer magic back and forth twice a day within a soulbond."

"Doesn't that leave you with no magic for half the day?" I asked.

Luc shook his head. "If I had no magic right now, I'd be dead. Most Azarasians have enough to survive and defend their own blood. The stronger among us can do more with what they have left."

"And if a wraith catches a Dusk vampire alone after dawn?"

"It was a risk we had to take," he said, uncharacteristically soft. "They'd have overrun us centuries ago otherwise."

A crack of underbrush split the air. Jules emerged from the forest a second later. His golden-white hair shone even under the dim light, a loose strand trailing against his cheek as he sighed dramatically. No blood on him. No dirt. Like he hadn't just fought four monsters and shoved his arms into their torsos.

"Find any?" Luc asked.

Jules sighed, forlorn. "No. We're still tied."

Luc nodded, then his gaze dropped to me. "In that case, you can cast the winning vote."

"What?" I nearly squawked. "Why me?"

Luc glanced back at Jules. The lords stared at each other for a second, an unspoken decision passing between them. When they turned their attention back to me, I knew they had reached a unanimous conclusion.

Luc smirked, that rare, arrogant half-smile that made me either want to slap him or fuck him. It was truly fifty-fifty. "It's only fair you decide, little curiosity. You're the prize, after all."

I had to stop my jaw from dropping. I was the prize. That was less shocking somehow than what he called me. Little curiosity? Because I asked questions or because I was an oddity? Perhaps both. Whatever the meaning, it stirred something inside me.

Part of me didn't mind the idea of being a prize at all.

I gave it a shake. *Focus, idiot.* "And what does that mean?"

"Pick, Nessa."

"I—I—" My tongue felt clumsy in my mouth, a useless lump of muscle that couldn't form an answer. Pick? The word sent panic lashing through me.

How did I *pick*?

Jules, with his golden smirks and teasing words, irresistible in his reckless charm. He made danger feel like a game, one I might even want to play.

Luc was entirely different. Steady. Calculated. An impenetrable wall of power and purpose. Where Jules teased, Luc studied. Where Jules taunted, Luc challenged.

And that challenge thrilled me just as much as it scared me.

A choice between fire and steel. Between playful destruction and something unshakable and overwhelming. My stomach tightened. They were vampires. I was a thrall. A human, collected as food like all the others in the harvest.

It didn't matter that Jules made me laugh or that Luc made my blood thrum with a single glance.

They were the predators.

I was the prey.

I couldn't pick.

I *shouldn't* pick.

And yet, something inside me ached to step closer. To let myself get caught between them. To feel what it would be like to be someone's prize.

A cold, round weight pressed into my palm. The sensation lured me from my panic and brought me back to a world of luminous eyes. Both lords watched me, but it was Luc who pressed something into my hand.

"Flip the coin."

I tossed it in the air, entranced by their gazes. If he had told me to eat the coin, I probably would've done that without hesitation, too. I didn't even bother trying to catch it. Luc told me to flip it. I flipped it. What happened to it after that wasn't my concern.

Jules flashed out a hand and caught the coin.

He held it up to the rising light. "Ha! I win. Told you the godstars love me."

He showed it to Luc, who sighed. Jules clapped him on the shoulder. "Don't cry, Lucey, you know I always share. Besides, you could have won if you spent less time flexing your big, sexy muscles—"

Luc wrapped a hand around Jules's throat. His arm flexed as he tightened his grip. "Like this?"

My jaw dropped. I resisted shuddering at Luc's deep growl. Jules didn't bother. Heat flared in his bright eyes. There was a delighted curve to his lips that paired too well with the Lord of Dusk's dark smolder.

Were they going to kiss again?

Did I *want* them to kiss again?

I swallowed. "Well, I'm going to go find my wagon."

"No," they said together. I went still, my pulse skittering.

Luc reluctantly let go of Jules's throat. The Lord of Dawn gave a small pout, but then turned on me and winked. I think my heart stopped.

Luc rolled his eyes. "There will be more wraiths the closer we get to Montaurère. You're riding with us until we reach the capital."

I COULDN'T STOP STARING at Montaurère.

Yesterday, when Jules had pointed out a sky-piercing mountain on the horizon, it had seemed impossibly distant. Weeks away, surely. But the road twisted through the cliffs and pine-thick slopes of a lower pass, and by this morning, that peak loomed far closer than it should have.

An hour ago, we had turned a bend in the road and nothing but a wide field separated us from the city.

I had spent most of that last hour with my jaw agape. Sprawling white villas clung to the mountainside, winding up from the base to the very tip. Ribbon-thin waterfalls spilled down the rock, catching the light like molten silver. In places too steep for natural paths, platform walkways stretched between buildings, delicate-looking but sturdy, linking the city like a web spun into stone. At the peak, a giant white castle with dozens of sharp, gold-tipped towers speared out from the earth.

How did a castle that massive even stay on a mountainside that steep? Any human-made structure would have crumbled long ago, sliding straight into the lake that glittered to my right.

Stars, a city of vampires had no right to be this breathtaking.

Or maybe it had every right. Montaurère was as dazzling as its immortal inhabitants.

I drank in every detail—the soaring spires, the intricate terraces, the bursts of color woven through the stone. Thousands of Azarasian flags snapped in the wind, their deep crimson and sapphire striking against white facades and patches of greenery. If each flag marked a home, then hundreds of thousands of vampires lived here. The last Corraidin census had counted only thirteen thousand humans within our entire boundary. I couldn't even fathom a city this vast.

But even Montaurère's splendor couldn't distract from my racing pulse and damp palms. If Jules hadn't refreshed my soothing runespell a few hours ago, I'd be doubled over from the sheer force of my anxiety. After the longest week of my life, we had finally arrived. What happened now? I knew little about what happened to the harvested beyond becoming blood thralls. Even less about Montaurère.

Karra hadn't visited the Capital of Dawn in volume one of *The Soulborne Queen*, but she had mentioned its extensive underground network, deeper than even Tenebra de Mar, where Azaras had once held his court. Vampires liked to hollow into the earth just like their demon and hellbeast brethren. Light meant nothing to them when their senses were far superior to mortal creatures.

I swallowed hard. Is that where they would take us? How many humans had gone missing within those dark caves? How many screamed in terror and agony—or *pleasure*—right now, a vampire's fangs buried in their throat?

"Are you well?"

Luc's voice rumbled through his chest, faint vibrations at my back. His breath brushed the tip of my ear. The deep spice of him invaded my senses.

"I'm fine," I said, managing to sound mostly normal.

I'd ridden with Luc during the last two days and switched to Jules's hellsteed at night, the lords passing me between them as their magic switched at dusk and dawn. Thankfully so, because I didn't think I could sleep in Luc's arms. Not that he wasn't as warm and solid as his soulbound, but Jules's presence at my back was all easy joy and brightness.

On the surface, at least. I didn't let myself think too hard about that.

With Luc, I couldn't stop picturing him fucking.

I shuffled in the saddle, heat curling low in my stomach. Not painful, thankfully. Just... persistent. Vampires were gorgeous, sure, but I'd never been this constantly attracted in my life. Not even before my illness, when other girls my age had started sighing over romance and stealing kisses.

Luc inhaled sharply. His grip tightened on my hip, fingers pressing through my cloak. His arms and thighs flexed around me, solid, immovable. I swallowed. Every time his muscles shifted beneath his leathers, my mind dragged up the blood thrall's expression. Bliss-shocked, broken apart. She had all but died from her orgasm. Would it feel that incredible if the Lord of Dusk thrust *me* down on his massive, pierced cock?

*When*. Not if.

Luc inhaled deeply, a slow, deep breath against the crown of my head. Was he... sniffing me? "It will take us much longer than a half-hour to reach Dawnspear if you don't stop thinking about fucking me, little curiosity."

"What?" I stiffened, back snapping straight. My voice came out embarrassingly high-pitched. "I wasn't—that's rather presumptuous of you."

"Is it?"

I shivered as the words tickled the exposed skin of my neck. I couldn't help it. Luc hummed, a smug, pleased noise. The kind that belonged alongside a smirk, the sharp curl of his mouth when he knew exactly what he was doing. Heat flared hotter in my core.

I drove my nails into my palms as we rode between two stone columns, each one etched with familiar runespells. *Protect. Shield. Barrier.* It was time for a subject change and there was one answer I still needed.

It would probably cool my rampant desire, too.

"You still haven't told me what I volunteered for," I said. "Every time I've asked, you evade the question."

Luc considered me. "If I tell you, will you run screaming?"

"I'd have to get off this hellsteed first."

Jules snorted, the sound carrying from where he rode ahead of us.

Though I knew the answer, I added, "Will I get very far?"

"Not very."

"Then no, I won't run," I said. "There's nothing I can say or do to stop this. Running isn't going to help."

"And knowing will?"

I wasn't going to like his answer, was I? "I can't see how it'd hurt."

Silence fell between us. The road widened into an empty square, the stone beneath us paling to match the buildings of Montaurère that had begun dotting the landscape on either side. A gilded arch rose from the square's center, grand and foreboding. As wide as two wagons, it framed a thin, black surface that was almost reflective, shifting like trapped smoke.

Luc finally spoke. "We don't usually tell our volunteer until the ceremony."

Ceremony? "Have any of them asked?"

"No."

"They usually don't speak at all." Jules glanced back over his shoulder, his eyes flickering between me and his soulbound. "I've decided you must be insane."

"I don't disagree," I muttered.

"I vote we tell her, Luc. What's the worst that could happen?" His gaze dipped, deliberate, to the pulse at my throat. Hunger flickered behind his golden irises, bright and sharp. "If she manages to run, that just means we get to chase her."

I repressed a shudder, but my heart stuttered. I hadn't witnessed the Lord of Dawn feed from any of the thralls, though he had admitted to it before the attack. And after spending so much magic killing wraiths, he must have done so again. How often did a vampire need blood?

"You're to be the next Mortal Bride."

I tore my gaze from Jules. Mortal *Bride*. The words rang hollow, unfamiliar. I hadn't come across the term before, but my skin tingled with unease. I inhaled slowly, intentionally. "And who exactly am I marrying?"

"It's not a real marriage," Luc said. "But the ceremony will bind you for life, so we stole the term."

Bind me for life. My stomach twisted. "Bind me to *whom*?"

The words came out sharper than I intended. Luc's gaze settled heavily on the back of my head. A weighted silence stretched between us. I refused to hunch my shoulders. I would not cower.

"It's not to a person," Luc finally said, "so much as to a spell."

"Let's not lie to our volunteer, Lucey. It's to a spell *through* a person." Jules paused and cocked his head. "Two persons. People? You get what I mean."

"That doesn't really answer my question."

Jules chuckled. "I guess it doesn't, no."

I sighed. Why had I expected the lords to give me a straight answer now, when they'd danced around it for days? I'd find out soon enough.

Luc surprised me by continuing. "The collective magic of our impire powers the runespell that transfers Azarasian magic between soulbound. But since it's a perpetual spell, it needs a constant supply of lifeforce. For lack of a better term, the runespell needs a sacrifice."

Sacrifice.

Every part of me went stiff.

Fuck.

Maybe I wasn't going to be anyone's bride. I'd once read about an ancient human culture that married a virgin to a godstar before stabbing her through the heart. It seemed a brutal practice, but what were vampires if not brutal?

"Are you going to sacrifice me?" I somehow kept the words steady.

What would I do if he said yes? What *could* I do? My chances of escape had always been low. Now they were nonexistent.

When I'd chosen my fate years ago, I had hoped to survive the Azarasians. But if I was a sacrifice, was I truly any better off? Maybe I should've married Patriarch Meallán and let him fuck me through my body's protests, clinging to the useless hope of meeting the birth quota.

"A single death wouldn't provide anywhere near enough energy," Luc said at last. "Even if you were overjoyed to offer us your life."

That wasn't a no. Shit. I had volunteered to be a *sacrifice.* I hadn't lied when I told Luc I wouldn't run, but stars, I wanted to. My heart had made no such promises, though. It thundered against my ribs, demanding I flee. "In what other way can you sacrifice someone?"

The lords exchanged a glance. Luc shifted his grip on his hellsteed's reins, steady and deliberate, before raising his free hand. "May I have your wrist?"

I swallowed down my fear and slowly held up my wrist. Luc traced his thumb over my pulse. His touch was warm, steady, measured. I tried to breathe, tried to slow the frantic beat beneath his fingers.

"See the arch?" he murmured.

I forced a frown to my lips. Better that than parting them. "Am I not supposed to? It's hard to miss."

Now that we were closer, I noticed tiny runes carved into every inch of the black, wavering surface. The material must have been daemium, same as the lords' weapons.

"Watch." Luc's thumb settled over my pulse. Pressed down, just slightly. "This will sting."

Before I could ask, Luc's thumbnail sharpened to a black point and sliced across my skin. A faint flash of pain struck as my flesh split with ease. I flinched as blood pooled at the small cut.

With a wave of his hand, Luc took control of my blood. The droplets rose, bubbling up like liquid pearls before merging into a swirling circle above our heads. I stared, transfixed. Would I ever stop marveling at this otherworldly power? I hoped not. My fate was grim, but if I held onto this wonder, maybe my soul would survive mostly intact.

Screams shattered the quiet.

I dropped my gaze. Jules had lifted his hands, and with them, blood burst from every Maboni. Tiny cuts at their arms, wrists, and hands seeped crimson. He didn't take enough from any one human to harm them, but together, my blood and theirs wove into a rushing stream three bodies wide, pulsing like a living artery in the sky.

As Jules directed the crimson river toward the arch, Luc raised my still-bleeding wrist. Like he meant to press his lips to my skin. Heat flared deep inside me.

Jules growled, dark and possessive. It was a noise much more suited to the Lord of Dusk.

Luc halted mid-motion and slowly arched a brow.

"Her blood is mine first."

My eyes widened. Wait, was that what the lords meant when they called me their prize? Had Jules won me *first*? As my thoughts spun, a moment stretched between the vampires. Then, slowly, Luc relented with a nod of his head. He had lost, after all. But I didn't think he'd yield to anyone but his soulbound.

Shadows coiled at his fingertips as he traced a pattern over my skin. *Heal.* The cut closed, not even a scar left behind.

Luc didn't linger. With a firm but deliberate touch, he tilted my head back toward the arch. "Watch."

Jules looped the floating river of blood around the arch's gilded rim, then splattered it across the daemium surface like an artist staining canvas. The grooves of the runes drank it in, flooding red. *Gate. Distance. Path. Arrival. Cross.* The gate shuddered, its dark surface rippling like disturbed water. The runes pulsed, devouring the blood—until suddenly, shadows erupted outward, a shockwave of energy blasting the air.

The daemium faded... into a white stone wall, climbing with roses.

I blinked. That wasn't what I expected. The wall didn't align with the surface. It seemed farther away, like I glanced through a window. I tilted my head, catching the gleam of gilded towers rising above.

Just beneath Dawnspear, a splash of red.

A wall of roses.

"Is that...?"

"It is," Jules said, grinning at the gateway. "Why climb a mountain when you can simply appear at the top?"

Oh. That was... amazing, actually. I hadn't read about any runespell like that in any book. "Isn't that a security risk? Invaders could breach the castle instantly."

Jules's smile fell. "You ruin all the fun, lovely."

I flinched. Didn't I always?

"No frowning," Jules said, instantly perking back up.

Luc kicked his hellsteed forward, Jules falling in beside us. "Yes, theoretically, if someone cracked the security wards on the Imperium Square's runegate, they could march an army on the castle."

"I, for one, welcome the challenge," Jules said. "Dawnspear's walls could use new decorations."

I frowned. Decorations? What?

The arch's shadow swallowed me whole as we reached the runegate's surface. I braced for impact, expecting... something. A lurch, a sensation of falling, a flash of magic piercing through me. Instead, warmth brushed my skin like a gentle caress.

And then we were through.

Sunlight flickered—gone in one second, tracing me from a different angle the next. The air felt no different. My ears didn't pop.

But my eyes nearly did.

Vampires in flowing silks and glistening jewels drifted across the pristine stone square, moving with effortless grace around the other gilded runegate. Their hair cascaded freely down their backs, their skin bare beneath the delicate shimmer of fabric.

Thralls followed their masters in silence, collars of iron, silver, or gold gleaming at their throats. They wore simple black uniforms, the thin fabric clinging to their forms, leaving little to the imagination.

At the first sign of the lords' hellsteeds, the crowd parted without hesitation, eyes lowered as they cleared a wide path.

Before us, Dawnspear loomed.

The castle was as wide as it was tall, a sheer wall of pale stone rising like a monument. I angled my head back, trying to take it all in. My neck ached from the effort. Sharp spires speared in the sky, circling a massive central keep, their gilded tips catching the late-afternoon sun. Hundreds of arched casement windows gleamed between carved turrets and intricate buttresses.

Beyond the keep, twisting vines of crimson roses climbed a formidable curtain wall. The wall projected outward at its corners into bastions before continuing in a straight line toward the gatehouse, where the main gate stood in solid gold, carved with the blazing image of a sun. The carving wasn't just decorative. Its position matched the exact location of the real sun, marking the time with eerie precision.

Near the gate, a heavy golden chain dropped from the parapet, its weight pulling at something pale and veined with black.

I squinted.

My stomach dropped. "Are those shadow-streaked *bones* hanging from the walls?"

"They are," Luc said.

So that was what Jules meant by decorations. "Why?"

"To send a message."

Now that I had seen one skeleton, I saw another. And another. Rib cages, femurs, skulls. Curled fingers frozen in their last moments. The vines had grown through them, twisting through hollow eye sockets, weaving around skeletal limbs like nature itself had claimed the bodies.

"That's a lot of messages."

Jules rode his hellsteed in a slow, lazy circle until we were face to face. His golden eyes gleamed, sharp as the spires above us. "It's one message, just in twenty-two parts."

The wonder I'd felt—Montaurère's beauty, the magic, the sheer breathtaking scope of it—shriveled to nothing. Cold, hard reality slammed back into me.

I was a living sacrifice.

What had the lords said before they distracted me with magic?

"So I'm a blood sacrifice?"

"No. Well, yes?" Jules shrugged, waving a hand as if my impending fate was hardly worth the concern. "All thralls are technically a blood sacrifice."

Luc was more direct. "It will be your life we sacrifice, but slowly, bit by bit every day. As you sleep and eat and laugh and come" —I stiffened, but Luc continued on as if the last item on his list were as ordinary as the first— "your lifeforce will replenish. You will become the covenant runespell's home, an endless well of magic in its purest sense."

"I see." I kept my voice calm, even as my mind screamed on the inside. Run. The word slashed through my thoughts. But where? Through the city of vampires? Into the forest of hellbeasts and wraiths?

No.

Defiance was pointless. A waste of time. A waste of breath. I could scream, struggle, curse their names, but that wouldn't change the fact that vampires were stronger. Faster. Deadlier. I'd read the history textbooks. I'd seen it myself. What could I possibly do against them?

Running wasn't an option.

Fighting wasn't an option.

But breathing? Staying whole? That was my choice.

I wasn't going to die. Not today. But my life would never be mine again. I would be fuel, woven into the heart of a runespell that empowered an *impire* of vampires.

Assuming my life was even enough.

The first wagon came through the runegate behind us. The lords kicked their hellsteeds back into motion, aiming for the castle's gilded gate. I stared down at my hands, twisting them together. The lords knew something wasn't right with me, but if I told them I was permanently broken, they might search for another volunteer. The illness of my body surely affected my lifeforce.

If I wasn't strong enough to host their spell, I'd probably die. Was becoming an ordinary thrall the better fate? My shoulders tensed at the thought of the runespell carved into my neck, forcing compliance.

Fate had offered me an escape, but I couldn't take it. I wasn't even good enough to be a *sacrifice*.

A hysterical laugh crawled up my throat, but I smothered it. "I don't know if I'm the best choice for that."

"You're currently the only choice."

I shuddered at the sudden chill in Luc's tone. "Surely you could find a human in the city to volunteer."

Luc's answer came without hesitation. "Anyone who's ever worn a thrall runespell isn't a willing volunteer, even if the runes are removed."

"But a branded Maboni is?"

"The brand didn't control you," he said.

"It would've killed me if I left the island."

"It would've, yes," he agreed. "But that's not the same as controlling you."

The distinction didn't make me feel any better. "I'm... not well. Sickly and weak. There are days where the pain and exhaustion confine me to my bed. If it's a strong lifeforce you need, I'm not the candidate for your covenant."

Luc was silent for a moment. "Your lifeforce is more than sufficient."

I blinked. "What?"

"The strength of a body doesn't always determine the strength of a lifeforce." Luc's voice was calm, matter-of-fact. "Perseverance and grit can fuel a person just as much as joy and pleasure."

"Oh." That didn't settle my stomach. I didn't think anything would. "So am I pretend-marrying the spell's casters? Who—"

I froze in Luc's arms.

The covenant runespell held the Impire together against the threat of the wraiths.

We stood before Dawnspear, home of the Court of Dawn.

The lords were powerful and respected, vampires who no doubt operated in the highest echelon of Azarasian society.

There were only two vampires they could possibly serve.

My breath caught. "Did your kings cast the covenant spell?"

Jules considered me. Something ancient and callous flicked behind his grin. A brief glimpse behind his jolly mask. "Yes."

I wracked my brain for what little I knew about the Conqueror and the Butcher. Not much. They had ruled for four centuries. They were soulbound. The Azarasians stationed in Mabon always referred to them collectively as the Imperium or by their epithets. Never their names. Never their genders.

But anyone called the Conqueror and the Butcher by vampires were monsters I should fear.

My heart pounded, a hard, erratic rhythm. Fuck, this was really happening.

Luc exhaled, almost amused. "Your heart is beating so loud I can nearly feel it against my chest. You aren't going to pass out, are you, Miss Halloran?"

My mouth dried. "No?"

"You don't sound sure about that," Jules said. "Is it really that terrifying to fake-marry two kings? You weren't as scared of the hellserpent or wraiths, and they'd have ripped you to shreds."

"And someone named the Butcher won't?"

"Of course not." Grinning, Jules pulled his curved lynx dagger from its sheath and flipped it easily in his hand. Daemium caught the light, gleaming darkly. "For humans, I much prefer a blade. It makes cleaner cuts."

I stared.

Stared longer.

He wasn't...?

He didn't mean...?

"You *what* now?"

Luc chuckled low in my ear. "Ah, yes. We never properly introduced ourselves."

"That was quite rude of us, wasn't it?" Jules twirled his dagger, the tip pointing to himself. "Julien Roche, King of Dawn, pleasure to meet you." The daemium tip swiveled toward Luc. "That brute breathing down your neck is Lucero Azaras, King of Dusk. You might know him better as the Conqueror, which makes me your friendly neighborhood Butcher."

My mouth gaped open and stayed that way. Jules—the motherfucking *Butcher*—continued grinning at me from the back of his hellsteed.

I was an idiot.

The way all the convoy warriors treated my traveling companions suddenly made perfect sense. I thought they were just in charge of the harvest. Not that they were the supreme rulers of the Azarasian Impire.

My stomach twisted. I'd spend the last week alternating between eye-fucking and glaring at the *Imperium*.

My vision spun. If Luc—the *Conqueror*—hadn't sat firmly at my back, I'd have slumped right off his hellsteed. Was I going to faint? I couldn't faint. Not now. I had to say something. Anything.

All that came to mind was, "Being chopped up with Thérèse doesn't sound much better." Followed by, "Wait, did you say Lucero *Azaras*?" And then, much later than it should have been, "Your Majesty?"

Jules burst into laughter. The red-cloaked vampires on the walkway above the gatehouse straightened at the sound.

"He did say Azaras," Luc answered, amusement lacing his voice. "The demon is my sire."

I twisted fully around to look at him. His gorgeous face was too close for comfort, but I didn't even care.

Luc was Azaras's *son*.

Demons were shapeshifters and didn't have any physical traits to pass to their children, so they probably didn't look alike. But my mental image of the Beast King changed nonetheless.

Jules wiped away the tears his laughter had wrung from him. "You know, most people stare less once they learn who we are."

I stiffened. Fuck. It had been insane to make eye contact with the vampires at my back and side when they were merely lords. I didn't know what was worse than insanity—but whatever it was, I had it. Because I was still staring directly into the Conqueror's eyes.

Luc slowly arched one brow. That arrogant, infuriating smirk twitched at the corner of his lips.

Right. Because I was still staring.

I wrenched my gaze forward as we approached the castle's gate. A lone skull, crowned in tarnished gold, dangled from chains above the entrance beneath the parapet. Jules flipped it off as we rode through.

The white stone road led through a garden, trimmed pear trees lining the path to Dawnspear's towering doors. If the lords—kings—hadn't just shared world-altering information, I'd be drinking in every manicured shrub and flower bed in the runic parterres. Instead, I traced my finger back and forth along my book's dulled edges within the satchel crossing my chest.

Questions crawled up my throat. I bit my lip. I needed to stop speaking. Making casual conversation with two murderous warlord kings who planned to fake-marry me as a living sacrifice wasn't smart. But they hadn't killed me yet for the offense. If they did, who would serve as their volunteer? If their covenant spell was as important as I thought, they wouldn't risk it.

When they didn't need my cooperation, it would be a different story.

Better to ask now, then.

I started with something easy. Hopefully. "Is Karra your mother?"

"She isn't."

"Oh." My shoulders slumped. Jules had said I'd have access to a library. I had hoped to find *The Soulborne Queen*'s remaining volumes and finally finish Karra's story, but did I want to anymore? Knowing what I knew? "I guess it's not a happy ending for them after all."

"You look heartbroken, curiosity."

"I shouldn't be. It's a historical romance. When does real life ever go well?" I cringed as a thought occurred. "Wait. You're telling me I've been yattering on about *erotica* written about your father?"

"Azaras is my sire, not my father," Luc said, voice suddenly flat. "I've never met him."

"Still. You're related."

"Azarasians aren't terrified by the idea of their relatives fucking," Jules said cheerfully. "That's very much a human issue."

Before us, the road split into two, leaving the garden behind for an open forecourt. We circled a fountain, its centerpiece a massive golden spear stabbing skyward between spurts of water. The gilded piece was as beautiful and deadly as its Butcher King.

Unlike Jules, it was slightly more bloody—at this moment, at least.

Trails of red streamed down the spear's shaft from the *flayed* body impaled on its sharp end. I clutched a hand over my mouth. My stomach tried to spin around and leave. I couldn't tell if they had been male or female, mortal or vampire. There was no skin left, just gleaming muscle, wet and raw. Their chest had been cracked open, ribs reaching outward like grasping fingers, a beating heart cradled in the center like a palm.

The *beating* heart.

It—they weren't dead. How could they not be dead? Even knowing vampires were near indestructible, this seemed too terrible to live through.

But if they were a vampire, why weren't they healing?

I saw my answer a second later. A line of runes floated before the heart, shadows sinking into the ruined body. *Imprison. Suspend. Endure.* The spell held them trapped in this state, bleeding and broken, neither living nor dead.

But it didn't halt the agony.

The only thing keeping the forecourt from filling with screams was a golden gag strapped tight over their mouth. Their lidless, bright blue eyes flickered, rimmed by a thin line of shadow. I jolted. Every vampire I had met so far had gold or silver eyes. Did he not have a soulbond? Azaras had cast the soulbond runespell across his kingdom *three* thousand years ago. I knew vampires were immortal, but the thought of living that long hurt my brain.

If you could call this living. There was nothing but pain and madness behind that gaze. Whoever this had been, they weren't anymore.

They weren't anything anymore.

I wanted to tear away, but I was trapped in that gaze. Even like this, the vampire mesmerized me. "Is your entire castle decorated with corpses?"

Jules snorted, like there wasn't a *skinless* body writhing a couple feet away. "Nah, just the outer wall and forecourt garden. I'm not letting the traitors inside."

Of course. Silly me.

When the hellsteeds reached the far side of the fountain, the angle finally forced my gaze away from the undying vampire. I swallowed and faced forward. There was nothing I could do for them. I couldn't even save myself.

I wracked my brain for what I planned to ask the kings next, but my thoughts had managed to escape where my stomach had not. Had it really mattered, if I couldn't remember? I knew the important parts of my fate.

Mortal Bride.

Fake marriage.

The Conqueror and the Butcher.

My nausea flared again.

The road merged into an open area for carriages and wagons. Vampires in navy and maroon livery stood waiting at the base of the broad staircase leading to an ornate set of red doors.

As one, they dropped into bows, a closed fist pressed to their hearts. "Imperium."

Jules was off his hellsteed in a blink. He gently patted Cala's nose and murmured, "Please don't bite anyone."

One of the attendants stepped forward—hesitant, but resigned—and took Cala's reins.

Jules walked to my side as Luc dismounted behind me. Without a word, the King of Dawn wrapped strong hands around my waist and lifted me down. Firm. Effortless. My knees nearly crumpled. I hadn't stood for more than a few minutes in days, and if not for healing runes, my thighs would be chafed raw.

Jules tightened his grip, keeping me upright before I could collapse at his feet. Golden eyes met mine. I ducked my head. Do. Not. Stare. At. The. Butcher. King.

Idiot.

"You're heeding my advice now?" His pretty mouth pouted in my periphery. "But I wanted to watch you bat your little eyes at me, your strong, beautiful, charming rescuer."

I resisted the urge to glare. "What exactly did you rescue me from?"

"Today? Falling off a hellsteed. Long term? A boring life without orgasms."

My gaze snapped up. "What?"

Fuck. He'd made me look. And now that I was looking, I couldn't stop. The afternoon sun lit his blond waves into pale gold, a perfect match for his eyes.

"Orgasms are a *great and terrible sin*, aren't they?" he asked, his voice going gruff in imitation of a patriarch. "Along with everything else enjoyable in life?"

"Well, yes." He wasn't wrong. Once our school curriculum began covering sex, we were required to attend church nightly to purify our minds of the Azarasians' wicked propaganda. By then, I'd already snuck a dozen romance novels past Deidre. "But I really don't think you can take credit for every... orgasm I'll have for the rest of my life."

Assuming I could even have one. If venom rid me of my pain, perhaps—

"Why not? I plan to give you at least the first dozen, starting tonight."

My jaw dropped. He planned to *what* now? *Tonight*?

Jules stuck out his tongue. A tiny ruby embedded in a gold stud caught the light, flashing red.

If my jaw could drop further, it would have. "Do you have a tongue piercing?"

Jules grinned. Shit, why had I said that aloud? "Do you like it?"

I opened my mouth. Closed it. Opened it again. I finally settled on a strangled, "Do you?"

His expression turned wicked. "It comes in handy at times."

"In what way?"

"Wouldn't you like to know?"

"Well, yes, that's why I..." Wait. Did he mean what I thought he meant?

His smile broadening, Jules winked and headed for the stairs. "You won't have to wait long to find out."

I stared. My heart started pounding loud enough that I heard it in my ears.

Oh, my fucking stars.

I forced my eyes to narrow. "Why is everything an innuendo with you people?"

"We're vampires," Luc said, halting at my side. "Unlike humans, we don't believe sex is something to hide in shame."

Heat flooded my face. At this stage, it was far beyond a flush. Why was I even debating this? And with the Conqueror and Butcher of all people? I'd left my common sense back in Mabon.

I hadn't realized it was something I needed to pack.

"It's not shame," I said weakly. "It's just... not proper."

"Why?"

"Because..." It was a duty to endure? Because the Church said so? "Just because."

Luc arched a brow. "That's terrible reasoning."

I sighed. "I know."

The King of Dusk gently shook his head before following his soulbound up the stairs. His steps were controlled, deliberate. Power contained in every stride. Both kings moved with confidence, but Luc commanded authority with a step next to Jules's effortless glide.

Without the kings beside me, one of the vampire attendants approached. To them, I was probably no different than the kings' hellsteeds and saddle bags. They reached out—

"No."

Luc didn't raise his voice, but the weight of his command snapped through the air. The vampire attendant dropped to their knees so fast that bone met stone with an audible crack.

"Forgive my overstep, Your Majesty."

Both kings had turned, but neither spared a glance at their kneeling subject. Their gazes locked on me instead. Luc reached out a hand and crooked a finger. No words. No expression. Just a silent command.

I straightened. I would not cower. If I repeated it enough times, maybe it would become true. I climbed the stairs to Luc's side, every step like walking toward my execution. The sense of impending doom had quieted on the road with the kings, but now it pounded against my breastbone, keeping time with my heart.

Jules strolled through the opened front door like he... well, like he owned the place. Which he did. "I'm hoooome. Did you miss me?"

The vampires bustling through the entrance hall bowed immediately. It gave me the perfect opportunity to gape unobserved.

The floor was a masterpiece of inlaid stone, obsidian, and ivory marble swirling in elaborate patterns that stretched across the impossibly vast hall. Crystal chandeliers the size of a person hung from every second coffered ceiling, twinkling in the sunlight spilling through the arched windows. White columns with gilded crown molding stretched toward a distant ceiling, its expanse painted in deep, bloody shades—not of dawn, but of slaughter.

In the mural, dozens of bodies lay broken and bleeding around a dark throne, its seat wide enough to fit two bloodied kings. Luc and Jules sat enthroned in carnage, every bit the Conqueror and the Butcher. There was no sign of the smirking, infuriating men I had come to know.

But I had only met the masks of the monsters. They had told me exactly who they were.

They had decorated the first room of Dawnspear with a reminder of how they built their impire.

"No," a male voice responded, grumpy and unafraid to share it.

Two dark-haired vampires had remained standing. I hadn't noticed them at first, too overwhelmed by the sheer majesty of the room. The man had the sleeves of his plum-colored doublet rolled to his elbows, his black hair cut short and utilitarian. Not a single strand fell across his pale face or sharp, silver eyes.

"That's not very nice, Sabas. I could have you killed for being mean to me."

"Please do. I've spent the last month doing Luc's paperwork." Sabas dragged a hand down his face. Like every other vampire, he was beautiful. But there was a shadow beneath his eyes I hadn't known immortals could get. "I'll stab myself if I see another grain report."

"It's not like Rox not to help," Luc said mildly.

"He lost a bet," the woman beside Sabas said. Her black uniform was a version of the kings' army leathers, elevated with silver thread and armored plates. Most vampires wore their hair loose, but hers was neatly braided, a long plait resting over her polished shoulder pauldrons. Her olive skin deepened the gold of her eyes. She stood nearly as tall as Sabas, both of them a couple inches shorter than Jules—and still a good three inches taller than me.

"You bet on paperwork and then *lost*?" Jules pulled Thérèse from her sheath. "We can't tell anyone this was a mercy killing. It will ruin my reputation."

"Put Thérèse away, Julien."

Jules frowned playfully over at Luc. "I'm not actually going to stab him, *Lucey*. Then Cédric would die, and Perry wouldn't ever forgive me for killing his favorite brother."

"Aren't you his favorite brother?" the woman asked dryly.

"Am I? He's always yelling at me, so it's hard to tell."

"We were attacked by wraiths near Widow's Lake," Luc said, ignoring his soulbound to address Sabas and the woman.

She turned to a maroon-cloaked vampire among the still-bowing attendants. "Send a squadron to sweep the area."

"Yes, General." The vampire dipped their head and strode from the hall.

Sabas pinched the bridge of his nose. "That's the closest a pack has traveled to Montaurère in a century."

"The bodies at the Dufresne Abattoir must have lured them from the wilds," Luc said. "Your last report said you found the last of the culprits?"

Sabas nodded. "Their tribunal concludes today."

"Schedule an audience for tomorrow morning." Luc stepped forward. Every vampire and thrall moved with him without hesitation. The motion was automatic. Jules lagged behind, but no one else dared. "We'll announce their sentences publically."

"Ugh." Jules waved a finger at his boots. *Unfasten*. With a flare of shadows, the laces came undone, and he kicked them off his feet. "How about the day after? I planned to spend tomorrow in bed."

He said that last bit while looking at me. Why was he looking at me? My blush had started to fade, but at that, heat rushed to my face again.

Jules winked and held out a hand for me. "Best not to get left behind, lovely. Montaurère is a dangerous place for humans without a collar."

I crossed the marble floor slowly, hesitating only a moment before placing my palm in his. Jules curled his fingers around mine and started after his soulbound at his own pace.

I glanced back at his boots, sitting abandoned in the middle of the entryway. "Won't someone steal them?"

Jules snorted. "I could leave them in a city square. They smell too much like me to risk touching."

"Everyone can't know what you smell like."

"They don't, but we can sense magic in a person's scent. By process of elimination, the boots are mine or Luc's."

I nodded and twisted around—

The kings' retinue had stopped. All the vampires stared at me like they were shocked I knew how to speak. Or maybe it was that their Butcher King chatted back. I went rigid under the intensity of those bright eyes.

"This is...?" Sabas asked reluctantly. His brow furrowed as his gaze flickered between Jules and me.

"Our new Mortal Bride," Luc said.

Sabas waited for further explanation, but neither king seemed willing to give it to him. "And?"

The kings shared one of those loaded glances. After a moment, Luc shrugged nonchalantly. "And Jules might keep her."

"Keep her?" Jules twirled a strand of hair that had escaped my braid around his finger, pulled it to his nose, and inhaled. His eyes fluttered shut. "I think I might breed her."

My stomach dropped. He might *what* now? A storm of emotions whirled at his words. Terror, obviously. Anticipation? I wasn't going to touch that one.

And then what always followed—shame and a muted flash of pain through my core.

*Human female, sixteen, likely infertile.*

I had told the kings I was ill, but they hadn't asked for details. They didn't know. But I did. The memory of that day, the vampire healer's clinical voice, still haunted me.

I hadn't ever had the chance to decide if I wanted children. For a Maboni woman, there was no choice. Marriage. Children. Obedience. The only path. It had terrified me. But when the verdict came, my relief had been short-lived.

Una had abandoned me. My stepmother barely looked at me. Patriarch Meallán had stared, eyes heavy with pity and perverse desire all at once.

I hadn't been worth much. No Maboni was. But that day, I became worthless.

But if I hadn't been infertile, would I be a mother now?

It didn't matter.

I would never be.

But I couldn't tell the kings that. Just in case Jules wasn't joking. He had to be. The offspring of a vampire and a human was always a witch, and the King of Dawn wouldn't want a witch child.

And if he wasn't joking... well, vampires had low fertility rates, like all demonbloods. He would surely blame it on that. Maybe, for once, my broken body was a blessing.

The General raised her dark brows. "That's a first."

"Fatherhood looks good on Cédric." Jules released my hair. "Might be time I give it a try."

Luc didn't acknowledge the remark. His gaze swept the thralls, assessing, discarding. A silent moment stretched, taut with expectation. When his eyes settled on a golden-haired thrall, she didn't flinch, but something in her posture shifted, as if bracing.

"Our volunteer needs to be bathed and dressed with the other Maboni," he said. "You know the rules, Maire."

"Yes, Your Majesty."

"Ready her for the ceremony."

Maire nodded and stepped to my side. Two chains of gold circled her neck. The first, a gilded collar. The second, a pendant necklace of a star. But instead of the star rising to the sky on a tail of dust, the symbol was flipped like the star was crashing into the ground. My stomach twisted at seeing the Church's symbol again, even if it was upside down.

She wore a sleeveless black gown of fine-quality linen, the material clinging to her flat stomach and perfect curves. Two slits ran up through the middle of the skirt, exposing flashes of bare skin with every step. Too much skin. Back home, a woman wouldn't dare show so much as an ankle outside her house. But every thrall I'd seen had worn this little.

As if their bodies didn't belong to them at all.

Maire gestured for me to follow her. I swallowed and took a step—

"Wait." We both stiffened at Luc's voice. His gaze had dropped to my chest—no, to the satchel over my chest. A flicker of something crossed his face, too brief to name. Not calculation. Not possession. Something closer to... reluctance? Then, just as quickly, his expression smoothed. He turned to Jules. "Take it."

"Ah, yes. Good call." The King of Dawn strolled back over and raised his hand. "Hand it over."

I hesitated. Then, slowly, I passed him the satchel and my book.

Jules bopped my chin with his knuckles. "I'll see you later, lovely."

Later. Tonight. The ceremony. I forced a breath out and turned to follow Maire before I panicked. We moved toward an empty section of wall between columns. She pressed on the wall. It clicked open, revealing a door worked seamlessly into the design. She ushered me into a narrow hallway.

When the door closed behind us, shielding us from vampire eyes, her head snapped up. Her soft, submissive expression was gone. She gripped my arm with surprising strength. "We don't have a lot of time. Listen well, and maybe this won't be the worst night of your life."

"WALK, NESSA."

I glared down the steep limestone staircase that cut into the earth like the gaping mouth of a beast. Distant music reverberated from the darkness and into my bones. My heartbeat quickened alongside the drumbeat. "You're not serious."

Maire had talked almost nonstop for the past hour. Through scrubbing me raw in a giant tub, dumping all of my clothes into the fire without a care, and tossing a ball of gauzy white fabric at my head. She had remained harsh and abrupt... until we reached the Staircase of Doom.

"Now, Nessa," she snapped. "Remember what I said? Keep your eyes down. Never let them see your expression. Follow all instructions quickly and silently. *Disobey* and there will be consequences."

I swallowed and took the first step. Then the second. Maire had repeated those four rules like they were core tenets. Maybe they were, given the utter silence of the Maboni who walked in a line behind us. A handful of black-clothed, collared thralls moved among the wave of white descending deeper into the earth, but I hadn't spoken to anyone except Maire. Like during the journey from Mabon, I stood apart.

Too bad I wasn't dressed differently.

A white gown slid down the softness of my belly and over the curve of my hips, flowing to the floor. Every inch of my skin was visible through the translucent waterfall of fabric. Maire had pierced my ears with quick, efficient movements, the sting barely registering before she slipped in a pair of simple gold studs. She had then brushed out my braid, leaving my brown hair loose and drifting down to my waist.

I had never felt so exposed.

"Why even bother dressing us?" I asked. "Why not just send us into their dens naked? We basically are."

"What color do they wear at Maboni weddings?"

Horror slowly rose within me. "...white?"

"Why?"

"To..." I swallowed. The sick fucks. "To show we're pure and untouched."

"Exactly."

Shivers danced across my skin. I wrapped my arms around myself. A sharp pain lanced through my core. I sucked in a breath. How many hours had passed since the kings last cast a soothing rune? Too many. Especially with terror pressing in, anxiety tightening around my throat, and the desire I refused to acknowledge burning beneath it all.

A murmur of voices reached my ears over the music. The runelight sconces along the walls had grown dim, fewer and farther between, but the next one illuminated a polished marble floor stretching into the darkness. A corner ahead bled soft light.

I squeezed my fist open and shut.

The end of the Staircase of Doom.

The start of the worst night of my life.

I didn't care what advice Maire thought she imparted upon me. None of it changed that simple truth.

"One foot in front of the other, Nessa," Maire said. "I'll be right behind you."

I reached the marble floor and turned the corner.

I stumbled.

Runelights carved into towering stalactites bathed the cavern in an eerie glow. The space was massive, easily the size of the castle aboveground. Multiple tiered floors stretched into the rock, each lined with chaises, cushions, pools, and tables piled with food. Five levels dropped below us, assuming we mirrored what I barely glimpsed on the other side of a yawning chasm. Narrow paths crisscrossed the gap, terrifyingly thin and without rails. A human would fall to their death trying to cross, but a vampire could probably walk it blindfolded.

Maire had called this space the Abyss. The sinister name fit perfectly.

But its majestic yet lethal architecture wasn't the easiest thing to focus on.

Not with all the writhing bodies.

A vampire man had his female thrall's legs around his neck, his fangs buried in her thigh. On the chaise beside them, a human male thrust into a vampire woman with reckless abandon. In the nearest pool, a vampire man fucked his male thrall from behind, licking a trail of blood on his shoulder. My gaze flickered from body to body to body. The wet slap of flesh and fervent cries of release joined the echoing music to create a debauched symphony.

I had witnessed glimpses of feedings on the road, but nothing like this. The depravity the Church warned about came to a terrible, sinful light. *Godstars, protect me from what is to come.* I hadn't prayed in years, but I couldn't stop the thought. This was the terrible fate that awaited all the Maboni. That awaited me.

But for ten thousand years, this was simply life. When the first demons fell to the earth, all of humanity became prey.

I exhaled slowly, forcing the hysteria down. *You will survive this.*

"Shit," Maire muttered behind me. "You're untried."

"I think this would be a shocking sight for anyone."

"That's not the problem. You're the property of the Imperium now." Maire fumbled around in her skirts. Where was she even hiding a pocket? "After they claim you as their Mortal Bride, they'll likely feed from you. They're both large enough that it will hurt if you're inexperienced."

Large? Make that massive. I bit my lip to stifle a strangled laugh. If I started, I didn't think I'd ever stop. "Won't their venom help?"

"Their venom is strong, stronger than most, but no venom will last long enough to help you when you walk tomorrow."

I nodded absently. Tomorrow. When I was Mortal Bride and thrall to the Conqueror and the Butcher. After they claimed me tonight. After they *fucked* me tonight. My mind spun, light and untethered. Huh. Was this what dissociation felt like? I'd only read about it.

Maire gave up her search with a sharp breath. "I didn't think to bring any salve. I'll bring it to you the first chance I get. Neither king is... overly cruel to their thralls, so I wouldn't worry too much."

"How do you know?"

"That the kings aren't overly cruel to their thralls?" she asked. When I nodded, she continued, "I've served the Imperial Family for nearly a decade. While I belong solely to the Crown Mage now, I didn't until three years ago."

Something unexpected flared in my chest. Anger? Jealousy? It didn't matter. I had no right to feel any of it. Only terror. "So you've fucked both of the kings?"

"I've fed both of them." Maire's grip on my arm tightened. We had stood still for too long, the line of humans waiting behind us. She pulled me forward. "While fucking and feeding are intertwined for vampires, we refer to it as feeding only. You'll do well to remember that. To say you fucked a vampire is to infer you're their lover. Most won't react kindly to that insinuation from a thrall."

"So we'll only have sex with them during feedings?"

Maire looked down. "I didn't say that."

I nodded slowly. I couldn't manage anything more for a reply.

Maire weaved us through the Abyss, past beautiful vampires in various stages of undress, their fangs sinking into mortal flesh. Hundreds of eyes flickered toward me as we moved deeper and deeper. I didn't turn to see if the Maboni followed.

If I looked anywhere except at the floor in front of me, I'd scream.

If I thought of all the eyes tracing my body, I'd run.

But it was impossible not to notice the Azarasians slowly abandoning their thralls and facing me—and the procession undoubtedly behind me. Unholy light gleamed in each luminous gaze.

Something tingled across my skin, a softer caress that chased away the scratches of attention and settled me firmly back in my body.

I peeked up through my lashes, only for my gaze to crash into molten silver and gold.

All Azarasians with soulbonds had the same colored eyes, but I recognized these in a heartbeat. We had reached the far corner, where a grand staircase carved into the rock rose beside a drop into nothingness. It led up to a platform holding a single black throne. Constructed entirely of daemium, it wafted shadows from its high back and curling armrests, every visible inch carved with tiny, shivering runes.

And probably every hidden inch, too.

But the Kings of Dusk and Dawn blocked my view.

The throne's seat was wide enough for both vampires, with room to spare. On the left, Luc lounged with the lazy confidence of a predator. His high-collared navy doublet fit his broad chest perfectly, fastened with two columns of silver buttons. Dark trousers and knee-high boots fit him with the same precision.

Jules sat cross-legged on the right, his elbow propped on his knee. He still hadn't found shoes, bare feet peeking from beneath dark slacks. His ruffled white shirt hung unbuttoned to his sternum, two thick golden chains crossing his chest between crimson epaulets threaded with gold. He'd traded out his rings for ones with larger gems, though none matched the teardrop-shaped rubies dangling from his ears.

Between us and the kings' platform, four vampires sprawled on gilded chaises and plush cushions. The Kings' Council. Maire had gone over their names quickly. On the left, Crown Enforcer Sabas spoke low to his soulbound, a golden-eyed, brown-haired man who bore a striking resemblance to Jules. Crown Mage Cédric Roche, Jules's brother and Maire's master.

To the right, General Isabeau reclined back, her fingers absently stroking the ringlets of the black-haired, dark-skinned beauty curled against her. Crown Chancellor Roxiana Vela, Luc's aunt through his deceased grandmother, Marisol Vela.

When Maire had said that, I'd startled. I recognized the name. Before Marisol became the Regent of Tenebra de Mar and grandmother to the Beast King's son and heir, she was a lieutenant under Azaras at the start of *The Soulborne Queen*. Karra hadn't liked her very much.

Isabeau murmured something, and Roxiana straightened, her silver eyes widening as they locked onto me. She didn't bother lowering her voice. "Really? *Her*?"

Luc snapped his fingers.

The music stopped.

The entire floor—no, the entire cavern—dropped into absolute silence.

All the vampires bowed. Maire nudged me sharply. Thralls had to drop to their knees before the Imperium. Only vampires were allowed to stand. I forced my legs to move, sinking down with the others to the cold, dark marble.

Roxiana stood with inhuman grace. She was about my height, easily making her one of the shortest vampires I'd encountered so far. Her dark ringlets cascaded to her waist and her ochre gown clung to her curves, its cut-outs perfectly placed to reveal flashes of her toned abs, arms, and legs.

Even in the middle of a vampire feast, I couldn't stop my envy. Starsdamned demonblood genetics.

Her voice boomed across the Abyss, amplified by a rune I couldn't see. "You stand before their Majesties Lucero Azaras and Julien Roche, Kings of Dusk and Dawn, Imperators of the Blood Legion, and Imperium of the Azarasians." A pause. "You may all rise."

We all did.

"Who presents the Maboni Harvest?" Roxiana asked.

All the attention turned to me. My throat went dry. The silence pressed in, thick and suffocating. They were all staring. The kings, their council, the gathered Azarasians, the harvested and collared thralls, hundreds upon hundreds of eyes dissecting me like a specimen in a laboratory.

I forced myself to breathe, but it wasn't enough. My hands clenched into the fabric of my gown, but there was no comfort in it.

Only the reminder of how little it covered.

Pain curled low in my abdomen, a familiar, unwelcome pressure. My tongue felt too thick. The words were there, but they stuck in my throat. No one moved.

Luc and Jules waited. The council waited. The entire cavern waited.

This was a nightmare.

Maire's fingers brushed mine.

I flinched. But it was enough.

"I will, Your Excellence," I said, my voice barely above a whisper.

It didn't matter. The silence carried it anyway.

"And who presents the Isauran Harvest?"

The Isauran Harvest? There were witches here, too? Movement sounded behind me. I finally twisted around. The Maboni cowered, a stark contrast to the line breaking off from the end of ours, approaching alongside.

The Isaurans looked human, if slightly taller. Unlike vampires, their demon blood didn't gift them inhuman beauty, though most were attractive. A faint shadow rim circled some of their otherwise ordinary irises, thin enough to be overlooked.

They wore collars already, marked with runes. *Suppress. Submit. Obey.* It almost looked like the thrall runespell. Why not carve it into their skin?

The first seven witches appeared in their everyday garments, but the twenty or so behind them were clad in the same white fabric I wore. They all walked with straight shoulders and raised chin, their lowered eyes the only sign of submission. Vampires leered as they passed, but the witches didn't shrink back.

When they reached the front, one separated from the group. A slim, dark-haired girl moved forward, a gilded cane tapping against the floor with every step.

No, not a woman. A *teenager.*

She was the youngest person in the Abyss. The youth from Mabon had been ushered from the thrall bathing chambers to their new quarters. Maire had said they wouldn't be spared, but they would only feed vampires of a similar age until adulthood.

The teenage witch folded both her hands on top of her cane. "I will, Imperium."

Luc arched one dark brow. "And you are?"

"Morrena, Exalted Daughter of Isaura, Your Majesty."

Luc stiffened.

Jules nearly slid off his seat, kicking his feet in glee. "Morrena? We didn't recognize you in your new body. How's that treating you?"

New body? What in the stars did Jules mean by that? Witches couldn't shapeshift like demons. Vampires could barely manage it, and their ancestry was more demon than human.

"Better than death, Your Majesty."

Jules cackled. "Very true. I forgot how hilarious you are."

"No one finds me as funny as you do, Your Majesty."

The smile slipped from his face. Something dark and terrifying moving behind the King of Dawn's golden eyes. "Careful. I don't enjoy strapping children to my Block, but I'll make an exception for you, given you're... what? Four thousand?"

Four thousand? But witches were mortal, living a couple hundred years on average. That was the whole reason they created the everlife runespell. Was it because she had a new body? How did that work?

I let the questions distract me. Otherwise, I'd have to consider the Butcher's Block, a thing of horror stories. I had hoped it wasn't real.

Morrena didn't react to the threat. "Four thousand one hundred and eighty-nine, Your Majesty."

Jules whistled. "Damn. You just refuse to die."

She almost frowned, but the Exalted Daughter wiped her expression quickly.

"You last presented the Isauran Harvest twenty years ago, did you not?" Luc asked, done with the pleasantries. If threatening to torture someone on the Butcher's Block could be considered a pleasantry.

"I did, Your Majesty."

"And last you were here, you attempted to surrender to us again."

"Yes, Your Majesty."

Luc's voice turned frigid. "Since then, have you heard from your sister, Exalted Allegra?"

Who was Exalted Allegra? The Queen Mother Luc had mentioned after the wraith attack? That explained the change in his tone. The air in the cavern dropped. It was never a good idea to piss off a vampire. But to anger the Conqueror? The entire harvest, witch and human, hunched their shoulders, making themselves smaller.

"Not since we last spoke, Your Majesty," Morrena said carefully.

"Then perhaps you should try again."

Morrena stared at the kings' feet for a long second. Then, with slow, creaking movements, she dropped back to her knees, clutching at her cane for balance. She pulled up her sleeve, exposing her forearm. "On behalf of Isaura and its High Council, I, Morrena, Exalted Daughter of Queen Isaura, surrender unconditionally to the Azarasian Impire. My country and our citizens are at your mercy."

The shadows of a runespell appeared. *Oath. Loyalty. Union. Retribute.* The first three runes matched the allegiance spell Azaras once used to bind his citizens to the throne. But I had only ever seen the retribution rune on Maboni brands.

The rune that killed the man who tried to leave our island.

Morrena had pledged her life to Isaura. Wouldn't surrender trigger the rune?

Tension thickened the air, every eye on the rune on Morrena's skin...

Nothing happened. Was something supposed to? If Allegra was dead, would the allegiance runespell have faded, since Morrena would have inherited her throne?

Jules sighed. "Nope. Bitch must still be alive."

Morrena remained on her knees. "Allegra is tenacious, Your Majesty."

"We will find her one day," Luc said darkly.

"One day," Morrena said. "But that day is not today, Your Majesty."

Luc glared, but Morrena didn't die instantly. She flirted the line between stupidity and bravery just as I did. Or skirted, more accurately. Exalted Morrena didn't seem the least bit interested in the kings.

That insanity was mine alone.

"Proceed with the harvest," Jules said, when it became apparent Luc would not.

He said the words to both of us, but his gaze was on me.

Morrena glanced over from where she kneeled and raised her brow. My jaw opened. What was I saying again? Maire had told me the words, but I couldn't for the life of me remember them.

There was another reason beyond my illness that I never left my bookshop. The crowd's gaze stabbed into me, as sharp as my illness and just as destructive to my thoughts.

Morrena faced the kings. "We thank the Impire for their generosity. You provide the clothes on our backs, the food in our bellies, and the roofs over our heads. In repayment of such kindness, we gift you twenty-five of our people to serve as your new thralls, from this day until they breathe no longer."

Ah, yes. Those were the words.

When the silence continued after Morrena spoke, a thousand waiting eyes on me, I exhaled deeply. "We thank the Impire for their generosity," I said, my voice only trembling slightly. "You provide the clothes on our backs, the food in our bellies, and the roofs over our heads. In repayment of such kindness, we gift you three hundred and five of our people to serve as your new thralls, from this day until they breathe no longer."

"And?"

I swallowed. "I gift you myself to serve as your new Mortal Bride, from this day until I breathe no longer."

"We accept your gifts," Luc said, a spark of heat flaring in his gaze. He completely ignored Morrena at my side, his eyes fixed on me as intently as Jules's. "Now come here, Miss Halloran."

My insides flipped. I forced myself to straighten. Every part of me wanted to cower, to fold into myself and disappear. My breath stuttered out.

I would survive.

I put one foot in front of the other. If I thought any further, I'd make a run for it. I had no interested in being fucked into the nearest chaise. I didn't know if walking toward the kings would stop that from happening, but hopefully it reduced the chances.

Tonight, at least.

Every vampire, witch, and human stared as I approached the kings. To them, I was just flesh. They'd use my body like any other thrall. Like what would've happened anyway if I'd let Aislin go and stayed behind, waiting to be harvested at thirty. They couldn't claim any more from me than that.

But a sudden rush of... everything washed through my chest. Rage. Fear. Resignation. Hope. I dug my fingers into my palms. There were too many emotions to sort through.

Beneath it all, my pulse throbbed between my legs.

I climbed each step in time with my breath, not too fast, not too slow. The kings' daemium throne sat in the center of a circle of runes only a couple steps away. *Dominion. Protect. Echo.* I frowned. The power and protection runes made sense, but what did echo mean?

Finally, I reached the top. My eyes flickered up slowly—

Two nearly black gazes ensnared me. A sharp ache formed in my chest.

Luc leaned back, taking in every nearly bare inch of me. "Hello again, little curiosity."

My nipples tightened, the sheer fabric grazing against them with every breath. Stars, what had they done to me? This couldn't be natural. A second ago, I had gifted myself to them. I had gifted three hundred of my people to them.

To be eaten and fucked.

Jules patted his knee, drawing me from my thoughts. "Sit."

"On you?"

"On my knee." His lip twitched. "It's one of the more innocuous places you'll find yourself sitting."

I shuddered, my heart skipping a beat. The corner of his lips twitched at the sight. I pushed the image of sitting on Jules's cock right out of my head and faced the problem at hand.

How did one go about sitting on another? Jules's thighs were sculpted to perfection but my ass still wouldn't fit. I hesitated, trapped in my own mind. I didn't know what to do. Worse, people were watching. How many were at my back?

Fuck, I was going to vomit... or cry.

If I was unlucky, maybe both.

A hand looped around my waist and tugged me down.

I fell into Jules's lap. My body locked up. I was *sitting* on the Butcher. Jules traced the outside of my thigh, the heat of him burning through the thin layers of fabric.

He leaned closer until his mouth brushed the ridge of my ear. "I can feel your pulse between your legs, lovely. Will you be drenched for us by the time we leave the dais?"

I gasped at the terrible, wicked, enticing words. Fuck. I managed a glare, aiming for aghast and landing on desperation.

Jules playfully nipped my chin, a faint brush of teeth.

I nearly jumped off his lap, but his arm around my waist tensed. Luc dropped a hand on my knee. I froze. The King of Dusk didn't look at me, but he didn't have to. His touch was a brand just like the one that once graced my neck.

"You're dismissed, Morrena," Luc said. "Return to the exit with your delegation and you'll be escorted to your rooms."

"Thank you, Your Majesty." Exalted Morrena finally rose to her feet, her knuckles white on her cane. She turned on her heels and walked back the way we came.

The six other witches in ordinary clothes followed her, one by one. We watched and watched and watched until they disappeared from view.

A lump formed in my throat.

The air in the cavern shifted, tension rising like a drawn bow.

The vampires stared, their bodies wound tight, coiled like beasts before the pounce.

Dread pooled in my belly, cold and suffocating.

*I will not cry.*

*I will not scream.*

*I will not let these monsters break me.*

I tried to shuffle out of the kings' oddly comforting touches, but their hands tightened on my knee and ass, holding me in place.

Luc glanced at their chancellor. "Roxiana?"

Roxiana sliced her hands through the air, and a rune flared into existence. *Count.* The shadows solidified into glowing numbers. I frowned at the giant 60, as confused as every other Maboni. What had the rune counted?

The Isaurans just looked grim.

59.

58.

57...

Oh.

Oh, fuck.

Roxiana grinned as the vampire horde circled like vultures. "I suggest you run."

FOR A MOMENT, EVERYONE stood still.

54.

53.

52.

Panic spread through the Maboni harvest thralls like a contagion. Almost as one, they turned on their heels and bolted for the door. The Azarasians surrounded them on three sides. There was nowhere else to run but the exit.

45.

44.

43.

The vampires shifted, subtly but deliberately, blocking the way to the doors Morrena and the other witches had used. The only path left was the gaping mouth of a tunnel, yawning open in the rock.

37.

36.

35.

Blindly, the Maboni ran for it.

"You're herding them," I said.

Jules absently traced circles on my hips. "My favorite part of the hunt."

A shudder rolled through me. At his words? His touch? Both? I shook off the thought. This was horror. I shouldn't desire its masterminds.

At the base of the dais, chaos churned. Some thralls understood there was no escape. Most of the Isaurans had stayed still, their eyes downcast. A handful of Maboni had made the same choice, but as hundreds of hungry, blackening gold and silver eyes fixed on them, their fragile resistance shattered into fear.

22.

21.

20.

One man made a break for the edge of the cavern floor. I couldn't turn away. Was he going to jump? Some would rather die than become a vampire's blood whore.

Instead, he scrambled onto one of the narrow walkways. One step. Two steps. A wobble. I slammed my hand over my mouth to hide my gasp—

Before he fell, Roxiana grabbed him by the scruff of his neck. The vampire was a head shorter than him, half his width, yet she lifted him back to solid ground like he weighed nothing.

13.

12.

11.

Roxiana let go. The man whirled, slamming his arm toward her—

A scream tore from his throat. His body convulsed. The thrall runespell at his neck flared with dark energy, binding him in place.

Luc scoffed lightly. "Fool."

Roxiana crouched, patting his head like a chastised pup. "There, there. I guess I should have added that attacks on us aren't tolerated, no matter how futile. It was in your best interest to run and submit." Roxiana bounced to her feet. "Your life is forfeit now. What a waste."

The man's head snapped up at that last bit, his eyes widening.

3.

2.

1.

The vampires struck.

Roxiana fisted a hand in the man's hair, jerked him upright, and sank her black-tipped fangs into his throat. Most of the others vanished in a blur, streaking into the tunnels after those who fled.

But on the cavern floor, nearly a hundred Azarasians pressed in. Hissing, growling, staking their claims. The strong pushed forward. The weak were shoved back, snapping at the edges. The already-collared thralls remained where their masters had left them, kneeling in obedient silence.

But the unclaimed were still outnumbered two to one.

Just the way vampires liked it.

Isabeau circled Roxiana and her thrall, their bodies gyrating on the ground. Whether she was waiting her turn or figuring out how to join her soulbound, I wasn't sure. Almost every other vampire pair in sight repeated the dance. Yelps and screams echoed through the cavern, from the floor, from the tunnel. Fear, momentary pain from the bite... and then pleasure.

Bodies crashed together. Clothes tore.

I tore my gaze away, staring into the drop beyond Luc's shoulder. I did not need to see this. I'd experience it soon enough. Maire had already warned me.

I scanned the crowd, tracking her down among the frenzy. I found her where I feared she'd be—sprawled across the lap of Sabas's soulbound, Cédric. His fangs were deep in her throat, his hands gripping her hips, guiding her as she rode him with reckless abandon.

Maire had spoken like she hated her vampire. But if the raw moans spilling from her lips were any indication, venom had made a liar of her.

My heart pounded. Fear swelled in my chest, heavy and cloying. I was minutes away from becoming a living sacrifice and thrall.

But beneath the terror, something else stirred.

What would it be like? To be claimed by the Conqueror and the Butcher? Would I moan like Maire did, reduced to nothing but a vessel of need?

My nausea spiked. But what if their venom wasn't enough to stop my broken body from clawing at me from the inside?

My lips parted. A whisper of air escaped. "What would happen if I wasn't willing to be your volunteer?"

Jules stilled beneath me, his fingertips halting on my hip. Though I didn't turn my attention from the cavern's darkness, the kings' attention pressed against my skin like a physical touch.

A warm hand traced across my chin and tilted my face away from the feast. I followed the strong arm across the throne to an ocean of black, the faintest sliver of silver gleaming between pupil and shadow rim.

"You'd still be our thrall," Luc said, his voice a low, dark caress, "albeit an alluring one with lust in her eyes."

"I'm not... that's not..." Words tangled in my throat. I should fight this. My mind fought it. But my body... my body didn't.

Luc studied me. Reading too much. Understanding too much. "Are you unwilling to be our volunteer, Miss Halloran?"

Something about the way he said the words sent another shiver through me, my skin prickling with a confusing mix of fear and desire. It wasn't really a choice. They would bite me either way. But there were benefits to being their Mortal Bride, the best of my limited options.

If they needed my lifeforce to recuperate to fuel their spell, then I couldn't be miserable, could I? In other lives, I was dashing through tunnels or warming Patriarch Meallán's bed, caring single-handedly for a brood of children.

I swallowed hard. Stars, I'd done a lot of that in the past few hours. It was a miracle I hadn't dropped dead from nerves yet.

"I'm willing."

Jules relaxed beneath me, that easy grin sliding back into place. Luc nodded once, rising to his feet with the slow, deliberate grace of a predator. "Then it's time to make you our bride."

*Our* bride. I breathed in through my nose. Out through my mouth.

When Luc extended his hand, I took it. His touch was warm, sending sparks along my skin. As the King of Dusk tugged me up, Jules lifted me from his lap. He stood beside us in a quick movement and wrapped my other hand in his. "You had me worried there for a second. All my hopes and dreams, dashed by a single sentence."

"A bit dramatic, don't you think?" I tried to match his light tone but sounded breathless.

"Not at all."

The kings led me around the throne, approaching the stone wall behind it. Only when we stood before it did I see the diagonal slash in the rock. It wasn't wide enough for all three of us shoulder to shoulder, so Jules moved in front of me, Luc at my back. Their hands held mine captive. My spine tingled—the monster luring me forward, the predator prowling behind.

Runes flashed in the air as we passed through. *Barrier.* Warmth tickled across my skin, but nothing stopped me from moving forward.

We entered a large alcove, the smooth rock polished to a gleaming finish. A gilded daemium runegate loomed against the far wall, large enough for a single person to step through. But my attention caught on the bed-sized crimson chaise piled high with silk pillows.

My fear spiked. Like a virgin on her wedding night, only this was so much worse. The burning desire in my core drowned beneath cold terror.

*Breathe, Nessa.* In. Out. In. Out. *You must stay calm.* My pulse steadied.

I would survive this.

But even if I didn't, Aislin and her baby would. That had to be enough.

Jules stopped at the edge of the chaise and spun to face me, his eyes alight with mischief. I stumbled back into Luc's chest. Both kings closed in, surrounding me with their inhuman warmth. Jules traced the line of my jaw, while Luc's fingers trailed up my spine. I gasped, my body singing with the touch.

I cleared my throat. "How does this work? The magic, I mean."

Jules's lips twitched. "What else would you mean?"

I shot him a glare. Luc answered, his voice steady, "We're part of the spell. As the ones who cast it, we control it. Our lives aren't intertwined with it like yours will be, but we use our connection to bind you."

I nodded. His words made sense, but that didn't explain how they'd cast the spell.

"All it requires on your part is a runespell," Jules said, reading the question on my face.

"Like the thrall one?"

"A little like the thrall one, but it will go here," he said, dropping his hand to the space above my breasts. My pulse jumped. "And it won't hurt."

Luc had reached the top of my spine. He drew a warm, twisting shape along my skin—

I lost all sensation below my neck.

My body crumbled. I slumped forward into the kings' waiting arms.

Panic crashed through me. Godstars, what the fuck? I tried to move, to fight, but I had no control. My mind thrashed, willing my arms to lift, my legs to work.

Nothing worked.

No sound left my lips.

Jules's voice cut through the rising terror. "Don't panic, lovely," he murmured, brushing my hair from my face. His touch was gentle, almost soothing. A mockery of comfort. "It's only temporary."

Only temporary? My pulse roared in my ears. They had *paralyzed* me. I couldn't feel anything below my neck and my starsdamned mouth didn't work—

Luc plucked me into his arms and laid me carefully on the chaise. Fuck. Fuck fuck fuck. But he didn't follow, didn't pin me beneath him. I lay sideways on the cushion, my body limp, positioned perpendicular to Luc as he kneeled at the edge. Jules stood above him, arms crossed, looking down at me.

No, not at me.

At my sternum. At the place where they planned to carve a fucking runespell into my skin.

I couldn't do this.

I didn't want to do this.

I needed to do this.

"Close your eyes and count to one hundred," Luc said.

His voice carried a quiet command. My body almost obeyed, lulled by his confident authority, but I forced my eyes to widen at him. I would *not* obey blindly.

Luc met my stare.

No, the Conqueror met my stare.

I refused to cower under it. I was already helpless in his hands. What more could he take from me?

"You won't feel a thing," he said softly after a long moment. "And when you open your eyes, your body will be your own again."

Would it?

Still, I glared up at him. At both of them. But the kings only stared back, their expressions serene and cold.

The Imperium, waiting for me to submit.

Did I have any other choice? They wouldn't begin until I calmed. And I needed to be calm. I needed to be their *willing* sacrifice. They hadn't told me what would happen if I resisted or changed my mind mid-way, but it couldn't be good.

More than anything, I wanted to live. So I closed my eyes.

1.

*I can do this.*

2.

*I will survive.*

3.

*I can do this.*

4.

*I will survive.*

The count to one hundred stretched into eternity and snapped past in an instant.

98.

*I can do this.*

99.

*I will survive.*

100.

Fingertips ghosted against my pulse.

I gasped at the sensation, the soft touch like a strike of lightning after the nothingness that floated through me. My chest was still numb, but everything else came rushing back. Two arms. Two hands. Ten fingers. Two legs. Ten toes.

My eyes fluttered open.

I bit my lips to stop my scream.

Blood drenched my chest, trickling across my collarbone and soaking into the neckline of my white gown. *Soothe. Soothe. Soothe.* The runes flared, but I barely noticed them with a giant runespell carved into my chest, pulsing black shadows. *Bind. Sustain. Conduit. Transfer. Dusk. Dawn. Endure. Glamour.* The runes repeated over and over, an intricate web of magic woven into my flesh.

I sat up, bending my legs and pressing the soles of my feet to the cushion. Trying to stand didn't seem the wisest idea. Blood slipped in thin rivulets over my ribs, pooling between my breasts before disappearing beneath the fabric.

"See? Was that so bad?" Jules asked.

Yes. Yes, it fucking was. But if I opened my mouth, I would scream, so I glared. Again.

Jules grinned like he found my defiance charming, like I was some adorable creature baring its teeth.

Luc didn't smile. He only studied his work. Cool, meticulous. Detached. His freaking shadow claws had carved a spell into my chest, and he looked at the marks like a scientist evaluating his latest experiment.

Then, ever so slowly, Luc extended his clawed hand to his soulbound. "Since she's yours first, Julien."

Jules's grin sharpened, like a child unwrapping a long-awaited gift. He leaned forward and took Luc's bloody finger into his mouth, his tongue flicking over the dark talon before he sucked. I breathed out shakily.

Luc held his gaze, unblinking.

When Jules finally pulled back, Luc's claws had faded to nothing, the last of the darkness dispersing into the air.

"Good boy." Luc caressed his cheek. "How does she taste?"

I shuddered. Jules did, too, but he still nipped at his soulbound's knuckles as he pulled away. "Delicious."

"Hmm." Luc refocused on me, the smolder not leaving his eyes. "There's one more thing we must do to activate the spell. Stay on the chaise until I tell you otherwise."

A part of me bristled at the command, but I didn't move. Instead, I curled in on myself, arms wrapping around my middle as if that could hold me together. *I can do this. I will survive.* Being a sacrifice was better than being a corpse.

Luc touched his inner wrist. A rune flared to life against his skin. *Relay.* It glowed briefly before disappearing back into his flesh. "Send him in, Estrella."

The runegate across the alcove shuddered. Its surface shuddered and then burst. *Gate. Distance. Path. Arrival. Cross.* A wavering figure stepped through—dark-haired, silver-eyed, draped in hardened leather and impire's insignia.

Estrella.

A human thrall followed her. He was an inch or two shorter than me, his graying hair cropped neatly, his face deeply lined with age. His black tunic and trousers were finely made, modest and opaque, unlike the thin silks draped over other thralls. Around his throat, a collar of gold and silver twisted into intricate patterns. It was far more elaborate a piece than Maire wore.

My breath caught. Oh. No, it couldn't be. They hadn't said... but I hadn't asked.

Where was the current Mortal Bride?

Dead, perhaps? I hadn't considered it. I should have. They had said the runespell needed a home, that it must always have one. Which meant... there had to be a living Mortal Bride now.

I stared at him, wide-eyed and speechless. He didn't look at me at all. Didn't even glance my way. Surely if he knew he was about to die, he would panic? Try to run? Unless... unless he didn't know.

Unless he couldn't see me at all.

A cold weight settled in my chest.

Estrella simply bowed, then turned back to the runegate. On the other side, Tristan waited. She stepped through... and the shadows swallowed her, crashing together like waves on the shore. The gate solidified once more into a smooth, unbroken sheet of daemium.

The man—the Mortal Bride—managed a slow, practiced bow. He kept his gaze lowered and respectful. "How may I serve you, Imperium?"

"Bare your throat," Luc said coldly, circling around the man.

A shudder ran through the Mortal Bride, so slight I might've imagined it. But he obeyed, closing his eyes and tilting his chin up, exposing the long, vulnerable line of his neck.

Jules approached him slowly and traced a line up his throat. "Such an obedient bride you are, Odran." His black gaze flickered over to me. "Oddly, I don't think I'll miss that."

Odran frowned slightly. "Your Majesty?"

Jules didn't answer.

Luc didn't either.

Instead, Luc fisted a hand in Odran's hair and yanked his head back farther. Jules smiled, a cruel expression. Then, together, their canines extended—long, black-tipped daggers.

They struck as one.

Luc and Jules plunged their fangs into either side of Odran's neck.

His body jerked. Once. Then slackened. Bliss washed over his face. His lips parted, a quiet moan escaping. With every swallow, his body trembled, swaying where he stood.

But the kings didn't move, didn't succumb to the lust that should have overtaken them. They only drank. And then, in a sharp, practiced motion—

They tore away.

Hot droplets splattered against my face.

Everything in me went quiet. Blood spurted from the Mortal Bride's neck.

From the two gaping *holes*.

The Conqueror and the Butcher had bitten his throat out.

The Mortal Bride twitched, eyes rolling back as he crumpled to the floor. Dying. Right in front of me. Luc and Jules stood over his twitching form, blood painting their lips, their chins, the silk of their shirts.

A searing heat pulsed through my chest.

I screamed.

# 17

THE SUDDEN PAIN SLAMMED into me, hard enough to knock me flat on the cushions. The dark runespell on my chest flared, shadows drinking my blood like it was water in the desert. The more it drank, the more it burned and twisted.

*Bind. Sustain. Conduit. Transfer. Dusk. Dawn. Endure. Glamour.*

It flashed into other shapes, other runes, running through the verses of the spell. Each flare of shadows seared into my vision.

Within seconds, the spell had absorbed every drop, from the cut in my skin to the stains in my gown. It cooled instantly. A weight pressed into my chest, *inside* my chest, like the magic had hardened and settled somewhere behind my ribs.

I pushed onto my elbow. Where the raw edges of the cut had been, a black imprint in the covenant spell's shape marred my skin. I traced a finger against it, expecting to feel something, but the runes faded the moment I touched them.

I exhaled, long and slow. I had survived.

The first part of this, at least.

*You can do this.* I lifted my face to the vampires before me. The Mortal Bride—the *former* Mortal Bride—slumped dead at their feet.

I stomped down on my panic. I would *not* become a blubbering mess on the floor before the Conqueror and the Butcher, no matter what horrors they committed.

"Is that... it?" I asked, managing to sound nonchalant. Almost.

"To make you the Mortal Bride, yes." Luc licked the blood from his lips. He drew a small rune against his own skin. *Clean.* It absorbed the remaining crimson drops.

"Oh."

"No need to be disappointed, lovely." Jules didn't care about the blood on him, letting the red run in slow rivulets down his chest. "I'm quite hungry after all that work. Aren't you, Lucey?"

"Absolutely starving," Luc replied, those black eyes on the fluttering pulse at my neck.

Everything in me froze. "But you just ate."

"Hardly," Jules said.

Without looking at the body, he drew the faint lines of a rune in the air. *Incinerate.* The former Mortal Bride turned to dust at his feet and then vanished entirely.

Just like that.

Gone in a second.

All that remained was his silver-gold collar, clattering against stone.

No matter the smiles and banter I shared with the kings, that was all I was. A single mortal in a long line of disposable brides. One day, it would be my body disintegrating at their feet while a new bride cowered on the cushions.

"Take off your dress, bride."

Luc's voice shocked me out of my grim thoughts, but my nipples pebbled instantly. "What?"

"You heard him," Jules said, dipping a finger in the blood on him. He brought it to his lips, eyes fixed on me.

Luc began unbuttoning his doublet. "If you want something to wear tomorrow, take off your dress."

I had just watched someone die and replaced them as the Mortal Bride, but my courage suddenly failed me. "What if I say no? I'm your willing volunteer—"

"You *were* our willing volunteer," Luc corrected. "Now you're our Mortal Bride. We can now do with you what we please."

Oh.

Shit.

The kings followed my every breath. I shivered at the weight of their black-eyed stares and couldn't stop. I was *trembling*. Had I ever truly done that before? But if there was ever a time to tremble, it was now. I was alone with two vicious vampire kings. There was nowhere to run. Even if there was, I wouldn't get far.

But did I want to get far? I wasn't trembling in fear alone.

Stars, I was deranged. Sick. Something was terribly, terribly wrong with me. They were the Imperium. They were murderers. One day, they would kill *me*.

But a part of me didn't care. I was so tired of suffering. The loneliness ached as much as the pain. For once, I wanted to feel good. I wanted *them* to make me feel good. I didn't believe the godstars were listening, but I prayed to Them anyway.

*Please let their venom make my pleasure stronger than my pain.*

*Please let me pretend they desire me for me.*

*Please let me have one moment of peace, no matter how brief.*

I shook my head and slid to the edge of the chaise. I was their Mortal Bride. Their thrall. They were hungry. This was a transaction, nothing more. I needed to keep all my silly hopes and feelings locked in my chest where they belonged.

I reached for the sleeves of my dress, but I paused a touch away. The kings had seen me naked, but this was different. This wasn't an almost-innocent bath in a lake.

The kings planned to feed on me.

The kings planned to *fuck* me.

I didn't care what distinction Maire made. To me, they were one and the same. The fear rose, washing away every other emotion.

"I don't..." I swallowed. "I don't think I can."

Luc flicked a finger in my direction. "Julien, assist our bride."

"With pleasure."

Jules approached, a bloody grin stretching across his face. He stripped his own tunic off with a quick flick of buttons. My heart pounded, the beat low in my core. He dropped the fabric without a care, baring the crimson-streaked, toned lines of his perfect chest.

He stretched out his arm and wiggled his finger. The dead Mortal Bride's collar flew off the ground and into his waiting hand.

I froze.

No.

Jules ran his thumb over the silver-gold band, inspecting it with a casual air, as if it hadn't just been wrapped around a corpse's throat. As if it wasn't still warm from another's skin. From someone whose body had disintegrated to nothing.

I couldn't breathe.

Jules stepped closer.

Panic clawed up my throat. My lips parted, but I couldn't speak. Couldn't move.

The cool weight of the collar brushed my throat, smooth metal gliding over my skin like a lover's touch. The pressure settled against my throat. The air in my lungs turned thin. My pulse thumped wildly beneath the metal, a frantic drumbeat in my ears.

*Click.*

The lock snapped shut.

Sealed. Done. Unbreakable.

Before I could start hyperventilating, Jules swept his hands across my shoulders. My gown parted, the straps sliding in a slow, traitorous glide down my arms. It didn't even bother putting up a fight.

One second, it was on me.

The next, a puddle on the ground.

Cold air rushed over me, raising goosebumps across my bare skin. I gasped.

Jules's stare dropped from the collar to my breasts. He licked his lips unabashedly. For my blood, not for me. But my nipples didn't care. Aching, humiliating peaks tightened under his attention.

*Wicked, sinful girl.*

I crossed my arms across my chest.

"No." The King of Dusk was behind me in a blink. Luc's fingers curled around my wrists, tugging them gently but firmly behind my back. "You are ours now, Nessa. We want to see our new bride."

*Ours.* Heat rushed in every direction—to my cheeks, to my chest, to my cunt. "You already have."

"You didn't let us look." Luc inhaled deeply against the back of my hair. "This time, we will have our fill."

Their black gazes traveled over me like a caress. Jules's focus lazed down to the expanse of my soft stomach, pressed kisses to the curves of my hips, and lingered at the tuft of curls between my legs.

Luc traced a slow, deliberate path down my spine. I couldn't see his eyes, but I felt them. Felt them fixed on the roundness of my ass. He ran his fingers through my long, loose hair at my waist, tugging just enough to make me shiver.

I writhed underneath the kings' devouring stares.

Why were they looking at me like that? I wasn't meant to be looked at like that. Not by anyone as gorgeous as them—

Jules cupped my left breast, rubbing his blood-stained thumb around my nipple. A trail of red smeared across my skin. I stuttered out an exhale as a spark jolted through me.

Every thought vacated my head.

He let loose a sigh. "Stars, I've wanted to touch these pretty pink nipples of yours for days."

He swirled his finger faster and faster. The blood—the *dead* Mortal Bride's blood, some part of me yelled—made his touch glide over me. Oh, fuck. I bit my lip to stop my moan—

Luc's knuckles closed around my right nipple and twisted. Another wave of heat burst through me. I yelped, flinching away. But I didn't get far, the King of Dusk's body at my back unyielding.

His breath tickled across my ear. "What an exquisite little sound you just made. Perhaps Jules had the right idea, keeping you to ourselves."

I forced a snort. Exquisite? Me? Not at all. Not in any reality. "There's no need to play games anymore."

Both kings' fingers stilled, though they remained hot on my flesh. Luc circled to my side, keeping his grip on my wrists. "Games?"

"The pet names. The quips. The... flirting, I guess?" I said, managing a flippant tone. "You were pretending so I'd be your willing volunteer. There's no need for that anymore."

There was a long pause.

Luc slowly arched a dark brow. "Why would we pretend?"

He wasn't serious. Was he? "You're the kings of an entire impire. If you hadn't wanted me to be your Mortal Bride, you never would have noticed me."

Luc arched his brow higher. Jules remained restlessly still, like a beast about to pounce on his prey.

Shit... they were serious?

No.

"I'm not interesting or young or pretty and if you aren't at least *one* of the three, you're nothing." I raised my chin and kept my voice firm. "So let's get this over with. Stop playing games with my feelings and fucking bite me already."

The kings just stared. They weren't even blinking. I clenched my fist and told my body to stay still under their scrutiny. But my pulse hadn't yet steadied from their touches, the pounding of my heart giving me away.

I wanted them to want me. I *shouldn't* have wanted them to want me.

It didn't matter. The Imperium could never want a shy, broken spinster who preferred books over people.

Then Jules shuddered. "Fuck, that made me hard."

My eyes widened—and dropped to his trousers. My mouth dried. He wasn't lying. Or maybe he was. Vampires controlled their own blood. If he could will away his erection on the hellsteed, he could as easily summon one.

I swallowed. "I'm not surprised distress does it for the Butcher."

Luc had his hand around my neck in a blink. Everything within me clenched.

"Being an insolent brat does it for the Butcher," Jules said, then grinned at Luc's hand. "And the Conqueror."

"Let me make something clear." Luc pulled me closer until my back pressed into his chest and slid his hand to my jaw, tilting my head back, back, back until I met his eyes. "We *are* the kings of an entire impire. We have no need to play games. What we want, we take."

It took everything in me to hold his dark, powerful gaze. "And what is it you want?"

"Right now? To fuck that defiant little mouth of yours while you come screaming on Jules's cock."

My mouth dropped open as the fire in me burned bright. Luc's dulcet tones summoned wicked images in my mind, ones I had buried in my sickest fantasies. My core was slick between my legs. I pressed my thighs together, a useless attempt to hide my reaction.

Jules breathed in and groaned. He pulled back his blond hair and tied the strands in a knot. "You'll have to wait your turn, Lucey. I need to taste her right now."

My brow furrowed. "You've already tasted me."

Luc smirked. "He didn't mean your blood."

What? But before I asked, Luc was gone from my back and my thighs hit the cushion. I tumbled onto the chaise. The question fled my brain alongside my insecurity.

Jules dropped to his knees in front of me.

Oh, fuck. I tried to scale back on the chaise, away from whatever he had planned. "What are you doing?"

"I need to see if the rest of you is as sweet."

"But..."

He looped his arms around my knees and pulled me closer to him. Odran's blood smeared from his chest to my knees. "But what?"

I still couldn't understand it. "You shouldn't want to touch someone like me."

"I shouldn't want to bury my head between the thighs of my soft, innocent bride?" Jules spread my legs wide until every glistening part of me was exposed.

Luc groaned at the sight over his shoulder.

My skin pebbled, my breath rushing out of me in fast pants.

Jules didn't give me a chance to reply.

It all happened at once.

As my butt hit the edge of the cushion, Jules dipped his head between my thighs. He lapped his tongue through my wet center. All thoughts vacated my head at the slow, languorous lick.

Oh my fucking stars.

I jerked in his hold as pleasure flashed through me. When he reached the top, the ball of his tongue piercing bumped against something hyper-sensitive. My clit. I squeaked, an embarrassingly high-pitched sound. My thighs whacked against his shoulders as I clenched. I felt his bloody smile—*felt*—before he rolled his tongue around and around.

"You... you... Ahh." I couldn't even form a sentence. My entire being focused on the jolts of pleasure shooting through me from that tiny nub I had searched for but never found.

I had touched myself before, but it hadn't felt like this. My pleasure was a muted trickle, a rarity. My pain was a forest fire and all too common. But this... this felt like... I whimpered. I didn't even know how to describe it.

Like death.

Like life.

I never wanted it to end.

I spread my legs wider. I didn't mean to. But I couldn't help myself. I needed his tongue deeper inside me. Jules chuckled, and I nearly screamed as the deep vibration traveled right through me. I grabbed for the cushion behind me, anything to hold me down to reality. My head dropped back as my body trembled.

A hand fisted in my hair and tugged my face back up. I met luminous black eyes, the King of Dusk towering behind the King of Dawn. "Eyes on me until you come."

Pain flared through my scalp, a quick rush before the soothing rune washed it away. But it made the pleasure between my legs stronger. I moaned.

"Does it feel how you imagined?" Luc asked. "While reading all those dirty little books of yours."

"I—I—" Jules's tongue leisurely swept toward my entrance before he came back to my clit. I swallowed. Stars, I'd get this sentence out if it killed me. "It was just one book."

"That doesn't answer my question," Luc said. "Julien."

Jules took the little bud into his mouth and sucked. A shout burst from my throat. My eyes nearly rolled back, stars flashing behind my eyelids.

Luc tightened his fist in my hair. I mewled, snapping my gaze back to the King of Dusk. "When I ask, you answer. When I command, you obey. Am I understood?"

I exhaled shakily. "Yes."

"Yes, what?"

Everything within me tightened even more somehow. "Yes, Your Majesty."

"Good girl."

I whimpered at the words.

His smirk became a grin, a rare and gorgeous sight. "Now, does your king's tongue *feel* how you imagined?"

Jules circled faster and faster around my clit, his piercing scraping against the edges. "N—no. I never could have—oh stars—imagined this."

My chest heaved, my words breathless, but I had answered. Jules continued his torturous pattern, spinning the heat higher and higher in me. The pleasure writhed under my skin, invading my every cell.

Through it all, Luc watched. My panting, flushed face. My heaving breasts. Jules buried in my cunt. His cock had hardened visibly beneath his trousers, but he didn't touch himself. The Conqueror wasn't ruled by his body. He ruled it—as he did the bodies at his feet.

Jules dipped his tongue lower again, this time circling the rim of my entrance. I gasped at the sensation. The building pressure. The shooting tendrils of heat. The way my body clenched in eager anticipation.

But I knew it wouldn't last. It couldn't. It never did. My body wasn't meant for pleasure, only pain. My panic spiked—

Jules dipped his tongue inside me.

I tensed, bracing. First, the stretch as my cunt expanded for him. And after that... after that... The heat in me built, but it didn't turn to shattered glass, scraping at my insides.

My nipples tightened.

My breath spiked.

My nerves tingled.

I cried out, a desperate whine. My legs jerked, but they were trapped within Jules's grasp, locked between his body and the chaise.

Without warning, the King of Dawn lifted my thighs and hefted them over his shoulders. Odran's blood smeared against my inner thighs, but I barely noticed. His tongue slipped deeper into me.

"Fuck, fuck, oh, fuck." My legs tried to snap closed, but they only looped tighter around Jules's back.

"What a loud, dirty mouth you have," Luc purred.

I clamped my jaw shut. Shame rushed through me. *Quiet, girl.* My stepmother's voice snapped through me. I was too loud. I was always too loud. Too tall. Too soft. Too big. Too much. I curled into myself, wishing the chaise would swallow me whole.

Jules's lidded black eyes flickered up to me. Something wicked flashed through them.

Luc had the same idea. "Make her scream louder."

I bit down on my lower lip, knowing it was in vain.

Jules pressed his tongue against my inner walls. The ball of his piercing rubbed against me. Pleasure lit my every cell and nerve as he grazed against a spot as sensitive as my clit.

I couldn't hold back my scream. I stood on the edge of a cliff, almost there, ready to jump off, ready to fall.

But I couldn't. Not only did my body turn pleasure into pain, but it denied it entirely. Jules pushed me higher and higher. I wanted to crash. Wanted the bliss to destroy me.

But it wasn't meant to be. I didn't work—

Luc tightened his fist in my hair. "Stop resisting."

"I can't," I whimpered.

"You most certainly can."

"No, no, I can't. Please, please please—ohhh..."

Jules slid one hand down my thigh. His fingers threaded through my curls to my clit. He didn't even need to search. He found it on the first try, the practiced hands of an expert. The begging trailed into an obscene moan.

He tweaked that aching bud. I shrieked. The drop started—

Luc chuckled. "That's it. Come on my soulbound's tongue for me, little curiosity."

Waves of ecstasy crashed into me. I shuddered, thrashing against the kings' hold on my legs, in my hair, but they held me firm, their grips unyielding. A shriek escaped my lips, the sound wanton as I buckled and thrashed and *came* on the Butcher's tongue.

My orgasm wrecked me, destroyed me, remade me.

I had never felt anything like this before. Never imagined something like this. And I never would've expected it here, little more than their thrall and sacrifice. But the King of Dawn lapped at me like a delicacy, like the best thing he had ever tasted. I whimpered as he guided me through the bliss with gentle strokes.

As I spasmed, Luc released my hair. I slumped back into the cushion, heaving and boneless. Aftershocks of pleasure fizzled through me. I stared hazily at the cave's ceiling.

Fucking godstars.

I rubbed my hands down my face. I lay naked on the chaise, the fabric soaked beneath my ass. I wished the pillows would swallow me whole.

I had *come* on the King of Dawn's tongue. He hadn't even bit me first. It felt like a betrayal to my whole country, to every thrall born and raised in the Impire. It was certainly a betrayal of the Church and the godstars.

But I couldn't force myself to care.

Jules gently removed my legs from his shoulders. I didn't resist him at all, little more than clay in his hands. My toes brushed the floor, a shock of cold. It wasn't enough to pull me from the haze.

Weight pressed down on the edge of the chaise. Light kisses trailed up my stomach and around my breasts. Breath ghosted across my left nipple before lips closed around the tight bud and sucked.

A strangled, exhausted cry escaped me.

The King of Dawn flickered his smug, black gaze to me from where he had crawled over my body. When he released my nipple, my cry turned into a pitiful whine.

"So demanding," Jules murmured against my chest.

He brushed his lips across my chest to my right nipple. I moaned as he rolled his piercing around and around the aching nub. With a faint brush of teeth, he pulled back with a wet pop. I shuddered.

Jules trailed kisses along my collarbone, to my pulse point, then across my jaw. I watched him move without reaction, floating in bliss. When his lips hovered over mine, he murmured, "I've never tasted anything like you, lovely. Melted sugar, with just the faintest spice of blood. You'll be writhing on my tongue daily."

Blood. He meant *my* blood.

I should have cared. Should have been mortified. I had come apart on the King of Dawn's tongue, and he had tasted the blood that always came with my arousal.

The thought barely registered. My mind was too slow, too soft, drifting in warmth.

All I managed was a hoarse, "Uh-huh."

He grinned at my response.

Large hands looped under my arms. I was pulled across the chaise from underneath Jules to between two thick, golden-brown thighs. I left a humiliating wet trail along the cushions.

Jules hadn't been the only one to climb onto the chaise. Luc now rested on the huge pillows propped against the wall. He settled me on top of him, his skin soft and warm. I melted into him—strong chest, smooth abdomen, and a hard length burning into my lower back.

I gasped. Seeing Luc's cock and feeling it were two different experiences. There was no way it would fit within me. He'd tear me in two.

Jules noticed my shock as he prowled forward. "Don't worry. You'll only take my cock tonight. Luc will have to fuck those beautiful, plump asscheeks of yours."

As Jules said the words, Luc pulled me closer, closing that last inch. He pinned his erect cock between us, the hard length burning into the curve of my ass. His piercings pressed against my skin. All five of them, little studs at the ends of thin bars. My head dropped back on his left shoulder.

The King of Dawn pushed onto his knees between my legs, his erection bobbing with the motion. My mouth watered. He lifted one of my calves and hooked it over Luc's thigh, then did the same with the other.

Spreading me wide and open for him.

I should have cared. I should have been terrified or embarrassed. He was going to bite me and fuck me.

But I remained loose and floating.

"You have one last choice," Luc said right into my ear. "Do you choose the bite of ecstasy or the bite of agony?"

"I prefer the ecstasy myself." Jules leaned over me until his nose brushed mine, trapping me between their powerful bodies. "As both the bitee and the biter."

"Most who choose the bite of agony the first time never choose it again," Luc continued. "But it is still a choice for you to make."

It wasn't a choice at all. I had experienced pain nearly every other day for a decade, the last week the one exception. I wouldn't ever choose agony when pleasure was the other option.

*Wicked, sinful girl.*

But I didn't care what my stepmother or the Church thought of me anymore. In their eyes, I was doomed the moment I decided not to marry.

"Ecstasy," I whispered.

"You'll have to repeat that," Jules said. "I didn't quite hear you. Did you, Lucey?"

"No, unfortunately not."

I swallowed and cleared my throat. I blinked some of the haze from my brain, just enough to respond. "I choose ecstasy."

The tip of Jules's nose brushed my earlobe. "Then consider this your warning."

Jules's canines morphed, the ivory stretching into faint, swaying shadows. I stared, entranced. I hadn't witnessed the transformation this close before.

Luc tilted back my head, baring my throat for Jules—and him. His lips brushed down the cord of my neck, the sharp tip of his fangs grazing my skin. They both planned to bury their fangs in me, like they had the former Mortal Bride.

Panic finally burst through my lust.

Two sets of fangs pierced my neck.

I gasped, my body locking tight. It burned. The pain licked up my spine, curled through my ribs like a fist squeezing my lungs—

But then it softened. Melted. The sharp, stabbing sting dulled to a languid pull, a heat that coiled through me, rich and dizzying. My nipples peaked. My clit throbbed. Fuck, I needed them. I had just come, but I needed to again. Now—

Everything shattered.

Sensation exploded in my veins.

Heat. Fire. A mind-breaking pulse. It slammed into me, wrapping around my bones, twisting through my blood. It filled every part of my body, from my head to my fingers to my toes.

It wasn't pain.

It wasn't pleasure.

It was something else.

Something *more*. It filled me up, my entire body prone in its grasp. It reached through me to the bodies above and below me. Luc and Jules's fangs were in my neck, blood dripping down my skin, but they didn't move, as entranced as I was.

I settled into the warmth, the otherness, letting it in.

And in.

And in.

It didn't stop. It just built more and more, higher and higher. I tried to shuffle under the sudden weight of it, but still I couldn't move. My wonder twisted, darkened.

I couldn't fucking move.

It wasn't like before, when Luc paralyzed me. I felt the kings around me, the hard press of their cocks, the softness of their skin, the tickle of their hair against my face. It was like something had pinned still my very soul.

And was now determined to crush it.

The pressure ground me down. Any second now, it would crack my bones, pulverizing me beneath it. I thrashed internally as it built and built, higher and higher.

I breathed out slowly through my nose. I couldn't control much, but I could control that. I knew pain. I survived pain. I would survive this, as well.

Sometimes the only way out was through. Resisting my illness only made my stress worse, which in turn made my pain worse. It was a vicious cycle that never ended. The only way to stop it from spinning on and on was to surrender. To let the pain wash over me and not worry about when it would end.

It *would* end.

I relaxed my every muscle, going slack in between the kings and the power whirling within all of us. I gasped as it filled through me, that agonizing pressure now a rush of warmth.

For a second, I was complete.

Unbroken.

Invincible.

Strong.

Then the power latched onto my very bones and pulled me into darkness.

# 18

I DRIFTED SLOWLY AWAKE through the fog of my mind. My dream—no, my nightmare—of blood and bodies and silver-gold eyes faded with every inhale. Beneath me, the softest, creamiest silk caressed my bare skin.

Strange. I'd never had a bed this fine, just like I never slept naked. My loft was always too cold for that. I blinked brown hair out of my eyes, strands twisted in every direction. That, at least, was normal—

A muscular, golden-brown arm looped across my chest.

My breath stilled. My heart stopped.

I followed the arm from wrist to elbow to shoulder to the perfectly sculpted chest of the dark-haired man pressed against my side, his strong features softened in sleep.

Luc.

At the sight of him, the entire night crashed back into me.

Yesterday—the harvest, the covenant runespell, the kings—had been real.

Oh my fucking godstars.

A soft, melodic sigh brushed against my stomach. I couldn't move, not with Lucero *fucking* Azaras holding me prisoner in a starsdamned cuddle, but I tilted my head, already knowing who I'd find.

Jules sprawled on his front, his torso nestled between my legs, using my stomach as a pillow. Dried blood marred his chin and throat. His hair was more tousled than usual but still tied back in a knot at the base of his neck.

From when he had stuck his tongue in my cunt.

His tongue.

My cunt.

Together.

Fuck.

That was really all there was to it.

I slumped back onto the chaise and stared at the cave's smooth ceiling. How was this my life? If I told the Nessa of a week ago that a blood-soaked Butcher King ate me out and then fucked me on *top* of the Conqueror King, we would have laughed hysterically.

At least... I thought he fucked me on top of Luc. Their fangs had plunged into my neck and then—

Then...

My thoughts stuttered. Slipped.

I blinked at the ceiling, suddenly blank. What was I just thinking about?

Luc shuffled against me, his nose brushing against my cheeks. Every fiber of me focused on him. My pulse hammered against my ribs. His lips settled over my throat, just above the new collar encircling my neck. Drawn to the scent of my pulse, to the panic surging through my veins. Every inch of me tingled where his warm skin touched mine.

Then Jules stirred in his sleep, his chest rubbing against my core.

I ignited.

Fuck. I needed to get out of here. But there was nowhere to go. Even if Jules wasn't lying on top of me, I'd still have to get past Luc hugging me like his favorite pillow. I was trapped under a pile of vampire kings.

I bit my lip to hold in a giggle. I, Nessa Halloran, who had spent her life with her nose in a book, was under a *pile of vampire kings*.

Just breathe. Yes, breathing I could do. If I breathed softly, maybe my heart would slow. Maybe the heat building in my belly would fade. Maybe the sparks dancing across my skin would slow.

Maybe the two fucking heavy vampires on top of me wouldn't bite me in their sleep.

Or when they woke up.

I swallowed. That was the real concern, wasn't it?

If anyone had sex for breakfast, it was vampires.

Assuming it was morning. Maybe we had only slept for ten minutes. But the cave was silent except for the soft, melodic whistle of Jules's snore. The echoes of music, laughter, and screams had faded. I felt refreshed, the exhaustion from sleeping on a wagon for the last week gone.

Hours had passed, I was sure of it.

I stiffened. Yup. Hours had definitely passed.

Now my bladder was awake, too.

I wiggled slightly. I couldn't help it. Now that I'd thought about it, I really, really needed to pee.

Jules nuzzled his head against me. "Five more minutes," he murmured, his voice thick with sleep.

I went rigid. Every muscle froze, but my heart did the opposite, racing as fast as a hellsteed. A small frown furrowed between Jules's flawless brows. In *The Soulborne Queen*, vampires could wake instantly if they sensed a threat. Jules obviously didn't consider me one, but if he was even half awake, that would be enough—

His eyes flashed open.

Luminous gold locked onto mine.

I yelped. It was a small sound, but it was enough to startle Luc out of sleep. His entire body went taut. His bright silver eyes scanned the cave in a single second, sharp and assessing.

Then that heavy gaze fixed on me, and I nearly died.

Not because they were vampires. Well. Partially because they were vampires.

More because we were all naked and had *sex* last night... last night—

Jules suddenly pushed up onto his hands and knees, still staring at me. The intensity of a predator had changed into the confusion of a man. "Huh."

I blinked slowly at him. I had lost my thought again. "Huh?"

"Yup," he said, popping out the word. "Huh. Best sums it up."

Luc exhaled and sat up, pulling his arm from me. He ran a hand through his dark, loose curls. His back rippled with the movement, muscles flexing under his flawless skin. I had to stop myself from licking my lips.

"What do you..." Luc's voice trailed off. A flicker of something crossed his face. He almost caught it, but then it was gone.

That wasn't like the Conqueror. Luc always had complete control over his words.

I shuffled, unnerved. Something was wrong, but I couldn't... I couldn't...

"Am I crushing you?" Jules flopped onto his side next to me, as if nothing was amiss. Because nothing *was* amiss. "Just wait until Luc gets his turn on top."

Blood rushed straight to my face. My mind instantly summoned the visual of the Conqueror scaling up my body. The breadth of his shoulders blocked out the world until everything was only him, glistening with sweat, his muscles rippling with each thrust.

Jules and I weren't the only ones imagining it. At his words, Luc's attention dropped, skimming across the soft lines of my body. His pupils dilated ever so slightly.

Because I was still naked, every inch of me on display.

I sat up, a quick movement. A wave of dizziness rushed over me, but I pushed through it. My inner thighs were a mess, sticky with the aftermath of last night. My desire. Odran's blood. My heart stuttered at the sight.

I needed to get out of here.

"Um..." I cleared my throat. "Is there a privy nearby?"

The Kings of Dusk and Dawn just stared.

Luc blinked once, twice. He shook his head, like he needed to physically force himself to focus. But his frown didn't ease as he finally answered, "Through the Abyss, in the Hall of Mirrors."

A straightforward answer, for once. Something was definitely off.

"Thanks?" With as little self-consciousness as I could muster, I shuffled to the chaise's edge. I reached for my gown puddled on the floor—

"No," Luc said, his tone sudden and cutting.

I dropped the gown, more from shock than obedience. "What?"

"You disobeyed last night."

I blinked. What did that have to do with anything?

"Luc told you if you didn't take off your dress, you'd have nothing to wear," Jules reminded me, the edge of his lip twitching. "Since I took it off, I guess it belongs to me now."

"But..."

Luc arched one dark brow. "But?"

I bit my tongue. I wasn't their willing volunteer anymore. I was their Mortal Bride and thrall, collared and claimed. Everything Maire had said came back to me.

*Keep your eyes down.*

*Never let them see your expression.*

*Follow all instructions quickly and silently.*

*Disobey and there will be consequences.*

I had always disagreed with rules, but that didn't mean I disobeyed all of them. I couldn't win every battle. I couldn't win most battles, even in Mabon.

But I didn't want to walk out of here naked. Every inch of me screamed against it. I wasn't a godstar carved from granite. I was soft, vulnerable, utterly human. But I had a feeling public nudity was something I'd need to adjust to unless I wanted to go insane. Vampires didn't care about nakedness.

At least my unbound hair was long. It would cover my breasts. But there wasn't any way to hide my ass.

I dropped my gaze. "But nothing."

A knuckle grazed my chin, tilting my head back up. My world became golden eyes. I expected Jules's carefree smile, but a dimmer but no less beautiful version graced his lips. Confusion softened his usual mischief. "Don't do that."

I blinked. "What... exactly?"

"Lower your gaze," he said, frowning. "I don't like it."

He didn't *like* it?

Jules twisted back toward Luc, who hadn't moved. The Conqueror simply watched us, impassive as stone. Jules gestured vaguely at me. "Why don't I like it? I usually love it."

Luc's silver eyes narrowed slightly. "I'm not sure."

Jules pursed his lips, brows drawing together like he might push further. Then, just as suddenly, the frustration slipped from him. In a blink, his usual mischief was back.

"Well," he said, hopping to his feet, brushing it off as easily as dust from his hands. "Might as well find some breakfast."

I tried not to look at his ass, but it was right there in front of me, just asking me to stare at its perfect, firm—

I shook my head. Nope.

My stomach chose that moment to betray me. A loud rumble echoed through the cave.

Jules turned, grin widening. "It seems you are as hungry as I am after last night."

I swallowed, my face heating. "So it seems."

What else was I supposed to say? Stars, I wished I'd spent less time with books and more with people. Not that it would have helped much. Luc and Jules weren't people. They were centuries-old vampire kings.

Jules, however, looked entirely delighted by my awkwardness. "Come, lovely."

He didn't even glance at his scattered clothes. A flick of two cleaning runes erased the dried blood from his skin and mine. Then, utterly at ease, he strolled for the archway. Completely naked.

He waved a hand at me.

I hesitated before slowly pushing to my feet. "Just because I'm not wearing anything doesn't mean you have to be naked, too."

"Best way to come, in my opinion."

I glared. He snickered, completely unrepentant.

Luc, however, still hadn't moved. But his frown had deepened even further, a storm cloud across his gorgeous face. Something about his expression held me in place. Not the usual intensity, not the predatory stillness. This was different.

Something was wrong.

He knew it, felt it, but he didn't know what. And he *hated* that. A muscle twitched in his jaw. For a fraction of a second, his control looked thin. Stretched. A crack in the mask.

Not rage. Not hunger.

Panic.

The Conqueror didn't grasp for control. He *was* control. He dictated, he commanded, and the world obeyed. Because it had to. Because the alternative was worse. They had all tried to wield him, so he made himself unwieldable. Not a pawn prince, but a king—

His gaze suddenly snapped to mine.

I jerked back into myself. Spinning on my heels, I strode after Jules, pulse hammering in my throat.

The Butcher was a psychopath, but his presence was nothing compared to his soulbound's. Even knowing Jules intentionally lured people into a false sense of security wasn't enough to keep me in that room with the frowning Conqueror.

I'd had enough trembling for the week.

That was the reason. Nothing else. It wasn't that I'd never been able to read Luc before. Not once.

But for that brief moment, I had.

I was clearly losing it.

I passed through the barrier rune, a gentle tickle across my skin, and stepped onto the dais behind the throne. Jules had confirmed it was morning, but the Abyss was just as dim as last night. No light, no time. Just an endless, eerie twilight. Stars knew how far underground we were.

My gaze flickered around the vast chamber. I didn't spot Maire among the thralls, awake or asleep. The chaises, cushions, and pools were empty of vampires, but thralls in bloody scraps of black and white scattered the space, most curled up in sleep. Two or three sat up, rubbing the sleep from their eyes and blinking around blearily.

Further back near the tables, a dozen black-clothed, collared thralls cleared tables of food, like this was any other morning. For them, maybe it was. If the feast-orgies happened frequently, they must have learned how to carry on.

There had to be at least two hundred of us missing.

How many were in the tunnels below?

How many others had woken up in a vampire's bed above?

Jules reached the top step but paused when he realized I hadn't followed. He held out his hand, wiggling his fingers. I swallowed. If I was going to survive this, being brave would have to become second nature.

As I stepped forward, the King of Dawn followed my every movement. I'd have to get used to that, too. People hadn't looked at me much in the bookshop. Here, I was prey among predators. Watching me seemed to be the kings' default.

When I reached his side, I pressed my palm into his. Jules started down the stairs without a word.

At the base of the steps, a male thrall sprawled on his side—

I stopped. Or, at least, I tried to. Jules kept his leisurely pace, my hand trapped in his. But I slowed just enough that Luc caught up. The heat of him pressed into my back, closing the space between us instantly.

If not for the corpse, I'd have scrambled away.

It was the Maboni man from last night. The one who had tried to run onto one of the narrow pathways across the dark drop. Roxiana had declared his life forfeit, but I had forgotten him in the chaos. The red puncture mark of fangs scarred both sides of his neck, his collarbone, his inner thighs.

I reached up, brushing my neck, but both marks were gone, like they had never happened. Vampire saliva healed surface wounds—or else everyone they bit would bleed out—but no one had bothered healing him.

They had *drained* him.

His skin had turned an unnatural shade, not just pale but empty. A color I had never seen on anything living. His bloodshot eyes stared, fixed and glassy.

His lips were frozen in a soft smile.

My eyes tingled. No. I wouldn't cry, not here. Not in front of the worst of the monsters. This was my reality now. I was the Mortal Bride. And I would be until the kings one day lured me back into that room, their new Mortal Bride runemarked and invisible on the chaise.

Death would walk beside me the entire way, my constant companion, always near but never touching.

Until the Conqueror and the Butcher tore out my throat.

# 19

MY FINGERS DRIFTED ACROSS the silver-gold collar encircling my neck. A single tear slipped free, racing down my cheek. How many Mortal Brides had worn this collar? Had carried their runespell inside their chest?

How many more would wear it after me?

Jules glanced back at me, at the body. "Ah, don't cry, lovely. He quite enjoyed his death."

I tore my gaze from the corpse. "That doesn't make it better."

"From your perspective, I suppose."

"From anyone's perspective."

"Any human perspective," he corrected, twisting around to walk backward as he tugged me along. "Coming to death is a goal of mine."

"Then why don't you offer yourself as the next meal? Spare some poor human if you're so eager." The words snapped free, sharp and angry. Against Maire's rules. But I didn't care.

"Careful, little curiosity." Luc's deep voice swept over me. He didn't touch me again, but I felt him there, at my back. "We're not above punishing our errant brides when they speak out of turn."

The hairs on my skin raised. I twisted, just enough to see his intimidating form in my periphery. "Punish how?"

His lip curled slightly. "Depends on the bride."

Jules sighed, almost dreamily. "I can't wait."

I shuddered... but I didn't think it was in fear. Stars, I was fucked in the head. I started to frown, to cover my perverse desire, then caught myself. *Never let them see your expression.* I didn't have to deny or disapprove of their sinful ways like the Church demanded. Not anymore. I needed to stay blank, unaffected.

I kept my steps steady, my gaze forward. I would *not* tremble.

The kings crossed the Abyss with me between them, weaving around furniture and thralls like they were one and the same. I didn't notice another dead body. The others from the harvest were splattered with dried blood, their clothing shredded, but otherwise appeared unharmed.

Physically, at least. Most of them now wore simple silver or gold collars like Maire and the other experienced thralls, though a few necks remained bare. More than one person we passed clawed at the metal, fingers desperate but useless against the solid band.

We reached a grand archway, massive wooden doors propped open to allow free movement between rooms. This wasn't the tiny door we had entered through last night, leading to a narrow hallway and that endless staircase. This space was different. Soft carpets muffled my steps, three twinkling chandeliers of rubies casting deep red light across gilded daemium gates. Nearly thirty of them hung like mirrors along the walls.

A silver-eyed vampire female in a slinky crimson gown bowed beside the entrance. On the table next to her, an open box revealed plain iron collars, like the ones I'd seen on some thralls outside Dawnspear. The different collar types meant something, but I couldn't bring myself to care.

There was only one other door in the room.

It better fucking lead to the privy.

"Imperium," the female said, dipping into a deep bow.

I pulled my hand from Jules's and crossed the room, head held high. The vampire female didn't even look at me. Her gaze remained fixed on the floor, unwavering, obedient. Even if she had looked up, who would stare at me when the Kings of Dusk and Dawn stood there like living sculptures?

"Rise, Luisa," Luc said. "How many unclaimed thralls have passed through?"

"Not many, Your Majesty. This quarter's harvest was quite popular with the High Courts..."

I pushed into the privy, her response fading away. Like the one I'd used before the revelry, runes kept the small chamber clean, disposing of waste instantly. I could get used to never needing an outhouse or chamber pot again.

By the time I finished, the kings were speaking softly as Luisa fastened an iron collar around an older Maboni man. He clutched the remnants of his torn outfit in front of his crotch, his knuckles white. Both kings looked up as I crossed the Hall of Mirrors toward them. Their gazes swept over me, assessing, unhurried. I kept my spine straight and my arms lowered, but the urge to cover myself itched at my skin.

Jules sighed wistfully. "I deeply regret not fucking you again before getting out of bed."

I didn't even blink. Saying wild, ridiculous things was just Jules.

The King of Dawn's gold eyes flickered to mine, his brows slightly raising as his lips quirked. "Not even a purse of those pretty lips. Have you adapted to me already?"

"Maybe I'm just tired."

Luisa's head whipped toward me in shock.

Jules pursed *his* lips. "That's not it."

"How do you know?"

"You're not hard to read."

It wasn't an insult. But it still hit like one. Simple. Boring. Ordinary. Not hard to read. I added Jules's words to the list, stacking them alongside my stepmother's taunts and the whispers of my neighbors in Corraidin.

I turned away before he could see it sink in. "Privy aside, why didn't we use the gate in your... private cave?"

Jules snorted. "Private cave?"

Luc's callous gaze didn't rise from me. Behind his icy facade, there was something sharp, biting. A trace of heat. He couldn't be disappointed about not fucking me, could he?

"That one is linked to a specific gate in our apartment," the King of Dusk said. "We've warded our apartment against intruders. If you were to step through, the spell would attack you instantly."

Their apartment. I hadn't asked where the Mortal Bride lived. I hadn't assumed *with* the kings, but if my lifeforce now powered their most important runespell, it made sense. I was a vulnerability for them. They would want to keep me close.

How close, exactly?

In the next room close?

Or in their bed close?

My nerves tried to grab my cunt and make a run for it. I stopped them both from going wild.

Jules raised his hand toward the end of the Hall of Mirrors, where an expanse of wall stood empty of daemium gates. Something rippled. I squinted, but my vision warped. Was that a glamour rune? There was one on my chest now, hiding the covenant, but seeing another on something that wasn't solid was... unsettling.

When the floating trail of blood touched the barrier, the glamour fell away.

Jules summoned blood from a *body* chained to the wall. Three gilded bars carved with runes looped around the unconscious thrall, a cage around their legs, torso, and neck. *Sleep. Soothe. Endure.* Thin, sharp blades erupted from the bottom of the neck piece, stabbing the thrall's chest below their collarbone. Blood trickled down from each puncture point.

I stared in horror. Even after Jules pulled all the blood he needed to activate the runegate, even as the glamour resettled, hiding them from view. Their face had been serene, peaceful. Like they weren't being drained, drop by drop, their lifeforce keeping the vampires' runegates running.

A hand looped through mine. Luc's. I barely had time to react before he dragged me forward, straight toward the daylight now spilling through the open gate.

A shiver wracked my body as I stepped through. Light hit my eyes, bright and disorienting after the Abyss's dim glow. I blinked, adjusting. This hallway was nothing like the ones below Dawnspear. Pale wallpaper framed elaborate crown molding and arched casement windows, polished marble floors gleaming in the sunlight. Behind me, the runegate settled back to solid daemium, blending seamlessly with gold-framed art of bloody battles and even bloodier revelries.

Beautiful and terrible, like almost everything in the Impire.

At least there weren't any bodies chained to the wall.

That I could see, at least.

Luc released my hand and approached a towering set of solid gold doors, their surface carved with hundreds of looping runes. *Ward. Protect. Shield. Barrier.* The power of the runespell hit me all at once. It wasn't nearly as searing as the covenant, but it radiated like banked fire, stronger than most magic I'd encountered.

Luc lifted a hand, expectant. "We'll need your blood to add you to the wards."

I swallowed but approached the kings and that intimidating door. The end of the hall behind me led to a set of stairs, but running wouldn't be an option again. Vampires treated chases like foreplay.

When I reached Luc, I placed my knuckles in his palm. His thumbnail darkened, sharpening to a wicked black edge. With a quick slice, blood welled from the shallow cut.

I waited for the instinct to pull away. It never came. I didn't react. Didn't have to force myself not to flinch. I had been trying to hide my fear, but this time, there was strangely nothing to hide. Moments ago, I had been thinking about death—about thralls drained dry, about what it meant to be a Mortal Bride. That fear still sat in my chest, cold and heavy.

But standing here alone, between the Conqueror and the Butcher, I felt... comfortable.

My brow furrowed. Jules was right. It was far too soon for me to have adapted to them. Ever since I met the kings, even when I boldly raised my eyes to theirs and spoke my mind, my nervous terror had beat beneath my skin.

Now, it didn't.

Was it because I was the Mortal Bride now?

No, that didn't make any sense. If it was, Jules wouldn't have asked.

Luc waved his hand over mine, pulling my blood into the air. He guided it to the runes on the door. With a flare of shadows, they drank up my blood.

Nothing happened.

"Is that all—"

Luc pushed open the doors.

I stopped short, breath catching. A collection of plush red chaises before a massive fireplace filled the center of a high-ceilinged room, even more elaborate than the hallway. But it was the massive window that stole my attention. Like a moth to flame, I drifted toward it.

Montaurère sprawled below, glittering in the morning sun. A terrace with overflowing planters of bright roses cut into my view, but from this vantage point at the top of the mountain, the entire city lay open before me. Spires rose from rooftops, their pointed tips reaching for the sky, casting long shadows over pale, vine-covered stone. Twisting streets carved through the city's expanse, leading toward the lake far below. Beyond its turquoise-blue depths, mountains rippled across the horizon.

My entire life had been spent in the streets of Corraidin and the inked pages of my books. I had traveled the world through those stories, but my imagination paled in comparison to reality.

My toes brushed something soft. A dark rug lay in a patch of sunlight, a stark contrast to the white, gold, and red that dominated the room.

I might have questioned the decorating.

Except the rug moved.

A massive black *wolf* uncoiled, paws the size of my face pressing against the floor. I stopped dead. Smooth black fur ruffled faintly with shadows, the beast four hundred pounds of prowling death. My body locked in place as the beast stretched, yawning, exposing a mouth full of wickedly sharp teeth.

The *hellwolf* moved to sniff me, its warm breath brushing my face. I leaned away. Or maybe I was falling over. I couldn't really tell.

Luc's arm looped around my waist. His thick, corded muscles pressed into my soft stomach. "Titus, don't eat our guests."

I don't know why, but I held out my hand. Titus was a hellbeast, not a pet, but I hoped this wasn't offensive. I really hoped the kings wouldn't let him rip my arm off.

The hellwolf's glowing black eyes pinned me in place. My heartbeat stuttered and a line of sweat dripped down my back.

A second later, Titus released me from his gaze and *nuzzled* my hand.

I almost dropped in relief. Thank the stars. I gave him a quick scratch behind the ear. It luckily didn't result in the loss of an appendage. I pulled back after the quick touch, not wanting to test another monster's patience—

Titus nudged my hand and whimpered.

"Gah, fine, I'll pet you." I raised my second hand, scratching behind both ears at once. His tongue lolled out, a monstrous thing acting like an overgrown dog.

The kings were silent behind me. I twisted around.

Luc was staring. Not cold or callous but sharp and focused like I had just done something impossible. Behind him, Jules gaped. The King of Dawn snapped his jaw shut a second later, hiding his shock behind an easy smile. But I still caught it, peeking out around the mask.

"It's generally ill-advised for anyone else to touch Titus," Jules said as he approached with his hand out.

Titus butted his head against the vampire in greeting, then immediately leaned back into my touch.

Jules eyed the hellwolf with exaggerated offense. "He seems to like you."

Befriending a hellwolf was the least weird thing to happen to me today. And it was still morning.

"How did you domesticate a hellwolf?" I asked into the silence.

"He's not domesticated." Luc's attention shifted to the hellwolf. "I told you not to follow us to Mabon."

Follow them? Was this the hellwolf I spotted in the woods that first night? When he had run off into the darkness, I imagined him returning to a cave or wherever hellwolves lived. Not to Dawnspear to sleep on the kings' floors.

The wolf shook my hand off his head and glared at Luc.

"Staying in the woods the whole time still counts," Luc said, like he understood the glare.

Titus huffed, affronted.

Wait. "Does he understand you?"

The hellwolf's shadowed gaze flickered back to me. Shit. He did. There was no doubt in my mind, staring into those dark eyes.

Luc nodded. "Which is why he shouldn't have followed us."

Titus turned wide, innocent eyes on the King of Dusk. After a moment, Luc sighed softly. He gave the wolf a scratch on the head. "Don't do it again."

Titus let out a low rumble, a far more agreeable sound. The hellwolf flopped back down into the beam of light and rolled onto his back, exposing his belly to the sun. I couldn't blame him, but it left me alone between the very naked, very intense kings.

"Um." I wracked my brain for something to say, but it was like they tried to stare *into* me. My thoughts scattered. "What now?"

The door slammed open in answer. Both kings twisted. Jules hissed through black-tipped fangs as Luc moved until his broad shoulders blocked my view. Or blocked me *from* view. Their reaction was immediate and possessive.

And arousing, but I ignored that.

I pressed onto my toes, but the only thing to balance on was Luc. I dropped back down, glared at those enormous shoulders, and leaned to one side to peek around.

Roxiana stood in the doorway, her body still and gaze lowered. A slight frown creased between her brows.

Luc relaxed and Jules stopped hissing. A faint flush tinted the King of Dawn's cheeks as his fangs dissolved into smoke. Was he embarrassed? I didn't think Jules was capable of something so human.

"Yes, Roxiana?" Luc asked smoothly.

"The Council session started fifteen minutes ago. Jules is sometimes late, but you never are. What's wrong?" She glanced between their naked forms, at me behind them. "I can cancel—"

"No." Luc looked to Jules, who nodded and turned for an open doorway on one side of the fireplace. "We haven't convened in over a month. There's much to discuss."

Luc turned, the Conqueror fully back in control. His silver eyes locked onto mine. "Starting with our new Mortal Bride."

JUST BECAUSE THE COUNCIL meeting was about me didn't mean I was invited.

I watched the gilded door close behind the kings and stared for a solid minute. For the first time in over a week, I was alone. Air rushed from my lungs, like I hadn't breathed since they called my sister's name in the harvest. My legs gave out, and I sank to the floor.

I was the Mortal Bride to the Kings of Dusk and Dawn.

I would never step foot in Mabon again.

The Butcher had eaten me out last night and had threatened to do so daily.

That last one wasn't *entirely* terrible. Still, I pressed a hand to my chest and tried to steady my breaths. Focused on the tangled knot of emotions unraveling inside me. I'd shoved them down when the kings woke, but now they surged back, raw and forceful. Terror. Anger. Grief. And... excitement?

Stars, I'd hoped that the last one would vanish once I was free of their alluring presences. But the pull of them lingered. Sometimes I thought I could get lost in their eyes. Just lean into that silver and gold and ignore the world.

Last night, I had let them lure me into tranquility, uncaring what they did with my body as long as it felt good. But if my desire for them wasn't entirely a lie, maybe my surrender wasn't either.

Maybe I had wanted them to fuck me.

*Wicked, sinful girl.*

My fingers traced the cool metal at my throat, curling around the silver-gold collar. My body was just confused. I had spent the last week in fear. The last couple years in isolation. Anyone would crave touch after that. Anyone would find it harder to resist comfort when everything around them had fallen apart. It was survival. Nothing more.

And their venom. That was surely warping my mind, too.

That was all. That had to be all. I was little more than their pet, their belonging—

A whine pulled me out of my head.

I dropped my hand and glanced down. Titus had rolled onto his back, fixing me with a pathetic, pleading look. If he were a normal dog and not a demon wolf, I'd assume he wanted belly scratches.

But since he *was* a demon wolf, I could just ask. "If I scratch your belly, will you eat my hand?"

Titus cocked his head to the side like I'd said something silly.

Well, if he killed me, at least I wouldn't have to worry about what the fuck to do next.

I didn't have many options. I couldn't leave. Even if I could slip through Dawnspear's labyrinthine streets, even if I made it past thousands of vampires, I'd still have to survive the forests of hellbeasts and wraiths beyond Montaurère's border stones.

Only to what? Go home to Mabon? Mabon belonged to the Azarasians. Flee somewhere new? There was a whole world beyond the Impire, but every inch of it belonged to demons and their spawn. Everything had since the First Godsfall.

Freedom was not an option for a human.

But that didn't mean I could let my captors seduce me. Falling into pleasure, into debauchery, was the easy way through this new life. I couldn't do it. They could have my blood and my body, but I couldn't give them my soul.

But what if I did? What if I wasn't strong enough to resist the easy way out? I had suffered for too long.

A sharp twinge lanced through my core, twisting deep and low. I hissed out a breath, pressing a hand to my lower belly. Damn illness, always answering its summons.

More accurately, the last soothing rune the kings had drawn was fading. They'd drawn one last night, and the rune had never lasted more than a day.

When they returned, would they draw another for me? Or had they only done that to lure me into being their Mortal Bride? My only option might be venom. How long did its effects last after the bite? My pain had been dulled so far this morning, but now it was creeping back.

So that was my answer. Their venom's effects lasted no more than seven or eight hours. That wasn't too terrible. But how often did thralls feed their masters? What if it was only every couple of days?

What if it was multiple times a day?

I didn't like either option.

I exhaled slowly, forcing my breath steady. Calm. No reason to panic. No reason to let my anxiety spiral. Whatever happened, everything would be fine. Completely fine.

I stretched my bare legs out on the sun-warmed floor, letting the heat soak into my skin. Distraction. That was the only option now. I focused all my attention on rubbing my hand across Titus's belly. The faint shadows of his coat tickled against my fingers, his warmth grounding me.

For a couple of minutes, nothing mattered but petting a hellwolf while sitting butt-naked in a collar on the floor of the Imperium's apartment.

When my shoulders finally loosened, a long sigh escaped me.

Titus arched his eyebrows at me. Well, not exactly, given he was a wolf, but it felt like he did.

"It's nothing," I said, rubbing large circles into his dark fur. "Well, not nothing, but it doesn't really matter."

Titus whined again.

I blinked down at him. He actually wanted to know? It was odd that I knew that, but I answered him anyway. "My life has changed irrevocably in a single week. I don't really know what to do about it. I don't even know if I can do anything about it."

Titus huffed like that was obvious. I took it back. This hellwolf was mostly prowling death, but the rest of him? Pure sass.

"If you're so smart, what should I do then?"

Titus flopped back onto the floor, stretching lazily in the sun.

A vote for the easy way, then. But Titus was a hellwolf. He could roam the halls, the streets, the wilds without fear.

I patted him gently on the head. His black eyes slipped shut. He might understand me, but he didn't know how to be human any more than I knew how to be a hellbeast.

Lying on the floor wasn't an option for me.

Not forever, at least.

I wasn't quick to stand. Even when my feet went numb, I lingered. When the pins and needles set in, I reluctantly pushed to my knees and wiggled my toes.

Titus glanced at me and whimpered.

"I'm just going to look around." Without waiting for the hellwolf's reply, I faced my new home—no, my new life. This wasn't my home. I hadn't had one of those since my mother was harvested. I never would again. I was the kings' living sacrifice. Their thrall. This apartment was *their* home.

It was my gilded prison.

And gilded it was. Far above, the ceiling shimmered in faint, frosted gold. The patterns on the walls weren't wallpaper but veins of solid metal. Gold-lined frames caged every painting, gold stars curled over the fireplace mantle, and the nearest chaise was backed in twisted gold. Yet, somehow, it wasn't garish. The kings had found the line between opulence and overindulgence, weaving the gold seamlessly with the white stone floors, deep red cushions, lush green plants, and flashes of color in the violent art.

I meandered toward the open doorway. The kings had left this first room dressed, so I wasn't surprised to step into a bedchamber. My eyes skipped past the towering windows and landed on the massive, four-poster bed carved from daemium.

The curtains were pulled back, exposing black, silky sheets and enough space for a dozen people. Shadows wafted from the frame, the surface carved with runes. Were the kings worried about assassins attacking in their sleep? I couldn't think of another reason to have a bed frame made of solidified magic ripped straight from a starcrater.

My gaze lifted. The gold-frosted ceiling continued here, except directly over the mattress, where the haze faded to a perfect reflection. Anyone lying in that bed would see themselves sprawled out, every moment on display. Heat flared in my cheeks. How obscene.

I quickly looked away. Did the kings share this room? This bed? They were clearly intimate, but I didn't know to what degree. Azaras hadn't let anyone so much as glance at Karra once they were soulbound. But the kings had said they were companions, the weakest of Azarasian soulbonds.

A few steps away, a small circular table sat with two chairs, an intimate place to share a meal. A maroon cloak draped over the nearest seat. I tugged it around myself, its fabric still holding the scent of smoked honey. Of Jules.

My eyes drifted back to that bed.

Would I be expected to sleep with them? I didn't want to sleep on the floor, but their bed wasn't a great alternative, no matter how soft it appeared.

I backed out of the room with a sharp shake of my head, shoving the thought aside. I would deal with it when it happened, not a moment before. If I let the stress in, it would drag my illness with it, and neither would let go easily.

I crossed before the fireplace to the next door. Maybe it would lead to a second, smaller bedchamber for me? If the godstars were kind.

I pushed open the second door... and into a cacophony of color and the harsh scent of paint.

"Stars." My eyes didn't know where to start first. An easel, holding a bare canvas over a paint-splattered floor. A table cluttered with sheets of paper, each marred with charcoal. A pottery wheel, abandoned mid-spin, a perfect vase left untouched in the center. A solid block of marble taller than me, a chisel stabbed deep into the wall beside it. A bejeweled—

Wait, was that a bejeweled *spine*?

Even from here, I could see the red stains on the bone. It wasn't hard to picture Jules tearing someone in half and encrusting their still-bloody spine with gemstones. Seemed like his level of derangement.

A deep growl cut through my thoughts. I spun around quickly. Titus had raised his head, dark eyes fixed on a figure in black standing by the entrance. Maire. I hadn't heard the door open. Where had she come from?

The thrall's blond hair was pinned up, strands of gold tumbling loosely down her back. It exposed the slender line of her gold-collared neck. Her gown was the same gauzy black as yesterday's, but today, instead of sleeves, the bodice twisted together and hooked into the base of her collar. She held another slip of black fabric over her arm, her green eyes cautious as they took me in.

For a moment, we simply stared at each other.

I cleared my throat. "Can I help you?"

Maire snorted, breaking the tension. "I attend to the Mortal Bride's needs during the day. I'm here to help *you*."

"Oh." I pulled the cloak tighter around me. "Aren't you Prince Cédric's thrall?"

Maire slowly crossed the space to the chaises arranged between us. "He has no need for me if I'm not warming his bed or feeding him or his son."

"Prince Cédric shares his thrall with his *son*?"

"Prince Rosier is six months old."

"Oh." I hadn't seen any vampire children yet, and Karra hadn't mentioned any in *The Soulborne Queen.* Vampires were born the same way as humans and witches, but I didn't know if they were loved and cherished or ignored until adulthood.

"What are you feeding him? Baby vampires don't bite, do they?"

Maire's smile was slight, but tight at the edges. "They do, but their venom doesn't cause pleasure until puberty. They don't take much lifeforce, so there's no need for it to mask the agony." She paused, then added, "But I meant that as infants, they drink their mother's milk, same as any human baby."

"Then why are you..." I stared and Maire stared back. "You're his *mother*?"

Maire's jaw tightened. Bitterness crossed her expression, but it vanished before I could be sure.

"Prince Rosier is a vampire," she said slowly, that pity for my ignorance back in her eyes. "I was never his mother, not even when I carried him inside me."

"But... how?" I struggled to make sense of it. "You're human. Cédric's a vampire. Shouldn't Prince Rosier be a witch?"

"The Azarasians have a runespell for that." Maire spoke flatly, like it was common knowledge. The Azarasians had never told us that, though. "That's how their population grew quicker than other vampire nations. The genesis runespell isn't easy to cast. Most vampires couldn't without the covenant."

I stared, my stomach twisting. More horrified by Maire's words than anything that had happened in the last day.

The room felt too warm. My breath came shallow, and the nausea that always lurked at the edges of my pain stirred awake. I had watched vampires descend on the terrified harvest, using them for their blood and bodies. The same had happened to me. But the kings had taken it further. They had bound my life to their covenant runespell.

But this?

Stealing our wombs? Taking our children? Refusing to let Maire even call the baby she carried hers?

My skin prickled, bile rising in my throat.

Maire raised her hands like I was a panicked animal. "Don't worry. You're the Mortal Bride. The kings have never bred a bride before."

"You obviously didn't hear what the Butcher said yesterday." Stars, Jules's threat to breed me took on a whole different meaning. I shook my head. "It doesn't matter. I'm... I can't have children."

Maire's expression didn't shift. "While that may be a curse in Mabon, that's a blessing here."

"Won't they get angry at me?" I had watched far too many women publicly shamed by the Church for failing to provide their husbands with the three children needed to avoid the harvest. It had happened to my mother. She had been blamed for the weakness that killed my infant brother, born a year before me. And again after she miscarried a second time, only weeks before her name was called.

My father had been overjoyed when she was gone.

He had remarried within a month. Aislin was born less than a year later, fulfilling his quota just weeks before his thirtieth birthday.

Her lips curled slightly, but it wasn't a smile. "Vampires are lucky to have one child a century. You won't take the blame if they can't plant their spawn in your womb."

Something about the way she said it, distant and clipped, made my stomach turn. The thrall runespell might have encouraged loyalty, but even that couldn't dull the horror of what she'd experienced.

Maire took two quick steps forward and placed something silvery on the low table between the chaises. Before Titus could growl, she quickly retreated. "The salve I promised. When you need a refill, let me know. Just because they can't get you pregnant doesn't mean they won't try their hardest."

I stared blankly at the tin.

"You can use it now, too. For the discomfort."

"The... discomfort?" My brow furrowed. She was right. Why wasn't I sore? There was no reality where I wouldn't be if Jules had fucked me as hard as he planned. The kings had bitten me last night. I remembered that, the rush of sensation... and then...

The thought slipped away.

Maire's brows lifted. "You don't ache at all? Stars, I misjudged you, Nessa. Most Maboni virgins can't take two vampire cocks in one night and walk straight the next day."

Heat flushed to my cheeks. "I'm not... I didn't..."

Her eyes widened. "Wait, they *didn't* fuck you?"

I swallowed. Opened my mouth. The answer was yes, but it didn't feel right. Why didn't it?

"But they bit you? Did you choose agony?"

Shame twisted in my gut. "Uh, no, they bit me and..." I hesitated. The kings had pinned my body between them, their fangs sinking into my throat and then...

I shook my head. Maire had asked something, hadn't she? I needed to answer. "None of it hurt then and it doesn't hurt now, either."

Her brows knit together. "Are you well, Nessa?"

I didn't know what to say to that. Jules had made me writhe and scream on his tongue, Luc's hand fisted in my hair. The Butcher had fucked me on top of the Conqueror. My face burned. "I'm fine."

Maire didn't look convinced, but after a moment, she let it go. She held out her arm, revealing the slip of fabric she carried. "This is for you. It doesn't cover much more than that cloak, but at least you won't have to hold it up."

I nodded. Getting dressed was a decent first step. I couldn't do much clutching Jules's cloak around me. I reached out, and Maire handed me the fabric.

Awkwardly, I maneuvered into the dress, keeping the cloak draped over my shoulders. When the black fabric finally covered most of my torso, I hesitated, then let the cloak fall aside. I fumbled with the top, twisting the fabric, trying to figure out what went where.

"Allow me." Maire slowly approached, gaze on Titus. The hellwolf didn't growl, but his eerie, shifting eyes stayed locked on her.

Maire moved carefully, finding two small metal loops in the fabric. She hooked one to the left side of my collar, then the right. The fabric draped in a deep V down my chest, pooling around my hips, leaving my back bare from my shoulders to the softness of my waist. I shook out my hair, letting my brown waves fall, covering as much skin as they could.

*Wicked, sinful girl.*

*Fuck off, Deidre.* I wasn't fond of Azarasian fashion, but I couldn't argue with wearing my hair loose.

"Thank you." I turned away from Maire, my skin still crawling. I needed to think about something else. Anything else. I gestured at the final door off the entry lounge. "What's in there?"

"The library. You can't..."

Maire's answer beyond *library* was a blur of words. I pushed open the door and forgot everything. Books. Thousands of them. Rows upon rows of gilded shelves stretched high into the grand room, easily twice the size of the bedchamber. Rolling ladders stood ready, waiting to be climbed, their gold fittings gleaming in the light pouring through a domed glass ceiling. The scent of aged parchment and leather filled the air, warm and familiar.

For a breath, I could almost pretend I was back in my shop. But *Books & Bows* had been small, cramped with uneven shelves and a bell that barely jingled. This place was towering, gilded, meant for the Imperium. It made my little shop feel like a closet.

I stepped inside, drawn forward by a power even greater than a vampire's enchantment. Maybe my life wouldn't be that terrible after all.

Maybe Titus had a point, taking the easy way.

Could life as a vampire fuck toy really be that terrible if I spent the rest of my hours *reading*?

# 21

I DRIFTED THROUGH THE shelves, tracing my finger along every spine. Each cover was smooth beneath my fingertips, the titles embossed in gleaming gold and silver. A faint rune, almost invisible, was etched into the leather. *Preserve*. That explained why every book was pristine, not a single cracked binding, frayed edge, or curling yellowed page in sight.

I sank into the shelves. Here, the world was quiet, peaceful. Just the hush of paper, the weight of knowledge, and the pull of stories, waiting to be chosen.

Fur brushed my shoulder. I flinched, but it was just Titus meandering past me, deeper into the library. I followed the hellwolf until we reached an open space in the room's center.

Titus dropped onto a thick rug in a patch of sunlight between a pair of sofas to my left, but my attention fixed on the large table to my right. I approached without thinking. This space belonged to the kings, same as the bedchamber and the art studio, but the books made it feel like home.

Scrolls, star charts, and neatly stacked books covered every inch. I circled the table, my gaze drifting across every stroke of ink, whether word, symbol, or sketch. There were calculations, something that looked like an angular diagram. Were they tracking the Blood Star's rising? Back in Mabon, we celebrated its return weeks ago, but I was further south now. I had no idea when it would appear here.

As I rounded the back, a desk tucked into the corner caught my eye. Expanding my loop around the space, I traced my fingers along its golden edge. A small, framed portrait sat on the desk. The beautiful vampire in the painting had dark, curling hair, deep brown skin, and luminous silver eyes. She smiled, her gaze soft with affection and locked with that of her observer. The brushwork resembled the chaotic style of the art studio next door, but this workspace was too meticulous to belong to the same person.

Assuming Jules was the artist, that meant this must have been Luc's desk.

Did the Conqueror have a queen? I didn't think so. Perhaps a paramour? If so, she hadn't attended last night's celebrations. Unless she had stood at the back of the room, watching.

Not that I was any sort of threat or competition. I was human, a thrall. It wouldn't even count as infidelity, assuming the Azarasians believed in such a thing. From what I'd learned and witnessed, monogamy wasn't common beyond heartmates and the occasional beloved pair. Companions took lovers freely, affection shared rather than claimed.

I shook my head. Stars, all their flirting had gotten to my head. I didn't want to be a threat or competition. The Imperium had *lured* me into becoming their Mortal Bride. Now that I was, I would surely meet the real Conqueror and the Butcher, the two brutal warlords an entire continent feared.

I turned to Maire, but she wasn't behind me. She wasn't in the library at all. I stepped away from the desk, circling back around the table toward the aisle. Maire stood in the open doorway, her lips pursed in a frown.

Was she waiting for me to invite her in? I wasn't her master, but she sort of served me. "Uh, come in?"

"I can't enter the Imperium's library without—" Maire paused, her hands raised and stepping forward. Then another step. Another. Her brow furrowed. "How odd."

"What?"

"I tried to follow you before and hit the apartment's wards. I should have hit it again by now."

"Oh." I didn't know what else to say. The kings had mentioned the apartment's wards, but they hadn't said anything more about them.

Maire hesitantly walked into the library, each step slow and simple like she expected the wards to sneak up on her. "Odran could only enter the bedchamber without the Imperium."

Memory flashed through me. The old man spasming as blood poured from his neck, coming as he died. I shuddered and grazed my fingers along the cold metal of our shared collar.

I cleared my throat, forcing the image away. "What does the Imperium expect of their Mortal Bride?"

"Not much," Maire said. "Most of your hours will be your own. I can bring you books, paints, anything you want. The... happier you are, the longer it will take the covenant to deplete your lifeforce."

My stomach dropped.

Maire must have noticed because she quickly added, "Odran was the Mortal Bride my entire lifespan. You won't live any shorter a life as their bride than you would as a thrall."

As a thrall. That wasn't exactly comforting.

"I see," I said. "I won't be expected to serve them?"

"Serve them, no." She paused at the edge of the last shelf before the open space. Her gaze flickered briefly to Titus, who remained seated, his dark eyes locked on her. "Feed them, yes."

My heart stuttered. "I figured that."

Maire studied me, her expression unreadable. "Odran fed the Imperium *and* the Imperial Council."

I inhaled sharply, but I forced my shoulders to stay still. A pit opened in my stomach. For some reason, fucking the kings didn't horrify me, not entirely, but the thought of touching their council did. My pulse quickened, nausea creeping up my throat.

But this was the life of a thrall. I had known that.

Maire had served the kings and their council for years before becoming Prince Cédric's personal thrall. If she could survive it, so would I.

I forced the thought aside. "Can you show me around? Where do all the thralls spend their—"

Maire cut me off. "The Mortal Bride can't leave the Imperium's apartment unless escorted by the kings, their council, or the Imperial Guard."

"Oh." I fiddled with the ends of my hair. "Will I ever get to leave?"

"If the kings decide to bring you to revelries or events, but otherwise... no."

I swallowed hard. I was *locked* in here. My stomach twisted, a strong turn that bordered on pain. My illness was creeping back, a quiet warning. If I let myself spiral, stress could turn it into something worse. But I couldn't keep changing the subject to avoid stressful things.

Everything Maire shared was stressful.

Maire narrowed her eyes, thinking. “But... you walked through one of their wards.”

“Do you think I can leave?”

She hesitated. “I’m not sure.”

“Can we try?” My voice was quiet, but insistent.

Maire’s lips parted slightly, like she wanted to say no. Like she should say no.

I pressed on. “If something’s wrong with their wards, they’ll figure it out eventually. This might be...” My throat tightened. “This might be my only chance to walk around without supervision ever again. For my entire lifetime.”

I had spent my whole life confined. To Corraidin since birth and my bookshop since my illness worsened. I wanted to see more. Even if it was just the thrall quarters. Even if it was ugly. I just wanted to know.

Maire didn’t respond right away.

Shit. I hurried to correct myself. “But I don’t want to get you in trouble. That was selfish of me—”

“No, you’re right.” Maire cut me off again, her voice firmer now. “This might be your only chance. You should see the thrall quarters. Odran never did, and... it made him difficult.”

Difficult? What did that mean? “Are you sure it’s not a risk?”

Maire exhaled, casting a wary glance toward the doorway. “Not if we stick to the thrall quarters,” she said. “We’ll have to hurry. The Imperium will return after their audience. But no one should notice otherwise. The Imperial Guard they leave at their door rarely check, and your scent should linger long enough that they won’t be able to tell you’ve left. The wards mute their senses, anyway.”

“How will we get out if there are guards at the door?”

Maire’s expression didn’t waver. “We’re not taking the hallway.”

I nodded, but doubt crawled up my spine. Was this worth the risk? The kings didn’t need me willing anymore. But Maire didn’t think we’d get caught. I barely knew the woman, but if I wanted to survive here, I had to trust someone. It wouldn’t be the vampire kings who *owned* me.

“Lead the way.”

Maire turned and exited the library. I lingered, glancing at Titus, but the hellwolf just watched.

I followed her into the sitting room as she approached the wall near the main entrance. With a tap to a section of patterned gold, a servant's door popped open silently. So that was where she had appeared from earlier.

Maire glanced over at me, about to say something. Her jaw snapped shut as her gaze flicked behind me and widened. Titus had followed us from the library. He sat in the doorway, silent, watching.

Waiting.

Disapproving?

But he wasn't growling. He had no intention of stopping me. I shouldn't have known that, but I did.

That didn't mean he intended to let me go alone.

"Stay here, Titus." I gave his snout a gentle stroke. "I'll be back soon."

The hellwolf stared, shadows swirling in his eyes.

"Please."

After a moment, Titus relented, dropping his head. I scratched behind his ears, digging both my fingers into the thick fur at his neck. The hellwolf closed his eyes, his tongue lolling out.

"Thank you." With one final scratch, I turned back around to Maire. She quickly masked her expression, but I had seen the shock. The same shock the kings had when Titus first let me touch him.

She shook herself and stepped through the servant's door. I followed, peering over her shoulder. The passageway was narrow, just wide enough for one person. A few steps in, the corridor twisted into a steep stairwell that plunged into darkness.

Maire reached for a wall sconce and pulled free a slender metal wand. Without hesitation, she pricked her finger. "Most runes in Dawnspear are useless to humans since we have no power to activate them. But the runelights have been spelled for us."

She brushed the wand against the sconce. A rune flared into shadows the second her blood touched the metal. The darkness sucked her blood down and flared against the wall. Then, golden light erupted, illuminating the stairwell.

We descended, the runelight following beside us, leaping from sconce to sconce. The kings' apartment was at the top of Dawnspear. Assuming the thrall quarters were near the bathing chambers, we had at least a few floors between us and our destination. Maire didn't speak. Neither did I. The only sound was the patter of our steps and the soft rumble of my stomach.

I hoped Maire planned to feed me during this trip.

A couple minutes later, the stairs curved sharply before straightening out. At the bottom, a half-closed door loomed ahead. A low thrum of voices seeped through the crack.

Maire halted and turned to me. "Keep your head down and don't speak to anyone." She grabbed a section of my hair and pulled it forward, letting the loose strands curtain my face. "You just became the Mortal Bride, so no one should recognize you, but we shouldn't risk it."

I swallowed. "Why? Are there vampires in the thrall quarters?"

"No. But half the thralls would report you if they thought it might earn them a favor." Maire kept her hands busy, fingers combing through my hair. "We're the lucky ones. We're fed, clothed. We don't get sent to the abattoirs or the workhouses. We help our masters dress, run their errands." A pause. Her hands stilled for just a breath. "The hardest thing we do is feed them."

I frowned. "And the other half of the thralls?"

Maire's voice was flat. "The other half worship demonbloods."

I had thought that was just something the Church said to scare us. My gaze dropped to Maire's falling star pendant. "Do you?"

"Vampires are less suspicious of those who wear the falling star."

I nodded. A practical choice, then. Maire finally finished fussing with my hair and continued down the stairs. I scurried after her. I wouldn't be able to navigate back on my own and that wasn't an option. The kings had already threatened me with punishment today. I wasn't eager to find out what that meant.

My pulse leaped.

Fine. A part of me wanted to know.

I ignored it.

When Maire reached the bottom step, she pushed through the door and kept walking. I forced myself to follow, head lowered just enough to avoid drawing attention. It took everything in me to put one foot in front of the other.

The thrall quarters weren't as extravagant as the rest of the castle, but they weren't dank and run-down either. The walls were smooth stone, the floors swept clean, but there was no mistaking what this place was—a barracks, not a home.

Dozens of thralls moved down the long hallway, their footsteps light, their murmured conversations a constant, shifting hum. Doorways lined the passage, some closed, others yawning open, revealing glimpses of the lives inside. I couldn't help but stare. Beds crammed the rooms, lining both walls, some stacked two or three high. Pallets were shoved into corners where beds wouldn't fit, thin blankets folded neatly at their ends. There was easily space for twenty to thirty thralls per room.

The murmur of voices thickened, turning into a low, steady drone. Underneath it, there was something else.

A slow, rhythmic sound.

A drum.

I frowned, listening hard, but as we turned a corner and passed another open door, I figured it out.

On the nearest bed to the doorway, a woman straddled a man, riding him with frenzied movements. I only just stopped myself from stumbling. My pulse jumped in my throat, my gut tightening. Not just from the display itself, but from the ease of it, the normalcy. I should have been witnessing something private, forbidden. But here? No one was hiding. No one was ashamed.

And once I noticed, I couldn't stop.

In every room we passed, thralls fucked in the open. Some in pairs, others tangled in groups, skin shining with sweat. One room was little more than a writhing mass of limbs. On a nearby bed, a thrall lay fully clothed, flipping through a book as if the gyrating bodies around her were nothing more than background noise.

No one reacted to them.

No one stared.

Because this was normal.

Maire must have noticed my discomfort because she grabbed my hand and tugged me forward, muttering, "You Maboni are so easily scandalized."

"You don't consider yourself Maboni anymore?" I kept my voice low, grateful for something—*anything*—to focus on.

"I've never set foot in Mabon," she said. "My mother was harvested years before I was born."

I faltered. Maire had been born into this—into servitude, into feeding them, into a life where even her body wasn't her own. I'd always guessed this happened to the Maboni taken as thralls. It's not like none of them would ever get pregnant. But I had never truly thought about what that meant.

Generation after generation, raised under vampire rule, never given the choice to be anything else.

"And your father?" I asked.

"I don't know who my father was," she said. "It doesn't matter anyway. We're not raised by our parents."

A cold knot formed in my stomach. I had willingly taken my sister's place to spare her and her unborn child from this same fate. But Maire had lived it her entire life. How many of Maboni descent had been born here, just like Maire? How many more would be?

Did the Azarasians encourage it? Expect it?

Were their birth quotas here, too?

I forced the words out, low and unsteady. "Do the Azarasians force you to reproduce?"

Maire didn't even blink. "Not exactly, but we aren't given contraceptive runes or herbs. The Azarasians could always use new thralls."

"Then why...?" I waved a hand awkwardly, trying to find the right words. "Why does no one resist?"

Maire only arched her brows at me. "Resist?"

I gestured vaguely around us. "This. All of it."

A bitter smirk tugged at the edge of her mouth. "You've only been bitten once. Give it a couple more times and you'll understand."

Maire didn't elaborate. She didn't need to. The Azarasians kept a lot from us, but we knew about their venom.

"But why should we?" she added. "It's one of the few things we can enjoy in this life. There's no marriage here, Nessa. No weddings, no wives and husbands, no families in little houses. Those rules bound you once, but in the Impire, they don't exist. Not for thralls. Not for most vampires, either."

Was that terrifying? Or freeing? "I've realized."

Maire slowed her pace, glancing at a closed doorway. "I need to check on something before we continue."

"Check on what?"

Instead of answering, Maire pushed open the door and stepped inside.

I hesitated. Standing idly in the hallway felt too exposed, too conspicuous. After a second, I stepped closer. The door remained slightly ajar. From the threshold, I could see little more than dim lighting and the shapes of beds.

Curiosity pulled me forward. I peeked through, craning my neck for a better look—

Into a room like all the others. Almost like all the others. This one was smaller, without any stacked beds, and sleeping women in iron collars occupied the closest three.

*Pregnant*, sleeping women.

I stopped dead—inside the room. I had wandered forward without thinking.

"What is this?" My voice came out hollow, barely above a whisper.

Maire didn't answer me. She was already moving, her steps quick, purposeful. On the fourth bed, a dark-haired thrall lay awake, her thin shift pasted to her sweat-drenched skin. The bulge of her stomach rose sharply beneath it, etched with thick, twisting lines of shadow.

I couldn't see the other women's bellies, but I knew if I could, they'd be marked the same.

Each of these thralls carried a demonblooded child.

My insides went cold.

"When did she wake, Éamon?" Maire asked the two thralls hovering at the panting woman's bedside.

The red-haired man at her bedside shifted slightly. "A couple of minutes ago."

The other thrall didn't speak, only continued patting the pregnant woman's brow with a damp cloth.

"Have you reported it to Healer Chastain yet?"

"No." The thrall glanced over at me, but there wasn't any recognition in his eyes. He placed a hand on Maire's arm and led her slightly away from the bed. "We thought... this is her only chance to say goodbye."

Maire flinched. I didn't know what was happening and didn't want to interrupt, but I itched to ask the question.

"I'm sorry, Maire."

Maire's throat bobbed. She glanced at me, as if recalculating something. Then, to Éamon, "I'll be back in ten minutes. Fifteen at most. Send for the healer when I return."

Éamon frowned. "Maire—"

She leaned closer, her whisper harsh. "She can't be here when the healer arrives."

The man's eyes flickered to me and widened with sudden recognition. "How in the stars did you bring the Mortal—?"

"It doesn't matter," Maire snapped, cutting him off. "Sophie is like a little sister to me, Éamon, but I need to return *her* first."

Éamon nodded slowly. "I have apartment access. Let me take her back."

"And if the kings return before I do?"

Éamon exhaled through his nose. "I've attended the..." he gestured at me "...before, when you're indisposed. If they notice and ask, I'll say you asked me to take over for you today. But they won't notice or ask."

Maire gripped his shoulder. "Thank you, Éamon."

"Of course, Maire. Anything."

Maire turned back to Sophie, leaned over, and pressed a kiss to the pregnant woman's damp forehead. "I'll be back in a second."

Sophie gritted her teeth, tears streaking her face, but managed a nod. Maire brushed back her damp hair, fingers gentle. Then she turned to me. She gestured for the door, and I followed her out into the hallway silently.

Éamon slipped out behind us. The moment the door closed, Maire slumped against the wall and bowed her head. Her breathing was unsteady.

"I'm sorry, Nessa," she murmured. "This wasn't the last thing I planned to show you. Sophie isn't due for another week. I didn't expect..."

I swallowed. "Is she... dying?"

Maire's glistening eyes met mine. "No human woman survives a vampire birth without help. Their little parasitic spawn are born hungry."

Little parasitic spawn. My stomach twisted. Maire had birthed a vampire child. She wasn't legally his mother as a thrall, but she had carried Prince Rosier and breastfed him like he was her own.

"But you're summoning a healer?" I pressed. "In Mabon, vampire healers help our mothers with their births."

Maire let out a humorless breath. "You're a delicacy, Nessa. Born and raised in near freedom, all to make your blood taste better. Sophie is just another Impire-born thrall. There are millions of us." Her voice hardened. "Vampire babies are as hard to kill as an adult. It's only the human or witch mother who's at threat during labor. Prince Cédric is the only reason I lived while his son tried to drain me."

Maire wiped her eyes and pushed herself to full height. "These thralls don't have a vampire who cares enough about them to ensure they survive. They don't even know who fathered their child. I was hoping..." She glanced away, swallowing thickly. "Some thralls never wake from the hibernation the baby forces their body into during the final weeks. I hoped Sophie would sleep through her death. It's the kinder fate."

I swallowed down my nausea. Sleeping through her *death* was the kinder fate? I glanced back at Éamon, who had stepped away to give us our privacy. "So you have to take me back upstairs."

Maire nodded. "We have to summon Healer Chastain. She might not know what the new Mortal Bride looks like, but she could sense the covenant in you."

"It's fine, Maire."

She blinked, surprised.

I forced a weak smile. "I'd do anything to see my sister again. You shouldn't miss any time with yours."

Maire studied me for a beat, then sighed. "You won't get another chance to see Dawnspear without a vampire a step behind you."

"I've seen enough." And I had. Whatever life the kings had planned for me, no matter how comfortable their apartment, it would remain a gilded prison, a home to the worst of the monsters. I couldn't look at it and see anything else. Not if this was how the rest of the thralls lived, packed into crowded rooms or left for dead while baby vampires ate them from the inside out.

Maire turned back to Éamon.

"Éamon will take you back."

Without another word, she turned and slipped back into the room. She kneeled beside Sophie as the door swung shut behind her.

Éamon stepped up beside me. His voice was quiet, but firm. "Come on. Let's get you back upstairs before you're missed."

I nodded, my throat dry, and followed him into the hallway. The scent of too many bodies pressed in from all sides, but I kept my head down. Don't look. Don't listen. Just keep moving.

This time, I didn't glance inside the open rooms. Didn't count the beds crammed together. Didn't listen to the voices, the low moans, the soft murmurs between thralls who had long since learned to find comfort where they could.

Éamon didn't speak at first. He moved quickly, his steps light but purposeful, his body tensed as though expecting an interruption at any moment.

"I'm glad you saw this."

I frowned, glancing at him. "What?"

Éamon's expression was grim. "Odran attended the occasional feast and revelry, but he was content to obey. He didn't know what it was like to really be a thrall." The narrow hallway twisted until finally we stopped at the servant's staircase. He pushed the door open, but his voice lowered, almost urgent. “But you’ll remember that this is all we are to them. Something to bite, fuck, use, and discard—”

A hand caught the door, stopping it mid-swing.

The world seemed to contract in an instant.

Pale fingers. A leather-clad arm. The brush of magic, featherlight but unmistakable. My heart stopped, then lurched as I felt them before I even saw them.

Estrella and Tristan towered over us.

Behind us, the thralls in the hallway dropped to their knees.

Estrella smiled, slow and sharp. “You better hope that isn’t true, human.” Her eyes flicked from Éamon to me. “Think the Imperium will bite, fuck, use, or discard you for endangering the covenant?”

I SLAMMED INTO OBSIDIAN marble, gasping for breath as Estrella released her grip on my collar. Pain flashed through my knees from the impact. The vampire female had carried me from the thrall quarters over her shoulder, her hold on the metal at my neck just tight enough to cut off my screams. It had been uncomfortable but not painful, not really.

Not compared to Éamon's experience.

Tristan dragged him behind like an afterthought, one finger looped through his collar. The vampire had stayed behind his soulbound the entire way, forcing me to watch every second. Éamon twitched, his eyes rolling back as the vampire cut off his air supply. The only reason he wasn't dead was the rune Tristan had drawn the second before he grabbed him. *Endure*. It was the same one on the body in the forecourt garden, the one capable of keeping a vampire alive through impalement and flaying.

What was a little strangulation in comparison?

Éamon went slack on the ground beside me, choking in a pained breath. His collar had bitten into his skin, the red mark around his neck bleeding where the silver had cut into him.

My collar suddenly felt too tight. A familiar ache curled in my lower stomach, the stress jabbing my illness's fingers into my gut.

"Are you causing trouble already, little curiosity?"

I forced myself onto an elbow, my breath uneven. Silver eyes glowed at the top of a long flight of white stairs. Luc. I had vaguely registered Estrella carrying me into a large room, but only now did I see where I had been brought.

We sprawled at the bottom of the grand staircase, the Imperial Throne rising before us. Four councilors stood as sentinels, while two kings watched from their daemium seat. Luc lounged on the left, the silver buttons of his high-collared, form-fitting doublet stark against black fabric. To his right, Jules grinned, draped in a gold-embroidered tunic, every inch the glittering, bejeweled King of Dawn.

But it was the crowns that held me captive.

Made of daemium, their sharp spires breathed shadows, the darkness drifting through the tousled strands of Luc's dark hair and Jules's pale gold waves. They were crowns forged for the Conqueror and the Butcher, imposing, otherworldly, brutal.

The dull pain in my stomach twisted harder.

I tore my gaze away, drifting upward. The audience hall was the antithesis of the Abyss, a bright, gilded room with solid marble columns stretching impossibly high. On the ceiling, a mural showed hundreds of meteors blazing through a midnight sky. Their golden flames trailed against a backdrop of stars. The godsfire dimmed the closer the meteors were to the ground until only the black of a demon's shadows remained. The artists had layered magic over their depiction of the Second Godsfall, the entire painting wavering like flame.

I gaped. How did Maire and the other thralls keep their heads bowed day after day when Dawnspear looked like this? Every single thing from the architecture to the art was a feat no human could ever achieve. Everything in Mabon was drab and dull in comparison. No wonder Lady Delphine and Lord Raul always looked angry.

Then again, the thralls didn't have much choice. The few I had witnessed in the hallways scurried along, terror in their steps. There were a thousand eyes on them, most silver and gold, but there were flashes of color here and there from vampires older than Mabon itself.

And now those thousand eyes were on me.

Two far brighter than the others.

I turned my focus back to the kings. A small curve tugged at Luc's lips at my distraction. Little curiosity, indeed. I shot a glare at the bastards as I slowly pushed onto my knees. I wished I could blame the decision entirely on oxygen deprivation, but I really couldn't.

Estrella stepped toward me. I closed my eyes, bracing for the hit—

"No," the kings said as one, the firm command of the Imperium.

Estrella stilled immediately. Within a blink, she kneeled, her head bowed toward her kings. "Forgive me, Imperators. She is yours to discipline, not mine."

Luc rose to his feet and prowled down the stairs, a predator approaching its prey. "And what exactly has our bride done to require discipline?"

"We found her in the thrall quarters."

Luc stilled.

A breathless silence swept through the courtiers, whispers strangled mid-sentence, shuffling footsteps frozen in place. Even the runelights seemed to hold their flickering breath.

Jules let out a low whistle, slicing through the hush. "Naughty girl. How did you manage that?"

I opened my mouth, but before I could find my voice, Estrella answered. "We believe she was led there by her thrall attendant. But as we were stationed outside your apartment, we can't be sure how she left."

Luc linked his hands behind his back. "Cédric, check the wards on the apartment."

"At once, Your Majesty." Without so much as a glance at me or Éamon, Cédric headed toward the open doors at the far side of the audience hall, the entryway wide enough to fit a wagon.

Luc approached slowly, his imposing frame blocking out the throne behind him. I glanced up, up, up until I met those molten eyes. I could have stared for minutes easily, but Luc slowly arched a single brow. The movement snapped me back to reality, dragging my attention down like a weight around my throat.

Shit.

I dropped my gaze immediately. I needed to ignore my strange comfort around the kings, especially in public. I was just something to bite, fuck, use, and discard. Nothing less, nothing more.

I knew that. I had always known that.

Luc's attention flickered to Éamon, motionless at my side. "This one is yours, Sabas?"

"He was," the vampire replied coldly.

I shuddered at the tone. *He was*. How did two simple words sound so final? Éamon flinched, but he didn't raise his head from the floor. Was that what they expected of their thralls? No wonder half the attention in the room was on my back.

I was about to command all of it.

A fresh wave of nausea crept up my throat, tangling with the pain curling in my gut. I swallowed hard, forcing both down. I didn't know what the punishment was for endangering the covenant, but it couldn't be good. If anyone was going to suffer for my choice, it should be me. I was the Mortal Bride. They couldn't kill me.

Not right away, at least. They'd need a replacement first.

If the kings disappeared for a couple weeks around the next harvest, then I'd worry.

I exhaled slowly, my pulse pounding as I forced my head back up. Luc's sharp jaw came into view first, then the faintest curl of his lips. Making eye contact with the Conqueror himself, I said, "This is my fault, Your Majesty. I should bear the punishment for it."

The chamber didn't stop this time. It *reacted*. A ripple of unease passed through the courtiers, an almost imperceptible shift in posture, a few quick inhales sucked between teeth. Hundreds of gazes pinned me to the marble floor. But no one spoke.

Luc tilted his head, imperious as ever, but the slight curl to his lip betrayed his amusement. "Who said we didn't intend to punish you?"

My heart rate spiked. In my periphery, Jules leaned forward in his seat, a wicked gleam in his eyes.

I dug my nails into my palm. "I asked him to take me. Éamon shouldn't be punished at all for that."

Luc cocked his head ever so slightly. "You're lying."

"I'm—I'm not." Shit, I was. I had asked Maire not Éamon. "Why would I lie?"

"To save your fellow human unimaginable pain?"

Éamon shuddered but didn't make a sound. I didn't know the man, not enough to try to comfort him. And even if I did, it would only make things worse.

So I didn't.

"I wasn't forced from your apartment. It *was* my decision."

"Which is why you'll *also* be punished."

Jules grinned at Luc's words. Shit. Anything that made that beautiful maniac happy was bound to be terrible.

I frowned, my chin lifting the barest inch. "But—"

"Careful, Miss Halloran." Luc's voice dropped to a rasp, something rough and predatory. A warning. "I'm not known for my mercy. You're expecting me to spare a thrall and allow your obstinance?"

Stars, I wanted to slap that smug arrogance off his face. "I'm not expecting anything. You're the Conqueror. I would only expect you to be a monster."

I regretted the words the moment they left my mouth. They weren't a lie. They weren't even rude, as far as I was concerned. Luc *was* a monster. But for a long moment, he didn't move or speak. Neither did anyone else. I hunched my shoulders as the King of Dusk simply loomed, the full weight of his attention entirely on me. The audience hall waited with bated breath for his response.

A whisper of breath ghosted against my ear.

Fuck.

I had been so focused on Luc that I forgot Jules. And now the Butcher crouched beside me, too close, too warm.

"A monster?" Jules murmured, brushing a strand of hair from my cheek. "What a cruel thing to say about my soulbound, lovely."

I turned and met the Butcher's golden eyes. "Did I speak falsely?"

Jules's pupils visibly and immediately dilated, stark hunger on his face. He traced along my jawline. "Not at all."

My stomach twisted, nausea curling at the edges of my awareness. This was not going well. What had I been thinking? Bargaining with the Imperium, demanding things as if I had any power here? As if I could outmaneuver them? I spent most of my time in a bookshop talking to my cat. I didn't belong in this world.

Pain twisted low in my stomach. I clenched my fists, digging my nails into my palms. What else did I have to offer them? Nothing. My body had already been claimed, marked, twisted into something they owned.

The realization slammed into me, cold and final.

I couldn't save Éamon.

The admission scraped like broken glass inside my ribs. I had sacrificed what little autonomy I had to save my sister. I had nothing else. I closed my eyes and breathed in. *I will not cry. I will not scream. I will not let these monsters break me.*

But I didn't even have the power to guarantee that.

I forced my eyes open, pulse hammering as I met the Imperium's gazes.

Luc remained poised, his quiet intrigue nearly imperceptible.

Jules...

Jules was grinning. Something dark flickered beneath his amusement, something sharpened by anticipation.

A chill licked down my spine. They were *enjoying* this.

"If you're going to punish me, let's get on with it."

Luc's lips curved into a smirk, but it was Jules who answered. "Oh, we will. But not in the way you're thinking."

His words alone should have cooled the heat creeping into my limbs, but then Jules traced a slow line to my neck. His knuckles settled against my thundering pulse.

Jules hummed. "Most people fear pain the most, but that's not true for you, is it, Nessa? You've lived such a painful life."

His fingers stroked along my throat, slow, deliberate, nefarious. A shudder rippled through me, straight to my core. A sharp flash of discomfort followed the desire. My illness was creeping closer, worsening with every second of stress.

Fuck. What were the chances the kings would replace my soothing rune now? Slim to none.

Being bitten, on the other hand...

I forced my voice steady. "I still fear pain."

"But not the most," Jules said. "That honor belongs to public humiliation."

A cold sweat broke across my skin. "Haven't you already humiliated me enough?"

Jules snorted and sprang to his feet. "Not at all."

"What—?"

A hand fisted in my hair—Jules's—and yanked me up. I screamed, pain lancing through my scalp. I stumbled forward, my hand landing hard on Jules's muscular arm under a layer of silk.

The King of Dawn leaned into me and brushed his thumb against my lip. "How about this? Your punishment will be a kiss."

I stopped breathing.

"Excuse me?" I gasped out as Luc arched a dark brow. Jules wanted me to kiss him? As a punishment? In front of hundreds of vampires? The thought was so ridiculous, so absurd, that I almost laughed.

Almost. Instead, nausea curled in my stomach. Maybe he was onto something.

Jules placed his hands on my shoulders and turned me ever so slightly toward the King of Dusk. "I want you to kiss Luc."

I blinked. The world tilted. "*What*?"

Fuck, how was that worse? Jules was friendly and approachable... for an absolute psychopath. Luc was sharp and cold and intimidating. I glanced over at Luc's hulking frame, my gaze catching his for half a second too long. The silver in his irises gleamed, but he only assessed me. Watchful and waiting.

I looked away fast. My stomach revolted, a tangle of emotion rising in me, twisting tight. Jules wasn't just punishing me, he was toying with me. He wanted me to *fail* at kissing his gorgeous, brooding soulbound. He had seen my nerves last night when he touched me. He knew I was inexperienced. Having sex once didn't change that.

My brow furrowed, something flickering at the edges of my mind. That was wrong. Like a thread I couldn't quite grasp—

Jules grinned. "You did call him a monster, after all."

"I was calling you both monsters technically," I mumbled.

"If you want to kiss me, too, you need only ask."

"I wasn't saying that."

He leaned in close, voice dipping into something lower. "Weren't you?"

I shot him a glare, but heat flooded my face, betraying me.

"But we're not entirely cruel—"

Luc chuckled. "Aren't we?"

"—so if you kiss Luc..." Jules glanced at his soulbound, his smile growing by the second until Luc nodded. The King of Dusk raised his wrist before me, and the King of Dawn drew a small rune on his skin. *Bargain.* "If you kiss Luc right now before the High Courts, he'll free Éamon."

Shadows flared from the rune before sinking into Luc's skin. My jaw dropped. Karra had used a bargaining rune once. It meant the kings couldn't break their word. I glanced down at Éamon, but he still hadn't looked up.

Shit.

I exhaled slowly. I could do this. To save a life, I *had* to do this. It didn't matter that a thousand mocking eyes were on me. It didn't matter that the kings were among them. It didn't matter that I had never kissed anyone and didn't know where to start.

I took one hesitant step toward the King of Dusk. Why did he have to be so huge? Just standing this close to him made my palms sweat. My eyes flashed to his, then dropped lower, but tracing the hard lines of his perfect jaw was no longer the safe choice, not with those soft, almost-smirking lips so close. My stomach twisted. I hoped I didn't puke on him.

After what felt like a thousand years, I stopped a foot away from him. Luc considered me, his irises almost entirely swallowed by black. Only a small line of silver appeared between his pupil and shadow rim.

"In my experience, kissing requires touching."

I winced. "If it was easy, it wouldn't be a punishment."

Luc chuckled softly. "That is true."

I wrung my hands before me. How did one even start kissing someone? I'd have to rest my hands on his broad shoulders and stand on my toes just to reach. Maboni women were expected to save their first kiss for their husband on their wedding day. Before my body decided it hated me, I'd never been bold enough to steal one in secret.

And now, I was expected to go from nothing to kissing a vampire king.

Jules yawned dramatically at our side. "Time's up."

"What?" I spun to him. "You didn't say there was a time limit."

"I just did."

Fuck me. I twisted back toward Luc, pressed onto my toes, closed my eyes, and quickly brushed my lips against his. A mere breath of contact. I dropped back down to my feet just as fast.

There. Done.

When I opened my eyes, the weight of silence pressed in on me. The kings stared, clearly unimpressed. A laugh rippled through the chamber. Not loud but unmistakable. Heat rushed to my cheeks. My skin prickled, warmth crawling up my neck.

A spectacle. That's all I was.

"What was that?" Luc asked.

I wished the ground would open and swallow me whole. It was a good thing we weren't in the Abyss, because I'd have thrown myself over the edge. "A kiss?"

"Was it?" Luc raised his gaze from mine. "What say the Kings' Council? Was that a kiss?"

Roxiana snorted. "Hardly."

"I have to agree," Isabeau added, arms crossed, expression sharp.

Sabas only shook his head. Possibly in exasperation, but it was an answer to Luc's question, too.

A part of me wanted to shrivel up inside. Laughter whispered through the hall, weaving into old memories, echoes from my youth. Judging voices, mocking smiles, the weight of my humiliation. But it was worth it, if it saved a life. I could handle the judgment, the embarrassment. No one had ever died from being mocked.

If that were possible, I wouldn't be here.

A large hand cupped my cheek. "This is a kiss, Miss Halloran."

I didn't have a chance to react, to process the words, before Luc leaned over me and *kissed* me. No hesitation. No softness. His lips claimed mine, not teasing but testing—an assessment, a demand.

One I had to obey.

One I *needed* to obey.

Luc didn't kiss. He conquered.

He swept in, taking, consuming, until all I could do was yield. Until yielding was the only thing I wanted to do. Heat coiled in my stomach, winding through my limbs, leaving me weightless. I didn't even notice my body's rebellion. My fingers dug into his doublet, the last anchor keeping me upright.

Kisses had always seemed like messy things. But Luc kissed with precision, with brutality, with the same meticulous control that ruled impires. I moaned into his mouth, melting into him.

Surrendering before he could even demand it.

It ended just as quickly as it started. Luc pulled back and released me. I almost stumbled into Jules, his gaze locked on us, the gold nearly overtaken by black. The King of Dusk smirked down at me, arrogantly confident.

I tensed my legs, determined to stay standing. The Conqueror wouldn't fell me with a single kiss, no matter his reputation. It was just a kiss. A punishment.

So why was my heart still racing? Why did my lips still burn?

"Did you kiss me, Miss Halloran?" Luc asked, voice measured.

I blinked at him. "What?"

"If that was a kiss, did you kiss me?"

"...no."

"I'm glad we agree." He turned, facing Éamon—

No.

My hand shot out to his shoulder, desperation drowning every ounce of self-preservation. The heat of him, the strength beneath his doublet, sent a shiver up my spine. But it worked. Luc stopped to stare down at where I touched him.

I snatched my hand back. "But I... we..." *Get it together, Nessa.* "My lips touched yours. You didn't specify anything else."

Jules's laughter cut through the air. "She's got us there, Lucey."

"You're right, Miss Halloran. My apologies." Luc's voice was smooth. Too smooth. My skin prickled in warning. Something wasn't right. "Rise, Éamon."

Éamon trembled as he pushed to his feet, his hands clenched tight, his shoulders curled inward. This time, when Luc turned toward the thrall, I didn't move to stop him. I liked my hands attached to my body.

Luc approached the redhead. With deft fingers, he unhooked Éamon's collar and let it fall to the floor. The sharp clatter rung through the hall.

"You're free to leave."

For a second, hope unfurled in my chest. I turned toward Éamon, willing him to run, to move, to seize his chance before the kings changed their minds.

He didn't.

He didn't even lift his head.

Why wasn't he *moving*?

I saw it before I understood it—the vampires courtiers watching, the cruel amusement in their gazes, the way Éamon's hands curled into fists.

My hope froze. Cracked. Shattered.

The whisper of fabric. Jules circled me, his presence heat and silk and menace. He trailed his fingers along my shoulder, sending a shudder through my body. "Would you like to tell her, Éamon?"

Éamon finally raised his head and met the Butcher's, his green eyes burning with raw hatred. "Fuck you."

My breath caught.

Those hateful green eyes disappeared behind a broad back clothed in fabric dark as midnight.

"Is that any way to speak to your king?"

I couldn't see Éamon through Luc's form, but I heard his response, a wet choking sound. Luc turned ever so slightly—and he brought Éamon with him. The thrall dangled two feet off the floor, Luc's grip around his throat unyielding.

Fuck, fuck, *fuck*. My heart beat faster with every curse.

"Since Éamon here is incapable of answering a simple question, I will," Luc said. "Outside of a harvest feast, an uncollared thrall can be hunted, captured, and killed without recompense."

A slow, dawning horror filled my chest.

"You said you'd free him." My voice was barely above a whisper. I turned to the King of Dawn, but Jules chose that exact moment to move, circling me like a predator until I couldn't keep them both in my line of sight. "You sealed it with a bargaining rune."

"And our bargain is concluded," Jules said. "Luc removed his collar and told him he was free."

"He wouldn't have gotten very far."

"That wasn't part of the bargain."

Fucking bastards. They hadn't lied to me. They had tricked me. Panic surged, clawing up my throat as Éamon thrashed, his fingers grasping in vain at Luc's wrist. I couldn't watch this. I couldn't.

"Instead he insulted my soulbound," Luc said. "And as he's uncollared..."

Luc's lips parted, shadows curling over his teeth, lengthening into black-tipped fangs.

He buried them in Éamon's throat.

Éamon's body arched in agony, his scream splitting through the chamber. A high, ragged sound. I flinched back, a sob rising in my throat. When Jules had bitten that man on the road, I hadn't known whether his screams were from the wound in his gut or the fangs in his neck.

Now I knew.

Luc had said most thralls only tried a dry bite once. If this was the pain it caused, it was no wonder why.

Tears burned down my cheeks. I didn't want to watch this. I didn't need to see another person die. And another and another. When would it fucking end? I turned my head—

Jules closed a hand on the back of my neck and forced my gaze to Éamon. "You'll watch the entire thing."

I shut my eyes. It didn't stop Éamon's fading scream, his wet choking, but I refused to watch. "No."

"Excuse me?"

"No. You can't make me."

That hand suddenly wrapped around the front of my throat. "I certainly can."

He didn't squeeze. His thumb stroked against my pulse. I shuddered. But still, I kept my eyes closed.

"What a brave thing you are." Jules's breath brushed my cheek. "Foolish, but brave."

"And for a second, I thought you were actually complimenting me."

"Do you need compliments?" he purred. "Will that endear you to me?"

I clenched my jaw. "A thousand compliments couldn't endear me to you."

The room around me had quieted, making Jules's reply all the more clear. "I do love a good challenge."

Something hit the floor, something soft and limp. My eyes flashed open. Luc stood over Éamon's pale body. The thrall's dead eyes were open, pain and terror etched onto his face. A sharp gasp ripped from my throat. I slapped a hand over my mouth, choking back bile.

Jules brushed my throat, a trace of heat at his fingertips. I barely had time to process before my nausea vanished, smothered in an instant. I met his piercing gold gaze for a fraction of a second before I turned away.

But the sight that greeted me wasn't any better.

Luc wiped away a thin trail of *blood* from his chin.

I didn't want to look at either of the murderous beasts who owned me.

But I didn't want to see Éamon's corpse, either.

I didn't have to for long. Luc dropped his hand and drew the lines of a shadowed rune. *Incinerate*. Éamon's body collapsed into dust. The particles scattered, swallowed by nothingness. Like he had never existed. Like nothing had happened. Like they hadn't killed a man to punish me.

Luc turned on his heels, climbing the stairs to the throne as if it were just another day. "What's next, Chancellor?"

Roxiana tapped on her wrist, activating a runespell. *Archive. Extract. Reveal*. Lines of text appeared in the air before her. "The tribunal on the anarchists who destroyed the Dufresne Abattoir has reached a verdict."

"Excellent." Jules looped an arm around my shoulder. "Up we go, bride."

My body locked up. But I didn't have the strength to fight the King of Dawn as he swept me up the stairs to the Imperial Throne. Estrella and Tristan had taken position at the bottom of the stairs, blocking my escape. Not that it mattered. Even if they weren't there, there was no escape. Not from this life.

Not from these vampires.

I felt the moment we reached the top, not from the shift in height but from the weight of attention. Four sets of silver-gold eyes locked onto me. I barely kept my footing under their scrutiny.

Roxiana. Isabeau. Sabas. Luc. Maire had said the former Mortal Bride fed the kings and their council. My stomach twisted, a dull ache curling low. Walking naked through the Abyss had been humiliating enough. But to be passed between six vampires?

I swallowed hard. I would have to find a way.

My gaze dropped to the daemium throne, shadows breathing from the stone. Anything but the kings. Anything but the council. Anything but the image of Éamon's face—

No.

Not here. Not now. I clenched my jaw, forcing my mind away from him. Was this a replica of the one in the Abyss? It looked identical, right down to the carved runes lining the wide base erupting from the floor. That the Azarasians had enough daemium to forge not one but two massive thrones spoke to the Impire's wealth.

"Bride."

Luc's firm voice ripped me back to the present. He gestured to the floor at his feet. "On your knees."

The words rang through me. They settled into my bones like they belonged there. My body resisted, muscles locking tight, but I swallowed past the lump in my throat. Slowly, carefully, I sank down until my knees pressed against the cold, unforgiving stone.

The kings' gazes followed me, a singular weight, a shared hunger.

The chill of the floor bit into my skin, grounding me. I latched onto the sensation, onto anything real. I was alive. I would remain alive.

I would not break.

I would not—

Luc's knuckles skimmed along my cheek. "Good girl."

My breath hitched as I shuddered at the touch. But not from fear. From something far worse.

My mad need for the Conqueror and the Butcher wouldn't break me, either.

Would it?

I repeated it over and over as the kings resumed their audience, their voices a melodic lull over my head.

Like if I thought it enough times, it might come true.

# 23

I DIDN'T KNOW HOW long I had kneeled at the base of the kings' throne.

I let time blur around me, sinking into myself. If I focused too hard on reality, the pain in my knees, in my core, in my soul, went from a low rumble to a stabbing ache. If I let myself listen to the conversation around me, every word from the kings made me think of another pair of dead human eyes.

Éamon.

The man from the harvest feast.

Fergus.

A fresh wave of sickly heat rolled through me, sudden and burning. Then, just as quickly, I felt cold, a slow, creeping chill. My body couldn't decide which way to go. Not good.

I clenched my hands in my lap, nails biting into my palms. *Breath, idiot. Ignore it.*

I leaned into the fog.

My response wasn't right. It wasn't normal. It was my mind's way of handling trauma, shutting down and curling inward to protect itself. I had done it before, but at least then I had a book to distract me.

Without one, I could only drift for so long.

"We're nineteen, Your Majesty." A light, female voice reached my ears. "It's our twentieth birthday in a few days."

The joy in her tone settled in me like rocks and dragged me down to my body. The constant hum of pain I ignored clawed its way back to the forefront of my mind. I dug my nails into my legs and let the sensation of it shoot through my skin.

I twisted slightly to glare at the fuckers at the base of the steps.

Two beautiful, dark-skinned vampires, a golden-eyed female and a silver-eyed male, stood hand in hand, her left arm tied to his right with a crimson sash. They looked so young. Almost innocent. Only a year older than Aislin.

"We wanted to have our heartbonding before we enlisted," said the man.

My glare turned into a frown. Heartbonding. Was that the Azarasian version of a wedding?

A wave of dizziness hit me, disrupting my thoughts. I almost swayed. I fought it, forcing my breaths even. I couldn't be weak. Not here. Not now.

The woman curled into the man's side, as if she could get even closer than being literally bound to him, body and soul. "That, and in time for the Red Queen's Rising tonight."

My brow furrowed. They must have called the Blood Star the Red Queen. Their celebration was tonight? A night of revelry, excess, and debauchery, no doubt. My stomach twisted at the thought. I hoped the kings wouldn't make me attend.

But I knew they would.

"Will you stay bound until the Red Queen graces our skies with her full court?" Luc asked. He sounded like he cared, but from where I sat at his feet, his agitation almost hummed beneath his skin. His finger tapped slowly against the throne's black armrest.

"We plan to, Your Majesty," the man said. "It would be a great blessing to our bond."

"That it would." Luc smiled without a hint of arrogance, the practiced grin of a politician. "May you and your heartmate's love last an eternity."

"Yes, an eternity," Jules echoed, not bothering to hide how bored he was. Legs crossed, he fidgeted as he used his curved dagger to pick under his nails.

Luc pinched Jules's thigh, the movement hidden from the watching High Courts by my shoulders. Jules didn't flinch but I did, imagining the sensation on my flesh.

The King of Dawn turned on his own charm. "Fate has given you a gift most Azarasians will never know. Your bond is already more than blessed."

"Thank you, Your Majesty," the woman replied, her fear *almost* disguised. It didn't help that Jules waved his dagger around as he spoke.

The Butcher's own citizens feared him and rightly so. Anyone who passed through the front gate saw his handiwork.

His *art*.

But then, just for a breath of a second, something flickered beneath his jovial cruelty.

The way he noticed their fear, the way he always noticed. How it clung to him, inevitable, unshakable, like a shadow cast too long ago to ever fade. And he had done it to himself. Better they fear him than think him less, a stain of a soulbound on the Azaras heir—

His gaze dropped to me, like he had heard the thought. Or, more likely, spotted me staring at him.

I didn't duck my head. I didn't fucking care. The exhaustion was getting to me.

Jules grinned, sharper than his blade, and flicked a speck of dirt from his dagger's tip. "That will be all for today."

Luc arched a brow at him before he followed his soulbound's gaze to me. "A wonderful idea, Julien."

My knees and spine should have rejoiced at their decision. The sooner their public audience came to a close, the sooner I could stop kneeling at the base of their throne, stiff-backed. The sooner I could climb into a bed to cry and scream into a pillow.

But I might have to cry and scream into a pillow for a very different reason first.

Luc looped his hand through my collar's handle at my nape.

Oh, fuck.

The pressure at my throat increased as Luc tugged me up. I clawed at the collar, but my fingers were useless against the silver-gold band. My ass hit the warm heat of the Conqueror's strong thigh. My hand slammed into his velvet-trimmed doublet over hard muscle.

The moment I was settled, he loosened his grip, and I sucked in a breath. Sweet, precious air. But his hand remained on the collar.

"Meet us in the throne room," Luc said.

What? I noticed Roxiana nod the second before my vision blurred.

I jolted, vision spinning and melting. I gave my head a hard shake, squeezing my eyes shut.

I opened them to an entirely different room.

My jaw dropped. Instead of the vast audience hall, I now sat with the kings on their throne in a smaller chamber. Afternoon sunlight streamed through tall windows, gold light dancing across another ceiling mural. This time, instead of the Second Godsfall, the Conqueror and the Butcher loomed over a battlefield of bodies and red-tinged snow, powerful and confident in black armor over hardened leather.

Unlike the audience hall, this room was empty.

The crowns atop the kings' heads flickered, shadows curling and rising like smoke. The shadows drifted toward the throne, where the daemium drank them down like water on soil.

My skin tingled in warning. A lightning strike of pain lanced low in my gut, but I ignored it in favor of curiosity. My gaze dropped to the throne beneath me. "This isn't a replica of the Abyss and audience throne, is it?"

I couldn't help but try to delay the inevitable. It wasn't hard to guess the kings' wonderful idea. Their stomachs didn't grumble like mine, but their hunger was almost tangible.

In the corner of my vision, Luc finally allowed a small smile. "It isn't. They're the same throne, spelled to be in multiple places at once. We have a second one in Duskfell, but there is only one throne in each of our cities."

Jules jumped to his feet, ignoring our conversation. "Stars, that last hour was dull. I need a drink. "

"Isn't that why we're here?"

I went stiff in Luc's lap. There it was, the inevitable.

"She's non-alcoholic." Jules approached a small cart tucked into a nook beside the throne. He grabbed a decanter, raised it at Luc in silent question, but the King of Dusk shook his head. Jules shrugged, poured himself a glass of dark red liquid, and took a slow sip.

A finger traced one side of my neck to the tip of my chin. My head whipped back around, away from Jules.

"Your choice, bride?" Luc asked, breath against my ear.

I swallowed audibly. I knew what Luc meant instantly. Pleasure or pain. Agony or ecstasy. My head tilted back, just enough to see the dark-eyed beast behind me lazing on his throne.

It wasn't a hard question. I was already in pain. I didn't want to be in any more.

Burying my shame, I whispered, "Ecstasy."

Luc nudged my chin, his fingers warm against my jaw. My neck stretched before him, exposing a long expanse of unblemished skin—

I had just enough time to inhale before fangs met my flesh.

Heat surged through me, racing from my neck to my tightening nipples, pooling between my thighs in a flood of raw need.

I gasped. Every ache faded, burned away by bliss. For once, my desire didn't turn on me. I tried to squeeze my thighs together, desperate to ease the pressure.

But before I could, Jules was there, sliding a knee between my legs and pressing in. The King of Dawn's lean, powerful body towered over us, black eyes fixed on me as I gasped and buckled against his soulbound's hold. He had tied his blond hair back into a knot, keeping the wavy strands from his face.

Godstars, I wanted them to touch me. Right fucking now. I wanted those long, perfect fingers inside me. I wanted—no, I *needed.* I was hopeless, breathless, burning slow, the fire consuming me from the inside out.

I ground back against Luc's hard length trapped between us, but that didn't sate my ache at all. My own hand snaked between my legs. I usually couldn't stand to touch the softness of my thighs, but I needed friction, needed something.

Jules caught my hand easily. "Uh-uh, bride. You're ours now. No one will touch you unless we say so. And that includes you."

A second later, an odd, warm sensation caressed my arms and knees. Wafting shadows from the *daemium* twisted around my limbs and pulled them taut. They pinned my hands to the throne, spreading my legs wide enough for Jules to kneel between them.

I couldn't resist. I wasn't even sure I tried. My head dropped back against the King of Dusk's muscled shoulder.

Luc swallowed another mouthful of my blood, the pull at my essence, my lifeforce, muted beneath the white-hot surge of pleasure. I squirmed, whimpering. Fuck, why wouldn't they touch me? The King of Dusk had fucked that thrall on the road, gripping her hips, dragging her down onto his cock without hesitation.

So why wouldn't he take me?

I could feel the tension coiling in him, the rigid strain of his body beneath mine. He wanted. I knew it. I *felt* it.

So why wouldn't he give in?

Luc traced his fingers up my body and unhooked my dress from my collar. The fabric slid down to my waist. My breasts heaved, my nipples sharp and aching.

Jules licked his lips at the sight.

Luc crawled his hand down my body, across my soft stomach, and slipped beneath my skirts.

Yes. No! Yes? My brain couldn't settle on a response.

He slid his hand between my spread legs. I jolted as his fingers threaded through my curls, ever so slowly.

He rubbed his fingertips through my wet center and landed on my clit.

Pleasure shot through me. I forgot everything. I started panting at the soft touch.

Jules's breathing turned harsh as he focused on the shape of his soulbound's hand under my thin gown. "Is Luc touching your clit without my permission, lovely?"

I didn't even try to answer. My muscles went slack, my eyes drifting half-shut. Luc lapped his tongue against my bloody skin, tugging at the tension between my legs. His fingers stroked it higher. I couldn't hold back my moan.

With a final, deep swallow and a brush of his tongue across the puncture marks, Luc pulled an inch away from my neck. His breath tickled against my skin. "I don't need your permission, Julien. You won her first, not forever"—Luc circled his fingers around my clit, and I choked on my breath—"so this is mine to do with as I please."

"Is—Is—" I swallowed. "Is this a game to you both?"

"Yes," Luc said without hesitation.

"I'm in the lead." Jules sipped at his wine, those golden eyes flickering to me before returning south. He pushed my skirt up another inch, exposing Luc's hand on my needy flesh. "Shall we give Luc a chance to catch up?"

Luc swiveled his fingers. The jolt made me forget the question. It made me forget my *name*. My lips parted, a pathetic whine escaping from them.

"I think she's open to the idea," Jules said with a chuckle. "Shh, there's no need to answer. I can see it on your face. The bliss, the wonder, the surprise..." His gilded gaze sharpened. "How many times have you come in your life?"

Luc's finger remained on my clit, but he went still. The sudden lack of movement left me aching, thrashing against the shadows around my limbs. "What?"

"It's a simple enough question." Luc's lips brushed the side of my face, his breath dancing across my skin. "We'll know if you lie."

"Twice," I said without hesitation. Anything to get those fingers moving again.

But wait. That wasn't right. I had come on my fingers, Jules's tongue, and then... then again after they bit me. "Or three times?"

I frowned. That answer didn't feel right either. Why didn't it feel right? Something was missing.

Then Luc's finger moved again, and all that mattered was pleasure. "You don't sound sure, little bride."

"It was three."

"Before last night, you had *one* orgasm in nearly thirty years?" His voice was smooth, but his silver eyes flickered, watching me too closely.

"That's a travesty," Jules said, his grin growing sharp. "Who made you come? Besides me, of course."

What was this, a fucking interrogation? At my lack of reply, Luc slowed his finger again. "No one," I gasped out quickly, the sound nearly shrill.

"So you came on your own fingers?"

"Yes."

The King of Dusk cocked his head. "And never tried again?"

I looked away. He didn't understand. He was a vampire, a perfect specimen of corded muscle and smooth skin. I was disgusting, broken. A wicked, sinful girl. "No."

"Why?" Jules asked.

Luc sped the circles around my clit with each answer. My back arched, a moan escaping my lips. "I'm not—ah... There's something wrong with me. It sometimes... oh, fuck... hurts. A lot."

"How does it feel right now?" Luc asked, circling and circling.

I shuddered as bolts of pleasure shot through me. "You know how it feels."

Luc's smug arrogance all but radiated into me as I whimpered on his fucking finger. He increased his pressure ever so slightly. "I did, but I still want you to say it."

I exhaled shakily, but managed to say, "Why do you even care?"

"Despite what some human men think," Luc said, "sex is far more pleasurable when your partners are enjoying themselves."

"We're not having sex. You're..." My gaze went from Luc in my periphery to Jules, kneeling between my legs and watching his soulbound pleasure me with rapture. "He's..."

Jules grinned madly. "It's called foreplay, lovely girl. As Luc said, you'll be a better fuck if you're soaking wet and sobbing for it."

I bit my lip to stop my mewl. Soaking wet and sobbing. I was already most of the way there. "Oh."

"Mine was far more eloquent."

"Fuck off, Lucey."

Luc continued working my clit, luring me to the peak with slow, measured, maddening steps. "You didn't answer me. How does it feel, bride?"

The words hovered on my tongue, but I held them there, trembling. Amazing. Life-altering. Transcendent. I never wanted to experience pain ever again. Just this intoxicating bliss.

"So stubborn," Luc murmured.

Luc swirled my clit faster, faster. The touch remained light, a quick brush of his fingertip. Little gasps escaped my throat, embarrassing noises.

I didn't care. His venom still rushed through my veins, muting my pain. Leaving me bathing in light and heat and perfection.

This was the way a body should've worked. Should've reacted. It didn't even matter that it was the Conqueror fingering me. As long as he made me come. He lured me up and up with gentle strokes, higher and higher—

He pulled his hand away. "Julien."

No! I almost cried out, but held the embarrassing noise in. But I couldn't stop twisting in his grasp. I couldn't move much, but my legs widened slightly. I glanced at the King of Dusk over my shoulder, ready to beg.

He smirked. "What a needy little creature you are."

"Please," I whispered. I didn't even feel any shame at the question.

"Not yet. You haven't earned it." His silver gaze released me and flickered down. "Isn't that right, dearest?"

I blinked away the fiery bliss and managed half a frown at Jules. He placed his half-full goblet on the throne's arm and removed the jeweled gold rings from his right hand. "Hold these for me."

The chill of the metal pressed into my trapped palm. I clenched my hand around them automatically. What was—?

Jules suddenly dropped lower. I gaped down my body and at the king crouching between my legs. When Jules exhaled, his breath brushed against my aching center. That single brush had me straining in Luc's lap, battling the shadows around my limbs.

The King of Dusk's hands dug into my hips, locking me in place, as golden eyes flickered to me. "Now, now," Jules murmured. "You wouldn't deprive a man his favorite meal?"

My mouth watered. "You… I… No?"

Jules grinned—and then locked his fangs into the soft skin of my mound.

The pleasure in me burst, like oil thrown on fire. Blood trickled down my skin, through my curls and over my clit.

Jules lapped his tongue through me, slow and hard.

I moaned, eyes slipping shut. His tongue piercing grazed against that sensitive nub and my moan turned into a yelp.

Luc's hands caged my legs in place as Jules groaned into my cunt. It was a desperate, hungry noise, half male and half beast. Jules started sucking and nipping and licking my blood-soaked clit, burrowing into my body. Devouring me.

My eyes rolled back as waves of heat thrummed through me. Would Jules really fuck me with his tongue every day for the rest of my life? He got better each time, learning what made me whimper and applying each lesson like a dedicated pupil.

"Please." I didn't know what I was begging for, not exactly, but I needed more.

Luc chuckled, a deep rumble. "Please, what?"

"Please, Your Majesty. I need to come. Please make me come."

"Not to me," Luc murmured against my ear. He reached out and brushed a knuckle along Jules's temple. "To him."

I whimpered but obeyed. "Please, please, please—"

Jules had no objections. He slid his finger toward my soaked center. I gasped at the sensation. The King of Dawn circled the rim of my entrance until the pad of his finger dipped inside me.

I tensed, bracing for the pain. There was a tinge of discomfort, but the building heat washed it away. It didn't turn to shattered glass, scraping at my insides.

My nipples tightened.

My breath spiked.

My nerves tingled.

My world narrowed to the pleasure between my legs.

Jules's knuckles brushed my entrance as he sunk deeper. Deeper. Deeper. The side of his palm brushed my curls as he buried his finger as far as he could inside me.

I exhaled in a long whine. Fuck, that felt... amazing. There was no blinding pain as my body turned against me. No curling into a ball as it radiated through my core. Only a warm wave of venom and tongue-induced pleasure, rushing through me.

"That's enough, Julien."

No, no, no. "Please, don't stop."

Jules glanced up, but his tongue and finger didn't stop their tantalizing dance. Those shadowed gold eyes flicked from his silver counterpart to me, flushed and heaving against his chest. The King of Dawn smirked against my cunt.

With one last swirl around my blood-stained clit, he healed my skin and pulled back. I nearly sobbed.

But he didn't stop rocking his hand back and forth as he licked his glistening lips. "My apologies, darling. I got carried away."

Luc hummed. He released my hip... and returned his fingers to my clit.

I groaned, embarrassingly loud.

*Both* of their hands were now between my legs.

"That's it, little curiosity," Luc said. "Surrender to your kings."

I had surrendered the moment Luc's fangs pierced my neck. Earlier even. Last night. At the lake. In Corraidin. My body arched until my head rested against Luc's shoulder, his sharp jawline, silver-rimmed shadow eyes, and tousled dark hair filling my entire vision.

The King of Dusk's expression was almost bored... if I ignored how hot it was. It was the lazy confidence of a predator, secure in his claim on his prey.

On me.

The kings sped their pace, each thrust harder, each swirl around my clit faster. The strain pushed me higher into intoxicating heat. It spread through my chest, my lungs heaving. Stars, this was going to kill me.

*They* were going to kill me.

How dare they touch me like this, together, after doing such wickedly horrible things.

How dare I crave it.

"Are you enjoying our fingers, lovely?"

A breathless moan escaped my throat, as good an answer as any.

"Are you going to come for us?" Luc's voice rumbled through his chest and into me, the sound satisfied and very male. I shuddered as it stirred the fire in my core higher.

Luc pressed hard against my clit. I shrieked at the burst of pleasure-pain. "Ye—ah, yes, Your Majesty. I'm going to... oh... going to come."

"Good girl." Luc rubbed faster and faster as Jules curled his finger. He brushed against a spot within me that made me jerk and mewl. "Come for us now."

My body obeyed him.

My eyes rolled back.

"Oh, fuck, stars, fuck!"

I jolted as I came, my body jostling between the two vampires holding me down. My back arched, my head slamming against Luc. My hands clenched, wishing they could wrap around Luc's thighs, my fingers wanting nothing more than to dig into his hard muscles. I bucked against them, their hand and their throne's shadows, as their venom stretched the orgasm on and on.

When it finally released me, I slumped down in Luc's lap and closed my eyes. I hadn't even noticed Jules's rings piercing my palm.

Was this what thralls went through every feeding? Stars. No wonder they became addicted.

I let out a soft, satisfied sigh. The pleasure still pulsed in my veins, hot and hazy, like the remnants of a fever. My skin tingled where their hands had been, my thighs trembling in the aftershocks. I should have felt relief. Instead, a slow, crawling awareness slithered down my spine.

The kings hadn't spoken.

That should have been a blessing. It wasn't. I blinked away the haze. Jules had gone completely still between my legs, one hand resting lightly on my thigh. Luc's fingers splayed against my belly and hadn't moved since I'd gone slack in his lap.

There was a tension in them, something barely restrained. They weren't teasing, weren't taunting, weren't moving at all.

This was different. Heavier.

Heat crawled up my throat, thick and cloying. My thighs pressed together, as if I could somehow hide from the weight of their attention. I had done something wrong. I must have.

My gaze flickered down to their hands. The smallest trace of blood marred Jules's skin, mixing with my desire.

Shame flooded me. I couldn't know for sure, but I doubted it came from the bite. Would there ever be a time I wouldn't bleed when aroused? Their venom had eliminated any discomfort, but my body still reacted.

Now that they knew about my pain and noticed my bleeding, did they regret choosing a broken bride?

"What?" I asked, voice shaking.

The silence deepened. But the kings finally turned their attention from me to each other.

"Did you..." Jules hesitated, his gaze flicking between me and his soulbound. His lips parted like he had something to say, but nothing came out.

The Butcher was *speechless*.

But Luc already knew the rest of the question. "Feel her come? Every second of it."

"You did *what* now?" I stared at the kings, the heat in my cheeks searing throughout my face. They had *felt* me come? What in the hells did that mean? Like *felt* it, felt it or...

I didn't know any other way to feel something, but surely they couldn't mean what I thought they meant.

Somehow, the idea of the kings feeling my orgasm was worse than having one in front of them.

The King of Dusk remained a rock at my back, but he slowly traced a line along the inside of my arm. I tried to breathe, to calm my racing pulse. When he reached my wrist, his fingertip heated—

"This will sting."

That was all the notice I had before Luc slid a *shadow-edged claw* through my soft flesh. Skin parted, blood welling instantly before it spilled down my arm. Pain shot through me. My instincts roared to life, screaming at me to run, to get away.

I wasn't safe, not here, not ever.

But also... I was.

My mind rejected the thought, but my body melted into Luc's, as if it trusted him. As if we were safe here.

I ignored it. My body didn't know a starsdamned thing. It turned against me daily.

The throne's shadows shackled my limbs. The kings' hands buried into my skin. The covenant runespell claimed my lifeforce.

I was *not* safe.

But if the kings wanted to slice me to pieces, I couldn't do anything about it.

Besides shouting, that is. "What the fuck—"

Daemium shadows lashed around my head, sealing over my lips. I let out a muffled scream, my voice smothered to nothing.

A second ago, they had looked at me with heat. Like I was something to be devoured. Now? That hunger had vanished.

Stupid. I had let myself forget who they were. What they were. Vampires were our masters, our captors. We would only ever be prey.

"Do you feel that?" Luc asked Jules, his focus entirely on his soulbound at our feet, like I wasn't shaking against him, bleeding on his lap.

"Maybe?" Jules raised his right hand, the same one that had stroked between my legs. He sucked his glistening fingertip into his mouth, licking away the taste of my blood-tinged pleasure. His eyes fluttered shut like he was savoring it. A second later, a rune flared. *Clean.* It wiped the remaining sheen from his skin. "It's too faint for me to tell, but it's an easy enough hypothesis to test."

Hypothesis? What hypothesis?

Then the King of Dawn shoved his finger *into* my open wound.

My vision went white. I shrieked into the gag, tears flooding my eyes. Just a couple minutes ago, the same move in a wildly different location had me moaning.

Now it was pure agony.

I had thought I knew pain. I was wrong.

Everything I had ever suffered was nothing compared to this. I jerked, but the shadows held me firm.

Jules pulled his finger out as fast as he shoved it in. His brows lifted. "I definitely felt *that.*"

"As did I, but it's still muted." Luc's voice was clinical, distant. "Perhaps a weak empathy runespell that only affects physical sensation."

A weak empathy runespell. On me.

No. No, that wasn't possible.

My breath came short and sharp through my nose. Someone had cast magic on me? Someone besides the kings? The thought twisted deep in my gut.

When?

Who?

And, most importantly—why?

Had the runespell always been there? Had I lived my whole life under the influence of it without knowing? My mind raced, clawing at memories, but nothing stood out.

During the harvest? No, the magistrate had only drawn the amplification runes, and no other vampire had approached me besides the kings.

Before that? Was it my father? My stepmother? Impossible. They hated magic.

A random stranger I passed in the market, then? A brush of magic against my skin, unnoticed? The questions churned inside me, frantic, desperate. But the gag choked them all down.

With a wave of his hand, Luc took control of the blood streaming down my arm. It rose from my flesh, forming a languid swirl above us. I should have been horrified, but a sick part of me found it mesmerizing.

"How would that benefit anyone?" Jules asked.

"I don't know yet." Luc dissipated his shadowed claw and lifted my arm.

The gag muffled my gasp as his tongue flicked across the cut, sealing it with deliberate pressure. Jules leaned in, dragging his mouth over my elbow, swallowing every drop that escaped. Goosebumps raced over my skin.

Even after they had cut me open. Even after Jules had shoved his *finger* inside my wound.

Those were important distinctions, but my body didn't care. If I wasn't gagged, I might have sighed.

Luc released my arm a second later. Daemium shadows wrapped around my wrist and wrenched it back down.

Jules licked his lips and stood in one smooth motion. His desire was obvious, but with a roll of his shoulders, his body obeyed his command. "Fuck, she's delicious. Think that's part of the spell?"

"She tastes the same as she did last night. Before we bit her and..." Luc's words faded, silver eyes going blank. A flicker of something crawled over his face, like he snatched for a thread, lost it, grabbed for it again. "Did you... Are you certain you fucked her last night?"

What were they talking about? Jules had slithered up my body, Luc had fisted a hand in my hair, their fangs had burrowed into my neck and then—

"Of course I did," Jules scoffed, shaking his head. "What kind of question is that?"

His grin was quick, automatic. But his voice stumbled just a fraction on the last word. The playful curve of his mouth faded a breath too late. "We bit her. And then I..."

They glanced at each other. Then down at me.

Then, suddenly, as one, they stiffened.

"Fuck," Jules breathed, letting out a low whistle. "The good ol' lifeforce trap."

Luc pinched the bridge of his nose. For once, he actually looked stressed. "It was a bloodborne runespell, then. It takes a lot of power to cast one of those. That might narrow it down, at least."

What were they talking about? I tried to demand answers through the gag, but only muffled sounds escaped. Jules had fucked me last night. He had. I... I...

I didn't remember it.

The hole in my memory gaped back at me. I had danced around it since waking, every attempt to focus slipping from my grasp. But now that the kings had noticed it, now that they had spoken it aloud, I couldn't *not* notice it.

Something had crushed me.

That was the last thing I remembered. A weight too vast, too immense, pressing against my chest, stealing my breath, like I had been buried alive. Like I had been drowning in power.

And then I woke in their arms. Naked and sweat-stained, but there was no pain, no soreness. No explicit memory, only the vague certainty that we must have fucked. Because that was the only logical explanation.

But if Jules had fucked me last night, I'd have felt different. Changed. And I did, slightly. But the change was something deeper, something more elusive than flesh.

Luc rose to his feet. I slid down his body and hit the floor hard, my gown bunching around my waist. Pain throbbed in my knees, but I barely noticed it. I grasped blindly for my gown, desperate to cover myself, but the throne's shadows snaked down my body. They winded around my wrists, binding me to the seat's base.

Luc crossed the hall. He didn't spare me a glance. Instead, he stopped beneath the floating swirls of crimson, silver gaze fixed and sharp.

"What do you do?" he murmured to my blood, barely audible. "And who would dare cast you?"

Was the Conqueror... was the Conqueror worried?

"Well, once you've figured that out, let me know who I need to kill." Jules's grin sharpened, but something about it was too casual, too forced. His gaze dropped to me, half-naked at his feet. "I hope it isn't you, lovely. That would be such a shame."

I flinched. But this time, I didn't glare. Jules wasn't joking. I didn't know what kind of magic bound us together, but if they decided I was responsible, I would die at the Butcher's hand.

I swallowed hard. Sweat trickled down the back of my neck. This time, pleasure or confusion didn't muddle my reaction. This time, it was all fear.

I forced myself to hold onto it. The Butcher didn't make idle threats.

I didn't even care if the stress of it dragged my illness from its orgasm-induced slumber. But nothing happened. No sudden cramps. No nausea crashing over me like a tide. Maybe it was chance, maybe it was their venom. I couldn't tell. I had felt the cut, but that was sharp pain, a literal hole in my arm.

Without turning from my floating blood, Luc snapped his fingers toward the doors. A carved rune flared black. *Open*. The gilded double doors to the throne room parted on their own.

A distant drone of sound sharpened into voices. The Kings' Council entered. I stiffened, shoulders slumping, instinctively trying to make myself small. Like that would hide the fact that I was half-naked, my breasts visible for all to see. They probably wouldn't notice given nudity was a frequent occurrence around here, but that didn't matter to me. Too many people had looked at me already.

I focused on breathing.

"If we send a Blade for her, another Tyrhari horde warlord will take her place within the week," Sabas said, mid-argument with Isabeau at his side. "We know how Vigdis thinks, how she fights. It's better to let her live. We can thwart any of her attempts on the Northern Wall."

Isabeau frowned, her serious expression becoming even more so. "It's been ten years since Luc and Jules last reinforced the protection runes."

Sabas crossed his arms as Cédric entered behind them, settling at his soulbound's side. "Then the answer is arranging a visit to the border, not sending a Blade."

"Vigdis split her horde and is coordinating attacks on Kotara," Cédric said. "We can't defend that territory as easily. Perry said—"

"If Perry and Jessenia actually thought the horde could breach Kotara's walls, they wouldn't spend half their reports bitching about the dry heat,"

Sabas said dismissively. "Vigdis is no more a threat to us than an Alvarese pirate."

Names. Strategies. Places I didn't know. The words blurred together. I knew the Butcher's assassin force was called the Blades, but a Tyrhari horde? Kotara? I had no idea where they were, who they fought, or why any of it mattered.

Isabeau's gaze flickered to the kings and I, the crease between her brow deepening as she took us in. "An Alvarese pirate nearly killed our kings once."

"He tried to kill me," Jules interjected, his grin nearly as bright as usual. "But I *actually* killed him. Important distinction."

Luc's voice cut through the conversation. "Vigdis Dauthrekkr will die on an Azarasian blade on the battlefield. Her body will decorate our walls until the hellcrows tear it apart."

Isabeau paused, considering. "We haven't made an example of someone in years."

The Conqueror's silver eyes glinted coldly again, but he couldn't hide his concern. Did I know that because of the empathy bond? "It's high time we do so again."

Sabas's gaze sharpened, finally tearing away from the debate long enough to take in the room. His dark eyes flicked from the kings to the blood spiraling above us.

Then, down to me.

"What's happened?"

Jules dropped onto the throne and patted my head. It wasn't a comforting touch, not after he'd just threatened to kill me. "We're not sure yet."

"What does that mean?" Isabeau asked.

The kings glanced at each other, coming to another one of their silent decisions, before Luc asked, "Cédric, what happened with the apartment's wards?"

The Prince of Dawn faced the throne, straight-backed and serious. I hadn't had the chance to study Jules's brother for long. His hair was a darker blond than the Butcher's, neatly trimmed over a handsome, composed face. They shared the same golden eyes, rimmed with just enough shadow to mark them as demonborn. While he resembled Jules, he seemed almost ordinary compared to the King of Dawn's glittering, sharp beauty.

If I wasn't gagged, I'd laugh at the idea of considering any vampire ordinary.

"Nothing, as far as I can tell," Cédric said. "They're intact and unaltered."

Luc lowered his attention from my blood. "Then how was our Mortal Bride wandering the thrall quarters?"

A flicker of something crossed Cédric's face. Hesitation. "I'm... not sure."

Luc arched a brow. Incredulously, maybe, like Cédric had never *not* had an answer for him. His gaze swept over the council, weighing them in an instant, before turning to me. "How did you break through our wards, Miss Halloran?"

As Luc asked the question, the shadow gag withered from my mouth, though it remained close, a threat lingering at the edge of my vision. I inhaled deeply, steadying myself. I had no idea when I'd be allowed to breathe freely again.

The kings and their council waited.

What was the right answer? Lying wouldn't help. I didn't know how I had walked through their wards or how this bond had happened. The wrong words would get me killed, but what if silence could, too?

"I walked, Your Majesty," I said, keeping my voice level.

"Hmm." The deep rumble was clearly skeptical. "And you also wouldn't happen to know why we felt an echo of your pleasure and pain?"

Three pairs of eyes widened.

A sharp inhale. A step back. Sabas's fingers curled into fists, while Cédric's brow furrowed, calculating. Isabeau's hand hovered over her sword hilt. No one spoke, but the shift in the air was unmistakable. Shock laced with something sharper. Fear, perhaps. Or worse—uncertainty.

My skin prickled with warning.

It was Sabas who spoke first. "You *what*?"

Luc didn't answer. His attention stayed on me. His silver eyes pinned me in place, the sheer authority in them making my breath stutter. Cold-eyed. Unshaken.

The Conqueror in full.

A tremor ran down my spine. I wrenched my stare away and ducked my head. I hated bowing before them, before anyone, but I wanted to live more. "I don't, Your Majesty."

Jules hummed and threaded a hand through my hair, twisting a loose strand around his finger. "That's a comfort to hear, bride. Here I thought we'd have to travel to Mabon again this year."

I didn't reply. Didn't flinch. I only just repressed a shudder at that gentle touch, so at odds with the threats to kill me. *I will not cry. I will not scream. I will not let these monsters break me.*

Sabas dragged a hand through his dark hair, looking one wrong answer away from tearing it out entirely. "What the fuck is happening?"

"We haven't thoroughly tested it, but we felt her pleasure when she came and her pain when we cut her arm," Luc explained, gesturing at my floating blood. "Both were faint sensations, but that could change with time."

"That doesn't answer my question," Sabas said.

"We got hit by a bloodborne spell last night when we both fed from her," Jules said matter-of-factly. "It knocked us out and made it hard to remember, as they're oft to do."

Cédric's brow furrowed. "Most bloodborne runespells that do that and create empathy links are rather permanent."

*Permanent.* My stomach clenched.

"That's assuming it's a known spell." At Luc's silent command, the swirls of my blood stopped spinning and weaved between the council. "What do you sense in her blood?"

A pause.

No one answered right away. The vampires studied my blood, their gazes sharp, their silence heavy. Like I wasn't even here. Like I was an object to be examined, a puzzle to be solved.

Except for Jules. It was entirely possible the Butcher was paying attention as he *braided* a thin strand of my hair. My fingers twitched, itching to slap his hand away. Did he play doll with all their brides or was I just unlucky?

I had to swallow the quip. The kings hadn't reformed the gag, and there was no need to remind them of that.

"I don't sense anything," Cédric said after a minute. He glanced at Sabas, who nodded in agreement. "Only blood."

"It's the same for me," Isabeau said.

Luc nodded once, like he had already expected that answer. "We all should be able to sense the covenant in her blood, as well as traces of this other spell. Which means she's glamoured."

Every eye snapped to me at once. I went rigid. Glamoured? I resisted the urge to touch my face. Did that mean I didn't look like this? Or that everyone around me saw something different? I grasped at the memories, trying to remember exactly how glamours worked in *The Soulborne Quee*n.

Jules dropped my finished braid. "Egh, power glamours are the worst."

"When was it cast?" Isabeau tapped her finger against the pommel of her belted sword. "You were with her the entire ride from Mabon?"

Luc nodded. "We didn't let her out of our sight until we reached Dawnspear."

The councilors all paused, visibly thinking through the problem.

Sabas raised a finger. "The Isauran delegation—"

Jules cut in smoothly. "The witches are bound. Even if they weren't, Exalted Morrena isn't powerful enough to cast a glamour that could fool us."

"We can discuss who cast the spell later," Luc said, waving the thought away. His attention returned to me. I lowered my eyes but not my face. The shadow of the Conqueror loomed in my periphery. "Its effects so far are a nuisance at best. I want to know what it really does. And to do that, I need the glamour off."

A simple statement. A calm statement.

The council reacted like he had suggested feeding himself to a hellbeast.

"Luc—" Sabas started.

"I insist—" Isabeau spoke over him.

Cédric cut them both off with a sharp glance. Surprisingly, they fell silent. But as Crown Mage, magic was his area of expertise. "It's a power glamour strong enough to trick you, created by someone with enough strength to cast a bloodborne spell on you. Who knows what else it's hiding?"

A flicker of something crawled up my spine. What else was it hiding? What could possibly be worse than what had already happened to me? I resisted the urge to touch my skin, like I might feel something different beneath my fingertips.

Luc was unmoved. "I can feel its edges. It was designed to hide powerful magic, but nothing nearly as strong as the covenant. If removing it triggers anything, we'll know."

Cédric's frown deepened. "I should still be the one to remove it."

"Jules and I are more likely to counter any traps, and if not, survive them," Luc said.

Isabeau scoffed. "You're the Imperium. We *can't* risk it. If we lose you, we lose the covenant, and we'll be invaded from every direction. Not to mention from the Trost and the Marsanians inside the Impire itself."

Jules snorted. "I think the worst part is that we'll be dead, Issie, but sure, the Impire getting royally fucked is the bigger concern."

Isabeau shot her King of Dawn a dry look. Jules only crossed his legs, twirling his foot in a circle.

"At least wait until after dusk," Sabas muttered, pinching the bridge of his nose.

"Rude." Jules glanced at Luc. "But not the worst idea. I don't want to untangle a power glamour and that's essentially a hobby of yours."

The words sent another shiver through me. I didn't mean to ask the question, but it slipped out before I could stop myself. "Untangling power glamours?"

The councilors turned their blank stares toward me. I resisted the urge to shy away. I was used to staying quiet and in the corner. I had for years. But after a week of the kings' attention, I didn't want to fade back into the wallpaper.

"Magic in general, more like," Luc said. His stare was intense and callous like his councilors, but there was a warmth to it... no, a heat, simmering right below the surface.

A ripple passed through the council. And this time, their unease wasn't directed at me. The way the kings treated me unnerved their councilors. Perhaps another element of this new spell?

But the kings thought it had activated last night, when they fed from me, transferred through my blood. They had always allowed me to speak my mind.

A soft knock sounded on the door.

Luc touched his inner wrist, which suddenly flickered with a shadow rune. *Relay*. The same rune he had used last night to communicate with his Imperial Guard. "Come in."

Estrella slipped through the doorway and bowed low. "The Crown Chancellor has brought the Isauran delegation here to speak with you, Imperator."

Jules curled his lip. "Why?"

Luc didn't glance at him. "We invited them."

Jules scoffed. "You and Roxiana invited them. I certainly did not."

Luc ignored his soulbound. "Send them in, Estrella."

Sabas let out a low breath. "Is now the best time?"

Luc turned toward his throne. I shuffled quickly to the side. The King of Dusk would undoubtedly remove me from his path if I remained in it. "It's excellent, actually. All the delegation witches can remove a fraying power glamour, and it's no great loss if it costs one of them their life."

No great loss. My stomach twisted, but I didn't outwardly react.

"You're going to release a witch?" Sabas asked incredulously. "What if they kill the Mortal Bride? What if the power glamour does when they remove it?"

"It won't and neither will the witches." Luc lowered himself into his throne like he was born to it. Which he was. "I'm more than capable of supervising without my full strength."

"And I'm more than capable of killing a witch instantly if they step out of line," Jules added.

With a single gesture from Estrella, the double doors swung open. In an instant, the council shifted, taking their positions along the throne's flanks.

I was still bound at its base, my gown bunched around my waist. I tried to flick my hair over my shoulder to cover my breasts. I failed. Five demonbloods in the room while I was half-naked was already too many. Now, there would be more and I couldn't do anything about it.

Roxiana sauntered through the open doors, her movements fluid grace. Behind her, the Isaurans walked with their heads bowed. Exalted Morrena led the six delegation witches, her cane tapping against the stone floor in steady, punctuated beats. The sound sent shivers down my spine.

When they reached the middle of the room, a respectable distance away, the witches stopped and lowered to their knees. Tristan followed them in, closing the doors with an echoing thud. A witch at the end of the line flinched.

The guards took up positions near the exit, forming an unspoken barrier. Roxiana continued until she reached Isabeau's side next to Luc. She bowed to the kings, kissed her soulbound quickly, and then settled into her place.

"We're honored, Imperium," Morrena said, her voice smooth but low. Her delegation mirrored her movement behind her, bowing deeply.

"The Isaurans have agreed to all our terms," Roxiana said.

I resisted a snort. The Isaurans might have been demonbloods, too, but if they were sending harvests, they had no power to refuse any of the Impire's terms.

Luc inclined his head slightly. "Excellent. Which of your delegation is best at glamour removal?"

Roxiana's brow furrowed. Her gaze flicked to Isabeau, who leaned in, whispering something low and urgent. The chancellor's silver eyes flickered to me and widened.

Morrena straightened ever so slightly, but didn't raise her head. "I am, Your Majesty."

Luc didn't hesitate. "Second best, then."

The witch paused, a flicker of something crossing her face. Annoyance? No. Frustration. She hesitated only a breath before asking, "May I ask why, Your Majesty?"

There was a beat of silence. The witches all seemed to hold their breaths, waiting to see if they'd be punished for Morrena's question.

But the kings had bigger concerns. "It seems our new Mortal Bride came with her own runespells," Luc said. "And one of them is a power glamour."

Morrena exhaled through her nose. "I see. I can—"

"You can't," Luc cut her off smoothly. "You're one of the Exalted Daughters of Isaura. You're more useful alive."

For a split second, something flashed in her expression. Annoyance again. But it was gone as quickly as it appeared.

Morrena nodded stiffly. "In that case..." She turned slightly, her gaze sweeping down the line of witches. "Edda?"

None of the witches reacted. Then, a second later, a blonde witch rose to her feet and stepped forward. She looked twice Morrena's age—at least, physically. Which meant she was likely centuries old. "Of course, Exalted Daughter."

But she didn't move immediately. Her eyes flickered to Luc, then Jules, then me. She visibly swallowed. "I'll need to touch her."

My pulse stuttered. My mouth went dry. Why did I suddenly feel like the subject of an experiment?

The shadows at my wrists uncoiled, releasing me. I exhaled slowly. As calmly as I could manage, I straightened my gown and hooked the top of it into my collar.

Luc flicked a hand toward the witch. "On you go, bride."

I stood. I had no choice but to obey. No choice but to move. Every eye in the room tracked me as I stepped forward. No one was speaking. Even Jules wasn't making a quip.

Was it really that dangerous to remove a hidden power glamour? What would happen when it was removed?

Was I going to die?

I forced my breathing to stay even. Forced my steps to be steady. My pleasure still dampened my inner thighs, but I kept my head held high.

I would *not* cower.

"You may use your magic to remove the glamour from our bride, nothing more," Luc said, a clear warning in his tone. Disobedience would mean death for the witch.

Edda nodded once. As the suppression rune on her collar dimmed, the air around her warmed. Luc had released her magic. She stepped closer and settled her hands lightly on my shoulders. My muscles tensed on instinct, like I could rip my arm back before she touched me. But there was nowhere to go. No way to refuse.

The witch closed her eyes in concentration. Her fingers started drawing runes against my skin, the heat from the spell rising. It sunk deeper and deeper into me.

I braced, but nothing happened.

This wasn't so bad. From the way the vampires talked about the removal, I had expected—

My world erupted into agony.

The kind that seared through every nerve ending, that shattered thought and reason. Worse than the cramps of my illness. Worse than Jules shoving a finger into my arm. I didn't even scream.

I couldn't.

My limbs went slack, but I didn't hit the floor. Edda held me upright, her grip unyielding. A thousand hands clawed at my skin, raking over my bones.

They weren't just peeling something off me.

They were peeling me apart.

The first layer ripped away easily, but the second wasn't just on me. It was *in* me, woven into my very flesh.

I had never noticed it before, but now that someone tugged on it, I knew. It was as essential to me as my own heart. I tried to push those hands away mentally, but I wasn't a witch. I might be able to read runes, but I had no power. Nothing happened beyond my soul splitting apart, my very existence unraveling—

Edda jerked violently.

The movement reverberated through her arms and into mine. I blinked back to reality right as her chest pulsed like something exploded within her. Blood gushed from her nose, her mouth, her ears. Like someone had reached inside her and yanked every drop from her veins. It splattered across my cheeks.

The light left her eyes.

She collapsed to the ground.
Completely and entirely dead.

# 25

Without Edda holding me upright, my legs collapsed beneath me. I landed with a wet, sickening squash on her body.

Her. Body.

Oh, stars.

I was sitting on a fucking corpse.

I sucked in air, but I didn't have enough to scream. Blood smeared my hands, my hips, my thighs. It was everywhere, warm and sticky against cooling, dead skin. I thrashed, scrambling to get off her, but the floor was slick with blood, my palms sliding uselessly. My vision swirled, the world fading in and out of focus.

Pain still clawed at my insides. It was like Edda had rooted around inside me, the damage she left scarring my very soul.

Tears streaming down my cheeks, I finally managed to crawl away. My nausea subsided slightly now that I wasn't touching a starsdamned *dead* person—

I bumped into Jules's legs.

My head went back until my vision became nothing but the King of Dawn. The afternoon light turned his hair into a pale halo, gilded and blinding. His golden eyes fixed on me at his feet. He brushed a fingertip through a splat of witch blood on my cheek and brought it to his lips.

"Hmm." He made a face. "Not bad, not great. Mediocre at best."

I didn't bother holding back my horror. "Are you rating how the witch you *murdered* tastes?"

"How dare you suggest something so barbaric, lovely? I was rating how the witch *Luc* murdered tastes." Jules's quip didn't have quite the same zest as normal. Something about it rang untrue? His joyful mask was flawless and yet somehow I *knew* his grin was strained.

"We mean no harm, Imperium," Exalted Morrena said, kneeling in my blurring periphery. The Kings' Council had surrounded the remaining witches, boxing them in with nothing but the threat of their power. "Edda acted without my knowledge—"

"Silence," Luc snapped.

I flinched at the harsh command, cowering down to the floor at Jules's feet. I hated this. Hated the way I instinctively curled inward, making myself small like I had for so many years. But I was in a room full of monsters. Monsters who had already killed two people today.

Survival was more important than pride.

But even through the terror, my curiosity stirred. I risked a glance to my left until a polished boot with silver clasps came into sight. My gaze followed upward, past dark, tailored trousers over hard muscle, past black velvet drawn tight across a broad chest. When I met silver eyes, my heart nearly stopped.

Luc cataloged every part of me, his burning gaze methodical. Whatever he saw, it must have satisfied him, because he turned. But as he did, he shifted subtly. He positioned himself between me and everyone else in the room except his soulbound.

Something in me stuttered at the possessive motion.

Stupid, gullible heart.

Even spattered in the blood of their latest victim, it still hadn't learned.

Luc let the moment stretch, watching the witch delegation tremble. Then, in a voice cold enough to silence the entire room, he said, "You will not repeat a word of this to anyone ever, not even to another soul in this room."

A word of what? But Exalted Morrena nodded quickly. "Yes, Your Majesty."

Luc stared for a moment longer, a chilling look, before he glanced toward the door. Estrella and Tristan stood at attention, flanked by four unfamiliar vampires. Black armor gleamed over hardened leather, the star insignia of the Impire stamped over their chests. They must have entered when the witch nearly killed me.

With a flick of his fingers, Luc issued his command. "Take the delegation back to their quarters."

The four guards moved instantly, surrounding the witches in a blink. They hauled the delegation to their feet with little care for dignity. Exalted Morrena barely had time to grab her cane, clutching the carved wood to her chest with bloodless knuckles as the guards ushered them out.

Estrella and Tristan closed the doors behind them, but they remained inside, their gazes locked on me.

Like I was a threat to the kings.

Fuck. There was more to this mess than weak empathy links and power glamours.

"What just happened?" My voice came out as a hoarse whisper, but in the throne room's silence, everyone heard.

Eight pairs of luminous eyes snapped to me at once. If I hadn't already been kneeling on the floor, I would have collapsed beneath the weight of their attention.

Jules circled me until he stood at his soulbound's side and drew a rune in the air over Edda's corpse. *Incinerate.* Her body to ash. The moment the witches had left, the mirth had disappeared from his face, replaced by calculated appraisal.

It wasn't an expression I'd ever seen from the smiling King of Dawn.

"I guess this shouldn't be a surprise," he said, without a hint of his usual effervescence.

Luc didn't lift his gaze from me. "I didn't figure it out, either."

"We're both idiots, then."

I frowned. Wonderful. They were ignoring me. Maybe Dawnspear would start to feel like home. The thought was bleak enough to make me snort aloud, only slightly delirious.

Luc arched a brow. His expression didn't change from controlled confidence, but there was turmoil behind those silver eyes. "Do you find this amusing, Nessa?"

My breath hitched. Nessa. Luc had never called me by my name. I was always *Miss Halloran* or *little curiosity* or *bride* to the King of Dusk. Never Nessa. "I don't know what *this* is."

"Don't you?"

The accusation was clear in his chilling tone. My crime, not so much. "Not at all."

The kings exchanged a look before turning to their council. Sabas, Cédric, Roxiana, and Isabeau stared like I had sprouted a second, dangerous head—and they each had a different plan for dealing with it. Sabas and Isabeau's hands hovered over their weapons, ready to strike. Cédric held a vial of crimson, my blood catching the light as he studied it. His brow furrowed, eyes sharp with quiet calculation. Roxiana's silver eyes remained narrowed and shrewd, considering.

Luc took in their reactions as thoroughly as he had taken in mine.

Then, he made a decision.

"Leave us."

Sabas tore his intense stare from me. "Estrella and Tristan should remain behind."

"She's no threat to us," Luc said.

Sabas's mouth thinned. "If she harms herself—"

Harm myself? I wasn't optimistic about my future, but my body had never felt more stable. The kings' magic and venom had stopped my pain and dulled my other symptoms. For the first time in years, I almost felt normal.

"She's no threat to us," Luc repeated, this time with finality. "Leave us."

This time, the Kings' Council obeyed without argument or hesitation. They all dropped into bows. Then, in the space of a breath, they were gone. The door clicked shut as Estrella and Tristan closed it behind them.

Leaving me alone with Luc and Jules. Again.

And this time, things were significantly colder.

The first three times I was alone with the kings, I had ended up naked within minutes.

Twice, they had made me come.

This time, I doubted that was the way things would go.

I wasn't kneeling before two regular vampires. I bowed before the Conqueror and the Butcher, and this was not a game to them anymore.

Jules, who always filled silences with sharp smiles and lazy quips, said nothing.

Luc, who usually dissected me with clinical interest, stared at me like I was something beyond even his understanding.

Stars, why couldn't they just say something? I would rather be threatened. I would rather be touched. Anything would be better than being studied like this.

Luc drew a quick, simple symbol in the air. The shadows flared in the breath of space between us before suddenly flinging toward me. *Truth.* I jerked back as the shadow rune crashed into my face and dissipated into nothing with a slight flare of heat. "Do you know how truth runes work, Nessa?"

My breathing hitched. "No?"

"You're now incapable of lying."

So this was an interrogation. I shouldn't have been surprised. "Can't you tell when a human's lying?"

"Normally, but that's less clear now with you," Luc said.

If this interrogation had any chance of ending with my death—and it did with the Imperium involved, even if it wasn't until they found my replacement—I might as well speak my mind. "What does that mean?"

But the King of Dusk ignored me. "Why didn't you try to fulfill the birth quota?"

I flinched. I had answered this question dozens of times over the last couple of years. No one ever understood my reasoning. I had stopped expecting them to, but for some reason, I had thought the kings would understand. I told them how touching myself brought pain. They had witnessed most of my illness's effects. The only point we hadn't addressed was my infertility.

I lowered my head, staring at my knees. The cold stone blurred beneath me. "I already told you. There's something... wrong with me. I'm in pain a lot and..." My cheeks flushed. "*Desire* can make it worse."

"Most Maboni consider a harvesting the worst fate imaginable," Jules said. "You really would rather become a thrall than experience the occasional, painful fuck?"

My gaze snapped upwards. The bastard. "It wouldn't have been *occasional*. It would have been always. It would be always now, if I wasn't wearing a soothing rune or filled with your venom."

"So you'd rather give your soul to a vampire?" Jules grinned, sharp and dangerous. "The godstars surely won't invite you to their paradise after death now."

My anger flared higher. I lifted my chin, forcing the words through clenched teeth. "You don't need to mock me. I've spent far more time reading history books than scripture. The godstars don't care about this world or any creature on it. There's no paradise after death. There's just death."

A flicker of something crossed Jules's face. Interest? Surprise? His brows rose, amusement curling at the edges of his mouth.

But my response only made Luc frown. "Why did you volunteer for the harvest, Nessa?"

"You were there," I said. "I volunteered in place of my sister."

"And if your sister hadn't been called, would you have still volunteered?"

I frowned. Why would anyone volunteer for the harvest for no reason? Though the question made sense, if I was in on the plan to... make them feel me come?

It didn't seem that serious an attack.

I shook my head. "No."

Luc paused, his surprise at that simple truth almost tangible. I expected Jules to break the silence, but for once, he remained still, arms crossed over his chest, jeweled fingers tapping against his sleeve.

After a moment, Luc continued, "So it was a coincidence that you volunteered for the harvest the same day we were in town seeking a new Mortal Bride?"

I opened my mouth, then paused. When he put it that way, my answer sounded ridiculous. But I couldn't lie. "I guess? It does sound like an awfully large coincidence, but if it was planned, I didn't know about it."

Luc's expression darkened. He didn't like that answer. "Who cast the power glamour on you?"

"I don't know."

The next question struck as fast and precise as a swing of his axe. "What does your second glamour hide?"

I frowned. A *second* glamour? "What second glamour?"

"The witch didn't trigger a defensive rune," Luc said. "She tried to remove another spell that felt like it was woven into your very bone. The other spell must be a glamour, too, since we didn't give the witch permission to remove anything else."

"I didn't know about either glamour." I really, really didn't. The closest I had ever come to magic before the harvest was watching magistrates cast runes to project their voices.

But that obviously wasn't true. I wasn't sure what terrified me more, being surrounded by an agitated Imperium or facing the possibility that my whole life was a lie.

Or was it whatever had shocked the Kings' Council and Imperial Guard?

"What happened earlier?" I asked, softly this time.

For a second, neither king moved nor answered. There was something... uneasy about them? Their expressions remained blank, but that was the word my instincts insisted on using.

"When the witch tried to remove your second glamour, she almost killed you." Luc's voice was deliberate, measured, slow. "The runespell was likely cast when you were very young, making it an integral part of you. She nearly tore your soul apart." His next words sent ice down my spine. "When you started to die, I started to die. Jules started to die."

My heartbeat pounded against my ribs. "Why... would my death cause yours?"

"You truly don't know, do you?" His silver eyes speared into me. It was like he was peeling away the layers of me until he reached the core of who I was. "We've been soulbound."

I stared.

Stared.

Stared harder.

I must have heard that wrong.

"We've been *what*?!"

Soulbound. They couldn't... They couldn't possibly be saying... No, no, no. A pulse of heat raced through me, my breath ragged, chest rising and falling faster than it had when Éamon died. I opened my mouth to say I didn't understand, but I couldn't form the words. They were lies.

I *did* understand.

I hadn't read beyond the first volume of Karra and Azaras's story, but I knew what happened.

Their bond snapped into place during a feeding, a soulborne spell activating when the demon latched into her lifeforce.

They had both collapsed, their bodies overwhelmed by the merge.

At first, Karra had only felt Azaras's strongest emotions, but she had seen past the mask he wore with his courtiers. She had *understood* him.

I hadn't put together the pieces. I nearly convinced myself I had imagined those few glimpses into the kings. It hadn't even crossed my mind this could be a soulbond.

With the fucking Imperium.

My world started spinning. Only the cold stone cold beneath me, biting into my bare skin, kept me grounded. "No."

Luc arched a dark brow down at me. "No?"

"That... no." Why was it suddenly hot? I was barely wearing anything. "This must be a dream. This can't be real."

Luc remained as calm, controlled, and intense as ever. As serious as ever. He wasn't joking. Neither was Jules. I stared up at them from my place on the floor.

Fuck, this was happening. Either that, or I had died or lost my mind. Were those the preferable options? I slumped down off my knees, my ass hitting the floor.

This changed everything.

The weight of it pressed in on me, thick and suffocating. I ducked my head, but if I wasn't looking at the vampires above me, I was looking at the blood splattered below me.

Stars, I should've been more disturbed by that.

But instead, my thoughts spiraled in another direction. "You're not lying, are you? That's why I've felt so..."

Comfortable?

At ease?

Safe?

The idea of admitting that aloud made my stomach swirl harder than at the sight of blood.

"Do you think we're lying?" Luc asked, his voice nearly soft.

My gaze flickered from luminous silver to gold and back. A day ago, I'd have said there was no way for me to know, but now I looked at them... and knew.

Just like how Karra had known.

"No, I don't," I said. "Why cast a truth rune if soulbound can't lie to each other?"

"The caster behind your glamour and soulbond was clearly talented and powerful." He spoke the words slowly, each one measured. "Perhaps they weaved something into the spell to allow you to lie to us."

"Do you think I'm lying?"

Luc considered me for a long moment. "The bond is telling me you aren't. But if you don't have any answers, we need to find someone who does."

Jules reached out a hand. "That woman in Corraidin wasn't your mother, correct?"

I stared at it for a second too long before hesitantly placing my palm in his. The King of Dawn easily pulled me to my feet, but he didn't let go.

Luc didn't step back, either.

I stood trapped in the space between them, their bodies bracketing mine, their presence a solid, unyielding wall of heat. My shoulders nearly brushed both their chests.

Oh, stars, I was soulbound to the *Imperium*.

Before I panicked, Jules tilted his head slightly. "If you don't have any answers for us, your parents might."

Shit.

I didn't know much about magic, but one did not accidentally cast a bloodborne soulbond. It had taken the demon Isaura hours to cast the spell on Karra. How had I not noticed?

Had someone erased my memory? Who? When? I didn't think so, but most of my childhood was a void I didn't poke at. The days in *Books & Bows* blurred into one, endless pages and pain, but before it was little more than darkness and fractured flashes.

Kneeling in church. The tight squeeze of my mother's hand. Sitting silently at the dinner table, always on the edge of my family. Telling stories to Aislin with her new dolls. The chill of the bedchamber Deidre had moved me to after Orrin's birth. Una and I giggling at the back of the classroom, years before it all went wrong.

Nothing about magic.

But if someone had cast these runespells years ago, how had they known I'd become the Mortal Bride?

How had my parents not noticed their child missing? My stepmother, I could believe. But my mother? No. That made no sense.

"She was selected for the harvest when I was nine," I said. "It's been nearly twenty years, so I'm sure she's long gone."

The kings shared a look.

"Despite whatever rumors you've heard in Mabon, most of the harvested thralls live long lives here," Luc said. "Maboni are collared during or after the harvest feast and can't be killed as long as they wear a collar."

Éamon's screams echoed in my head. "I noticed. How kind of you."

"Kind?" Jules snorted. "We have thousands of fangs to feed. The blood has to come from somewhere."

The words scraped against my mind, their casual cruelty catching on every raw edge. I licked my suddenly dry lips. I would get through this conversation without running away screaming.

"That's not a guarantee," I muttered. "Maybe she was eaten by a hellserpent on the way here or killed by your chancellor for fighting back."

"It's possible but unlikely," Luc said. "Most of the humans we import live until they're seventy."

"Seventy?" The eldest Maboni I had ever met, Great-Aunt Cloda, passed at seventy-one. Most were lucky to see sixty.

Luc nodded. "Vampire venom, sweat, blood, and cum improve a human's health and lifespan."

My mind ground to a halt. Sweat? Cum? My body knew to be repulsed, but my curiosity twisted in the opposite direction. Just existing around vampires stretched a human's life? I swallowed, my throat dry. "That's... disturbing."

Luc's lips twitched. "Your mother would be in her late forties?"

"About." I crossed my arms, holding myself together. "It doesn't really matter, does it? She could be anywhere in your Impire."

"We keep detailed ownership records, so it should only take Sabas a day or two to track her down," Luc said smoothly. "We can send a message to Mabon and have Delphine question your father."

Alarm spiked through me. My father had only ever tolerated me, but I still didn't want him to be interrogated by vampires. Not even my bitch of a stepmother deserved that. "I doubt my father knows anything," I said quickly. "He thinks magic is a blasphemous affront to the godstars."

Jules snorted. "The godstars are magic, just like their former kin."

"I didn't say it made sense."

But the King of Dusk wasn't one to be side-tracked. "He'll answer my questions nonetheless."

How were they being so... practical about this? "Shouldn't you be upset that you're soulbound to a human?"

The shift was instant. The look in their eyes went from examination to possession.

I shuddered. I couldn't help it. The kings had always looked at me like I belonged to them. But before, it had been the distant, indulgent gaze of a vampire with a favored thrall. I hadn't realized it then, but it was so clear in comparison.

Now they looked at me like I was theirs and theirs alone.

Luc's voice was low and steady when he finally spoke. "All Azarasian children are taught from a young age that there's no point in resisting or denying their bond. Once souls merge, they can't be untangled."

"At all?" My voice barely rose above a whisper.

Jules tilted his head, his golden gaze sharp. "Not by magic, distance, or death." A slow, knowing smile curved his lips. "Might as well get used to us. We're going to be spending a *lot* of time together."

I swallowed hard. Their every sentence felt like the closing of a door I hadn't even realized was open.

It slammed shut forever with Luc's next words. "Enemy or a pawn, you're ours for eternity now, bride."

# INTERLUDE 1

*"That explains how she left the apartment, at least," Cédric said into the silence growing thick in the Council Chamber. My brother's brows had raised, but curiosity burned in his gaze. "It's keyed to your soul, not your blood."*

*Sabas massaged his temples and leaned back into his chair, looking on the edge of a meltdown. "That's the only thing it fucking explains. How did a human survive a soulbond with the Imperium? Your power alone should have crushed her, never mind the obvious soul incompatibility."*

*"Given she's alive, they're obviously not that incompatible," Roxiana mused into her full goblet.*

*Sabas shot her a glare. "They're so fucking incompatible, they didn't even realize it was a soulbond until she nearly died."*

*Luc arched a brow at our Crown Enforcer's tone from where he stood by the windows overlooking Montaurère, his hair gleaming blue-black in the afternoon sun. "It's not like either of us has ever experienced a new soulbond. It'll take time for it to settle and feel like our previous bond."*

*"And it's only a little past noon." I said the words lightly, even as my thoughts spun. "Didn't take us that long."*

*I had known something was... not wrong, but different the second I woke on Nessa's soft stomach from the deepest sleep in my life. I wanted to wake that way every morning, buried in her and Luc's scents.*

*And I would.*

*The spell had affected all three of us, merging us together into one. Luc had always been mine, my soulbound, my companion, my lover. But now she was also mine, my soulbound, my... heartmate.*

*My heartmates.*

*I couldn't believe it. Me, with heartmates. The vampire they called the Butcher. I had killed too much. Laughed too much while I did it. I took and I took and I took. Maybe I could play at devotion, but love? Real love? The kind Luc had once, the kind Nessa read about in that worn book of hers?*

*I hadn't been built for it.*

*But that didn't matter. Fate had handed it to me anyway.*

*Glee bubbled through me. My companion was now my fucking heartmate. We had a lovely, soft wife to share. And I would spend an eternity wrapped in them, the only two creatures in existence who would be mine, truly mine, forever.*

*The godstars really did love me.*

*Sabas's voice droned on in the back of my awareness. "Only because she almost died and then you almost died."*

*"I'm aware, Sabas," Luc said, but his attention was on me. He arched one brow at the delirious grin on my face.*

*I winked at him, at my heartmate, my fucking heartmate—*

Luc's face flashed out of view, my entire world shifting, changing—

*My other brow raised to join the first as Jules winked at me. Companions couldn't feel their soulbound's emotions like they were their own, but Jules's whirled at the edge of my consciousness, stark against his easy sprawl at the council table. My soulbound loved to flirt, fuck, drink, and live, but this was different.*

*This changed everything.*

*We had been companions for centuries. Jules was my closest friend and sometimes lover, the only family I'd ever wanted or needed... but now we were three.*

*Three souls entwined.*

*Three souls changed.*

*He would always be my closest friend, but as our new bond settled, he would be my heartmate above all else.*

*If I weren't controlling my pulse, my heart would be flitting around in my chest like Nessa's whenever we approached her.*

*"Are you sure it's a soulbond and not a lifebond?" Isabeau asked.*

*I reluctantly tore my gaze from Jules to watch our Crown General pacing between the table and the windows. Sitting during a crisis wasn't in either of our natures.*

*I shook my head. "A lifebond may explain us nearly dying when she did, but it wouldn't let us feel her pleasure and pain."*

*I had felt the cold claws of death through the soulbond once before, when Jules was hunting Allegra after the massacre at Duskfell. That witch had almost succeeded in killing the both of us, the closest anyone had ever come. I'd never wanted to feel helpless again after Corinne, after my bloody succession. And then to almost die months later, Jules suppressing his pain but unable to hide his panic, I made myself a vow. One I had kept... until today.*

*But only for a second.*

*In the next, Jules and I had struck as one.*

*We had felt her dying, our soul fading with her, and knew.*

*"It's a soulbond," Jules said. "I haven't been able to stop thinking about our bride since we met her—"*

*"The standard attraction rune lure," Cédric muttered.*

*"—but it's a hundred times worse now that the bond is formed," he continued, ignoring his brother. "If this weren't a relatively serious problem, I'd have taken her back to the apartment instead of handing her off to Estrella and Tristan."*

*The council all turned to me, as if expecting a similar proclamation. Nessa had occupied too many of my thoughts in the last week—and in most of them, she was naked beneath me, panting, legs spread wide, her pleasure-glazed eyes locked onto mine. She had made such beautiful little squeaks as I fucked her.*

*As Jules fucked her.*

*As we fucked her.*

*I had fantasized about every combination, as obsessed with sex as a starsdamned teenager. Even when she was awake, staring hesitantly at me with her wide brown eyes, I couldn't banish the sounds of her cries.*

*My jaw clenched. The hunger worsened every day. Worse still when she was near. A lesser vampire would have taken her that first day on the ship, bent her over the table, and fucked her until she couldn't stand.*

*Fucked her until she overflowed with cum.*

*Jules had joked about breeding her, but it wasn't a joke anymore. The blood moons were coming, a little over a month away. Their urges had never clawed this deep.*

*The need to rut. To claim. To knot my fingers in her hair, drive her to her knees, and spill into her until she drowned in my scent.*

*I exhaled slowly through my nose, shoving the monster prowling behind my ribcage down. Its craving didn't own me.*

*I was in control.*

*All I said aloud was, "It's a soulbond."*

*"Her eyes didn't change color," Cédric said, tapping his chin. "I've never met a non-Azarasian soulbound pair, but all the texts we have report that even demons get streaks of silver or gold in their eyes from a soulbond. The second glamour must be affecting her appearance, but what else is it hiding?"*

*"We might not be able to remove the second glamour from her, but we can try removing it from her blood," I said. "Any clue could lead to the answers we seek."*

*All gazes dropped to the small, runed vial in front of Cédric, filled with Nessa's blood. It had nearly splattered against the floor when the witch almost killed my new soulbound, but Cédric had caught enough of it to examine more thoroughly. Traces of magic sparked in it still, from the covenant, from the soulbond, from old layers of spell.*

*"That might take a couple days," Cédric said.*

*"Did you have other plans?" Jules asked dryly.*

*"Beyond tonight's revelry? It's Rosier's bond rite tomorrow."*

*"I'm aware." Jules slithered to his feet and strolled to the bar cart. It was impressive he had lasted this long before joining Roxiana on her path to utter intoxication. "The ceremony doesn't take more than an hour. Sabas can give Vérène's parents the tour of your suite, his first official duty as a bonduncle."*

*"I've been a bonduncle for six months."*

*"Exactly," Jules said, willfully misunderstanding him. "It's about time for him to get in some practice."*

*Sabas flipped him off.*

*The levity faded as I turned to Cédric, cutting straight through the humor. "You'll make time, Cédric. Whoever cast this spell on our bride must have known the soulbond wouldn't stay secret for long. They'll make their next move soon."*

*"And what is your next move?" Roxiana asked.*

*Jules raised his golden eyes to mine.*

*Then, my heartmate grinned.*

*"We have a wife to claim."*

Aches flared through my body, dragging me back to consciousness. My dream faded into fog as I groaned. It had been about the kings, discussing something with their council. How... mundane. But no matter how hard I reached for it, the conversation blurred and twisted, slipping through my grasp.

Not that it mattered. It was just a dream. Better that than a nightmare—

It took a second for my mind to fully wake. Memory slammed into me like a storm. The ceremony. The agony. The impossible connection snapping into place, binding me to the two monsters who had stolen my life.

I was *soulbound* to the Imperium.

Godstars save me.

A sharp breath shuddered from my lips. It was real. There was a spell woven into my very being, a link I couldn't break. It couldn't be undone. It could never be undone.

But that meant... had that been an ordinary dream? Once Karra was soulbound to Azaras, she sometimes slipped into his mind whenever she was asleep and he was awake. Which was almost always, since demons didn't need to rest. Vampires did, but during our week on the road, they had only slept once.

Did that mean even my dreams would no longer be my own?

A strange chill crept down my spine. I had no control over it. No control over them. I hadn't chosen this bond, hadn't asked for it. But now, it was inside me, chaining me to the Conqueror and the Butcher. I would never be alone again.

My stomach twisted. No need to panic. Not yet. There were too many unknowns. I forced my fingers to unclench from the sheets, grounding myself in the present. Grounding myself in my body. Every part of me hurt, from the bruises on my knees to the cramp in my back to the pounding headache pressing against my skull.

All perfectly normal after kneeling for hours on cold stone, feeding two murderous vampire kings, orgasming on their fingers, having one of the aforementioned fingers shoved into a wound, nearly dying, falling on a corpse, and discovering a fucking soulbond of all things.

I let my head fall back and sank into something sinfully soft—

A large snout nudged the back of my hand.

Every part of me went stiff. I turned ever so slowly...

Titus panted at me from the end of a gilded bed, piled with pillows. Ah. Yes. After Estrella and Tristan had all but locked me in the Mortal Bride's bedchamber, exhaustion had crashed over me like a wave. Vampire venom might have numbed my pain temporarily, but it hadn't fully erased my other symptoms. I had crawled into bed immediately, uncaring that Titus snuggled into my side.

It had been nice, to be honest. I had spent too many nights shivering in my loft. With Titus at my side, it was like sleeping next to a fire that never burned out, no careful rationing of firewood required.

The hellwolf shuffled closer to me with a low whimper when I didn't respond. The bedframe creaked with the movement. The Mortal Bride's bed wasn't designed to hold a four hundred pound hellwolf.

When the legs didn't snap beneath us, I exhaled and reached out. Titus slid his head beneath my palm. I snorted, but my fingers automatically dug into his thick ruff, giving him a thorough scratch.

I stared into those dark, shadowed eyes as his tail started wagging back and forth like the dog he wasn't. "You knew I was soulbound to them, didn't you? That's why you like me, since you sense I'm bound to your masters."

Titus huffed like I had asked something obvious.

I wished he could actually speak. I had a thousand questions about my new life, and the hellwolf didn't see any need to keep me in the dark. But there was only so much we could cover through yes-and-no questions.

As I scratched Titus's ruff, I finally blinked around at the room I'd barely noticed earlier. The ceiling was a pale, frosted gold, the walls papered in a soft, neutral pattern that matched the rest of the kings' apartment. None of the murder art had made its way in here, thankfully. An armoire stood beside a full-length mirror, and in the opposite corner, there was a row of bookshelves. Along with a bedside table, those were the only furnishings in my new prison.

My gaze snagged on a scuffed leather-bound book resting on the nightstand.

*The Soulborne Queen: Volume I by Katalina Estevez* shined a dull silver on the cover.

I jolted upright. Titus huffed at my sudden movement. That hadn't been there when I passed out. I had handed my book off to Jules at Luc's command when we first arrived in Dawnspear and hadn't thought of it since. There hadn't been time.

Tingles crawled my spine. One of them had been in here. One of them had stood over me while I slept, placing my book at my bedside.

I clenched my fingers around the worn cover and hugged it to my chest. Tears pricked at my eyes. Returning it didn't make up for treating my people as livestock. It didn't undo what they had done to me. But I couldn't see how it benefited them, and that had to mean something.

Or maybe it was just a trick, meant to lull me into compliance.

I shook my head. Whatever it was, I wouldn't turn away one positive thing in this terrible place.

Titus's gaze snapped toward the door, sudden and sharp, as quick and terrifying as any vampire. I nearly yelped, startled.

It clicked open a second later.

I dropped my book and pulled the bed sheet tight against my body as Maire entered, her head bowed. Long strands of delicate silver and gold chains draped over her arm. A petite, dark-haired thrall with warm brown skin followed at her side, carrying a platter of jewelry and two small tins.

Before the door shut behind them, I caught a glimpse of Estrella and Tristan stationed outside. Not outside the apartment. *Inside.*

So I couldn't run off again.

Titus huffed and flopped back onto the mattress, wholly unconcerned. The two thralls flinched at the movement.

I cleared my throat. "Maire?"

She didn't meet my eyes, stepping closer over the blood-stained gown I had torn off before passing out. "The Imperium requests your presence for dinner before the revelry for the Red Queen's Rising."

Every muscle in me tensed from my neck to my core to my toes. Dinner. I had slept for only a few hours then.

I exhaled slowly. The kings had fed from me once already today. Vampires only needed blood every few days to survive, but the kings weren't merely surviving. They were thriving. This world was their playground, and humans their playthings.

If they wanted to consume my blood ten times a day, there was nothing I could do or say to stop them. I might have been their soulbound now, but I was human first and foremost.

When I didn't reply, Maire finally flicked her gaze up to me. The green of her irises made the red veins from her tears even more noticeable. Had Maire cried for Sophie and Éamon? Her sister and friend were claimed in terrible ways, one after the other.

"This is Riona," Maire said into the silence, gesturing to the thrall at her side. "She serves General Isabeau and Chancellor Roxiana. She'll be taking over for Éamon."

I flinched. "Maire, I'm so sorry—"

"Why? That traitor faced the Imperium's justice for his actions." There was contempt in her tone, but her expression was somber.

Two vampires stood outside the door, listening to every word. Maire couldn't say anything more without revealing her true loyalties. And I couldn't, either, without exposing her as the one who had actually led me from the apartment.

I nodded, hoping my eyes conveyed what my words couldn't. But Maire dropped her gaze a second later.

Stars. Was this what Odran went through every day? Ignored by the vampires protecting him, avoided by the fearful thralls serving him?

How had he not gone insane?

How would I not go insane?

But that was a problem for another day.

I gestured at the chains she held. "Is that for me?"

Maire and Riona moved to dress me in silence. It wasn't a two-person job, but I wasn't going to say anything. I had already gotten a thrall and a witch killed today.

I stomped down on the guilt before it overwhelmed me. I hadn't killed them. The kings had.

I did *not* control the kings.

Perhaps that would need to become a new mantra of mine.

When I spun and faced the mirror, I nearly fainted. The gown was little more than silver and gold chains, but there were enough of them that I'd hoped they would cover most of my skin. The thigh-length skirt covered enough... as long as I didn't move.

The top, however, didn't even try.

My pink, flushed skin peeked between the strands that fell loosely over my chest before cinching together with a ruby-encrusted clasp between my breasts. I tried to adjust the chains, shifting them over my important bits, but there wasn't enough metal to hide them.

Maybe Aislin could've managed, but I couldn't even cover a single nipple.

I hadn't thought I had any shame left over my nudity, not after every eyeball that had traced my skin this last week. Apparently, I was wrong.

"Where is the, uh, rest of the outfit?"

Maire carefully placed a headdress of chains and rubies over my loose brown waves. A red, teardrop-shaped jewel the size of my thumb hung over my forehead. "There isn't any."

"Oh." I nervously looped a strand of hair around my finger. I literally glimmered in the dim light of my new bedchamber. I didn't look terrible but... "So I'm wearing what is essentially a large necklace?"

Maire held my gaze solemnly in the mirror and nodded.

My cheeks warmed. "And I don't get any say?"

"No." Maire brushed back my hair and added dangling silver-and-gold earrings, almost tame compared to the rest of the ensemble. Her expression didn't change. "This is what the Imperium wants you to wear, so this is what you'll wear."

I swallowed but nodded. The message couldn't be clearer.

Tonight, the kings planned to fuck me, and nothing would stand in their way.

I shuddered... and not just from fear. What would Maire say if she knew I craved the kings' touches? What would any thrall? I was wet and desperate for my *captors*. I dropped my gaze to hide my reaction, but Riona kneeled at my feet, looping massive pale pearl bracelets around my ankles to match the ones circling my wrists.

I forced a slow, steady breath. There was something clearly wrong with me.

And that something was the soulbond.

Karra had known what was happening to her, had bravely sacrificed herself to slay a demon. But even she hadn't been able to resist the overwhelming need the spell created for Azaras. If a determined witch couldn't fight the demon who had *eaten* her family, what hope did a tired human have against the vampires who had made her their living sacrifice?

But I had to resist. I had to.

If I even had the choice.

When I was harvested, survival had been my only goal. Now, I was soulbound to the Imperium. It should have meant freedom, but instead, it was just a different kind of cage. Choice had never been mine, then or now.

I didn't choose this outfit.

I didn't choose to attend a revelry where vampires would gorge themselves on blood and pleasure.

I didn't choose any of this. I'd have much preferred to read a book, curled up with a story instead of wrapped in chains, preparing to be devoured.

The soft tip of a finger traced along my spine.

I stiffened, my heartbeat stuttering. My eyes flashed open to meet Jules's bright, gold gaze in the mirror.

The King of Dawn was draped in rubies and pearls, a headdress matching mine resting over his pale blond waves. Massive ruby earrings framed his sharp jaw, while an intricate cuff embedded with gemstones gleamed over his biceps. A length of deep maroon fabric hung from his shoulders, the rich color a striking contrast to his ivory chest, dusted with faint gold glitter beneath matching body chains spaced even further apart than mine. Loose slacks hung low on his hips, completing the effortless display of decadence.

"When I saw this dress, I knew it was the right choice," Jules said, his finger tracing along my shoulder. I resisted a shudder. "Didn't I make an excellent choice, Lucey?"

Luc leaned against the doorway, broad shoulders filling the space. "I wouldn't know. You're blocking my view."

"My apologies, darling. I'll have to rectify that." Jules dropped his hand from my shoulder and entwined his fingers with mine. Before I could process the movement, he spun me with effortless grace.

My chained skirts swept apart as I twirled. I resisted the urge to slap them down. I wouldn't give them the pleasure of watching me squirm, no matter if it made me a wicked, sinful whore.

When everything stopped spinning, my world narrowed to silver eyes.

The King of Dusk had shed his dark doublet for a navy-blue robe, silver buttons sparkling like the night sky. Two silver chains crossed his chest, each side ending in a massive ruby. Lines of glittering silver dust traced his neck and jaw, swirling over the sharp ridges of his cheekbones, but the rest of him remained unadorned. His simple silver rings lined his knuckles, his dark curls tousled and effortlessly regal.

Jules circled me, my hand still trapped in his. "Is this more to His Majesty's satisfaction?"

"It's better." Luc pushed off the doorframe and approached with slow, measured steps.

My heartbeat kicked faster, but I held his gaze. I wanted to melt beneath it, to cower, to hide. But I wouldn't. I steeled my spine.

I was his soulbound now. He couldn't hurt me.

I wouldn't let him intimidate me.

"Better?" Jules's golden eyes traced my bare skin, his gaze a lazy caress. "She's perfect."

My breath hitched. Perfect. He was insane. I certainly wasn't perfect. *They* were perfect.

Luc stopped beside Jules, towering over me. The heat of them became a fire, radiating into me. I'd had both of their eyes on me before, but this was different. They were... enjoying me. Admiring me. Something fluttered low in my stomach.

I wanted to curl into a ball.

I wanted to run.

I wanted to beg them to fuck me until I couldn't think anymore.

I hadn't said anything aloud, but Jules's grin widened and Luc let that arrogant smirk play over his lips. Their intensity changed with their expressions, simmering interest turning to a slow, smoldering boil. I wanted to lean into them, to press my hands against their chests. The next inhale drowned me in their scent, thick spice and smoked honey.

Stars, I was soaking my inner thighs.

I clenched my legs together.

"You're dismissed for the night, Captains," Luc said.

Captains? I blinked, my small, crowded room returning to focus. Maire and Riona kneeled, heads bowed. Estrella and Tristan remained by the door, watching. Blood rushed to my chest and cheeks. I had completely forgotten about all of them.

The two Imperial Guard nodded and bowed. "As you wish, Imperator."

In a blink, Estrella and Tristan were gone, speeding from the room quicker than I could see. But Maire and Riona remained in place. How long would they stay there, kneeling, if the kings didn't dismiss them?

I didn't really want to know the answer.

But the kings weren't interested in having an audience this time.

Jules flicked his fingers toward the thralls. "Leave the tins. Take everything else."

"Yes, Your Majesty," they murmured in unison. With quick, efficient movements, they collected my discarded gown and the empty jewelry tray without daring to meet my gaze. Maire and Riona disappeared as quickly as they had entered.

Neither looked back.

I was on my own.

But I always had been on my own. I could face this. I *would* face this. I straightened my shoulders and kept them that way, even when the chains slid over my nipple, grazing sensitive skin.

"You look ready for battle." Luc brushed a knuckle against my chin, tilting my gaze up to his.

I narrowed my eyes, pretending the fire in me was rage instead of need. "Shouldn't I be?"

Jules cackled. "You're such a little spitfire when you're mock-angry."

This time, my glare was real. Mock-angry. Asshole. The soulbond made everything I did and said painfully obvious to them. I'd never be able to hide my true feelings again, not from them.

"I never shy away from a fight," Luc murmured, "but I think I'll enjoy delaying a win for once."

"Who said you'll win?"

The corner of Luc's lip crooked. "I always win, little curiosity."

# 27

IT WASN'T LIKE I could glare any harder, but I tried anyway as the King of Dusk smirked down at me, as infuriating as he was arousing.

"She's not wrong, you know." Jules slunk forward and leaned back against the door to hold it open. "She'll come twice as much as us, and that might make *her* the winner tonight."

Luc looped his arm around my waist. "I get to watch her beg every time she comes. Therefore, I win."

Tingles sparked along my spine at the touch. "You don't even know me."

"People don't need to know each other to fuck, lovely."

More heat flooded my cheeks. "But..."

"We have an eternity to learn everything about you." The King of Dusk led me from the room with a firm hand on my lower back. "Tonight, the only thing I wish to know is how best to make you scream."

I almost stumbled. Oh, my fucking godstars. My heart thundered at that terrifyingly confident statement.

*I will not cry. I will not scream. I will not let these monsters seduce me.*

I didn't even believe myself.

I kept my head held high as we walked into the fading sunlight shining into their bedchamber, Titus at our heels. When I'd looked around the apartment earlier, I hadn't imagined one of the three massive doors within their bedchamber led to my future residence. But it shouldn't have surprised me. I was their pet, their possession. To get to the Mortal Bride, an intruder would have to go through the Conqueror and the Butcher first.

The rich, buttery scent of freshly baked bread filled the air, warm and inviting. I'd smelled it countless times drifting from the bakery near *Books & Bows*, but fresh loaves had never been in my budget.

All my focus went to the small table, now laden with steaming platters and a silver case. When Maire said the kings had summoned me for dinner, I thought I was the meal. I hadn't expected food. I hadn't expected a seat. But a gilded stool with a soft red cushion sat waiting for me. They wouldn't expect me to kneel at their feet again.

But I didn't care where I sat, so long as I got to eat.

My last meal had been yesterday before the harvest feast. My stomach clenched at the sight of the spread. The dark-gold skin of what looked almost like roast chicken crackled under a thin layer of juices. The vegetables—carrots and something leafy I didn't recognize—glistened with melted butter. A small wheel of pale, soft cheese sat beside thick slices of crusty bread, its scent tangy and rich.

It was a verifiable feast... to me. The thralls had thrown out five times this much food from a single banquet table this morning in the Abyss.

Luc guided me to my seat, but I'd have found my way there even without his touch. I plopped down onto the stool in front of the only empty plate. The chains dug into my ass, but I ignored them, too busy salivating. I leaned forward to inhale.

Luc settled into the chair at my side and poured brandy into his goblet. "Eat."

I stared at him for a second. Was this a test? They were the Imperium. Deidre had always made us wait until my father started eating and that same deference had to apply here. But Luc didn't have a plate, and Jules wasn't even sitting. He stood beside me, just within my periphery.

"That was an order, Nessa," Luc said. "I won't have you passing out on us tonight."

I bristled at the command—and the implication.

I picked up the fork and stabbed a carrot. I raised it to my mouth, holding the Conqueror's gaze.

His pupils dilated slightly, shadow expanding to devour the silver. It was a stupidly dangerous game to challenge these vampires. Luc's grip tightened around his goblet, but he didn't move, didn't speak. He just watched as I slowly, deliberately plopped the carrot in my mouth—

Flavor exploded on my tongue.

Fuck. This was delicious.

How had they made a carrot taste this good?

I hadn't realized my eyes had closed, my face slackening as I savored the taste until Jules sighed, his breath brushing the top of my head. "We're going to break so much furniture, aren't we?"

It took me a second to process his words. I straightened in my seat—

A sharp flare of pain stabbed through my core. I twitched. Damn. I had hoped the kings' venom and the nap would have kept my illness at bay longer. But my desire had awoken it, luring it back to ruin my life.

The kings' attention snapped to me, sharp and assessing. Jules froze midway through unscrewing the first of the two tins Maire and Riona had left behind. Luc's scrutiny settled on me like a weight, pressing tight around my ribs. I forced myself to breathe through it, but the nerves only fed the ache.

After a moment of waiting silence, Luc said, "You're in pain again."

I clenched my jaw. "I'm fine."

Luc arched a brow. "You aren't."

"It's just a little pain." A cold snout touched my arm as Titus huffed at my side. Even the hellwolf was concerned for me. I gave him a quick scratch behind the ears. "You barely noticed it."

"Our bond is new." Luc held out his hand, palm up on the table. "I can't feel your pain like it's my own yet, but I see no reason to make you suffer it when the solution is simple."

With a short exhale, I hesitantly lowered my left hand to his. That didn't stop me from spearing another carrot with the fork. Luc traced a rune onto my forearm with slow, precise strokes. This one was more elaborate, layered, but my brain still interpreted it as *Soothe*. Intriguing.

When he finished, the rune flared with burning shadows before settling into my skin. Warmth spread through me, easing my aches and banishing my waking illness back to slumber. Neither king visibly reacted, but Titus let out a satisfied huff and curled up at Luc's feet, his massive head dropping onto his paws.

I tried to pull back my arm, but Luc tightened his grip on my wrist.

Swallowing my food, I said into the silence, "You altered the rune."

"This one will last longer." His thumb brushed absently over the new mark. "I see no need to recast it tonight or tomorrow morning."

"Why not make it constant? I'll always need it."

"Not all pain is bad," Jules said. "It's your body telling you something is wrong and sometimes you need to listen."

"Says the Butcher."

"Exactly. Pain is my specialty."

I exhaled sharply, but a different thought nagged at me. "Then how do you know I'll need it tomorrow morning? My pain doesn't happen every day. Just most of them."

Luc arched a brow. "You're untried, are you not?"

Heat rushed to my cheeks.

Oh.

Because my cunt would be sore, he meant.

I tore my gaze from Luc, only to land on Jules. The King of Dawn had remained standing, lowering the first unscrewed tin to the table beside me. Inside was... silver dust? The same shimmer Luc wore on his neck and jaw.

Not what I had expected.

I frowned. "What is that?"

"Edible body glitter."

The blush burned its way down my neck. "*Edible* body glitter?"

"Mh-hmm." Jules dipped a finger into the dust. "There's a reason Luc and I don't have a plate, wife. We don't want to fill up before the main course."

I almost dropped the fork as my heart stopped. For once, not at their promises to fuck me.

He had called me *wife*.

"I thought you said this was a fake marriage."

"That was before you triggered a bloodborne soulbond on us and made it real." Jules pushed aside the thin chain strap of my top. But unlike at the ceremony, he didn't push it entirely from my shoulder. Just... aside. He trailed his finger along my collarbone to my neck, drawing a glittering line directly to my pounding pulse.

"I didn't trigger anything." My voice came out tight. Did I? The soulbond might have been cast on me, but I hadn't known. Hadn't asked for it. "And I'm not your wife."

"Except under our laws, you are," Luc said. "*Wife*."

A shiver ripped through me at the deep, steady rumble of his voice. "There are different levels of soulbonds, aren't there? You're companions. Maybe I'll be that for you, too."

Even as I said the words, they felt wrong. Flickers of the dream came back to me, slipping just out of reach. I grabbed for them, but they were hazy.

Jules dipped his finger in the second tin of gold dust and traced another line on my skin. Mapping the paths he planned to *lick*. "Azarasian soulbonds can settle at different intensities because they're formed in the womb. But when the soulbond is cast on those with grown souls, they can only be blended in their entirety."

I paled. That meant... Luc and Jules weren't just my soulbound.

They were my *heartmates*.

The strongest of soulbonds.

My stomach churned. Estrella and Tristan were heartmates. I had seen the way they moved, effortless and synchronized, acting in perfect tandem without a word. They never had to speak, never had to guess what the other was thinking. They simply knew.

Their wills weren't just aligned. They were *fused*, one thought and one purpose.

I wasn't like them. I couldn't be like them.

I didn't want to be swallowed whole.

My hands clenched into fists. I wanted to run. I wanted to scream. I wanted to tear at my skin until this thing inside me was gone.

But I couldn't undo it. I couldn't escape it.

It wouldn't happen all at once. Even in *The Soulborne Queen*, months had passed before Karra stopped feeling like herself. But the bond was inside me even now, putting roots in my soul.

Growing like ivy until I was covered in *them*.

Forever.

I licked my suddenly dry lips. "Well, I'm Maboni. Maybe I don't recognize your laws."

"And what exactly are Mabon's laws?" Luc asked. "You have to have a ceremony binding yourselves together? We did that."

"You made me your sacrifice, not your wife," I muttered. "And that's just one part of it."

Luc tilted his head, studying me. "And what's the other part? That we have to consummate the marriage?"

"That's..." not what I meant. But the words couldn't leave my lips.

Because they were true.

The only two requirements in a Maboni marriage were the ceremony and consummation. A couple was married in front of a church patriarch, then escorted to a bedchamber to seal the union.

The silence stretched.

Jules smirked. "That's what?"

I stiffened. "Fuck you."

Jules sighed dramatically. He extended the gold and silver lines around my shoulders. "Isn't that what we're talking about?"

I gaped for a second. I wanted to be upset. I should have been upset.

But my heart raced more with anticipation than fear.

Maybe it was time to admit to myself I wasn't petrified. Of the sex, at least. Not the whole soulbound-to-the-Imperium thing. If my first two experiences were any indication, the kings weren't over-promising when they said I'd be orgasming hard tonight.

Luc's lip curled at me, but he dropped his gaze back to my wrist. His finger pressed to my flesh, right above the soothing rune, and started tracing another. Heat prickled along my skin.

I wanted to watch, magic still enthralling despite all I'd witnessed the last week, but Jules dropped to a crouch at my side. He traced spiraling lines of dust along the curve of my hips, down the side of my thighs.

Their every touch burned.

I only just resisted a shudder.

I cleared my throat, scooped some maybe-chicken onto my plate, and tried to ignore the writhing energy beneath my skin. "What spell are you drawing?"

"This one is a guardian runespell," Luc explained, layering rune after rune on top of each other. *Alert. Relay. Locate. Glamour.* "Jules and I both have them. The Imperial Guard will now sense your location and if you're in danger. If you rub your finger against the runemark, you can communicate with them across short distances."

"Is my life fueling these spells, too?"

"Our power is," Luc said. "The spells would drain your entire lifeforce under prolonged attack."

"But the covenant won't?"

Luc repeated the guardian runespell a second time, then pulled back just before the markings settled into a tiny black mark on my wrist. Within a blink, it faded from sight. "You're the covenant's home, not its primary power source."

Jules reached my calves and looped around to the inside of my thigh. His fingers dusted gold in looping patterns, dangerously close to where I ached most. He hummed lightly as he worked.

My heartbeat kicked up. "Can I even carry the covenant if I'm your soulbound?"

"You still have a lifeforce it can use." Luc traced his fingers to my elbow and started another rune. *Prevent. Cleanse.* "It's simply a little more... permanent than we'd prefer."

I repressed a flinch. Of course it was more permanent than they wanted. I was meant to be their human sacrifice, not their human wife.

"What's this one?" I asked quickly, desperate to banish the thought. It wasn't personal. I had no reason to be offended if the Conqueror and the Butcher didn't want me.

I didn't want them.

Physically, sure, but not romantically.

Luc didn't look up as he finished the final rune. *Nullify. Regulate.* "A contraceptive runespell."

My body clenched with need while my heart wrenched with something far uglier. "Oh."

Jules stopped humming, his pout deepening as he flicked a look at Luc. "Boo, Lucey. You're ruining all our fun."

Luc arched a brow but didn't dignify it with a response. He kept working, his fingers tracing precise strokes, while Jules trailed his own patterns in dust, absentminded and slow.

"Fine, you're right." Jules sighed, long-suffering. Then his nostrils flared as he dragged in a deep inhale. Lips curling, he winked at me. "Unless you disagree. If you want me to put a baby in you, all you have to do is ask."

I gaped at him. Stars, why was the idea so arousing? It wasn't even possible. "I don't want you to put anything in me."

Wait. Shit. My stomach dropped. The second the words left my mouth, I knew my mistake. Heat flared even hotter in my face, mortification curling tight in my chest.

The bond wouldn't let me deceive them, not even with an offhand remark.

"Lying already, are we?" Jules's grin sharpened. He dropped a hand on my knee and twisted me toward him. "What do you want more? My finger, my tongue, or my cock?"

I put my fork down with a deliberate click. "There's no need to be so crude."

"I'm sorry, lovely. I just can't wait to fuck you tonight." Jules lifted his hands, now dusted with gold and silver, and traced two thick lines from my hips to my waist to my stomach, his touch slow, lingering. "I haven't decided how I'll take you for your first time yet. On your hands and knees, perhaps."

The heat of his words and fingers sent a shiver up my spine, but it wasn't just the sensations. He touched a part of me I hated, soft flesh laid bare beneath the chains. My throat tightened, but I forced a frown to my face. "Well, you still have time to decide."

Jules leaned in until his nose almost brushed my breasts. "Not that much."

"You—" My words cut off as Jules slid his hands under the chains of my top and circled my nipples. I gasped, my eyes flashing open. The King of Dawn's smile widened as he painted one silver and the other gold.

Oh, stars. The thought of them licking this glitter off my skin instantly lit the fire in my core to scalding.

Jules rose, stepped back, and surveyed his work. Like him and Luc, I was now covered in swirling loops of dust, though mine shimmered in silver and gold. A satisfied hum rumbled in his throat.

"Almost there," he murmured, head tilting as he studied me. "But something's missing."

Before I could ask what, he reached out, his gold-dusted thumb dragging slowly across my lower lip. I shuddered. A faint sweetness bloomed on my tongue, rich and indulgent.

Jules smirked, admiring his final touch. "There. Now you're perfect."

My heart stuttered. *Perfect.* I was no such thing.

Luc stood behind me. Even if I wasn't looking, it was impossible not to sense the tall vampire's movements. Something clicked, perhaps the locks on the silver case that had remained untouched.

"Pull back your hair."

My hands lifted automatically, gathering my loose waves before I even registered the command.

A pulse of panic tightened in my throat. I hadn't thought about it. I hadn't questioned it. I had just... obeyed. The soulbond wasn't just making me crave them. It was making obedience feel natural, like they were something I didn't need to resist. The realization slammed into me, cold and suffocating.

Before I could lower them, Luc reached around my neck and unclasped my collar. My pulse stuttered. The last time I'd watched Luc remove a collar, he'd killed Éamon a minute later. But he wouldn't kill me. I was his soulbound.

I rubbed at my too-bare neck and looked back at him. "What are you doing?"

Luc discarded the Mortal Bride's collar on the table and pulled out a new one from the case. Unlike the first, this one wasn't a simple strand of twisted metal. A flower made of silver and gold bloomed in the center, with a dangling sapphire and ruby glinting at its base. Two delicate chains drooped from the centerpiece and looped toward either side, connected by silverwork. Tiny sapphires and rubies dotted the metal, flashes of blue and red woven together in a hypnotic pattern.

Something this intricate must have taken weeks to commission. Who had they intended this collar for?

Something flickered. I squinted closer at the pattern carved into the metal. Runes. I could just make out their markings, buried in the ornamentation. *Protect. Shield.* The Mortal Bride's collar had meant ownership, a claim stamped in metal. This one was different. This one was meant to *protect* me.

Luc fastened the new collar around my neck. The weight of it settled against my throat, heavier than the last.

"You're more than our Mortal Bride now." Luc's voice was soft, almost reverent. "You're our human soulbound."

I reached out and touched the collar, my fingertips tracing along the metal and jewels. "Don't you want to figure out who cast the soulbond before sharing that with your courts?"

"We do," Luc said. "But assuming whoever cast this soulbond did so in order to kill us, you're vulnerable to attack. You need more protective spells than the Mortal Bride's collar provided."

Jules pulled me to my feet. "Besides, when we tell everyone, I don't want them thinking we were treating our new soulbound poorly. That's uncouth."

I hesitated. "Even if I'm human?"

"Even so."

Luc stepped closer until my back almost pressed against his chest. He reached out a hand to Jules, who passed him the silver dust. My mouth went dry.

Luc dipped his fingers into the glitter until it coated his skin. "We might receive a challenge since you're human, but there won't be more than one and after, they'll accept you since you survived the bond."

"After what—"

Luc's hand curved around my hip. Slow. Deliberate. He slid it beneath the chains of my skirt. Every part of me went still.

His palm cupped my mound.

For a second, he just held me. His thumb brushed over the top of my curls, light and fleeting, as my pulse dropped between my legs. Then Luc pressed down, his touch firm and claiming, smearing silver dust over my most sensitive flesh.

My breath stuttered.

Jules's eyes darkened, gold swallowed by shadow as he watched Luc paint me in silver. Marking me. Claiming me. I felt something slither against my senses. A flicker of satisfaction, sharp as a blade, and something deeper, a heavy, simmering hunger.

I didn't think they were mine.

Then they were gone.

And Luc's fingers were there instead, circling my clit. I gasped as the silver dust on his hand mixed with my wet need. The stress, the tension, the fear all melted out of me. If Luc weren't standing behind me, my weak knees would have dropped me to the floor.

He stroked me once, twice—

Luc pulled back. Cold air rushed in where his heat had been. I bit my lip to hold in a whimper. The King of Dusk had all but promised I'd beg him tonight. I didn't see the need to prove him right immediately.

I pushed off him and stepped away, putting space between myself and the vampires who owned my soul.

Catching my gaze, Luc slowly, deliberately, licked the glittering damp from his fingers and groaned.

Fuck. My cunt was doomed.

"You shouldn't have, Julien."

Jules grinned brightly at Luc. When he spotted my raised brows, he said, "Your silver dust is chocolate-flavored, Luc's favorite. He has a very sensitive tongue. It's quite talented, too."

"I'll be the judge of that," I muttered before my brain caught up with my mouth. My eyes widened. What the fuck was wrong with me?

"You certainly will," Jules purred.

"One more finishing touch," Luc said. "Lean over the table."

I nearly choked on my next breath. "What?"

Luc pulled the silver case closer. Inside, my new collar had taken up most of the space, but four cones of silver and gold remained inside. The smallest was no wider than my pinkie. The largest—my wrist. They gleamed in the low light, smooth except for the single rune carved at each tapered end.

Jules plucked the smallest out. Rubbed his thumb over a runespell. *Glide. Heat. Soothe.* A flash of black pulsed beneath his touch before it faded.

It looked no different.

Jules turned the piece in his hand and passed it to Luc with a flourish. "The honor is yours, darling."

I swallowed. "What are you doing with that?"

"It's for your ass."

I stopped breathing. Every part of me locked. "*Excuse me*?"

I knew what anal was. The Church would have preferred we stay uneducated about sex, but the Azarasians set our curriculum. I couldn't imagine how anyone found it pleasant.

Luc's lips twitched. "You'll wear it throughout the revelry. Lean over the table, bride."

For a moment, I didn't move. The air felt too thick to breathe. How had this become my life? A dress of chains, a collar, and a *plug*. But before my brain could settle on a decision, my body made it for me. I stepped closer to the table, placed my hands on the surface, and leaned forward. The chains of my skirt shifted, sliding forward.

My ass, already dusted in silver and gold, was laid bare to the kings.

What was I doing? The kings had a pretty collar and matching butt plugs ready to go at a moment's notice. I should have had questions. Complaints. Something.

Luc's warm hand spread my cheeks apart and pressed—

I flinched as his fingers caressed my second hole. Fuck. Nope. I couldn't do this. I tried to pull away, but Jules was suddenly there, pinning me in place. My wide eyes met his but he only smiled back, heat in that golden gaze.

"Relax, bride." Luc pressed the tip of his finger into my ass. A small intrusion, just a whisper of pressure, but even that made me gasp. "Your ass will take a cock soon enough."

"And one day, Luc and I will fuck you together," Jules said as Luc's finger pressed a fraction deeper. "You want to be ready for us, don't you?"

I shuddered. My breath came fast. The stretch of Luc's finger wasn't much. But the thought of what he was preparing me for sent heat curling low in my stomach. I should have been horrified. I should have refused.

Luc's breath grazed my neck. "Answer him."

Through a deep inhale, I found myself nodding.

Luc hummed in approval. “Good girl.”

My body heated at the praise. Not because I wanted it. I didn’t. But... stars, it did something to me anyway.

The next second, a smooth, tapered tip pressed against my entrance. I expected the chill of metal, but it was warm and slick. So that was what the runes had done.

“It will sting at first,” Luc said. “But your ass will adapt just like your wet cunt did to Jules’s finger.”

I tried to slacken, to relax, but my muscles clenched anyway. The Conqueror didn’t care. This was as much mercy as he was capable.

He pushed.

The plug slipped inside me. A moment of pressure. A stretch. Muted pain flared. The plug nudged past the tightest part, the flared base slipping into place, and a startled yelp tore from my throat.

My body tried to expel the foreign object, but it was no contest. Luc pressed the plug deeper until the narrow base nestled snug against me.

A strangled sound left my throat. Not pain. Not exactly. Just... too much.

“Breathe.” Luc’s hand remained firm on the plug, as if waiting for me to adjust.

I exhaled in a rush. The pressure shifted as my muscles fluttered around the plug, trying to make sense of it.

Jules brushed a strand of hair from my face. “You took that plug beautifully.”

The kings released me as one, pulling back. I swallowed and slowly straightened. The plug shot sensation through me at the movement. I bit my tongue to hold in my reaction.

How would I survive the revelry with a piece of metal lodged in my ass?

Jules held out his arm. “Are you ready?”

“I guess,” I said, my voice rough.

Luc settled at my other side and gripped my palm. The touch broke the mesmerizing effect of Jules’s gaze. I twisted toward the King of Dusk.

“Come, little curiosity.” His lips curved. “I’m eager to start the evening.”

The rest of Luc’s meaning glowed in his silver eyes. The sooner our evening started, the sooner it ended in their bed.

*Breathe in. Breathe out. Breathe in.*

The sound of my stifled huffing joined with the rising melody of laughing voices and otherworldly music. I should have cared more about whatever depraved hell of a party we were about to attend, but every step jolted the plug inside me. A spark of pleasure warred with the settling discomfort. I bit my lip to hide my whimper, but a desperate noise escaped.

Luc's lip twitched in my periphery, but Jules didn't bother holding in his satisfied grin. "We haven't even reached the revelry yet."

"Is this part of your plan?" I aimed to sound stern and faintly annoyed, like I wasn't awkwardly waddling through the halls of Dawnspear. All that came out was breathlessness. "Torment me until I beg you to take me back to your apartment, even knowing what you have planned for me there?"

Luc's massive hand slid lower, squeezing my ass. "What exactly do we have planned?"

I straightened, my entire body tensing—

Oh, *fuck*. My ass clenched down on the plug again. I gasped and choked at the same time, a mess of a noise.

Luc chuckled. I glared at him to my right, but the King of Dusk kept his focus on the hallway ahead.

"Funny," a new voice muttered. "That was my exact question."

I yelped, an embarrassingly high-pitched sound. Sabas now walked beside Luc, a step or two behind. If the kings hadn't boxed me in, I'd have fallen flat on my face. But as I stumbled over my bare feet, pearls clattering around my ankles, Luc's hand at my hip and Jules's on my shoulder tightened, holding me effortlessly in place.

Luc didn't turn, but Jules did. Those heavy ruby earrings swayed between the strands of his pale blond hair as his head moved. "How long have you been prowling the hall waiting for us?"

"Too long." Sabas had switched into an elevated version of his usual black doublet and trousers, the addition of a star-shaped ruby brooch his only embellishment. He somehow looked even more exhausted than yesterday, but the weight of it still didn't tarnish his immortal good looks. "Are you telling the courts?"

"Not tonight," Luc said.

Sabas didn't wait for Luc to explain or elaborate. The Conqueror didn't do that. "If someone were to ask?"

"No one's going to ask us directly if she's our soulbound. And since they won't, whatever answer we give won't be a lie." Luc's voice remained cool. "Why can't we keep our hands off our bride? Because she's ours to *touch*."

"Why did we growl at someone who stared too long?" Jules continued smoothly. "Because she's ours to *admire*."

Luc delivered the final blow, his voice silk over steel. "Why did we ditch the party early to hunt her through the halls? Because she's ours to *fuck*."

Heat rushed through my entire body. I should have been disturbed. The kings didn't know me. They only claimed me now because of the bond between us. But my body didn't care.

I had never been anyone's before. No one's daughter. Barely Aislin's sister. Certainly no one's lover.

Something unfamiliar fluttered through my chest.

The kings' hands on me tightened at the same moment. Had they heard the sudden rush of my heartbeat? Or glimpsed my tumultuous emotions through our bond? I hadn't noticed anything from them... until I thought about it.

Luc's expression was serene and confident, but underneath it swirled a storm of emotions. Concern. Determination. A smidge of wariness. And, new to the mix, a growing excitement. Jules was far less conflicted, burning with impatience and mad glee all at once, though his bright smile only showed the second emotion.

"But if someone did?" Sabas pressed. "You've never been this possessive with a previous Mortal Bride."

"Then we'll tell them." Luc took my hand as we started down a stairwell. I flushed, somehow more flustered by the quiet chivalry of the gesture than when his palm was on my ass. "I'm not breaking the allegiance runespell with an unnecessary lie. But this is our castle, in our city, in our impire, Sabas. If anyone dares to challenge us because we're bound to a human, I will kill them and then go on with my evening."

"They'll want to know who cast it."

"They aren't the only ones."

Sabas exhaled sharply. "What if—"

"Enough with the hypotheticals, Sabs," Jules said. "Go find a vat of blood wine and someone to bury yourself in until you stop thinking. We'll talk tomorrow morning about whatever worries of yours survive that."

Sabas didn't reply.

After a moment, I twisted around. The Crown Enforcer was gone. Had he gone back up the stairs? There was nowhere else for him to go, but the revelry sounded like it was ahead of us.

Did it really matter? I had more important things to worry about.

Namely, the kings at my side.

Jules let out a long sigh. "I love Sabs, truly. The paranoia makes him great at his job. But I think he may need a vacation."

"We'd have to haul him there ourselves and then sit on him to make him stay," Luc said, amusement lacing his voice. "I doubt any of us would find that relaxing."

"Maybe we can get Cédric to lace his drink?"

My eyebrows raised. "You want your brother to drug his soulbound to help him relax?"

Jules tilted his head against mine with a dramatic sigh. How we were still walking straight when he clung to me like a six-foot-four leech was a mystery. "What other option is there? We can order him to take a leave of absence, but he'll never do it."

"It won't be a request."

I shuddered at the callous authority in Luc's tone. Another spark shot through me from the plug.

Oh, stars, I needed to stop doing that. At this rate, I wouldn't last an hour before begging them to touch me. To hunt me through the halls. To fuck me hard.

*Wicked, sinful girl.*

I shook my head, shoving the thoughts down. If the increasing noise was any indication, we had almost reached—

The kings turned a corner and led me through an open doorway to a terrace of pale stone and gilded columns. My jaw dropped. A garden sprawled below us, manicured trees framing a hedge maze, the greenery expanding into the distance before the sharp drop of a cliff. The city sparkled on the mountainside below us, the twinkling lights of other fires, other revelries. High above, the Blood Star peeked over the horizon, a bright spear of red surrounded by four dimmer lights.

My imagination couldn't have conjured this sight if it tried.

But neither would it have conjured a thousand half-intoxicated Azarasians. They had draped themselves in their finest silks and brightest rubies, hair unbound and threaded with gems like my own. Dust painted nearly every inch of exposed skin—and there was a lot of it, more than I had ever seen. Even the thralls shimmered under their black uniforms, collars and simple ruby jewelry reflecting the flickering light.

Everywhere I looked, there was indulgence.

Goblets in hand, arms intertwined, fangs sinking into bared throats. Vampires spun across the open terrace floor, flitted between velvet lounge chairs, and surrounded tables heaped with food. The air was heavy with the scent of roasted meat, spiced wine, and the cloying sweetness of melting sugar.

Beyond the terrace, two vampires wrestled in their finery, a silver-eyed female taking down a green-eyed male as a circle of spectators jeered and cheered. Bodies writhed together in the open, in pairs and trios and quartets and... however many that cluster was, a mass of glittering skin and shifting limbs.

In Mabon, we gathered around fires, passing cups of mulled cider, hands brushing but never lingering. Here, there was no restraint. No whispered flirting behind clasped hands. No stolen kisses in the dark. Here, pleasure was taken openly, offered in full view of anyone who cared to watch.

It made my skin crawl. It made something in my stomach twist. And yet... my pulse still quickened in the kings' hands.

I tore my gaze from the depravity, but Luc simply watched me, his impassive expression a stark contrast to the intensity simmering behind his eyes. He missed nothing. The red glow of the Blood Star caught my eye, and I lifted my gaze from his, letting its light anchor me.

I inhaled the open night air.

Just me and the Blood Star.

And the vampires at my sides.

"You call the Blood Star the Red Queen?" It was a silly question, the answer obvious, but I had to say something to ease this tension.

"The Red Queen and her court," Luc said, his breath against my ear. "Your people only care about the queen, but she has four handmaids in the two silver stars to her right and the two gold stars to her left."

I nodded. We called the other stars the Blood Star's Guard, but we didn't mention them much during our spring celebration.

Without waiting for anyone to acknowledge them, the kings moved forward in perfect sync. Shit. I scrambled so they weren't pulling me between them.

The weight of a dozen luminous silver and gold stares flickered to me. To the kings. The closest vampires cleared a path and bowed as we passed, their thralls dropping all the way to their knees. But I had expected something more... elaborate. The Church made a bigger fuss about Patriarch Meallán entering a sermon than the High Courts did for their brutal rulers.

"Shouldn't someone announce you or something?"

"Why would they?" Luc arched a dark brow. "It's not like they've forgotten who we are."

"The regents enjoyed copious bowing and groveling when they entered a room," Jules said, plucking a goblet from a serving tray carried by a thrall. He offered one to Luc, who took it without ceremony and lifted it to his lips.

I glanced at the tray, half-expecting Jules to hand one to me as well. But of course, he didn't. It wasn't ordinary wine inside those goblets. The metallic scent of blood hit me a second later. I swallowed hard. Right.

"Alphonse mainly, but even Marisol had her days," Jules continued. "After a couple of centuries, it gets a bit dull. We try to save the spectacle for special occasions now, like when we're entertaining dignitaries or ambassadors from our vassal states."

I frowned. I didn't know much about the regents who ruled before Luc and Jules took the throne, but from the way Jules spoke, they must have relished their power. But if they only reserved grand displays for dignitaries now, that meant—

"The Isaurans are here, aren't they?" Unless they had thrown the witch delegation in their dungeon for almost accidentally killing me... or eaten them.

"Oh, they are." Jules waved lazily over his shoulder toward the towering walls of Dawnspear, where numerous balconies lined the floors above. "They have the best view for tonight's festivities."

I shuddered. Some thralls had runed collars, marking them as harvested witches. Only a handful of vampires were feeding on the terrace, their intertwined bodies almost easy to ignore over the cacophony, but that would surely change as the revelry went on. The Isaurans would be forced to watch their own people succumb to the bite one by one for hours, helpless to stop it.

My voice came quieter than I meant. "I guess that's one way to remind them of your power."

"They're reminded every day by the collars around their neck," Luc said.

I brushed my fingers against my collar. It was impossible to ignore.... both as a wearer and a witness. More than one Azarasian widened their eyes at the sight of the new collar around my neck. No one whispered. No one pointed. But the weight of their attention settled on me all the same.

I exhaled slowly. Only the Kings' Council and the Imperial Guard knew about the soulbond right now. To the High Courts, I was no better than a human thrall, barely worth notice. But when they found out? That attention wouldn't slide off me.

It would *devour* me.

If I couldn't handle this, how would I survive that?

"Imperium." A red-haired beauty clad in nothing but dust and strings of rubies stepped forward before she bowed. Godstars, she was absolutely stunning. Her golden eyes flickered halfway up to Jules, demure and respectful. "It's been too many nights since you last visited our bed, Your Majesty."

I tried to keep my face neutral, but my eyebrows lifted before I could stop them. How... forward. My fist curled. The motion set off a chain reaction—muscles tensing, sensation jolting through me from the plug. I swallowed my sharp inhale, refusing to give anything away.

A handsome, silver-eyed male wrapped an arm around the redhead's shoulder. Unlike his soulbound, his gaze was on me. On my collar. On the chains and dust that barely concealed my breasts.. "And we'd be honored if your new bride joined us—"

"Eyes on me, Lord Étienne, unless you want me to remove them." Luc's voice cracked through the air like a whip. "Our bride's for us, not you."

Lord Étienne and his soulbound dropped to their knees in a blink. "I apologize for my overstep, Imperium," she said. "If we displeased you—"

"You did not, Sylvie." Jules didn't hide the sharp edges under his kind, soothing smile. All the vampires in the vicinity had hunched their shoulders at Luc's outburst, and reassurances from the Butcher weren't exactly comforting. "Lucero and I have other plans tonight, and they don't involve anyone but our Mortal Bride."

"Of course, Your Majesty," Lady Sylvie said.

The kings didn't reply. Wouldn't reply. The two vampires backed away, and the rest of the High Courts followed, carving out even more space for the kings as we cut across the terrace. No one dared glance at me or my collar again, but the weight of their attention somehow grew heavier.

There was something about it that almost felt... disbelieving.

And why wouldn't it be? The kings had turned down two beautiful vampires for me. Lady Sylvie's red hair gleamed like polished rubies, her body honed and sculpted in ways mine could never be.

*She has hips for whoring.* I tensed as my stepmother's voice whispered in my mind again. My stepmother and sister were as thin as the vampire, but they could never match her beauty. Their jealousy always twisted into judgment, and now that same judgment sat like a stone in my chest.

"Ooh, what was that?" Jules stopped abruptly, spinning to block my path at the edge of the open dance floor. He extended his goblet, and a thrall scurried over to take their empty cups. His golden eyes locked onto mine, gleaming with intrigue. "It burns so hot in your chest, I can almost feel it in mine."

Fuck. Of course the one emotion that could match the strength of my pain and pleasure would be my insecurity. "It doesn't matter. It's not about you."

The heat of Luc radiated into my back. "Then what is it about?"

I frowned over my shoulder at the King of Dusk, at the arrogant smirk curving his lips. Half of me wanted to slap it off his face... and the other half wanted to kiss him. I did neither. Instead, I twisted forward and glared at Jules's chin.

A hand fisted in my hair.

I yelped as Luc yanked my head back, forcing my vision skyward, straight into the molten silver of his gaze. "I asked a question."

"You did. I don't have to answer." I somehow kept my voice steady, even as my nipples pebbled and need pooled in my core. "You own my blood and body, not my thoughts."

Luc's grip didn't tighten, but his hold remained firm. "I wasn't asking to own them, I was asking to know them."

"Why?"

"I believe that's how relationships evolve," he said dryly.

"We don't have a relationship."

"Don't we?" Jules traced a finger along my bare throat, down to my collarbone. "I seem to have quite a few memories of our *relationship*."

Jules's head between my legs. Luc's lips on mine. Their fingers stroking inside me, touching me together. I shuddered at the flash of memories and clenched my thighs together, but I doubt it did much to hide the scent of my desire. It didn't help me ignore it, either. "You don't have a relationship with your Mortal Bride."

"You know you've become much more than that," Jules murmured, his voice a soft caress under the music and laughter.

I swallowed. These were monsters who ate people. They were my captors, my owners, my tyrant kings. They had killed a thrall and a witch in front of me today. If Luc and Jules felt anything, it was only the result of the bond tying us unwillingly together. They didn't care for me as anything more than their possession.

Tonight, they planned to fuck me. I planned to... let them. Beg them, probably. None of that meant I had to let their beautiful smiles and heated touches lure me into complacency. We didn't have a relationship. We couldn't *ever* have a relationship.

This was an exchange, nothing more. They'd get to claim me. I'd get to come, my nerves sparking with pleasure instead of pain. They were still the villains in my story, no matter how good they made me feel if we started fucking.

*When* we started fucking.

Luc tugged harder. "Answer, Nessa."

Pain flashed through my scalp. I yelped, the sound nearly a breathless moan. Godstars, what was wrong with me?

"Fine." I tried to snarl at the King of Dusk, tried to twist my confliction into rage, but I couldn't hide the rasp of my desire. "I wished I looked like Lady Sylvie. If I looked like her, I wouldn't care that you're parading me around naked for your courts to mock."

Luc slowly arched a brow, equal parts unimpressed and amused. "That's not judgment in their eyes, little curiosity."

I scoffed. "What else would it be?"

Luc didn't answer immediately. Instead, he released my hair, letting the silence stretch between us. But I knew what he wanted instantly, instinctively, his intent like a whispered command through the bond.

A challenge to look.

I didn't want to. Didn't need to. I already knew what I would find. But... when I let my gaze drift, I caught the way a few vampires watched us. Not with disdain. Not with amusement.

With *longing*.

They weren't laughing at me, the soft, unremarkable human caught between two godstars made flesh. They were imagining themselves in my place.

A single word dropped from Luc's lips, a brush against my ear. "Envy."

I shuddered. Envy? No. That couldn't be right. What in the stars would any vampire be envious of me?

But Luc wasn't lying. Not even slightly. But he had to be... right?

His fingers ghosted down my spine. "You're in the arms of two of the strongest vampires in the world, who can't keep their hands off you, wearing a collar and gown worth more than most country estates. Is that not something to covet?"

"But... they're all beautiful and immortal and I'm just..." I flapped a hand down at myself "...me."

Jules snorted and shook his head. "You say such ridiculous things sometimes." His golden gaze flickered to Luc. "Perhaps we should call it a night? I think our bride might need to ride both our cocks to believe we desire her."

I straightened. "We just arrived."

"A decision I'm regretting already."

My heart stuttered and twisted. Desire and fear tangled in my stomach, a nauseating mix. Minutes ago, I thought I'd beg them to fuck me.

But now that it might actually happen...

Stars, I couldn't do this.

My world started spinning.

Luc's hand tightened around my hips. "Breathe."

"I can't."

"You can."

I forced myself to exhale slowly. Not on my own. Because the Conqueror commanded it. But my heart didn't stop racing, my skin heating and sweating and pebbling.

Jules wrapped both of his bejeweled hands around mine. "I have a better idea. Let's dance."

My brain stopped. Dance?

My eyes drifted from Jules to the scene behind him. Vampires twirled and twisted to the thud of the music. In the corner by the balustrade, some musicians even danced, their flutes played flawlessly throughout. It wasn't like anything I had ever seen, so far removed from the stiff dances of Mabon.

No.

Dancing was somehow even worse than sex. At least I wouldn't have an audience for that... today. But dozens of eyes still flicked to the kings, watching their Imperium interact with me. If I danced with them, the gazes would follow.

I didn't know how to dance. My stepmother had attempted to teach me the steps to the stiff, measured line dances popular in Mabon. I had only ever managed to trip over my own feet. My body wasn't meant to move the way a dancer's did. It just wasn't.

My head started shaking before I could even manage any words.

Jules tugged gently at my hands. "That wasn't a request."

I didn't stop shaking my head. I dug my heels in, not that it would help. "Even if I could dance, I'm not going to twirl around in front of the entire Courts of Dusk and Dawn *naked.*"

Warm fingertips brushed along the curve of my ass under the chains—and nudged the tapered end of the plug.

I yelped, nearly jumping in Luc's arms.

"Would you rather stay here alone with me then?" Luc's voice was smooth, teasing. "When Jules wants to dance, nothing can stop him."

I almost flung myself at Jules.

"Ha! I win, Lucey." The King of Dawn twirled me away in his arms as Luc chuckled darkly behind us.

Jules cut through the swirling, sensuous dancing with ease, the other Azarasians stepping aside for their Butcher King. When we reached the center, he spun me around. A sharp jolt of pleasure shot through me from the plug. I barely bit back a gasp, my knees threatening to buckle, and tripped over my feet.

And we hadn't even started yet.

I tried half-heartedly to pull away. "I can't dance."

"Everyone can dance."

I shook my head, flushing. Behind Jules, Luc settled into a cushioned chair at the floor's edge. A thrall approached with another tray of blood wine and dropped to their knees at his feet to offer him a goblet. He took one without glancing away from us and leaned back into his seat. The way he sprawled, effortlessly commanding, turned the chair into a throne.

Godstars, was he going to watch the entire time?

Panic clawed at my ribs. "I can't. I'm not... I'm too big to be graceful."

Jules gave a gentle yank. I crashed into his arms. His arms skimmed between the chains at my hips, around the softness of my stomach. "You're the perfect size."

My pulse dropped between my legs. "I'm not—"

"You're a tiny, soft morsel that I want writhing on my tongue daily for as long as we live," Jules crooned. "And you can dance."

My mouth watered.

Jules grinned and pressed a finger to my chin. With a light tap, he popped my gaping jaw closed. Heat burned my cheeks.

Before I could counter, Jules slid his hands up, one settling on my waist, the other taking my hand. "So let's dance, lovely."

I REALLY, REALLY COULDN'T dance.

But somehow, in Jules's arms, I did.

The King of Dawn twirled me across the dance floor, between the Azarasians whirling around us in every direction. I had no idea how we weren't crashing into people. No idea how I hadn't fallen flat on my face, only to be trampled under vampire feet. No idea why I seemed to... enjoy myself?

I couldn't stop the laugh that bubbled to my lips. The Azarasians danced like they lived, free to do as they pleased. There were no rules, no steps. No ulterior motives. There were no disapproving parents watching from the sidelines, whispering as I stepped on their son's toes and made a fool of myself.

There was just me, Jules, and the music, living for the here and now.

Jules grinned. "See? It's not that hard when you have an excellent partner."

I snorted. "How modest of you."

Jules's smile widened at my jab. I hadn't said it with any vitriol. For once, I was joking *with* the King of Dawn. It was hard not to when my every muscle relaxed at his touch, my skin tingling.

"I don't think I've ever been modest a day in my life," Jules said. "Despite what your patriarchs may say, there's no shame in taking pride in your achievements."

*Wicked, sinful girl.* The voice in my head wasn't my stepmother's this time, but Patriarch Meallán's, loud and righteous.

My foot landed wrong, but Jules didn't miss a step. His grip tightened, steadying me effortlessly. "So you don't worship the godstars *and* patriarchs are a sore subject? The Church of the Rising Stars hasn't changed at all in the last four centuries."

I frowned at him. "You know, for a second, I was enjoying myself."

"You still are."

My frown deepened. He wasn't wrong. He couldn't be wrong, not about what I was feeling. "But I'd be enjoying myself *more* if we weren't talking about starsdamned patriarchs."

"I think they're supposed to be the opposite of starsdamned," Jules said, his eyes sparking with mischief. "Starsblessed?"

"That's not a word."

"How would you know? Have you read the entire dictionary?"

"Yes."

Jules's brows shot up. "Why would you do such a dreadfully boring thing?"

Heat flashed to my cheeks. Stars, why couldn't I have a conversation without turning a progressively worse shade of red? "I ran out of stuff to read."

His hands slid lower, wrapping around my hips. "Surely that's an impossible task."

Before I could react, he lifted me off the floor and spun me in a dizzying circle. My breath hitched as twinkling lights blurred around us, my head tipping back. I squealed, half exhilaration and half sharp pleasure from the plug.

When my feet once again touched the floor, Jules chuckled, low and pleased. "Luc reads something new every week, and we're five hundred years old."

I glanced over Jules's shoulder... and my world narrowed to a single pair of darkening silver eyes. I shuddered. Luc's gaze had been burning into us this entire dance, but I'd grown used to the heat against my skin. But like the sun, now that I looked at him directly, my vision became him and only him.

I had to breathe deeply to steady my heart rate. *You need to calm down, Nessa.* But it was near impossible when two hunters had their sights set on me.

"I didn't have... nearly as many books as Luc has," I said, trying to shift my focus.

Jules's lips twitched at my breathlessness. "That's only a quarter of his collection, too."

My eyes widened. The library in their apartment must have held thousands of books. "A quarter?"

Jules laughed. "You're going to die when you see the library in Duskfell. Ooh, and the university." His head tilted slightly toward the towering castle above us. "Hells, the one on the second floor here might do it, too."

There was an even larger library in Dawnspear? I almost dropped Jules's hand and demanded he take me there this instant. But if it was as grand as the rest of the castle, I wanted my first memory there to be of the books, not getting railed into a shelf.

Right?

I frowned. I didn't know anymore.

"Nah, ah," Jules pinched the dust-painted skin of my hip, a playful reprimand. "No frowning. If you start, I'll have to make you smile again."

I yelped, my heart stuttering. If he only knew why I was frowning. Thank the stars the bond hadn't shared my exact thoughts… just everything else. If my face wasn't already flushed red to match the cape draped over his shoulder, he'd probably have noticed and lured the truth out of me.

"I can't spend all my time smiling, Jules."

"Why not?"

"That's not how life works."

"That's not how your life worked," he corrected smoothly. "As our wife, smiling all the time is the goal."

Wife. I flinched at the word. The movement turned into a shudder as sensation rippled through my core from the plug. I bit back a moan, inhaling sharply. Jules wouldn't stop saying ridiculous things, not when he knew exactly how his words affected me. Wife. Wife, wife, wife. Maybe if I thought about it enough, I'd become desensitized to it.

But I wasn't meant to be anyone's wife. Especially not *after* the harvest.

I glanced around, but none of the vampires twirling around us stopped to stare. "Won't someone hear you?"

"Luc and I have a permanent privacy runespell."

"Oh." That explained those times on the journey here where I heard them speak but couldn't understand, no matter how hard I tried to listen.

"We'll have to add you to that, too, once we tell the courts," Jules said. "But it excludes anyone not part of our conversation, so only Luc can overhear us now, *wife*."

I kept my body loose, refusing to react this time. "Stop calling me that."

Jules leaned in, his breath warm as his lips hovered just over mine. "Make me."

A flutter shook through my chest. Bastard. I glared at him, that beautiful, wicked face less than an inch away. "I can't."

Jules clicked his tongue. "Probably not, but you didn't even try."

"Why waste time trying to achieve the impossible?"

"If you never try, it will always remain impossible."

Of course a vampire would think that. Jules had been born powerful. If he set his mind to something, he could bend the world to his will. Meanwhile, I had spent a decade just trying to survive without a future, a family, or even a working body.

"Stars, you're infuriating."

Jules chuckled. "That's what Lucey says all the time. But am I wrong?"

I narrowed my eyes—

"I said no frowning."

My hands tightened on his shoulders. "You—"

Jules crawled his fingers up my bare spine to my upper back and dipped me.

I tumbled back, a short scream escaping my lips. But Jules's hands remained hot on my skin, guiding my fall. For a moment, my world flipped into the twinkling night sky above.

What a sight.

Then warm lips pressed to my throat. Jules kissed a slow, teasing path up my neck... then found my mouth.

Every thought vanished.

His lips moved against mine, soft and coaxing. I melted into him. Jules teased the seam of my lips with his tongue, seducing his way in where Luc had commanded. I opened just as easily.

He instantly deepened the kiss, claiming me, devouring me. I dug my hands into his silken blond hair. A low, desperate sound escaped my throat.

As his tongue dominated mine, he pulled me upright and tight to his chest. His skin was hot, solid, perfect. My nipples rubbed against him, dragging another shudder from deep inside me.

Jules swallowed the sound.

His hands slid lower, over my waist, over my hips. The dust on my skin smeared beneath his touch, marking him just as much as me. Through his thin trousers and the chains of skirt, he hardened against me, thick and long and hot.

Stars, his cock would be *inside* me tonight. Another flare of pleasure ricocheted through me as my ass clenched around the plug. I fisted my hands in his headdress—

Jules gasped softly, breaking the kiss.

Luc had wrapped a hand around the back of his neck.

The King of Dusk held him in place, his back to his chest. For once, I wasn't the one trapped between two bodies, but Jules sank into it, entirely at ease. His tongue flicked out, licking away a smear of gold dust.

I couldn't help but do the same. A sweet taste exploded on my tongue, some exotic fruit I had never tried but desperately craved now.

Jules leaned into Luc and smirked over his shoulder. "No cheating, darling. We promised not to interfere with each other's orgasms."

Luc must have tightened his fist, since Jules shuddered. "Your cock's still in your pants, Julien. You're nowhere near orgasm."

"Are you sure?" Jules angled his head until his lips nearly brushed Luc's jawline. "Why don't you reach down and check?"

"It would be far easier to ask our bride."

Jules hummed, dragging his heated gaze back to mine. Then he ground his hips, slow and deliberate. I couldn't hold in my gasp. His thick length rubbed against me, the friction of his trousers sliding through the delicate chains and against my skin. "Tell Luc how hard I am for you, lovely."

Luc released his grasp on Jules's neck before I could figure out how to form a sentence. He wrapped that hand around his soulbound's jaw, wrenched Jules's head to the side, and claimed his lips.

My mouth dried.

Fuck.

My world became their lips, battling and nipping and licking. It had always been impossible to ignore the kings, but now they overwhelmed my every sense. *Became* my every sense. Jules bit Luc's bottom lip, luring a growl from the King of Dusk.

The brat. He couldn't help but misbehave.

Luc deepened the kiss, a stark reminder of Jules's place. But the King of Dawn *never submitted easily. He always made me work for it. Always made sure I knew his control was a gift, one he could reclaim at any moment.*

*But when he did surrender, it was perfection.*

*Jules melted into my chest with a sensual groan—*

I shuddered back into myself at the sound, my skin prickling as heat washed through me. I had leaned into the soulbond again. But this time, I hadn't just known what Luc was thinking.

Those *were* his thoughts.

I should have been afraid. I tried to be. We had been soulbound for less than a day and I was already slipping into their minds. But the bond drowned out every fear, refusing me any emotion beyond lust and safety when I was wrapped in the Butcher's arms like the Conqueror had him in his.

Our connection was new and blossoming. If this was how I felt now, what would it be like when our soulbond settled? When we became true heartmates? My craving for these monstrous kings already itched under my skin.

Nothing else in the world mattered.

Only that I *needed* them.

Luc pulled away slowly, gold dust brushing his lips. From my lips to Jules's to his. I shuddered at the sight.

Jules tightened his arms around me, leaning lazily into Luc. "Now can we go?"

Luc smiled fondly down at his soulbound, so at odds with the unyielding mask of the Conqueror. "You'll have to ask our bride."

Both luminous gazes turned to me, their pupils swallowing more of their irises with every passing second.

I swallowed. "Does it matter what I want?"

"We're asking, aren't we?" was Luc's silken reply.

Yes. No. Maybe. Stars, I wanted them. But no matter how many times the soulbond suppressed my fear, it flared back again.

What would it be like when the kings' bodies were over mine, rocking into me, claiming me? Would I be too enraptured with their skin brushing mine to care that they were murderers? That they were the Conqueror and the Butcher, Imperium of the Azarasian Impire?

Would that finally be enough to silent the stubborn emotions for good?

Did I even want them silenced?

"Nessa." I stiffened at the rumble of Luc's voice. "Your answer?"

I opened my mouth to say something, but I didn't even know what. An answer slipped out before I could stop it—

"Yes."

Jules grinned, delighted. "*Yes*?"

Fuck. I had said *yes*. I tried to step back. I knew I shouldn't. Never run from a vampire. But Jules's hands were already on my hips. I didn't get far. That didn't stop the kings' luminous irises from darkening, shadow swallowing the remaining silver and gold.

I forced myself to go still, but it was too late for that.

I had said yes.

Someone cleared their throat.

All three of us frowned instantly, a hint of the kings' irritation sizzling across the bond, intertwining with my own. I glanced past their shoulders. Behind them, Cédric bowed, the golden stars stitched into his scarlet overcoat a perfect complement to Sabas's ruby brooch.

But instead of his soulbound at his side, Maire curled into her master's arms, draped in a gauzy black gown that didn't hide the shimmering gold painted over her lithe body. Her gaze caught mine for a moment before returning to the floor. It took her a second longer to hide her shock.

Because of the new collar around my neck, one no Mortal Bride had ever worn before?

Or because the Kings of Dusk and Dawn held me in their arms as they held each other?

Cédric didn't let the silence stretch. "Your guest is here."

Guest? There were already a thousand vampires here at least. But whoever the kings had invited, Jules's brother deemed it important enough to interrupt.

Jules released a long sigh and reluctantly untangled himself from Luc's arms. "Sorry, lovely," he drawled, smoothing a hand down my side before stepping away. "We'll have to delay the fucking ever so slightly. It does give you more time to run, though."

The faint chill of the night tickled my skin without his warmth, but the moment his words sank in, it disappeared just as fast.

More time to *run*.

"Excuse me?"

He brushed his thumb against my dusted bottom lip. "We'll give you a ten-minute head start."

"Twenty," Luc interrupted. "You can't just throw your Rising gift at the courts."

Jules pouted. "Why not?"

Luc only arched a brow in reply.

The expression made Jules release another forlorn sigh. “Fine. Twenty minutes.”

I didn’t want to know. I did want to know. “Twenty minutes to run where?”

“The game is simple, bride.” Luc circled me, black eyes intent on my face. His voice was pure, dark promise. “Where we catch you is where we fuck you.”

I gaped. My face flushed scarlet all the way to the tips of my ears. Damn skin, always giving me away. Not that my galloping heartbeat wouldn’t betray me just as easily. “What?”

The corner of Luc’s lips quirked. “I don’t repeat myself.”

“I—you—what—”

Jules huffed a laugh. “Don’t pretend you’re not intrigued by the idea.”

I twisted sharply to shoot him a glare, but his eyes weren’t on my face. They were on the painted buds of my hard nipples, peeking out between the chains. I had been aroused half the day, but Luc’s words were fuel to the fire.

I crossed my arms across my chest. “We’re outside at night in spring.”

“It’s nearly summer,” Jules said, his grin widening. If Luc wasn’t standing behind me, I was sure I’d see his smirk sharpen, too.

“Stay here if you wish,” Luc said, his breath against the back of my head. “Jules and I have no qualms about taking you before our courts.”

I spun back, this time with a jolt—

I whimpered. Damn plug.

Those silver-lined black eyes heated to blazing.

Getting fucked in public, in front of the entire Courts of Dusk and Dawn, was another inevitability in this new life of mine. Over the past hour, more and more vampires had stripped their thralls and fellow Azarasians of what little clothing they wore, their bodies pressed together on chaises, against tables, on the floor.

Even heartmates, monogamous as they were, had joined the revelry. In the corner of my vision, Tristan had Estrella pushed against a marble column, their bodies moving in perfect synchronicity. The revelry raged on around them, but they didn’t care.

But I couldn’t. Just couldn’t. The kings were gorgeous, their bodies carved perfection, and next to them, my flawed, soft flesh would be painfully apparent. My stomach swirled at the thought, a jumble of nerves and fear... and the tiniest smidge of interest.

But only the tiniest smidge.

"It's closer to nineteen minutes now, bride," Luc said.

"How is she supposed to know that, Lucey?" Jules traced a finger along my bare arm, but I didn't turn back again. "Help our poor bride out."

Luc flicked his fingers in the air. *Count.* When he pulsed his power into the rune, the shadows flared and twisted, turning into numbers.

18:53.

18:52.

18:51.

Shit.

My very own countdown.

The chase had begun.

# 30

I FLED THE DANCEFLOOR.

The kings' attention burned into my back. I didn't run, but only just. If I ran, they might ignore their own countdown.

But I certainly couldn't. Unlike at last night's harvest feast, Luc had somehow tied the shadowed numbers to me. No matter which way I turned, they were there, blinking in the corner of my visions.

18:31.

18:30.

18:29.

Shit. Fuck. Shit.

I quickened my pace. A hundred curious eyes flickered to me as I wove through the revelry, slipping between tables stacked with food. Had we passed these on the way in? I had never had this much issue navigating a crowd. Normally I could see over everyone's head, but all the vampires towered over me. Even the shortest Azarasian women were my height.

It didn't matter. I aimed for Dawnspear, the castle looming ahead impossible to miss. Eventually I'd find a door. At this point, even a window would do. For once, I wouldn't care if the courts laughed at me as long as they didn't get to watch their kings fuck me.

*Fuck* me.

It was finally happening. I'd always known it would. I thought I'd have another three months until my birthday and harvesting. I thought it'd be with a stranger. Some unknown vampire who wouldn't introduce himself or care about the pain stabbing through my core. Who'd just grab my head and plunge his fangs into my neck as roughly as his cock split me open. My only hope had been that his venom would numb both my illness and my inexperience at once.

And it would have. But I didn't even need a vampire's venom when the soothing rune on my arm kept the aching, clenching, throbbing agony away.

Instead, I was a bundle of aching, clenching, throbbing *need.*

I spotted an open door and nearly cried out in relief.

The high-ceilinged hall was empty of vampires and thralls, the runelights lining the walls between the murder art dimmed. I hesitated, nibbling at my lip, a jittery buzz rattling through my bones. Left or right?

Since the right hall overlooked the terrace, left won the competition. I started down the corridor.

16:37.

16:36.

16:35.

I picked up the pace. If I didn't have a plug in my ass, jolting through me with every step, I'd probably be running. I didn't even care what that would look like, given I was practically naked. There was no one around anyway. I turned a corner, heading deeper into the castle—

And walked into a wide hall full of writhing bodies.

My jaw dropped. I'd heard the noises, the moaning and groaning and wet slap of flesh, but I had thought it all echoed in from the terrace and garden. Bodies twisted together on sofas and cushions lining the walls, pressing into each other in alcoves and shadowed corners. Vampires. Witches. Humans. All tangled in sin.

And my only way out was through.

I swallowed. No one turned. No one acknowledged me. I doubted they would. They were all... busy. I breathed in, then out. I could do this. Keep my eyes forward, move fast, and get out.

16:01.

16:00.

15:59.

I weaved through the depravity, my gaze locked ahead. Around a dark-haired female vampire riding a male witch, a goblet of dark red blood wine still clutched in her hand. Around a vampire fucking a human thrall into an Azarasian on her knees, his fangs in the thrall's throat. Around two male vampires sharing a red-haired woman, both their massive cocks thrusting into her as her eyes rolled back, body limp—

I ripped my gaze upward. The kings didn't plan to do that to me tonight, did they?

When Luc had slid the plug into my ass, he implied it would happen soon... but soon wasn't tonight, right? I couldn't go from a virgin who'd had three whole orgasms in her life—two of which happened in the last twenty-four hours—to taking both of the kings at once.

I veered around a mass of too many bodies to count—

And met a pair of familiar blue eyes.

Una.

I hadn't seen her since we arrived in Dawnspear. A silver-eyed vampire had her pinned to his chest, his fangs in her neck over her iron collar. They were on their knees, bodies rocking together. Una moaned, her fingers clutching his forearm, as a golden-eyed woman approached. The Dawn vampire stroked her cheek.

The man pulled his fangs from Una's neck and nipped her ear. "Lick my beloved's cunt for me, pet?"

Una didn't hesitate. She slid her hands up the vampire woman's thighs, gripping her ass as she leaned forward, licking a slow, eager path between her legs. The vampire sighed, fisting Una's golden hair as she sucked and nipped—

*Wicked, sinful girl.* I rushed the last few steps out of the hall, shaking my stepmother's voice out of my head. What would she really say, if she could see the perfect Una now, eagerly eating out one vampire while another fucked her? Would her tone be horrified? Judgmental?

No.

It wouldn't be either.

If my stepmother were here, she'd be a sinner like the rest of us. Her veins would be flooded with a vampire's venom. It didn't matter how holy she thought she was. Una was just as pious—*had been* just as pious.

And now she was a blood thrall, a vampire's eager whore.

Like I would be before the night ended.

I shuddered, but the tension between my legs built. I slid my hand between the chains of my skirt, pressing down, as if pressure alone could offer relief.

Instead, I only soaked my fingers.

I whimpered. Stars, a part of me wanted the kings to find me. Wanted them to bend me over the nearest chaise and make me theirs forever. I couldn't tell if it was the soulbond or the kings' venom clouding my mind.

Maybe it was both.

Worst of all, maybe it was neither.

A high-pitched scream of ecstasy rang out behind me. I ripped my hand away and strode forward, pulse hammering. I was still far too close to others. I had no chance of finding my way to the kings' apartment, but there had to be somewhere empty. Maybe if I went up a floor?

A melodic laugh echoed through the hallway. I stiffened mid-step, but the countdown ticking away in the corner of my vision forced me to keep moving. Ahead, two black-haired vampire females cuddled on a wide sofa, one's skin a lighter olive and the others a deep golden brown—

Bright gold and silver eyes swung toward me.

Roxiana and Isabeau. The general's sword leaned against the couch's arm, her burgundy pantsuit with gilded buttons discarded in a puddle on the floor. Roxiana hadn't removed anything, but her gown was little more than rubies strung together, smudged silver swirls painted into her skin.

I stared at them.

They stared at me.

11:42.

11:41.

11:40.

"Stairs to the apartment are that way," Roxiana said, breaking the silence. She pointed to the end of the hall, slightly to the left. "When you're up two floors, head south until you reach another staircase. Stay on that one until you reach the apartment."

I opened my mouth. Closed it. Opened it again. I didn't know these vampires. They'd never addressed me directly before. They were the kings' trusted councilors, but my comfort with my new soulbound didn't extend to their friends.

Fuck it. They couldn't punish me for speaking my mind. "Why are you helping me?"

"Why not?" Roxiana shrugged. "It doesn't harm anyone or hinder my kings' plans. Besides, I doubt you'll make it to the second staircase."

The general stroked a hand down her beloved's shoulder. "Might be a better idea to stop at the lounge next to it. Those stairs can be hard on the knees."

I gaped. Isabeau simply watched, unreadable, but the corner of Roxiana's lips twitched. The smirk mirrored Luc's perfectly, the family resemblance uncanny. My stomach flipped at the sight.

But unlike her nephew's, Roxiana's easily grew into a full-fledged smile. "Tick-tock, bride."

I jumped at the words and rushed down the hall. Roxiana's laughter followed me past runelight after runelight.

At least she hadn't lied.

A stairwell opened to my left. I all but lunged for it, biting my lip as the plug shuffled within me. Two floors up, the pulsing music from the revelry had faded slightly, the moans and laughter dampened beneath it.

Now to go south... But without the stars to guide me, I had no idea which way was south.

Moonlight streamed through open balcony doors at the end of the hall. I still had a little over ten minutes, more than enough time to check and orient myself. Worth the risk if it got me closer to privacy.

I rushed to the end as quick as I could and swung into the open air—

And met six widening gazes, each belonging to a witch, their irises rimmed with the faintest line of shadow.

The Isauran delegation.

I stared at the witches.

The witches stared at me.

"Oh." When Jules said the Isaurans were watching from a balcony, I had assumed he meant under guard, but there wasn't a vampire in sight. "Sorry, wrong door. Obviously. I'm just going to—"

I cut off and backed away before I blubbered more stupidity out into the world.

"Nessa, was it?" On the other side of a stone bench, Exalted Morrena leaned against the balustrade, hands folded in front of her. Like the Azarasians below, the Isaurans were dressed in red to celebrate the Blood Star's rising, but here the color felt different.

Somber.

Like I'd walked into a funeral.

"Uh, yes?"

"You are without king, council, or guard?"

I awkwardly turned to glance behind me, but the hall remained as empty as it was when I walked through it. A shiver prickled up my spine. "Maybe? I doubt they'd just let me wander the halls alone."

Morrena's unnervingly young face remained unreadable, but her gaze dropped to my collar. "They would if you wore some of the most intricate defensive spells I've ever seen."

I stiffened. My fingers brushed along the collar, the cool metal grounding me. Was that supposed to be a reassurance? A threat?

Morrena noticed my wariness. "My collar is marked with an obedience rune drawn by the Conqueror himself. We were all ordered not to harm any Azarasian or their property, so I can't hurt you, Nessa."

An obedience rune. Not a thrall runespell.

Why not? Thrall runespells didn't just enforce obedience. They bound the bearer to the Impire itself, limiting movement, decisions, even thought. That would've been a far more effective way to control a powerful witch.

Was it because of the allegiance runespell? Did the two interfere? Was that why the kings needed her to surrender?

Not that it mattered. Morrena had just implied she'd kill me if she wasn't wearing an obedience rune. That wasn't at all comforting.

Neither was the time.

8:49.

I swallowed, the flutter in my stomach returning to the forefront of my mind. Over half my time was gone, and I hadn't made it far, the revelry right below us. "Um, I should go. The kings will be... following me soon."

"Hunting you." Her words made me stop again. "I'm aware. I've been watching."

I flinched. Of course she had. That was why the Azarasians had left them here. Ordered them here, no doubt.

I hesitated. "I'm... sorry."

"What for?"

"That they make you watch."

Morrena nodded slowly, her gaze returning to the balcony's edge. "I have visited the Azarasian capitals every three years since they conquered us centuries ago. They always make each Exalted Daughter or Son watch after delivering a harvest."

8:01.

My stomach dipped. More than half my time was gone, and I'd barely made it anywhere. But I couldn't stop myself from asking. "How? You look fifteen. From what the kings told me about wraiths and the everlife runespell, I didn't think witches had found a way to be immortal yet."

"We haven't."

My brows raised. "Then how...?"

Her expression didn't change. "My sister developed a runespell that powerful female witches can cast when pregnant. When it's time, we... transfer into the new body, and our old one dies. The kings graciously allowed me to cast the soulshift spell sixteen years ago."

"That— I— Wow." I took a step closer, my curiosity burning brighter than even my desire or fear. "Why?"

She shrugged. "I assume the Imperium will keep me alive until they find Allegra or confirm she's dead."

Allegra. The sister Morrena and the kings had spoken of last night. The one responsible for gifting a harvest full of witches wearing the everlife rune to the Azarasian court nearly four hundred years ago. "Your sister, right?"

Morrena nodded. "In that, you and I are similar. We are both here suffering because of our sisters."

A chill slid through me. My heart pounded, but I held her gaze. "How do you know that?"

"I asked the right thrall," Morrena said simply. "I wanted to know more about the human woman who will be the Queen of Dusk and Dawn."

I stiffened. So they'd figured out what happened earlier. "I'm not a queen."

"You are according to Azarasian law," she said. "Soulbound heartmates share one fully merged soul. That means you share every title with your husbands."

My *husbands*? I wasn't touching that. It was somehow worse than them calling me their wife. "I couldn't even decide what to wear tonight. I doubt I'll rule much of anything."

Morrena's lips twitched. "Your bond is new. Right now, it's lust and obsession. But one day, you will own the Kings of Dusk and Dawn's hearts and bodies as much as they own yours. I'm sure you'll resist, but soulbonds are inevitable."

I closed the final few steps to Morrena's side and looked over the balcony's edge, heart pounding, mind racing. Vampires feasted and fucked and fought, a sea of beautiful faces, glittering dust and too many rubies. "What point are you trying to make, Morrena?"

The Exalted Daughter finally turned, her hazel eyes piercing. "You'll have something no human has had since the First Godsfall. You'll have *power*."

I barely breathed. "And what are you expecting I do with this power—?"

The music below cut off mid-note.

Silence crashed over the revelry. I stiffened, but no one below was looking at us. Every Azarasian had turned to the grand staircase, their collective focus locking onto one figure standing at the top.

Jules.

The King of Dawn grinned and raised his hands with a flourish. "Don't you all look fabulous tonight?"

His voice rippled through the terrace and garden, amplified by a rune I couldn't see. The courtiers tittered and simpered over the compliment, even coming from the Butcher King.

"We have a treat for you tonight, my friends." Jules paced the top step like a performer on stage. "One better than even last night's harvest and worthy of our Red Queen's Rising."

The crowd's attention shifted to the open doors behind him.

A vampire woman in a flowing crimson gown emerged, two gilded leashes raised in her hands. The chains trailed down to eight thralls, collared, gagged, and dusted in gold, moving in unison behind her.

My pulse slammed into my ribs.

Jules kept speaking, his tone light, indulgent. "When Lady Renée came to us a hundred years ago and asked for twenty Maboni from our harvest, I laughed in her face. We had never claimed over two humans ourselves."

The woman descended the steps, her thralls following obediently. They were led past the buffet to a circle of eight poles surrounding a low table lined with empty goblets.

Jules smirked. "But Lady Renée had a vision of a delicacy bred across centuries, perfected by the discerning hand of its mistress." He gestured grandly. "She is quite the salesman."

Luc strolled to Jules's side. "Her expertise in genetics didn't convince you, Julien?" The words were dry, amused. "I'm shocked."

Jules waved a hand. "This isn't the Colloquium, darling. This is a revelry. And revel we shall. Tonight, my friends, you will be the first to sample Lady Renée's long-awaited vintage." His golden eyes gleamed. "And should you find a favorite—well, she'll be accepting bids until midnight."

Bids.

On humans.

Bred. Sold. Like livestock.

My stomach twisted, nausea surging.

Lady Renée slid her finger along the leashes' ends, and the chain clattered to the floor. I expected at least one thrall to try to resist, but each moved with lowered heads to stand before the poles. The moment they stopped, their collars snapped back, locking their heads at an angle that exposed their necks.

I couldn't look away.

A vampire stepped forward, tray in hand, holding eight slender, curved instruments gilded in gold and etched with tiny runes. *Soothe. Endure. Stream.* Lady Renée plucked one without hesitation and clasped the chin of the gagged thrall before her.

I couldn't breathe. I couldn't move.

All I could do was watch as she plunged the curved device into the first thrall's throat.

My stomach seized, nausea clawing up my throat. The thrall flinched—just barely. A minuscule shudder that his soothing runes and servitude didn't let him complete. But his eyes flickered wide, some discomfort remaining. His mouth worked against the gag, but no sound escaped.

The only noise was the slow, wet drip, drip, drip of blood filling the goblet below.

A tap.

Lady Renée had added a fucking *tap* to his throat.

I slapped a hand over my mouth, bile surging at the back of my tongue. The woman beside him was next. Then the next. Each new snap of metal sent shocks through my bones, my vision blurring.

None of the thralls fought. They stood limp, blank-eyed. They would continue to stand there, bleeding, until the vampires drained them dry.

Lady Renée lifted the first full goblet and turned, approaching Jules. She bowed low. "It's only fitting you have the first taste, Imperium."

Jules plucked the goblet from her grasp and inhaled, breathing in the scent of the fresh blood. My stomach twisted.

He lowered the goblet and offered it to Luc. "After you, darling. I've already gone first so many times this week."

Luc took the goblet from Jules and brought it to his lips. His throat bobbed as he swallowed down the blood. When he pulled away, his tongue flickered out to catch a missed drop on his lips.

My horror burned into something twisted and sick and wrong. Because I couldn't look away from Luc's tongue catching that stray drop.

Because I still wanted him.

And that made me feel worse than anything else.

Luc exhaled, considering. "A smooth vintage. Rich, decadent. Well worth the effort, Lady Renée."

Jules snatched the goblet back and took a sip. "Hmm. That's amazing." The King of Dawn raised the goblet. "May the Red Queen and her court reign over another year of prosperity and health in our lands. Long live the Impire."

The crowd raised their goblets in unison.

"Long live the Imperium."

A thousand voices.

A thousand monsters.

Jules lowered his cup and turned his head.

His eyes locked onto mine instantly. "Now you'll have to excuse us, my friends."

My breath hitched. I jolted back, the enchantment of his voice shattering.

4:14.

4:13.

4:12.

The King of Dawn winked. "We have a bride to hunt down."

# 31

4:10.

4:09.

4:08.

I jolted away from the balustrade. How had I let the countdown tick down that low? It was in my starsdamned line of sight. "I need to go."

"Nessa—"

"No, Morrena." I backed away from the balcony's edge, from the witches, from the kings below promising sinful pleasure. "I can't help you. Not now. I don't even know how to help myself."

Morrena's expression softened into pity. "There is nothing you can do now but submit and let the Imperium have you. You're their soulbound. That means something to the Azarasians, so they will take care not to harm you. But as their soulbound, you alone will one day be able to stand against them."

"Stop saying that." Rebellious speech against our vampire overlords in Corraidin ended with a trip to the nearest garrison to feed the troops. I couldn't imagine a different fate awaited humans and witches within Montaurère.

"I will not." Morrena closed the distance between us, her cane tapping against the stone. "And I will make sure every Exalted Daughter and Son who visits after me will repeat it."

I scurried back through the doorway. The witch stopped at its opening, like she couldn't pass any further. I threw my hands up in the air, panic clear in my voice. "Do whatever you want, Morrena. I can't help you and I really, really need to go."

Morrena's eyes widened, but I was already turning. I hadn't exactly been polite, but I didn't really have time to worry about a witch's feelings. My words surely weren't the worst she'd heard today.

3:22.

3:21.

3:20.

The hunt had well and truly begun. I couldn't see or hear the kings, but I knew with certainty that they followed me. An awareness prickled down my back. Even without the soulbond, the prey in me sensed her hunters.

I raced down the hall, turning blindly. Roxiana and Isabeau's advice to head south from the staircase couldn't help me now. There was no way I'd find my way upstairs. Just like the councilors had said.

I turned another corner—

Luc stood in the middle of the hallway, watching me with burning black eyes.

Fuck. I backtracked and continued straight.

2:49.

2:48.

2:47.

Stars, I was running out of time. To do what, I didn't know. I couldn't escape this. Did I want to escape this? Even after what I had just witnessed, my pulse pounded between my legs, my desire wetting my inner thighs.

Godstars forgive me. I wanted to fuck these monsters.

But that was all it was. All it ever could be.

"Nessa." Jules's voice echoed eerily through the halls as he sang my name. "Where are you running, lovely?"

"I'm not running," I muttered. "All I can manage with this starsdamned plug is a brisk walk."

He cackled. "It looks like running to me."

This time, his voice didn't echo.

It came from directly behind me.

I twisted around—

And met luminous black eyes, the pupils swallowing all but a single line of gold.

Oh, fuck.

1:22.

1:21.

1:20.

My heart pounded as something within me screamed to run, even though it was meaningless.

The monsters had already caught me.

As Jules stalked toward me, my mouth went dry. I fell under his spell, entranced by the hunter's cold, inhuman beauty, the luminous sheen to his eyes, the sinuous sway of corded muscles under twinkling chains.

I shook myself out of it right before he reached me. My heart exploded in my chest, releasing a flood of panic. My foot hit the softness of a rug. I twisted—

And slammed into something warm and solid. I froze as Luc's breath brushed my forehead. "Uh-uh, little bride. You can't escape us now."

My nipples peaked. My body had always been a traitor. I shouldn't have expected anything else from it. Still, I weakly tried to scramble away. But Jules had continued forward, trapping me between his body and Luc's.

0:47.

0:46.

0:45.

"There's still time on the countdown," I said weakly.

"There is," Luc agreed. "Just enough time to do this."

Before me, Luc drew a small rune on his forehead, the flare of shadows gone in a blink. *Remember*. Jules must have done the same, judging by the familiar heat of magic at my back.

Jules rested his cheek against my head. "After you, Lucey."

The tip of Luc's finger brushed my temple in a quick, curving pattern.

"What does it do?" I asked, my voice hoarse.

"Over centuries, memories dull, even for demons and their ilk," Luc said. "We want to remember this and now we all will."

"I—"

But I was out of time.

0:03.

0:02.

0:01.

0:00.

The shadows of the countdown faded as a large hand wrapped around my throat, fingers weaving through the collar's decorative chains. A shuddering breath escaped me at the touch.

Luc tilted my head back and kissed me. Claimed me. Conquered me. I melted into his strong chest, the heat of him branding my skin. His grip firmed at my throat, at my waist, fingers just shy of bruising as he deepened the kiss. His tongue swept against mine, dragging me under like a tide I couldn't fight.

Jules pressed closer, his hard length jabbing against my lower back through his trousers. His nose brushed my neck, breath warm as his lips skimmed down to my shoulder. Soft, teasing, as though he had all the time in the world to enjoy unraveling me.

Luc released my lips... then twisted me around and yanked me backward, arching my spine. "After you, dearest."

Jules wasn't one to turn down a gift. His breath traced over my chest as he cupped my breasts, only delicate chains separating his skin and mine. His thumbs brushed over my nipples, the chilled metal contrasting with the heat of his fingers. I shuddered out a breath.

I grasped Luc's arm, his hand still firm at my throat, but my gaze was trapped in gilded shadows. Jules took that aching gold-dusted bud into his mouth and sucked—

"Ahhh." I couldn't help the breathless cry. Pleasure coiled tight in my belly, flaring up from my core and the plug. Jules circled his tongue around my nipple, licking every bit of dust from my skin. Slow, thorough, tormenting. The bump of his piercing sent a sharp jolt through me. I yelped, knees buckling, but Jules pinned me between his body and Luc's. Holding me up.

Holding me *trapped.*

Jules pulled back an inch. Cold air brushed my abandoned nipple. My breath gasped out.

The King of Dawn slipped his fingers through the chains of my top. "This is in my way. Remove it."

Me? I blinked hazily. My mind lagged behind, drowning in sensation. But before I managed a reply, Luc's free hand ghosted around my waist, threading through the chains.

Then he tore.

The silver and gold brassière snapped. Half of the chains slid over my shoulders before clattering to the floor. The sound was sharp, final. I jolted at the noise. The remainder of the metal looped around my shoulders, covering nothing. The kings had lured me into an alcove off the main hall, but we were still out in the open for anyone to see—

Luc disappeared from my back in the same breath that my legs hit the edge of a cushion. I tumbled onto a chaise so decadently large it might as well have been a bed. Above my head, I met my own wide eyes in a *mirrored* ceiling.

Oh. That was why the kings had herded me to this alcove.

But I only held my gaze for a moment.

A second later, two vampires were crawling on top of me.

On my left, Jules had stripped off his trousers and maroon drape, but the delicate chains of his shirt still ghosted against my fevered skin. Most of his pale hair was now gathered into a messy knot, but loose strands tumbled free, the rubies of his headdress swaying between them. On my right, Luc had shed his navy-blue robe before lowering his head, his tongue tracing a path of silver dust from my arm to my shoulder.

My skin tingled where it touched theirs. Every inhale enveloped me in Jules's smoked honey and Luc's heady spice. My world narrowed until my every sense was them.

Stars, I needed them. I didn't mean to arch into them, but my nipples ached, needy and tender. Their mouths could soothe them and—

Jules's lips closed over my left breast.

I inhaled sharply, heat ripping through my chest and shooting down my spine, straight to my core. The plug only heightened the pleasure, amplifying every touch. My fingers dug into the King of Dawn's biceps, desperate, grounding.

Then another mouth brushed over my silver-dusted right breast.

My gaze ricocheted from Jules as I gasped.

Luc smirked at me.

"Poor little bride," he said, exhaling against my sensitive skin. "So desperate for our mouths."

*Our* mouths? My brain halted at those words.

Luc's black eyes held mine as he leaned in and took my right nipple into his mouth.

I moaned, the sound a long, helpless *ahhh*. Sensation lashed through me, curling hot to my clit, to the plug, to my toes. My eyes flickered madly between the two vampires on either side of me. Jules mouthed me wildly, his piercing ripping gasps from my lips. Luc sucked leisurely, his tongue lapping slow, maddening circles around my nipple.

I shuddered, writhed. Stars, I wouldn't survive this. There was no way. My thighs clenched, my body straining, bracing for something inevitable.

Then Luc pulled back abruptly, licking silver dust from his lips. He inhaled, slow and deep, and his lips twitched. "Did I get it wrong? Are you not desperate for our mouths?"

When I didn't answer, he nipped at my aching skin. "Answer me."

"You're not wrong," I nearly yelped the words. "I need you."

"Where do you need me?" he all but purred.

Mortification flared, sharp and unbearable. My thighs pressed together, as though I could hide the truth, hide the wet heat between my legs. "You know where," I whispered.

"Do I?" Luc's smirk turned into a wolfish grin. "I'd ask Julien, but he seems otherwise occupied."

Jules smiled against my breast, but he didn't stop swirling his tongue.

Luc rubbed his thumb against my lonely nipple. "Here?"

"No."

He dropped his hands lower, across the softness of my belly. "Here?"

I shuddered. "No."

Luc slipped his fingers between the chains of my skirt and through my silver-dusted damp curls... but no further. "Here?"

Stars, I was going to explode. I shook my head, words failing me.

Luc slid a finger into my soaked center.

I cried out, my hips jerking. His touch was unbearably light, teasing, just a soft, circling stroke against my clit. So much like before. When he'd painted my skin in silver dust, when he'd marked me.

"Here, little curiosity?"

I nodded, breathless, useless, lost. My chest heaved, straining beneath the pressure of these teasing touches.

He put the slightest bit of pressure on my clit. "Say it."

A strangled cry ripped from my throat. "Yes. There. Touch me, please."

Luc hummed, satisfied. "I didn't plan to touch you."

Then he withdrew.

A sharp, desperate whimper escaped me. I grabbed for his arm to stop him, but before I could—

Jules reached across me, pinning my wrist to the cushion.

The King of Dusk chuckled darkly. "I planned to taste you."

Luc disappeared. Literally, between one blink and the next. Fuck, vampires were fast. Where had he even—?

A warm hand landed on the inside of my thigh. "Spread your legs for me, wife."

Every inch of me froze. I had already ridden Luc's fingers and Jules's tongue, already been laid bare beneath their hands, their mouths, their hunger. But Luc ordering me to expose myself, to spread my legs slower and slower until my cunt opened for him...

I gave a sharp shake of my head.

It was the most *lewd* thing anyone had ever said to me.

I wanted to do it. I wanted to welcome him inside me. But to say yes, to surrender...

Godstars forgive me.

I let my legs droop open until my knees bounced against the cushion.

Luc groaned, his black eyes focused on the soft, pink flesh of my cunt. His gaze was nearly a touch. I shuddered, growing wetter, hotter. His hands slid up my thighs, spreading me wider, stretching me until my body clenched in desperate anticipation. His fingers grazed over my skin, circling the plush curve of my hips, tracing lazy, taunting lines before his palms cupped my ass.

Luc's hands were large, possessive, consuming. Still, my flesh overflowed between his fingers. I flushed and squirmed, totally exposed—

Then he squeezed.

I yelped, body jolting as he hooked my thighs around his shoulders. His breath trickled over my drenched, aching cunt. My gaze flickered wildly from the beautiful pale-haired godstar nestled at my side to the gorgeous dark shadow between my knees.

Jules's arm rested firm against my chest, keeping me in place.

But I could still see.

Luc's dark eyes glinted as he breathed me in. "Jules has had you on his tongue twice, and I haven't gotten a single taste. It's time to rectify that."

His head of black tousled curls dipped between my legs.

Luc pressed a light kiss to my clit. I gasped, the sound tearing out of me.

Then the Conqueror devoured me.

Luc licked me like a man starved. Fuck. My back arched violently, a cry ripping free. Jules had buried his face between my legs like my cunt was his favorite food, but Luc was a man on a mission.

His mission? Making me scream.

He twisted his tongue—

I convulsed, shattered, another cry punched from my lungs. My one hand dug into Jules's shoulder and my other clamped shut, clamoring for something to hold.

Jules released my wrist. "Grab his hair."

His command was a groan of words said against my skin, but I obeyed instantly. My fingers fisted in Luc's curls, tugging, shaking. He chose that exact second to plunge his tongue into my cunt. I moaned, my eyes rolling back. The King of Dusk's grip on my thighs tightened, keeping me still as he feasted.

Jules's mouth wandered, releasing my nipple to trail slow kisses across my chest. He circled a finger around my right nipple, a teasing touch. "Luc is rather good with his mouth, isn't he?"

I couldn't answer. Not beyond a pitched, keening whimper. Luc circled my clit with the rough pad of his thumb, pressing his tongue against that achingly sensitive spot inside me.

I shuddered.

Fuck. Oh, stars.

"Ah, poor, sweet Nessa, having your wits tongued out of you." Jules rested his chin on my sternum, his wicked golden gaze never leaving me. Waiting for my answer.

The longer I stayed silent, the more my abandoned nipples ached.

The softer Jules traced his fingers along my right breast.

The slower Luc rubbed my clit, his tongue dragging torturously slow out of me.

The bastards. "What was the question again?"

Jules's grin was all satisfaction. "Don't play coy."

"I— I—" I tried to reply, I really did, but the pleasure thrumming through me had melted my brain. The Conqueror had his fucking head buried between my legs. The Butcher had a hand on my breast, his cock hard against my thigh.

I was little more than a writhing mess between them.

Jules flicked my nipple.

I yipped. "His mouth is amazing," I nearly shouted, desperation stripping my voice raw. "I've never felt anything like it. Please. Touch me."

Jules chuckled. "I think you just insulted me, but since you begged so nicely..."

The King of Dawn lowered his head back to my left breast. His eyes closed as he wrapped his mouth around my sore nipple, his free hand gripping my other breast, rolling the aching bud between his fingers.

Godstars, this was perfect.

Almost perfect. Luc's tongue only swiped soft, teasing strokes through my heat.

Like they heard my thoughts, Luc sucked in my clit at the same time Jules clamped his lips around my nipple.

My back arched. Pleasure pulsed through me, a wicked crescendo of twisting tongues and skilled fingers.

When Luc circled my clit, Jules grazed his teeth against my skin.

When Jules pressed kisses to my nipple, Luc sucked harder, a sharp, dizzying contrast. My head slumped back into the cushion—

Only to meet my glazed eyes in the mirror over the chaise.

Fuck. Luc's dark head rocked between my legs, his powerful back flexing, muscles rippling with every movement. Jules curved himself around me, a naked godstar with pale hair. My body trembled, my face slack and flushed, the image in the mirror utterly debauched.

When I had worried about them eating me, I hadn't imagined it like this.

The mirror was like oil on a fire. Pleasure burst, then clawed at my skin, unbearable in its intensity. My squirming increased. I couldn't survive this. Surely this much pleasure would kill a person.

But Luc didn't even tense his hands on my thighs to hold me in place. I was trapped. Shit. Fuck. It spiked higher and higher... I spiked higher and higher. Luc slipped his tongue back into me—

I burst with a scream. Jules caressed my nipple one last time, then leaned back, watching me break. My eyes rolled back. My thighs clenched down, locking Luc's head in place. Locking the Conqueror's head in place.

I should've released him, but I did *not* care.

Each aftershock sent fresh ripples of pleasure through me. Ricocheting. Building. Echoing. My ass clenched around the plug, doubling every feeling. I writhed and shuddered and moaned and made so much noise as I *came* on his tongue.

Fuck, that was embarassing. But the emotion was quickly washed away by the haze of pleasure, the thick, warm weight of satisfaction. I sank into the cushion, boneless.

When the kings had said they were going to fuck me, I had assumed they meant with their cocks.

I had no complaints about their tongues, though.

I met my glazed eyes in the mirror above me. Slack lips. Flushed cheeks. My legs sprawled. I was utterly ruined. I should have panicked. Should have felt the old, nagging voices creeping in.

There was nothing but silent, warm peace.

Jules burrowed into my side and nibbled at my earlobe. "Roll over onto your hands and knees."

My entire body went stiff. I wouldn't have thought it possible, not after the orgasm they had wrung from me. The kings didn't plan to stop here, like they had the last two times. No activating soulbond would save me. No shock revelation would interrupt.

Tonight they would make me theirs.

Jules wanted to *fuck* me on my hands and knees.

I hesitantly pushed onto my elbow. Luc still lay between my legs, resting on his forearms, watching me with hooded eyes. Not even his broad shoulders could block out the open hallway behind him. I couldn't flush any harder, but my body certainly tried. Anyone who walked by would have noticed the Conqueror and the Butcher pinning me down, their hands and mouths everywhere.

"Can we..." I swallowed, suddenly nervous. It was hard not to be with those two pairs of bright eyes on me, watching me more intensely than a human ever could. "Can we go somewhere more... private?"

Jules absentmindedly drew circles on my shoulder. "Where did you have in mind?"

Godstars, how did he make such simple words sound so sinful? "Your bed," I whispered hoarsely.

Jules's gaze flickered down as he arched a brow at Luc. Almost immediately, the King of Dusk shrugged at the silent question. I was Jules's first, so the final decision belonged to him.

The king who didn't care at all about anyone staring at him, naked or otherwise.

The king who treated the world as his stage, all of us a captive audience to his show.

I breathed out slowly. I would survive this, whatever the choice. I probably wouldn't even think about my embarrassment until later. Just looking at the kings had the soulbond sinking its claws back into me, erasing everything but the bodies touching mine.

Jules studied me with a predatory patience I hadn't realized he possessed. Did the soulbond show him glimpses of me, like it had shown me pieces of them? Did he see my shame? My fear?

Would he care?

He traced his fingers idly over my bare hip. "What will you give me in return?"

I tensed. "I don't have..." I swallowed. If he asked, I must have had something left to give. "What do you want?"

"Everything," he breathed out, letting the word linger. "But for now? Your willing and eager submission."

Fuck. My breath hitched. I wished it didn't. But he could see everything, into my very soul.

Cheeks burning, I nodded.

"Say it," Luc murmured.

I swallowed again. "I'll... submit. Willingly and eagerly."

Jules hummed, clearly pleased. "Very well. Since you're our soulbound and all, I suppose we can make an exception."

"And if I wasn't?" The question slipped out before I could stop it. I already knew the answer. They were indulging me, accommodating me, only because I was theirs. And if I weren't...

Luc chuckled. "If you weren't, we'd already be inside you."

Jules's grin sharpened against my skin. "But if our wife wants privacy, our wife will get privacy. I'll gladly fuck you in *our* bed." He pressed a slow, open-mouthed kiss to my jaw. "The High Courts will hear you scream either way."

I WAS A DESPERATE, needy mess.

When Luc finally reached the top of the final staircase to the Imperial Apartment, I nearly whimpered with relief. With every step between the alcove three stories below and here, my cunt had slid across his bare abs.

I bit my lips with his every movement.

Tightened my legs around his waist.

Dug my fingers deep into his shoulders.

*Breathe, Nessa.* I said the words to myself, but Luc and Jules's voices echoed in my mind, low and knowing. I shuddered at their dulcet murmurs.

The King of Dawn slithered along behind us, his grin widening with every squeak I kept down and every one I didn't. Jules hadn't bothered plucking our abandoned clothing from the floor, nor did he use his blood control to lessen his straining erection. I was far closer to the bulge in Luc's trousers, but it was *that* monstrosity I'd feel first.

I swallowed hard, smothering both a whimper and the betrayal of my watering mouth.

In no time at all, the Conqueror crossed the hall, pushed through the golden, runed door, and cut through the sitting room. Titus glanced up from where he lay by the fireplace, the flickering blaze painting lazy light across the room. He quickly flopped his head back down, not the least bit interested or concerned.

The second we passed into the kings' bedchamber, all thoughts of Titus fled my mind.

This was it.

This was happening.

Fuck.

I had never both wanted and feared something this badly. Wanted the pleasure, the touch of skin, the intensity of those luminous gazes. Feared what it meant. To them? Nothing. How many thousands of vampires and thralls—human, witch, and Mortal Bride alike—had shared their bed? To them, I was one of a million, a routine indulgence after a revelry.

To me, they were the first men to touch me, to pleasure me, to claim me. I had known this was the world I lived in, where sex meant nothing, but I had spent too long with my head in a book, trapped in romances and unrealistic expectations.

I wanted them to fuck me. I wanted it to mean something, more than just magic binding us together… and at the same time, I didn't.

I didn't know which was more pathetic.

At least the first was reasonable.

I closed my eyes and inhaled deeply… and by the time I exhaled, Luc was lowering me to the ground at the end of their bed. My feet sunk into soft rugs.

It wouldn't ever be *my* bed, no matter how many times they fucked me on it. Tonight would surely be the first of many.

Luc turned toward a dresser positioned between the door to my bedchamber and the bathing chamber. As he did, Jules looped around my back, the heat of him a caress across my dust-smeared skin. He breathed in my scent. I clenched—and moaned as pleasure pulsed through me.

Jules hummed, his fingers tapping against my lower back and down my spine. Down, down, down… until he tweaked the end of the silver plug.

I jolted with a yip, but he caught me with a loose arm around my hips, keeping me close. "You've been such a good girl for us, wearing this all night without complaint."

Luc twisted one of the silver rings from his fingers. It clattered onto a tray on the dresser. Then another. "She complained twice."

"With little complaint," Jules amended.

"Sit, Julien," Luc said without turning. Another ring clattered.

Without a word, Jules released me and dropped onto the end of the bed. He loosened his pale hair from its knot, letting it spill over his shoulders as he sprawled back with a grin.

"I said sit, not lounge."

I shuddered at the rumble of Luc's voice, but Jules only pouted. "You're mean, Lucey."

The King of Dawn pushed back up, but his eyes stayed on me, standing in front of him wearing nothing but a skirt of chains, a couple strands of necklaces, and a collar.

I drank in every inch of his ivory skin in return, but my gaze kept flickering to his cock, achingly hard and impossibly long. He hadn't bothered removing any of his jewelry, from the headdress woven into his pale blond waves to his heavy earrings and the rings on his fingers.

Stars, he was a sight to behold. All bright gold and glittering rubies and perfect, carved muscle.

The bastard knew it, too. He loved the way everyone always stared, enraptured by his beauty. But even his lovers never entirely forgot their fear, forgot that Jules's hands and *the Butcher's hands were one and the same. And while she was afraid, she didn't fear me, couldn't ever fear me. Only lust shined in her dilated eyes, a deep, warm mahogany—*

"You better get over here quickly," Jules drawled. "Our bride is eye-fucking me hard."

I ripped out of the bond, my cheeks burning red. "So are you."

"Exactly why Luc should hurry the fuck up."

Two more rings clinked onto the tray. "Hands on his shoulder, Nessa."

I stiffened at the command and glanced back at Jules, but he only watched me with that pleased, infuriating grin.

I had agreed to submit. There was no backing out now.

With a deep breath, I stepped closer until my knees bumped his and placed my hands on his strong shoulders. Jules's black eyes dropped to my breasts and stayed there. I repressed a shiver.

"Take a step back."

I frowned. Step back? But then I'd be... leaning over Jules, bent just enough, leaving myself wide open.

I obeyed before I thought too hard about it.

"Spread your legs."

My head snapped toward Luc. "What—?"

Luc had stripped from his trousers, his toned, bronze ass on full display. My mouth dropped open slightly. The muscles of his back rippled as he removed the last of his rings. I didn't think I'd ever get used to the sight of the Conqueror naked.

"You have your orders," Luc said, turning.

I snapped my jaw shut. "Why?"

The King of Dusk closed the distance between us. It took everything in me not to bolt from the powerful, gorgeous, obviously aroused vampire prowling toward me.

Not that I'd make it far if I did.

"Because you need to be wetter to take Julien's cock," Luc said. "I'm going to make you come again."

Now my jaw dropped all the way. How the fuck was I supposed to respond to that? I just stared as Luc reached my side, a towering shadow of golden-brown skin and dark hair—

A spark flashed against my ass. *Through* my ass. I yelped, spine snapping straight, nipples tightening almost painfully. My nails dug into Jules's shoulders as I forced out a breath.

Luc had *spanked* me.

I met black eyes lined with silver, the hungry gaze of a vampire. My core clenched. The memory of Luc's fingers between my legs hit me so vividly, I nearly gasped. I clenched my thighs together.

Luc smirked, his nostrils flaring. "Obey, Nessa."

Damned vampire noses. I clenched my thighs tighter, as if that would change a thing—

*Smack.*

Luc slapped my ass again, harder this time. His voice turned razor sharp. "*Now.*"

I mewled, a strange pleasure flooding through me. I'd felt that touch all the way through to my clit. A part of me was furious that anyone dared spank me, the act demeaning and wrong in the eyes of the godstars. But the depraved part of me won out, heart fluttering so hard I couldn't bring myself to care.

I spread my legs.

Luc hummed in approval. He brushed his fingertips around the curve of my ass and grazed the silver plug. I shuddered at the touch.

He tugged it from me in one smooth motion. I yelped. The heat of magic flared almost immediately behind me, no doubt sterilizing the silver. Would he step away to put it back in its case? My body began to relax—

Luc slid a finger all the way into me.

"Oh," I gasped, clenching down on Jules's shoulders. Luc's sudden invasion should have felt jarring, but my body welcomed him without resistance, slick and aching.

Luc aimed to somehow make me wetter.

He pulled out—then pulsed back in.

In.

Out.

Luc went from nothing to fucking me with his hand in a second flat.

I moaned. Jules licked his lips. I nearly buckled from the building heat in that gaze, the building heat between my thighs.

Luc slid a second finger into me.

I choked on my next moan. Oh, stars. My nails dug into Jules's skin.

"Fuck, she's tight." Luc pulsed his fingers apart slightly. I squeaked at the sensation. Thanks to the soothing rune, it wasn't anything compared to the cramps and bloating I used to suffer daily, but neither was it comfortable.

Before discomfort could dampen my pleasure, Luc returned to his rhythm, stoking the fire in me, hotter and hotter.

I had just come less than ten minutes ago. It wasn't going to take that much to push me over the edge again. My chest heaved, my entire body trembling.

"You look overwhelmed," Jules murmured, watching me intently. The shadows in his pupils swirled. "Are you going to come on Luc's fingers for us?"

"I—I—I—probably."

"Shh." He pressed a finger to my lips. "You'll hurt Luc's feelings if you're still capable of speech."

"How many fingers will stop her from forming sentences, do you think?" Luc asked with a rumble. "Let's try three."

"Wai—ahh."

Luc didn't wait. He slid a third finger inside me, stretching me open. My knees actually buckled this time—but Jules caught me with steady hands, holding me upright.

I squeezed my eyes shut. Luc stroked and stroked and stroked, spreading me open deeper and deeper. Oh, stars, I couldn't... I shouldn't... Every part of me clenched.

Something warm brushed my fingertips. My eyes jolted open. A drop of blood dribbled down Jules's chest.

My nails had pierced his *skin*.

The King of Dawn didn't even notice. "Don't fight it. Let yourself come. Luc won't stop until you do."

I couldn't speak, so I just shook my head. I wasn't saying no, not really. I wasn't saying much of anything, barely capable of speech anymore.

But Luc took it as a denial. "Stubborn brides get a fourth finger."

Nope.

My legs snapped shut instantly, trapping his hand between my thighs. Though not really. No human strength could stop a vampire from doing whatever he wanted.

Luc didn't move. "Release my hand."

I shuddered at the sinful promises in his voice.

"I'd do what he says," Jules whispered conspiratorially. "Luc always gets what he wants."

"He... It won't fit."

"I will," Luc said. "Breathe, little curiosity."

I shook my head. "You won't."

"You are my soulbound." He straightened his fourth finger slowly, the sensation a brush against my inner thigh. "We have to fit together, in every way. I know you can take four fingers because you'll take my cock."

Luc's hand slid forward until his fingertips met my wet center... and kept going, nudging into me. Past the first knuckle, then the second—

"Oh, fuck." I tried to swallow the moan that followed the words, but it slipped free, raw and unrestrained.

Luc pumped his hand deep inside me. Each thrust strummed the tension in me higher and higher. Stars, I shouldn't have enjoyed this. Shouldn't be on the edge of another orgasm, so soon after coming on their tongues.

Jules smirked up at me, enjoying the show as I fought against the orgasm Luc was fixated on giving me.

The King of Dusk chuckled softly. "I love a good challenge. You've put up a valiant fight... but now, you're going to come for me."

Luc twisted his hand, palm facing the floor, and curled his fingers.

Once.

Twice.

Thrice—

I shrieked as the pleasure burst, my body clamping down on Luc's fingers. My back arched. I whimpered, tears streaming down my face. Oh, stars. Their touches shouldn't feel this good. It wasn't right.

But how could I resist this bliss? This ecstasy that shattered every thought, every fear, until only they remained?

Luc's fingers stayed deep inside me, coaxing me through the aftershocks, slow and unrelenting, stretching out my orgasm until it turned unbearable. Until I was raw and open and trembling. A wreck in their hands.

My breath stuttered as another pulse rolled through me, weaker this time but no less consuming.

Jules hummed in satisfaction. "Look at you, lovely. You're beautiful."

I wanted to deny him. Wanted to protest.

But I could barely breathe.

The last remnants of my orgasm shuddered through me, wringing me dry. My bones melted, muscles going liquid, useless. I sank into Jules's chest, sagging against him, panting and spent.

And they hadn't even fucked me yet.

The King of Dawn stroked a hand down my back, the touch surprisingly gentle for the Butcher. I considered burying my face against his glittering chest, but Luc's triumphant satisfaction almost warmed my skin. I twisted around, intent on glaring at the Conqueror, taking far too much pride in his victory.

My attention snagged on his hand and stayed there. His fingers glistened, a faint pink tinge to my desire. I'd started bleeding again. More lightly than before, but still enough that I noticed it.

I cringed. Would there ever be a time I wouldn't bleed when aroused? At least there hadn't been any pain. I didn't even want to know how much agony I'd be in without magic.

Holding my gaze, Luc sucked his forefinger and middle finger into his mouth. My jaw popped open in a soft breath of shock. There wasn't much dust on his fingers, but Luc made it seem like he was licking melted chocolate from his skin instead of my blood-tinged wetness.

Jules whined. "You really love making me suffer, don't you?"

Luc only arched a brow. Then, without a word, he offered his ring finger and little finger to Jules. The King of Dawn didn't hesitate. With a low noise, Jules seized Luc's wrist and dragged his fingers into his mouth. He moaned at the taste of me.

When he finally released Luc's hand, his black eyes were darker. Hungrier. Jules pushed to a stand, easily lifting me in his arms—

And dropped me onto the mattress, face first.

I stiffened, returning to reality with a sharp burst of adrenaline.

Luc had moved in a blink to the head of the bed, relaxing back into the mass of black, silky pillows. I couldn't see Jules, but I knew he was behind me. Even without the soulbond, I'd have felt his gaze trailing my bare skin, the curve of my thighs and ass and hips. I stayed still, my heart galloping as fast as a hellsteed. Frozen under the gaze of two vampires.

Jules ran a finger along the back of my thigh, a touch so light I almost thought I imagined it. "Crawl across the mattress to Luc."

I swallowed, but didn't move. I didn't think I could. "Across the mattress?"

"Yes," Jules purred. "Slowly."

A shiver traced my spine. My nipples peaked. "This wasn't..."

"This wasn't what you meant when you agreed to be fucked?" Luc asked. "Did you imagine you'd just lie back and close your eyes? I fear I have a few more expectations than your human men."

I bristled and pushed onto my knees, scrambling further onto the mattress. "I don't exactly know what I'm doing—"

Jules put a hand on the small of my back and pushed me over.

My hands hit the sheets right as the mattress dipped behind me. My skirt of chains surrendered to gravity, slipping down my thighs, hanging loose from my waist. My body screamed at me to run. To escape the intensity of those luminous, shadow-rimmed eyes.

To escape the agony they would cause when they fucked me.

Because it *had* to hurt. How couldn't it? For a second, my body locked. I was stuck in the past, in the life I had resigned myself to living. I wasn't meant to experience pleasure. Only pain.

"Shh, lovely. Breathe." Jules nuzzled my back. His body caged me in as his hands stroked slow paths up my dust-painted sides. The soothing pattern didn't settle the racing of my heart, not when his hard length brushed my ass and Luc's gaze trapped me like iron. "Nothing is going to hurt tonight."

"What about tomorrow?"

"Nothing is going to hurt *ever*." Jules pressed a gentle kiss to my shoulder blade. My heartbeat steadied. "Crawl, bride."

My breath hitched, but I obeyed, crawling toward Luc. He raised his arms to prop them against the pillows. This must have been how his subjects felt when they approached his throne. Those dark eyes trailed down my chin to where my body swayed beneath me, watching with obscene interest.

*Cover up, Nessa,* my stepmother's voice snapped. She had pulled at the neckline of my gowns to cover my cleavage too often when my breasts had first developed. My fingers dug into the cushion. My shoulders curled. No one could ever possibly desire my body.

But Luc's cock only hardened as he devoured the sight of me.

Too soon, my knees brushed against his thighs. I leaned back, unsure where to put my hands, unsure what to do—

Jules pushed me down again. I crashed into Luc's hard, silver-smeared chest with a yelp. The King of Dusk brushed his knuckles across my chin. Jules slid his palms down my soft thighs. He hooked his hands under my knees and lifted, spreading me until I straddled Luc's legs. Cold air brushed my opening cunt. I shuddered.

"Aww, you shouldn't have," Jules said, swiping a finger through my drenched slit. He popped two fingers into me with ease. I gasped. "She's soaked for me."

The corner of Luc's lip twisted into that arrogant smirk. "She's soaked for *us*."

"Yes, sure, us." Jules pulled his fingers out. Something hard and thick and hot brushed the swell of my wet center. "But I get to feel that wet grip on my cock first, so right now, she's all for me."

I FLINCHED AS THE head of Jules's cock glided through me. Panic flooded my system. The soulbond fought to smother it, but even magic couldn't contain this.

I couldn't do this. My body couldn't handle my fingers without cramping, much less a huge cock. My brain didn't care that I wore a soothing rune, or that Luc had just had his fingers in me. I was broken, irreparable in the eyes of the godstars long before the harvest.

I scrambled forward, crawling up Luc. "I can't—"

Luc's hand wrapped around my throat, threading through the chains of my collar. I stilled like prey in the jaws of a predator. His thumb traced the frantic rhythm of my pulse. My fingers dug into his chest, my entire body taut, muscles screaming for me to run—

I should have run.

I should have—

Jules shifted behind me. His cock nudged against my entrance, just enough for my body to recognize what was happening—

And I clenched.

Jules stopped.

Luc's gaze burned into mine. His grip tightened just enough to ground me, to remind me who was in control.

"Pick a cock," he said into the lengthening silence. "Dusk or dawn?"

The mattress bounced. Jules fell back onto his heels with a sigh. "No fair. We flipped for her."

"That was before she was our soulbound."

"Fine." Jules sighed again, dragging it out for effect. "Pick a cock."

I licked my lips. My gaze dropped to Luc's cock. Jules was longer, but Luc was thicker and pierced. Godstars, neither of them would fit. I didn't care what they said, I wouldn't believe it.

Luc jerked my chin upwards, drawing my eyes back to me. "Your choice?"

I swallowed. "Dawn," I whispered with shame.

"What was that?"

"Dawn."

"I need a full sentence."

I narrowed my eyes at him, but obeyed. "I pick Jules's cock."

"Thank fuck," Jules exhaled with pure relief.

Luc's thumbs flashed up to my lower lip. "Glare at me all you want. You won't be glaring in a minute."

Jules shuffled behind me, his weight moving closer. He gripped my hips and pulled me back.

The head of his cock split me open.

A sharp gasp broke from my lips. Sensation flooded through me, a twisting ocean of sparking heat and aching pressure. My breath hitched. I ducked my head, eyes squeezing shut—

Luc tangled his fingers in my hair and yanked. My breath left me in a yelp as I jerked forward, locked into his gaze.

"Eyes on me, little curiosity. I want to watch Jules come inside you for the first time."

"I—"

Luc tightened his grasp on my throat, my collar, cutting off the sound. Behind me, Jules slowly slid deeper. A tremor racked my frame as the first inch of him sank into me. My cunt clenched around his hard length.

Luc loosened his grip a second before Jules rolled his hips. A tiny thrust.

Just enough.

I yelped. Fire pulsed through my nerve endings, pleasure and discomfort tangled together. But it didn't edge into pain. Luc's rune spread its heat through me, soothing the stretch.

Jules chuckled. The sound vibrated through him, into me. The tingles turned my yelp into a moan.

"Good girl." Luc stroked my temple with his thumb. "Moan for Jules as he fucks open your tight cunt."

Jules took Luc's words as a command. His thumbs brushed up and down my spine, every motion in sync with the slow, deliberate thrusts of his hips.

He slid deeper an inch, spearing me open. Then he slid back, retreating halfway before pushing in again.

I whimpered with each shallow thrust.

Moaned when he pulled back, sliding against my sensitive walls.

Yelped when he increased his pressure, his depth, filling me more.

My eyes watered as the sensation swelled within me. Tears trailed down my cheeks and across Luc's fingers on my throat. I stayed locked in his black gaze, but every cell in my body focused on where Jules *fucked* me. Every stroke built a tense storm of pressure within me.

My nipples ached.

My clit throbbed.

Jules sank deeper. Then deeper still.

My vision dotted with sparks, aching and wonderful. My back arched, my breath hitching.

Fuck, how much further did he have to go? Jules wasn't going to take me halfway. I was soaked for him, but not even... oh, stars... not even that could save me from the devastating length of him.

With a groan, Jules slammed his cock once more and his thighs smacking against my ass. His fingers dug into my hips like handles. My breath hitched, but the sound was drowned out by Jules's long sigh.

"Ah, fuck, you feel divine." His voice was husky, roughened by pleasure. "It's like your cunt was made for me."

My eyes widened. His cock stretched me from clit to navel, a deep, consuming fullness. I spasmed around him. Jules shuddered. I trembled, my arms weak where I braced against Luc's chest. My vision spun and blurred.

The King of Dusk brushed his lips against mine. "Remember to breathe."

I sucked in a huge breath. The moment my diaphragm expanded, my cunt clenched. I nearly choked.

Jules traced a line up my spine. "Are you ready?"

"Ready for...?" I wet my lips, not recognizing the rasp of my voice. "Ready for what?"

"For me to fuck you?"

"Have you—?" He moved, and I jolted. "Have you not been fucking me already?"

Luc's smirk was pure indulgence. "I fear Jules has only warmed you up."

I whimpered.

Luc studied me for a second before his gaze flickered over my shoulder to Jules. "She's ready. Fuck her."

I couldn't see Jules's grin, but I didn't need to. I heard it in his voice. "Let's see how much she can take before she screams."

Jules pulled out suddenly. A strangled noise caught in my throat. My body felt surprisingly empty without him. My lip started to twitch into a frown—

He slammed back in. His skin slapped against mine.

*Oh.*

Then he was gone again... and back before I even adjusted.

Oh! The fire inside me roared, licking up my spine. Another thrust. Then another. Each thrust pushed a moan from my lips, my thighs rocking forward.

His fingers dug into my hips, hard enough to bruise. I mewled, a pathetic, desperate noise. It didn't sound like me. I never sounded like that. Never so pitched. So wanton.

So pleasured.

Luc released a deep groan. He caressed my thundering pulse in my neck, those dark eyes devouring my face. He lowered his hand from my hair. The tips of his fingers traced a path down my throat.

He wrapped his fist around his rock-hard cock.

With Jules's next thrust, Luc stroked himself. Like it was his cock stretching me, marking me.

Like I was being claimed by both of them.

My jaw dropped. Luc's glowing gaze held mine for a moment before lowering. His attention dragged down my throat, over my collarbone, lingering on my heaving breasts. Down, down, following the soft curves of my stomach, to the place where Jules split me open.

Luc groaned, tightening his fist. "Fucking exquisite."

Exquisite? If Jules weren't fucking me senseless, I might have laughed.

"I'm—oh!" The word fractured into a cry as Jules drove into me, hard. "I'm not."

"Was I lying?" Luc rumbled.

No. Stars, no, he wasn't. My fingers dug into his skin. Jules's hips smacked against mine, relentless. Luc's hand stroked faster, his fist working over his thick cock.

Savoring me as much as the King of Dawn.

I arched, my back bowing. My eyes nearly rolled back. I was going to combust. I didn't even care. Nothing had ever felt more right in the world.

Like I was meant for this.

Meant for them.

Meant for Jules to pound into as Luc gripped my throat in one hand and his cock in the other.

I hadn't spent my life lonely, but waiting. Waiting for this, waiting for *them*.

My hips tilted, almost instinctively. Jules slid even deeper, bottoming out inside me.

He gasped. "Stars, wife."

The pleasure in me spiked at his words.

Jules pulsed into me again with a groan, his balls slapping against my clit. I pitched forward, my breath stuttering as the jolt spread through me. Luc's fingers slipped from my throat. He reached for Jules's hand, gripping his soulbound to steady him.

Jules squeezed back, breathless. "She feels so fucking good, Lucey."

Luc only smiled.

Jules's thrusts turned ruthless. He rammed into me, forcing me to meet every stroke, fucking me deeper. "Fuck, I'm going to come."

Luc's brow furrowed. His strokes quickened over his cock. "Not yet, Julien."

"Luc—"

"No." Luc's growl was low, commanding. Absolute. "Our bride is going to milk your cock when *she* comes."

Jules shuddered. "Fuck."

His pace turned brutal. My limbs trembled, unable to hold myself up. I crashed into Luc, my lips brushing his chest. Jules kept moving. Didn't stop. I screamed into Luc's skin as the fire in me roared, brighter and hotter. Luc's knuckles brushed my breasts with every stroke of his fist, each pass a wicked tease against my skin.

Luc's dark gaze dipped to me. "Beg for it."

I blinked at him through hooded eyes. "Wha—at?"

"Stop, Julien."

Jules froze. His cock twitched inside me, his breath ragged. His fingers dug so tightly into my hips I knew I'd bruise. His body shook, stopped at the very edge of release. "Fuck, you bastard."

Luc exhaled slowly. Perfectly in control, even as Jules fucked me on my knees on top of him. "Our bride can't come until she's begged for it."

Jules's hand slipped from Luc's. He tangled his fingers in my hair and yanked my head back. Pain flashed at my scalp. I yelped.

"You heard him. Neither of us are coming until you beg."

Stars, I needed to come. The desperation clawed up my throat. I barely recognized my voice as I croaked, "Please."

"Please what?" Luc brushed his fingers along my jaw. "Don't think. Just answer."

"Please make me come."

Luc smiled, slow and devastating. A rare and beautiful sight. "As you wish."

That was all Jules needed to hear. His cock slid free before slamming back into me. Oh. Oh! I was so close, teetering on the edge. My world narrowed to the pleasure between my legs and the dark eyes holding me prisoner.

*Stars, make me come. Please make me come.*

Luc released his cock. "Your godstars aren't going to make you come, little curiosity. Your kings are."

"Please, please, please." The word punched out of me with every thrust.

Luc crawled his fingers across the softness of my stomach and threaded them through my soaked curls. He circled my clit—

A cry ripped from my throat as I shattered.

Pleasure crashed over me, drowning me, dragging me under. I screamed. Complete and utter bliss. My cunt clenched around Jules. The King of Dawn snarled behind me as his hips jerked. A second wave rolled through me. Not mine, but an echo of his. A spurt of warmth flooded me.

His *cum* flooded me.

Jules groaned, the sound raw and guttural. I bit Luc's collarbone, the sensations overpowering. Luc fisted a hand in my hair and pulled my face up. My teeth ripped his skin. A burst of metallic heat exploded across my tongue.

Luc's mouth crashed into mine, licking his own blood from my lips. His hand had returned to his cock, working himself harder, faster—

A third wave slammed into me.

Into *us*.

Jules and I groaned together. Luc's hot seed spilled across my breasts, my stomach. His growl rumbled from his chest through to my mouth, through to where his lips claimed me. He nipped my tongue.

Pleasure ricocheted within me, battering me from all sides.

I think I blacked out.

Jules's thrusts slowed, drawing it out, fucking us through the final aftershocks. Little tremors rolled through me, weaker now, but still enough to steal my breath.

When the fire in me settled into a gentle warmth, Jules pulled out. A gush of his cum dribbled down my thighs. He hummed, pleased. His hands trailed over my ass, squeezed, and then dropped away.

Luc's grip on my jaw vanished at the same second. My limbs collapsed beneath me. I slumped against him, spent, wrung dry. I didn't care that I was sprawled across a vampire in a wet spot. The runes woven into the fabric whisked away the mess, but they did nothing for the sweat and cum clinging to my skin.

My eyes fluttered shut. The warm spice of Luc soaked into me. I breathed him in, lungs still struggling for air. My heartbeat needed another couple minutes to calm down, too.

How had I gone from one orgasm in my entire lifetime to five in less than twenty-four hours?

But I suddenly understood why demons had spent all their time fucking since the Godsfalls.

"Fuck," I gasped, nearly breathing out the word.

Luc hummed. His fingers brushed a damp strand of hair from my cheek, untangling it from where it clung to my slick skin. Stars, the kings really did make every part of me sopping wet.

"Fuck indeed," Jules chuckled, still a little breathless. The mattress jostled as he moved. I peeked weakly over my shoulder, but I didn't really care what he did, too busy floating in a thick fog of bliss.

A hard length pressed against my side. I stiffened. Luc had come, his release still cooling on my skin, but he was already achingly hard again.

Something warm coiled around my wrists. I blinked. Daemium shadows from the bedframe weaved between my arms—

The shadows tugged.

I suddenly slid up Luc's body until my nose brushed his. My eyes widened. The haze I floated in vanished, ripped away by pure shock. Luc smirked at my expression. The shadows twined higher, wrapping my arms above my head, holding me aloft by the four posters of the bed.

Jules's hands settled on my hips. He twisted me around, shifting me with ease. My body moved like putty in his hands. His cock, still slick and faintly smeared with my blood, brushed against my thigh. The shadows continued twirling down my arms, around my neck, around my shoulder.

The top of my head bumped the King of Dusk's chin. Freed from the press of my body, his cock bounced beneath me, the thick tip tracing my wet center.

I shuddered. Jules's pupils dilated as Luc groaned.

"What...?" I croaked out the word through dry lips.

Luc's breath brushed my ear. "You don't belong to Jules alone, little curiosity. You're *ours*."

Jules slipped his hands under my knees, hooking my legs over Luc's bent legs. I was sprawled wide, indecently exposed. He traced one hand along my inner thighs before gripping Luc's cock. He stroked the King of Dusk once. Twice.

Luc growled, growing even harder beneath me.

Jules's grin turned sharp, almost maniacal. He lined Luc up with my entrance. "I'm quite proud of my cock, but Luc's going to split you right open."

My jaw dropped. Oh, stars, I couldn't—

Fingers looped through the back of my collar, through a chain I'd thought was decorative. But it wasn't. It was a starsdamned *handle*—

Luc jerked me down.

I yelped as the head of his cock speared into me. The King of Dawn had the longer cock, but he didn't match the King of Dusk's girth. A deep ache flared through me, stretching, burning. I strained against the shadows binding me, but they didn't give. I couldn't do anything as Luc dragged me down, Jules's hands on my hips guiding me onto his cock.

The first of his piercing slipped into me, rubbing against my inner walls. My yelp turned into a long whine.

"That's it," Luc murmured against my neck. "You can take me."

A second bar of metal slipped into me. My eyes rolled back. Stars, I'd thought Jules had stretched me, but Luc *stretched* me. If I'd taken the King of Dusk first, I might have died.

And with every inch Luc claimed, I still wasn't sure I wouldn't.

Could a person be fucked to death?

His third piercing pressed inside. I whimpered, shaking. Fuck, how many were left? Five in total, I thought. One every two or so inches.

Jules's bright gaze flickered from my eyes to where Luc disappeared inside me. "You're doing so well, wife."

The fourth piercing breached me. Tension spread through my body. I cried out—

Luc tightened his grip on my collar. The sound cut off. For a second, my *air* cut off. My eyes rolled back.

His fifth piercing pushed in, ever so slowly...

My ass bounced against his thighs. At the exact same moment, Luc loosened his grip. I sucked in a deep breath. My cunt spasmed around him.

The Conqueror was buried deep inside me.

Luc groaned, his head dropping to my shoulder. "Fuck."

A smear of gold dust brushed his chin. I didn't even think. I turned my head, my tongue snaking out. I licked the gold from his chin. It was sweet against my tongue, almost like a berry.

His dark eyes flashed to me, just in my periphery, the beast stalking me, out of sight. They promised sin. They promised bliss.

"See?" Jules released my hips and grazed his fingers through my cunt, to where Luc speared into me. The King of Dusk and I shuddered as one at the featherlight touch. "She's divine."

Jules's voice dropped lower, thick with something dark and wicked. "And I'm going to use her divine cunt to fuck the life out of both of you."

That was all the warning I had. The shadows tightened. They yanked me off Luc's cock—and then slammed me back down.

A sharp cry tore from my throat. Luc's piercings ground against my inner walls, every metal bar hitting that spot deep inside me. I shuddered. Luc tightened his hold on the back of my neck.

My head lolled back against Luc's chest as Jules slid me up and down, using the daemium shadows to fuck me onto the King of Dusk. He watched with glee. His dark gaze flickered from our faces to my bouncing breasts to the place where Luc stretched me wide. The King of Dawn's blood-stained erection thickened at the sight.

"Julien."

Jules stopped at just his name. I sank further onto the King of Dusk's cock, but the shadows didn't pull me up.

Luc's hands settled on my hips, his grip firm, possessive. His fingers curled into my soft curves, his thumbs resting just at the swell of my ass.

They tightened as he thrust me down onto him, mirroring Jules's pace. I yelped.

Ah.

Ah.

Ah!

Luc bounced me on his cock. Harder. Harder. I was screaming, sobbing, shaking against the shadowy restraints. Fuck, I couldn't do this. I couldn't survive—

Jules dropped his fingers to my clit.

I almost passed out. I almost died. My spine arched, a strangled gasp wrenching from my chest.

Jules leaned down and kissed me. The silver dust on his lips melted against my tongue, sweet and sinful. His thumb worked in slow circles, never lifting, never relenting.

I writhed.

I twisted.

Luc thrust.

Jules stroked.

This was the fucking end.

Jules's teeth found my lip, scraping the edge of pain. I sucked in a sharp breath, like I'd forgotten how. "Stay with us, Nessa."

"I don't..." Neither king slowed their pace. Not the fingers on my clit. Not the cock driving into me. I clawed for words, gripping them in desperation. My entire body clenched with the effort.

Luc growled as my cunt squeezed him, an inhuman sound. Oh, gods, why did that make me wetter?

I gasped, but Jules swallowed the sound.

"It's too much," I rasped against his lips.

Jules grinned. "You can take it."

"I can't."

Luc kissed my ear. "Shall we grant you mercy?"

"Luc—ahh." His name escaped my lips in a broken whine.

"You *will* come for us."

"Oh, stars."

Luc lowering his hands, gripping my ass and smearing silver-gold dust. He pulled one of my thighs up from where it rested over his leg. Jules pulled back, gripped my calf. He bent his head and brushed his lips against my skin, then his tongue. He licked a slow, deliberate swath of gold from my leg. His fingers didn't stop their dance between my legs.

Luc's angle shifted, his piercings rubbing against every nerve inside me—

Fuck, I was going to come again. "Fuck, fuck, oh, fuck."

Jules chuckled. That one breath tipped me over the edge. My entire body tensed—

Jules's teeth sank into my calf at the same moment Luc's fangs pierced my neck.

My world exploded into three. The force of it nearly knocked me out. I arched, spine bowing, fingers clawing into my palms. My cunt clenched down as Luc's seed flushed into me. As Jules came hot and wet across my stomach. Blood trickled down my skin, mingling with smeared dust and cum.

Luc lapped and sucked at my throat, slow and thorough, drinking me down. Jules mirrored him, his lips and teeth at my ankle. With each swallow, more of their venom flooded me, flooded them. It stretched out the pleasure, made it endless.

I bucked, writhing beneath their mouths, but the shadows at my arms and the hands on my waist held me still. The King of Dusk's palm found my throat, pressing me down. Holding me exactly where he wanted me. I struggled—

His grip firmed, cutting off my air.

If I fought too hard, he'd choke me.

I went slack.

Gripped by pleasure. Letting myself drown.

I shattered into specks, like the smears of silver and gold on our skin.

I sunk back down to reality. Into warm skin. The silk of sheets. The familiar rumble of two voices.

My vision focused from the haze of bliss on something glittering and gold. The ceiling. I sprawled between them, my body a limp, exhausted weight against the sheets. My chest puffed with my slow breaths. If the mirrored surface weren't gold, I'd bet my body was flushed red beneath the glittering dust.

I should have been ashamed.

But all I felt was—

Safe.

Held.

Claimed.

Jules slid a blanket of black silk over my hips.

My blinks slowed.

I drifted into warm, gentle darkness.

# INTERLUDE 2

*I lazed against the headboard and raised my goblet to my lips. Blood wine coated my tongue—smooth and full-bodied, carrying the warmth of spiced oak. Jules had always favored the vineyards in the eastern reaches of the Impire, where the wines were laced with florals, but I had long preferred the vintages of the south.*

*Until recently.*

*The sweetness of blood lingered as always, but the only flavor I craved now was our bride.*

*"She bled even more on your cock than she did mine."*

*I arched a brow at Jules. My soulbound leaned against the bedpost, a half-full bottle dangling from his grip. Moonlight turned the sheen of glitter and sweat on his hard, sculpted ivory skin into a dewy glow.*

*He was fucking perfection.*

*"Lucey?" My gaze flicked up his body to darkening gold eyes. "You're ogling."*

*I sipped my blood wine again. "Are you not mine to ogle?"*

*Jules grinned slowly. Still gripping the bottle, he crawled across our bed until he kneeled before me. His gaze dipped to the sleeping human at my side, her shoulder brushing against my thigh.*

*Nessa remained slack in the depths of sleep, her face smooth, her brilliant copper hair a tangled mess beneath her. Jules had tossed a sheet across her lower half earlier, but her stomach and breasts remained bare. Her nipples were red from where we had sucked, the remaining dust on her chest smeared with sweat.*

*"She's certainly ours to ogle," Jules said, his gaze just as fixed on our bride.*

*"She's certainly ours." If our bride hadn't passed out straight after coming on my cock, we'd have fucked her until dawn. I craved her small, soft body*

*pinned under me, her fingers twisted in the sheets, and her cries echoing through Dawnspear's gilded halls.*

*But humans were fragile creatures. Sleeping every night, their bodies folding under pleasure long before ours would. It was an incompatibility we'd have to work around.*

*But we'd break her in soon enough.*

*Perhaps I'd wake her in an hour for her first lesson—*

*Jules reached out and ran his finger along my cock. I twitched at the touch, but kept myself soft as he swirled through the red-streaked wetness drenching my shaft. "Do you think she'll bleed every time we fuck her?"*

*She had so far, whether it was our tongues, fingers, or cocks inside her. I had fucked my fair share of virgins over the centuries, but none had bled quite like our bride. But none of those virgins had experienced pain at the first sign of stress or arousal. The soothing rune had kept it pleasurable for her, if her whimpers and the waves of bliss pulsing through our new bond were any indication, but it wasn't a cure.*

*"Probably," I said, my voice all rasp. "We should consult a healer."*

*"That wasn't what I was saying." Jules raised his stained finger and sucked it into his mouth, his lips closing around his knuckle. With a wet pop, he pulled it free. "But you're right. She's our soulbound now. It'd be cruel to make her spend an eternity in pain just so we can lick the blood from her cunt daily."*

*This time, I didn't bother stopping the rush of blood to my cock. "It would be, wouldn't it?"*

*"At least human women bleed monthly." Jules lifted the bottle to his lips, taking a long, indulgent swig before holding it out to me. "Still, I can't waste this opportunity."*

*I stared at the wine for a moment. When he didn't pull it back, I plucked it from his grasp.*

*My soulbound reached back, tied his golden-white hair into a knot at the base of his neck, and then lowered his head—*

*Until my cock was in his mouth.*

*A low groan escaped my throat. His tongue glided against the underside of my length, swirling around my piercings as he took me deeper. Deeper. His lips sealed around my base, the tip of me nudging into his throat. I dropped my head back against the daemium headboard.*

*Then Jules sucked hard, devouring our bride's desire and blood from my skin.*

*Pressure built in my palm, my fingers curling too tight. The bottle cracked. Then splintered. Then shattered. Fuck. Wine and glass splattered. Our bride was on my other side, so the mess only fell onto our silk sheets. The runes woven into the fabric absorbed it instantly.*

*I barely noticed. Jules's mouth was still on me. His tongue slid slow and deliberate along me, lapping up the remnants of blood and wine as if savoring both. My hips twitched up, but he took my length easily, letting me sink deeper like I had a thousand times before.*

*Slowly, Jules dragged his mouth up, stretching around my sensitive tip before releasing me. He licked a stray drop of red from his lips and pouted. "That was my favorite red."*

*"I'll buy you another." My skin had already healed the damage from the glass, but I wrapped my wet fist around my length and stroked, spreading a fresh sheen of bloody wine. "Take me back into your mouth, Julien."*

*"You're not the boss of me, Lucey." But my King of Dawn smiled as he said it. He grabbed the goblet from my other hand, swallowed the remaining wine with one gulp, and tossed it over his head. It clanged in the distance, but our bride didn't stir from her sex-induced slumber.*

*Jules dropped his head back down and wrapped that infuriating mouth around me.*

*I sank back into the pillows as his head began to bob. Perhaps I'd let our bride sleep through the night. She could use the rest. Poor, little thing had already had four orgasms in the last couple hours.*

*Jules and I could entertain ourselves well enough until she recovered.*

I DRIFTED AWAKE, THE world returning in fragments as the vivid dream faded. Curling onto my side, I buried my face in plush sheets. Tingles ran up my skin, dancing from my spine to the languid muscles in my back. They settled low, between my legs, a slow, insistent throb. It wasn't a painful sensation, but I had never felt anything like it before. I shifted my hips, pushing up a leg—

Discomfort flared through me.

From *between* my legs.

From where the kings had hollowed out a place inside me for their *cocks*.

My eyes shot open. Morning light danced across the black sheets tangled around my limbs in a massive daemium bed. The Imperium's bed. The night returned in a rush, a blur of bliss, sweat, and shuddering breaths.

Blood rushed to my cheeks.

Oh, stars. I fucked two beautiful, terrifying, alluring vampire kings.

Or, more accurately, had been fucked by them. It wasn't like I had done much more than scream as Jules first pounded into me and then bounced me on Luc's impossibly thick cock.

I had enjoyed every second of it.

I threaded my fingers through my mess of brown hair and tugged. Shit. The ache between my legs pulsed in time with my heartbeat, a constant reminder of what had happened.

Of who had been inside me.

I pressed my palms against my face. It changed nothing, right? It was just a little sex. People had sex all the time. I was now one of those people.

I, Nessa Halloran, who had spent the last decade hiding in my bookshop in pain, had been railed by two vampires into multiple mind-blowing, sleep-inducing orgasms—

*Stop thinking about it.*

This couldn't change anything. This *didn't* change anything. I was still the Mortal Bride, a living sacrifice and home to the Impire's most important spell. The kings had forced me from my shop, my sister, my life like they did hundreds of Maboni every year. Vampires were terrible, evil creatures who killed millions, including my mother.

Probably. The kings had said they'd find her. But not because they were helping me out of kindness or affection. They wanted to know who had cast the soulbond and why. Nothing more.

I inhaled to calm my wild heart—

And nearly moaned. The sheets smelled of smoked honey and thick spice, sweat and sex. It smelled like *them*. Obviously. The kings hadn't only fucked me. After I fell asleep, the debauchery had continued.

Flashes of the dream returned.

Luc's back against the headboard, goblet of blood wine in hand.

Jules kneeling between his legs, pale hair tied in a knot.

The lazy glow of moonlight glinting off damp skin, the slow drag of a pierced tongue along a pierced length.

The softness of Jules's hair on my knuckles and the tug of Luc's fingers in my scalp as the Conqueror held the Butcher steady, guiding him deeper.

I shook my head. I needed to get out of here. But their scent wasn't just on the sheets. It clung to me, from the dried sweat on my skin to the...

To the unmistakable stain of our combined *pleasure* streaking my inner thighs, tinged pink with my blood.

A bath. That would solve it.

I rolled onto my side and crawled toward the bed's edge, eyes locked on the door leading to the kings' bathing chamber. I didn't know if it was mine to use, but right now, I didn't care. Nothing would stand in my way—

"Going somewhere, little curiosity?"

My throat went dry. My nipples hardened. A flutter tightened my stomach. Pressure increased between my legs. I turned ever so slowly toward the sound of that alluring voice, already knowing what I'd find. As soon as the question formed in my mind, I *sensed* them.

Across the expanse of fine carpets before the bed, Luc and Jules sat around the cozy circular table. The King of Dusk clutched a book in his hand, a silver ring once again on each finger. Every strand of his blue-black curls lay perfectly in place, the silver buttons on his dark violet doublet fastened all the way to his throat.

Across the table, Jules had an open sketchbook propped against the table's edge, resting on his crossed legs. His pale blond hair was swept into a messy bun, and his maroon robe hung loosely at his middle, the belt barely tied, exposing a sliver of his perfect chest.

Those bright silver and gold eyes were already fixed on me.

They probably had been since the moment I awoke.

I swallowed. "I just... to the bathing chamber?"

I didn't mean for it to be a question, but it became one anyway. Luc arched a dark brow. My heartbeat stuttered.

"I have to pee and..." I waved a hand vaguely, my face heating even more "...bathe."

"No." Luc returned to his reading, flipping to the next page.

I stiffened. "You can't just—"

"Just what?" Jules cut in, tilting his head. "Mark you? Claim you? Lovely, that's exactly what we *plan* to do daily."

I gritted my teeth. "You don't get to decide how I smell."

"Don't we?" Luc asked.

"So if I try to bathe, you'll stop me?"

"Not at all. But if you wash our scents off you, we'll be forced to reapply them." Luc's gaze flicked to mine, intent. "And given our packed schedule today, we'll only have a half-hour to do so."

"I don't think our sweet bride is ready for that, Lucey," Jules said, twirling his pencil through his fingers, the movement quick, dexterous. "If she thought one-on-one was overwhelming, how would she survive two-on-one? We'd have to carry her limp body around for the rest of the day."

"But I'm... sticky." Even if I ignored the sweat and cum, glitter smeared across my neck, breasts and stomach.

"Sticky?" Jules repeated with a slow grin.

I bristled. "Oh, fuck off."

Jules suddenly leaned over me, close enough that our noses nearly touched. "How about I fuck you again instead?"

I yelped and clutched a sheet to my chest, even though the kings had seen every inch of me.

"If you think you're sticky now, give us that half-hour and we'll show you sticky."

I forced my expression into a glare. The kings had cleaned the night from their skin, a flawless bronze and ivory, but they'd force me to walk around reeking of sex. Reeking of *them.*

That sounded exactly like something they'd do, didn't it?

"I don't like being dirty."

Luc turned another page. "You aren't dirty. You're scent-marked."

Blood rushed to my cheeks. The kings had claimed me as Azaras had Karra, scent-marking me with their cum like I was their possession. Because I was *their* possession. The small parts of me that had succumbed to the soulbond hummed in satisfaction. But the rest of me was embarrassed and confused and panicked and enraged.

I swallowed down every rampant emotion. "For how long?"

"You can bathe tonight." Jules stretched back to full height and slid his pencil into the groove above his ear. My gaze dropped to his exposed chest, the muscles rippling faintly with the simple movement. "We should have more than enough time after that to mark you again."

Heat rushed from my face down my neck, creeping lower. *Focus, Nessa.* I forced my expression into a glare, but my displeasure wouldn't change anything. The kings had made up their minds. I was their soulbound, but I had little sway over them. I was just a warm body to house their spell, their soul, and now their cocks.

Exalted Morrena's implication that I could change things in the Azarasian Impire seemed even more ridiculous in the light of day.

Jules held out his hand. "Join us."

Join them? I frowned... and only then did I notice the food on the table. Croissants sat in a gilded basket beside a platter of soft cheese and cured meat. A small dish held eggs, their tops cracked open to reveal golden yolks. Nearby, steam curled from a delicate porcelain pot, the scent unmistakable. Coffee, a delicacy from the east. Aislin had tried it once, a gift from the magistrates at her wedding to Donal.

It was a breakfast fit for kings, extravagant and excessive.

Hunger crashed into me. My belly growled, the sound echoing through the room. Luc didn't react, but an unnerving twinkle entered Jules's eye. "I do love a woman with an insatiable appetite."

"I'm hardly insatiable," I muttered.

"No?" His grin widened, all teeth. "Then what was all that begging about last night?"

Heat surged up from my chest. I swallowed hard, willing my body to stay still, willing my already overheated face not to betray me even more. I raised my chin ever slightly.

Jules found my prim response endearing, if the deepening of his grin was any indicator. He wiggled his fingers.

With a sigh, I placed my hand in his. There wasn't any other option. Sparks flared to life where our skin met. I leaned into the touch.

One night, and I was addicted.

Straightening my shoulders, I pushed to a stand, wrapping the bedsheet around me—

"Leave the sheet," Luc said impassively.

I froze for a moment. *They've already seen every inch of you, idiot.* With a slow exhale, I let the sheet flutter down beside me.

Luc's gaze dropped, unhurried, to my breasts, my hips, the curve of my ass. Jules's eyes didn't even flick past my nipples. But both their irises darkened, silver and gold swallowed by hunger.

I cleared my throat.

Bright eyes flicked back to me. Jules cocked his brows. "Yes, wife?"

My shoulders tensed. I couldn't deny that word, not any longer. We might not have married, but the only man a Maboni woman touched like I had the kings was her husband. "I thought we were on a tight schedule."

He sighed and led me to the table. "I guess."

"You don't guess, Julien," Luc said, flipping another page with infuriating calmness. "You know."

"Ignore him. He's not a morning person."

I snorted. The Conqueror wasn't a morning person? What an asinine thing to know. "And you are?"

Jules hooked his foot around a stool and dragged it out for me. "I'm an anytime person."

I gingerly dropped into the seat, trying to keep my head held high despite sitting naked between two clothed kings. The ache between my legs flared as my ass sank into the cushioned seat. I flinched. How much pain would I be in without magic? I didn't want to imagine.

Without looking up from his book, Luc reached over and traced the shadowy lines of the rune on my arm. *Soothe.* The discomfort faded instantly, replaced only by the tingling heat of his skin against mine. My nipples peaked at the touch.

For once, neither of the kings had any sly remarks.

Luc nudged a teacup closer to my empty plate. "This will help, as well."

I plucked the porcelain from the table. Instead of coffee, dark red tea steamed in the cup, releasing a light floral scent. "What is it?"

"Willowroot tea," Luc said. "It has restorative properties. Most thralls drink it daily to counter blood loss and increase stamina."

Ah. While thralls had duties beyond serving their masters, not all seemed physically demanding. There was only one reason they'd need more stamina. "I see."

I took a sip, the warmth spreading through my chest. The taste was pleasant enough, but something lurked beneath the floral notes, something nearly bitter.

"Luc also spiked it with his blood," Jules added.

I almost choked. "He *what*?"

Jules snorted. "You'll get used to it. After all, you'll be drinking our blood for the rest of your life."

"Why?"

Jules met my gaze and grinned. "You're mortal, remember?"

I blinked at him. Right. That.

The soulbond tied our *lives* together.

Karra had been a witch, but she had still been mortal. Her lifespan was measured in centuries, unlike Azaras's eternity. If Karra couldn't kill herself to kill the demon king, all she had to do was stay away from him until she aged and died. And he would have, even if he were in perfect health.

But I didn't see how drinking blood would solve that issue.

It was like Luc heard the question. "Drinking our blood will halt your aging, like Azaras's blood did for Karra."

"I've only read Volume I," I said faintly. "I haven't gotten to that part of the story."

"Give us a spoiler warning next time, Lucey," Jules said, flicking his pencil across the table.

Luc caught the pencil without looking and tossed it right back.

I ignored their antics. Boys. "So vampire blood makes mortals immortal?"

"Not all vampire blood," Luc said. "Blood from a vampire of average power can only heal a mortal's illnesses and wounds."

"But *your* blood...?"

"Will make you effectively immortal."

I nodded, my head bobbing slowly for far longer than it should.

*Immortal.*

The word settled in my gut like a stone. I had spent years preparing for death. The harvest, the unknown fate that awaited me in the Impire, the certainty of becoming a blood thrall—I had made peace with all of it, because I had to.

Now?

Now, I would never die. Not naturally. Not in a few decades, not even in a few centuries.

Eternal. Unchanging.

Just like them.

My stomach twisted. I would outlive my sister. Outlive her children. *Their* children. Would I even remember Aislin's face in a hundred years? Would she still be real to me when time stretched so long I couldn't see its end?

A shiver crawled through me. I had never wanted to be their Mortal Bride. But at least mortality had given me an escape from the pain, whether emotional or physical.

There was no escape from this.

I pressed my lips together, setting the cup down before I could taste the blood in it again. Jules was still grinning. Luc was still reading. Like the entire world hadn't just shifted beneath my feet.

I exhaled sharply and reached for a pastry instead.

Because what else was there to do?

The room drifted into a somehow comfortable silence. Jules rubbed the base of his pencil against his temple, his gaze as intent on his sketchbook as Luc's was on his book. Was this how they spent every morning? It was surprisingly peaceful, almost mundane, for two vampires known as the Conqueror and the Butcher.

I should have welcomed the quiet, the peace, but my foot jiggled as I bit into the pastry. I wasn't comfortable in this new life. This new *immortal* life. Who knew if I ever would be?

I tilted my head, my gaze catching on the spine of Luc's book. *Irrevocable Tethers: The Magical, Biological, and Psychological Consequences of Soulbonding* by Crown Mage Rafael Valcázar. Consequences? What consequences? A prickle of unease tightened my throat.

I knew the author's name, though. Rafael was in *The Soulborne Queen*. As Azaras's Crown Mage, he'd witnessed the first soulbond. Studied it. Warned Azaras how it would change him. My fingers curled against my thigh.

Rather intense reading for the morning.

On my other side, Jules had his sketchbook once again propped at an angle, only the vague impression of lines visible from my seat. I leaned forward—

"Nah-ah, no peeking." He pulled his sketchbook closer until I couldn't see a thing. "It's not done yet."

Fair enough. Aislin had been the same way, refusing to show me the gowns she made until they were finished.

A pang shot through my chest. It had been a little over a week since the harvest. Now that I was the kings' soulbound, would I get to see my sister again? Or was I still doomed to the fate of every thrall, parted from their loved ones forever?

But if they let me visit home, what would I even say? I had fucked the Conqueror and the Butcher, our terrifying, unholy Imperium. Only once, sure, but given it would take a week to get there, we'd easily be in the double digits by then. Maybe even triple. The bond pulsed between my legs already, a damning reminder.

I was their Mortal Bride, their eternal blood thrall. And I wanted to hate it, needed to hate it, couldn't hate it, and *did* hate it all in one breath.

I was finally the wicked, sinful whore my stepmother always thought I was.

I shook my head sharply. It didn't matter right now. I pulled apart a croissant and scrambled for any topic that would stop my thoughts of home and damnation. "What's on this packed schedule of yours?"

"There's an execution at half past ten," Luc said. "Then our bondnephew, Rosier, has his bond rite ceremony—"

"*Our* bondnephew?" I had flinched at the mention of an execution, but now I twisted toward Jules. "Isn't he your blood nephew?"

"Yes, which makes him your and Luc's bondnephew."

I opened my mouth... and snapped it closed. I now had more claim to the young Prince of Dawn than his own mother did.

I flinched inwardly at the thought of Maire. The way she had stared at me last night returned to me vividly. Maire and I weren't friends. We'd had a handful of conversations. But we were both humans in an empire ruled by monsters. A *world* ruled by monsters. I had thought her an ally. She obviously had, as well.

But last night, I looked like the Conqueror and Butcher's pampered thrall, wearing their gems and begging for their touches. In her mind, just as bad as Odran.

If only she knew how much worse it was.

Maybe today she'd find out. "Am I attending all these events with you?"

"Did you have other plans?" Luc asked sardonically.

"No." I hadn't really thought much about what I'd do in this new life. I had spent the first half of yesterday in survival mode and the second half wildly and inappropriately aroused.

Today, my survival was almost guaranteed... as was my arousal. The second I refused to consider. But the first opened a world of possibilities, ones I had never allowed myself to consider. Wishing for the impossible only brought pain and misery. I had let go of all my dreams a decade ago, so long ago that I couldn't even remember what they were.

There were too many unknowns to start dreaming again right away. Who had cast the soulbond on me? What did they want? What would they do next? What would the *kings* do next? But what I did know was that I didn't want to spend my new life being paraded around. Yesterday and the night before had been difficult enough.

I needed time alone to think.

"But no one besides your council and guard knows I'm your soulbound," I said. "Won't someone get suspicious?"

"You're our Mortal Bride and thrall."

Damn. That was a yes. I stabbed my fork into a slice of poached pear. "Doesn't your Mortal Bride usually stay in your apartment?"

Luc closed his book and set it carefully on the table. "Who told you that?"

"It—" I almost said Éamon.

Stars, I had fucked his murderers.

I pushed down the sudden burst of panic... or maybe the soulbond did. Either way, I let it go. The kings couldn't harm Éamon anymore, but they would know if I lied.

And I couldn't watch Maire die, too. "Does it matter?"

"We didn't always bring our past Mortal Brides with us, but not because we were hiding them," Jules said with a small frown at me. "If someone tried to break the covenant runespell, I just killed them."

I shuddered. Of course. The Butcher wouldn't turn down an opportunity to cut someone into pieces.

A gentle knock sounded at the door.

I went stiff. Dozens of the thralls had seen me naked yesterday morning, but today was different. With one look at my tangled hair and dust-smeared body, whoever was at the door would know the kings had fucked me.

Luc watched me intently, his eyes not even flickering to the door when he said, "Come in, Tristan."

"But..." I started.

"But?" Luc repeated.

"It's just..." I glanced down at my lap on habit, but that only made things worse. My thighs were a mess. "It's very... obvious and—I—it—"

Luc arched a brow. "It?"

I stammered. "I—you—we—"

Jules put me out of my misery. "They already know Luc and I fucked you. I'm sure all of Dawnspear knows." His smile grew wide, wicked. "You're quite the screamer."

My flush spread through every inch of my face.

After a moment of silence, the double doors clicked open, like Tristan had waited for us to finish. He stepped through and bowed. Behind him, Maire and Riona dropped to their knees as Estrella mirrored her soulbound from where she stood behind the thralls.

All of them remained that way even as Tristan said, "Your bride's attendants, as requested, Imperium."

"You may rise." The vampires did as Luc commanded, but Maire and Riona stayed on their knees.

"Maire and Riona will dress you for the day." Luc glanced at the thralls, every bit of heat in his gaze freezing. "You may wash her face, but nothing else."

"Yes, Your Majesty," they both murmured instantly.

"We leave in fifteen minutes."

I remained seated until four pairs of bright eyes focused on me.

Luc tilted his head, a slow, assessing look. "But if you insist, we can clear our schedule."

Jules grinned. "I love spending all day in bed."

I jolted to my feet. "I didn't say that."

"Then go," Jules said. "If you stand there any longer, you'll end up face first on the table with a cock in your cunt." He winked at Luc. "Whose, I'm not sure. I guess it depends on who's faster."

I glared, but stepped away from the table. "You don't need to be so crude."

Maire's eyes ricocheted up to me in shock. She must have thought me insane to speak to the Butcher that way.

"I don't," Jules admitted. "But it's quite entertaining to watch you flush."

With a final glare, I turned on my heels and marched for the Mortal Bride's bedchamber. Chills slivered down my back as too many eyes focused on my bare skin. But I didn't run or scream. I kept my head held high until I pushed through the door into the small room.

The moment it closed behind me, my knees almost buckled.

I pressed my back against the wall and closed my eyes. Breathe in. Breathe out. The kings were no longer watching me, but I wasn't alone. I wouldn't ever be alone again. Even if Maire, Riona, and Estrella hadn't followed behind me, two faint presences hovered in the back of my mind. I frowned, trying to shrug off the ghostly sensation, but they didn't fade.

It wasn't my imagination.

It was the soulbond settling into my bones.

"My lady?" Maire asked hesitantly.

I flinched and turned to her. Riona stood at her side, Estrella lingering near the doorframe. Past them, I caught sight of my reflection in the mirror.

I thought I'd look different. Changed. But I was exactly the same, if slightly more mussed and only wearing my collar and a skirt of tangled chains. Gold and silver dust smeared across my skin, nipples, and inner thighs nearly bare of the glitter. There weren't any marks on my skin, as if the kings hadn't bitten me as I clenched down on Luc's cock.

I shuddered.

Maire's eyes flicked down my body, then back to my face. Her mouth opened, then shut. Her expression softened with... pity? She should hate me, hate everything I represented.

But she didn't know I was a traitor to my people, to all humans trapped on this cursed world overrun by demons and their monstrous spawn.

There was something else in her expression, too. A question she wouldn't dare ask.

The kings didn't treat their Mortal Brides this way.

She might not know why yet, but she would soon.

*Everyone* would soon.

I swallowed. My hands clenched into fists.

"It's alright, my lady," Maire said, misreading my panic. "Let's get you dressed."

But Maire didn't know.

It wasn't alright.

And I wasn't sure it ever would be again.

# 35

SHADOWS ENVELOPED MY SKIN as I followed Luc through a runegate into the heart of Montaurère. My slippered feet pressed into polished limestone, a stark contrast from the soft rugs of the kings' apartment. A rush of brightness blurred my vision. I blinked hard, stepping to Luc's side, disoriented by the shift in light.

My stomach clenched like a thread pulled taut. Not nausea. Not quite. But something close. Luc's palm settled against the small of my back. My body started to relax before I even noticed, but the moment I did, I stiffened.

Luc didn't acknowledge it. He only let his hand linger, like it belonged there.

Around me, the city stirred. Voices melded together in a pleasant hum, blending with the distant clatter of wheels over stone, the rhythmic footsteps of a waking city.

When my vision cleared, I inhaled sharply.

The runegate exited into a bustling square. The daemium surface was embedded in the base of a grand statue, a stern-looking vampire warrior frozen in stone. Gilded buildings of pale stone gleamed beneath the morning light, so pristine they nearly hurt my eyes. Flashes of color broke the endless white—burgundy awnings shading storefronts, scarlet gowns draped in window displays, maroon shutters over wrought-iron balconies. Manicured greenery softened the stark perfection, placed at careful intervals.

All around us, vampires moved through the square and the winding streets criss-crossing the mountainside with effortless grace. Clad in silks and embroidered brocades, they were as unbothered by their Imperium's arrival as the High Courts had been last night. Collared thralls in black followed their masters with bowed heads.

"That's exactly how I looked the first time I saw Montaurère." Jules stepped from the runegate behind us. He draped an arm around my shoulders, hard muscle encased in silk.

I snapped my jaw shut.

Luc hadn't moved his hand from my back. Now they were both touching me, one a lingering weight at the base of my spine and the other wrapped lazily across my shoulders.

My heart nearly imploded.

Jules's waist-length cape brushed against my back as we started forward. The crimson silk was embroidered with golden thread, gems glittering along the seams. On top of his usual rings, heavy teardrop earrings, and gilded daggers, strung rubies encircled his wrists and a golden bar pierced the rim of his ear, capped with tiny pearls.

The King of Dawn was as ostentatious as his city.

And just like his city, he was the preface to death.

A twinge shot through my belly, neither sharp nor dull. Stars. Not now. Was Luc's new soothing rune wearing off already? I exhaled through my nose, slow and steady.

This was nothing more than a walk through a city out of a storybook, accompanied by two gorgeous vampires who had never, ever harmed a soul. I was here of my own will. My body was *not* on the verge of panic. My insides weren't unraveling.

What would I say if that fiction were true? If I weren't heading toward an execution on the arms of the Imperium? If the men on either side of me were simply showing me their beautiful city?

"Were you not raised here?" I asked, forcing my voice steady.

There was too long a pause between Jules's comment and my reply, but he ignored the awkward silence. "Luc and I were born in Tenebra de Mar and spent our first half-century there. Azaras was one kingdom in name only then, our two halves ruled by opposing regents left in charge by the Beast King. There wasn't much travel between the cities."

I glanced at Luc on my other side, the dark violet of his doublet resplendent in the sunshine. He had strapped his axe to his back. It was the first time I had seen the terrifying weapon since we arrived in the city. "Even for their king's son?"

"Maybe if I were only Azaras's son," Luc said. "But I was also Marisol's grandson, so Alphonse never sent a formal invitation."

Alphonse must have been Montaurère's former regent. He wasn't in *The Soulborne Queen* like Marisol. "So you just showed up?"

A small smirk curved the King of Dusk's lips. "With a retinue of intoxicated courtiers and thralls, not a warrior in sight. I grew tired of the insult and thought to deliver one right back."

"Luc demanded entry at the gate," Jules said. "Alphonse took one look at him, decided he didn't want to die, and treated us like treasured, expected guests." He released a wistful sigh. "Ah, the good old days. I can't shock anyone with my power like that anymore. The one downside to having a reputation. Rue the day you have one."

"Me?" I nearly squealed. No. I wouldn't ever have a reputation. Not like the Conqueror and the Butcher.

The Bookworm didn't quite have the same ring.

"Who else?" Jules asked, waving at the empty space around. Estrella and Tristan followed distantly behind. "It's just you, me and Luc, lovely."

I shot him an exasperated glare. Like I needed the reminder. All the passing vampires bowed low, murmuring *Imperium*, but none approached. One or two pairs had started to approach, only to flare their nostrils and not dare any closer.

I didn't even need to ask why. The emerald gown I wore was a similar cut to the white one from the harvest feast, but the slits up the front and back were higher, almost to my navel. With every step, the layered fabric parted. Not enough for anyone to see anything, but enough for air to brush against my stained thighs. It was a constant reminder to everyone—including me—that I was scent-marked.

Riona had snuck me a towel, but she hadn't dared put any water on it. I had merely rubbed my sweat and slick and the kings' cum into my skin. I didn't know why I bothered. The Azarasians clearly still smelled the kings on me.

I'd be lucky to end up the Bookworm. Right now, I was the Conqueror and Butcher's Whore. "Whatever my reputation, I'm sure it will pale in comparison to yours."

"Maybe," Jules said. "But maybe not. Wouldn't that be fun?"

I aimed a frown at Jules, but the King of Dawn only winked at me. I twisted away, facing forward.

We approached another square, where Azarasians lounged on stone benches and vendors called out from painted carts of carved wood, hawking sweet treats and sizzling meats. I let my gaze wander. The people. The buildings. The colors, the clothes. I drank in the foreign sights—

My gaze landed on a massive falling star carved into white stone.

Nausea welled in my gut. Out of all things I'd expected to see in the vampire capital, a church wasn't one of them. Maire wore a pendant with the falling star and had mentioned thralls who worshipped all demonbloods as gods, but I never thought they'd have a church in the city's center.

The star burned into me. I shriveled under its eyes. Even though it was falling instead of rising, I was back in the Corraidin church before the godstar murals. Kneeling for hours as Patriarch Meallán droned on, while my stepmother and sister prayed fervently beside me.

And now I stood before the star stained with vampire cum.

A sinner, come before the godstars's light to be judged.

How could I have ever contemplated going home? I barely tolerated walking past a church. No one had ever returned to Corraidin after becoming a thrall, but if they had, I could easily imagine the reception they'd receive.

I was now broken, marred, and *used*. I would be shamed out of town.

My insides twisted, a hard wrench.

The kings' hands tensed on me. I jolted, giving my head a sharp shake. I should have pulled away from their touches, but the soulbond didn't think it was anything out of the ordinary. If anything, my wiggle of anxiety eased when the kings tucked me tighter between them.

*Breathe, Nessa.* I meant the words to be in my voice, but it was Luc's that whispered through me. The pounding need that thudded through the bond like a constant drumbeat since I woke became all that harder to ignore. The memory of his hand around my throat as Jules rocked deeper and deeper into me filled my mind with alarming clarity—

"Nessa?"

My hands clenched together at my sides, anything to distract from the beat between my legs. "I'm fine."

For a second, the kings just watched me, seeing right through the indifference I wore. Then their expressions were gone, hidden under the Conqueror's impassive stare and the Butcher's playful grin.

For once, the kings wouldn't question me.

Perhaps because we had an audience.

Beneath my feet, veins of black daemium split through the pale limestone slabs as we entered the square. A small crowd of vampires gathered around a dark, smoking stage carved with runes. *Imprison. Shield. Endure.* In the center, two vampires were bound to a post with shadows, one a dark-haired, pale-skinned male and the other a brunette with a golden-brown tan. They looked vaguely familiar, but I hadn't paid much attention to yesterday's court session.

When their verdict was announced.

When their execution was announced.

I swallowed.

I couldn't pretend anymore. Today I'd watch even more people die.

As we approached the stage, the murmurs of the crowd faltered, the air thickening with anticipation. Vampires backed away and bowed, parting for their Imperium. I scanned the gathered vampires, looking for the executioner. Surely there was one. We didn't have the role in Mabon, as the magistrates were more than happy to handle any criminals. But it had been a position in the Beast King's time.

No one seemed to have any weapons.

Beyond the axe at Luc's back and the daggers at Jules's hips.

My throat went dry. "You're going on that stage, aren't you?"

The kings' gazes met over my head. "*We're* going on that stage," Luc corrected. "Our decision condemned them so it's only right we take their life, whether on their knees or their feet, weapon in hand."

"Wait, you're going to *fight* them?"

Luc ascended the stairs in a measured stride, his polished boots clicking against the daemium. The entire square sank into silence without a command from the Conqueror. "If they choose it."

"Most choose it," Jules added. "Those two certainly will. Not that it will be much of a fight."

The two prisoners stiffened at Jules's words as the crowd tittered. Their privacy runespell had likely muted most of our conversation, but everyone heard that last bit.

Jules stood aside for me to take the stairs before him. At the base, Estrella and Tristan settled into their places, standing guard. They didn't follow, their only duty to ensure no one else did either.

"Then why bother?"

"All citizens of the Azarasian Impire have the right to challenge us," Luc said, offering me a hand as I reached the top. "It's been centuries since anyone *not* slated for death has done so, but sentenced criminals have little left to lose."

Dozens of eyes tracked our every move, from Luc's fingers laced with mine to Jules slipping behind me. All I could focus on were the kings. "Do they have to fight both of you?"

"Usually Luc and I flip for it, but I'm oddly not in the mood for murder." Jules wrapped his arm around my shoulders again. "You can have them, Lucey."

"But it's daylight," I said, unsure why I was arguing. I couldn't be *worried* for the Conqueror. "He doesn't have all his power. That Dawn vampire does—"

"That Dawn vampire does not." Luc released my hand and unholstered his axe, shadows rising from the polished daemium of the blade. "When our citizens swear the allegiance runespell to the Impire, we don't demand their life like the Isaurans do. They join the covenant spell, gaining power and protection as long as they remain loyal. But if they break their oaths, they must return the strength we gave them."

The shadows holding the two prisoners dissipated into smoke. The dark-haired male with golden eyes remained standing, but his silver-eyed soulbound staggered forward. If I thought Sabas appeared tired, these two looked nearly human in their exhaustion. Not even their immortal beauty could counter the dull pallor of their skin and the dark circles around their eyes.

On the inner part of their forearm, runes blared with shadows. *Oath. Loyalty. Union. Transfer. Dusk. Dawn. Retribute.* It was in the same spot as Morrena's, but theirs looked freshly burned into the skin. Angry and raw. The retribution rune exacting its punishment.

"Then won't they die anyway?" I asked slowly. "Vampires need power to survive, right? You could simply wait for them to die."

Jules brushed his thumb along my skin, eliciting a shudder down my spine. "Where's the fun in that?"

"It's death," I said. "It's not *meant* to be fun."

"There's not a bloodthirsty cell in your body, is there?"

I glanced away. "That's not entirely true."

I had imagined my stepmother dead. Una. The magistrates. Donal, once or twice. Patriarch Meallán far more than that. Only in comparison to the kings did I look like a saint.

Jules turned his head, his lips against my ear. "Our cum doesn't count."

Blood burned through my face.

Luc stepped forward with his axe before him, the curved edge of the blade pointing between the two prisoners. "Mateo Herrera and Théodore Fontaine, you have been found guilty of treason against the Azarasian Impire. For the last seven years, you have worked with the anarchists to defy our nation, culminating in the deaths of six vampires and the destruction of the Dufresne Abattoir and its three thousand thralls.

"For these crimes, we have sentenced you to death." His deep voice was a crack of thunder through the square. "As is your right, if you disagree with our verdict, you may challenge us to combat, soulbond to soulbond."

My eyes widened. "Excuse me?" I whispered to Jules.

"To challenge one part of a soulbond is to challenge a soulbond in its whole," he said. "But the two of us only need to stand here, lovely. Luc will do all the work."

"Why bring me at all?"

"If we didn't, we'd be the ones breaking our allegiance runespell," Jules said. "I like being alive, so that's not an option."

The Dawn vampire, Mateo, lumbered forward, rage and hatred clear on his face. I had glared at Luc and Jules a dozen times over the last week, but at least I could blame the awakening soulbond spell for my bold insanity. These vampires had no such excuse.

Excluding their inevitable death at the kings' hands.

"Fuck you and your verdict." Mateo spat at Luc's feet, but his hands clenched at his sides, shaking. His fingers curled, then uncurled, like he was debating lunging now.

Before the kings could cut him down like a human.

Luc didn't react. He stared, the unflinching face of Death, of the Conqueror King. Mateo took the smallest step back toward his soulbound before clenching his fist tight and standing his ground.

But it was too late for that.

A smirk cracked the ice. "So be it."

I shuddered at the darkness in those words, in his expression. It was a movement echoed by every living creature in the square. But where terror rushed through them, intoxicating need flowed through me. I clenched my thighs together, forcing out an exhale. The swirl of stress, shame, and desire pressed against my ribs like a vise. It was like my body wanted to revolt.

A crack split the air as Luc rammed his axe into the ground. Shadows writhed where his daemium blade cut into the stage. If I thought it had been quiet before, it was nothing compared to now. Half the audience had stopped breathing, the prisoners among them.

Luc slowly walked around his axe and rolled his left sleeve to his elbow, followed by his right. The precise, methodical movements of a man utterly unconcerned.

"What's happening?"

Jules grinned down at me. "Lucey's pissed."

"Pick up your axe, bastard," Mateo snarled, but a tremor laced his voice. "We choose combat."

"I'm aware." Luc stretched out his hand as he approached, the confident gait of a predator. His voice lowered. "But you're not worthy of dying on my blade."

The tips of his fingers blackened, sharpened, turning into terrifying claws of shadow. The darkness covered his knuckles like armor. I expected him to flash forward and tear into the vampire, but all he did was clench his fists.

A sting of pain surged through my hand as Luc cut into his *own* flesh. Why—?

His blood wet tiny runes carved into his silver rings. Shadows flared. *Fuse. Sharpen. Break.* The metal twisted and merged, thickening at the top. The smooth silver sharpened into sharp points.

My stomach rolled. Fuck. Those weren't rings. Not anymore. Maybe not ever.

They were weapons. Metal knuckles made to inflict pain and nothing else.

A sharp lance of discomfort curled through my belly. I almost hunched, arms curling around my stomach. Jules's wide grin faded slightly. He turned, his arm still over my shoulder, and pressed a finger against the faded soothing rune on my arm. *Soothe.* Heat pulsed through my chest, chasing away the discomfort.

All the physical discomfort, at least.

The prisoners stretched their fingers, summoning shadow claws that barely extended past their knuckles. Compared to Luc's, they were pathetic. A vampire's fangs and claws were a gift of biology from their demon ancestry, but the same power that fueled their magic fueled their strength. And these two had none.

Stars, I wished I could look at this clinically, analyzing it as if it were just another passage in a book. The bits and pieces of knowledge I had cobbled together finally took a shape that made sense.

But I couldn't.

Luc planned to beat these vampires to death.

He stopped a couple feet away and crooked his claws, summoning the traitors to their end.

Mateo snarled and charged.

I flinched at the speed of him, the flash of movement blurring in my vision. He swiped for Luc's throat with shadowed claws. He might have landed the hit if Luc hadn't shifted to the side. Not dodging, but stepping, just enough that Mateo brushed the fabric of his doublet.

A flicker of hope flashed in the vampire's golden eyes.

But there wasn't a trace of fear in the Conqueror King.

His fist collided with Mateo's face.

His silver-ringed knuckles cracked bone on impact. Blood burst across the stage, splattering the King of Dusk's bronze skin. The crowd cheered and hollered as Mateo's skull caved in under the pressure. Blood and brain leaked down his chin. I tried to scramble back, but Jules held me still.

Chunky crimson droplets rained across my face.

I slapped my hand across my mouth. Jules's finger on my arms changed from an aimless circle to another shape I recognized well now. *Settle.* My nausea faded as quickly as it reared its head.

When Luc pulled back, the vampire dropped. His head—what remained of it—splattered against the ground, little more than a mess of blood and brain matter.

Tears streamed down my face. Fuck, that was nasty. I did *not* want to see mashed vampire bits. But I couldn't tear my eyes from the gore.

A strangled scream split the silence.

Théodore, the Dusk vampire. His soulbound twitched at Luc's feet, dying, choking, still aware. Luc stepped over the twitching corpse just as the brunette launched himself forward with the last bit of strength he had.

He swiped at Luc, a clumsy strike that might have split a human in two. Luc dodged it with ease. With boredom, even.

Luc tilted his head. "Try again."

Théodore bared his fangs, his breathing ragged. His hands twitched at his sides, but his power was gone, drained.

He knew it.

Luc knew it.

But Luc wanted him to try anyway.

He snarled and swung wildly. Luc dodged with almost lazy precision. Once. Twice. Again.

"Pathetic," Luc muttered.

Then he struck.

His claws sank into Théodore's throat, wrapping around his spine. The vampire choked. His fingers clawed uselessly at Luc's wrist, grasping, grasping—

Luc sighed. Then tore his spine free.

Théodore's body lurched, back arching, mouth gaping in a silent scream. His spine tore through the soft flesh of his throat, vertebrae snapping, ligaments stretching until they severed.

His limbs stopped moving.

But he could still scream. A horrible garbled noise rasped in his throat.

Luc clenched his fist, a wet squeeze. A pulse of heat rippled through the square as shadows crawled his arm, twisting and twining through that broken body like dark vines. Midday, in the bright sun, his reduced power burned hotter than most of the Dawn vampires in the square.

When he released his fist, the tendrils of shadow tore Théodore to bits.

The screams cut off.

Silence, for just a beat.

Then the crowd erupted.

Azarasians whooped and hollered, their cheers swelling around us. The air vibrated with triumph, with the thrill of violence well executed. Luc had ended it in under a minute, and the vampires reveled in him, in their terrible Conqueror King.

At our feet, the daemium stage soaked up the blood, gobbling it down like soil after a drought. But the scent still clung to the air, thick and metallic, worming its way into my throat.

Stars, that was disgusting.

I swallowed hard, blinking away the sting in my eyes. I really wanted to puke. Instead, I turned away. Fuck it if it made me a coward. I did *not* need to see this.

But in the corner of my vision, Mateo continued to twitch.

I shut my eyes. "Why isn't he dead?"

"Only heartmates die instantly when their soulbound dies," Jules said nonchalantly. "Companions can survive a few hours, though they turn rather feral."

Luc turned, glancing down at the broken thing on the stage. The Dawn vampire's face hadn't healed much, but the ragged flesh of his skull twitched, reforming. With a smooth wave of his hand, daemium spikes speared from the stage. They impaled Mateo through the chest, arms, legs, throat. His body finally stilled.

The crowd roared louder.

I breathed slowly through my nose, then out through my mouth. Minutes ago, I had basked in the city's beauty. The white stone buildings were as bright, gilded, and divinely stunning as the vampires who inhabited them.

But the wonder and awe only hid the truth. This was a home to monsters, as brutal as they were beautiful. They were the beasts who owned me, who had owned me and every human I had ever known.

And no matter how much blood their kings spilled, how many bodies fell at their feet, they would own me forever.

# 36

I SHOULD HAVE TAKEN the kings up on their offer to clear the schedule and spend the day in bed.

My feet dragged as we moved through the halls of Dawnspear. Hours had passed since the execution, the time spent in a haze of political discussions with the mage guild over new runespells for the Azarasian war efforts. I had listened eagerly for the first few minutes, but when a mage started describing a rune that melted an opposing army's flesh from their bones, I retreated inward. The rest blurred into places, names, and casually described horrors.

If only the image of the prisoners' mangled bodies had faded so easily.

I dug my nails into my palm. By the time the daemium had swallowed the corpses, they had been little more than pulp. Not a speck of blood or brain matter remained on me, but the ghost of it lingered. If I closed my eyes, the warmth of the droplets dripped down my cheeks.

Luc's rings burned through my gown where his palm rested against my lower back, his touch a silent reminder. The execution. The polished lie of Montaurère, pristine and golden on the surface, rotten beneath. The unshakable truth that I belonged to the Imperium.

I couldn't forget. Maybe those criminals had deserved death. Three thousand thralls, dead because of their actions. But the Conqueror and the Butcher had caused far more destruction than that. Their actions had killed hundreds of thousands.

And yet... I didn't hate them.

I should have. But the soulbond had stripped that from me.

All I had left was exhaustion. It coiled through me like smoke, curling into the spaces between my ribs. My pulse felt too slow. My limbs, too heavy. The kings' runes had kept away the pain and nausea, but my illness had never been that merciful. It could be so much more when it wanted to ruin my life.

My symptoms hadn't flared like this since the day I was harvested. It was long overdue.

"Good night, brother?"

Cédric's voice pulled me back. We had remained on the ground floor, navigating stars knew where, and now paused at a junction as Sabas and Cédric approached. But I barely noticed them.

I could only gape at the *baby* the Crown Mage held.

Prince Rosier looked like his father, a Roche through and through. His ivory cheeks were plump, his golden hair soft wisps. He tugged at the lapels of Cédric's maroon coat with a gurgling laugh, fascinated by the light catching on the gilded trim. If not for the luminous gold of his irises, I might have thought him any other six-month-old human child.

Behind him, Maire and another thrall followed in silence, their eyes on the floor. Maire didn't even glance at the child she had carried, but her shoulders were too stiff, her posture too rigid. She could pretend all she wanted, speaking of Rosier like he was a curse instead of a son, but it wasn't the truth.

"You could say that," Jules answered his brother jovially, but his arm tensed around my shoulders at the same instant Luc's grip tightened at my waist.

I frowned between them. I didn't think any of my emotions or sensations were strong enough for them to notice. But they weren't looking at me. They didn't even notice how I stared at the infant prince.

They were glaring down their councilors.

Sabas and Cédric slowed. Their gazes flicked to the way I was tucked between the kings, the way their fingers pressed in—

They stopped a few feet away, hesitating.

Before last night, they wouldn't have.

I'd thought the kings claiming me might ease their possessiveness, not intensify it. But that was delusional thinking. Azaras had only grown more obsessed with Karra the longer they were together.

A twinge shot through my torso. Without the soothing rune, that cramp probably would've sent me crumpling to the ground.

The King of Dawn nipped at my earlobe. I jumped, pushing into Luc's chest with the movement. Everyone around me besides the kings disappeared. "Couldn't you, lovely?"

I blinked at him, pulse hammering. Couldn't I what? "Huh?"

His golden eyes gleamed with mischief. "Say we had a good night?"

It took me a second to retrace the conversation. All the blood in my body rushed to my face. "I guess."

Luc chuckled, a deep rumble against my back. "You guess?"

Heat flared between my legs, unwelcome and insistent. Not now. Gods, I shouldn't have felt like this. Not when my anxiety and my illness swirled within me, sinking deeper by the minute. I had hoped the leftover desire from last night's bout of insanity would fade. Instead, it worsened.

Karra had thought the soulbond's effects maddening, and I suddenly understood why with perfect clarity.

"That's not the resounding feedback I was expecting," Jules said, his fingers tracing the curve of my shoulder. "Maybe we reschedule the security deliberation this afternoon—"

Sabas shot his king a flat look. "No."

Jules winked at his Crown Enforcer. "What's the difference if we do it in a day or two?"

"Your entire life has changed in a day or two, so stars fucking know."

Jules groaned. "Egh, fine. We'll come to your little meeting, Sabas."

"It's *your* little meeting," Sabas muttered. "The security of the Impire is your purview."

Jules sighed dramatically. "Don't remind me."

"Stop teasing him, Julien," Luc said, his voice edged with exasperation and amusement. Then to Sabas, he added, "He'll attend even if I have to drag him there."

Jules huffed, affronted. "You'll do no such thing." He leaned into me, his lips brushing the curve of my ear. "I will, however, be taking a lunch break after the bond rite. But we shouldn't be too late."

I stiffened. But if their venom could ease my body's betrayal and push away this exhaustion, I wouldn't object.

If I knew for sure, I'd probably be begging for their fangs right now.

"You should push it an hour," Cédric said to his soulbound.

Sabas scoffed. "I'll push it two."

Jules slapped his hands over his ears. "Don't tell me that! Now I'll be late for your new time."

"You weren't late for the bond rite." Cédric smiled down at his son, his sharp features softening. Pure, unadulterated love. A heartless Azarasian had managed more tenderness for his child than my father ever had.

"Yeah, because Luc's in charge," Jules said with a pat to the King of Dusk's shoulder over mine. "But also, we technically haven't reached the bond rite, so we're all late."

Cédric frowned at his brother.

Luc shook his head slightly, then waved an arm, gesturing for Sabas and Cédric to lead. "After you. It's Rosier's bond rite, after all."

Sabas and Cédric nodded before striding ahead. When they had put enough distance between us, the kings fell into step behind them, guiding me forward.

A cloying heat suddenly flashed through me. Pressure swelled in my center. It wasn't desire this time. How long would the bond rite take? How long until I could sit, or better, leave? But I had no idea what it even entailed.

Luc's sharp gaze flicked to me. "You aren't feeling well."

Not a question. A fact.

"I'll survive." The words scraped my throat. I had to keep moving. I wouldn't dare ask the kings for reprieve. They had already noticed my flashes of pain, the nausea, but exhaustion? That was quieter. Too soft to transfer across our new bond. They didn't feel the slow drag of it pulling at my bones.

"That's not a reassuring reply." Jules squeezed my shoulder, his inhuman warmth bleeding into my skin. "We can give Cédric our apologies—"

"No." I cut him off, sharper than intended. I couldn't afford to be seen as weak. Not before these vampires, my captors and soulbound. "Rosier's your nephew. This seems important, so you shouldn't miss it."

Jules hesitated, but Luc didn't. "What you're feeling should be important to you, too."

I flinched. My feelings were *not* important. They had never been.

It hadn't mattered when the pain was tearing through my gut, but Deidre still expected me to kneel in church for hours. It hadn't mattered when I wanted to collapse after running *Books & Bows* alone for days, but the ledgers still needed balancing. Being tired wasn't an excuse.

I forced my spine straight. "I can handle it."

Was that true? Didn't matter.

Luc held my stare for a beat longer, then nodded once. "Very well."

A few steps later, the soft strains of music reached my ears.

We passed through an open doorway into a long, elegant hall. Tall windows lined one side, the late morning sun spilling through like liquid gold. Crystal chandeliers hung overhead, refracting the light into bursts of color. On the other side, richly painted murals stretched from floor to ceiling, too grand and intricate for my exhausted mind to process.

On the far side of the hall, a figure sat at a gilded instrument, hands drifting over an array of ivory and black keys. The sound that poured from it was unlike anything I'd ever heard. Laughter and hushed conversation wove between the notes of music. Thralls moved through the crowd, balancing trays of gilded goblets, while clusters of vampires sipped their drinks.

I didn't realize I had slowed until Luc's hand pressed against the small of my back, guiding me forward again.

Some Azarasians dipped their heads when the kings entered, but many didn't even pause their conversations. Instead, the focus was entirely on Rosier and another infant held by a dark-skinned woman. The prince's soulbound, I assumed.

It made sense. A bond rite probably had something to do with soulbonds. The name all but confirmed it, but what exactly did it involve?

"What exactly is a bond rite?" I asked, my voice lower than intended. I should have asked before now. If my mind weren't fraying at the edges, I probably would have.

"Every soulbound pair has one at six months," Luc said, waving over a thrall. The human bowed smoothly, balancing the tray before him. "It's primarily to determine the type of bond Rosier and Vérène have. It will end with Vérène's parents giving her to Sabas and Cédric to raise and protect."

My brain stuttered. Give their daughter away? "What? Why?"

Luc plucked one goblet for himself and a second for Jules. "Once soulbound turn six months old, the bond becomes more pronounced. It's difficult for a soulbound pair to sleep when apart."

That explained why Karra had struggled to sleep without Azaras in Volume I. But that was fiction. This was my life. I clenched my fingers against the fabric of my gown. I hadn't considered that the kings' absence wouldn't just be an ache, but a physical inability. Would I be able to sleep at all without them?

"Vampire babies are much like human babies in that regard," Jules added, snatching his drink from Luc. He leaned into me as he did so, his half-buttoned shirt gaping open, silk warm against my cheek. I inhaled, smoke and honey. Not even that comforting scent was enough to settle the unease in my bones. "If they can't sleep, no one can."

Then, casually, effortlessly, Jules brushed his lips across Luc's.

Stars.

I snapped back to reality.

I had seen the kings kiss before—far more passionately, far more possessively. In my dreams, I had watched them go beyond kisses. Yet this? This was nothing more than the ghost of a touch.

And somehow, it was the most sensual thing I had ever witnessed.

My breath slipped out in a slow exhale.

Jules pulled back with a satisfied hum and clinked his goblet against Luc's. "Thanks, darling."

Then he winked down at me.

I flushed and cleared my throat. "So... they're expected to hand over their child?"

"It's only symbolic," Jules said. "Vérène's parents, Lord Martien and Lady Alix, moved into Sabas and Cédric's guest suite weeks ago. They'll live together, raise their children together, until Rosier and Vérène are grown and capable of living on their own."

They'd live together? Raise their children as a unit? How... strange. But I guess it made sense if soulbound needed to be together to sleep restfully. For their parents to rearrange their entire lives like that, it had to be necessary.

The thought lodged like a stone in my throat. That kind of dependence wasn't just uncomfortable. It was suffocating. A sharp ache crawled through my muscles, curling tight. My bones felt too heavy, like they carried the weight of centuries instead of decades. Only the soothing rune kept me from keeling over.

Still, I forced myself to stay calm. "So you've slept in the same bed since you were six months old?"

"Before that," Luc said, voice even but edged with something colder. "Marisol wouldn't risk anything happening to her precious grandson and heir."

Jules scoffed, sharing in the bitterness. "The moment she found out who carried his soulbound, my mother was whisked away to live in Duskfell."

I couldn't help my curiosity. The kings had told me so little about themselves. I knew Luc was Azaras's son, but not Karra's. His mother was one of Marisol Vela's daughters, Roxiana's sister. It was clear neither he nor

Jules had much love for the former Regent of Tenebra de Mar. They never called her Grandmother, only Marisol.

But I knew even less about Jules's family. He had two brothers—that was all. It was strange to think of him with a mother. Of course, he had one. Vampires didn't spring fully formed from the ether. I knew that. But that somehow made much more sense than the Butcher having something as mundane as a mother.

"And your father?" I asked.

Jules scoffed, swirling his blood wine. "My father had no choice in the matter, much to his dismay."

"They separated him from his soulbound?"

"My parents weren't soulbound," Jules said, too smooth. A deliberate kind of detachment. "My mother was his witch thrall."

I gaped. His mother was a what now? "And you call her your mother?"

He shrugged casually, but the movement was forced... and only to my eye. "That's what she was."

"But..." My gaze flicked past him, where Maire stood with three other thralls a few feet behind their masters. "She was a thrall."

Jules smiled, a perfect, practiced mask, but to me, it lacked its usual spark. It was unnerving, knowing his expression was flawless, convincing to anyone else, yet feeling the truth beneath it. Not just in my gut, but in *our* soul. "She didn't have any parental rights to me, but Titus was rather protective of her, so Marisol had no choice but to let her stay."

I swallowed. So that wasn't the norm. I had imagined it earlier, when Maire first told me about Rosier, but seeing it in practice... It was different. It was worse. The vampires cooed over the infants, Cédric and Vérène's parents beaming.

Maire? She stared at the floor.

A good, obedient thrall.

*That* was the norm.

Would that happen to me one day? Would I stand behind them, silent, while the High Courts praised my child like I wasn't even there?

It didn't matter. I couldn't have children.

Well... I *likely* couldn't have children. My fertility scores were so low I was essentially infertile. But the healers had said I could possibly have a child if I tried. A slim chance. One in a decade, maybe, just like my mother. Vampires had difficulty conceiving, so the odds would be even lower, but my lifespan was measured in centuries now.

Maybe one day, it would happen.

And I couldn't do anything about it. The kings had always owned my body and now they owned my soul. Jules had joked about breeding me before we were soulbound. It wouldn't be a joke anymore, even if it didn't happen right away. My exhaustion worsened, like the fatigue of a flu, but without the sniffling and coughing. A dull heaviness bloated in my belly.

Warm fingers brushed my jawline. "Breathe, curiosity," Luc murmured. "You're our soulbound. We won't be taking our children from you."

I flinched and pulled back, but Jules was at my other side. I was trapped between them. "That's rather presumptuous of you."

Luc arched a brow. "And why is that?"

The arrogant bastard. I clenched my fists. Fuck it. They'd find out eventually. They might as well hear it from me. "Because I'm infertile, that's why," I snapped.

I braced for their reaction. Shock. Disappointment. Something.

But Luc only tilted his head slightly, like I'd told him something mundane. "Your fertility scores are rather low for a human, but with magic and the aid of a healer, it's possible."

I blinked at him.

What?

"Wait. You know?" My voice came out too thin, too breathless.

Jules grinned like I'd asked if the sky was blue. "Did you think we wouldn't read the file of our new Mortal Bride? Or, well, that Luc wouldn't read it and then summarize it for me?"

"I..." My throat closed. I had no response.

They'd known this entire time.

Luc's voice was steady, unshaken. "It's nothing you need to concern yourself with."

Nothing to concern myself with? Like it was that simple?

"You're ours now," he continued, "but that doesn't mean we'll force a child on our soulbound."

I let out a sharp breath. "But my choices didn't matter when it came to the collar or sharing your bed?"

"The collar is for your own protection." Luc met my glare without hesitation. "And you came to our bed willingly."

I crossed my arms, lips pressing into a thin line. I couldn't argue with that.

Before I could dwell on it, the gentle music faded, the final notes lingering. I turned as Cédric, Sabas, and Vérène's parents approached the grand instrument at the front of the hall. Sabas lifted a hand, fingers tracing a rune in the air. *Chime.* A crisp, twinkling sound echoed through the room, cutting through conversations like a subtle command.

Vampires stilled, shifting their attention toward the dais.

Cédric stepped forward, his voice smooth and regal. "Thank you for joining us to celebrate Rosier and Vérène's bond rite. Today, we honor the sacred bond that ties them together, the foundation of our strength, the force that has shaped our Impire. Through the rite, we will witness what kind of bond fate has woven between them."

Before I could process what was happening, movement at my side drew my attention. Roxiana sidled up beside Jules, draped in a sheer, rose-colored gown that clung to every curve. Beside her, Isabeau cut a stark contrast in her fitted black leathers, the General once more after last night's revelry.

"Have you placed your bets?" Roxiana whispered to the King of Dawn. "I'm thinking they're beloveds."

"Companions are still the most likely option," Isabeau said.

"But Vérène's parents are heartmates," Roxiana countered, gesturing subtly toward Lord Martien and Lady Alix. "It's possible. Companions plus heartmates usually equals beloveds. Am I wrong?"

Luc's lips twitched into a smirk. I frowned at him. I didn't get what was funny.

Jules tipped his head toward Luc, the picture of barely restrained amusement. "If you really want to know, Roxi—"

Roxiana shot him a warning look. "No, don't ruin it. Let them cast their spell. It's tradition, after all."

I had no idea what was happening.

Jules must have caught the confusion in my expression because he reached out, brushing a thumb against the crease in my brow, smoothing it away with a touch. "Azaras cast the Azarasian soulbond runespell. Luc can sense their bond type, just like the Beast King."

Oh. I narrowed my eyes at Luc. "So you win every bet, then?"

Luc merely lifted his goblet to his lips. "I don't place them anymore."

"We made a killing the first few decades, but people caught on eventually," Jules said. "Not that I need their money, but stars, do I love winning. Now I have to place bets in secret just for the thrill."

A hush fell over the room as Cédric, Sabas, Martien, and Alix raised their hands, fingers tracing a series of precise runes in the air. *Reveal. Illuminate. Merge.* Shadows pulsed in response. As the spell activated, two glowing masses flickered into existence—one golden and the other silver, shimmering with barely contained energy.

The entire hall held its breath as the glows drifted closer, drawn by an invisible force. I watched, captivated despite everything, as the golden light surged just past the halfway point with the silver.

Then it stopped.

The audience released a collective exhale, murmurs rippling through the hall. It was a beautiful display—

The dam holding me upright broke.

A fresh wave of heat crashed through my torso. My vision wavered, the glowing masses blurring into streaks of light. The weight in my bones turned crushing, exhaustion dragging at my limbs like a current pulling me under. My head swam.

I had endured pain, nausea, exhaustion that would have left others collapsed in bed for days. But my body had finally betrayed me. I'd burned through the last scraps of strength keeping me upright, the sheer force of will that had carried me through the day crumbling beneath the weight of it all.

Weak.

I hated the fragility of my body, hated that I couldn't endure longer. Hated that no matter how much I fought, I would always lose to this.

Now, my singular focus became surviving until I could get out of here.

I'd settle for the Mortal Bride's bedchamber, even if it didn't have a lock.

A chaise would do at this point.

"Yes!" Roxiana cheered, her voice slicing through the haze, along with a few others throughout the room. The vampires who had bet on beloveds. "I told you, Is."

"Go collect your prize, dove," Isabeau said with a pat to her soulbound's hand. "Then you can collect what you bet me."

A flush tinged Roxiana's dark bronze cheeks. "Can I now?"

Isabeau smiled at her, a full, wicked grin.

"Oh, a sex bet. I love it." Jules glanced down at me, eyes gleaming. "What do you want to wager, bride?"

I frowned at him, barely processing his words.

"We'll see what the—" Jules started, stepping forward with me on his arm—

The room lurched.

Light fractured, the chandeliers overhead turning into spinning, blinding stars. The floor tilted beneath me. Too fast. Too sudden. My knees buckled.

I would've caught myself. But two arms wrapped around me instead, one at my waist and another across my chest. A spike of panic, of fierce concern, stabbed through me. I swayed, my vision narrowing, everything around me warping into streaks of color and sound. The music cut off abruptly.

Then—

"Back the fuck up unless you want to die," Roxiana's voice cut through the void, sharp and commanding.

Someone nearby gasped. The shuffle of feet. The weight of a hundred eyes pressed in. But I couldn't focus. The space around me wavered, voices distant, blurred like sound through water.

"Fuck." Jules's grip on me tightened, no trace of his usual teasing left. "Should've known you were pushing too hard."

Luc exhaled sharply through his nose, a slow, measured sound. Too measured. Like he was holding something back. His voice was deep, controlled, but sharper than usual. "Nessa. What do you need?"

"I just..." The words felt too big in my mouth. "I need to lie down."

Luc moved before I could register it, arms locking around me before my body could betray me further. He lifted me effortlessly, cradling me against his chest like he had carried me a thousand times before.

Jules stepped in front of us, his posture shifting in an instant. The sharp gleam in his golden eyes, the tension in his frame, the way his fingers twitched at his sides. For once, he wasn't putting on a show. He was clearing a path.

And if anyone was foolish enough to stand in the Butcher's way, they wouldn't live long enough to regret it.

The silk of his back was right there, within reach. I touched him. I barely had the awareness to think about it.

But the moment my fingers brushed him, the tension in my muscles eased slightly. My body recognized them both. Their warmth. Their strength. The anchor they had become against my will.

I couldn't even hate the relief that settled into my bones.

# INTERLUDE 3

*"THIS CONDITION ISN'T UNHEARD of in human and witch females, Your Majesty," Healer Chastain said from where she kneeled on the floor at the foot of our bed. "Since her system is now clear of your blood, the adverse effects should subside within a few hours."*

*"And?"*

*Healer Chastain's shoulders hunched at the chill in Luc's voice. My soulbound stood before the healer, a wall between the room and our unconscious bride. Nessa lay tangled in the sheets, her breath softened from its earlier harsh rattle, but sweat still marred her too-pale skin.*

*I brushed a strand of copper-brown hair from her face and imagined her fever lessening.* **Soothe**. *If I focused, the cloying heat of it trickled weakly through the bond. It felt almost akin to the humid air of the Alvarese rainforests, heavy and exhausting on my shoulders. It wasn't anything I had ever experienced myself. I'd been gutted a time or two, but vampires didn't get sick, more like our demon ancestors in that regard.*

*What a delicate little creature we found ourselves bound to.*

*I traced my finger along the soft edges of her face. I had always been aware of our differences. I had killed enough mortals to know how easily they crumbled. But healing them? Stitching them back together? That had never been a concern of mine.*

*"I will have to consult my colleagues, Your Majesty," Healer Chastain continued, her voice careful. "Our healing runes aren't effective against the condition. We can't target the misplaced cells since they aren't abnormal. And our*

*blood only increases the immune system response, which results in inflammation and worsens the symptoms."*

*Luc stared down at her for a moment. Healer Chastain lost control of her heartbeat under the Conqueror's glare. Most people did. It was impressive she had lasted as long as she did.*

*"None of that sounded like a solution," he said.*

*Healer Chastain ducked her head. "I apologize, Your Majesty. We haven't had much reason to study the illness, so I'm not sure if there is a cure. But I can gather the brightest minds from the healer guild and create one, if not. I have no doubts about that, Your Majesty."*

*Luc gave a sharp nod and waved her away. "Consider it your guild's top priority."*

*"Yes, Your Majesty." Healer Chastain backed away, remaining on her knees. When she was far enough away, the healer climbed to her feet, Estrella holding the door for her on the way out.*

*Luc turned his attention back to Nessa, cuddled into my chest. I patted the space on her other side, but he shook his head. He hadn't relaxed since our bride stumbled hours ago. I doubted he would again until she woke.*

*After a heavy pause, Sabas cleared his throat. "Imperium?"*

*My gaze snapped to him. Our council and guard had watched the healer examine our bride from the far side of the room, their backs nearly against the wall. It was strange to see them so distant and wary... yet entirely necessary. Cédric had approached a step closer earlier out of curiosity at Healer Chastain's discovery spell, and it had taken everything in me not to rip my brother's heart out. Before my nails could fully sharpen, Luc had growled and Cédric quickly scrambled back.*

*I didn't even want to imagine what would have happened if my soulbound hadn't warned him away from our bed and our ill bride. What the fuck would I have told Perry?* Hope you enjoyed Kotara, I murdered our brother and then had to mercy-kill Sabas before his broken bond drove him insane. Do you want to raise Rosier and Vérène or should I?

*When Luc didn't respond, I said, "Yes, Sabas?"*

*Our Crown Enforcer hesitated. "If she doesn't consume your blood, she'll age."*

*"I'm aware," Luc said coldly. "I think we're all aware."*

*"Of course, Your Majesty. I meant no offense."*

*Luc inhaled, trying to steady himself, to bring back his ironclad control. "It wasn't offensive. Speak plainly, Sabas. Neither of us considers your words as an attack, even in this... heightened state."*

*My gaze locked with Luc's. The same intensity that burned through me scorched through him. To protect, to defend, to shield. If we hadn't spent centuries mastering our self-discipline, how would we have reacted when Nessa nearly collapsed in public?*

*Everyone at the bond rite would be in pieces, scattered across the castle.*

*Hells, today was only our second day as heartmates. I had known being bound to a human would cause problems, but I hadn't imagined senselessly slaughtering my friends and courtiers among them. Senseless slaughter had never been an issue for me. I played the role of the impulsive king well, but I had never killed anyone accidentally.*

*Only intentionally.*

*"What if this is their play?" Isabeau asked carefully. Her arms were crossed, hands far from the hilt of her sword. A deliberate precaution. "An assassin isn't needed to kill your bride if she can't consume your blood to make her immortal. They can simply wait fifty years."*

*"It's not that she can't consume their blood," Cédric said. "It's that doing so will cause her agony."*

*Roxiana, the most at ease among our councilors, leaned against the table and scoffed. "It's like you've never met heartmates, Cédric. Even if her agony wouldn't one day feel like theirs, do you really think they'd keep feeding her their blood when they know it will harm her?"*

*Cédric narrowed his eyes. "Her dying of old age would harm her more."*

*"It won't get that far," Luc mused, keeping his eyes on me and Nessa. The ghost of his tension in my shoulder faded when he looked at her, safe and whole in my arms. "There are other ways to get vampire blood in a human."*

*The room dropped into silence at the implications. Especially coming from Luc.*

*Cédric cleared his throat. "Birthing a vampire only extends a human life by a decade. You can't spend eternity knocking up your bride every ten years."*

*My eyes dropped to the faded mark of the contraceptive runespell on her arm. Luc had been right to place it on her. Though the chances were always low—lower still with her fertility issues—it wouldn't make any of our lives easier to navigate a pregnancy while our new bond settled.*

*Pity.*

*"Why not?" I quipped. "I've always wanted a dozen kids."*

*"You'll have surpassed number twelve two centuries in," Roxiana muttered.*

*"I've always wanted a couple hundred kids, then. Happy?" A hundred was far too many, but I hadn't been joking when I said I'd gladly put a baby in our bride*

*as soon as she asked. If she woke this second with the demand, that rune would be gone and I'd be balls deep inside her.*

*I barely swallowed a shudder. Stars, this new soulbond made me want to fuck even more than usual.*

*And I wasn't alone in that. Luc's pupils had blown wide, his irises reduced to slivers of silver. I didn't even need to ask. I knew exactly what he was imagining.*

*Fucking her until she was limp and sated.*

*Filling her up with his cum until she was round with* our *child.*

*If she was even remotely fertile when the blood moons rose next month, nothing would stop my darling's Beasty from breeding her.*

*The urge already pounded through his veins, my veins. Ours, ours, ours. No one would take her away. If she died, I would* follow. I wouldn't have to mourn her, the loss clawing a hole in my chest. My jaw clenched as I looked down at her. But she wouldn't die. I wouldn't let her. I had failed Corinne, but I wouldn't fail her or Jules, my heartmates—

*I wrenched myself out of Luc's head with a ragged breath. Fuck. That would take some getting used to. I had always been aware of my soulbound, but I had never slipped into his head like that. Never felt what he felt as if I were him. I had done it with Nessa, too. And Luc had done it with both of us, though he hadn't mentioned it. It was surely as unsettling to him as it was to me.*

*"Exactly what we need in the world," Sabas grumbled. "An army of little Juliens."*

*"It'd be more of a temporary fix than a permanent solution," Cédric said. "You'd have to start sacrificing vampires to create fertility runespells powerful enough to conceive that frequently."*

*I traced a finger along Nessa's cheekbone. "I think our bride might object after a handful of births, too."*

*Luc's voice cut through the conversation. "I trust the healer guild will find a solution. But if they don't, we will do what we must to survive."*

*I couldn't help the small smirk that played along my lips. Bright silver-edged eyes flickered to me, a question in the slight tilt of Luc's brows.*

*I shrugged innocently. "If knocking our new wife up would be such a hardship for you, darling, I'm more than happy to play stud."*

*Luc was on the bed in an instant, hovering over Nessa with one hand gripping my jaw. "I will surrender some things to you, Julien," he murmured, voice dark and edged with need. "But that will never be one of them."*

*I shuddered, but a wicked grin spread across my face. "I look forward to the challenge."*

THE DRAINING FOG RECEDED from my mind, reluctantly releasing me from my fitful half-slumber. Silver eyes. Gold eyes. Fingers brushing along my temple, my chin. A deep growl. The warmth of their power, followed by the cooling wave of a rune. Voices whispering things I couldn't understand until they turned into clear words in my dreams.

Then peace.

Silence.

The press of a body at my side while another's hand wiped the sweat from my brow.

Then nothing.

Nothing.

Nothing.

Rising light.

For the second day in a row, I woke to dark sheets, the kings' tantalizing, male scents invading my every sense. I moaned, my thighs clenching slightly—

I stiffened at the sudden bloom of desire. But it wasn't followed by a flash of agony, the deep, stabbing ache that usually accompanied my haze and stayed past its welcome.

It was just... gone.

No lingering exhaustion and uncomfortable bloating in my belly. I pressed a hand over my lower stomach. My illness never left so quickly. It always lingered, clawing at me for days. But it was entirely gone, like I had imagined it sinking its claws into me at the bond rite. The kings' must have cast a soothing rune, one strong enough to force my body into this unnatural peace.

Something moved, something in black.

I flinched, yanking the sheets to my chin. Riona approached with downcast eyes, a tray in hand. What? My brain couldn't make sense of it, even as she lowered the gilded tray to the side of the bed. My gaze dropped. Fresh crusty bread. More cheese than one person could possibly eat. She set a familiar leather-bound book beside it, then quickly backed away, her gaze still averted.

I blinked hazily. At the food. At the book. At Riona.

The thrall cleared her throat, brown eyes flickering to the door. Like someone stood right outside, listening. Estrella and Tristan, no doubt.

"Yes, Riona?" I asked when the silence stretched on.

"His Majesty, The King of Dusk, insists you spend the morning in bed, reading and resting." Riona hesitated, licking her lips. She turned to face the dresser, where a swath of crimson lace cascaded down its side. "But if you decide to rise, His Majesty, The King of Dawn, wishes you to wear the dress he selected."

I stared. Blinked. Processed.

They wanted me to do... nothing?

Well, nothing or play dress-up for Jules.

"Where—" I didn't even need to finish the question. Luc was beneath me, floors below, but Jules was close. Not right outside the bedchamber but in the apartment, likely in one of the rooms I had yet to explore.

"Yes, my lady?"

"Never mind." I pushed onto my elbow, the dangling jewels on my collar tinking against the metal. "Thank you, Riona."

She dipped into a bow before backing toward the door and leaving me alone.

I picked at the food as my brain returned to life at a snail's pace. Whenever I woke from days of pain and exhaustion, I always had to force myself up. Wash the dried sweat from my face. Dress and flip the sign on the shop door. Pray for enough customers that I could purchase a slice of cheese that would last a week without molding.

Now I had a full platter of cheese, eight different types arranged artfully before me. I didn't need to stand or bathe or dress or work.

I just needed to *rest*.

When was the last time I had simply rested? If I wasn't in agonizing pain, I was up and about. Even when I was in agonizing pain, I was up and about. My stepmother hadn't tolerated laziness. When my body first started fighting me, she refused to let me lie down, no matter how much I cramped and ached.

She was merciless after my fertility results. If I couldn't have a child, I could at least know how to clean and cook. Even then, she had been preparing me for Patriarch Meallán.

But the kings wanted me to rest.

A swirl of emotions rose within me, too many to distinguish between. It was a burst so strong my eyes watered.

I pushed up until my back rested against a pillow propped against the daemium headboard and grabbed *The Soulborne Queen*. Losing myself in its pages was a balm I had used for years. Whether my mind spiraled toward doom or tangled itself in hope, fear, and shame, a book always helped.

But the moment Azaras made his grand debut, the character I had imagined for years twisted into Luc. Demons were shapeshifters. They didn't have physical traits to pass down to their offspring, but both sire and son were tall and dark-haired. Their arrogant confidence matched, too, though Azaras was a bit more unruly. My brain didn't care about the other conflicting descriptions.

I closed the book. There wasn't any reading or resting happening anymore, not in this bed.

My gaze caught on the crimson gown.

Ten minutes later, I gently turned the doorknob and peeked into the sitting room.

Jules's chosen gown had gone over my head effortlessly, the kings' magic having already cleaned me. A straight waterfall of crimson, it rippled to my feet until I cinched it at the waist with a matching sash. My hair was slightly tangled, but after a quick brush, it was passable by Azarasian standards. I resisted the urge to braid it tightly, like the good Maboni woman I wasn't. I was ready to go in under four minutes, but it had taken the remainder to work up the courage to open the door.

How had Jules found a gown even more sheer than the harvest dress?

Swirls of a maroon pattern twisted through the crimson lace, but the darker bits strategically avoided anything of importance. Every part of me was visible—the peaks of my nipples, the faint marks on my soft stomach, the curls between my thighs. I had tried to enter the kings' wardrobe, then my tiny chamber, searching for something else. But neither door had opened for me.

It was either this gown or a bedsheet. And if I wore a bedsheet, Jules would laugh at me. I shouldn't have cared, but I knew he would. I couldn't let him have the satisfaction.

But I had almost done it anyway.

Estrella and Tristan flanked the doorway, the Impire's star insignia glinting in the light from the center of their dark leathers. They turned as I stepped forward, my chin raised, my eyes lowered out of habit.

"Are... the kings around?" I asked, unsure what else to say. Neither had moved much since I woke, but I didn't know what they were doing, only where they were located. Their emotions weren't strong enough to leak over, and I didn't reach out and check, lest they sense me looking.

It was already embarrassing enough that my first instinct upon standing was to go to them.

"His Majesty, The King of Dusk, is meeting with the Crown Chancellor and Crown Enforcer in the throne room," Estrella said. "But His Majesty, The King of Dawn, remained behind. He's in the apartment's private garden, Your Majesty."

Estrella gestured down the hall past the library doors, but my eyes remained wide on her. She had used Majesty so many times. Had I hallucinated that last part?

"Your what now?" Estrella had barely spoken to me on the journey from Mabon. The few times she had, she had called me human. Exalted Morrena had called me the Queen of Dusk and Dawn, though no one else had acknowledged it. Not even the kings.

Until now.

"The Imperium have requested we not call you by your title in public until they announce you to the courts," Estrella said, gaze lowered in deference when she turned back to face me. "But in the privacy of your apartment, we will show you the respect your new soulbond entails."

Sweat broke out along the back of my neck. "I'm not anyone's Majesty."

"You are now, Your Majesty," Tristan said like it was that simple. He gestured me forward. "Please follow us."

Estrella led the way down a long hallway lined with murder art in gilded frames. We passed a handful of doors, but I didn't ask what lay behind them.

My gaze fixed on the bright windows ahead.

Dawnspear was built into the mountainside. The southern half of the palace overlooked the sprawling city below. The northern half was embedded into solid rock—at least, until the floor beneath us. Whether the mountain had curved naturally or the vampires had carved it away, a small garden occupied a plateau level with the kings' apartment.

On the balcony overlooking the greenery, Jules sat before an easel, his back to me.

If Estrella or Tristan said anything, I didn't hear them. I stepped through the doorway into the morning light, lured forward by the King of Dawn's mere existence. The closer I got to him, the more the anxious twisting in my belly calmed.

Jules didn't turn, though he undoubtedly heard me. Humming as he worked, he dipped his gilded brush in more paint. I stepped closer, circling his side until the canvas came into view.

And froze.

My breath caught. Smooth skin over thick thighs and a plump ass. A long back, sweat dripping through the rivulets of soft flesh. Artfully tousled hair like copper streaked with dark gold. The woman lay collapsed against Luc's bronze chest, the King of Dusk watching her with starved intensity, his gaze locked on her as she panted, her lips parted. Her eyes were gold and green and brown and somehow beautiful—

Fucking stars, was that supposed to be *me*?

My jaw gaped. Heat rushed to my cheeks until I was surely as flushed as I was in the painting. The painting of me. After getting my brain fucked out.

*Before* getting my brain fucked out again.

I had seen Luc's expression in the throes of pleasure, had witnessed his desire as I came undone. But I still couldn't imagine someone looking at me the way Luc did the woman in the painting.

I couldn't imagine someone painting my ass either, but here I stood, staring at it.

"I couldn't decide which to add to my collection next. After I fucked you or after Luc fucked you." Jules pressed his brush to the canvas, stroking lines of pink across the woman's back. *My* back. "Your eyes made the decision for me."

My throat constricted. I didn't know what to say to that. I didn't know what to say to any of this.

What came out was, "Those aren't my eyes."

Jules's hand stilled. A shiver trailed down my spine. I knew a predator now listened to my every heartbeat. My every breath. When those golden eyes slid to me, I forced myself to stay still.

Jules let his darkening gaze drop. Hunger flickered over his face, devouring me in the sheer lace gown he had selected.

His grin turned wicked.

Fuck.

The King of Dawn patted his right thigh. "Sit, lovely. If I have your eyes so wrong, let me gaze into the beauties themselves."

My jaw dropped. Liquid warmth flushed through me. He wanted me to sit on his fucking lap while he painted my ass?

Stars, why was that so... arousing?

"Nessa," he all but purred.

My feet betrayed me. I blamed them entirely for the movement. I wouldn't. Ever. But I did. His attention stayed fixed on me, waiting and watching, the sensuous hunter ready to pounce. I circled his left leg until I stood between his muscular thighs, then twisted awkwardly to sit, stiff-backed.

Far too slow.

Jules struck. His teeth grazed against my nipple through the thin lace of my gown. I yelped, lightning striking through me. Before I pulled away—did I *want* to pull away?—he sucked the clothed, aching peak into his perfect mouth.

Heat surged through my veins. My knees weakened. His hands flashed to my hips as mine clutched his shoulders, nails digging into the hard muscle beneath the white silk of his tunic. His tongue flicked over the bud—

Stars, his tongue piercing had a *pointed* edge now, and the fabric didn't mute a damn thing. I moaned, a loud, desperate sound.

Jules smirked against my breast before releasing my abused flesh. He batted his eyelids at me, somehow innocent and sinful all at once. "If you shove your tits in my face, I *will* put them in my mouth. Fair warning, from now on."

I gaped down at him. Just gaped. No thoughts traveled through my brain. Only shock—

Every so slowly, Jules dropped his gaze. Tracing my throat. The collar at my neck. The weight of my breasts beneath the sheer crimson. His pupils darkened as they narrowed on my nipples, still stiff through the fabric. "And if you leave them in my face, I will put them in my mouth *again*—"

I sat my ass down. Hard. The plushness of my thighs pressed against the firm muscle of his leg, my skirts nowhere near thick enough to mask the feel of him. His eyes met mine and trapped me deep within liquid gold.

"Perfect," Jules murmured.

My flush crawled up my neck, the heat noticeable all the way to my ears. I must have been as red as a rose. Jules quirked his lips, but returned to his masterpiece and stroked that brush once again along the curve of my ass. A shiver chased down my spine, the ghost of his fingers tracing the same path.

"How are you feeling?"

I stiffened at the sudden, serious question. His voice had softened, the teasing gone. "Don't you know the answer?"

"Doesn't mean I can't ask."

Blood rushed to my cheeks. Why did he say things like that? It was easier to hate him when he was slaughtering innocents. Still, I found myself answering honestly.

"Usually when my illness flares like that, I feel it for days afterwards," I started, hesitant. "But this time, it's like... I'm already back to normal. Better than normal, actually. My normal is constant discomfort, but with the soothing rune, I don't even feel that."

He nodded, eyes still on his painting. "I'm glad to hear it."

I fiddled with the loose ends of the sash around my waist. "What happened?"

"Our blood increased your immune system response and your body began attacking itself," he said. "I can summon Healer Chastain to explain it all, if you wish."

"No, that's..." Words rose unbidden in my mind, an echo from my vivid dreams. "It caused inflammation, but that only irritated the misplaced cells and worsened the pain."

He smirked. "Eavesdropping on us while you're sleeping, are we?"

"No!" I nearly shouted in his ear. He chuckled, low and deep, the warmth of it brushing my cheek. "Maybe. I barely remember it, like any ordinary dream."

"We haven't done anything exciting while you're sleeping, so there isn't much to remember."

*My bronze hands, tangled in white-blond hair. The stretch of his lips around the base of my cock, the glint of his tongue piercing as he took me deep—*

I jerked my head, as if I could shake the image loose. Of course, that would be the dream I remembered best. My pulse dropped between my legs.

Jules inhaled against my hair and groaned. "Stars, you smell divine when you're aroused. What are you thinking about?"

"I'm..." I trailed off before I could voice a lie. I shifted on his thigh instead, pressing my nails into my skin.

Hours ago, my body had been fighting itself. Now I ached for his touch. I shouldn't have craved anyone's touch right now, much less the Butcher's. I shouldn't have wished his hands glided across me instead of his paintbrush against canvas.

But the craving wasn't mine. Wasn't *just* mine. The soulbond screamed within me. The kings hadn't left my side most of yesterday, but that wasn't enough. It wanted them closer. Needed them closer.

Jules dipped his brush, circling a fresh stroke of pink across the canvas, right where my thighs parted. I shuddered. When he pulled back, a sheen of pink-tinged gloss coated my inner thighs. Wet, glistening. Evidence of our pleasure, of my bleeding, captured in oil and shadow.

"If I got your eyes wrong, I might have made other mistakes. Best we check, don't you think?"

My mouth dried. I met those bright eyes, wicked and knowing. He didn't mean...?

His lips brushed my temple, deceptively chaste. "Stand," he whispered, his lips moving down to my cheekbone. "Pull up your skirts." He breathed against my lips. "And bend over the balustrade for me."

Shit. That was exactly what he meant.

I jerked back and straightened my shoulders. This was just the soulbond. It had writhed in me since I woke, filling my lungs with the kings' lingering scents from the bedsheets. It wasn't real. I had to resist.

My core clenched. I stiffened in his lap. *That* was certainly real. "Do you always come on this strong?"

Jules's brows lifted, his smirk lazy. "Don't I always?"

"I guess I just thought..."

His brows rose. "Hmm?"

I licked my lips and cleared my throat. "We had... sex two nights ago."

"Thirty-six hours ago, to be exact."

My eyes widened. "You're counting?"

His smile grew. "I think I'm setting a new record for myself."

"Thirty-six hours is a record? You're hundreds of years old."

"I'm a bit of a slut, even by vampire standards." He turned back to his work and breathed his next words against my earlobe. "We're soulbound heartmates, Nessa. Even once we settle into our bond, we'll crave each other. But right now, it's new. It needs... reassurance."

I swallowed. I didn't need to ask what he meant by reassurance. Karra and Azaras hadn't been able to keep their hands off each other, their soul seeking closeness in the only way it could.

"Don't you have things to do?"

"None besides you."

I somehow managed a glare as I grasped for another excuse. "There's still so much you don't know. About me. About who cast this bond."

His lips brushed the curve of my ear. "We have eternity to figure that out."

"Do we though?" I sorted through the blur of dreams. "If I can't drink your blood, I'm not immortal."

"That's a problem for another day."

"But—"

"Stop procrastinating and stand, Nessa."

I sucked in a breath. Fuck. I reached for another excuse, but none came to mind.

But why did I need an excuse? I could say no. I could walk away. I could return to the Mortal Bride's bedchamber and read the afternoon away.

But I wanted him.

No, the *soulbond* wanted him. It wasn't me.

It couldn't be me.

A question couldn't be a lie, right? "What if I don't want to?"

"Do you not want to?" he murmured. "If you can tell me no and mean it, I'll have to paint from memory."

I opened my mouth, but no sound escaped my lips. I could say no... but it wouldn't be the truth.

Jules's fingers found my chin, tilting my face toward his. Our noses brushed, his breath warm against my lips. "Tell me no, lovely girl."

I jerked to my feet and stepped back too quickly, as if his hands might follow me, as if I couldn't trust my own body to stay in place. His arm dropped, letting me go. His other hand still held the brush to the canvas, perfectly still.

Did I stay? Did I go?

I twisted around until I faced the garden. My pulse pounded, my body half-expecting him to pounce. Jules inhaled sharply at the sight of my backside through the lace, the sound nearly a hiss. I wanted to scoff in disbelief, but I knew his appreciation was real.

I stared at the wide white stone of the balustrade.

I imagined lifting my skirts, the air kissing the ample skin of my ass, and leaning over until my aching nipples pressed against sun-warmed stone—

What the fuck was I doing?

What was wrong with me?

Jules was the Butcher King. He owned my people. He owned *me.* I had to get out of here before I did something I regretted.

Something *else* I regretted.

I backed away, but his gaze stayed fixed on me. Something in me screamed to run. *Needed* to run. Estrella and Tristan remained inside by the door, but if I went down to the garden, I could get away. I could breathe. I could think—

"Nessa," Jules rasped, trapping me with a single syllable. "If you run, I *will* chase you. Not even Luc has the willpower to resist that instinct."

The heat in me flared. I was a handful of steps from the stairs leading down into the greenery. It would be easy to turn and dash down them. But once I got away, I wouldn't be able to stay away. I couldn't evade a vampire on the hunt.

Most of me didn't really want to evade a vampire on the hunt.

"And what will you do when you catch me?" I whispered.

Jules's pupils dilated at the question. He lowered his paintbrush and stood, the slow uncoiling of a snake preparing to strike. "Bury my fangs and cock so deep inside you that you'll feel me for days."

My nipples hardened to near-painful peaks. "So if I run, you're threatening to eat me and then fuck me?"

Jules's smile was slow. Lethal. Amused.

"Or fuck you and then eat you." He tilted his head, considering. "Yes, I think I prefer that order."

"Do I get a say in the matter?"

"Can I fuck you, wife?"

I shuddered. "I... I don't know."

Jules's gaze swept over me, lingering where the lace clung to my hard nipples and soft curves. "Don't you?"

I swallowed. What had I told myself the nights of the harvest feast and the revelry? That fucking the king was inevitable. It was a transaction between master and thrall, nothing more.

Now it was all those things *and* an itch I needed to scratch.

Once I did...

Stars, I couldn't even lie to myself. Once I did, I might pretend to resist, but I'd do it again and again and again. I couldn't fight the venom coursing through my veins. I couldn't fight the soulbond. I couldn't fight the craving.

I was so tired of fighting battles doomed from the start.

And why should I fight this one? I had already surrendered my body and my soul. More than once. I was damned from the moment Jules dropped his head between my legs and made me scream on his tongue.

Before that even.

Might as well enjoy my damnation.

Before I talked myself out of it, I spun on my bare feet and fled down the stairs.

# 38

MY BARE FEET SANK into the grass as I hopped from the stairs to the garden. What was I doing? I didn't know. I stomped on that voice inside of me and the soulbond kicked it from my mind.

I had made my choice.

I couldn't take it back.

I twisted, expecting to see Jules a step behind me. But he remained at the top of the stairs, luminous black eyes fixed on me. His entire body was tensed and coiled, a predator about to pounce. My heart stuttered.

Every instinct yelled at me to *run, now*.

That was a terrible idea.

I did it anyway.

I dashed across the grass, aiming for a row of tall hedges carved into an arched pathway. A stone bench piled with pillows blurred in my periphery as I sprinted past it. If I made it through the greenery, we'd be out of sight from the windows—

Jules appeared before the hedges in the blink of an eye. "I tried, I really did. But I don't have the patience for a hunt today. I need you."

I stumbled back. Oh, shit. I whipped my head around, but there was only open space at my back, a long stretch of lawn. Nowhere to run. Estrella, Tristan, and any thrall in the apartment would be able to see us.

Jules prowled toward me.

Fuck.

He crossed the space between us faster than I could process. He plucked one of the maroon pillows from the stone bench, not breaking his stride or his gaze with the movement. I twisted, knowing there was nowhere to go but needing to desperately get—

Jules pounced.

He crashed into me, arms locking around my waist as his weight sent us both tumbling. I screamed as we went down—

He slammed one hand out, catching us a mere inch off the ground. The other still gripped my waist. His breath huffed against my ear, in time with mine, in time with the wild pounding of our hearts.

For a moment, we just breathed together.

Then his teeth grazed my ear. "You never answered my question. Can I fuck you, wife?"

Stars forgive me.

I had sinned.

I would sin again.

I wanted to sin right now.

I wanted him to make me feel alive.

"Yes."

He released me. I dropped to the ground. My breasts pressed into the soft grass, shielded only by that thin layer of lace.

Above me, the shade flickered as Jules pushed onto his knees between my legs. His hands found my skirts, gathering the flowing fabric in a rough fist. He shoved the layers up over my hips, baring me to the open air.

I barely had time to gasp before the garden breeze kissed my naked ass.

"Hips up."

The command cut through my daze, instinct overriding thought. I pressed my knees into the grass automatically, lifting my hips. Jules jammed a pillow beneath me.

To keep my ass propped up for him.

More heat flushed through my face.

Then his palm cracked against one cheek.

I yelped, jerking forward at the sharp smack. The soothing rune dulled the pain, but I still felt every bit of the impact.

A low chuckle sounded behind me. I glanced back just in time to see Jules's smile widen, his shadowed eyes dark with something hotter than mischief. "Luc isn't the only one who likes this pretty, plump ass of ours."

His other hand came down, gripping the opposite cheek, kneading. Possessive. Pleased. My breath hitched.

With an approving hum, Jules shifted behind me, bracketing my legs with his own. A bit of pressure and he had my thighs pressed together, trapping me beneath him.

The clink of a buckle.

My heart jumped. My fingers dug into the dirt.

I had said yes, a moment of temporary insanity that I still floated in, but it didn't stop the spike of fear. "We're in the middle of a lawn. Anyone in the apartment could see us."

"It's our lawn. Our apartment. Our castle."

"Jules—"

A shadow fell over me.

Jules leaned forward, caging me beneath him. His hands found my wrists, pinning them down. His body—solid, powerful, all-encompassing—settled over mine. I was completely at his mercy. The heat of his cock burned against the curve of my ass.

His breath brushed the back of my head. "Our council, guards, and thralls have seen your beautiful, naked body already, Nessa."

I didn't have an argument for that. He was right.

And then he raised one hand from my wrists, snaked it between our bodies, and slid a finger deep into me. My thoughts fled. A cry tore from my lips.

"Stars, you're so fucking wet for me." He drew his finger out. "I don't even need to warm you up."

"Jules—"

The King of Dawn nocked his cock at my entrance and thrust.

"Oh, stars—" The words spilled from me as his length split me open.

As he filled me.

Filled me.

Filled me.

Fuck. I was going to burst. He was going to kill me. I would smile as I died. I had known that the minute I volunteered for the harvest. But I'd imagined dying from fangs, not a cock.

He hissed at the grip of my body, the pressure of his legs pining mine together and keeping me tight. When the head of his cock bumped against my ending, his fingers flexed around my wrists, a deep, wrecked groan escaping into my ear. "Fuck, I love your cunt."

A helpless whimper slid from my throat. The only sound I was capable of making. My entire body trembled, nerves sparking like wildfire.

Fuck. Was he always this massive?

I couldn't believe he fit inside me. How had I taken him *and* Luc back to back two days ago? I dug my fingers into the dirt, grasping for something to tether me as he let my body adjust to him.

Jules nuzzled into the back of my head. "Do you have trouble believing that, bride? That I love your cunt?"

"Yes." I managed to stutter out. There wasn't room in my mind for arguments, not with his cock impaling me like this.

"Just like you have trouble believing I'd want to paint your heaving, naked body as you whimper under me?" he asked, a smile in his voice.

A short, choked laugh escaped me. It cut off quickly into a groan. I hadn't meant to laugh, but it was such a ridiculous thing to say. What a sight we must have made. The brilliant godstar of ivory and gold buried deep in a pink puddle of a woman.

Divinity fucking mortality.

Jules slid out, then pulsed his hips. Our flesh slapping together. *Stars.*

"Answer the question, Nessa."

"Yes!" I shouted.

Sparks exploded behind my eyelids as he filled me again.

And again.

"Ohhh."

And again.

"Jules!"

His patience had reached his limit. With each thrust, his hips rocked mine into the pillow. Each time he bottomed out, he pressed me deep into the plush fabric.

I jolted with each touch.

My cries became an unending mewl.

Stars, I couldn't survive this.

I tried to squirm away, to escape the rising pleasure. His fist tightened around my wrists, his legs a cage to mine.

"Why?" he asked, voice hoarse.

Why? Oh. Yes. Why didn't I believe him? I fought the wave to form an answer. "Because I'm not... ah... I'm just..."

"Just..." He thrust. "...what?"

"Just Nessa!"

Suddenly, I was on my back. Jules's arms caged me in, his weight pressing me into the earth, our chests brushing through the thin layer of rumpled lace.

Those shadowed eyes captured mine. "What does that mean?"

I was dizzy from the sudden shift, dizzy from the wave of bliss clawing inside me, demanding him back. I glanced down between us. His thick, throbbing length lay heavy against my belly, soaked with my lust. His cock looked just as frustrated as I felt. "What?"

"Just Nessa."

I flushed. "It's… I'm…" I waved my hand around, gesturing vaguely at my entire form. "I'm just me. I'm… boring. Average in every way. Ordinary."

His eyes narrowed. "Who told you that?"

Everyone I had ever met. Even if they didn't say it like my stepmother, I had seen it. Had watched too many eyes glaze over, suffered too many interruptions while I tattered on about books and facts. "Does it matter?"

"It does."

"Can you…" I shifted beneath him, aching for friction, but his knees still trapped me. I snaked my hand down my body, over the lace. I needed something. Anything.

Jules caught my wrist in a lightning-fast grip. A second later, both my arms were pinned above my head again. Damn vampire.

"Can't we…" I couldn't believe I was saying this. "Can't we just fuck? Why do we need to talk?"

His smile was slow. "You said I don't know enough about you. I'm simply trying to rectify that."

Fucker. "Why do you care?"

Jules cocked his head. "Why don't you want to answer?"

I sighed and tried to squirm out from underneath him. His grip on me tightened, trapping me in place.

"Answer the question, bride."

"My stepmother," I blurted out. "She and my sister are beautiful, like little dolls with vibrant red hair, the greenest eyes and tiny, lithe bodies. I'm…"

Muddy brown hair.

Muddy brown eyes.

Plain features and a lumbering frame.

Large breasts and a soft stomach and thick thighs.

I swallowed. "I'm just Nessa."

Jules stared. "I think I'm going to kill your family."

My eyes widened. "What?"

"You heard me."

I pushed uselessly against his hold, wrists twisting beneath his grasp. "You can't kill my family."

Jules snorted. "I can quite easily kill your family." He said it like it was the simplest thing in the world. Like ordering wine or summoning a tailor. "I don't even need to do it myself. I'll have a message sent to Corraidin's magistrates. They'll gladly kill anyone I request." He pursed his lips, as if considering it. "Though it'd be far more enjoyable if I did it myself."

My heartbeat stuttered. If Jules wanted to kill my family, I couldn't stop him. I didn't care about my stepmother or father's well-being any more than they had cared for mine, but Aislin didn't deserve to die. Neither did Orrin, Saraid, Finola, or Urrick. They were *children*. "Please don't kill my family."

"Why?" he asked, like he genuinely didn't understand. "They don't deserve to breathe."

"For saying I'm just Nessa?"

"For making you hate yourself."

I flinched at the blunt words. "I don't hate myself."

Jules raised his brows. "Don't you? You can't lie to me."

My eyes burned. I hated *him* sometimes. At least, I tried. I blinked hard, shoving back the tears threatening to spill over, but that didn't stop my core from pulsing, desperate for relief. "Let go of me."

"No." Jules shoved his knees between mine, his free arm hooking under my thigh. He spread me wide with easy, practiced strength. He rolled his hips. I yelped as his cock slid over my clit. "You're not running away from this."

"Jules," I moaned.

"You aren't just Nessa anymore. You're *my* Nessa." He slid the head of his cock through my slick heat, slow, teasing. "My soulbound." Then, without warning, he thrust inside me. A single, deep stroke. "My *wife*."

A low moan escaped my throat. Finally. Back where he belonged. My ankles locked around his thighs, like I could hold him inside me forever. My cunt clenched around him. Jules groaned, dropping his head into the crook of my neck, his breath hot against my skin.

"You entranced me the second you first met my eyes, you brave, wild thing. How could there ever be anything ordinary about you?" He pressed a soft kiss to my chest, right above the neckline of the lace. Right where Luc had carved the covenant runespell. "I will thank the godstars every day for blessing me with an eternity in your soft body. And one day, in your heart."

My mouth popped open. A shudder rolled through me. How could he say things like that? How could he sound so utterly certain? I knew love between soulbound heartmates was as inevitable as sex between vampire and thrall. I had nearly accepted one, but the other...

How could I fall in love with the Butcher? The Conqueror?

Had it already started?

Jules smirked, as if he read the question on my face. He nipped my bottom lip. "Lock your ankles behind my back, lovely. Let's take you for a ride."

I obeyed. Without a second's hesitation.

Jules didn't give me another moment to prepare.

He thrust into me like he had never stopped. His rhythm picked up effortlessly, like his body had been waiting for this moment, aching for it. I clung to him, and he took me apart.

Oh, stars. He was everything, everywhere, all at once. My world was his swirling black eyes. His soft, pale skin. The strands of his white-gold hair grazing my cheek. The raw, breathtaking pleasure he wove through me. His nose brushed mine, our breaths mingling.

But he didn't close that last inch between our lips.

He wanted to watch every flicker across my face.

I knew because I wanted to watch his.

A pretty flush stained Jules's cheeks. His lips were parted, his eyes lidded. His brow furrowed as he released a low groan. He had never been more beautiful. Cresting on a wave of bliss, utterly lost to it. If I focused, I could nearly feel that building heat coiling in his gut, mirroring my own.

"I was—ah... wrong."

My fingers dug into the muscles of his back, holding on for life. I didn't even process what he said. *Couldn't.* "What?"

Jules pumped into me... then stopped. I whimpered. He lowered his face until he brushed my lips. Gold-lined black irises burned into me, trapping *me in their gravity. I sunk into the heat of her, her cunt around my cock, her soft skin beneath my chest, but that gaze of hers ensnared me. I didn't need the bond to read her, not when she looked at me like that.*

*She couldn't hide from me. Not in any way.*

*"This," I murmured, "is the best view of your eyes."*

I jerked back to myself at the words. Oh. *Oh.* I don't know how I flushed harder, given I was a few thrusts away from coming, but I managed—

Jules shifted, holding himself up on one forearm as he reached behind him. His fingers curled around my locked ankles. I gasped as he pulled them along his body, dragging them up from his ass to the small of his back.

My knees bent, my body stretching.

My hips lifted from the ground.

I moaned.

The King of Dawn pulled out of me before pushing back in. All thoughts left my head. I screamed. He sank deep. Deeper. Oh, fuck, this angle. My entire body arched, my eyelids flickering shut as heat rippled through me—

Jules nipped my chin. "Look at me. I *need* your eyes."

"Oh." I licked my lips, but my eyes blinked open. "Okay?"

His grip returned around my wrists, his other hand clawing into the dirt, grounding himself as he fucked me with punishing precision.

I tensed beneath him, my body clenching around his cock, sucking him deeper—

"Fuck," Jules groaned.

I watched, enraptured, as his orgasm shattered through him. He let it take him, surrendering with ease. Succumbing to his pleasure. Such beautiful bliss. It echoed through the bond, a faint aftershock curling through my senses.

But it didn't stop him. Jules kept thrusting, kept filling me, fucking me full of his cum.

Marking me.

Claiming me.

The wet slap of our bodies was indecent, obscene. He didn't pause, even once his eyes cleared, dark as night but wickedly alive. I whimpered, a pathetic, desperate, hot noise. I was closer, closer, closer.

But still not there.

*Of course not. You're broken, Nessa.* The thought slithered through my mind, taunting and laughing. I clenched, and not in a good way this time. A hint of pain flared through me with the movement, flaring through where Jules speared me open for him.

Jules didn't feel it, but he saw it, watching my every move beneath him.

He dropped his lips to mine.

I yelped, but he caught my mouth, swallowing the sound. His tongue overtook mine. Domineering. Possessing. His hips were all but ramming into mine, rocking forward to grind against my clit. Pleasure sparked through my nerves, the heat rising and rising.

Fuck, I was so close. I could see the edge, the fall into wonder. But I couldn't move, couldn't get there. So frustratingly, devastatingly close—

Words whispered against my lips. "Agony or ecstasy?"

I didn't even hesitate. "Ecstasy. Please, stars, make me come—"

He chuckled. "The godstars have nothing to do with this. *I'm* going to make you come."

"Yes, please, Jules—ohhh."

His fangs pierced my neck.

His venom met my bloodstream.

His next thrust shoved me off the cliff.

I buckled. Screaming. Sobbing. Begging. Pleasure tore through me, violent, punishing, divine. I clenched down around him, my cunt a vice grip around his cock.

Jules shuddered, a curse ripping from his throat as another orgasm dragged him under. His second release flooded inside me, hot and thick, his cock jerking with every pulse of pleasure.

I was wrecked.

Ruined.

*His.*

He swallowed a deep gulp of my blood, forcing another screech from my throat. The Butcher fucked and fed. Fed and fucked. And the explosion in me raged on and on.

When we floated down from the high together, Jules's hips slowed to a gentle roll, rocking me through the last aftershocks. The world stitched itself back together. Speck by speck. A sky of soft blue and white clouds stretched above us. The sunlight poured over the king, turning him into a gold-haloed masterpiece.

With a sigh, Jules collapsed on top of me. Even as the shocks of pleasure faded, my body twitched and trembled, completely wrung out. I melted under him.

I had thought of myself as a puddle of a woman before.

Now, I truly was one.

Before I complained about the bulk of him, Jules rolled off, dropping onto the grass. His black trousers were pushed down around his thighs, his softening, glistening cock visible to anyone watching. Our pleasure mixed with streaks of my blood.

My blush turned from bliss to mortified horror. Of course, I had bled. Even if I couldn't feel it now, my body still hated me. But Jules just went slack in the grass, throwing an arm over his face, completely unbothered. Like my blood didn't matter. Like lying half-naked in the sun didn't matter.

If I looked like him, I probably wouldn't care either.

I didn't turn toward the castle. I didn't need to know who watched the King of Dawn claim me in the middle of a lawn. In their private garden, yes, but the kings' apartment was hardly what I'd call private.

I yanked my lace gown over me like a pathetic excuse for a blanket. Something clattered, like metal against metal. Jules's gilded hellynx daggers clattered against his belt from where it scattered across the red fabric.

I couldn't resist. I traced the edge of the daemium blade's hilt, following the sheath of the short, wide blade that ended in a gentle curve. His other blade was curved and longer, made for quick slashes like with Fergus on the road.

"Why is this one a different shape?" I asked, my voice quiet.

Jules dropped his arm from his face and blew a strand of pale hair off his face. "Adé."

"What?"

He grinned lazily over at me. "Why is *Adé* a different shape?"

I managed an unimpressed expression, but it didn't change his smile. "Fine. Why is *Adé* a different shape?"

He reached out, tracing the blade where my finger had been a moment ago. "The shallow curve and extended belly allows for cuts precise enough to sever skin from flesh."

I dropped the blade. Stars, that was the Butcher's *skinning* knife.

...and I had fucked its owner.

Again.

I lay my hands over my face and groaned.

Jules snorted. "At least wait a couple minutes before regretting me. A lesser man might take it personally."

I didn't reply. I couldn't look at him ever again. Couldn't look at myself. Why had I done that? The bond had resonated through me like a bell, demanding and demanding since the moment I woke.

But I couldn't blame it all on the bond.

The moment he asked to paint my eyes, *I* had wanted him.

A shadow flickered above me, breaking through the gaps between my fingers. Everything in me tightened.

The press of undeniable power.

The weight of five centuries.

The might of the warlord king.

Oh, gods. Of course *he* was here.

I opened my eyes to a pair of black boots. I trailed my gaze up strong calves, over sculpted thighs, past a thick silver belt glinting in the sunlight. A solid black doublet stretched across his broad shoulders, ever the stature of a warrior.

I met darkening silver eyes. I went still beneath their luminous glow, like a child caught doing something naughty.

But Luc wasn't angry.

He was hungry.

I was lying naked before him in the sun, sweat-stained and scent-marked, and he wanted to devour me whole. He *did* devour me whole, luring me deep into his gaze until I was lost in him—

I tore my eyes away, halting the trance, before the bond dragged me into his head—

And met Maire's hardened expression.

I tensed.

The thrall dipped out of the gilded window frame a second later, but I had seen enough. The cold shock. The righteous anger. The... betrayal?

"This doesn't look very restful," Luc said, the deep rumble of his voice cutting through my thoughts of Maire.

"I assure you it was, Lucey." Jules tugged the pillow out from under me. My ass hit the grass with a splat. "See, look, a pillow."

Luc arched an unimpressed brow.

"She barely moved a muscle."

His other brow joined the first.

"I did all the work," Jules said, sitting up. "It still counts."

Luc's expression didn't change, didn't flicker from Jules. But his words were for me. "Do you feel rested, bride?"

I glanced between the kings. "What if I say no?"

"Ah, the betrayal," Jules exclaimed, draping a dramatic hand over his forehead.

Luc ignored him. "Then Julien disobeyed. When you disobey, you're punished."

Jules dropped his hand instantly. “Never mind. Tell him you're exhausted. I wore you out, didn't I?”

He—what? “You want to be punished?”

“Only by Luc.” A wild gleam filled his gaze. “Though you could give it a try, if you want. Bet you'd have me coming for you in minutes.”

Heat flushed from my cheeks down to my chest. “What? You—no—“

“Well, the offer is always there.” He turned his attention to Luc. “Speaking of coming, who's in the lead?”

The kings brushed their fingers against their wrists in perfect synchronization. A runespell flared into shadowy existence on their skin. *Archive. Extract. Reveal.* But the shadows didn't fade. They spread and rose, becoming shapes in the air above the kings' arms.

Words in the air.

And numbers underneath them.

The words were blurred, but I knew a tally when I saw one. Columns and rows of corresponding competitions, tracking their wins in an endless game.

Luc examined a specific tally. “We're tied again.”

My brow creased. “Tied?”

Jules cackled. “Our newest challenge. Take a guess. Luc was winning four-three until about five minutes ago.”

My face instantly heated. No. They couldn't... he couldn't...

Were the Imperium tracking my orgasms?

“Don't be shy.” Jules bopped my chin with his fingers. “Share your answer with your soulbound.”

I swallowed. “It's how many times you've each made me... come.”

“Exactly!” Jules grinned up at Luc. “Here to retake your lead?”

Luc let his eyes linger on me. My breath hitched at the heat in his gaze. If he wanted to fuck me, it wouldn't take much to make me spread my legs. The soulbond was sated for now, but underneath that was an endless hunger for the two vampires to whom I was irrevocably bound.

With the slightest nudge, I'd be desperate and needy all over again.

Wicked, sinful girl.

Luc offered me a hand. “Perhaps later.”

Jules pouted. “Why not now?”

I stared at his palm, silver rings glinting in the light. Luc only waited, knowing I'd obey.

Everyone obeyed.

With a swallow, I placed my hand in his, dainty in comparison, and let him pull me up. I held my dress before me, the pathetic barrier of fabric *slightly* harder to see through when folded.

Luc's lips twitched. I probably wasn't very successful at hiding anything.

Jules groaned at my back, at the sight of my entire ass in his face.

Or maybe it was his cum dripping down my thighs.

Then Luc spoke, this time directly to me. "Sabas found your mother."

# 39

My mother was alive.

My mother.

Alive.

Nearly twenty years had passed since the harvest that took her from me. I had been so sure she'd died ages ago. Patriarch Meallán always said it was better to imagine our loved ones dead than the damnation they actually resided in.

I straightened in the saddle, my back brushing Luc's wall of a chest. We followed a path down the eastern side of the mountain, beneath towering trees crowned with pale green leaves. Titus padded silently beside us like we were going for a leisurely ride.

One that would end with seeing my *mother*.

What would I say to her?

What would *she* say to me?

Would she say she missed me?

Would she judge me for not even trying to meet the birth quota, as she had tried and tried and tried?

Would she hate me for falling willingly into the bed of the Imperium?

I clenched my fists in my lap. There was no point ruminating over what would happen. I didn't even really remember her as a person. I had only been nine when she left. When I closed my eyes and pictured her, all I remembered was her widened brown eyes before she turned from her silent husband and sobbing child, toward town hall and the waiting magistrates.

The rest of her face? A blur.

Her voice? Long since faded from memory.

But even if I did remember her, she wouldn't be the same person she was when she left. I had only spent a little over a week in the Impire proper, and already I was a stranger to the Nessa of a month ago.

The trees thinned, giving way to sunlit rolling hills dappled with wildflowers. Titus dashed ahead into the open field, his huge paws crushing the scattered violet blooms. Jules's hellsteed, Cala, released a jealous huff that sounded almost like a growl. I shied back instinctively from the sound—and into Luc's chest. I shuddered at the touch of satin over solid muscle, the brush of his chin against my head. I forced my spine to go stiff. It wasn't wise to get too comfortable in these arms, no matter the bond's urging.

The King of Dawn patted his hellsteed's neck. "You can run once we get to Tenebra de Mar, Wrath."

I cleared my throat. *Don't think about Luc's body, don't think about Luc's body.* "You still haven't explained how we're getting to Tenebra de Mar in a day."

When Luc had told me Sabas had found my mother but that she wasn't in Montaurère, my heart had sunk. Her masters had left her behind as part of the staff maintaining their Tenebra de Mar home while they spent the spring and summer in Montaurère. Apparently, most of the Azarasians moved between their two cities, depending on the season.

It had taken six days to get from Mabon to Montaurère. Tenebra de Mar was in the south of the Impire, easily twice that distance, but the kings had assured me we'd arrive within the hour.

Jules glanced over his shoulder. "You'll see in a minute."

I frowned at him, then at Luc, but only enough to catch the quirk of his lips. He wasn't going to spoil the surprise, either.

I whipped back around before I gave into temptation and met those silver eyes. "What if my mother doesn't have any answers? Will you return to Mabon to speak with my father?"

"Sabas had the magistrates of your city speak with him yesterday," Luc said. I went still. "Your father doesn't know anything about glamours or soulbonds."

"Oh." My father must have been cursing my name, my stepmother adding another item to the mental sin list she had started for me at age ten.

Assuming they were alive.

How many bodies had I seen ravaged by the magistrates? They didn't attack indiscriminately, but if the Imperium had sent them to gather answers, there weren't any lines they wouldn't cross.

I didn't want to know.

I *had* to know.

"Did the magistrates... hurt them?"

Luc's heavy gaze settled on the back of my head. "Your family remained unharmed."

The tension fled from me. Thank the stars. I didn't care about my father or stepmother, but I didn't want them hurt. Aislin loved her parents and had already suffered enough loss.

My heart panged. Stars, I missed my sister. Did she blame herself for me leaving? Did she pray for my soul every morning and night? Or had she already forgotten me, thinking me better off dead like the Church preached?

It didn't matter. I'd never know.

Luc tensed his legs, urging his hellsteed into a trot. My pulse dropped into my lower belly at the feel of those strong thighs. I had ridden with both kings multiple times on the trip to Montaurère, my nerves and desire at war then. Now, after the soulbond, only lust remained.

How had Jules put it? The soulbond was *insistent*. It was content enough to be a few feet away from the King of Dawn after sating its craving in the garden, but its need for Luc had only grown wilder. I kept my breathing even as panic spiked in me. The emotion quickly faded away, suppressed by the bond and replaced with anticipation.

It was only a matter of time before Luc reclaimed his lead. And we *both* knew it. His attention on me had grown heavier on my shoulders. A shiver tracing my spine—

"If you had someone else question my father, why are we going to Tenebra de Mar ourselves?" I blurted out.

The kings glanced at each other, a quick flicker of their eyes that I sensed instead of saw. Both of them were... amused. Heat rushed to my cheeks. I wasn't being very subtle in my attempts to ignore the rising lust.

"Do you not wish to see your mother?" Luc asked.

"Well, yes, but I—"

Wait.

*Wait.*

Were they doing this for me? Why the fuck would they do that? They didn't know me. I didn't know them. I was only meant to be their Mortal

Bride and thrall until a soulbond tied us together. We didn't have a real connection.

Not *today*.

I exhaled slowly as we edged around the mountain, a rough face of rock to my right—

I choked on my breath.

Behind Montaurère, expanding northwest for miles into the hills, was a starcrater. Dark shadows steamed from the unrefined daemium, twisting up into the sky. I gaped at the expanse of darkness. It was nearly the size of a city, putting the one we had seen on the road to shame.

I didn't even have to ask.

"This is Toreth's starcrater," Luc said. "He was part of the First Godsfall almost ten thousand years ago."

Toreth. I didn't know that name. The Divine Host had only banished a hundred godstars during the First Godsfall, but I had never stumbled across a list. "It's... huge."

I couldn't come up with any better descriptor, but the wonder in my voice was clear.

Luc chuckled softly. "It's one of the largest starcraters on the planet. Toreth was a general of the rebellious godstars and incredibly powerful, even after he fell."

"Then why was Azaras the ruler of this region and not him?" Azaras was part of the Second Godsfall, when thousands of godstars streaked across the skies and littered the earth with starcraters. That didn't necessarily make him weaker than Toreth, but many of the First had held onto their domains during the centuries-long territory battles that followed.

"Toreth disappeared right after the First Godsfall," Luc said. "We don't have many records from then, so no one knows exactly what happened. He's alive, though. The shadows from his crater would stop if he were dead."

"That's... slightly terrifying."

Jules snorted from his place a few strides ahead of us, turning slightly in his saddle. "Wherever he is, he isn't bothering anyone. He's the least terrifying demon, in my opinion."

"Maybe he kills everyone he bothers, so they're never heard from again and no one knows he's running around committing unspeakable horrors."

There was a slight pause before Luc said, a smile evident in his voice, "You have quite the imagination, little curiosity."

I shuddered. No matter how far I ran from my desire, I always ended back in the thick of it. I straightened, clearing my throat. "How is Toreth's starcrater related to Tenebra de Mar?"

"We're going to use it as a runegate," Luc said.

"You can do that?" If a small hunk of daemium could transport us to the top of the mountain, how far could a runegate carved into a starcrater go?

Apparently, all the way to Tenebra de Mar at least.

"Once the runes are carved, it's not that difficult," Jules said before twisting around toward the green fields to our left. "You coming, Titus?"

The hellwolf stopped and glanced back. His shadow eyes flickered from us to the crater like he was weighing his options. After a second, he huffed and dashed for the treeline in the opposite direction.

I couldn't help but smile after the wolf. "I take that as a no?"

"Probably for the best," Luc said. "He and the hellcat who lives in Duskfell were at each other's throats all winter. I had to pry them apart too many times to count."

"That's what you get for being the responsible sibling." Jules smiled over at us. "I've nominated Cédric for that role. He's lucky Perry's off in Kotara, otherwise he'd have to spend half his time as our referee."

I stared for a long second. He couldn't possibly mean… "Wait." I spun toward Luc. "Are you saying that Titus is a *child* of Azaras? You have a wolf for a brother?"

Luc's lips twitched. "That is what he said."

"I have a whale for an uncle," Jules added.

"You *what*?"

"Thaddeus fucked a whale once."

I blinked at him. "Excuse me?"

"In his defense, he was also a whale at the time." Jules's brows furrowed in thought. "Or perhaps a kraken. Whatever he was, he was whale-sized, too."

"It's still messed up."

"It's not the oddest pairing," Luc said. "Do you know why the Tyrhari have never brought an army to our northern border?"

I frowned. "I don't know anything about your northern border. Books on geography aren't allowed in Mabon."

There was a beat of silence, just enough to notice, before Luc murmured, "We'll have to rectify that."

"A hellbeast is terrifying enough," Jules said. "Let's not give her nightmares by starting off her lessons with the Salathien Hellwood."

Hellwood? Nope. No thank you. Jules was right. I did *not* want to know what monster resulted from a demon and a starsdamned tree. A hellwolf and hellwhale were terrifying enough.

"Do you both have other hellbeast... relatives?"

Luc nodded. "You might meet Saffira, the hellcat, but she and Titus are the only two I know."

"He has more," Jules said casually. "Azaras's Beast infamously fucked anything that moved."

Luc stiffened slightly behind me, almost imperceptible if not for the soulbond. Jules didn't even pause.

"But all demonblood have hellbeast relatives," he continued. "So sharing a demon for a sire or grandsire doesn't mean much in our world."

Luc remained silent for a fraction too long. I felt it in the shift of his breathing, the brief tension locking his muscles. Why had that comment rattled him? Nothing rattled the Conqueror.

Then, just as quickly, he forced himself to relax.

"Titus and Saffira have the intelligence to choose to live in harmony with us," Luc said, his voice smooth and measured. "Our other hellbeast relatives are far more likely to attempt to eat us."

"Just like Azaras's hellbat children in *The Soulborne Queen*." I had read that scene more times than I cared to admit. Karra's first introduction to Azaras's hell realm almost ended with her being devoured by a bat the size of a dog.

"Ugh, hellbats." Jules visibly shuddered. "Fuckers will try to eat anything, demons included."

"Good to—" My voice trailed off as we crested the last hill between us and the expanse of shadow.

Were there... people kneeling at the starcrater's edge?

A cold, crawling dread spread through my limbs. I had wondered where Estrella and Tristan went. When we had returned to the apartment from the garden, they were nowhere to be found. Luc dismissing them wasn't too surprising, but they hadn't returned as we made our way through Dawnspear to the stables.

Instead, they had gone off to collect sacrifices.

There was no other reason for nearly twenty thralls to kneel around a starcrater.

The fluttering in my stomach twisted into nausea. If Jules hadn't reapplied the soothing rune before we left, I'd be doubled over at the sight. I wanted to be wrong, but I wasn't. Blood had activated all the runegates I'd witnessed. Those smaller gates hadn't even taken us far. If this one would bring us all the way to Tenebra de Mar, it would need far more power than a few drops could provide.

No wonder we hadn't used a starcrater to travel from Mabon. The kings would've had to kill half the harvest, maybe more.

"No." I nearly grabbed the reins from Luc's hands. I didn't know how to steer a horse—and Wrath was a hellsteed, likely to ignore my commands—but I would've tried if I thought it had a chance of stopping this.

"Relax, lovely," Jules said. "They're all prisoners, slated for death either way."

"And what crimes did they commit? Were they as guilty as Éamon?"

Jules cocked his head, frowning.

"The human who removed her from our apartment," Luc reminded him.

"It only happened two days ago," I nearly hissed.

Jules shrugged. "If I had to remember all the humans who died in front of me, I wouldn't have room in my mind for anything else."

"Maybe that's a problem."

Jules directed a grimace at Luc. "Darling, this was supposed to make our wife happy and now she's yelling at me."

"She is right here," I snapped. At the Butcher. Fuck him. "And she will continue yelling at you—"

Luc gripped the bar at the back of my collar and tugged lightly, just enough to make me stutter and stop. My clit throbbed, a sudden, short burst. If I could yell at my poorly timed desire, I would do that, too.

"Their crimes are irrelevant, bride," Luc said firmly. "They will die either way and if we can use their deaths to fulfill a greater purpose, we will always take that path."

I shuddered at the ruthless practicality of it. "Well, I don't even want to go to Tenebra de Mar anymore, so it's a *wasted* purpose."

"Liar," he murmured against my ear.

I flinched, pulling forward. Luc released his hold on my collar. "I don't want to go if it means someone will *die*."

Stars, please don't let that be a lie. Please, please, please.

Luc didn't contradict me.

I went slack in his arms. I wasn't completely lost.

"If your father didn't know about the runespells, your mother must. She'd have noticed her child missing otherwise." Luc blanked his expression, the Conqueror returning to his bright eyes. "I don't trust this conversation to anyone but us, and we can't waste a week traveling there on hellsteed."

Estrella and Tristan glanced at their King of Dusk, who nodded in reply. They moved in opposite directions, each unsheathing a steel blade.

The thralls trembled, their cries muffled by runed iron mouthpieces. None of them tried to run, but I knew they all wanted to. More than one thrall runespell flared as we approached from behind. Their faces would surely show their fear. But did I want to see their faces? Did I want to remember their terror as they died?

As one, in perfect sync as only soulbound could be, Estrella and Tristan slashed their blades across the bare throats of their first victims.

Blood sprayed in a crimson arc, splattering across the blackened earth. In a heartbeat, the guards twisted their blades downward, cutting from throat to navel. The bodies barely had time to crumple before their organs slipped free, swallowed whole by the shifting shadows.

The runespell carved deep into the soil flared with a surge of power as the pooling blood filled the grooves. I slammed a hand over my mouth. Luc drew a rune against my shoulder, stopping my nausea, but it did nothing for my horror.

Slash. Eviscerate. Repeat.

Again and again. The rhythm of butchery.

By the time the last body hit the ground, the runes were slick with blood, the soil greedily soaking in the sacrifice. The air grew thick with iron.

*Gate. Distance. Path. Arrival. Cross.*

The shadows over the crater writhed and stretched, thickening as they absorbed the strength of twenty stolen lives. A rancid smell reached my nose as the kings' hellsteeds stepped over the nearest corpse. Something crunched beneath their hooves. Not even a rune could stop me from gagging.

I swallowed the bile in my throat. Jules had said they were criminals... by Azarasian standards. Whatever their crime, they would have died anyway. But that didn't change the tremor in my breath, the way it shuddered past my lips as I fought to suppress it. Luc made no move to comfort me. His grip around my waist remained steady. Unyielding. Unrelenting.

Like I'd need to get used to death.

Luc clicked his tongue, and Wrath surged forward, running straight into the shadows. Heat washed over my skin—

And stayed, the sun suddenly burning in the sky. It crashed down on my shoulders, like we were in the thick of a Maboni summer. Stars, how hot would it get here if this was the temperature in spring?

We'd gone through a runegate on one edge of a starcrater and emerged from another. This one stretched just as far as Toreth's, but the landscape was harsher—a flat, grassy savanna sprawling beyond the steep cliff to my left. The stench of blood and rot was gone, replaced by the sharp tang of salt, a scent I had only encountered once before on the Thaddeian Ocean's breeze.

I turned, following my nose.

Turquoise blue water crashed against a shore of black, wafting sand. A shorter cliff of dark rocks rose on the other side of the beach, a city perched on its back. The Capital of Dusk was built on top of Azaras's starcrater, the twisting roads threaded between sandstone buildings like veins of shadow. Further inland, at the city's edge, the silver dome of a palace shimmered under the sun. Duskfell's famed tiered gardens cascaded down in a defiant burst of green, a stark contrast against the sand and smoke.

It was all beautiful. But my gaze was drawn past all of it, to the impossibly tall tower of daemium looming over the city center.

The Beast's Roost.

My imagination had paled in comparison to the real thing. From its peak, Azaras would have had all of his starcrater in his sight. I suddenly understood the terror that had gripped people every night for centuries, knowing their demon king's curse had turned him into a winged monster.

No one could forget the Beast hunted from the starlit skies, not with one look up. I judged Karra a little less for nearly wetting herself when she first looked over the edge.

A breath rushed out of me, long and slow.

I had stepped from brutal reality directly into the pages of *The Soulborne Queen*.

Karra's former home.

Azaras's former capital.

Tenebra de Mar, in the flesh.

# 40

By the time we rode into the palace's square, my wonder had trampled my anger and horror into dust. It was unfair that monsters this terrible created cities of such stunning beauty. Very few vampires and thralls remained in Tenebra de Mar right now, so I had no audience beyond the kings as I gaped at every intersection, every storefront, every grand house and manor.

And now I gaped at Duskfell.

The palace was plucked right out of *The Soulborne Queen.* Rusticated arches framed the thousands of sapphire blue doors and silver-paned windows embedded into the façade of black stone, nearly as dark as the daemium tower in the city center behind me. Towering columns stretched from the ground to the cornices crowning the building five stories overhead. From this angle, only the spire on top of the massive dome was visible, a glint of silver in the sunlight.

I barely noticed Luc dismounting his hellsteed, too busy drinking in every detail. I had imagined this city, this palace, a hundred times over, and not once had I come close to its true magnificence.

Large hands settled on my waist, plucking me from the saddle and my thoughts. Luc set me on my feet as a small contingent of vampire attendants spilled from the palace doors. I tried to keep my shoulders straight, but I couldn't help but hunch the slightest bit, even if none of them met my gaze directly.

"Imperium," a male vampire said as he dropped into a low bow. "We weren't expecting you. Please forgive our poor greeting—"

"It's of no concern, Barros," Luc said, twisting toward the vampire, one hand still resting on my hip. "This wasn't a planned trip."

Tristan slid from his hellsteed's back, but Estrella remained seated, like Jules. The King of Dawn nudged Cala forward until I was nearly forehead-to-snout with his white-spotted sable mare. "I'll collect Orlagh Halloran. Are we doing this in the throne room?"

"I think something less formal will suffice." Luc examined me coolly for a moment before glancing back to Jules. "The library?"

"Which one? Main floor, third floor, or the apartment?"

My gaping returned like it had never left. "Duskfell has *three* libraries?"

The corner of Luc's lip twitched. "I consider the third floor more of a laboratory."

Jules scoffed. "There's too many books for me to count, so it's a library."

"I don't think that's how it works," I said.

"It works how I want it to work." Jules winked down at me. "It's like you forget I'm a king, lovely."

I didn't dignify that with a response, but my grimace only seemed to amuse him.

"First floor it is, then," Jules said. "Try not to have too much fun without me."

I went stiff. The King of Dusk's hand burned into me through the thin layer of my gown. Jules didn't necessarily mean sex. Surely, there were other fun things to do in a palace. Not that the bond and I were in agreement on that one.

Luc only lifted an arrogant brow. "Don't be gone too long then, Julien."

Jules shuddered slightly at his full name in Luc's dulcet tones. "A fucking minute will be too long."

"You'll survive."

Jules straightened suddenly, a wicked light entering his eyes. "You know what would help?" He had his hellsteed turn until he loomed over me. "May I ask a boon of you, sweet bride?"

"A boon?"

"Something to warm my heart when we're parted."

I narrowed my eyes instantly. "How long will you be gone?"

"An hour," he sighed, like he'd said a year.

Or, given he was immortal, a century.

I glanced down at myself, as if a suitable gift might suddenly appear tucked into the folds of my riding gown. The emerald fabric was sturdier than the lace from this morning and paired with a contraption Jules had called a brassière. The matching drawers were made of silk and smaller than any undergarments I'd ever worn.

Apparently, traveling meant I gained extra layers—but none of them hid secret pockets.

"I don't have anything to give you."

His grin widened. "You do."

"Like what?"

Luc gave a small smirk. "He wants your panties."

I blinked at him. Panties? Jules had called the tiny drawers I wore panties...

"You want my *undergarments*?" I squeaked. The gathered vampires remained silent, their expressions unreadable, but I swore I caught the faintest flicker of amusement in Tristan's gaze before he schooled his features. "You just gave them to me two hours ago."

"Mm-hmm," Jules purred. "Just enough time."

Just enough time? I opened my mouth to ask... then snapped it shut. I didn't want to know. More importantly, I didn't want the entirety of Duskfell's palace staff to know. Though they likely already did.

I stared at Jules.

He stared back. He was entirely serious... and waiting for me to hand over my panties, like every other vampire in the palace's plaza.

I swallowed. Okay. This was happening. Honestly, it didn't even make the list of most embarrassing things that had happened to me in the last week. Breathe in. Breathe out. The quicker I got this over with, the quicker we could get inside.

To the *library*.

But how exactly did one gracefully remove their undergarments in public?

As if he heard the thought—or felt my panic through the bond—Luc offered me his hand. I stared at his bronze palm. That didn't answer my question.

"For balance," he added.

Oh. It did answer my question, then.

With a deep breath, I placed my hand in his. Luc steadied me as I bent and reached up my skirt. My gaze fixed on the stone tiles as I eased my panties down and stepped out of them. A little pink-tinged wet spot stained the center. Magic had kept away the pain, but my ailing body still reacted to the desire thudding through me. It always had, yet it still managed to shock me every time.

I bundled the fabric in my fist as I straightened, heat flooding my face. The blush deepened when Jules held out his hand, the rubies on his fingers catching the light. I all but tossed them at him.

The King of Dawn immediately brought them to his nose and inhaled.

My jaw dropped. My stomach flipped. My thighs clenched in vain against the wave of pooling heat.

"Delicious." Jules tucked my panties in his trouser pocket. "I'll make sure to return them in one piece."

I frowned. Why was returning them in more than one piece even an option?

The next second, Jules kicked Cala into motion. He guided her in a wide loop through the plaza before heading toward the gates leading into the city, Estrella and her hellsteed in his wake.

Leaving me alone with the Conqueror.

"Come, bride." Luc released my hand and lowered it to the small of my back. Without a word to the staff, he led me through the towering doors and into the palace's high-ceiling halls.

Where Dawnspear was gold and white and bloody paintings, Duskfell was silver and black and bloody paintings. But here, the ceiling murals depicted twinkling stars, not massacres. Instead of rigid symmetry and towering grandeur, the palace had arched corridors, recessed alcoves, and balconies draped in wrought iron. The doorways were rounded instead of square, their frames adorned with intricate filigree, and some hallways led through open-air courtyards. Each time we passed through an entryway into the interior, the temperature dropped, as if magic were warding off the worst of the heat.

What would the library be like? Karra hadn't visited any library in Duskfell in Volume I, so I had no idea what to expect. I glanced up at Luc—then dropped my gaze just as quickly. He radiated authority and confidence, an ease that I had never experienced once in my life. It was always difficult not to wilt into a stuttering moron before him.

Jules always made it so easy.

The King of Dusk didn't know the meaning of the word.

The silence only thickened the tension between us. *Within* us. Luc wouldn't breach it. His lips stayed in that small, knowing smirk, somehow as chilling as it was heated, a predator watching its prey squirm at the edges of its vision. He wouldn't have to wait long.

*Do it, idiot. He's literally been inside you.* "Why the library? Don't you have a dozen sitting rooms?"

His brow arched. "Would you prefer a sitting room?"

"No?"

That dark brow inched higher.

"No," I said, firmly this time.

He squeezed my hip, a small reward. And it was a reward, no matter how much I wished it wasn't. My skin tingled. My nipples peaked. My breath hitched.

Damn bond.

"That doesn't answer why." I didn't even know what I was getting at. Did I want to know if this was for me? Because I was his soulbound? Because he wanted to fuck me? Both?

The answer couldn't change anything. In the handful of hours after becoming their Mortal Bride—before they learned I was their soulbound—I had glimpsed the real Conqueror and the Butcher. Even if I hadn't, their kind, alluring personas had always had sharp edges.

Luc's deep, rumbling voice pierced my thoughts. "I want to watch your expression when you first see the library."

Oh.

I didn't know how to respond to that.

Before I managed some sort of reply, Luc guided us around a corner, through an archway—

And straight into darkness.

The runelights in silver chandeliers flickered to life the second our feet touched the tiled floors. A long hall stretched ahead, bookshelves lining the walls all the way to the barrel-vaulted ceiling. The rolling ladders only climbed so high, so a narrow walkway ran the length of the room a story up, accessible via two spiral staircases at either end. Pedestals bearing artifacts filled the empty space in the center, leading toward the back, where dark azure sofas were arranged around a richly woven carpet.

I stopped so abruptly Luc nearly dragged me forward.

Shit. I needed to sit down.

Would the rest of my life—whether mortal or immortal—just be the kings showing me progressively grander and grander libraries?

I wouldn't object.

Luc turned fully to face me as I took in the majesty of our surroundings. He drank in my reaction, the same way he'd watched Jules fuck me on my knees, his lips a breath away.

Heat tinged my cheeks, but I kept my gaze moving, roaming, absorbing, memorizing. What did I want to explore first?

My feet already knew.

I drifted toward a large silver-framed globe, nearly as tall as me. Luc followed at my side, just out of my line of sight, but even if I weren't bound to him, I'd have felt his imposing presence.

I didn't even know where to start. I spun the globe. It kept turning, stretching farther and farther, mountains turning into plains, into deserts, into lakes and oceans, and then somehow even more land beyond that.

"It's so... big." I didn't have a better word. No word could capture the weight of our entire world laid bare before me.

Luc reached out, steadying the spin with a single finger. It landed directly on a small island off the coast of a larger landmass.

*Mabon Farm.*

I repressed a flinch at my home being referred to as a farm rather than just a country, but I had known that was how the Impire saw us. I had read it in the books they provided. I swallowed and traced the familiar shape of my homeland to the Impire's shores.

"We were here, in Montaurère." Luc lowered his hand slightly, catching mine as it moved. A slow spark of tingling awareness traveled through my skin. He guided our hands over a mountain deep in the heart of the Azarasian Impire—slightly south of Mabon, a handful of miles inland. Then lower, to the tip of a peninsula surrounded by the Thaddeian Ocean. "And now we're here, in Tenebra de Mar."

I gently pulled my hand from his and continued tracing the borders of the Azarasian Impire. While cities were marked in the conquered territories under the Impire's banner, the only other settlements in Azarasian lands were fortresses dotting the coastline and a wall spanning Salathien's Bridge. The narrow isthmus connected our vast continent to another across Callistan Bay.

"Why are there only two cities marked in the Azarasian homeland?" The words left me before I even thought to hesitate. Knowledge was a safe space, one Luc and I had in common. Likely one of the *only* things a powerful king had in common with a broken bookworm.

He answered easily. "Because there's only two cities in the Azarasian homeland."

I twisted, my eyes widening. "You only have *two* cities?"

"We don't need more than two cities," he said, gaze steady on me instead of the globe. "There are fewer than three hundred thousand Azarasians. We usually welcome no more than a hundred children a year, so our population doesn't grow quickly."

I swallowed. Of course, it had only taken moments for our conversation to veer into the topic of children.

Flashes of my fever dream returned. Luc standing over me, Jules at my side. *There are other ways to get vampire blood in a human.* Jules had explained the reaction their blood caused, but neither of them had addressed the problem it created.

If I couldn't consume vampire blood, I'd age and die, dragging the Imperium with me.

If the healers didn't find a solution...

How long would it be before I contributed to that hundred?

Cheeks heating, I circled the globe, quickly leaving it and our topic of conversation behind.

The next pedestal held a clock encased in gilded brass, its delicate gears visible behind a panel of polished glass. A faint ticking filled the space around it, steady and precise. The one after bore a compact printing press, its iron frame smaller and sleeker than the massive machines I'd seen sketched in books. Rows of movable metal type were meticulously arranged on a tray.

The fourth object was slightly more familiar. A large rectangular instrument made of dark, hand-carved mahogany stood on four sturdy legs. It was the same type a vampire had played during Rosier's bond rite. This instrument wasn't as ornate, but something about its simplicity made it even more striking.

I drifted my fingers along those ivory rectangles and pressed down—

A musical note rang through the space, sharp and unexpected. I had anticipated the sound, but I still flinched, startled by the way it cut through the hush of the library. It didn't sound anywhere near as pleasant as when the musician had played the instrument.

"It's called a fortepiano," Luc said. His voice was as smooth as the polished keys beneath my fingertips. "The first was designed around fifty or so years ago. I watched the inventor make the one in Dawnspear and then put this one together myself."

I turned to him. "You built this?"

"I built the clock and printing press, too."

That took me a second to process. I glanced back at the instrument, the gleaming wood and delicate keys. It wasn't just a relic Luc had acquired. It was something he had crafted with his own hands.

"Can you play?"

Luc sat on the long bench, his movements as fluid as they were deliberate. He lifted his hands to the keys. A slow, mournful melody rose from the fortepiano's hollowed body, notes drifting through the library like whispers.

It was soft. Gentle. A story of something lost. Something long buried. Something that had no place in the presence of the Conqueror. He wasn't wearing his axe, but he didn't need it to be hard and unyielding.

When the melody finished, Luc's fingers hovered over the keys for a moment and then lowered to his lap. A flicker passed through the bond, a familiar ache. Grief, old and scabbed over.

I swallowed, my chest tight. "That was beautiful. Does it have a name?"

He didn't look at me when he answered. "It's a lullaby Jules's mother used to sing to us. Anyone who knew its name died centuries ago."

"Oh." I didn't know what to say to that. The silence hung between us, thick and weighted.

Before I breached it, Luc pushed from the bench and turned toward the shelves. "I have something to show you."

He led me to the towering bookcases, his steps silent on the marble tiles. My gaze trailed over the spines—histories, records, books bound in rich leather and embossed in silver script. Then Luc stopped before a particular shelf and gestured toward it.

My pulse kicked up before I even knew why. Then I saw it.

*The Soulborne Queen: Volume I* by Katalina Estevez.

And beside it—

My breath caught.

*Volume II.*

My hands moved before I could think, plucking it from the shelf and flipping it open in the same motion. The pages were smooth beneath my fingertips, the ink still crisp as if it were brand new. I scanned the first few lines, my pulse pounding in my ears.

This was it. The words I had longed for, hunted for, despaired I would never read.

I barely noticed Luc watching me from a step away. Not until I felt the weight of his gaze, intense, assessing, amused.

I looked up, cheeks flushing. "Oh. Sorry. I—"

"Never apologize for the things you love."

I swallowed. "Right. Of course. Sorry."

Luc arched a brow.

I clamped my mouth shut. If I didn't, I'd just end up apologizing for apologizing about apologizing.

His expression softened slightly. Then, without a word, he took the book from my hands. "Come."

Luc led me toward the seating area near the back of the library, to the dark azure sofas. To the left, a corridor led to an open-air courtyard bathed in soft, golden light. The breeze carried in a faint trace of salt through the archway.

He gestured to the sofa. "Sit."

I sat.

Luc handed me the book, his silver gaze steady. "Read."

I hesitated, clutching the book tight. "Are you sure?"

"Why wouldn't I be sure?" Luc tilted his head slightly, his gaze molten. "Did you have something else planned while we waited for Jules?"

Heat bloomed in my chest. "I—uh—no?"

Luc's smirk deepened, knowing. He had caught the lie.

He'd always catch the lie.

"Enjoy your book, little curiosity."

# 41

IF I THOUGHT READING a romance novel about Luc's sire while he sat across from me might be difficult, I was only partially right.

I had dreamed about getting my hands on Volume II since I found and finished Volume I years ago. Now, with the book in my lap and the words unraveling before me, it was ridiculously easy to sink into the story. Azaras looked exactly like Luc in my mind's eye, but I could ignore that... until things heated up.

*The Beast crashed into the dirt, a few shadowed feathers spiraling down from the wide span of his wings. The villagers had fled at his screech overhead, now cowering in their homes and hollows as the monstrous side of my soulbound prowled forward. I held my ground, even as those pitch-black eyes locked onto me, more animal than man. There was little anyone could do to reason with Azaras, but the Beast was truly impossible to sway.*

*Except by me.*

*His soulbound.*

*I swallowed. He hadn't been wrong. I could stop his destruction. Save thousands of lives.*

*And all I had to do was orgasm a dozen or so times between dusk and dawn.*

*A shiver trailed over my skin, a zap to my nipples and core. The Beast's nostrils flared—*

*And then he was on me.*

*His wings closed around me, sealing me in utter darkness. His clawed hands tore through the fabric around my waist. His shadows peeled the tattered remnants clinging to me—*

The book was snatched from my hands.

I jerked, ripped from Azaras's hell realm three thousand years ago to Luc looming over me in the present. Volume II was tilted toward him, silver eyes darkening as he scanned the page.

Reading the rest of the scene.

My heart nearly exploded from sheer mortification. I lunged instinctively, reaching for the book.

Luc only raised it higher. His face stayed impassive, but I felt the bastard's amusement.

The flush in my cheeks burned through my face. "Give that back."

Luc didn't even glance at me. "No."

"Do you really want to read smut about your sire?" I almost hissed.

The King of Dusk lifted a brow at my tone. I glared at him, willing my expression to hold firm instead of crumpling into a pout. Only Jules could pull off a pout.

Luc's smirk turned downright devious.

Oh, shit.

"*The Beast spun me around before my lips could touch his, shadowed fangs bared.*"

My jaw dropped. Was he... why was he reading the smut about his sire aloud? "What are you doing?"

Luc barely looked up from the page. *"I had almost kissed the monster who killed my parents. What was wrong with me? But the thought fled from my head a moment later when that clawed hand wrapped around my throat and tugged me off the ground."*

He turned the page. His smirk sharpened at the next paragraph.

Oh, stars. He was enjoying this.

*"My back slid up the feathers on his chest, so soft against my skin, but I barely noticed as his shadows tightened around my thighs and spread me wide open."* Luc's voice dropped lower, richer. He flicked a glance at me, silver eyes dilated. *"With a small jerk down, the Beast impaled me on his cock."*

"Stop it," I said, but I couldn't hide my shudder.

*"My vision flickered. I released a pathetic whine that only made the dark-haired, gorgeous predator that lurked behind me growl. With that hand around my neck, he had his shadows jerk me from his length and then back down again. The spines around the base of his cursed form rubbed against my sensitive walls—"* Luc suddenly snapped the book shut. "What a naughty little book you're reading, bride."

"There's nothing wrong with romance novels," I muttered, trying to remember how to breathe.

"I never said there was." Luc traced the small rune on the book's spine. *Return.* With a flare of shadows, Volume II lifted from his palm and shot back to its place on the shelf. "But all this reading has me parched."

Every part of me stiffened. My back, my nipples, my cunt.

The soulbond.

"Stand."

I glanced at Luc through my eyelashes. "But..."

"But what?"

I brushed my hair over my ear nervously. "Jules and I..."

"You and Jules fucked this morning?" His voice was a whisper across my skin, deep and sensual. "You didn't wash his cum off your thighs, did you?"

Our knees almost brushed. "No."

"Do you like smelling like him?"

I swallowed. "I don't... maybe."

His gaze darkened. "Do you want to smell like me, Nessa? Do you want both our cum staining your beautiful thighs?"

A fresh wave of heat rolled through me. Through *us*. My pulse kicked hard, and I started sweating instantly. Luc arched a brow. Slowly, he crooked a finger upward, a slight curved motion that instantly made my cunt clench.

I swallowed again, but still obeyed, rising carefully. As if being quiet would somehow help me evade the predator whose gaze followed my every move.

The predator I wanted to catch me, no matter how much I hated admitting it.

Luc put his hands on my waist, a gentle touch.

With effortless strength, he spun us, switching our places, so my back was to the library and his to the sofa. He dropped onto the seat and hooked one arm over the backrest, reclining like a king on his throne. Luc turned every seat he touched into a throne.

Those darkening silver eyes pierced into me, through me. The Conqueror. The man I was eternally bound to. I tried not to tremble, but I couldn't stop it. But now, instead of falling to my knees in fear, I wanted to drop in supplication, his heated gaze pleased with me as he murmured, "Good gi—"

I gave my head a sharp shake. Nope. I wasn't surrendering to the soulbond that easily.

All these orgasms were messing with my brain.

"You're wearing far too much." He reached out and tugged a sleeve from my shoulder. His fingers barely touched me, but I felt it everywhere. "Take this off."

I let out a slow, shuddering breath. My rational mind screamed at me to resist, to push back. But my body had never obeyed me. My heart thundered. My nipples ached. Heat pooled between my legs.

Stars, I needed to come.

Maybe after, I'd be able to think clearly. Maybe the pressure would ease, and I'd remember who I was before the bond.

Who was I trying to fool? I wasn't going to think clearly afterward. I wasn't going to fight this.

This was who I was. A woman too tired to keep resisting, too lonely to pretend she didn't want to be touched.

Hands shaking, I reached around and unlaced the back of my dress. The trembling slowed me down, but Luc waited, patient and poised. He stretched out his other arm along the cushions, his posture casual, his stare anything but.

When I finally loosened the last inch of fabric, the bodice drooped on me. Luc's eyes flicked to the peaks of my breasts, barely concealed by the brassière. I slipped my arms out of the frilly slip of silk. The moment my bare skin met the chilled air, my nipples pricked. Luc devoured every inch of my skin, memorizing each curve. Every soft expanse I had spent years knowing I wasn't supposed to show.

Like I was as beautiful as my stepmother or sister.

I stayed still, letting him look. Not rushing or coaxing him. The king took me in leisurely.

Just like how he planned to fuck me.

I swallowed. Luc's eyes flashed to my pulse. Slowly, he lifted his eyes to mine. He held me there, pinned in place, bound in darkening silver. Then, with a flick of his hand, he gestured to the gown still bunched around my waist.

A silent order.

I hooked my thumbs into the fabric and pushed. I had to quickly shuffle my hips to get the gown down—

Luc growled. I stiffened from cunt to nipple.

"Slower," he murmured.

Something twisted inside of me. Not heat, not lust. Something colder. A sinking weight. I couldn't do this. I wasn't beautiful. I wasn't made for this. I was fat and plain and Nessa. "Luc, I—"

He flicked one of my nipples. A spark flashed through me. I yelped, hands jerking up to shield myself. Luc growled again. This time, lower. Rougher. A sound of displeasure.

I froze.

He glared at my hips, where the fabric still clung, hiding me from his sight. His lips curled. Not quite a snarl. Not quite a smirk. "*Slower.*"

I closed my eyes and took a steadying breath before returning my hands to the gown. Rocking my hips gently from side to side, I obeyed.

Inch by inch, I bared myself to the King of Dusk.

Luc's gaze turned molten. His cock strained against his trousers, thick and pressing against the fabric. The heat in my core changed, a hunger that wasn't mine. I tried not to tremble and failed miserably. Hundreds had laid eyes on my body in the last week, but I would rather stand naked before an entire city than under his gaze.

When the gown slipped past the curve of my hips, gravity took over. It pooled at my feet.

In a blink, I stood bare before the Conqueror in the Imperial Library of Dusk.

Luc drank in the sight of me. He traced the slope of my hips, the dip of my waist, the soft curves and the dark curls between my legs. His cock somehow thickened further, pressing against the constraints of his trousers as he stared at my dripping, aching center.

Luc reached down, slow and deliberate, and freed himself. My mouth went dry. His cock was thick and heavy. The first time I saw it, I hadn't been prepared. I still wasn't. I never would be.

He patted the cushion on either side of his thighs. "On your knees."

My heartbeat stuttered, then kicked up a notch. I met his eyes, but they were heated steel. There was to be no disobeying him. I moved slowly, as if hesitating might somehow make me invisible.

But this vampire had caught me long ago. There was no escaping him.

I'd spend the rest of my maybe-immortal life riding his cock.

My body spasmed at the thought.

I placed my hands on his silk-clad shoulders and straddled his knees. My skin prickled as the cool air brushed over my open, aching cunt. The thick head of his cock brushed against me. My legs stiffened, holding me just high enough to keep from sinking onto his length. A heartbeat of resistance. A last, fleeting rebellion.

Luc trailed his hands up my thighs and around to the globes of my ass. He squeezed, palming the weight of them. I flinched, startled by the touch. His brow arched, as if challenging me to ask the question on the tip of my tongue.

I had a feeling if I did, I'd quickly end up on his cock.

Something about the way his fingers slipped between my legs, traced the slick heat of me, made me think I would either way.

He rubbed his fingers through me. I arched against him. Shuddered. The moan escaped before I could catch it.

Luc's breath tickled against my collarbone. "I've never doubted your desire for me. How could I, when you are this wet every time I approach?"

Before I could think, before I could brace, he plunged two fingers inside me.

I jolted, breath hitching.

He filled me.

Stretched me.

Proved his point.

"Yet I can tell by that look in your eyes that you doubt mine."

He leaned back suddenly, taking his warmth with him, his hands, his skin. I whimpered at the loss, the sudden empty space between my thighs.

For a minute, he only watched. The heat of his thighs spread through mine, amplifying the ache, the slow build between my legs. But he didn't speak. He watched me tremble. Watched me wait. Watched me simmer.

I couldn't. I cracked under the pressure. "Luc—"

"Hush, bride," he murmured. "Who said you could talk?"

I bit my lip and whimpered.

His hand brushed my inner thigh as he pulled something from his pocket. A flicker of heat kissed the air between us, faint but undeniable. I tensed, pulling back slightly—

Luc held the second of the silver plugs.

I gaped. "Were you carrying that in your pocket?"

"This one is only a quarter the width of Jules's cock." His fingers traced the warm, slick tip of the plug along my inner thigh, higher, higher. "He'll be fucking your beautiful ass within the week. You want to be ready for him, don't you?"

My stomach clenched, my thighs trembling. "I… I guess."

His thumb suddenly pressed into my clit.

I almost screamed. My hips bucked into his hand, but he held me firm, pinned in place. "Yes, Your Majesty! I want to be ready."

"Good girl."

Luc dragged the metal along the crease where my thigh met my core, a brush against flushed heat. The tip pressed against my tight entrance. I clenched instinctively, my body resisting the intrusion.

But Luc was patient. He rubbed slow, soothing circles along my hip. "Relax, little curiosity. Breathe for me."

I sucked in a breath and let it out in a trembling exhale. Luc didn't push further. He let me adjust, let my body learn to accept the pressure. The stretch.

When I finally exhaled again, he eased the plug deeper. Deeper. Deeper. A gasp punched from my throat. My nails dug into his shoulders, silk slipping under my grip.

The plug settled fully inside me, a perfect, sinful weight. It pressed against something impossibly sensitive. I let out a shuddering breath. My eyes slipped closed as my muscles fluttered around the metal, adjusting to the fullness.

Luc traced his fingers along the dip of my spine. "That's it. You were perfect."

I swallowed hard. My legs almost went slack. My tight ring clenched around the plug, but I inhaled slowly.

"Now sit."

My eyes flashed open. "Sit?"

He pulled my thighs abruptly forward. I jolted, tightening my grip on his shoulder. The movement shifted the plug inside me, a sharp burst of sensation sparking through my core.

Luc brushed his knuckles up the curve of my ass and wrapped his hands around the soft flesh of my hips. He pulled me down ever so slightly.

The hard tip of him brushed against my entrance.

Ah.

Sit.

I hesitated. Just for a second.

Luc's hold tightened. "Don't make me repeat myself."

Heat licked up my spine. I exhaled, let my legs go soft, until his cock nudged at my entrance. I yelped. My nerves ignited, pleasure spiking sharp and dizzying.

I couldn't do this. It'd kill me. He would split me right in two. I had taken his cock for the first time two nights ago, but my cunt clenched at the memory of the stretch.

A crack echoed through the library as Luc's palm struck my asscheek. Magic stopped the sting, but the jolt still made me flinch. I gasped, the impact sending another pulse of sensation straight to my cunt. My body jerked in shock, lost balance. I started to slip down his cock—

Luc caught me under my arms, holding me up with ease. "I said sit, not fall."

I licked my lips. "Well, maybe if you hadn't spanked me—"

With a harsh yank, he jerked me halfway onto his cock.

I shrieked as the first of his piercings nudged inside me. The plug shifted, amplifying every sensation, making me shake.

Luc groaned, the sound low and satisfied. The bond pulsed in time with his pleasure. "That was a beautiful noise, wife. Now sit on my cock and do it again."

I huffed and dropped my chin, gaze trailing down between us, to where Luc's thick cock speared into the curls between my legs. His thumb drew soft circles on my skin, but he didn't pull me down further. Didn't drive me deeper onto him. He didn't move at all.

He was waiting.

For me.

I wouldn't feel any resistance from his hands.

But his cock wouldn't be as easy to conquer.

My hands clenched tighter on his shoulders. My cunt fluttered around the thick intrusion, stretched but still needing, still wanting. Closing my eyes, I lowered—

A shuddering whimper broke free as Luc filled me, inch by torturous inch. His third piercing dragged along my walls, sending a jolt through my spine. But I couldn't stop. If I stopped, I'd never find the courage to take him all the way.

Another inch. Another stretch. Another brand of pleasure that seared through my nerves.

I let gravity guide me, my back arching as he filled every part of me. By the time his fourth piercing pressed inside, I couldn't breathe. Couldn't think.

The pressure within me nearly burst, but I still had a couple inches of him to go. I pulsed my knees slightly, tiny movements along his cock.

His eyes fixated on the subtle jiggle of my breasts, my stomach, my thighs, his black eyes bright as I lured him deeper and deeper into me.

And then—

I sat.

My ass pressed flush to his thighs, my body impaled completely on his cock. He spread through me, up into my belly, the crown of his length pressing against my ending. A perfect, tight fit.

Like I was made for him.

My head fell forward onto his broad, muscled shoulder, a moan tearing from my lips. The plug in my ass pressed deep, heightening the sensation. My toes curled, the heat in my core dangerously close to spilling over. It echoed through our connection. My harsh breathing rattled the still air of the library and mixed with Luc's growl.

His fingers skimmed the peaks of my breasts, the soft swell of my stomach, tracing the curves he owned. He gripped the wings of my hips, perfect handles for his large hands. He brushed a kiss against the edge of my ear. "Now up."

I stiffened. Pulled back slightly. Blinking at him through the haze of pleasure. "What?"

Luc flicked his finger toward the library's vaulted ceilings. "Up."

I stared. He couldn't... he didn't... I swallowed. My entire body seized at the thought of pulling off him. But I obeyed. Slowly, I tensed my legs, pushing myself off his cock. Every inch of him that left me made my breath stutter.

Shit.

Fuck.

*Stars.*

More and more of him slipped from my wet heat, my walls clutching at his length as if begging him not to leave—

"Stop."

I went still instantly, obediently. Only the tip of him remained inside me, barely nestled against my entrance, just enough to tease. The thick head of his cock was slick, flushed, poised on the edge of taking me all over again.

"Good bride," Luc murmured, a deep rumble. A slow, wicked smirk curved his lips. "Now you're going to do it again."

I tensed, my skin prickling in a sudden wave of cold. "Luc—"

"But faster this time." His fingers tightened on my hips. "And then faster and faster until you're bouncing on my cock. Am I understood?"

I swallowed, trapped in the sheer command in his gaze, but I still found myself asking, "And what if I don't?"

Luc's pupils devoured the remaining silver. His face didn't change. His hold didn't tighten. But the air around us thickened, humming with inevitability.

When he spoke, his voice was pure hunger. "Then I'll pin you to the floor and fuck you until I'm done with you."

A shudder tore through me. Was it really a punishment if I flushed just thinking about it? About Luc pushing me down, spreading me open, his frame enveloping me as he rutted me into the floor, each thrust a branding claim?

Luc's arm slid up between my breasts, fingers weaving through the delicate chains of my collar. He wrapped them gently around his knuckles, the gesture deceptively soft. "Am I understood, wife?"

My mouth went dry. My thoughts tangled. How did I want the Conqueror to fuck me? He won either way, whether I rode him or he rode me. Did I lose either way? Not in terms of orgasms but...

I wanted to please him. Wanted to please both of them. A hollow ache spread through my chest. I didn't know what I was doing, but if I could please them, then maybe I could forget they didn't have a choice. We were bound together by a spell none of us had agreed to.

I was their Mortal Bride. More sacrifice than wife, no matter what they called me. The only reason I was still breathing was because they couldn't kill me. I shouldn't have wanted to *please* the Imperium. What was wrong with me—

Luc's hand tightened around my throat, just enough to notice. My nipples pebbled. My clit throbbed. My cunt clenched around nothing.

"Answer now," Luc said. "No more thinking."

A helpless whimper slipped free. I looked down, where his thick cock glistened between my thighs. Stars, why did looking at him make him feel bigger?

I closed my eyes and dropped onto his cock. A gasp strangled in my throat as I sank onto him. Luc groaned, his fingers tightening around my throat, his grip anchoring me as I took him to the root.

"That's it," he murmured.

I braced myself, hand clutching at his rock-hard arms. I started to ride him, slow at first, testing, teasing, feeling each inch of him as I moved. It was nowhere close to how fast and hard Jules had bounced me on Luc's cock.

But this slow, deliberate pace was torture of a different kind.

"Look at you." His voice was thick with approval. "Riding my cock so well."

I tried not to mewl, but the pathetic gasp left my lips. My body clenched at his words, at the raw pride behind them. I tried not to writhe too obviously, tried to hold onto some sliver of dignity, but the pleasure coiled in my gut, hot and unbearable.

Fuck, I was going to come. Not right away, but soon. There was no way I could survive this. I scrunched my eyes shut as I pulsed on him—

Luc fisted a hand in my hair and tugged, my back arching. My eyes flashed open, clashing with his. Lips brushing my cheekbones, he devoured every flicker of expression across my face. "Eyes on me."

"Wha—what?" I barely managed the word without losing the rhythm of my hips.

Luc's breath tickled my lips. "If you're going to fuck me as a wife does her husband, you're going to look at me. If not, then you're my thrall and I will treat you as such."

Stars, why did a shock of need tear through me at those words? What was wrong with me? I was already fucking the Conqueror. Why did I want him to bend me over and use me—

I moaned, the pleasure in me heightened at the thought.

Luc smirked. Like he had slipped into my mind and seen every filthy thought I'd tried to bury. The surge of his dark satisfaction rushed through my chest. His grip on my throat eased slightly, enough to let my breath hitch, enough to let the anticipation stretch between us. "Do you want me to fuck you like a thrall?"

"Yes." I didn't even hesitate. There was nothing left of Nessa Halloran in this wave of bliss.

"Say please. Beg your king."

I was already drowning, already breaking.

My nails scraped against his shoulders. My lips parted, desperate, needy. "Please, Your Majesty," I sobbed his title. "Please fuck me like a thrall."

Luc's smirk turned sharp. "Such a good girl."

He pulled me off his cock. I gasped, the sudden emptiness a violent shock.

Luc's hands caught under my knees and jerked me forward like I weighed nothing.

The world tilted. My vision spun—ceiling, bookshelves, vaulted arches. My back hit his knees. I barely had time to inhale before Luc widened his stance and dropped me.

I hit the sofa. My bent legs jerked up, spread wide.

Luc straightened them with a firm push, forcing my thighs against his chest. My calves brushed his shoulders, my heels digging into the solid wall of his body. Before I could adapt, before I could even breathe—

Luc gripped my thighs and drove into me.

A ragged scream tore from my throat.

My spine arched off the cushions. My breath caught. My thoughts burned away to nothing.

Luc fucked me. Or used me to fuck himself.

Hard, fast, relentless.

He dragged me along his length, forcing every inch of me to feel him, to take him, to be reshaped by him. I wasn't riding him. I was a weapon in his hands, a means to his pleasure, a toy to be used.

And I loved it.

His cock slammed into me, again and again, the wet slap of our bodies echoing through the library. He thrust deep, so deep I thought I might break apart, that I might split open from the force of him.

He rubbed against a sensitive spot inside me. I groaned. His fingers shifted. The third time his cock hit that spot in a row, my eyes watered. My nails dug so deep into his knees that I pierced through his trousers. Hot blood welled to the surface.

That just made Luc bounce me on him faster.

He slammed me onto his cock at a speed no mortal could match. Again. And again. My breasts jiggled obscenely. My soft flesh trembled from the force of his thrusts. My legs spasmed at the flood of feelings. My bliss. His bliss. I wailed, gasping at each quick, deep thrust.

"Luc," I moaned as I arched even further, my head off the side of the sofa as my hair brushed the floor. I *needed* to come. I released Luc's thighs and reached for my clit—

Luc growled. A second later, my knees hit the floor. He pressed my face to the library's rug, caging my arms beneath me.

And then he *mounted* me.

There was no other word for it.

Luc claimed me the way a beast mated in the wild. With his entire body. With his entire strength. My thighs trembled as he rocked forward, pinning me under him, each brutal thrust pushing me deeper into the rug. Each deep stroke vibrated through my belly, through the plug in my ass, through every part of me.

The force punched a cry from my lips, a pitched *ah, ah, ah* that echoed through the vaulted chamber.

Luc fisted the handle at the back of my collar. With a sharp tug, he pulled me up. Slowly. The pressure flared in my neck and sent lightning through my body. My airway constricted partway. My body gently arched. My hands clenched in the rug.

Luc held me off the floor, halfway to his chest. Our bodies collided. Flesh slapped. A choir of choked moans and deep grunts filled the air. My vision waved. The heady scent of sex mixed with old parchment and leather.

Luc fucked every single one of my senses until everything I was rode his cock into euphoria.

He plunged into me—

And stopped. His hold on my throat loosened slightly.

I sucked in a full breath, my exhale escaping as a desperate whimper. Why had he stopped? I tried to roll my hips, to take more of him, but I didn't have the leverage. Luc stayed sheathed within my throbbing heat.

"Open your eyes, wife."

I hadn't even realized I'd closed them again. My eyes opened to meet a glowing, gold-rimmed black gaze.

Jules stood by the edge of the sofas, his eyes fixed on me. He drank in the sight of my flushed face, of Luc's fist woven through my collar, of the way my body trembled beneath his soulbound's grip. His lips twitched at my helpless mewl.

But when his gaze dropped, that smile slipped off his face.

Luc held me at just the right angle. The King of Dawn had a full view of my body. Of how I shook. Of how my thighs quivered. Of how my breasts bounced when Luc fucked me.

And Jules responded to the sight.

His arousal brushed against my senses, a sharp throb of heat. His cock strained against his trousers. When he caught my gaze lingering, he groaned and gripped himself through the fabric.

"Any..." Luc tightened his hold on my collar and I shuddered "...requests for the finale?"

My jaw dropped. Because Luc wasn't speaking to me.

He was asking Jules.

"Harder."

Harder? Luc couldn't possibly go harder—

Luc obeyed instantly. His next thrust slammed into my belly, the force jarring the plug inside me. Fire flared in my core, pleasure so sharp it blurred into something unbearable.

I screamed. My nails dug into my palms. Tears escaped my eyes, but the King of Dusk didn't slow. Didn't falter.

He. Only. Fucked. Me. Harder.

Each thrust was a possessive brand. His. His. His. Everything in the world narrowed down to the climbing pleasure in my core, the fist at my nape, the gold-rimmed black eyes devouring every slap of our flesh.

Oh, stars, I was going to come, I was going to come so hard—

Luc yanked on the collar, cutting off my air. At the same moment, he slid the hand clenching my hip between my legs and strummed my clit harshly—

I came.

I convulsed.

I *died.*

Every part of me clenched around Luc, but he ripped his cock from my grip and fucked me back open. He rode me as I came and suffocated and somehow came ever harder, tears streaming down my face as the orgasm rocked my body. As the orgasm *destroyed* my body. A person couldn't feel this much and survive.

Then he released the pressure on my throat. Air rushed back into my lungs. The bliss twisted higher, tighter.

A strangled scream tore from me.

Jules hissed. His trousers hung loose, his hand stroking along his hard shaft. "Shit, she's so beautiful when she comes, Lucey."

Beautiful. The word punched through me. Raw, real. Spoken with undeniable truth. My cunt squeezed Luc's cock tighter—

With a groan, Luc burst within me. His hot seed flooded into my body. His pleasure rushed through the bond, extending my orgasm. With every buck of his hips, he filled me. Marked me. Claimed me just as thoroughly as Jules had. My body greedily clenched down around him, wanting more and more.

*Needing* more and more.

Luc yanked on my collar, this time pulling me up. He closed the distance between my back and his chest. I slammed into hard muscle under silk. I went slack against him, my head lolled onto his shoulder.

He plunged his fangs into my neck.

Another orgasm hit like lightning. A devastated cry caught in my throat. The rush of his venom streaked through my veins. My first orgasm hadn't even faded yet, but I was pulled back to the peak in a second. The pleasure whited out my vision. I went slack. His tongue swept against my neck, swallowing me down like my cunt did his cock.

He fucked us through the ecstasy. My world narrowed. The soft roll of his hips. The tease of his fingers on my clit. The pressure of his hand on my collar. The kiss of his lips at my throat.

The soulbond inside of us, nearly reunited and whole.

When the bliss faded to a trickle, an aftershock, Luc pulled his fangs from me. He licked over my skin, sealing the wounds. Then he released my collar, my body.

I slid off his cock, my limbs boneless, useless. I collapsed onto the rug, my elbows catching me just before I sank into the soft fabric. The swaying ocean of pleasure swept away the pain.

I didn't think I'd stand ever again.

"Fuck," Jules panted out the word.

I rolled my head the slightest bit, glancing blearily through the strands of my tangled hair. The King of Dawn stood a couple feet away from us, his hard cock in hand. His strokes grew faster, sharper, chasing his own orgasm on the tail end of ours.

I blinked slowly. When I next opened my eyes, Luc stood before him, a masterpiece in dark silk.

Luc pushed Jules's hand aside and gripped his cock.

Jules tensed, his gaze dropping to where Luc held him prisoner. For a moment, I could almost feel the warmth of his palm. The King of Dusk stroked from tip to base, brushing the light dusting of blond over the King of Dawn's balls.

Jules jerked in his hand and grunted. "Fuck, Lucey—"

Luc lunged forward, swallowing the sound with his lips. The Conqueror claimed the Butcher's mouth the way he claimed everything else. He glided his palm over him, slow, teasing, until Jules shuddered against him. The King of Dawn nipped at his lip, but Luc squeezed him tighter.

Jules groaned and gave in. Opened wider. Let Luc plunder and claim.

My jaw popped open at the sight. Stars, if anyone was beautiful, it was them.

Something ignited within me, my lust climbing back from the brink. I didn't know how it had recovered already. The space between my legs pulsed, a pleasant ache that Jules had started and Luc had only intensified.

I almost sobbed at the rising desperation. Would nothing satisfy this craving in me? But the soulbond brushed the edge of my panic aside, leaving only heat.

Our unending need.

Luc released Jules suddenly and stepped back.

The King of Dawn growled, a low, frustrated sound. "Luc, you bastard—"

Luc snapped his finger, silencing and summoning all in one. He circled to Jules's side and pointed at their feet. "Come here, little curiosity. It's time you learned how to suck a king's cock."

My heart nearly stopped. "What?"

Jules grinned, almost deliriously. "You mean it?"

But Luc wouldn't repeat himself. He slowly arched one of those dark brows at the both of us, but only responded to Jules. "You won her firsts. The sooner you come down her throat, the sooner I can fuck her mouth."

My whole body was already flushed, but I somehow turned so scarlet I was maroon, a shade to match the top half of the Azarasian flag. Heat spread from my cheeks to my chest, sinking low into my belly, pooling between my legs. The plug throbbed inside me. My stomach twisted.

Not with fear.

With anticipation.

I couldn't lie anymore, not even to myself.

"Bride," Luc said, the order clear in his tone.

I pushed onto my knees on the rug. My body hadn't come all the way down from the orgasm. Wetness dripped down my legs, my pleasure and Luc's combined. Streaks of pink tainted my release. I quickly looked away. I couldn't think about that now. My main priority was standing. It wouldn't be easy, but I started to climb to my feet—

"Crawl."

I tensed, the movement echoed by my cunt. Crawl. Like I had across the bed toward Luc, Jules a waiting shadow at my back. This time, I stared into both their black eyes.

Before I let the idea intimidate me, I crawled across the rug. The plug inside me rubbed deeper with every movement. My thighs trembled. My breath hitched in rough, ragged pants. I must have looked a mess.

Stars, I wasn't meant for this. To be wanted. To be desired.

But Jules groaned, his cock twitching. His eyes burned, devouring me. Luc returned his hand to his length and slid—

Jules caught his wrist. "Do you want me to come in her mouth or on her face *right* this fucking second?"

Luc's smirk curved slowly. "I'm amenable to both."

"Well, I want to come in her mouth."

"Of course, dearest." Luc pressed a kiss to Jules's temple. "Anything for you." His attention flickered down to me, his burning gaze hardening. "Now."

I sped my movements until I reached their feet. Sitting back on my heels, I stared up at the kings' perfect bodies. At Jules's hard cock straining between us, a glistening bead of liquid on his tip.

Fuck, he was even more intimidating from this angle.

My mouth went dry. I licked my lips, almost unconsciously. Godstars, I really was the whore my stepmother always believed.

Jules groaned. "Oh, do that again."

Luc smirked.

My heart rate stuttered. "I don't know..."

"Neither did Jules nor I, centuries ago," Luc said, tracing a finger along my chin, a sudden soft edge to his hard voice. "Open your mouth."

My jaw popped open, more in shock than obedience. Luc stuck his thumb in my mouth a second later. Pressed. Back. Back. Back—

I almost gagged.

"Breathe through your nose."

I inhaled quickly. Tears flooded my eyes, but I kept my head raised.

"Now suck on my thumb."

I closed my lips around that digit and sucked obediently. Tears watered my eyes as I did. As I gazed up into two sets of luminous, black eyes in two terribly perfect faces.

Approval lit the King of Dusk's gaze, a faint glimmer that the bond rushed through me. He pulled his thumb from my mouth. "You don't need to know how. Keep your mouth open. Relax your throat. Remember to breathe."

Jules snorted. "You could even skip that last one. Doubt I'll need more than a minute."

I blinked up at them. "Men don't usually joke about not lasting."

"Human men need breaks," Jules said with a grin. "Vampires can stay hard all day."

A shudder wracked my body.

Luc's fingers skated down my jaw. "Take his cock into your mouth."

Jules shuddered at Luc's words across his cheek. I swallowed down my nerves. The soulbond dissolved what remained, leaving only heat. Only hunger. Trapped in two pairs of burning eyes, I pressed my hands to Jules's thighs for balance and slowly took the tip of him into my mouth.

The salt-sweet taste of him burst across my tongue.

Jules moaned.

Loud.

My eyes widened. The sound sent a pulse straight to my cunt.

I flicked my tongue across his tip, then pressed it along the underside of his cock. His skin was velvety smooth, hot, achingly stiff. The taste of him was almost... pleasant. Not at all what I expected, even after all the romance novels I had read.

Or was that the taste of me? Luc had touched him with the same hand that had been between my legs. My eyes widened with shock, my body clenching around the plug—

Jules's hips jerked. He rammed an inch deeper into my mouth. I choked. Too thick. Too deep. Too much.

This wouldn't work.

Luc threaded a hand through the back of my hair, halting my retreat. He traced a rune lightly on my neck. My gag reflex eased. It did nothing to help with the sudden return of my panic.

I didn't know how to do this. Fuck. Books made it seem so easy.

"Look at me, Nessa."

My eyes shot up to the King of Dusk at his command. Those bright eyes smoldered in the dim runelights, like two silver-streaked godstars fallen to the ground. I sunk into him, even with the tip of the King of Dawn's length heavy in *her mouth. She looked so delicate, crouched at our feet, struggling to take all of Jules. But her nerves scraped against my skin, a growing itch under the thudding pleasure building in our King of Dawn.*

*I'd let her try. Now it was my turn—*

I slammed back into my own mind. My body moved on instinct.

I let go. My spine slackened. My jaw relaxed.

Luc tightened his hand in my hair and tugged me off Jules's cock.

"Open wide."

I had a second to obey before he thrust my face forward. Jules's cock speared into my mouth and edged into my throat. My cry came out as a wet gag.

Jules hissed, fisting his hands at his sides. "Oh, fuck."

I closed my eyes and breathed through my nose, relaxing my muscles.

Giving in.

Letting the kings use me.

Succumbing to the pleasure and heat that tickled beneath my skin, through our bond, through the plug.

"That's it." Luc's praise curled dark and smooth in my ears. "Good girl, surrender just like that."

Before I even had time to adjust, Luc pulled my face back. Jules's cock slipped from my lips.

His groan vibrated through the room. "Fucking hells—"

Luc guided my head down again.

I sucked in a breath—

Jules choked as his length brushed against my lips. The crown of his cock nudged my throat. Light burst behind my eyes as my vision wobbled. Saliva trailed down my chin.

But I had only taken half of him into my mouth, the rest of him untouched. He wouldn't fit. He *couldn't* fit.

And I couldn't do this. I wasn't built to please anyone. Too fat, too broken, too ordinary—

"Wrap your fist around the base of him." Luc grabbed my right hand and lifted it to where he wanted. "Stroke him, just like this."

With Luc's hand guiding mine, I slid Jules's cock through my grip. His velvet skin twitched under my touch. The tips of my fingers just barely touched around the girth of him. Luc guided my strokes slow, teasing. Drawing out every inch of torment.

Jules groaned, his head tipping back.

Luc's other hand curled in my hair. He tugged.

I gasped in a breath.

A single breath—

Then Luc pushed me forward. Jules's cock thrust even deeper this time, his tip ramming into my throat. Luc stroked my hand along his base. The heat of the King of Dawn was in my mouth, in my palm. Shadows crawled into my vision as my lungs cried for air.

Jules's eyes flashed down to me. "Oh, stars. Lucey, I can't—"

His voice broke on a moan. His self-control frayed, splintering. For a second, I felt how difficult it was to not fuck my face with wild abandon, but his self-control was solid as stone, supported even further by Luc's iron grip.

Luc nipped his jaw. "Then don't."

Jules's breath hitched. His eyes flared wide, desperate on Luc, on me.

With an arrogant smirk, the King of Dusk glanced down at me. "Jules is going to fuck your throat now." To Jules, he added, "But gently, dearest. We don't want to break our bride's jaw."

Break my jaw? My eyes widened with alarm.

Luc released me and caressed my cheekbone, a light brush. "It's usually not an issue, but you're driving us crazy with that mouth of yours. Isn't that right, Julien?"

"Fuck, yes!" With the shout, Jules's self-control splintered, a crack of stone. He threaded his hands through my hair the next second, loosening Luc's hold and claiming his place.

When he bobbed my head forward, his hips snapped.

His cock shot deeper into my throat. I jolted, the sensation traveling through me to my clit. To the plug. A smothered moan tried to escape me.

His thrusts built, steady, rhythmic. His balls slapped against my chin. My eyes watered. His every movement jolted through me, pushing him in and out of my throat. His every thrust stoked the ache between my legs.

My left hand dropped, snaking down my stomach—

"No."

I stopped. Jules stopped. He was still lodged deep in my mouth, but we both obeyed instantly, attention on Luc.

Awaiting the King of Dusk's decree.

Luc's arm curled around Jules's waist. His lips brushed his temple. "I wasn't talking to you this time, Julien."

Jules whimpered.

Luc's gaze snapped to me. "Raise your hands above your head, little curiosity."

My fingers twitched. My cunt cried out in protest, but I raised my hands above my head without thinking.

Luc wrapped a single hand around my wrists, holding me bound.

"Continue."

Jules rocked his hips forward.

No hesitation.

No mercy.

His cock slid deeper. My eyes rolled back. My lungs screamed for air. But the burning pressure between my legs kept me conscious. Not just mine... but also an echo of Jules's. The sensation of his tension building in me was unfamiliar and yet not.

I clenched my thighs together, the only movement I had left.

Luc's voice dropped. "Are you going to come down our bride's throat?"

I barely heard Jules's strangled reply, my focus on his soft, urgent thrusts. "Yes."

"Is she going to swallow you down?"

A breathless chuckle. Jules's lips tipped into a smirk, even as he trembled. "She better."

"And if she doesn't?"

Jules tightened his hold on my hair. My wavering vision focused, narrowing on those two gorgeous faces. "Then I'll fuck her mouth until she does."

The King of Dusk chuckled. "As you wish."

I automatically sucked in a breath at the dark rumble of a sound. My throat clenched around Jules's cock.

He gasped, fist tightening almost painfully in my hair. "Oh, fuck, stars, Lucey, I'm going to—"

He thrust in again and again and again. His hips picked up the pace, losing his rhythm.

Jules released a deep groan. His hot seed spilled into my mouth. *Down* my throat. The taste of his release was salty. Thick. Heavy on my tongue.

I swallowed it without thinking.

Jules shuddered violently. His cock throbbed against my tongue. "Fuck, lovely."

His bliss washed through me like a warm wave. My own body tightened in response. My cunt clenched. My ass flexed around the plug—

A white-hot pulse of pleasure shot through me, spreading, tightening, bursting. I choked on his cock as I came again. I shuddered and cried and writhed against Luc's hold on my wrists. My eyes rolled back. Everything inside me cracked open—

I think I blacked out.

When I blinked through the bliss, Jules had slowed the roll of his hips, thrusting once, twice more. With a long, sated sigh, he pulled his cock from my mouth and released my hair. He dropped that hand down my face, across my cheek. The gesture was so like the one Luc had made moments ago.

Gentle.

Intimate.

My lashes fluttered.

Rolling his head back, Jules brushed his lips across Luc's. "She was perfect, darling. Thank you."

A part of me preened at the praise. I tried to drown it with shame and guilt, but it kept rising, floating through me. I couldn't stop it, not buoyed by the soft waves of pleasure flowing through the soulbond on all sides.

Luc's voice cut through the haze. "But was she perfect?"

*That* certainly stopped it. The Conqueror had spoken, the ever-calm authority. My stomach dropped. My shoulders curled, even as Luc still held my wrists.

What an idiot. Of course I wasn't perfect. Of course I had failed—

"Open your mouth."

I blinked up. What? Luc brushed my chin, tilting it up before he tugged at my jaw.

I didn't resist.

My mouth popped open.

Both of their luminous eyes dropped to my parted lips. Stars. They were checking if I had *swallowed* Jules's cum. Heat rushed from my cheeks to my chest, but I slackened my jaw. Letting them see. I had obeyed. I had swallowed every last drop of the King of Dawn.

Luc grunted in satisfaction. "Good girl."

I shuddered.

Luc released my jaw and my wrists. My bones collapsed. I went slack on the rug at their feet, utterly spent. Through hooded eyes, I watched Luc squeeze Jules's ass. The King of Dawn nipped at his lips in response.

Luc pulled back and turned away, strolling toward the sofa with his usual unhurried ease. He passed over me, his shadow falling across my trembling form. I couldn't see his movements, but I sensed him lean over—

A firm tug. An obscene slide.

A sharp gasp tore from my throat as he pulled the plug from my ass. I released a humiliating yip before I could swallow it down.

Jules chuckled. "Is that also for me?"

Luc hummed as he examined the glistening toy between his fingers. "Later."

With a flick of magic, the plug vanished from his hands, cleaned and tucked away in his pocket. Luc continued to the sofa and dropped back onto the cushion. A king reclaiming his throne. He raised an arm along the seat's backrest, taking up the same position he had earlier. But this time, his cock wasn't hard and waiting. It was soft, glistened with my bloody lust.

He smoothed his tousled doublet, lacing his trousers with maddening ease. "Where is she?"

I pushed up onto a shaky elbow and stared. She? Who was—?

Oh.

Oh shit.

Oh fucking shit.

My mother.

Jules fastened the buckle on his trousers with a click. "I left her near the door with Estrella and Tristan."

Wait. Wait. My brain froze. "Outside the door?"

"No, lovely. *In* the library."

I stopped breathing. My face flamed. My mother—the woman I hadn't seen in nearly twenty years—had heard Luc fuck me. Had heard me scream and whimper and moan. Had heard Luc's instruction as I gagged on Jules's cock.

Part of me wanted to jump to my feet and glance across the length of the library. The other, larger part wanted the rug to swallow me whole.

I settled for scrambling for my gown, tugging it over me like a shield.

Jules fished something from his pocket. With a lazy flick of his wrist, he tossed it at me. My rolled panties landed on top of the dress.

I gaped at Jules.

He winked. “Saved those from Luc for you.”

# 43

"Bring her over."

Luc's voice cleaved through my stupor. Bring her over. I blinked up at Jules as he straightened his shirt, the silk smoothing beneath his fingers. His brows lifted slightly at me.

Oh, fuck.

Her. My mother.

Over. To where I still crouched, naked and cum-streaked.

Estrella and Tristan were bringing over my mother *now*.

I grabbed my gown, twisting, yanking, shoving the fabric over my head. Too tight—no, the wrong way—shit, where was the hole for my torso—

I found it and dragged the dress over my body, frantic fingers clawing at the laces.

Wait. Where did I toss the brassière?

I spun around. I didn't see the scrap of silk. I didn't really need it, but if it was just lying about and my mother noticed it—

Luc cleared his throat.

My gaze snapped to him. The silk contraption dangled from those long, silver-ringed fingers. Cheeks aflame, I snatched the brassière and strapped it over my chest before fixing the riding gown over top of it. I shimmied on the panties as I stood.

A tangled mass of reddish-brown hair fell into my face. Like the thump of Patriarch Meallán's fist against the pulpit, I jolted to attention. I ran my fingers through the knots, yanking, smoothing. I was marred. Wicked. Sinful. I needed to be clean, to be proper, to be tidy—

The kings were staring at me.

I swallowed.

Jules grinned. "You'll need to do far more than that to convince someone you weren't just thoroughly fucked."

Heat flashed under my skin, panic curling tight in my ribs. Oh stars, oh stars. My fingers worked harder. Strand by strand, I pulled my hair back, getting it out of my face, where it was unruly and untamed and wild—

"Sit," Luc said, patting the sofa. His voice was an order, not a suggestion.

My hands twitched, but they didn't stop fidgeting as Jules sprawled onto the sofa beside Luc. He leaned into the King of Dusk. My fingers slowed. What a sight they made. Jules's blond hair wasn't as tousled as mine, but his waves brushed at his shoulder, the faint sheen of sweat on his pale skin evidence of his own release. Luc remained pristine, his forehead curl untouched, his doublet only slightly creased. But there was a looseness to him, so at odds with the Conqueror's usual manner.

Thoroughly fucked indeed.

"Nessa."

The Conqueror's voice, however, hadn't relaxed at all.

I snapped upright, my fingers falling limp from my hair. The urge to twist it into a tight, aching braid itched beneath my skin.

Was this what it was like? Returning from the marital altar in the Church's cloister, dragged into a celebration of the sin you'd spent your life avoiding? I'd never had a wedding, never been pulled from a chamber with a blood-stained sheet, the proof my innocence was dead. But I remembered Aislin's pink cheeks as Donal dragged her before the congregation, proclaiming her his.

This was that but worse. I was the Imperium's, officially and eternally. Their blood whore, their obedient thrall, their Mortal Bride.

And my mother would be the first from my old life to witness it. Perhaps the only one—

A low growl cut through my spiraling thoughts, a warning rumble. I straightened like the warriors had at the city gate when we arrived, instantly at attention.

Luc stared, solid and unblinking.

I had disobeyed the Conqueror.

Twice.

Fuck. I hurried forward, my movements stiff, as Jules fought back a smirk.

My foot caught on a fold in the rug.

I tumbled forward—

Directly into them.

Silk. Hard muscle. A wall of heat and power.

Jules let out a delighted cackle. "No need to throw yourself at us."

I narrowed a glare at him. "I—"

Luc moved me without effort, shifting my body like I weighed nothing. Suddenly, I was half in Jules's lap, my calves brushing Luc's thighs. My brain stuttered even as my body betrayed me, relaxing into their warmth. A shiver zapped through my spine. Heat tinged my cheeks.

"Imperium."

The world tilted, expanding outward in an instant. Tristan's voice. I jolted, gaze snapping past the kings to the Imperial Guard. He and Estrella stood at attention, watching us from lowered eyes.

Between them, a human woman kneeled. Her silver collar gleamed against her skin, her thin black gown draped like mourning attire.

My heart nearly stopped.

*My mother.*

Luc's voice cut clean through the silence. "Do you know why you're here, Mrs. Halloran?"

My mother—my *mother*—couldn't stop her gaze from flickering to me between the strands of her brown hair. I met eyes the same muddy shade as mine. "I assume you have questions, Your Majesty."

She barely hid the bitter edge to her words.

Jules rested his chin against my shoulder, the grinning face of the Butcher in the curve of his lips. "I see where you got your attitude from, lovely." His eyes went flat as he focused on my mother. "I find it less endearing in you, thrall."

Where Jules's words made me wet, my mother only trembled.

"If you know we have questions, I assume you can guess what they are," Luc continued like Jules hadn't just threatened my mother with a smile.

This time, she chose not to respond.

Luc let out a deliberate sigh. "You'll tell us eventually, one way or the other. Offer the information freely and you can go back to your life."

"Life?" The harsh whisper escaped my mother like a rattle. "This existence isn't my life. You stole me from my life twenty years ago."

The kings both leaned forward, a soft brush of pressure where their bodies touched mine.

The prey had captured the predators' interest.

Fuck. This wasn't going to end well.

"Returning to Mabon isn't part of our offer," Luc said. "It's your life here or your death here."

Death? I whipped toward Luc, my movement jostling Jules from my shoulder. He pouted at the disturbance, but I barely registered it, my pulse pounding in my ears. "You aren't killing my mother."

Luc's pupils dilated slightly. "I don't allow my enemies to live."

"It's bad practice," Jules said, gently tracing his knuckles along my arm.

"She's my mother."

"I'm aware," Luc said, unmoved.

The bastard. Crossing my arms, I sat straight-backed. Holding myself apart. It didn't work, given I was still perched across their laps. Luc's lips curled, the smallest flicker of a smirk.

Then it was gone.

His attention shifted back to my kneeling mother. "What will it be, Mrs. Halloran? Life or death?"

My mother snorted. "It will be death either way."

I flinched. No. It wouldn't come to that. I had barely even processed *my mother* stood before me. They couldn't kill her before me, just as I got her back. "Mother—"

"So you're our enemy?" Luc asked.

"I am." Her eyes met mine directly this time. Her terror remained, but rage coiled beneath it. A flicker of something restrained, something waiting. "So is she."

My jaw dropped.

Wait.

"What?" I said the word so softly my mother didn't even hear me.

She aimed her next barbed sentence at Luc. "Shall you kill her, too, Conqueror?"

The breath in my lungs stilled. *What*? How had this progressed to killing me? I didn't have the slightest idea why I'd carried a soulbond under a glamour. On top of another glamour and stars knew what other magic. If I was a pawn in some enemy's plan, I didn't know anything about it.

But even if I had known, even if I had willingly played my part, I wasn't their enemy.

I should have been. The kings were vampires, our Azarasian masters. I had feared them. A part of me had hated them for years. They were the villains who had lorded over my entire life.

Had, had, had.

I *couldn't* feel it anymore. Just like the kings couldn't kill me.

Luc only slowly arched a brow at my mother, woefully unimpressed. "You know I can't."

My mother paused at that. Licked her lips. "I didn't know for sure."

Luc tilted his head, studying her. "Your daughter just tried to command me without consequence. I would've thought it was obvious."

"And she keeps on glaring," Jules added. "We wouldn't tolerate an ordinary human glaring at us."

I scowled. "I glared at you before the soulbond."

"You were our volunteer." Jules nipped my shoulder. "And it was adorable."

I nearly jumped at the light brush of his teeth on my skin. A small, embarrassing squeak escaped me. A blush stained my cheeks, but my mother didn't react. If she had lived here for twenty years, where it wasn't rude to watch someone fuck at a feast, what was a little sexual tension between her daughter and her soulbound in a library?

I squirmed, my legs shuffling in discomfort. But that only made it worse. The stain down my thighs was unignorable. How could I just sit here, minutes after the Butcher had his cock in my mouth, the Conqueror's cum drying on my inner thighs, while the mother I had dreamed of for two decades sat across from me?

I couldn't think straight with this starsdamned soulbond.

I squirmed harder, trying to wiggle out of their laps.

Two different hands clamped around my waist.

Luc's breath brushed my ear. "I have no reservations about bending you over again, little curiosity. Even in front of your mother."

I forced myself to go still, every part of me.

Luc hummed, his voice dipping against my skin. "Pity."

"It really did work, didn't it?" my mother asked.

This time, it was the kings' turn to stiffen. Lust burned away. Something sharper, heavier, deadlier, took its place. Their eyes cut toward my mother.

Luc's voice was quiet. "If you're aware of the soulbond, then the spell wasn't cast recently."

My mother didn't reply.

Luc's fingers tapped against my hip. "Was it?"

Her gaze dropped. Not entirely to the floor in respect and fear, but partway, enough that she could gauge their reactions.

Luc's gaze pinned her in place. "Tristan."

The Imperial Guard stepped closer to my mother as one. Estrella fisted the back of her hair and yanked her head up. I gasped alongside my mother.

She had only shown me half her profile, but now I saw all of her. An hour ago, her face in my mind's eye was a blur, but now it was clear, right in front of me. She had aged, wrinkles marking the peach skin we shared, but there was a glow of health to her skin I wouldn't have expected after spending twenty years as a thrall.

What had Luc said? Vampire venom, sweat, blood, and cum all improved a human's health and lifespan.

I didn't want to think of that.

And I didn't have to.

Tristan drew a small rune on her neck, the same pattern the kings had drawn on me only two days ago. *Truth.* But that alone wouldn't get my mother to talk.

Estrella drew a new rune over her thrall runespell at the top of her spine. *Torment.*

Jules snapped his fingers.

The effect was instant. A sharp convulsion wracked my mother's body, her spine snapping taut. A ragged, animal scream tore from her lips. Her limbs seized violently, her fingers curling into claws as she twisted against the invisible force raking through her nerves.

I lunged before I could think, before I could weigh my options. I didn't even make it a step. Jules's arm hooked around my waist.

I tried again. I thrashed against him, elbowed hard into his ribs. It was like slamming into stone. His grip tightened. I shoved against his hold. Pulled, twisted, pushed—

Nothing.

No give. No movement. No escape.

"Stop it! Stop it, you fucking monsters!" my voice rang in my ears, raw with rage.

Jules didn't even look at me.

Luc's expression remained utterly composed.

My mother convulsed again. Her eyes, wide and unseeing, reflected nothing but agony. Veins stood out on her throat, her mouth open as that terrible wail rose in pitch. My stomach lurched. I had never heard anything like it before. Her fingers scrabbled at the back of her neck, nails digging at the rune as if she could peel it from her skin.

I couldn't breathe.

"Stop it," I said again, weaker this time. But my voice barely felt like my own. My ears rang. My pulse slammed against my ribs like a trapped thing, desperate to escape.

This was what it was to be powerless. Not just outmatched in strength, but crushed under it. Nothing I said, nothing I did, would change this.

Another jolt wracked my mother's body. Her scream splintered, fading into a keening sound that hit something primal in my chest.

This wasn't just punishment. This wasn't just pain. It was *torment.* It reached deep, searing into her marrow, overriding thought, identity. Everything but the unbearable, relentless sensation—

Luc snapped his fingers.

The rune cut off in an instant. My mother collapsed forward like a puppet with cut strings, her panting breaths sharp.

I shoved forward with all my strength. My pulse hammered like drums, deafening in my ears. A second ago, the kings had held me steady, had torn me apart with pleasure. Now, they were tearing my mother apart with pain.

I fought. Hard. My muscles strained against their grip, but I was nothing against them.

It didn't matter.

This time, they let me go.

In three frantic steps, I was across the rug and dropping to my knees at her side. My hands trembled over her, unsure where to touch, what to do, how to fix this.

She flinched.

My chest caved inward. I stopped. Pulled back. Swallowed. Was she... scared of *me*? I had imagined this moment a thousand times—the reunion, the relief, the sobbing embrace. Not this. Not her shaking beneath my hands. Not her flinching at my touch.

But I'd sat on our captors' laps. I let them hold me. I let them use me.

My insides twisted, nausea creeping up my throat. I sat back on my heels, utterly helpless. This was wrong. All of this was wrong. I couldn't stop the kings. I couldn't make my mother tell the truth.

I couldn't do anything.

My mother pushed onto her elbows, her breath shallow, sharp. Her gaze flickered past me to glare at the Imperium. Not looking at me. Not even acknowledging me.

Awaiting her torture.

No, no, no—

"When was the soulbond cast?" Luc asked.

My mother didn't reply. Why wasn't she replying?

I swallowed hard, my throat aching, burning. They would find out, even if they had to peel her apart and stitch her back together again. They would do it. They had the strength. The power. The ruthlessness. She had to know that.

Resistance wasn't an option.

"Tell them, please," I whispered.

She glanced at me.

Nothing.

Stars, no—

Luc snapped his fingers.

My mother shrieked. Her back bowed violently, her body contorting as if something had reached inside her and twisted her spine into knots. I had to crawl back to avoid her flailing limbs. Tears burned down my face, but I couldn't move. I couldn't breathe.

I couldn't stop this. I could only watch.

And through it all, my body still tingled, still trembled in the aftershocks of their touch. The warmth of them still lingered on my skin. It was wrong, it was vile, it was sick. How could I have let them touch me?

How could I still feel them?

"Please—" My voice cracked.

Jules cut me off. "No, lovely," he said, his tone almost fond. Like my mother wasn't writhing in agony at his feet. "We need answers. It's either this or my Block."

The air was punched from my lungs. The Butcher's Block, where the Imperium's enemies begged to die. Jules was threatening to torture my mother, like they weren't already. To the kings, this was simply foreplay.

She still had all her skin, after all.

I curled my shoulders and prayed for it to end.

One.

Two.

Three.

When I reached fifty-four, a full, unbearable eternity later, Luc snapped his fingers again. My mother collapsed, her wail cutting off.

She didn't move.

Silence rang in my ears. Was she... was she dead?

"Your answer, Mrs. Halloran?" Luc's tone was clipped this time, his patience fading. I didn't know him well, but I could feel it, sharp and fraying at the edges. He was worn, but he *refused to yield—*

I caught myself before I slipped further into his mind. I did not want to spend any time in the Conqueror's head while he interrogated my mother.

Slowly, painfully, my mother pushed onto a shaking elbow. Bloody scratches welled at her forearms, her shoulders. The crimson congealed under her fingernails. Her gaze flickered to mine again. This time, there was something else there, something I couldn't name. She exhaled slowly, reluctantly.

"Before she was born," she rasped, the words grated out of her. "The soulbond was cast before she was born."

My breath caught.

*Before* I was born? Not after. Not recently. Not by accident.

"Curious." Luc drummed his fingers against the sofa's backrest. "How long before?"

"During conception."

"Who cast the spell?" Luc asked immediately.

My mother gritted her teeth. "I can't tell you."

Jules snapped his fingers.

My mother dropped. Pain ripped through her. She clawed at the rune, at herself, turning the small cuts in her skin into gaping holes.

My pulse pounded in my skull. I whirled toward Jules. "She was answering you, asshole!"

Jules only grinned. "That didn't sound like an answer to me."

"She can't lie, can she?" My voice came sharp, desperate. "She *can't* tell you."

"She has a point, Julien," Luc said.

Jules huffed out a sigh. "Fine."

With another snap, my mother was panting on the rug again. A thin sheen of sweat glistened across her skin, but she didn't look at me. She didn't look at anyone.

Jules slouched back into the sofa's cushion. Like nothing had happened.

Luc eyed him before leaning forward. "Why can't you tell us, Mrs. Halloran?"

She blew matted hair from her face, a tremor in her breath. "If I try... to tell you... I'll die."

Jules tilted his head, something thoughtful in his gaze. Luc only watched. "So a vampire or witch swore you to secrecy?"

She gave a jerky nod to her head.

Luc's gaze flickered. His mind was moving, calculating, considering. "And why did this vampire or witch cast the soulbond during conception?"

"It was... hypothesized to improve compatibility, both for the merge of your souls and improving the attraction rune's odds."

A beat. Then another. The weight in the room changed. The kings didn't move, didn't speak, but something slammed into me. A wave of fire, anger and possession, both all-consuming. It flooded through the bond, surging from two directions at once, wrapping around me like shackles.

I turned.

Two pairs of black eyes burned into me. Both watching me. Both holding me in place with nothing but their presence.

Hunger coiled between us, inescapable.

Exactly like they were... even before we met?

Something surged through my limbs. My chest heaved, my breath caught. Not fear. Not panic. Something deeper. Hotter. Needier.

Arousal.

Pleasure at being claimed.

No. *No.*

A shudder ran down my spine, wrong in every way. My body clenched with want, my mind with revulsion. I crushed the lust, stomped it into the dark, buried it deep where it belonged. Where it couldn't touch me. I forced myself to turn. I needed to focus. I needed to understand.

"What do you mean?" My voice was too thin, too fragile, but I forced it out. "By compatibility?"

My mother frowned, but she caught herself quickly. Her expression went blank.

"You're not going to answer me, either?"

Luc answered instead. "If two souls are incompatible, they'll reject the soulbond, killing one or both parties depending on their variance in power. But if you cast a bloodborne or soulborne soulbond on an unborn child, it could theoretically influence their development to be more compatible with the target."

Development. My brain halted on the word.

"It would mean altering the spell," Luc continued, like he was already dissecting the magic in his mind. "And it would be far more difficult to cast."

"We already knew we were dealing with an expert, darling," Jules murmured. He was smiling again, but it didn't reach his eyes.

The weight in my stomach grew heavier. "And by influence my development, you mean...?"

Luc didn't hesitate.

Didn't blink.

He stared directly into me, into *our* soul. "You were made to be ours."

*You were made to be ours.*

The kings continued questioning my mother, but their voices blurred into a murmur at the edges of my mind.

*You were made to be ours.*

My insides recoiled. I didn't know what to do with that information. I was my own person. Wasn't I?

I had never questioned that before. If I wasn't, I would have bowed to my stepmother's wishes and married Patriarch Meallán. Allowed him to use my body no matter how much it hurt, in the pathetic hope of birthing three children before I turned thirty.

But I hadn't. I had forged ahead, alone.

And the kings liked that about me. My defiance had endeared them right away. My stubborn refusal to bow to the path set for me was a point of intrigue.

But if I were made for them, my entire development influenced by the soulbond, then this *was* the path set for me. I hadn't escaped it at all.

It explained too much. I had no overwhelming urge to share my thoughts with any other Azarasian. Luc and Jules weren't just ordinary vampires, they were the Conqueror and the Butcher. I had found them petrifying even before I knew that, but my terror hadn't dissuaded my interest. The rush I felt for them had been instant and surprising.

I hadn't experienced that desire with any human man. I think I would've been instantly intrigued even without the influence of magic, but the kings had been interested in me, too. That had never made any sense. I wasn't ugly, but I wasn't a great beauty, not one who could ensnare a vampire with a single glance.

An attraction rune on its own couldn't do that. Karra had knowingly entered her soulbond, intending to seduce the Beast King. The magic had helped her lure Azaras to her the moment she was in his proximity, but I hadn't tried to seduce the kings.

But if I were made for them...

I swallowed a laugh.

None of this had been natural.

None of this had been true.

None of this had been *real*.

But of course it hadn't. I couldn't believe I had actually thought two vampires could desire me naturally. My own family hadn't wanted me. Why would strangers? Without the soulbond, I was just another thrall to them, someone to fuck and discard like Éamon had said.

Only one person in the world had ever truly loved me—or so I thought.

"Did you even want me?"

The library went deathly silent. Four sets of luminous eyes landed on me, but I ignored them all for the pair that matched mine, a dull human brown.

My mother.

I had missed her for twenty years. Dreamed of the childhood I remembered in flickers. But had she ever loved me? Had she ever wanted me?

Or had it just seemed like it in comparison to my father's indifference and Deidre's disdain?

My mother met my gaze. "I never wanted any children."

I nodded stiffly. I couldn't blame her for that. It wasn't a choice people in Mabon were allowed to make. Not without severe consequences. "But after I was born? Did you... want me then?"

*Did you love me then?* But I couldn't ask that. It was too pathetic, too fragile, too hopeful—

The furrow in my mother's brow deepened. "I chose to care for you, but I never wanted a child. You were... a responsibility."

I held my flinch back this time. Of course. That was all I ever was. Another mouth to feed and body to clothe.

I exhaled slowly, voice trembling. "So after I was born to meet your quota, you would what? Convince me to volunteer so I could be bound to the Imperium? So that my death could kill them?"

My mother didn't reply.

I stared at her, willing her to answer me. To say she didn't mean it, that she lied, even though she couldn't with the truth rune on her skin. She stared back, her gaze equally intense. I couldn't read her expression. I didn't know her. It was like she expected something from me... and found me lacking.

A disappointing, unwanted responsibility.

Why had I expected anything else?

The shattering inside me was quiet at first. But then it cracked wide open, and I was breaking, breaking, breaking. I was standing before I even realized I'd moved. My eyes tingled. My insides writhed, wanting to escape. I backed away from my mother, the kings, the guards.

From everything and everyone.

"I need to... I need air."

I didn't wait for permission. Fuck their permission. I turned on bare feet and walked away. Just away. If the corridor leading to a courtyard wasn't before me, I don't know where I would've turned.

The open archway revealed vibrant green gardens. There was no door, but the humidity of Tenebra de Mar didn't touch me—or the precious parchment stored in the library. I stepped through. As soon as I touched the walkway, the heat crashed down onto me.

My tears followed a second later.

I inhaled deeply, the sound near a sob, as I pushed from the path leading to some other archway and into the depths of Duskfell's hanging gardens.

Sun-warmed stone gave way to terraces of greenery, spilling over the edges of carved balustrades. Bright fruit in shades of vibrant orange and deep red dangled from dark-leaved trees, the air heavy with their unfamiliar sweetness. Ivy coiled around pale columns, creeping along the walls of the tiers below. Bursts of red and violet blossoms broke through the green. Water trickled in fountains, the soft sound swallowed by the cries of birds wheeling overhead.

It was beautiful and otherworldly.

I didn't care.

My heart cracked open in my chest, fracturing with every step. I wrapped my arms around myself, like I could hold the pieces of me together.

My mother had been cold, distant, aloof. Maybe it was her situation. She had been a thrall for twenty years. I couldn't imagine what she had gone through, what she had witnessed. Terrible, terrible things, surely.

But that wasn't enough of an excuse for me.

She didn't care. She had never cared.

I was just a pawn in a larger game.

A game I had been made to play before I was even born.

A game I had been made to *lose.*

The kings had always owned my body, but I had thought, at the very least, that my soul was mine.

It never was.

My breath hitched. My lungs squeezed tight. I didn't know what to do. I didn't know what to feel. My mother didn't care. The soulbond had influenced me my entire life. I couldn't trust anything, not my senses, not my thoughts, not my emotions. They weren't mine.

How much of me was? I had clung to my sense of self for so long, determined not to let my stepmother or the Church or my illness turn me into someone I didn't recognize. But all along, what I recognized wasn't truly me.

Stars, what the fuck was I going to do?

I entered a clearing, the greenery giving way to a stretch of grass before a statue. The figure of a woman was carved into a block of daemium, red carnations in bloom at her feet. I almost walked right past it. But then the blur of my vision cleared—

And I saw her.

I stopped.

It was the dark-haired woman from the portrait on Luc's desk. This time, she was dressed in her finest gown, exposing sinuous peaks of her toned body. Her expression was fierce, overlooking the garden like it was the field of battle.

I hadn't thought about her much, given all that had happened, but jealousy washed through me. I was a rock next to a gemstone, dull and boring beside something gleaming and twinkling.

That was the type of woman the kings could actually love, a beautiful vampire warrior.

Not me. I was a pitiful trap—

I dug my nails into my elbows. The pain didn't register, but the pressure did. It jolted me out of my jealously, my insecurity. None of that mattered.

I did *not* want the kings.

But I had thought that before, and I'd think it again. Because I had been made by the soulbond for them. The core of my being was made to want them. There was nothing I could do.

I was trapped forever.

Bound for eternity.

My breath started escaping me in shallow pants. My head spun.

I couldn't do this.

I couldn't do this.

I couldn't—

My knees buckled. Carnations crumbled beneath me as I hit the ground, the scent of crushed petals mixing with the salt of my tears. My thighs pressed together—*stuck* together.

Because I was stained with the Conqueror's cum. A sickening tingle crawled over my skin, like a thousand ants skittering along my inner thighs.

I needed it off.

I grabbed at my skirts, yanking the fabric up as I scrubbed at my skin, harder and harder. It wouldn't come off. I was marred. I was stained. Deidre had been right. She had sensed it the moment she looked at me. I was a wicked, sinful whore, meant for our terrible Imperium. That was all I had ever been.

That was all I ever would be.

I rubbed and rubbed and rubbed, but I could still feel them.

Their fingers on my skin.

Their cocks burning inside me.

Their presences hovering at the edges of my mind. Getting closer and closer with each passing hour until nothing would be left of me.

A violent shudder wracked through me. My stomach lurched. Oh, stars, I was going to puke. I curled into myself, clutching my chest—

Two shadows shifted overhead, the ominous swirl of a storm and a cackling wildfire. I couldn't see them, but I didn't need to look to know. Their gazes met over my head, something passing between them. Something I could also know, if I wanted.

But I didn't want to.

I didn't want this bond.

I didn't want this life.

The kings settled around me, surrounding me like they always did. Like they always would. Luc's grip was firm as he pulled my hands away from my scraped skin. The welts between my thighs burned, an angry red from where I had rubbed myself raw.

But I could still feel it, feel them.

I pulled against his hold, but he didn't budge in the slightest. It was like I hadn't even tried.

Because I was trapped by them eternally. My vision wavered. The birdsong and breeze faded beneath the suffocating weight of my heartbeat.

On my other side, Jules stroked a hand down my back. "Shh, just breathe."

Luc's fingers over mine drew two small shapes on my hand. *Heal. Clean.* Magic coated me in a wave of warmth. The skin between my thighs faded from angry red to regular pink. The sweat, the dirt, the cum all disappeared from my skin.

But it didn't matter. Because the kings' soul was still inside of me, merged with mine. The heat of them didn't just press in from all angles.

It radiated from within.

I jolted back, ripping myself from their hold. They let me go.

My ass hit the grass, a sharp jolt of pain that barely registered as I scrambled away. "Don't touch me."

"Lovely—"

"Don't call me that." I tried to snap the words, but they came out half a sob. "I'm not your lovely, your little curiosity, your wife. My name is Nessa."

Neither of the kings moved closer, but their eyes didn't leave me.

"We know that, Nessa." Luc's voice was calm. Too fucking calm.

I laughed, short and sharp. "Do you?" I glared at the King of Dusk, the terrifying Conqueror. Even kneeling in the grass at my side, he was intimidating. "To you, I've always been your possession. I was made to be your possession."

Jules exhaled through his nose, reclining back as he plucked at a crushed carnation. "All Maboni are our possessions," he said, offhand.

My vision went red.

If I had something to throw, I would have hurled it at his smug face. But my slippers were gone, lost somewhere in the library. "That's not helping."

"And what will help?" Luc asked, leaning forward, silver eyes sharp as a blade. "This is your life now. You can spend the rest of it resenting us... or you can accept it."

Anger welled in me. What a cold-hearted bastard. "Fuck you."

Luc's jaw twitched. If I was anyone else, I'd be dead now. If I weren't in the middle of a breakdown, he'd have bent me over his knee.

Instead, all he said was, "It's the truth, Nessa. A harsh truth, but the truth nonetheless."

I tugged at my hair. Why weren't they angry? They had been angry. I had felt their fury when they realized how deeply they'd been manipulated. But now? Nothing. They weren't unaffected, I knew that much. But they weren't fighting it either.

"How are you so calm about this?"

"Why wouldn't we be calm?" Luc asked.

"You just said there's no choice. We're trapped together."

Jules didn't move. But something in his expression shifted.

"Trapped," he repeated, flatly.

"You know what I mean."

"Yes." The King of Dawn held my gaze. "You meant trapped."

He wasn't smiling. Had I... had I actually offended him? I hadn't thought it was possible to insult the Butcher.

"That's not..." But that *was* what I meant.

I dragged my hands down my face, feeling the weight of my exhaustion settle into my bones. Whoever had cast the spell that made me for the kings had done a shit job at it. I couldn't even excel at the one thing I had been designed to do.

I stared at the grass at my knees. Watched it sway in the breeze. Tried to let it calm my mind.

Failed miserably.

The kings waited. They always waited. I could maybe outthink them, but I could never outlast them. I couldn't stomp away again. They had let me do that once already. I had been given all the space they could allow me.

My next words came out so softly, I barely heard them. "I can't do this."

They didn't ask what I meant. They knew.

This life. This soulbond. This fate.

Luc's response was steady, unshaken. "You can."

I aimed another glare at him. "You're fucking terrible at comforting people."

Jules sighed dramatically. "What did you expect from the Conqueror?"

He crawled closer, crushing carnations without a care. His smile had returned, but it wasn't real. He was still thinking about what I'd said. Trapped. He shouldn't have cared. He was the Butcher. He skinned *people for fun. But I couldn't stop the pesky emotion. She thought us a cage. She wasn't wrong. We would always be her cage, her captors.*

*But... I thought maybe, just maybe, she could actually learn to love me. But that had been an insane idea. No one could love—*

I jolted out of Jules's thoughts, my breath catching. My brow furrowed. What the fuck was that? Those couldn't have been the Butcher's thoughts. They were too vulnerable.

I was losing my mind.

"He isn't wrong, though," Jules continued once he slithered to my side. "You can't change this. You can't change that the soulbond was placed on you before birth. You can't change that it's bound us together. But that doesn't mean you're out of choices."

I let out a bitter laugh. "I've always been out of choices. I didn't pick this life."

Luc tilted his head. "Neither did we."

I flinched. How was I still offended by their rejection, even as I tried to reject them? "I'm well aware. You wouldn't ever pick me." My gaze flickered up toward the statue watching over us. "You picked her."

Luc didn't look at the statue, but a quiet reminisce passed over his face. "Corinne died during Isaura's wraith attack on Duskfell."

Something deep inside me—some bitter, jealous knot—uncoiled just a little. There wasn't a beautiful vampire somewhere out there, waiting to drop in on my new soulbond unannounced.

Shit, I didn't mean to be grateful she had died. And at a wraith's claws? That was horrible. Would the soulbond make me horrible?

"Someone like her, then," I said, voice hollow. "Beautiful. Perfect—"

Luc moved faster than I could react. He suddenly kneeled an inch away, his hand catching my jaw, stopping the words from forming. "You were made for us. *You* are the perfect choice."

A tremor crawled through my body. Heat spread through me in a slow, treacherous pulse. My nipples peaked.

I ignored it all. "Then there's something fucking wrong with you."

Jules smirked like I'd said something hilarious. "We've never denied that."

Luc didn't laugh. His thumb brushed against my lower lip, his touch softening from a restraint to a caress. Just for a second, he looked... no, *felt* tired. "I didn't mean you," he said after a pause. "I meant this life."

I snorted. The Conqueror didn't choose this life? What other life could he live? I couldn't see Luc as anything but a king.

He saw the disbelief in my eyes, in my soul. "I didn't choose to be Azaras's son. I didn't choose to be his heir and Marisol's pawn."

*Pawn.* Something sharp and cold pressed against my gut. I was a pawn, but I couldn't imagine the word applied to him. What exactly had his grandmother done to him?

I shouldn't have cared.

But I did.

I shifted, my voice hushed but steady. "Then why are you here?"

His eyes flickered toward Jules, just for a moment. The King of Dawn only watched, tracing slow, lazy lines down my arm. "Just because the path was picked for me doesn't mean my want for it was a lie."

I swallowed. "I don't know what I want."

The words came automatically. A reflex. But that wasn't true, was it?

Luc didn't challenge my statement. He released my jaw. "You don't need to decide now."

But I had. I had always known what I wanted.

An impossibility.

A wild dream.

A *home.*

I wanted somewhere to belong, somewhere to rest, somewhere to be at peace. Someone to share it with, to make the days and nights a little less lonely.

I wanted what I had never had.

The soulbond whispered they were the answer. With the kings, I wouldn't have to fear. I could be safe and warm, cherished and kept. Their pampered little wife, adored and protected. My body leaned into their heat—

Wrong.

I jerked back, sharply shaking my head. The Imperium couldn't be the answer. No matter what every fiber of my being screamed at me.

Because they weren't safe. Because I would never be cherished. Because I would never—*could* never—find peace in their arms, stained with the blood of thousands.

It wasn't real.

It would never be real.

# INTERLUDE 4

*"WHEN WAS THE LAST time you slept, Luc?"*

*My soulbound didn't turn from where he stared out the windows overlooking Duskfell's gardens and the city beyond. "When the soulbond activated."*

*Moonlight framed the blue-black of his tousled curls and the bronze of his bare skin. He'd removed his doublet, but his trousers remained, hiding that perfect ass of his from view.*

*I meandered across the rugs at the end of our daemium bed, wearing nothing beyond my favorite rings and the rubies in my ears. "That was five nights ago."*

*"We stayed awake for a week at the siege of Trost." Luc's gaze flickered briefly to me as I slid into his periphery. "What's four days?"*

*I sighed. The turmoil within him was like a distant storm, flickering on the horizon. I hadn't noticed it clearly while Nessa was awake. Her pain had been fresh, jagged tears in her heart that consumed my attention until she'd finally fallen asleep. Luc's wounds were centuries old, injuries reopened by Orlagh Halloran's revelations and the mere sight of our new bride standing before Corinne's grave in the falling light. "Luc—"*

*"I'm fine, Jules."*

*Things were truly dire if Luc had resorted to lying to me. I stepped around until I blocked whatever shrub he'd been glaring at. Instantly, tension flared in my shoulders. I tried to roll out the sensation, but it was nothing more than an echo through the bond.*

*Stars, the man shouldn't have been this tense, especially after his orgasm in the library. I'd never seen him come that hard before.*

*But I'd never seen him this stressed before, either. He'd weathered inheriting his throne on the eve of tragedy, Marisol and Corinne's blood still warm on his skin. He'd persevered through the century of war and conquest that followed, building our kingdom into an impire. He'd navigated court politics and backstabbing with ease, ever the ruthless warlord.*

*Only to be bested by a soulbond with a human.*

*"You need to sleep, darling," I murmured, with a light brush of my knuckles against his chin. "I can guard us tonight. I've had more than my fair share of rest these last few days."*

*He didn't respond, but at least he stopped trying to glare through me. Those shadow-rimmed silver eyes met mine. In the comfort of our apartment, of our soulbond, the cold mask of the Conqueror slipped, his fear and grief suddenly clear in his gaze.*

*"Oh, Lucey." I wrapped an arm around his shoulder and closed the final inch between us until our chests touched. If only we could share our godcurses through our bond. Luc deserved the peace of an hour without emotions.*

*He tensed, even though I had been creeping closer for minutes now. My two soulbound were similar in that regard, both requiring a gentle approach. Though their reactions, if I weren't careful, were polar opposites. Nessa only blushed and stuttered, but Luc snapped and snarled.*

*"Do you not trust me to keep us safe, darling?" I asked, my words soft. "To protect our small, vulnerable bride?"*

*He let out a long sigh, a deep rush of breath. "You're the only one I trust with that."*

*"But?" If he wouldn't say it, then I would. "She's not Corinne, Luc."*

*He flinched, the smallest twitch. His rage thundered briefly through the bond—then disappeared just as quickly, without even the slightest growl. He dropped his forehead to mine. "I know that."*

*"Do you? Then why are you guarding us in the depths of our very own palace? An enemy would have to penetrate layers of wards to get in here."*

*Luc frowned. "Corinne died in this palace, protected by layers of wards."*

*"A bad comparison." I nipped at those soft lips of his, banishing his frown. "Luc, I'm not going anywhere and neither is our new wife. I am yours forever. Have been yours forever. And now she's ours forever, too. Though she's deliciously soft, she won't suffer any harm. Nothing will get past the two of us, not this time."*

*"Jules—"*

*I kissed him gently. "No more arguments, darling. It's time to come to bed."*

*When I laced my fingers through his, he didn't resist. I pulled him toward the bed. Our bride curled up in the center of the large mattress, a flash of copper and peach amidst black silk, dwarfed by the imposing daemium headboard. It stretched up the entire wall and curved gently onto the ceiling.*

*Nessa had drifted to sleep on a sofa almost immediately upon entering our Duskfell apartment, the poor thing utterly exhausted. It wasn't a surprise given the week she'd had. She had only just recovered from her illness, too. I'd smelled hints of blood when we both fucked her today, but I hadn't noticed any pain through the bond. But we'd taken it slow, gentle.*

*Not that she'd necessarily agree.*

*But if she hadn't been bedbound just yesterday, I'd have fucked her in so many other places. Coming on my tongue as she woke. On the floor in the closet as we dressed. In the stables, bent over a barrel of hay. In an alley off Tenebra de Mar's market square, her nails digging into Luc's back as I watched him rail her against the wall.*

*He'd have his turns, of course.*

*Garden. Table. Shower. Bed. Bed again. Stars, I'd be fucking her now—*

*Luc pressed into my back and his warm hand circled my hardening cock.*

*I stilled. Fuck. But my expression didn't even twitch as I twisted to Luc and slowly raised my brows. "You're such a tease, Lucey."*

*"Tease?" My soulbound gave me a rough stroke. Pleasure flared through me, but I only smirked at him. The pain was still there in his eyes, but his lust rose alongside mine, slowly sweeping everything else away. "Don't be silly, Julien. You know I don't tease."*

*Holding my gaze, our breaths mingling, Luc stroked me from base to tip, again and again. This time, I allowed my gasp to slip free.*

*"I take," Luc whispered.*

*I grinned. Now there was my Conqueror King. "If you're taking, why am I the one that gets to come in your hand?"*

*Luc growled before he claimed my lips, plunging his tongue into my mouth. I broke the kiss a second later to turn in his arms. A rumble started in his throat, but I swallowed it eagerly, burying my hands in his soft, dark curls. Claiming him back. Wanting him as fiercely as he wanted me.*

*Luc and I had always been equals, neither besting the other. Didn't matter if it was in the fighting arena or the bedchamber. Every inch he conquered, I swiftly reclaimed. Even now with his hand stroking, stroking, stroking...*

*He stepped forward, the backs of my thighs brushing the sheets, and nudged a hard thigh between my legs.*

*I bit his lip.*

*Luc pushed me down onto the mattress with a small snarl. "You coming in my hand and me taking your ass aren't mutually exclusive things, Julien."*

*He had his trousers unlaced and on the floor a second later, his cock hard and thick for me. My mouth went dry at the sight. He crawled forward, herding me backward, pressing me deeper onto the mattress. Nessa didn't stir, even as Luc pushed me down an arm's length away from her, settling his knees between my spread legs.*

*His hand reclaimed my cock as his lips brushed against my abs, my chest, my collarbone, my chin. I groaned loudly. Uncaring if it woke our bride. I had watched Luc fuck her earlier. She could watch Luc fuck me this time around.*

*With a wide grin, I spread my legs and bent my knees until my calves brushed his ass. "Prove it."*

*Luc pulled back. A grin spread across his face, one that promised bliss. My heart skipped a beat. Stars, he was gorgeous when he smiled like that. He needed to do so more often. Just like he needed to fuck me more often. How long had it been since we'd last had sex? Two weeks? As companions, we'd tended to share thralls more often than each other.*

*But he was mine now. Forever. I didn't have to share him with anyone outside our soulbond again.*

*I raised my feet, resting them on his shoulders, open and waiting just for him.*

*The shadow of his eyes swallowed the remaining line of silver. Luc nudged the thick head of his cock against the tight ring of my ass. Heat blossomed across my skin as his finger traced a small rune, making me slick for him.*

*If he didn't fuck me soon, I was wrapping a leg around that torso and claiming that cock myself—*

*Luc thrust into me in one powerful stroke.*

*Fucking finally.*

*I groaned, my back arching. "Oh, fuck, Lucey."*

*My hands clenched in the sheets as Luc started fucking me. His hand didn't leave my cock, stroking me up and down in perfect rhythm with his possessive thrusts. I moaned, stars bursting across my vision.*

*With every ram of his hips against my ass, his piercings rubbed through my tight channel.*

*With every stroke of his skin against mine, I saw a flash of divinity.*

*With every grunt from his lips, our bodies shuddered in tandem.*

*Fuck, I was going to come.*

*I wanted to come so hard it felt like dying. "Harder."*

*"Ask nicely, Julien."*

*I almost whimpered. The bastard loved nothing more than pathetic begging.*

*And I wanted to orgasm, so I begged pathetically. "Please fuck me harder, Lucey. I want you to make me come."*

*Luc's grin darkened. "Again."*

*"Please fuck me so hard, darling," I groaned out the words. "I want to come for you. Please make me come for you."*

*Luc managed a soft chuckle. "Very well."*

*With his next thrust, I nearly slid up the silk sheets, my hand slamming out to catch myself just before I hit the headboard. Shadows coiled around my wrist. I could have shaken off Luc's control, commanded the shadows to release me, but I didn't.*

*Instead, I raised my other hand.*

*Shadows seized my wrists, pinning them back against the headboard. With every pulse of his hips, I inched closer and closer. Again, again, again. I had asked Luc for harder and he delivered. He always delivered. My head fell back into the pillow, my hair a mess of blond waves over black silk.*

*Luc grunted, the sound shifting into a growl as he took in every inch of my glistening, pale skin beneath him. Stars, I loved when he looked at me like that, like I was the most beautiful thing that existed. He was every bit my perfect match above me, a dark-haired warrior godstar made of bronze. I ached to thread my fingers through those tousled dark curls, to kiss him breathless until we both came, gasping against each other's lips.*

*Fuck, he needed to make me come. Now. My hands tightened into fists against the daemium. Perhaps I'd surrendered a bit too hastily.*

*A soft gasp sounded to my left. Nessa had twisted toward us in her sleep, her brow furrowed ever so slightly. Her nipples were hard rosebuds against the black of the sheets. Her hand slipped between her legs at the tension. At the echo of our pleasure. The sensations from our bond were far stronger when her sleeping mind couldn't stop our soul from drifting closer, bridging the distance between its pieces.*

*Was she watching us fuck in her dreams right now?*

*Stars, I hoped so.*

*Luc grasped my jaw, pulling my gaze sharply back to him. "This is just you and me, dearest. If any naughty voyeurs wake, they'll have to fuck themselves."*

*I almost shook Nessa awake at the thought. The only thing that could make this better would be watching our proper Maboni bride touch herself to the sight of Luc fucking me. I wanted her to come on her fingers so I could lick the nectar from her skin.*

*Fuck, no, wait. I wanted her to ride my face as Luc took my ass. That would be true divinity.*

*Luc tightened his fist, drawing my attention back to him, to the present. "Pay attention when I fuck you, Julien."*

*True divinity would have to wait for another day. "Yes, darling."*

*The pleasure spiked in me, reaching and reaching crescendo—*

*I fell.*

*"Fuck, I love you," I nearly shouted, my nails digging into my palms as I came. My body arched sharply, trembling with every pulse as my release spilled hot over Luc's hand and across my abs. My vision went white, my senses overwhelmed by the blinding intensity of my climax. I closed my eyes, surrendering as wave after wave of bliss dragged me down, drowning me in pleasure.*

*Luc followed me a second later. The warmth of his bliss and his cum flooded deep inside me. Marking me as his. Forever. Always.*

*When the euphoria finally receded, I sank limply into the mattress beside Nessa, breathing heavily. Our bride whimpered softly in her sleep, reacting to the lingering ripples of our pleasure. The scent of her arousal mixed intoxicatingly with our own.*

*One day, when our bond was closer to settling, the sensation would be strong enough to make her come alongside us without a single touch.*

*I couldn't fucking wait for that day.*

*Luc collapsed at my side. His expression had already shifted back to seriousness. I almost frowned. Was he fucking kidding me? If another orgasm couldn't make him relax, nothing could.*

*"Jules..." he began quietly.*

*Oh. He didn't need to say anymore. I knew exactly why he was frowning.*

*I'd said I loved him.*

*We'd exchanged those words before, of course, but always as companions. Brothers-in-arms. Lovers, occasionally. Eternal soulbound. Even when my heart had longed for something deeper, I'd held myself back.*

*It meant something different this time.*

*"You don't need to say it, Lucey." My gaze remained locked on his, wanting him to feel the truth of my words. Not that we could lie to each other, but our bond had only changed days ago. Love took time even for heartmates. Even if we had teetered on the edge of it for centuries. "It's okay if you don't—"*

*Luc kissed me, cutting off my words. "Of course I love you, you fool. I've always loved you and I always will."*

*A fluttering filled my chest. He loved me. He had always loved me. He always would love me. I smiled against his lips. "Say it again."*

*The Conqueror obeyed without hesitation. "I love you, Jules."*

# 45

DAWNSPEAR GLITTERED IN THE morning light.

My gaze followed the elegant line of its tallest tower to the golden spire piercing the sky, luminous against the blue. Around us, Imperium Square buzzed with activity, the chaos a stark contrast to the serene grandeur of the castle rising above it all.

Dawnspear remained just as magnificent and awe-inspiring as it was the first time I laid eyes on it six days ago. How had it only been six days? It didn't seem possible. Almost everything had changed.

No dread or terror rose in me at the sight of the bright castle. I wasn't passing through the wall of climbing roses and shadow-streaked bone as a captive thrall, heart in my throat, stomach a pit of dread. I wasn't scared for my future, my life, or even my body.

None were at risk. Not from the Kings of Dusk and Dawn.

That should have been a relief.

It wasn't.

It wasn't anything.

I wasn't anything. I was hollow. That was the only way to describe the sensation in my chest. Like I had been scooped out and left empty. My limbs moved, my heart beat, my lungs filled, but something was missing.

I had been born to be compatible with the kings.

I wasn't someone's daughter, but someone's pawn.

I couldn't stop my gaze from flickering back to Estrella and Tristan, riding behind us. My mother perched in front of Estrella, small and frail in her thin black gown and simple cloak. Unlike yesterday, her gaze remained firmly on the ground. Whatever bravery had possessed her had fled overnight.

My anger and anxiety had gone with it. But the emptiness they left behind settled deeper with every breath. It crept in slowly, cold and quiet, spreading through my chest. Even Jules at my back, radiating warmth and quiet happiness, wasn't enough to push it away.

My mother didn't want me.

She had never wanted me.

She had birthed me for the quota and for the kings.

Well, for the soulbond and whatever plan the demonblood she was allied with had, but the result was the same. My entire life had been influenced by the soulbond, warping me into something I wasn't.

Something for *them.*

But how could I ever be right for the Conqueror and the Butcher? That had to be a mistake. A severe miscalculation on part of the soulbond.

*I've always loved you and I always will.* Luc's words came back to me, a low murmur from the dream. I shouldn't have witnessed his and Jules's whispered confessions. The moment had felt... private. Intimate. Not for my eyes.

If I said that aloud, I'd only get a smirk from Luc and a laugh from Jules. We were soulbound. Their emotions had itched at the edges of my mind since I woke. One day, I'd feel them like they were my own, just like their bodies would feel like my own. We couldn't get more intimate than that.

But I still shouldn't have witnessed any of it. I had known the kings for a mere twelve days. Twelve days to their five hundred years. Who was I to watch the moment the Conqueror confessed his love for the Butcher? Who was I to feel the Butcher's elation, his dream coming true after so many centuries?

I was an invader in their soulbond. Even with the help of magic, I could never belong. Luc and Jules were gorgeous and powerful and confident. I was plain and broken and shy. Whatever emotion they one day felt for me, it wouldn't be real. Not compared to the love they shared.

They were a perfect match for each other.

And maybe that was the root of the issue. It wasn't that I felt safe in the arms of murderers. It wasn't that my existence was manufactured. It wasn't that I didn't want to fall for the vicious Imperium.

What if this new life was just like the old?

I'd forever be on the outside, watching others experience the love and belonging I'd always craved. Only this time, there was no end date. I couldn't drink the kings' blood now, but they would ensure their survival, no matter what.

This would be my eternity.

Surrounded but alone.

Needed but not wanted.

Perhaps loved, but not truly.

No warm bed, endless food, or mind-shattering orgasms could fill that empty place in me.

But it was an improvement, at least. I wasn't cold or hungry. I didn't have to count my stipend or patch the same rip in my shawl over and over. I wasn't in agony every day, my own body turned against me. Maybe this was the best life had to offer me. Maybe I should accept—

Teeth nipped at the ridge of my ear.

I yelped, pulling away from Jules. The sharp sting snapped me back to the present, to my reality, as sudden as a knife to the throat. I shot him a glare, but the King of Dawn only grinned. There was mischief in his eyes, but also something keener, something quietly assessing.

When I kept staring, he winked.

The heated promise behind it shivered along his skin, my skin. The soulbond dragged the sensation straight through my chest, past my hardening nipples, down to the low pulse between my legs.

Revulsion followed it, clawing up my throat.

My body wasn't mine. It had been shaped for *them*, made to crave their touch, even when I wanted to shrink away. But the bond quickly smothered the feeling. It had been less than twenty-four hours since Luc and the library. The bond thought that was long enough.

It *needed* them.

Clenching my thighs tighter around Cala's saddle, I spun back around. My pulse pounded in my ears, but I ignored it. We had already passed through the Sun Gate, but the road to the palace lined with pear trees wasn't exactly short. Courtiers strolling the garden dropped into bows when they spotted their Imperium.

I latched onto them, onto anything to ground me. I traced the runic parterres with forced focus, willing myself to slip away, to find that void of feeling again.

Jules chuckled, his breath against my cheek. "You'll have to try harder than that, lovely."

Heat rushed to my cheeks. Was he teasing me about my failed attempt to drift off or the want I couldn't hide? Maybe both. "I don't know what you're talking about."

"Liar."

I resisted the urge to glare at him again, but my gaze betrayed me, sliding to Luc astride his hellsteed ahead of us. He wasn't laughing. He was watching, not with amusement, but with quiet certainty. He was waiting for the moment I stopped fighting. The moment *she gave in, whether she wanted to or not—*

I dug my nails into my palms. I refused to slip into either of their heads. Just like I refused to feel this need.

Jules's macabre fountain decoration would come into view soon. I forced myself to picture it, to brace for the sight of flayed flesh and exposed ribs. But not even a flayed body was enough to dampen my arousal.

"The sweet scent of your desire is certainly an improvement from the panic or dissociation," Jules said. "But it ruins my plans for the day just the same."

I couldn't help it. My head snapped back around. The King of Dawn's grin widened, immensely satisfied. He'd baited me into reacting, but I didn't care. Jules had plans that didn't involve me naked, wet, and begging? My lips almost twisted into a frown.

That was *not* disappointment I felt. Not at all.

*Liar*, my brain whispered in Jules's voice.

I ignored it. "What exactly do you have planned for the day?"

"Luc and I spent the last month in Mabon, so we have far too much work for my liking," Jules said with a sigh. "Meetings with the council, the Blood Legion High Command, the Merchant Syndicate. Impires don't run themselves, unfortunately."

"You only planned to attend half those meetings," Luc said without even glancing back.

"Well, yes. I didn't say I was attending them all, just that they were happening."

I nodded, but my focus was on crushing the rising disappointment. I didn't want them. I didn't need them. But the bond whispered otherwise, curling warmth through my chest, tricking me into believing their absence would leave me cold.

But could I blame it entirely on the soulbond? Without the kings by my side, I was nothing more than a fragile human in a city of vampires. The ease I felt wasn't from the towering walls of their castle or the safety of their apartment.

It was them.

Their presence. Their attention. Their touches.

But that was the bond. It wasn't real—

"Don't worry, I had a lunch break planned," Jules said, cutting off my thoughts. "Figured Luc and I could take turns licking your sweet cunt. Winner gets to fuck you, loser has to watch." Jules paused. "Or maybe the winner gets to fuck the loser and *you* have to watch."

My breath hitched. The heat that had been slowly spreading through my cheeks jolted through my entire body. It was absurd. Vulgar. Exactly the kind of thing that should've made me recoil. But Jules knew exactly what he was doing. He saw me slipping away again and lured me back with the one thing the bond wouldn't let me ignore. My distress didn't stand a chance against the wave of unadulterated lust that crashed over me.

Jules leaned in, his lips brushing against my ear, warm breath sending shivers down my spine. "You'd like that, wouldn't you?"

My body went stiff and straight. Jules knew. I didn't know how, but he knew I had watched Luc and him fuck in my dream.

"You weren't very inconspicuous this morning," he continued, answering the question clear on my face. "Blushed the second you looked at me."

My stomach twisted. Heat. Mortification. Arousal. All at once.

"I plan to win this, though, so you'll get a little variety in your new hobby. Any preference for how I should fuck our Conqueror King?"

"Don't bother answering him," Luc said before I could cobble together an answer. "Jules won't be winning. Assuming I even agree to the wager."

"You'll agree and you'll lose, Lucey."

Luc glanced over his shoulder and arched an impervious brow.

Jules stuck out his tongue, the gold of his piercing catching the light.

My clit pulsed hard enough that I nearly whimpered. My fingers twitched with the urge to cup myself, to relieve even an ounce of the tension coiling inside me.

"You wouldn't know it, since Luc loves to be in control," Jules said, golden gaze fixed on the King of Dusk. "But every once in a while, he wants me to tie him up and fuck him like a dirty slut."

Luc's expression didn't change, but something sharp pulsed across the bond. It tingled through me like sparks, buzzing just beneath my skin.

Jules obviously sensed it, too, since his grin went sly. "Keep in mind, the bondage part is mandatory with Luc. Can't keep him in line otherwise."

My mouth dried. It wasn't hard to conjure the image of Luc leaning back against a mattress, black eyes locked and focused on me. But imagining shadows shackling his wrists, his ankles... My stomach clenched, interest sparking just as sharply as Luc's did at Jules's wicked words.

The kings had said they had meetings to attend. But they weren't thinking about politics anymore. Just like I wasn't thinking about what my mother had said anymore. Heat flooded me, stoking the ravenous beast the kings had awoken inside of me, the one that craved pleasure and despised pain. She wanted me to grab Jules's hand, guide it between our legs, and beg him to make us feel good.

Another part of me screamed. This wasn't natural, this wasn't right, this wasn't real—

A muted moan of agony reached my ears.

The sound spread through me like a splash of cold water. My desire died instantly.

We had reached the loop before the steps to Dawnspear's red door, vampire attendants preparing for their kings' arrival in the warming Montaurère air. Behind them, Sabas and Cédric waited. The Crown Enforcer's arms were crossed and his face fixed into a glare while the Crown Mage waited patiently.

Overseeing it all, the flayed body writhed on the fountain's golden spear.

Nausea surged in my gut. The impaled vampire's gaping chest was a ruin of torn flesh, twitching muscle, and exposed ribs, just like last time. I twisted my head away until Jules's earring came into focus, the heavy ruby drop swaying with his movement.

Jules narrowed his eyes at my swift change in mood, glancing between me and his prisoner. "It's been a long time since I've been tempted to kill good ol' Pops, but your repulsion is a compelling argument."

I blinked. I had not expected that response. "That's your *father*?"

"Unfortunately," Jules said.

It was such a Jules answer, I couldn't help but snort. "For you or him?"

The King of Dawn pursed his lips. "I used to say me, but I think this might beat anything he ever did."

"You've kept him on the edge of death for centuries," Luc said, quiet approval beneath his words. "That's quite a feat."

"I do love a good edge."

Luc's lips twitched in a smirk. I narrowed my eyes at him, at Jules, not understanding the joke but knowing one was there. I wouldn't ask. Admitting my inexperience in front of the kings during yesterday's trysts in the apartment garden and library had been embarrassing enough.

When we reached the steps, the vampire attendants scurried forward. Sabas and Cédric started down to meet us, their long shadows cast by the rising sun. Jules's brother's expression hadn't changed at all, unbothered by the shuddering corpse. By his *father*.

Were they only half-siblings? Did they even know? With all the orgies happening, some vampires surely had no idea who fathered them.

"What did he do to be worthy of centuries of torture?" I asked, trying to ignore all those quietly curious eyes.

For a long moment, Jules didn't answer. He dismounted Cala, his movements fluid, easy. Luc circled Wrath, his dark brow arching slightly in an otherwise stern expression. Shit, was that too forward of me—

"He killed my mother," Jules said simply.

"Oh." I gaped at him. I hadn't expected a reason. A good reason, at least. "Was it... intentional?"

"Plotted and planned. He chose her death, so I've made him beg for his." A terrifying smile bloomed on that beautiful face, but his triumph behind it was thin, like an echo of justice that had lost its edge long ago. "Not that he's sane enough to beg anymore."

I shuddered hard. I had always known the Butcher was cruel. But this? He had devoted *centuries* to his father's suffering. Not out of necessity, not as a punishment, but as a hobby. "That's awful."

"I know," he replied.

Luc stopped at Jules's side beside Cala. "Hands on the pommel, bride."

I blinked at him. "What?"

He tapped the pommel before me. "Hold that and swing your far leg over Cala's back." His hand lowered to the stirrup closest to him, a light brush over my skin. "You'll settle both feet here."

"And then?" I asked incredulously, glaring down at Luc. *Down*. I was sitting at the height of his starsdamned face. The Conqueror was the tallest person I had ever met, but the hellsteed dwarfed him.

And he wanted me to do what? Jump off? I'd break both my ankles... if I was lucky.

I glanced over my shoulder. Behind us, Tristan had unceremoniously dropped my mother to the ground. "Why can't you just lower me to the ground?"

Jules huffed a laugh. "And deny us the pleasure of watching you struggle?"

Luc's lips barely twitched. Not a smile. Not quite.

I narrowed my eyes.

"Do what he says, then he'll help you off," Jules said. "No one's expecting you to leap off a hellsteed on the first try. You're much too short."

I scowled.

The skinned body rattled on the spear.

Egh, that was disgusting. Teeth gritted, I grabbed the pommel and tossed my legs over without hesitation. Luc lowered me to the ground a second later, before I could even panic about how high off the ground I was.

Jules spun on his heel, already grinning as he faced Sabas. "Miss us, Sabs?" he drawled. "You didn't have to meet us at the door when we were only gone for a day."

Sabas didn't return the amusement.

"We need to talk," he said. No greeting. No pleasantries.

Both kings' brows lifted.

Something in the air shifted.

Cédric cleared his throat. "I discovered a signature in her blood."

# 46

My eyes didn't know where to fall first.

Floor-to-ceiling windows stretched across the right wall, opening onto a terrace that overlooked the distant blue expanse of the lake. Shelves of pale wood lined the room, meticulously arranged with hundreds of books and scrolls. On a recessed stretch of parquet flooring, eight plush red lounge chairs surrounded a circular gilded table. Bodies twisted in strokes of gold, white, and red on the ceiling, like an artist had rendered a revelry in paint.

Stars, I would never tire of simply *looking*. After a lifetime of dull human constructions, every room I entered was like stepping into a dream.

Even if this one was more of a nightmare.

Isabeau and Roxiana rose from their seats as the kings entered, dipping into shallow bows. But their attention flickered to me almost immediately, examining me with the cold interest of a predator.

A shiver crawled down my spine. Something was wrong. The creeping sense of unease coiled tighter. What had Cédric discovered from analyzing my blood? It couldn't be good if the entire Kings' Council was staring at me like I was their enemy. We didn't know each other, but our few interactions had been cordial until this point.

Now, hostility thickened the air of the Council Chamber.

Luc pressed a hand lightly against my lower back. I had stopped near the doorway, caught in the weight of those unreadable, silver-gold stares.

Estrella and Tristan shut the chamber doors with a thud.

Without a word, Luc guided me forward toward the table, where the council had reclaimed their seats. No chair looked more important than the others, but we rounded the table toward the two directly facing the entrance. Luc pulled a chair back for me.

As soon as I sank into the plush cushion, Jules took the seat beside me. The council followed his lead, settling back into place.

Luc remained standing. He didn't fidget or shift, only studying the gathered council like he would a battlefield. But beneath that stillness, a muted thrum of apprehension ran through him.

Then, finally, he spoke. "You discovered a signature?"

"I did," Cédric said with an incline of his head, those golden eyes flickering to Luc before cutting briefly to Jules.

The King of Dawn lifted a brow. If I noticed the council's intensity—and hesitation—then they certainly had, too.

"And?" Luc asked with a hint of annoyance. His tone was as even and unaffected as usual, but it itched through the bond.

Sabas exhaled through his nose, already impatient. He wasn't one to tiptoe around unpleasant truths. "It was Allegra Isaura."

The kings went predatorily still. Their reaction was so visceral that my entire body clenched, too. But within, my heart kicked into a hard, erratic rhythm.

Allegra Isaura.

The name echoed through my mind, ice sinking into my bones.

He had to be mistaken. How? Why? When? But that didn't matter now.

This was *not* good.

Rage slammed through my chest. I sucked in a sharp breath, caught off guard. I had never felt anything that intense from either of the kings besides their pleasure. It didn't feel like my emotion, but it battered against me.

Six sets of luminous eyes locked onto me, but I saw only one. Luc's. His silver gaze burned, bright as molten light, sharp as his *axe's blade. She had been given to us by the one person I wanted dead more than anything.*

*The woman we'd hunted for centuries, since we silenced the Isauran rebellion.*

*The woman we'd hated since she sent witches carrying the everlife rune into Duskfell and caused the deaths of hundreds, Corinne included—*

I yanked myself from Luc's mind. Sweat beaded along the back of my neck. "I didn't know."

My words were soft, barely a whisper. I was nervous, but I should have been terrified. The bond fought to push that terror down, muffling it beneath a manufactured sense of safety. It told me I was fine. I was protected. But out of all the enemies Luc and Jules had, Allegra was the worst possible option for who cast the soulbond and glamour rune on me.

She wanted the kings dead.

They wanted her dead.

And I was standing in between them.

Cédric cleared his throat. “There’s more.”

“Is it worse?” The softness of Jules’s tone sent another chill through me. I forced my gaze away from Luc. The King of Dawn sat perfectly still at my side. He wasn’t smiling. He wasn’t laughing. There wasn’t even a glint of wicked amusement in his golden eyes.

Cédric winced. “Yes.”

“What could be worse than Allegra?” Luc almost growled.

Cédric hesitated.

Luc’s irritation sharpened. “Cédric.”

The Crown Mage straightened. “Allegra cast more than a soulbond on her. I can’t tell for sure what’s under the second glamour rune, but...”

Roxiana leaned back in her chair, arms folding across her chest. “Cédric, if you don’t spit it out, I will.”

Cédric shot her a flat look. “Allegra was an expert at casting. She wove the first glamour rune over the soulbond, and then the second glamour over a secondary rune.”

Before Luc could snap at the Crown Mage again, he reached into his pocket and pulled out a vial of blood. The same one he’d used to collect my blood in the throne room? Probably. He handed it to Luc.

With a slight crease between his brows, Luc lifted the vial, his silver eyes fixed on me. I couldn’t breathe. The room was too quiet, too still.

He unstoppered the vial.

He went stiff as the dead.

The rage stopped. Gone in an instant as Luc inhaled. It was like the bond had gone numb. But that wasn’t possible, was it? I tentatively reached out to it, but in place of any emotion, I only found a glacial, endless void.

The chair beneath me jerked violently back.

I yelped, gripping the armrests in a desperate attempt to steady myself. A large hand slammed down over mine, pinning it in place. Luc leaned in, his towering frame blotting out the room.

The Conqueror looked out from his eyes.

From the nothingness of the bond came a burst of anger so scorching it burned. In his other hand, the vial of blood gleamed between his fingers. "Is there anything you'd like to *confess*, bride?"

Confess? There was a bite to the word I didn't like. Something sharp and dangerous beneath the smooth, patient tone. Stars, why couldn't I feel petrified? The dissonance was as disturbing as the unnatural quiet now leaching through the soulbond from Jules. Usually the King of Dawn was all fire and passion, the King of Dusk ice and intensity, but they had swapped.

"No?" My voice came out uncertain. I glanced over my shoulder at Jules. He had risen from his seat, no longer lounging but standing behind me. A shiver trailed my spine at his silence. "What's wrong?"

Luc's stare remained locked on me. "This is a vial of witch's blood."

My heart attempted to gallop out of my chest. Then it couldn't be my blood. Why had it upset the kings so much? I fought to keep my voice even. "Okay?"

Luc didn't waver. "It's also a vial of your blood."

I stared.

And stared.

And stared.

The floor felt too far away, like I was floating, untethered.

"What... do you mean?" I whispered.

Luc released my hand, once again towering over me. The moment he let go, I clenched my fists on the chair's armrest. I had nothing to hide. Nothing to fear. But stars save me, I couldn't stop myself from shifting under their gazes.

The silence stretched.

I licked my lips. "I'm not a witch."

Luc didn't react, but the bond fluttered with surprise. He could tell if I was lying. He had to be able to tell. My statement had been simple and clear. I was *not* a witch. There was no way to twist that.

Still, no response.

"That can't be my blood."

"We can all smell it," Jules said at my back.

The hairs on my neck stood at his eerily soft tone. "But—"

Luc put the vial to his lips... and tilted it back. He swallowed my blood in one bob of his throat. Then, without breaking eye contact, he flicked the empty vial toward Cédric.

The Crown Mage caught it easily.

"It's your blood," Luc confirmed.

My stomach dropped.

No.

No, no, no. "But you... you've consumed my blood before."

"We consumed your glamoured blood," he said. "Cédric stripped all the runes from this sample."

I opened my mouth, struggling to form words. "I think I'd remember if I was a witch."

But even as I said it, doubt slithered in. Demonic couldn't be taught. Only those with demon blood knew the language, reading runes as innately as their once-divine ancestors.

I'd always been able to read runes. Not fully. Not clearly. But the meanings had always been there, like whispers curling at the edge of my mind. Karra had described them as screams, so I assumed I only carried traces of demon blood like many humans did.

The kings didn't need to know I could read runes. I'd never revealed it, and now was the worst possible time. But I needed to know. A question couldn't be a lie, right?

I wet my lips. "If I were a witch, I'd have magic and be able to understand runes, right?"

Luc ignored the question. His silver gaze flicked to Cédric. "The secondary rune is a suppression rune?"

A suppression rune? Like what they carved on witch collars? Why would I...?

Oh, shit.

I barely heard the reply over the rushing in my ears.

"A strong suppression rune," Cédric said. "Stronger than I'd ever advise casting on someone for a prolonged period. But if it wasn't, she would have been discovered during her physicals when she healed too fast for a human."

Luc met Jules's gaze over my head. "Take it off."

"Gladly." Jules grabbed my wrist and pulled my hand up, my knuckles facing him. I tried to tug from his grasp. He was too strong. Shadows flared from his fingers, but they didn't turn to claws. Instead, he traced a rune through the air.

*Halt.*

My every muscle stiffened. I couldn't move at all.

A slice of metal split the air.

My heart jumped into my throat. I couldn't turn, but in my periphery, the glint of a blade appeared, blackened metal drinking in the light. The Butcher's dagger. It wasn't his skinning blade, Adé, but the other one. Thérèse, with her sharp tip and curve for slashing.

Fuck. A fresh wave of panic clawed up my throat. Jules wasn't going to cast a rune with shadows, he was going to—

Jules started carving.

I braced for the pain. A sharp flare, a burn, something. But Luc had refreshed his soothing rune on me before we left the palace this morning. The numbing magic still held. But I saw the blood. It dripped down my arm, obscuring most of the runes, but I felt the shape in my skin.

Jules started with a curve at the top, the tip of his blade pressing just deep enough to catch on flesh. Then, a steady downward stroke. The bond between us remained empty. He felt nothing. Not satisfaction. Not anger. Not even cruelty. Just that terrifying, unreadable calm.

He pulsed magic into my hand. The twisting shadows gobbled up my blood.

*Unravel. Suppress. Unravel. Soothe.*

Pain ripped down my arm, sudden and blinding. A scream attempted to rip from my throat. But I couldn't open my mouth, couldn't move anything beyond my eyes. All I could do was sit there, tears spilling silently down my cheeks, as my nerves caught fire.

With a final burst of heat, it stopped. I opened my eyes. The magic had devoured all the blood down my arm, but my skin still screamed, the rune cut into my open flesh.

***Unravel. Suppress. Unravel. Soothe.***

I blinked rapidly at the shapes. They were different now, not whispers against my mind, but stronger.

Like screams.

My chest rose and fell in short, frantic bursts. Pain twisted in my gut. No. This wasn't happening. That still didn't mean I was a witch. Maybe these were just... stronger runes.

But deep down, I knew.

Blood started seeping from the open wound. Jules hadn't drawn a healing rune. Was he going to leave me with the cut? Daemium injuries didn't heal on their own. I would bleed forever—or until an infection killed me—

Before I could spiral further, Jules lifted my hand. His grip was almost gentle now, his breath warm against my skin. He swiped his tongue over the wound. When he released it, my flesh was healed, not a trace or scar left behind.

Luc moved at last. He lifted a hand, drawing a final rune into the air. ***Release.***

My body unlocked. I slumped forward, sucking in a sharp, desperate breath.

Stars save me. I was a witch?

Oh, no. No, no, no. I couldn't be a witch. How the fuck did that make any sense? My breath rushed out of my lungs in heavy pants. The walls of the Council Chamber pressed in. The scent of blood—*my blood*—still clung to the air, coppery and thick.

This wasn't real.

It couldn't be real.

But I knew it was.

Witch. The word echoed over and over, rattling inside my skull. Allegra. The soulbond. The suppression rune. The room was suddenly too small to fit all these revelations.

I couldn't breathe. I couldn't fucking breathe. My fingers clawed at my chest, trying to loosen something—anything—beneath my ribs.

I squeezed my eyes shut. Tried to focus. Tried to count.

One, two, three—

My vision swam. My stomach clenched. My nausea rose.

Four, five, six—

My ears buzzed.

I was falling apart.

And they were all watching me do it.

"Is that it?" Isabeau asked, her tone as dry as ever.

I jerked. The council had all watched the kings remove the suppression rune with stoic expressions. Now they were all staring. Isabeau's slight frown. Roxiana's furrowed brow. Sabas's narrowed gaze. Cédric's wide golden eyes, a mix of curiosity in his confusion.

My stomach swirled again, a harder twist. "Is what it?"

"I'd have thought she'd have more power, too, given she survived the bonding," Cédric said, ignoring me.

More power? "What are you talking about?"

"The suppression rune was strong enough to suppress every trait passed along by her demonblood," Luc said. "If she's been wearing it since infancy, it might have caused permanent damage to her power."

Cédric nodded. "Possibly."

Sabas leaned back in his chair, crossing his arms. "Then how did she survive the onslaught of your power during the bonding? That part never made sense to me, but her being a witch clearly wasn't the answer."

"Her mother revealed the soulbond was cast during pregnancy to improve compatibility," Luc said. "Even though she has little power now, she was likely born strong enough to survive the bonding."

"Wait." My voice came out strangled, barely a breath. "Are you saying my magic is broken?"

Luc finally looked at me, tension still rigid in his jaw, the bond straining to dull his fury into something softer. "It appears that way. You still look entirely human because of the second glamour, but without the suppression rune, we can sense your power... or what little remains of it."

The words landed like a slap.

My magic was broken.

*Broken.*

Just like the rest of me.

A laugh bubbled up, sharp and wrong. Then another. Then another. My head tipped back against the chair as I tried to stifle it, tried to press my lips together, but it kept slipping out between gasps.

"Is something funny, witch?" Luc's words were calm, but his wrath simmered.

"No, not at all. Not at all," I said, choking back another laugh. But it didn't stop. "It's just... it's just my luck that I turned out to be a witch with *broken* magic."

Cédric tilted his head, the faintest trace of a frown between his brows. "It's damaged power—"

"Same thing," I hissed, cutting him off.

A hand fisted in the back of my hair and tugged. A sharp squeal tore from my lips at the flash of pain, my head jerking back.

Jules stared down at me, detached and composed. "Such attitude, witch. It's like you've forgotten who you're speaking with."

I tried to turn my head, to twist from his grip, but he held firm. "You can't hurt me."

"We can't *kill* you." Jules's fingers untangled from my hair, his knuckles grazing my jaw as he circled my chair. "There are so many options between here and death."

I shuddered. "You can feel my pain."

His smile widened. "Mhm-hmm. But our bond is new, so it won't hurt us that much." He flicked his gaze to Luc, who gave a single nod. "What's a little pain if it gets us the answers we want?"

My heart thundered at the chill in his voice. He grinned, but the emptiness behind it made my blood run cold. It went beyond ice. Not even Luc could numb himself like that.

I had been wrong. I thought I had witnessed every part of Jules.

It was time I really met the Butcher.

I swallowed. The bond tried to smother my panic down, but I clung to it. "You haven't asked me any questions."

"We have before." The Butcher crouched smoothly before me, all predatory grace. "I don't know how you lied, but this time, you'll tell us all your truths."

"I didn't know." My voice shook. My eyes darted between them. Safe. Unsafe. Safe. Unsafe. I couldn't decide which they were anymore. "I can't... I can't be a witch."

"Except for the fact that you are." The Butcher stroked his fingers through my hair, tucking a loose strand behind my ear. It was the only gentle thing left in the King of Dawn. The usual warmth, the levity, was gone from within him.

It was a lie. It wasn't right. What had he done to himself?

I met his eyes, pleading. "But I didn't know."

"Give me your hand."

"Jules—"

"You have no right to use his name anymore, witch," Luc cut in.

I swallowed and raised my hand from the chair's armrest. It trembled slightly. But when the Butcher took my hand in his, the shaking stilled. The panic in me started to ease.

Safe. Safe. Safe.

Lie. Lie. Lie.

His fingertips trailed along my index finger, slow and *deliberate. My thumb pressed lightly against the side of her knuckle, my other fingers tracing the delicate bones beneath her skin. So soft. So breakable. "Why did you volunteer for the harvest?"*

*"I already told you—"*

*I sighed. What a shame. Why did they always start with lies? Predictable. Luc and I braced for her pain. If only my godcurse could dull the sensations my soulbound felt. But it was no matter. Pain and I were old friends.*

*My grip shifted. My thumb dug in, my fingers wrenched, and with a sharp, practiced twist—*

Snap.

Agony burst through my hand, dragging me back into my body. White-hot. Blinding. A ragged scream tore from my throat.

Jules broke my fucking *finger*.

I jerked violently, but I didn't get far. Luc was behind me in an instant, his hands slamming down onto my shoulders, forcing me still. My muscles locked beneath his grip, trapped between them.

My vision blurred.

My breath stuttered.

The Butcher's grip only gentled. His thumb brushed slow circles over my palm, as if he hadn't just shattered something inside me. "See, we don't trust you. When you were just a human, we could maybe believe your innocence."

Luc's voice was a dark cut of sound behind me. "We wanted to believe it."

"But you're a witch." The Butcher almost sounded fond. "And Allegra cast the spells on you."

"I didn't know," I whimpered.

The Butcher hummed as if considering that. "Why did you volunteer for the harvest?"

"Jules, please."

He leaned in, his lips trailing along my jaw, my cheek—

He *licked* the path of my tears.

When he reached my forehead, he murmured, "Why?"

I sucked in a breath, forcing the pain down. I would survive this. I had to. "To save my sister."

"She's not your sister," Luc said. "If you're a witch and your mother's human, your father can't be human, too."

The words landed like his axe in my ribs. I stared at him, stunned. Disoriented. My breath slowed. My pulse didn't.

No. That wasn't...

Aislin *was* my sister.

She had to be.

But the math was simple. Two humans couldn't make a witch. My stomach twisted violently.

"Why, Nessa?" The Butcher's voice was soft, almost coaxing.

I swallowed hard, steeling my spine even as my breath shuddered in my lungs. "My answer hasn't changed."

His touch drifted, a deliberate caress over my middle finger.

My stomach clenched. "No, please don't—"

A sharp snap.

Pain exploded through my hand. It didn't come in waves. It was immediate, all-consuming, radiating from the broken joint in brutal pulses. I screamed, the sound raw and ragged. "You fucking bastards—"

Luc's hand slid from my shoulder to my throat. My voice cut off with a strangled gasp.

The Butcher sighed. "You're usually such a good girl for us, witch. When we ask a question, we expect an answer."

"What does your Exalted Mother have planned?" Luc asked, his hatred spiking at the mention of Allegra.

"I don't know." I didn't want to sob the words, but I couldn't hold them in. "You know I'm telling the truth. And if you didn't, I've spent far too many days in pain to ever choose it when there's another option. Please don't—"

Snap.

A fresh bolt of agony splintered through my bones. A broken, gasping sound tore from my throat. I clenched my jaw, but the tears still fell.

I couldn't get away.

I couldn't stop this.

I was held in place by my soulbound, surrounded by four other vampires in the center of a castle filled with them. An *impire* filled with them.

The kings didn't believe me. I couldn't even blame them. I wouldn't believe me, either. But I didn't know Allegra. I didn't know her plans. I didn't know why she'd placed a soulbond on me before I was even born or what she hoped to gain by binding me to the Imperium.

I was entirely helpless to stop this pain—both the kind radiating through my hand and the kind crushing my soul.

I wasn't special. The kings wouldn't change. The happily ever afters of my romance books weren't real, were never real, not in this world, not for me. *Never* for me. My fate was sealed, no matter which path I took.

All that awaited me was agony and apathy.

I didn't want to fucking do this.

"What does—"

"I don't fucking know what Allegra has planned," I said, cutting Luc off. "I've never met her. I didn't even know her name two weeks ago. I volunteered to save my *sister*. I understand that's too much of a coincidence for you to accept, and maybe Allegra planned it somehow, but from my perspective? I was saving my fucking sister from *you*."

The Butcher didn't move, but his focus sharpened, unwavering as he kneeled before me. Behind me, Luc's grip remained firm on my throat. A silent warning. A reminder of who held me in place.

Both of their eyes darkened.

My breath hitched, my mangled hand pulsing. But fuck it, I had already started yelling. "Why doom Aislin when this was my fate either way? I couldn't fulfill your stupid, fucking child quota. Even if I wasn't fucking infertile, it hurts just to get aroused." A bitter laugh choked me. "Maybe if it didn't, I'd have at least tried, like my mother did. But I couldn't even do that, so it wasn't a choice. It was an inevitability. One I couldn't do anything about.

"Just like I can't do any-fucking-thing about this. Someone else made the choice, and I just pay the price." I lifted my chin, glaring down at the Butcher even as Luc's hand pressed tighter against my pulse. "Just break the rest of my fucking fingers already. I don't know anything, and I'm fucking tired of this."

My chest rose and fell, breath shuddering past clenched teeth. Beyond it, silence. The council didn't seem to be breathing. The Butcher didn't answer. The Conqueror didn't move.

I could feel them, though. Watching. Processing. Deciding.

I had given them everything.

Still pinned beneath Luc's grip, I felt it the moment he made the decision. His fingers loosened a fraction, just enough to tell me the worst was over.

The Butcher exhaled slowly. Then, with the same care he'd taken before, he stroked his thumb over my shattered hand. As if he'd merely bruised it, as if the bones beneath my skin hadn't been twisted and ruined by his hands.

The torture was done.

For now.

His thumb finally stilled over my palm. "Very well, witch. We can pick this up later."

A fresh shudder ran through me.

Luc let go of my throat. I gasped, air rushing back into my lungs as I sagged back against the chair. My mind reeled from the abrupt shift.

I barely had time to think before Luc snapped his fingers toward the door. It opened. Estrella and Tristan walked in and bowed.

"Take her to our chambers," Luc said, his voice smooth and cold. "Lock her in the Mortal Bride's bedchamber."

The Butcher leaned back on his heels, still crouched before me, his golden eyes a strange mix of satisfaction and something darker. He lifted my hand between us and inspected his work. His lips twitched slightly, as if debating whether to say more.

But in the end, he didn't. He only kissed the back of my knuckles, his mouth brushing over broken bones. I flinched, pain shooting through my hand. I barely held in my whimper.

But even my ragged inhale was loud enough for a vampire to hear.

The Butcher traced a quick pattern. ***Heal.*** The pain vanished in an instant, bones snapping back into place as if they'd never been broken. He'd mended my fingers just as easily as he'd shattered them.

I glared at him. I wouldn't thank him for healing me, not after he injured me in the first place.

A faint frown tugged at his mouth. No other emotion surfaced, but if one had, it might've been confusion. Like he didn't know why he'd healed me.

I didn't have time to question it. A second later, strong arms lifted me out of my chair. Tristan. His grip was firm, careful, but not gentle. I didn't have the strength to fight him. Didn't have the will.

The kings looked away as Tristan carried me out, Estrella at his side. Luc turned his focus to the council, his expression carved from ice. The Butcher lingered a beat longer before he exhaled, the void in him thawing suddenly.

When he rose, he was once again the smiling charmer. "Well. That was illuminating."

Sabas leaned forward, fingers steepled. "Was it? She didn't tell us anything."

"She told us plenty." Luc's silver eyes cut toward the Crown Enforcer. "But our bride isn't the priority now. Allegra is—"

The door shut with a heavy thud, like the closing of a coffin.

# 47

SALT STAINED MY CHEEKS, wet streaks sliding over my chin and down my neck.

I'd tried not to cry. I really had. I'd already screamed and begged and bled. And still, the kings had tortured me without a hint of remorse. Like I wasn't their soulbound. Like I wasn't even a person. Like I had never mattered at all.

Because I hadn't. I never had.

I was their Mortal Bride, forced onto them for eternity less than a week ago.

I was a pawn, my entire life a lie.

I was unloved, a stranger at the Hallorans' table when I thought myself a daughter.

I was cursed, broken inside and out, forever and always.

Of course this would happen to me. I shouldn't have been surprised. I shouldn't have cried. The kings had smiled at me, protected me, touched me like I was wanted... but I wasn't. I'd known it wasn't real.

But the moment Tristan had dropped me on the floor of the Mortal Bride's bedchamber like I was little more than lumber, I couldn't stop the tears from flowing. Estrella slamming the door in my face hadn't helped either.

I was to stay in my room—out of sight, out of the way. I was a stain on the Imperium as much as I was on Deidre's perfect life. They wouldn't want me out there for the whole world to see.

Would my eternity be these four walls? I'd go mad. This room wasn't cold like my loft, like my childhood room. The sheets I curled into were soft. The mattress was made of feathers, not straw. But just because it was a beautiful prison didn't mean it wasn't a prison.

What had I called their apartment that first day of the bond, hours before I knew? A gilded cage? That hadn't changed.

I was trapped. Stuck. Powerless.

The seconds dragged to minutes, dragged to hours. The cramps in my belly clawed. I had only lived without the constant pain of my illness for two weeks, but its return felt so much worse. I couldn't do anything about it.

All I could do was wait.

I couldn't run from this room and demand... whatever Karra would've demanded. I was a witch some-fucking-how, but I had no magic. No power. None whatsoever.

And even if I did, I wouldn't know how to use it. All demonblood could read and cast runes, but turning raw lifeforce into magic took training. Precision. Skill.

I snorted. Even if I had that, what then? Barging out of this room wouldn't change anything. What would I do? Fight two Imperial Guard and however many vampires were between me and the kings? Force the Imperium to listen? They didn't want to talk.

And I couldn't make them want me.

What was there to want?

I gave a sharp shake of my head and buried it in the pillows. Even if something about me was appealing, I did *not* want them. My vampire warlord kings, beautiful and cruel. Monster and captor and lover, all in one.

I. Did. Not. Want. Them.

But the bond disagreed. It had sunk into my heart, threading through my veins like poison. It wanted them. It needed them. It didn't know why they were angry. It didn't understand why we weren't with them, soothing them.

Luc's dark rage battered the edges of my mind. Jules's chaos had tangled and twisted for an hour before vanishing into stark emptiness again.

There was more beyond the feral storm, beyond the terrifying void—but I couldn't wade through it.

I didn't want to.

I didn't want to feel them. I didn't want to slip into my mind and become them.

But I couldn't fucking ignore them. It wasn't like I had anything else to think about beyond pain. Pain that they had taken away, only to cast me back down to the pit. I couldn't even get the satisfaction of them feeling it with me. If they hadn't flinched when my fingers broke, what would cramps do?

My belly twisted like it was insulted.

I shook my head. Thinking about the pain made it worse. How many hours had passed? There was no way to judge time in this windowless coffin.

Fuck it. I couldn't fucking do this. I didn't know how to fight, lacked any charm, and apparently enjoyed being fucked like a whore, but I couldn't just sit here while those bastards decided my fate.

If I never tried, it would always remain impossible.

I paused at the thought. Had I just quoted Jules?

I gave my head a sharp shake. Whether the advice came from the Butcher didn't matter. I had to try. I sat up—

A sharp twist stabbed through my core. Nausea surged up my throat. Fuck. I slumped back onto the bed, clammy sweat breaking across my skin from the effort alone.

I closed my eyes. Inhaled. Exhaled.

I could do this. I could push through.

I *had* to do this. I *had* to push through.

I sat.

I stayed sitting.

I glared at the floor beside the bed.

I blew out a long breath and twisted, throwing my legs over the edge. I pushed to my feet. My muscles buckled for a second, my body swaying. I tensed. I would *not* fall.

Smoothing a hand down my skirt, I forced myself upright. Shoulders back, like a proper Maboni woman. Not that I was any such thing—my tangled, unbound hair, the scandalously cut emerald riding gown, my cunt still tingling from the pounding it had taken yesterday. I ignored that all and smoothed my hand down my back—

And froze.

My hands grazed a small circle of wet at the back of my gown.

I stiffened. I didn't even need to check. I was spotting. Not a surprise, given the way my illness thrashed inside me, unleashed after so long. I twisted and tugged at the skirt, but the runes woven into the fabric slowly cleaned the stains away.

But my illness was the least of my concerns.

The first was how in the hells I planned to get through the door.

I stepped toward it slowly. Even if it was unlocked, Estrella and Tristan were likely just outside. What would I do when I faced them? They couldn't hurt me, but I was no match for them.

I clenched my fists, my heart pounding as I approached the door. I had to at least try. Could I live with myself if I didn't even do that?

I reached out—

The doorknob turned.

I stumbled back. Shit. Had they heard me?

Of course they had. They were fucking vampires.

But it wasn't Estrella and Tristan who entered.

It was Maire, carrying a small tray with cured meat, wedges of soft-ripened cheese, a crusty bun glazed with honey, and clusters of sugared berries nestled in a porcelain dish. It was the smallest portion I'd ever seen in the Impire, but somehow bigger than most of my meals back home.

Was this what they served all their prisoners? Or did it mean something more? Something good or something nefarious? I stared at the little bowl of berries like it could answer my questions.

Maire stiffened when she spotted me, standing only a few feet away. I stared at her. She stared back.

"You have five minutes," Estrella said gruffly, before slamming the door.

We continued staring in silence.

The last time I'd seen Maire had been a quick glimpse of her face in the window yesterday, after Jules fucked me in the garden. After she'd *watched* him fuck me. Given the betrayal I saw flash across her face, she had witnessed long before the bite, when his venom flooded my veins. The only moment it became acceptable to enjoy a vampire's touch.

Maire raised the tray ever so slightly. "Your dinner, my lady."

I swallowed. "Thank you."

I didn't say anything else. She didn't either. With Estrella and Tristan outside, nothing we said would be private.

"Is there anything else?" The guards had said she had five minutes. That felt like a long time to deliver a tray of food.

"I'm to take the tray when I leave," she said. "The Imperium insisted."

Ah. So I only had five minutes to eat. I grabbed the tray and dropped back onto the bed. Pain shot through my core. I couldn't repress the flinch.

"Are you... well?" Maire asked.

It was an innocent enough question.

I didn't care to give a fake answer. "No."

Maire only nodded sharply, like my reply wasn't a surprise.

I tore into the bread. I hadn't eaten since this morning in Tenebra de Mar, an entire lifetime ago. But now my nausea hovered at the edges, peeking out with every whiff of meat and cheese. I breathed through it, through the pain, and swallowed.

I'd need what little strength I could cobble together.

Maire watched me eat for a minute before pursing her lip. Some decision crossed her expression.

She reached into the pocket of her skirt. Whatever was in there was light enough to avoid notice. She pulled out... a scrap of bark?

I frowned, gnawing on a crust of bread. Why in the stars did she have bark in her pocket?

Maire turned it over.

Two runes were carved crudely into the surface. ***Silence. Obscure.*** I nearly flinched. The runespell wasn't even active, but my mind yelled the meanings at me. That would take some getting used to.

So would the concept of Maire holding a rune. Where had a human thrall even gotten one? And what exactly did she plan on doing with it? Without magic or blood, Maire couldn't activate it. She didn't possess the first, and the vampires would smell the second.

She reached out... and handed it to me.

I stared. Why the fuck was she giving it to me? I took it anyway. My thumb traced the grooves.

My gaze snapped to her face. Did she know I was a witch? She was Cédric's thrall. Maybe she'd overheard him discussing it or making the discovery.

But I didn't have any magic. There was nothing inside me, no heat I could draw from.

But... I did have blood. Too easily accessible.

I bit my lip to stop a sudden hysterical laugh. Was I really going to rub the blood from my *spotting* on the rune? That was gross.

It was my only option.

Stars, I hoped this rune was like the runelights and would activate with blood alone. If it wasn't, I wouldn't even be able to explain what I'd tried to do.

I pushed to shaking legs and held up a finger to Maire, asking her to wait.

Spinning around, I jolted at the sight of my reflection. Red-veined eyes. Puffy cheeks. Fuck, I looked awful. I was taller and broader than Maire, only the crown of her blond head visible in the mirror over my shoulder. She wouldn't be able to see what I was doing.

I glanced at the ceiling and forced myself to take a deep breath. I couldn't let my feelings slip out. If Luc or Jules sensed even a flicker of surprise or hope, they'd know something was happening. I pressed everything in me down, burying it deep under the pain.

*Don't think, Nessa. Just do.*

I bunched my skirts in one hand and reached between my legs. My fingers came away smeared with pink. Eww. I swallowed, sent up a momentary prayer, and smeared the bloody ick across the rune. Please, please, please—

***Silence. Obscure.***

The rune flared with a flash of darkness, a gentle wave of heat brushing my skin. It burned through the bark, disintegrating in my hand until nothing remained.

I spun around. "Where did you get a rune?"

Her eyes widened, dropping to my hand—only to find me wiping at my skirts, the rune gone. She sighed out a relieved breath. "Exalted Morrena cast it."

"How? All the delegation and thrall witches wear collars."

"You, Nessa."

My brows shot up. "*Me*?"

"At the Red Queen revelry, you told Exalted Morrena she could do whatever she wanted," Maire said. "You're the Imperium, so those words deactivated her collar. That's how I walked through the wards in the kings' library. *You* invited me in."

I gaped at her. Oh. That... made sense. Soulbonds were designed to make multiple individuals one. The magic wouldn't be able to tell the difference between the kings and me. "You know I'm soulbound to the kings?"

She nodded. "And that you're a witch. When I shared that I overheard Prince Cédric telling Enforcer Sabas this morning, the Isaurans told me about your bond."

"Oh." I sank back onto the bed, more from exhaustion than shock. "And why did they give you a privacy rune?"

"In case I got the chance to speak with you." She glanced over her shoulder at the door. "We only have another couple minutes."

I shoved another piece of bread into my mouth at the words. I didn't know when I'd get another meal. "And what does Morrena want you to say to me?"

Marie's lips twitched, almost into a frown, but she smoothed it away. "*We* want you to free all the witches in Dawnspear."

I stared. All the witches? I didn't know how many witches were in Dawnspear, but it was probably a hundred at least. I couldn't leave this room. Maire couldn't sneak them in. "How would I do that?"

"She said all you need to do is say it aloud." Maire peeked back at the door again. "You're the Imperium, whether anyone knows it or not. You could free every thrall in the Impire."

My eyes widened. Every thrall? With just a couple words? I didn't have any power myself, but I wasn't powerless after all. I could use the kings' own authority against them.

"But you shouldn't," Maire blurted, seeing the look on my face. "Someone will notice that and inform the kings. Or worse, the kings will notice it themselves."

"And then they could reactivate the runespells?"

She nodded. "Just as easily as you can deactivate them."

She was right. Once the kings realized I had this ability—or realized I *knew* I had it—they also might find a way to strip it from me. I might only get one chance. "And what does Morrena plan to do once I free her?"

Maire grinned suddenly. Almost maniacal. "Burn this castle to the ground."

"Ah." That was... extreme. But against immortal vampires, extreme was the only option. "But what will that achieve? You aren't going to kill the kings with a fire, even if they were in the castle." I frowned, brushing against the bond I'd tried hard to ignore. "Which they aren't."

"I know," Maire said. "They left for a feast at the Blood Legion High Command."

I flinched. A feast? Jealousy flared, sharp enough to pierce through pain and exhaustion.

Were they feeding from someone else?

Were they fucking someone else?

I leaned back into the bond instinctively. I had to know. But no pleasure pulsed through our connection. No ghostly sensation tingled across my skin. Luc was practiced calm wrapped around a churning storm. Jules was still an empty pit of darkness wearing a smile, his emotions scooped clean from his chest.

They weren't focused on me.

Until I focused on them.

It was like they turned in my mind, facing me—

I yanked back from the bond and imagined slamming a door in their faces. It stayed shut. But they were there on the other side.

They'd always be there.

I shuddered. That didn't matter. I didn't care that we were bonded for eternity. I could ignore them like I ignored my pain. Like they ignored *my* pain.

Fuck. Them.

I raised my chin, staring at Maire with a confidence I didn't feel. "I want to leave."

Maire's green eyes widened. "You want to *leave*?"

"Yes."

"I..." She opened her mouth, closed it again. Clearly, she and Morrena hadn't discussed this option.

"Do you know what they did to me, Maire?" I held out my hand, even though the wounds Jules left were long healed. "They broke my fingers. I told them I didn't know anything. They knew I wasn't lying and did it anyway. So yes, I want to leave and I want to leave *now*."

"Exalted Morrena thought I would have to convince you to release them," Maire said. "We didn't... didn't discuss if you wanted to leave."

"Then go ask her." I plucked the last piece of bread from the tray. "I free all the witches in Dawnspear from the runes placed on them by the Impire. There. Now they can use their magic to get me the *fuck* out of here."

"I'll..." She hesitated, thinking. "I'll need to speak with them. I'm not sure that's possible. It would mean getting through the wards. You'd have to add their blood to the door to allow them entry."

My heart dropped. Shit. She was right. There was too much magic guarding me, never mind the two Imperial Guard outside the door.

"You can at least ask." My voice cracked. "I don't want to stay here, Maire."

Her expression softened at the ache in my voice. "After I take your plate and return it to the kitchen, I have to nurse Rosier. Riona will attend to you for the rest of the night."

"Is Riona loyal to the Azarasians?"

"She isn't."

"Then she can bring me their answer." I lowered the tray and reached for her hand. I'd beg if I had to. "Please, Maire—"

The doorknob turned.

Maire and I pulled back at the same time. But the guards barely looked at us, unconcerned with what a human and a powerless witch could do.

"Time's up," Tristan said.

Maire nodded and took the tray.

I stared up at her, pleading with my eyes.

After a moment, she sighed. "Have a good night, my lady. Riona will attend to you later." She widened her eyes, holding my gaze like we could speak without words. "I'm sure she'll care for any need you have."

*Any* need I had. Thank the fucking stars. Maire would ask the question. Riona would deliver my answer, whatever it was.

I gave a small nod. "Thank you, Maire."

She left the room without a second glance. Estrella pulled the door closed behind her.

I sunk into the mattress.

All I had left to do was wait.

# 48

When the doorknob twisted again, I nearly jumped from the bed. Hours had passed since Maire left. Or at least, it felt like hours. I had tried to lose myself in *The Soulborne Queen*, but the pain in my gut twisted and ached, growing stronger and stronger with every anxious thought that swirled through my head.

Was this the right choice?

What would the Isaurans say?

If they said yes, would we succeed?

What would the kings do if we didn't?

What would the kings do if we *did*?

Why couldn't I just return home, curl up with my cat and my books, and ignore the world for the rest of my life?

I laid *The Soulborne Queen* down with trembling hands and shook the thought away. If this was Riona, she might have an answer for me. The privacy runespell from earlier had faded to ash, but maybe she'd have another one so we could speak freely.

It wasn't like I'd run out of blood. My bleeding had only worsened with the stress. After Maire left, I had rifled through the wardrobe for a cloth and changed my outfit. The sapphire-blue dress wasn't as substantial as the riding gown, but at least it didn't carry the memories of the last day.

Riona stepped inside, but Estrella and Tristan didn't close the door this time. They didn't enter, either. I glanced at them, then back to the human thrall.

She kept her head bowed, but her gaze flickered around nervously. "The Imperium will return to Dawnspear within the hour, my lady. I'm to ready you for them."

I stared at her. Ready me for them?

The kings hadn't moved far from wherever they were in the mountainside city below, nor had their emotions changed. They'd put on their kingly masks, fulfilling their roles as the Conqueror and the Butcher. Luc still seethed. Jules remained numb. They'd been there all day, a steady pulse beneath my thoughts, as constant as my heartbeat.

But they'd return soon. Were they planning to torture me again? A cold sweat broke out over my already clammy skin.

I nodded stiffly. "And how exactly does one prepare to be tortured?"

Riona glanced up at that. "That's not..."

She faltered. Stars, why was she the nervous one? I was the one about to be tortured by my soulbound.

Without another word, she walked over to the wardrobe, threw it open, and pulled out a frilly bit of white lace I'd briefly considered using for my bleeding, then tossed aside. It wasn't like I could stain the expensive fabric in spite, given the tiny runes woven into every outfit I'd encountered so far.

She held it out. Beyond its sheer transparency, it was a short gown, probably meant for sleeping. It would barely cover my ass...

Oh. She wasn't preparing me for torture. Not the painful kind, anyway. "You're preparing me for their meal."

Riona nodded, a quick bob. "Yes, my lady."

I wanted to be annoyed by that. Disturbed and angry at being used. At my opinions being entirely disregarded. Stars forbid a little torture session this afternoon get in the way of the kings *fucking* me. But my heart only leaped, heat rushing to my cheeks. The fire in me erupted from pain to pain *and* desire.

How could I still want them this much after everything they had done?

Riona swallowed, then gestured toward the wardrobe. "Is there anything else you'd like, my lady?"

Her tone hadn't changed, but she stared directly at me now. Like she wanted to say something else but couldn't. I clenched my fist to steady myself against the pain in my belly and crossed the room to her side. My legs shook with exhaustion, the kind that rooted itself in my bones, but I managed. The wardrobe door obscured Estrella and Tristan's view.

Riona pulled something gently from her pocket. A small scrap of fabric, stained with six drops of still-wet blood. ***Conceal. Preserve.***

My stomach clenched, a sharp throb cutting through the cramps already twisting in my core. A prickle of awareness shimmered through the bond. Shit. My anxiety must have spiked across our connection. I forced my breaths to slow, quieting my thoughts before either of the kings noticed any more.

I stared at Riona, but she just shoved the scrap at me and gestured toward the bed.

No. Not the bed. My nightstand?

I frowned. She gestured again, more pointedly this time. Like she was... oh. She wanted me to take the scrap and hide it. Was this blood from the witches? For the wards on the door? How in the hells was I supposed to get it anywhere near the front when I couldn't even leave the bedchamber?

But I grabbed it from her anyway.

"No, I think that will do just fine, Riona." As calmly as I could muster, I approached the bed. I had no reason to open the nightstand, but I'd tossed *The Soulborne Queen* aside earlier, lying open on the sheets.

With my back to the guards and the thrall, the mirror reflecting only my shoulder, I leaned over and picked up the book. As I closed it, I shoved the scrap of fabric inside. The blood might stain the pages, but the rune would preserve it.

I placed the closed book on the nightstand and turned back around. My hands twisted together. I'd have to go through with tonight, then. Of course I would. It was unreasonable to expect the Isaurans to break me out immediately. Most of them had only been freed from obedience hours ago.

I exhaled slowly. As long as the kings didn't torture me, I would be fine. Surely they'd use a soothing rune or flood my bloodstream with their venom before fucking me. I could find it in me to enjoy their touches if they were meant to bring me pleasure.

If they chased my illness away, I'd even beg for it.

Riona gestured toward the door. "I'm to bathe you, my lady. In the kings' bathing chambers."

Her hand trembled slightly. Whatever the witches had planned, it had scared the thrall. Maybe it would happen sooner than anticipated. Not that I could add their blood to the door's runes if I were in a bathtub.

But I wouldn't resist Riona's request. I couldn't get out of here alone. I'd have to trust Maire, Riona, and Morrena, despite barely knowing any of them. Riona wanted me in the bathing chamber, so to the bathing chamber we would go.

I walked through the doorway with my shoulders straight and my head held high. Estrella and Tristan didn't react, but their eyes didn't leave me. Nightfall had come to Dawnspear, turning the sight out the windows across the kings' bedchamber into a scattering of stars and the glow of the moons over distant mountains. If I weren't a prisoner, perhaps I'd be out there, soaking in the view.

Titus rose from the rugs at the end of the kings' bed and shook himself out. Had the giant hellwolf been waiting out here for me this entire time? He padded over to me, a monster with dark fur and shadowed eyes, death made flesh—

And nudged my shoulder, his tongue lolling out in a happy pant.

"Did the mean Imperial Guard make you sit outside, Titus?" I buried my fingers in the thick ruff of his neck and began to scratch. The hellwolf leaned into my touch. "Yes, they're so mean, aren't they?"

Estrella and Tristan didn't respond. I hadn't expected them to. They were centuries-old vampire warriors. Nothing I said or did could hurt them.

With a final scratch to Titus, I twisted around. "Bathing chamber, right—"

Riona stared at me solemnly. It was such a change in expression, I stopped mid-step. Her nerves had been swept away by steel determination.

The thrall raised her hand and bit into her palm hard enough to draw blood.

My breath caught in my chest, a soft gasp. Unease pulsed through the bond in response. Estrella and Tristan closed ranks in front of me without turning as a low growl rumbled in Titus's throat.

Riona smeared the blood in a line down her chin, over her neck, and past her collarbones to the center of her chest—

Shadows flared over her heart. A giant rune bloomed across her skin.

***Stun.***

Magic exploded outward. The wave of heat rammed into me. A rune at my collar flared, and shadows burst through the room. ***Shield.*** They caught the worst of the impact, softening the blow, but it still hurled me off my feet. I hit the rugs. The impact ricocheted through my bones like I had slammed into stone. The breath whooshed from my lungs. My head snapped back, colliding with something solid.

Something warm.

Titus.

For a moment, I couldn't move. A high-pitched whine pierced my ears, drowning everything out. The world blurred at the edges, distant and vibrating, like I'd been knocked loose from reality.

I pushed onto an elbow, teeth gritted against the pain. My body screamed in protest, fire blooming deep in my core *and* rattling through my bones.

Titus lay sprawled beside me, motionless.

Alarm spread like ice through my chest. I reached for him with trembling hands and shook his massive shoulder. His body was heavy, too still. No groan, no snarl, no twitch of his paws. "Titus."

Panic built sharp and fast, echoed through the bond. I leaned over him, shaking harder now. "Come on, come on—"

He didn't move.

No. No, no, no.

I'd wanted out. Wanted freedom. Wanted to be anywhere but here. But I hadn't meant this. I hadn't wished anyone harm. Especially not Titus.

But how could the Mortal Bride, the new third of the Imperium, ever leave otherwise?

I spun toward where Riona, Estrella, and Tristan had stood. The two vampire guards were sprawled across the floor—Estrella on her back and Tristan half over her, like he had tried to shield his heartmate. Neither of them moved.

I slammed a hand over my mouth. Oh, stars. What had I done? Were they dead too? I crawled forward, ignoring the aches in my limbs and the twisting in my center.

Silver eyes met mine.

I jolted. My heart stuttered. Riona's rune had failed... or not? Estrella remained completely still, Tristan unmoving on top of her. Everything except her eyes.

I almost went slack with relief. Maybe that meant Titus wasn't dead, either? Oh, thank fuck. I couldn't handle if someone—

I finally noticed Riona.

The thrall had collapsed just as we had, but her tanned skin had gone pale. Beyond sickly. Beyond injured. It was a color no living thing could ever be. The rune faded slowly from her chest. Her eyes stared, unblinking, at the ceiling.

Completely and entirely dead.

Sacrificed to power the rune that stunned the vampires and hellwolf but left me unharmed.

Oh, stars.

Fuck, this was happening.

Of course it was happening. What had I expected when I told Maire I wanted to leave? It might take fewer lives than setting Dawnspear on fire, but nothing came without a cost. A cost Riona had chosen to pay.

Why? I couldn't answer the question. I didn't know what reason she had to lay down her life in defiance of the Imperium.

The Imperium who were rushing back to the castle at this very moment, their emotions a violent mix of fury and fear slamming into my chest like a punch.

Shit. They must have noticed my panic and pain. I forced myself to my feet. Riona was dead. I couldn't reverse that. I could only waste it.

I stepped around Estrella and Tristan and over the thrall's crumpled body in the doorway. She hadn't told me what the witches had planned next, but it wasn't hard to guess.

I rushed into the Mortal Bride's bedchamber and snatched my book from the nightstand. I didn't know how long the stun rune would hold the Imperial Guard. I didn't know how long it would take the kings to arrive. With a runegate in their apartment, perhaps not long.

Pain rippled through, but I had to move.

I didn't look at Riona on my way out—or at Estrella, Tristan, or Titus, either. Guilt flared through me, but I stomped it down.

But it was strong enough that the kings felt it.

Their rage crashed over me, from both of them this time.

Fuck. If this didn't work, I couldn't play the fool. The kings knew I was involved. How far would they think my deception went? I'd never convince them I hadn't known I was a witch. Or known Allegra's plan.

I passed through the bedchamber into the sitting room, heading straight for the gilded door. Hundreds of tiny runes were carved into the back, just like the front. ***Ward. Protect. Shield. Barrier.*** When Luc had added my blood to the runespell, he had used his power, but he hadn't activated any special rune or spell. Simply the act of the Imperium adding new blood to the wards had been enough.

Hopefully. If that wasn't how this worked, I'd suffer for it tonight.

I pulled the piece of fabric from my book. The six drops of blood were still glistening, suspended in time, yet drying blood stained the pages. Here went nothing. I reached out and rubbed the bloody cloth against the door. With a flare of shadows, the little symbols devoured the blood.

Nothing else happened. Just like the last time. Had that worked? I hope so.

Now what? I stepped back. Stars, I hated not knowing the plan—

A warm hand dropped onto my shoulders.

I dropped my book with a yip as Estrella spun me around, a terrifying glare on her face. "What did you do?"

Tristan leaned in the bedchamber doorway like he was struggling to stay upright. Both guards looked as haggard as those traitorous vampires had before their execution. But they were up. Standing. The stun rune hadn't even held them for three minutes.

Fuck. "I—"

Another wave of heat pulsed through the room. This time, it didn't knock any of us over.

Estrella spun away, unsheathing her sword in one fluid motion. Shadows coiled and twisted in the center of the room—

***Distance. Path. Cross.***

The Isauran delegation ran out of the swirling darkness. Their collars were gone and runespells glowed on their chests. ***Shield. Protect. Endure.***

And at their fingertips.

***Strike.***

Oh, shit. I jumped out of the way just as the rune's force slammed into Estrella. The vampire woman crashed into the wall, then bounced off with a snarl. Another rune hit her before she landed.

Three witches surrounded her.

The other three lunged for Tristan.

Morrena led the charge against Estrella. ***Strike. Strike. Strike.*** The vampire dropped to her knees under the onslaught of magic. I pressed against the wall, torn between the urge to flee and the awful compulsion to keep watching.

"Hold her," Morrena cried. "I'll bind her—"

Estrella didn't like the sound of that. She pushed back to her feet with all her might. One of the witches yelped, losing hold of their striking rune mid-cast. The shadows faded into darkness.

Estrella crossed the space in a blink and drove her hand through the witch's chest. The shielding rune etched beneath the witch's collarbones flared, but Estrella pierced right through it. The jagged edges of the spell cut into her arm, shredding her flesh as she twisted—

And pulled the witch's heart straight out.

I slammed a hand over my mouth as the dead witch collapsed. Blood rose from the heart in slow spirals, pulled toward Estrella, the vampire siphoning it to heal herself.

But Morrena didn't falter. ***Strike. Burn. Imprison. Imprison. Imprison.***

Estrella staggered back toward the windows, the heart flying from her grip. Her left arm was a wreck—still slick with gore from the kill, torn wide open by the shielding rune. Her skin had already begun to knit, but when Morrena's burning rune slammed into her shoulder, it ate straight through the raw flesh.

Estrella roared, a sound of pain and defiance. Across the room, Tristan echoed it, but he couldn't get to his soulbound. The three other witches hurled binding runes at him, confining the vampire to the floor in shadow.

***Imprison. Imprison. Imprison.***

Morrena and her remaining witch unleashed imprisonment rune after imprisonment rune. Shadows coiled around Estrella's limbs, tightening and tightening. She snarled and strained, muscles trembling against the magic. They pulsed brighter, tightening with every breath, but it still took two more layers before she hit the floor.

Morrena's brow furrowed deeply in concentration as she held the rune. "Eral?"

One of the witches turned, a dark-haired man who looked about my age.

"Help Ilenia hold her."

Eral nodded and released his binding rune on Tristan. The vampire man jolted, but the other two witches held him tight. Eral crossed to Morrena's side. The shadows twirling around his fingers turned into a familiar rune. ***Imprison***.

Morrena dropped her rune the second Eral took her place. She spun, searching, and found me pressed against the wall.

"Where's the kings' runegate?"

I opened my mouth. No sound came out. My heart beat so loud, I was sure it would explode. But I could turn my head. My trembling hand lifted, pointing.

Morrena crossed the room quickly, a muscle in her cheek twitching each time she put weight on her right leg. She nearly lost her balance when she stepped into the hallway before the runegate. Her cane landed with a hard thunk. Her other hand moved fast.

***Annihilate.***

The rune slammed into the runegate, shattering the daemium like glass. It didn't fall to the ground, but the cracks were absolute. The inactive runes carved into its surface faded to nothing.

Morrena went slack against the opposite wall, panting hard. "That should slow them down slightly, but we don't have much time."

I opened my mouth. Closed it. Opened my mouth. Barely five minutes had passed since Riona died. How was that even possible? "Time for what?"

"To cast another transportation spell." Morrena jerked her chin toward the wall beside me. "Open the servant's door."

I frowned, but did as I was told. I skimmed my hands along the wall where Maire had touched last time. My fingers caught on an invisible knob. With a twist, the door slid open—

Revealing nearly a dozen thralls, human and witch, jammed into the tiny space all the way down the stairs into the dark. I staggered back, breath catching. Where had they all come from?

"We'll need their help," Morrena said into the moment of silence. "If you could allow them entry?"

I stepped back. Right. "Come in."

None of the thralls moved, but the one at the front raised something in her hand—a small scrap of fabric dotted with blood. Ah. Yes. I grabbed it from her and returned to the door. I nearly stumbled. My fatigue hit me hard, my vision wavering. I braced a hand against the frame, breathing through the weakness. Just for long enough to steady myself. Then I rubbed the blood into the ward runespells. The second the runes' shadows absorbed it, the first new arrival stepped through.

Morrena pushed from the wall, leaning heavily on her cane. "Quickly now. If we're here when the Imperium arrives, we're all dead."

Her words got the thralls moving faster. Four witches darted to where Morrena and her delegation had first transported in. They removed their inactive collars, dropped to their knees, and quickly began drawing runes onto the floor. ***Distance. Path. Cross.***

The eight humans all stared at me.

I stared back.

Morrena approached. "You'll need to free them from their thrall runespells so they can help."

"Oh, right." I faced all the humans. "You're free from all runespells cast on you by the Azarasian Impire."

The words came too easily, but the magic obeyed. Their shoulders slackened at once, as if an invisible weight had lifted. A few of them gasped, blinking rapidly, like they'd forgotten what it was to exist without the spell. If they'd been born here, maybe they'd never known.

An older man reached back and touched the nape of his neck. "The rune's still there."

"Removing the runespell is a far more difficult process, which we don't have time for now," Morrena said. "Once we get to Isaura, we can attempt it."

The man didn't look pleased, but he gave a curt nod. I hid my frown. The sealing rune within the thrall runespell made it nearly impossible to break. Karra had once watched a human die when a witch tried to remove theirs—and that one had only been powered by a single vampire. The Azarasian spell drew its power from the combined might of the entire Impire.

"To the circle." When Morrena gestured forward, they all obeyed. "You as well, Nessa."

I swallowed. Something wasn't right. "I didn't know you could use the transport runespell without a daemium gate."

Morrena's lip twitched, like she was holding back a frown. I had gotten used to Luc patiently answering all my questions. "It's riskier, and the range is limited, but we should have enough power to reach the forest on the mountain's eastern slope, just inside the border stones," Morrena said. "From there, we'll use Toreth's starcrater to put distance behind us, then make the rest of the journey to Isaura on foot."

"Won't we need sacrifices for that?"

Morrena turned to the humans gathering around the circle and stared.

I swallowed. Oh. She had her sacrifices. Did they know? I suspected not, if that man had asked about having his thrall runespell removed. Had Riona not known she was going to die, either?

Witches were mortal, but they were still demonbloods. In Karra's time, they'd thought us lesser, and that hadn't seemed to change.

Thought *them* lesser. I wasn't human. I hadn't ever been human. But I'd been raised as a human. I couldn't stand by and watch Morrena sacrifice these human thralls to the starcrater. Even if that meant the kings got their hands on me again.

But if the kings caught me, they caught the witches and the thralls too. They wouldn't survive that either.

There wasn't time to argue now. Morrena was right about one thing. If we stayed in this apartment any longer, the kings would stop us. I focused on them. They were right outside the castle.

If our soulbond developed anything like Karra and Azaras's, there'd come a time when I would know all that instantly, instinctively. Even if I ran, there was no way to undo our soulbond.

But I had to go.

I couldn't stay.

I pulled away from the kings, from the tempest of emotion thundering across the bond. I reached back and unlatched my collar. The warmth of a rune brushed my fingers, but the kings hadn't thought to seal it with anything other than their authority. *Our* authority. I dropped it with a clatter to the floor.

As I crossed the room, I plucked *The Soulborne Queen* from the floor. I drifted my hands down its worn cover and frayed edges. I'd chosen it as the one thing I'd take if my name were called in the harvest. So much had changed in the two weeks since then.

But when it came to leave again without planning to ever return, I still wanted my book. I didn't know if I'd ever be able to read it without thinking of Luc and Jules. But even if I never cracked it open again, at least I'd have one thing that was mine.

I joined the others at the circle of transport runes. Every step jarred my insides, but I kept walking. I couldn't collapse now, not when we were so close. Morrena followed behind.

"Everyone within the circle," Morrena said.

We hastened to obey, even the four witches still casting binding runes on Estrella and Tristan. The two Imperial Guard lay pressed to the floor, straining against the shadows that held them. I was glad I couldn't see the betrayal in their eyes. I could barely handle the kings' rage, much less the anger of someone right in front of me.

Estrella and Tristan would get over it. Once we were gone, the Isaurans would stop the runes, and they'd be none the worse—

Morrena raised her hands, as did two of the witches behind her. Shadows flared at her fingers.

***Terminate.***

As one, the witches aimed the rune at Estrella.

*No.* "What are you—?"

The rune flared. The magic hit Estrella like a hammer. She screamed, a high, piercing sound. Tristan echoed it, the pain tearing through their bond. I slammed a hand over my mouth as her body convulsed, twisted, seized. Again and again, the magic wracked her—

She slumped down to the floor.

Still.

Solid.

Dead.

Across the room, Tristan was just as silent.

They were heartmates. He'd died the moment she had.

Oh, stars, what had I done?

The transport runes at my feet flared, their shadows intensifying. Devouring Estrella and Tristan's life energy as *fuel.* I couldn't move. My hand stayed pressed over my mouth, frozen in horror.

The shadows burst upward, curling like smoke. Warm tendrils wrapped around my limbs, my torso, my neck, my head.

The door slammed open.

I couldn't see the kings, but I knew it was them. Close, wrathful, closing the distance between us—

The shadows exploded outward.

THE QUICK BURST OF dark heat ended within a blink. I stumbled forward, the shadows gone from my limbs. My bare feet pressed into night-chilled grass. The light had changed, from the brightness of the apartment to moonlight piercing through a forest's thick canopy. Wind ruffled my hair, carrying the scent of damp earth and spring blossoms. In the distance, owls hooted and unseen creatures rustled through the underbrush.

The kings were no longer close. The length of a mountain now stretched between us.

We had done it. We had transported out of Dawnspear, out of Montaurère entirely.

It had cost Estrella and Tristan their lives.

I spun around, my glare aimed squarely at Morrena. "You didn't tell me—"

The Exalted Daughter's fingers moved fast. I barely saw the shadows in the dark before the rune flared.

***Block.***

A sharp pain exploded inside me. Not my illness. Not even anything physical. It was a quick tear, a cleave through something deeper, more essential—

Everything went numb. My mind. My thoughts. My limbs.

My book slipped from my grasp as I slumped to the ground like a puppet with its strings cut. Grass tickled my legs, arms, and shoulders, but it didn't feel right. Voices snapped above my head, but the sound was muffled. It was like a thick layer of fog had dropped over the world.

The only thing that felt real was the gaping hole inside me.

Where the fuck was it?

Where was my fucking *soul*?

A piece of it remained, a sliver I clung to with everything I had. But all I had left was a third. Could a person survive with a third of a soul? Did I want to? The rest of it was out there somewhere, but when I reached for it, there was nothing. There should have been something.

But there was *nothing.*

It was gone.

*Gone.*

Morrena had done it. She had severed the unseverable. Oh, godstars, I was going to die. I was going to cease existing. Ohgodsstarswhatwashappening—

*Calm the fuck down.* Some part of me shouted the words, distant and ragged. I barely heard them over the emptiness, the place where my soul had once lived. Not entirely in me, not anymore. It had lived in them, too, in my soulbound kings.

Now there was only silence.

*Breathe, idiot.* It wasn't gone. It was blocked.

Soulbonds couldn't be severed.

Morrena had used a blocking rune. Almost like the one that suppressed a witch's magic. Hers was obviously cast with the intention of blocking a soulbond. I wasn't going to die.

Not from that spell, at least.

Hands gripped my arms and pulled me up roughly. My head lolled forward. I tried to focus on my limbs. I could feel them, just there, but I let go of my soul to do it.

The emptiness turned sharp and jagged. I snatched the tattered piece of soul back, abandoning my limbs. It was my anchor in the storm, the only thread between me and the abyss. If I let it go, I'd drown in the darkness, battering me from all sides.

A hand gripped my chin and wrenched my face upward. Morrena. The witch peered into my eyes. The fucking bitch. Why had I trusted her? Was I stupid?

I might have been a witch, but I was the Conqueror and the Butcher's soulbound first. Of course I wouldn't find freedom with the Isaurans. I would become their prisoner. If I were lucky. If they killed me, they could kill the kings. They could shatter the power source behind every thrall runespell, every suppression collar.

Fuck, were they going to kill me?

Morrena's lips moved, but the sounds melted before they reached my brain. I tried to focus while clinging to my soul, but I couldn't—

Morrena slapped me.

The pain was sharp, momentary. But it worked, for just an instant.

"...aren't going to kill you," she said. "But we can't have the kings tracking you through..."

Oh, thank fuck. They weren't going to kill me. My expression must have conveyed that, because Morrena let go of my chin. I sagged back into the arms of whoever held me. My vision was nothing but grass.

A second later, the ground moved.

*We* moved.

Where were we going? Away from the rest of my soul, that much I knew. I couldn't tell where the other pieces were, but they weren't near.

Oh, stars. I had doubted we'd even make it to the starcrater, but if this was happening to me... then the kings must've felt it, too. They were missing a third of their soul, the part I clung to.

I couldn't picture the Conqueror and the Butcher collapsing, limbs loose and unresponsive, but that's what must've happened. Their council and remaining guard would defend them, but no one would know where to even start looking for me.

I hadn't wanted them to find me. I didn't want to be tortured or imprisoned or used for my blood and body.

But if this was the alternative, it was much worse a fate.

Fuck.

Fuck, fuck, fuck.

*Breathe for me, Nessa.* This time, the voice in my head wasn't mine. It was theirs. A deep rumble and a dulcet purr.

I obeyed.

*Breathe in.*

*Breathe out.*

*Breathe in.*

The more I tried to calm my mind, the more I sank into that fragment of soul I still had. And the more the world returned.

My limp foot rammed against a rock, pain shooting through my leg. I embraced it. Let it tether me. Let myself feel it. My arms ached from where the two human thralls held me between them. Something hot burned at my wrist. A sharp stab jolted through my core, the stress and fear fuel for my illness.

I let myself feel that, too.

And I kept breathing, gentle and slow.

"We should kill her," someone hissed in front of us, their voice echoing but audible. "I doubt your rune slowed the Azarasians down that much."

"We can't, Ilenia." Morrena's voice came through next, heavy with exhaustion. This pace must've been brutal on her leg. How far had we traveled already? Were we even close to Toreth's starcrater? The ground beneath me was still grass—no blackened stone, no twisted volcanic brush. Just the ordinary woods surrounding Montaurère.

"Sacrifices must be made if we want to overthrow an impire."

"We can't overthrow an impire," Morrena snapped at her. "If the kings die, someone else will take their place. She's more valuable alive, as a hostage."

Ilenia scoffed. "Without the covenant runespell, the Impire won't have the strength to keep Isaura's witches and millions of humans under control. The new rulers won't carry the Conqueror and the Butcher's power to cast another."

"Perhaps they will," Morrena murmured. "If we kill Azaras's son, we'll have to deal with the Beast King himself."

A pause.

Then Ilenia's voice, scornful. "Azaras might have given the Conqueror his throne, but Lucero Azaras isn't Karra's son, so he's not Azaras's *son*—"

"You know nothing, Ilenia," Morrena said flatly. "Trust me when I say, if we kill the Imperium, it will be Azaras we answer—"

The witch cut off mid-sentence. So did everyone else. The ground beneath me stopped moving.

"Is that...?"

I heard it then—faint at first, but unmistakable. The pounding of hooves thundering through dirt and underbrush. Dread and hope flared in the same breath.

"Fuck." A second after Morrena's curse, we were moving again, faster now. My feet dragged harder through the grass, my whole body jolting with each jarring step. "They caught up."

"But you put a blocking rune on her! The kings can't sense her. She's not wearing a collar—"

Someone tripped behind us. A witch cursed. Branches snapped as the pace faltered, then picked up again.

My heartbeat pounded in time with the hellsteeds. The kings were coming. Or their council and guard, if they were indisposed like me. I had never been so overjoyed and terrified at once.

I would be whole.

I would be a prisoner again.

*Their* prisoner again.

But I was a prisoner either way.

Morrena and her witches kept arguing, kept running, but I couldn't hear their words anymore. My sliver of soul writhed and twisted inside me, like it could tear free and dash in the opposite direction.

We wanted to be whole. *Needed* to be whole.

The man on my left jerked. His hold slackened. I flopped into the other man's side, my weight nearly dragging him down with me. My knees hit the dirt as he threw an arm around my torso to keep me up. In my periphery, the first man bled out in the grass. A gold-hilted throwing dagger jutted from the nape of his neck, driven straight through the center of his thrall runespell.

Shouts erupted around me as the pounding in my chest and the ringing in my ears changed. It came from all around now. A storm closing in. But I couldn't move. Couldn't see.

All I noticed was the man dying in the grass.

A blade pressed to my throat, sharp and cold. A male voice barked over my head, some threat wrapped in panic, but I couldn't make out the words. I was barely holding on, clinging to my soul—

"Release our wife, or we'll ensure your death takes centuries."

My head jerked up, suddenly mine again. That voice. Nothing else was clear, but it reverberated through me.

I fucking *needed* it.

On the backs of two towering hellsteeds, Luc and Jules glared down at the human holding a knife to my throat. Their eyes were black, their expressions merciless. Death incarnate, radiating fury and command.

Around them, more vampires circled on horseback like vultures waiting to feed. Four of them wore the insignia of the Imperial Guard, a faint rune glowing on their wrists.

The guardian runespell. Of course. The kings had tied me to their Imperial Guard. The spell was cloaked beneath a glamour, but that's what was searing the delicate skin of my inner wrist.

"Liar," the human holding me snarled. The dagger bit deeper into my skin as his grip tightened.

Jules growled, a guttural sound that sent a chill through me. I hadn't known he could make that noise. He was going to rip this fucker apart, no matter what Luc said.

Half of the eyes in the moonlit clearing flickered to me.

Jules grinned. Just for a moment. Just for me. Then he turned that expression back to the humans and witches, its edges sharpening. "She's right, my friends. No matter what my king says, I will be murdering you slowly."

I should've been terrified. I should've feared the horrors to come, done in my name. But I didn't care.

There was the rest of my *soul.*

I jerked against the arms holding me. Sensation had returned to my limbs, but they weren't mine to control. They belonged to my soul, to the part of me that screamed for them. I needed to move. Needed to go. I didn't even care that a blade was still pressed to my throat. It cut into my skin—

"Release her." Luc's voice wasn't a bargain this time. It was a command.

And the hands on me obeyed. Instantly.

Something in me snapped. Not strength exactly. *Need.* The fractured soul still inside me surged toward its other pieces, and my body followed before I could think. My legs kicked into motion. My arms shoved. Hands grabbed at me, fingers tearing at fabric, but I wrenched free with a ragged gasp.

The only thing that mattered was my soul.

For once, the kings and I were in agreement. They were off their hellsteeds in a flash of movement, moving forward as one—

I slammed into them. Arms and legs wrapped tight around them both. I pressed my face to them, my body, every part of me, clinging to the heat radiating from the soul we shared.

*Yes.*

This was right. This was better. But I wasn't whole, not yet. I needed to get closer. My hands slid under a dark navy cloak, under a half-buttoned white tunic, hunting for skin. Gods, I needed to be closer. Needed it.

Tears streamed down my face. Still, it wasn't close enough.

Luc gently pulled me from beneath his cloak, his bare hand finding mine. I sighed so hard it was nearly a moan. With one hand over Jules's heart and the other in Luc's grasp, I could almost feel it.

*Our* soul.

I brought Luc's hand to my face and nuzzled his knuckles. Literally nuzzled him.

"Hold her," Luc said, speaking over my head. "I'll take care of this."

Jules's arms locked around my waist. In one fluid motion, he stepped behind Luc and pulled me with him, drawing me around the King of Dusk until we were back to back. Jules pressed into me, pinning me between them.

I sunk into the heat. This. This was right. This was...

Almost perfect.

But not entirely. Because even now, I could feel it. Our soul, radiating out from the kings, just beyond my reach. I clawed at Jules, whimpering. I needed to get closer. I yanked at his tunic, but the runes woven into the fabric refused to tear. Stars, why was he wearing so many clothes all of a sudden? It was never this hard to get him naked.

The King of Dawn chuckled. "Battlefields aren't always nudity-friendly, lovely."

I blinked at him. Wait a minute. Fuck, had I said all that aloud?

And what battlefield?

My world had narrowed to my soulbound, the rest fading away. I spun in his arms, my back still pressed to Luc's. Around his shoulder, I met Morrena's tight gaze as the vampires continued their slow circling.

"Step forward," Luc commanded.

All the humans obeyed, but the witches didn't move. I'd told the humans they were free, but the thrall runespells remained on their necks. Luc only needed to speak to reactivate them. But the witches had removed their collars. Without them, they were the only ones capable of disobeying.

Luc pointed at the older man. The one who had helped carry me, then pressed a blade to my throat. "Only you."

The human took another step forward alone.

And again.

And again until he stood before the King of Dusk. His eyes were wide. His entire body trembled.

Luc held out a hand. "Your blade?"

The man handed it over without hesitation. Luc examined the weapon. It was partially rusted steel. Hardly fit for a king, but fitting for a runaway human thrall.

He returned it to where it belonged, pointy end first.

The blade slid straight into the man's chest. His breath escaped in a soft whoosh, his knees starting to give—

But before he could fall, Luc's other hand moved. Fingers twisted.

***Endure. Silence.***

The man slumped, but he didn't die. He didn't scream. A dagger pierced his heart, but he remained conscious. Aware.

And would through the massacre to come.

Morrena glared. "Fuck you—"

"Kill the humans," Luc said, smoothly cutting her off. "You may feed from the witches, but leave them alive. In either case,"—he smirked, cold and cruel—"there's no need to make it pleasant."

The vampires all dismounted. Sabas. Cédric. Isabeau. Roxiana. The other Imperial Guard. A few other vampires I didn't recognize and a few I did. They moved forward slowly.

Eral and Ilenia broke. They bolted into the trees, sprinting toward an empty patch of forest. Sabas was nearest, but he didn't move forward. He let them pass him—

And turned slowly on his heels, following them into the brush.

They wouldn't get away.

But predators liked the hunt.

Jules brushed my chin, drawing my attention back to him. "Let's get this rune off you, lovely."

***Unravel. Block.***

Everything flooded back. The pain in my knees, my heels, my core. Sudden nausea and the crash of exhaustion.

And rising above it all—burning red lust.

My nipples tightened. My core twisted low in my belly, a terrible yet wonderful burn. I didn't even care that the desire made my illness worse. My soul had found its other pieces.

It *rejoiced.*

Their emotions slammed into me a heartbeat later. I braced for Luc's rage. For Jules's emptiness. But what hit me was heat. *Hunger.* Like even after my betrayal, they wanted me. Maybe even more because of it. It surged through Luc, through Jules, through me.

Overwhelming. All-consuming. Mine.

My hands were on Jules's belt before I realized what I was doing, desperate for more, desperate to be closer—

This time, his hands caught mine. "Uh-uh, lovely witch."

"Please, please, please." The begging slipped out before I could stop it.

"Not yet." Jules traced his finger along my hand. ***Soothe***. The pain in me faded. Bruises, aches, the angry fire in my center. All of it dulled. "But soon."

Jules released me at the same moment Luc stepped aside. With a gasp, I crumpled to the ground, landing beside the dying man.

Luc settled beside Jules, his blackened eyes locked on mine. "You wanted to run, little witch. So I suggest you run."

# 50

I DIDN'T HESITATE. I pushed to my feet and ran in the opposite direction. The clearing behind me had already emptied of everyone but the corpses and the hellsteeds. The vampires had let the witches and thralls go for their game. I plunged into the trees, branches scraping my skin. My heart pounded, a steady rhythm the soulbond echoed back in chorus.

*Find me.*

*Fuck me.*

*Claim me.*

An hour ago, I'd planned to leave the kings for my freedom. But now, all I wanted was them. I wanted them to chase me. I wanted them to throw me to the ground, rip off my gown, and ravage me until I felt whole again.

This wasn't me. This was the bond. But that didn't matter.

The path to my left led deeper into darkness, so I turned right. A vampire could see in the dark, but a witch or human was as good as blind. We were within the city's border stones. Hellbeasts and wraiths weren't a problem, but I still wanted to see what monsters stalked me. My feet pounded into grass as I crested a small incline—

And I nearly tumbled down it as I stumbled back. Ilenia whimpered in Roxiana's arms, the Crown Chancellor's fangs in her neck. Isabeau crouched between her thighs, sucking on her gushing femoral artery. The witch was pale and limp, a drugged grin on her face as they drained her nearly to death.

It hit me like ice water. A jolt straight through my soulbond-induced lust.

The night wouldn't end in death for me or the witches, but it would for all the humans. Luc had ordered them killed. The vampire I ran from, the vampire I wanted *inside* me. I strained past the thunder of my heartbeat, and the forest answered with screams, moans, and grunts.

I tore my gaze away from the councilors and stumbled back into the trees. I needed to get out of here.

But I couldn't outrun this.

A few paces more and I spotted Sabas with a witch pinned against a tree. Eral. He moaned, his hands clawing at the bark as Sabas fucked him, fangs buried in his throat. Another few steps and two Imperial Guard had a human woman between them, her body slack and paling as they fed and fucked.

Everywhere I turned, witches and humans were writhing and moaning and dying as the vampires feasted.

Oh, stars. This wasn't a fun little run anymore, no matter how hard the soulbond tried to make it feel like one. I needed the kings, but they weren't here. Only carnage committed with their blessings.

I couldn't escape. I *couldn't* ever escape. I had tried and failed. The humans and witches all chose to flee the Capital of Dawn for themselves, but if they hadn't brought me along, would they have escaped? Had I doomed them all?

I had begged for escape, and they paid the price.

I leaned against a tree, trying to catch my breath. There was nowhere to go. Nowhere to run. Even though I was a witch, I couldn't outrun a vampire. I didn't know a thing about magic. Not that it mattered, since I didn't have any power to use.

The only choice I had was where the kings caught me.

And there were no good choices.

I pushed off the tree and stepped forward—

And everything changed.

A towering hedge rose an inch from my face. I jerked back. What the fuck? I glanced up, up, up to the distant sky, stars twinkling overhead. It was still night. My feet still sunk into grass. Screams and moans still echoed around me. But the air was warmer now, thicker, like it was now summer instead of spring. I backed away—

And bumped into another hedge. It prickled against my bare skin. I glanced downward.

Where the fuck were my clothes?

My collar had returned, but my gown was gone, replaced by a few dangling chains of silver and gold. Rubies and sapphires the size of a grape brushed my skin. I had thought my outfit to the Red Queen revelry was little more than a necklace, but this was *actually* little more than a necklace.

Why was I naked in what looked like a hedge maze?

My heart was already pounding with terror and excitement, but now confusion surged to join them.

What the fuck?

“Surrendering already, little witch?”

I yelped as the words ghosted across my ear. I tried to spin, but Luc looped a finger through the handle at the back of my collar. My airway constricted. I froze, the heat of him pressing into my back. The soulbond flared so strongly I nearly mewled.

“What’s—” My question choked off as Luc tugged the collar tighter.

“No speaking.”

I tried to disobey. What the fuck was happening? Why weren’t we in a forest anymore? Where had my clothes gone? But I couldn’t even gasp out the words. My mouth refused my commands.

A dark glow caught my eye.

Two cuffs circled my wrists, one silver and the other gold. A rune glowed on one of them. ***Obey***. Like the rune on the witch’s collars. What the—

A scream rang out ahead of me. No, a battle cry. My head snapped up.

The pressure around my neck vanished. Luc’s heat disappeared. The collar, the cuffs, the hedge maze—gone. I stood in the center of a small clearing, back in the forest.

And one of the human thralls was charging out of the trees, wild-eyed, a rusted blade raised in her hand.

I stumbled backward—

Silver rings glinted in the moonlight.

A large hand closed around hers, catching the blade mid-swing. Her eyes widened as Luc appeared from out of nowhere. Again. With a gentle squeeze of his hand, bone cracked. Her scream shifted from fury to agony. The blade slipped from her grip... and was caught by another familiar hand wearing gilded ruby rings.

“Bad thrall,” Jules purred, as if planning a seduction, not a murder. Blood splattered across his pale skin, his gold-embroidered tunic more red than white now. The runes in the fabric struggled to deal with the mess.

Blood dribbled down Luc's chin, too. I'd only been running for a couple minutes. Hadn't I? I couldn't really tell, not after that hedge maze. Had it been a hallucination? Psychosis? Whatever it was, Luc and Jules had used the time to eat a thrall or two.

Jules tossed his blade carelessly over his shoulder. It embedded in the dirt next to me. I flinched, but didn't move. It took everything I had not to run forward. Not to tear that ruined shirt from his shoulders and claw my way closer.

*Fuck me. Claim me. Fill me.*

The soulbond pulsed louder, its message changed. It had gotten its chase. Now it wanted surrender. My terror dulled beneath its song.

Luc reached for the thrall, like he planned to snap her throat and be done with it.

Jules swatted him away. "Not yet, darling. I want to play."

Luc arched a brow. "I want to fuck our wife."

My heart leaped. The soulbond jumped with it.

"Well, yes, I want to fuck our wife, too, but I can play first." Jules glanced over at me, lips curling into a sly smile. "How about you start without me? I'll join you when I'm done."

Heat rushed to my cheeks. Luc turned toward me, the silver in his eyes swallowed by his shadowed pupil. "Very well."

He started forward.

The Conqueror. Lucero Azaras. Luc. For once, all three sides of the King of Dusk stood before me. His walk was the seductive lure of a predator. There was no fear in his stride, no hesitation. Only the certainty that anything he desired in this world was already his.

I suddenly understood why people cowered when Luc walked toward them. He wasn't a man. He was an unrelenting force of nature, a storm on the horizon. One that would crash against the shores of your life, claiming everything in its path. No amount of begging or bargaining would change its course.

The Conqueror took what he wanted.

And what he wanted right now was me.

My skin prickled. Stars, my cunt was dripping. There was something very, very wrong with me.

But then I met his eyes again. His anger hit me like a gust. This wasn't a joyful reunion after the *blocking rune's removal. She had tried to run. Tried to escape with witches after insisting she knew nothing about being one. It had been centuries since someone had tricked me, tricked Jules. If she wasn't ours, she'd be killed for the offense.*

*But she was ours. And all the bond wanted was for me to fuck the betrayal out of her.*

*And I wouldn't object—*

I yanked out of Luc's head. He might not object, but I did. The King of Dusk might have called me his wife, but tonight I would be his whore. His captive. His plaything.

I bent down, grabbed the hilt of the thrall's blade, and raised it.

Not toward Luc. There was no point aiming it at him. I wouldn't win a fight. I wouldn't even land a blow.

I raised it to my throat.

Luc halted instantly, the stillness of a hunter sighting prey. Behind him, Jules kept his hand on the whimpering thrall, but his dark gaze fixed on me. "What exactly do you plan to do with that, little witch?"

I swallowed. "Don't come any closer."

Luc grinned, slow and dark. "Coming closer is exactly what your body wants me to do."

I swallowed again. He wasn't wrong. My nipples ached so hard they hurt. My clit throbbed. I needed them. Needed to be whole—

*Shut up.*

Holding my gaze, Luc started forward again, leisurely, confidently.

Challenge accepted.

Which meant I needed to follow through.

My throat brushed against the blade's tip. I didn't want to die. Not now. Not last week. Not this entire year. Not really. I wanted control of my fate, not out of my life. But I would never control my fate, not after tonight.

My gilded cage would become a prison.

Still, I didn't want to die.

My hand trembled as I pressed the blade's cold edge to my skin—

Before it even nicked me, Luc was there. His hand closed around the sharp metal. He pulled. The dagger ripped from my grasp as pain flared, echoed across the bond as the blade cut into Luc's flesh. He didn't flinch as he flung my meager weapon. It spun end over end, embedding in a nearby tree.

Then his bloodied hand wrapped around my throat.

I grabbed his wrist, but he yanked me back, slamming my spine into his chest. The breath rushed out of me in a single gasp. His grip wasn't bruising, but I was trapped, held too firmly to fight. Not that my body wanted to fight.

My hips shifted before I could stop them, thighs pressing together as desire coiled in my core.

*Traitor.*

Behind us, a scream split the air. The crack of bone. A wet tearing sound. Jules's melodic laugh. Oh, stars. He was going to *torture* the thrall to death while Luc fucked me.

"If you ever threaten your own life again," Luc whispered in my ear, "you'll get a cuff on each wrist that stops you from holding anything that could be used as a weapon. You'd be surprised how many things it won't let you touch."

A cuff on each wrist. Like in the hedge maze hallucination. My confusion cut clean through the fog of lust. "What—"

Luc tightened his grip around my neck, cutting off my words. Just like he had minutes ago in the maze with the collar I no longer wore.

For a second, he just held me. I writhed in his arms, not ready to surrender even though I was already caught. Like a fox thrashing in the snare, fighting against the inevitable. My back brushed the strong planes of his chest, smooth velvet over corded muscle. I shuddered, heat unfurling low in my belly.

Another scream behind us. Something soft and wet hit the forest floor. My desire tried to shrivel—

Luc growled. The sound rumbled through his chest and into mine. My nipples tightened to hard peaks. He nipped the top of my ear and rolled his hips against mine. The thick, hard press of him against my ass made me whimper. The blood on his chin smeared my forehead.

I stopped moving. Stopped struggling. I drew in a shaky breath, eyes fluttering closed. My pulse beat between my legs, a drum of need through my whole body. I hated how good it felt to be caught. Hated that my body arched for him, even after everything.

But the soulbond didn't care what I'd done. What they'd done. What they were still doing—Luc's heat at my back, Jules humming over a low gurgle.

It only cared that I was theirs.

I melted into Luc's hold in a heady, intoxicating surrender. I wasn't giving in. Not really. Just... accepting. There was a difference.

There had to be.

His breath brushed my ear. He held me there for another eternal moment, but I stayed still and waited.

"Good girl."

I shuddered. A soft moan escaped me at the rumble of those words. Luc's hand slid to my chin. With a firm squeeze, he twisted my head—and claimed my mouth.

My lips parted, helpless to resist the way he kissed me. His tongue conquered and plundered. Droplets of warm blood stained even hotter skin. I gasped, but he swallowed the sound.

His other hand traced around my waist, then up to my chest. He found my nipple beneath the thin fabric of my gown and circled it. Once. Slowly.

Then he fisted the fabric of my dress and tore it from my body.

I gasped. Cold air brushed my bare skin while his body burned behind me, heat radiating from his chest to my spine. The shock of it cracked through the haze of want, sharp and real. A flash of panic. A reminder that this wasn't safe.

But Luc didn't stop.

His free hand drifted lower, knuckles brushing down my stomach. He threaded his fingers through my damp curls. His palm settled over my mound. He cupped me. For a second, he just held me. Gently. Possessively.

Then two fingers slid into my wet heat and landed on my clit.

"Luc—" His name tore from my lips.

The thrall echoed my cry, a shriek of agony.

He nipped my lips. "Silence, witch."

Pleasure burst like lightning as his fingers started to swirl. I bucked in his grasp. "You don't... you can't..."

"I can," he murmured. "You are mine. If I want you to come on my fingers, that's what you'll do."

"Luc," I moaned. Stars, I shouldn't have felt this way. I had tried to run. I was his *captive* bride. Jules was torturing someone a couple feet away.

"With every day that passes, I feel more and more from you through the bond." His voice darkened. "I know how desperate you are for me, little witch. It fills you with such..."

I arched back against him. "Fear."

"Shame," he corrected, licking the line of my throat. "You really do want to be my toy and you hate that."

"Go fuck yourself, Luc."

He pulled his fingers out of me. I tried not to whimper and squirm. Luc's grip tightened at my throat. My vision flickered. His knuckles brushed my ass as he—

As he unlaced his trousers and stroked himself, my slick coating his fingers.

He jerked my head back until I met luminous eyes, his gaze a sliver of molten silver swallowed by black. "I will. With you."

My vision blurred. The world tilted. Within a blink, I was on my back, my legs in the air. Luc had dropped to his knees in front of me, pulled my ass up from the ground, and hooked my ankles over his shoulders. His pants slunk low on his thighs. His perfect, erect cock nocked at my entrance.

I pushed onto my elbows, my pulse fluttering in a sudden panic. I was too exposed, too out of control. Entirely at the Conqueror's mercy.

And the Conqueror didn't have any mercy.

In one hard thrust, Luc sunk into me to the hilt.

# 51

My back arched, a scream splitting my lips. The sound joined the chorus of pleasure and death around me, a harmony of ecstasy and violence. I gripped the grass beneath me, scrambling until I found a root. I curled my fingers around it, desperate for an anchor.

But Luc didn't move. He just held there, stretching me wide, keeping me filled and trembling. I writhed on his cock, trying to force friction. His piercings pressed into my inner walls, but I couldn't get him to nudge.

"Who do you belong to, wife?"

The word sent a thrill down my spine, brutal and undeniable. My nerve endings tingled, sensation dancing across my skin. "You?"

His hands dug into the groves at my hips, holding me effortlessly. "Was that a question?"

I shook my head quickly, nearly whimpering with need.

"Say it."

"I belong to you."

"And?"

A wet gurgling sound reached my ears, followed by the King of Dawn's soft chuckle. My stomach turned. Shame and arousal tangled in my gut. I hated the answer, especially now, but it was the truth. "Jules."

"Good girl." His hands squeezed as his thumbs kneaded over my hipbones. "And whose name will you shout as I fill you with my seed?"

"Yours."

He grinned. Not cruel, not kind. Certain. He brushed his mouth across my calf. His tongue flicked out, wetting my skin. I froze, mesmerized by the motion. He sucked my flesh into his mouth—

Shadows swirled from his incisors, forming sharp fangs.

He withdrew his cock, then bit down just as he thrust forward.

I dug my fingers deeper into the dirt as ecstasy tore through me. It struck down my legs like lightning, tightening my cunt, squeezing my clit, twisting at my nipples. The world blurred into white. I shuddered in Luc's grip.

He slammed me forward to meet his next thrust. And his next. And his next. With every move, he sunk deeper and deeper, claiming more of me, body and soul.

Working me open.

Undoing me.

Stars, it was terrible.

Stars, it was perfect.

His throat bobbed as he swallowed another mouthful of my blood. The suction alone made my cunt clench, pleasure spiking to a peak. I shuddered in Luc's grip. His name burst from my throat, raw and ragged. "Luc—ah!"

Tension corded the king's neck. His thrusts turned deeper, harder. He sucked down one last pull of blood before his tongue flicked out, sealing the wound with a soft swipe.

But his hips didn't stop.

He *branded* me with his cock.

My hands trailed up my belly, trembling, as if I could feel him through my flesh. I stared between my thighs. Where Luc buried his thick cock within my tight cunt, the length of him disappearing into my dark curls only to come out glistening wet.

In.

Out.

In.

Out.

My breath caught. I was enraptured, fascinated.

*His.*

Luc's gaze darkened as he watched me watch him fuck me.

A shadow settled over me. I didn't care. The forest could burn down around me. All the councilors, guards, and courtiers could watch, as long as Luc keep fucking me raw.

"Lovely."

I tore my gaze from between my thighs, from the mesmerizing rhythm of Luc's body claiming mine. Jules crouched at my head, his white-gold hair a wild, tangled crown. Blood painted his skin, his tunic undone nearly to his navel.

His gaze dragged over my body, slow as a caress. Those black-gold eyes devoured every jiggle of my breasts with Luc's thrusts, every pant from my lips, every twist of my hands in the dirt.

Luc slid his hands up my calves. His fingers hooked under my knees. With a jerk, he spread me wider. His next flick of hips thrust his cock deeper. A desperate wail escaped my lips. With every quick pulse, my cry grew wilder.

Luc fucked like he fought.

Mercilessly.

My hands tore the root beneath me from the ground. My head scraped against the dirt with his next brutal thrust. My arms scrambled outward, reaching for something, anything, before I floated away on a wave of bliss.

I met the warmth of a bare ankle.

Jules's ankle.

My gaze locked with the King of Dawn's at the touch. My fists tightened around his ankle as I dug my heels into Luc's back.

With his next thrust, I *pushed* into the movement.

Our bodies slammed together. Jules's pupils swallowed the remaining gold. I moaned. Luc released a deep grunt, his fingers denting my thighs.

The King of Dusk's rhythm turned punishing. He increased his speed, his strength, but my legs locked and I matched his pace instinctively.

The *soulbond* matched his pace instinctively.

It guided my hips.

It screamed in delight.

It didn't care if Luc fucked me until I broke.

Each cry from my lips became a breathless whine. We went from Luc fucking me to us rutting on the ground, a desperate, hard dance. I'd be sore for days, but I didn't care.

It felt *amazing*.

Jules licked his bloodied lips like a man starved.

The sight was the final straw. I pushed over the edge, falling into a waterfall of desire that crashed through me, unstoppable. My legs twitched in Luc's grasp as I flailed and shuddered, the tension exploding out of me in waves. My cunt clenched greedily on the King of Dusk's cock, sucking him deeper, desperate for more. My hands tightened on Jules's ankle, nails digging into his skin. I held on as stars burst behind my eyes, blinding and endless.

I never wanted to come down.

I didn't think I could.

With a roar, Luc followed me into the wave of bliss. His hot seed shot deep inside of me. The force of his pleasure slammed into the bond, flooding me with heat. It poured through every frayed nerve ending, addicting and overwhelming.

He didn't release my legs, but my entire torso slackened into the dirt. My lungs dragged in the air like I'd been running for miles. My solid bones now resembled little more than puddles. The night sky flickered and spun above, silver stars wheeling as the world kept moving, even though I couldn't.

Then Jules dropped to his knees. "I want to fuck her ass."

My eyes widened. He couldn't—Luc hadn't even pulled out yet. He hadn't softened, either, still thick and hard inside me. I didn't know how my eyes could widen further, but they did.

Jules's lips twisted into a cruel smile, promising mind-numbing pleasure. "If we want to fuck you all night, witch, we will."

The soulbond didn't flinch at the words. It purred. Welcoming. Greedy. As if this was what it had been building toward all along.

Luc wrapped one hand around my throat and settled the other at my hips. He pulled me up. I gagged, unable to breathe for a second. My chest slammed into his. My nipples brushed the soft fabric of his doublet, already painfully sensitive.

His dark eyes became my whole world, his lips an inch away.

My heart thundered. My body trembled. My cheeks flushed. Out of everything, that was what embarrassed me? Not that I was being shared between two vampire kings in the middle of a bloody death orgy in the woods.

Not that the dead thrall lay a few feet behind Luc, her body covered in slashes, her neck torn out, her face frozen in terror. I hadn't even noticed when she'd stopped screaming.

Not that a dozen witches and thralls were being fed upon in the trees around me. Their moans. Their cries. I couldn't tell which were pain and which were pleasure.

No, none of that. Only the King of Dusk's dark eyes.

Jules's bloody chest pressed against my back.

The head of his cock brushed my asscheeks—and settled at the tight ring of my asshole.

Cold sweat broke over my skin. I couldn't breathe. I couldn't think. Every instinct screamed. *Stop, continue, fuck me, claim me, fill me.*

My eyes widened. "Jules—"

"No." His hand drew a small pattern across my lower back. A rune of some kind. "What did you think would happen when you trapped yourself in a soulbond with the Imperium? That you wouldn't ride both of our cocks?"

"I didn't—"

Jules shifted his hips. The head of his cock pressed into me, stretching me slowly. An ache flared up my spine before the soothing rune dulled it.

Oh, *stars.*

The kings had been preparing me for this, but the plug Luc had used on me in the library was minuscule compared to Jules's cock. And Luc was still inside my cunt, stretching me open.

I was already full. I couldn't take more. I shouldn't have wanted more.

But stars help me, I did.

"We showed you mercy I didn't think either of us were capable of," Jules murmured in my ear as he pressed deeper and deeper into my ass. "You were so soft, so delicate. The perfect prey."

*I didn't know!* But I couldn't speak the words. I could barely breathe. I tried to squirm away from the pressure, a whimper catching in my throat.

Luc's hands clamped down on my ass, holding me still. "That ends now. You're a witch. Demon blood runs in your veins. Your body can withstand us taking you whenever and however we want." His gaze flicked over my shoulder. "I want to hear her scream."

Jules gripped my hips and thrust into me, seating half his cock in one smooth strike.

I squealed, literally squealed, my entire body tensing. Pain shot through my core before the soothing rune washed it away. The pleasure followed like a wave, cruel and hot, licking at the edges of my shame. My hands tightened around Luc's forearms.

This wasn't going to work. They wouldn't—*couldn't*—both fit.

I continued to squirm upwards, trying to ease the pressure, but I couldn't escape their grasps. "I can't... it won't fit—ah... I can't."

"You can."

"And you will right now," Jules said, giving his hips a quick thrust.

I shrieked as he sunk deeper. My vision flashed. My eyes watered.

In three hard pulses, he seated himself fully.

My vision waved as my nerves tingled. I went slack in the kings' arms. They speared into me—Luc in my cunt, Jules in my ass—forcing me to stretch around the impossible. My body tensed, trying to fight it. Trying to accept it. Trying to survive it.

Luc brushed my chin. "Stay with us, witch. We're going to fuck you now."

"You—ah!" Jules's hand wrapped around me, sliding between my stomach and Luc's chest. He lifted me slightly, freeing me from their cocks—

Luc's fingers dug into my hips as he rocked me back down.

The kings invaded me together. A whining gasp escaped me. My body convulsed. My vision shattered like glass. I thrashed as fire tore through me. The ecstasy was exquisite, unbearable, laced with pain their magic kept washing away. Before I could adapt, they withdrew—

—and slammed back in, deeper.

A scream ripped from my throat.

"That's it, lovely," Jules grunted. "You can take us. Cry for us. I want—uh—to hear every sob wrung from your lips as we claim your ass and cunt."

I dropped my head with a shuddering cry. It was too much. Too much sensation. Too much pleasure.

Too much *them.*

My arms and legs went limp. The kings fucked me up and down their lengths, a rhythm so punishing and precise it stripped me of thought.

My world narrowed to their cocks.

Jules's hands bruising my hips.

Luc's fingers digging into my ass. His dark eyes holding me prisoner, just as he and his soulbound did my body.

Blood slicked my back from where Jules's tunic brushed me, streaks smearing across my skin with every thrust. My hair clung to my temples with sweat, tangled from the dirt and the gore.

They had finally claimed me. *All* of me.

Every stroke wrung a cry of ecstasy from my lips. My fingers dug into muscled forearms as I screamed. Oh, fuck. Stars forgive me, I had never felt anything this perfect and terrible at once.

I whimpered, trying to arch again, but their hands held me immobile. But I could move my legs. I wrapped my thighs around Luc's hips and pulled him to me, calves pressing to the curve of his ass. The shift made the three of us moan as the kings' angles changed.

But they didn't miss a thrust. Our bodies moved in sync, led by instinct, by the soulbond, by a dance I didn't know but felt in my bones.

My breaths tore out in ragged gasps. With their next thrust, the sound broke into a pitched moan. I slumped back, head resting on Jules's shoulder. His chest slid against my back, slicked with blood and sweat.

He huffed, the profile of his face near impassive but for the fire burning in his eyes. "Are you enjoying this, witch? Being fucked by the Imperium?"

"This was what you wanted, wasn't it?" Luc reached up, Jules's hand taking his place at my hips. He twisted roughly at my nipples. "There's a price to accessing our power. You're ours forever. This is your eternity, Nessa."

My breath caught. The word hit deeper than it should have. Eternity. As if they weren't just claiming my body, but my future, too. My fate.

No escape. Not today. Not ever.

I should've been terrified. My body shuddered, betraying me.

Luc chuckled. "You like the sound of that, don't you? You're such a good little slut for us."

Something twisted in my chest at his words. *Slut.* I hated that he called me that, hated that it thrilled me. That it made the bond purr and the heat in my core spike. It wasn't love, but it was possession, and some traitorous part of me bloomed under it.

I wanted to spit in his face.

I wanted to deny it.

I wanted to snarl that I wasn't their anything.

But my body arched between them, already begging to come. The bond surged in response, greedy and overwhelming. It didn't care about shame. It only cared about being claimed.

I buckled as my orgasm tore through me like a storm finally cresting, violent and blinding. My muscles locked around them, trembling. My fingers dug into Luc's back, anchoring me as my spine bowed and the starry sky split open behind my eyes. I screamed, a raw, wordless cry that wasn't just pleasure, but something deeper.

I wasn't just climaxing. I was breaking. Coming apart.

The bond howled its delight.

It pulsed with triumph, flooding every nerve with ecstasy. This was what it had wanted all along. Both kings inside me, claiming me completely. Not just flesh, but soul.

I felt it in them, too. Their pleasure. Their possession. Their satisfaction. It was too much. Too overwhelming. Too perfect. I hated it. I loved it. I didn't know who I was under the weight of it.

I wanted to sob.

I wanted to beg for more.

My cunt clenched around Luc, my ass around Jules, as the bond burned through all my resistance and left only one truth.

I was *theirs.*

Their bodies tensed around me, their thrusting turning wild. With a groan from Luc and a moan from Jules, the kings came together, filling me with heat.

Jules threaded a hand through Luc's hair, leaned over me, and claimed his soulbound's lips in a kiss. Their bodies crushed me, smooth skin and gleaming muscle wrapped in velvet, pressing into my soft flesh.

My pleasure thrummed not only through my body, but through the bodies surrounding me. I came so hard I think my soul left my body.

My soul was *outside* my body, divided in three.

It hurt to be ripped into pieces.

It was euphoric to finally be whole again.

The kings released me as one, freeing me from their softening lengths. I slumped, sliding down their bodies. Neither king stopped me from collapsing to the grass at their knees.

I dug my nails into my palm and breathed, praying not to float away. Jules's hot seed dribbled down my leg, mixing with the damp of mine and Luc's pleasure. Blood stained my chin, my neck, my back. I was soaked in cum and sweat, filthy and oh-so-satisfied.

Everything blurred around me. I floated blissfully, the aftershocks of my orgasms a bobbing tide. Around me, the forest echoed with the sounds of dying. Screams. Moans. Gurgles. Pleasure and death, so tightly tangled I couldn't tell where one ended and the other began. The kings didn't care.

And neither did I.

Soft hands slid across my hips, up the curve of my stomach. Jules flipped me onto my back. My shoulders rested against Luc's hard torso.

My legs were spread. The cold air on my cunt sent a shock through my system. I jerked in Luc's arms. He held me down. He probably didn't even notice, my movements were so weak.

Jules licked along my inner thigh, his tongue slow and reverent. He stopped just shy of my wet heat, circling the throb of my femoral pulse.

"Jules, I—eh..." My brain couldn't even form words. Every thought had melted.

His dark eyes flicked to mine. Luc's grip tightened. Moonlight caught the glimmer of shadow-tipped fangs—

And Jules bit straight into my thigh.

My world exploded into an instant orgasm. I screamed. I thrashed. I prayed to every godstar that'd listen for mercy, for deliverance. My body couldn't take this.

With a deep pull, Jules lapped at my skin, devouring every drop of blood. My clit and cunt tingled at the sensation.

The world went darker. For a second, I thought I'd passed out. But it was just Luc leaning over me, taking one of my nipples into his mouth. He scraped his teeth against the oversensitive flesh as he cupped one soft, heavy mound. I shuddered and twisted—

Luc's fangs sank into my breast.

The waves crested again. I drowned in the depths of exquisite pleasure. My back bowed, my body seized, my throat ripped open with a cry I didn't recognize as my own.

But even as my body shattered, a scream built in the back of my mind, raw and furious. *This isn't me. This can't be me.* Not the girl who curled up with books. Not the one who hid in the shadows of her shop. Not the human sacrifice who once swore she'd never want this.

The bond devoured the scream whole. It turned horror into heat. Turned fear into fire. Turned me into something unrecognizable. I was unraveling, all dissolving into the dark.

And it felt so fucking good.

The world went dim, my limbs numb. All that existed was fangs and blood and shuddering pleasure swirling through my soul, whole once again.

# INTERLUDE 5

*The hooves of a dozen hellsteeds cracked like thunder across the stone roadways leading to Montaurère's peak. Bright, curious eyes watched from windows, stoops, terraces, and patios, all bustling with activity even this late into the night. They had watched us race from the city mere hours ago. What rumors and gossip would swirl through our courts tomorrow, first at our quick departure and then at our bloody return, unconscious witches thrown over our saddles?*

*Jules had a hand fisted in the torn fabric of Exalted Morrena's gown, the witch slung over Cala's back like a sack of grain. He didn't glance at her as she bounced against the hellsteed's flank with every jolt of movement. A spike of delight flared through our bond with each smack. If he hadn't been pulsing his weakened magic into the sleeping rune writhing on her skin, she would surely be awake and screaming. Like all our cargo would be.*

*Except for mine.*

*My arms tensed around our unconscious bride cradled in my arms, her naked, blood-splattered body wrapped in a cloak. After our rough claiming and feeding, she had melted into me with a sigh and fallen asleep instantly. As if I were the safest place in the world.*

*Even now, jostled by the hellsteed's steady canter, she didn't stir. Only once had she neared the surface, when Jules moved away to mount his own steed. She had reached out, seeking the touch of the man who carried the other third of our soul. It was almost enough to get Jules to stop, but he had shaken off the bond's influence.*

*I stared down at Nessa, tracing the shape of her plump lips, the curve of her soft cheeks, the shadow of her lashes against the pale peach of her skin. I had found her comely and pleasing to look at that first day we met only two short weeks ago.*

*Now I was enchanted, intoxicated, bewitched.*

*Which was only fitting, given she was, in fact, a witch.*

*A witch in league with Allegra Isaura herself.*

*That deep anger rolling in my chest surged to the surface. It hadn't faded since we learned the awful truth earlier today, but the blocking rune on our bond had made it inconsequential in comparison. Now that the rune was gone and our wife reclaimed, there was nothing standing in the rage's way.*

*Allegra fucking Isaura.*

*Stars, I'd kill that witch when I found her. I had vowed as much long ago, after she arranged the massacre at Duskfell. Bodies strewn across the hallways, vampires and thralls torn apart and their flesh devoured, Corinne among them—*

*I gave my head a sharp shake. Now was not the time to remember that night.*

*Jules had nearly caught Allegra once, months after our army seized Isaura's capital. They had both limped away from the fight clinging to their lives. In the years since, we hadn't encountered her once, but she still lived, even now. Morrena's failed surrender five days ago had proved that much. If Allegra was dead, Morrena's allegiance runespell would've faded, allowing us to finally cast a thrall runespell on the Isaurans.*

*But Allegra hadn't spent her centuries merely hiding—she'd spent them planning.*

*And now, three hundred years later, she had finally put her plan into action.*

*Whatever it entailed.*

*"If you frown any harder, you might make the expression permanent," Jules said, glancing my way as we finally turned into Imperium Square before Dawnspear's rose-covered wall.*

*My soulbound's words had the intended effect. My scowl sharpened into a glare. It was a look that made most vampires drop to their knees to beg for mercy, but Jules only rolled his eyes.*

*"You've never doubted yourself before, Luc. Don't start now. Whatever Allegra has planned, we will survive and prevail, as we always have."*

*"Will we? She's already succeeded in the first part of her plan," I grumbled with a pointed look at our bride.*

*Jules shrugged. "Sure, but we've survived and prevailed, have we not?"*

*I shot him a dry look. "Our bride nearly escaped us a mere hour ago, Julien."*

*"But she didn't," he said. "And she won't, even if she tries again."*

*"Allegra or our bride?"*

*"Both." His gaze drifted to Nessa. "Stars, we might even benefit from that bitch of a witch's plan."*

*I watched his eyes trace the lines of her throat, her shoulders, her chest. Almost... tenderly. His quiet yearning rippled through the bond. It was an emotion I rarely glimpsed on my soulbound's starstouched face. Jules was wild abandon and wicked glee, no part of him gentle. His lovers either feared him or bored him—or both. And with good reason, since he toyed with them like a cat with a mouse, the hunter in him too vicious to suppress even around other vampires.*

*But that didn't mean he didn't want.*

*Didn't crave.*

*Didn't covet.*

*He'd never been anything but happy for me when I had Corinne, but his envy had burned beneath his smile. It was always brief, always followed by that familiar shadow of grim acceptance, as if what he wanted most would always be out of reach. The few times those fears crept too close, he simply shut it all off.*

*My Butcher didn't believe himself capable of love.*

*But now we were heartmates, tied together by the little witch in my arms. And there was only one path for heartmates. I had accepted it days ago, but Jules had done more than accept. He had celebrated.*

*He finally had what he wanted, and it was inevitable.*

*"You always wanted a heartmate," I murmured.*

*"I did." His golden gaze flashed to me. "I always wanted you, too."*

*I arched a brow. "You had me."*

*"Did I?"*

*The words were quiet. Uncharacteristically soft. The Sun Gate loomed ahead, its massive doors already swinging open. Silence stretched between us as we passed through.*

*How could he question us? Of course he'd had me. We had been like brothers from birth, lovers for nearly as long, like all soulbound Azarasians. But if he had to ask—if that doubt had lingered for centuries—then he hadn't known it.*

*And that was my fault.*

*I had always been careful with emotion. Always controlled. Always distant. Emotion was weakness, something my enemies could use against me. Something Marisol had used against me, over and over again, when we were young. Sometimes, I wished my inherited godcurse were as useful as Jules's. I'd numb it all, quieting the storm beneath my skin and matching the ice I wore on the surface.*

*But I had no such escape.*

*I inhaled slowly, then exhaled. "You have me now."*

*"And we have her." Jules let a small smile play over his lips, his joy warming my chest. "Do you intend to let Allegra Isaura take us from you?"*

*My rage flared again, sharp and unyielding. My grip on Nessa tightened. "No," I nearly growled the word. "Never."*

*Jules chuckled. "There's the Lucero Azaras I know and love. I wouldn't expect anything less from you, darling."*

# 52

THE BRIGHT GOLD OF daylight lured me back to the world. I buried my head deeper into silk sheets, breathing in smoked honey and rich spice. The scents made my muscles go lax, drifting back to content sleep—

Then my heart kicked.

A sharp, sudden reminder.

I shot upright, breath caught in my throat as the room came into focus.

The kings' bedchamber. Empty. Still.

Memories surged in, sluggish at first, then crashing like a wave. I had tried to escape. Tried to run with the witches... only for them to turn on me, take me hostage.

Luc and Jules had crushed their plans without breaking a sweat.

Unless you included the sweat that had lined their brows when they *fucked* me together.

I slumped back and pressed a hand to my lower belly, like I could still feel them inside me. It didn't ache like it had after my first time. Only a low, pleasant throb pulsed through my core. They must have reapplied a soothing rune. Even without my illness, I'd surely hurt after taking both their cocks at once.

I shuffled my legs, but the sensations didn't change. My inner thighs rubbed together. I stiffened. They'd cleaned me of blood, but our dried pleasure still stained my skin.

I swallowed. The kings weren't in the bedchamber, but Luc was within the apartment, a quiet hum in my mind. If he heard me trying to bathe, I had no doubt he'd fuck me again. And he wouldn't be gentle about it.

Not that I had considered their treatment of me before they discovered I was a witch gentle. But after last night, I knew it had been.

Their bodies, pressing into me from both sides. Their grunts, a sensual chorus in my ears. Their cocks, stretching me wide together. The rub of Luc's piercings against my inner walls eliciting shudders as Jules fucked my ass, only a thin barrier within me holding them apart—

I gave a sharp shake of my head. It wasn't time to fantasize about the kings fucking me.

I had tried to *run* from them.

They wouldn't let that go unpunished.

When that time came, I didn't want to be a naked mess with tangled hair in their bed.

I crawled to the edge of the mattress and rose slowly. My body protested, begging for another day or two of sleep. The kings' runes dulled the pain and nausea, but they couldn't fully erase the fatigue.

No clothes waited for me this time.

Of course not. Riona was dead.

I flinched at the thought. The doorway to my bedchamber looked unchanged, but from the corner of my eye, I swore I could still see the thrall's pale corpse.

Her sacrifice wasted.

After another sharp shake of my head, I crossed to the kings' bathing chamber. Riona was dead, as were all the other human thralls who had come with us last night. But I wasn't. I couldn't change what had happened, no matter how much I fretted about it.

I stepped into the bathing chamber. A long marble counter stretched to my left, two deep basins Maire had called sinks embedded in its surface. A tub large enough for five stood to my right on gilded feet. Before the back wall, a section was walled off with gold-edged glass. An inactive rune glowed faintly on the ceiling, another mirroring it on the floor. Both matched the pair in the tub. ***Pour. Drain.*** There hadn't been a contraption like that in the thrall bathing chambers, so I didn't have the slightest idea what it was. Some sort of standing bath?

After relieving myself, I finally faced my reflection in the mirrors over the counter. My brown hair was a matted mess, but my upper body had at least been cleaned of blood and sweat. Only the tuft of hair between my legs and the skin of my inner thighs remained dirty, streaked with dry cum and the remnants of desire.

I clenched my fists to resist the urge to scrub myself raw. It wasn't worth it.

And oddly enough, that was actually true. My clit didn't pulse at the thought of Luc scent-marking me. Heat didn't flare in my core. My nipples didn't peak and tingle. I remained... unaffected. The soulbond hadn't just stopped urging me toward the kings. It slumbered entirely.

Like it was finally satisfied.

I gasped. Of course it was finally satisfied. I had taken *both* the kings last night. I'd thought something was wrong with me, my hunger for Luc and Jules seemingly endless. Karra has craved Azaras, but it hadn't been constant every second of the day.

But I didn't have one soulbound. I had *two*. For our soul to be whole again, I couldn't just fuck one of them.

I had to fuck both.

A sharp laugh almost escaped my lips. When Luc had said fucking them would be my eternity, I'd thought it a threat.

It wasn't a threat. It was just the truth.

My life would never be mine again. I was trapped. Caged by the kings, both physically and magically. Running last night had been a moment of desperation, of lunacy. There was no running. Just like there was no escaping my illness.

It simply was, and there was nothing I could do to change that.

The air in the bathing chamber thinned, every breath tight in my chest. This would be my existence. Wife to the Imperium. Queen in name only. Whore in reality.

I would serve them with my blood and body forever. Their captive. Their property. The *mother* of their children. My palms slicked with sweat, a chill sliding down my spine. There was no denying it anymore. When they decided they wanted an heir, they'd have all the time, all the magic, all the power in the world to plant their child in my belly.

And I couldn't stop it.

I couldn't stop any of this.

I'd thought I had no control of my life before, but now I truly had none. The floor tilted beneath my feet. Or maybe I was tilting. I couldn't tell.

A sharp pain shot through my core. I glanced down. My heart nearly stopped. Dark blood coated my thighs, thick and heavy, dripping all the way to my ankles. I didn't even care that I was suddenly wearing a thin nightgown, not in the face of all that blood. Not with the twisting in my belly.

It was like the pain of my illness, only far worse. A deep, relentless cramp that stabbed hard and didn't stop.

A wave of dizziness hit me. I grabbed the edge of the counter, gripping it like it was the only thing anchoring me to the world. What the fuck? Was I dying? Had the kings broken something in me? Why had it happened so fast, so sudden? I raised my head to meet my reflection—and flinched back.

My eyes were no longer brown, but a shade so dark they looked black. But more than the color of my iris had changed. They were flecked with silver on the right and gold on the left, luminous specks that spilled over my pupils. The asymmetry itched at something deep in me, unsettling and almost mesmerizing.

I swallowed back my nausea. They were so... foreign.

Inhuman.

"Nessa?"

I jerked around, spinning toward the sound of Luc's voice. The King of Dusk stood behind me, dressed all in black. His gaze swept over my trembling form, blood still streaking down my legs.

Something shifted in his expression. A realization flickered across his face. It twisted in his chest, sharp and sudden. An emotion I felt so clearly, I thought for a second it was my own.

Was that... sorrow?

I hadn't known Luc was capable of a sorrow like this. Not this sharp. Not this deep. Even his rage, his pain, his pleasure hadn't hit me this hard.

He closed the distance between us quickly, the terrifyingly cold Conqueror from last night replaced by someone else entirely. His expression was soft. I had only ever seen him look at Jules like that.

He took me into his arms like I was something delicate. *Precious.* It was such an insane concept that my breath caught. Something welled in my chest, something aching. A craving I had never dared acknowledge.

No one had ever touched me like this before.

Like I *mattered.*

Tears pricked at my eyes. I tried to force them down, to bury them like always, but they broke loose, spurred on by the pain in my center. I didn't know what was happening, but I leaned into his chest anyway, needing his warmth and comfort.

He pressed a kiss to my temple. "All will be well, my love—"

And everything changed.

Luc was gone, the kings' bathing chamber and the morning light with him. Runelight flickered across rough stone walls, their texture unmistakably that of a cave. Above me, the ceiling was perfectly flat, a jarring contrast to the uneven rock. I lay in the center of an enormous bed, under soft maroon blankets, completely naked and—

The bond blazed with joy, radiant from both sides. It pulsed through my chest, too warm to be real, too intense to be mine alone. For a moment, I let myself sink into it, let it cradle me.

Then the pain hit.

I yelped as a fresh wave tore through my center. Not the pain of my illness. Not the sharp cramp from moments ago, blood streaming down my thighs. This was far worse, like I had been ripped in two.

Had I been injured last night, after they fed from me? Was waking in the kings' apartment and walking to the bathing chamber the fever dream? Or was this? Luc holding me. Calling me his love. The cave. The bed. The pain—

"Nessa?"

This time, it was Jules who spoke. The King of Dawn pushed upright from the mattress beside me, golden gaze glowing like sunrise. "Lie back, lovely. You're healed, but—"

"What happened to your hair?" I blurted, my gaze finally taking in his short blond hair, a few wild pieces falling across his forehead.

He wore it well, but it wasn't Jules. Even tousled, it was too neat. Too... tame.

His brow furrowed, ever so slightly. "What?"

"What happened to your..." I reached up to gesture toward my hair, but my fingers met empty air. I froze. My hair fell to my waist, I should have reached it by now—

But instead, I brushed against soft curls just above my ear.

I jolted once in shock. Then again as pain shot through me. Why the fuck was my hair short? And why did it hurt so much—?

Soft fingers grazed my chin. Jules tilted my face toward his. He leaned over me, propped on an elbow, golden gaze scanning every inch of my expression. His eyes were still keen, the calculating mind behind the Butcher's wicked joy. But like with Luc, there was something new beneath it now.

Something brighter.

Something softer.

Something that shouldn't have existed.

The pressure in my chest swelled.

"Ah," he murmured, the word brushing warm against my cheek. "This is a poor time for a skip."

I stared at him. Were those words supposed to make sense? "What?"

Something split the air. A high-pitched cry that pulled at something deep within me.

My head snapped toward the sound. Luc stood at the end of the bed, bare-chested in dark slacks, his bronzed skin glistening in runelight. His silver eyes were locked on me. But I didn't meet them for once, too busy gaping at the bundle of lace and silk cradled in his arms.

I tried to press up onto my elbow. Was that a fucking—?

My vision wobbled.

I slumped back to the bed and slapped a hand against my face. No, no, no. That wasn't right. I squished my eyes shut. I inhaled, sinking into the cushion—

And exhaled, now leaning against something solid. My palms gripped the edge of a cold surface as water trickled in the background. The pitched cry had cut out. The light had changed from dim gold to the white of morning again.

I opened my eyes to my reflection, once again naked and cum-stained in the bathing chamber. My widened eyes stared back at me, the familiar brown of a shocked mortal. My face was wet, like I'd splashed water on it.

I didn't remember doing that.

"What the fuck?" I muttered.

"I believe that's my question, bride."

I jumped a foot in the air.

Luc stood in the doorway. But this wasn't the Luc I had seen moments ago. The long stretch of him was clad in a navy doublet embroidered with silver thread, his posture rigid and unreadable. There was no softness in his gaze—only heat, and something as hard as steel beneath it.

Like a king staring down a subject who'd disobeyed him.

Like I had.

I should have been concerned, but I was only terribly confused. Terribly, desperately confused. "What was that?"

He arched a brow. "What was what?"

"That!" I waved my hand vaguely at the room, like the room would become a cave again.

Luc only stared. He had no idea what I was talking about. None whatsoever. His expression didn't change, but the bond between us whispered the truth.

I swallowed. First the hedge maze, now this. My mind was breaking. But that was normal, right? Who wouldn't, after everything I'd seen and felt and suffered? I didn't know why my brain had conjured blood on my thighs, a concerned Luc, Jules and me with shorter hair, and a different Luc cradling a starsdamned *baby.*

I was sure it had a reason. I had been panicking about them breeding me. That was surely why.

I turned back to the mirror, leaned over, and splashed more cold water onto my face. The chill bit into my skin, just what I needed. A shock to bring me back.

*I will not cry. I will not scream. I will not let these monsters break me.*

I didn't believe the words. I was already fracturing, bit by bit.

"How long before the witches betrayed you?"

I glanced up to find Luc staring at me impassively. He wanted to jump straight into the interrogation? I could do that, as long as no one broke a bone.

"The moment we transported out of Dawnspear."

He nodded. "That's not surprising."

I winced. Of course it wasn't surprising to him. He was the bloody Conqueror. Plotting and maneuvering people was his entire existence. "I was surprised."

"Of course you were," he said. "You have a kind heart. You want to believe the best of people, despite the disdain you experienced your entire childhood."

I repressed a flinch. "I'm an idiot, I know—"

Luc's large hand suddenly encompassed my jaw. He tilted my head until I looked over my shoulder at him. The look he gave me was flat and unblinking, like my self-loathing was blasphemy. "Do *not* call yourself an idiot. Am I understood?"

I shuddered, my shoulders pressing back against his wide expanse of chest. "Yes."

He arched his brow.

I swallowed. "Yes, Your Majesty."

At that, he released me and stepped back, putting space between us once again. I wrapped my arms around myself, a shield and a support all in one.

Luc glanced down, like he'd just noticed I was still naked. Without a word, he turned and exited the bathing chamber.

He didn't need to give the order. He wanted me to follow him. I didn't have it in me to resist. I was tired. Confused. Defeated. And what would it accomplish, if I defied him? He could just stomp back in here and carry me out.

I glanced back at the mirror one last time, but my eyes were still a normal brown. No silver, no gold. No black. Just me.

Shaking my head, I followed Luc into his bedchamber. I didn't have time for hallucinations now. I still waited for the noose to tighten. And it would tighten. I needed to survive that.

Luc passed the long dresser between doors. A swash of black fabric lay across the surface, next to a familiar silver-gold collar.

But I didn't care.

A massive hellwolf stood in the doorway to the sitting room.

"Titus!" I launched forward, reaching out to bury my hands in his thick fur. "You're alive."

The hellwolf bared fangs as long as my hand and growled low in his throat.

I froze mid-step, blood draining from my face. Terror snapped through me. But that was fair. Titus wasn't a dog. He was a hellwolf. He understood exactly what I had done yesterday.

My shoulder slumped, the breath leaking out of me.

Even when I was a stranger in this place, Titus had let me curl into him and pretend I wasn't alone. But now, he looked at me like I was a threat. My stomach twisted, shame crawling up my throat.

I hadn't meant to hurt him. But I had anyway.

Luc stood motionless across the room, hands linked behind his back. He said nothing of Titus's reaction. Only tilted his head and said, "Get dressed."

I inhaled deeply and backed away until I stood beside the dresser. I picked up the fabric first. The gown was the standard black slip all thralls wore. That I hadn't since the soulbond was discovered. A pang shot through my chest, but I ignored it.

What else had I expected?

I slid the dress over my head. Whatever came my way, I would endure. Even if I was little more than their thrall again.

"And the collar," Luc said.

My hands hovered over the silver-gold metal. This was equally symbolic. I had to return myself to my shackles. I breathed in. Breathed out. Before I could hesitate longer, I wrapped the collar around my neck with a clink of metal. The tiny jewels dangling from its chains traced my collarbones. The contraption settled heavy on my shoulders.

I was the Mortal Bride once more.

Forevermore.

Luc crooked a finger. "Come here, bride."

Straightening my shoulders, I closed the distance between us. Luc's pupils darkened with my every step. Something hot tickled under *my skin, a desire I couldn't repress. Stars, I loved every time she obeyed me with that defiant glare.*

*Loved.*

*No.*

*It was too soon for that. Before I could dwell on it, I gave a slow spin of my finger. "Turn—"*

I jolted back to myself, Luc mere inches away. I held his gaze for a heartbeat. Just one. His shadowed pupil only swallowed more and more iris, that itch *under my skin growing—*

I turned before I slipped back into his head.

Luc's hands settled over the back of my neck, right over the latch to the collar. A moment later, the heat of magic flared across my skin, sharp enough to make me flinch.

"You're now unable to remove your collar without permission," Luc said. "Nor can you say the words to free any thrall."

Something inside me twisted. Cold and furious. I clenched my hands tight together. It was either that or yank at the metal choking my throat. Or scream. Or both.

"What now?" I asked, voice flat.

"Jules is nearly finished interrogating the Isauran delegation." Luc lowered his hand from my neck, but didn't step back. He didn't touch me, simply standing there at my back, out of sight but never outside my senses. "Once he's complete, they'll be tried and sentenced before the High Courts."

I closed my eyes. A trial. I didn't know much about Azarasian justice beyond what I had witnessed. The kings were judge and executioner, all in one. The delegation wouldn't survive the day.

If they were currently strapped to the Butcher's Block, that was likely preferable.

When Luc didn't say anything else, I managed a nod. "I see."

"Do you?"

I twisted at that, meeting his bright eyes over my shoulder. "I know you don't let your enemies live. It isn't hard to guess what will happen next."

Luc just hummed, a noncommittal reply. He didn't believe me.

I turned back toward the dresser and the wall.

Luc didn't speak. Like he was waiting. For what, I wasn't sure. I stared at the wall, harder and harder, until I couldn't anymore. I threw out the first question that came to mind. "Where's my mother?"

"Imprisoned, as well. Jules spoke with her yesterday afternoon."

I flinched. While I had sobbed and curled on my bed in pain, Jules had tortured my mother. She might not love me, but I didn't want to imagine her at the end of the Butcher's blades. "Did she tell him anything?"

"Nothing helpful. The rune binding her to secrecy cares not about pain." Luc paused. "Jules found it cathartic, at least."

Bastard. I narrowed my eyes. "I'm sure he did."

"Your betrayal upset him gravely."

I spun around, nearly barring my teeth. "Him breaking my *fingers* upset me gravely—"

A low snarl cut me off. Titus had crossed the room in a flash of black fur, now stationed at Luc's side. His shadowed eyes and gaping maw hovered inches from my face. Everything in me screamed to run.

But I only stiffened my spine. Titus couldn't kill me without killing the kings. He knew that. Had known that long before Luc and Jules did. And letting a hellwolf ravish me was a far cry from breaking fingers.

Luc didn't react visibly to Titus or me, but that squirming heat rose in him again. "Jules healed you right away."

Jules healed me right away? I'd stayed standing, but my thoughts had certainly fled at Titus's advance. I pursed my lips, retracing our conversation—

Fucking *asshole.* Like breaking my fingers was nothing. Stars, why couldn't I throttle him? He liked to have his hand around my throat. Let him see how he liked it in return. "That doesn't negate him *breaking* my fucking fingers."

Luc arched a brow, faintly amused. "The Butcher doesn't consider breaking a finger torture, little witch. The fact he took mercy on you when his emotions were repressed is only because you're his soulbound. When he's in that state, he usually does much worse."

Repressed emotions? That explained the hollowness I had felt in Jules yesterday… and felt in him again right now.

But that wasn't an excuse. For any of their actions.

I crossed my arms. "So he was so distraught he had to lock his emotions away, but not distraught enough to stop himself from fucking me."

Luc's features shuttered, his emotions dimming behind his mask. "Neither of us wanted to fuck you. The bond demanded it."

My fists clenched. They had certainly seemed like they wanted to fuck me. But then again… I had certainly seemed like I wanted to fuck them, too.

The soulbond wasn't just riding me hard. It controlled the kings, as well. Obviously. But I had never let myself think about it. I knew their desire for me couldn't be real—had never been real—but they had acted so accepting of the bond. Like every action was still their own. Like it was a choice.

In truth, they were just better at pretending it wasn't one forced on them.

"You didn't seem to feel its… insistence after the blocking rune was gone."

"Jules and I have experienced blocking runes before. All Azarasians must learn to endure, no matter what we feel from our soulbound, whether it's pleasure, pain, or nothing at all." Luc brushed his fingers through Titus's fur, soothing the hellwolf. "But there's no resisting what the bond demands when a blocking rune is removed. We could only delay it."

"You could've delayed it until we got back to Dawnspear."

"And why would we do that?" He cocked his head, genuinely confused. "We granted your wishes for privacy the first time we claimed you, but you shouldn't expect it often. Shame isn't in our nature."

Neither was decency. "I'm aware."

A spark flashed within me. Jules. His emotions surged through the bond, no longer sealed away. Whatever shield he'd built had fallen, and now the full weight of him crashed back into me.

Luc straightened. "Jules is finished. He'll be escorting the witches to the throne room for judgment."

I nodded, throat tight. "And I'm attending?"

Luc reached into his pocket… and pulled out a silver chain?

My stomach dropped. "What is—?"

He didn't answer. Just stepped forward and latched the chain to a small loop at the base of my collar.

My jaw dropped. He just put a *leash* on me. I stared at the chain in disbelief, everything in me recoiling. And yet… not all in fear. A terrible, shameful thrill twirled in my gut. I stiffened, fists curling at my sides, trying to fight it.

"You're not simply attending, little witch." Luc gave the leash a slow, deliberate tug that sent a jolt through my spine. "You ran just like they did. This is your trial, too."

I FOLLOWED LUC IN silence through the halls of Dawnspear, the leash between us glinting in the sunlight every time we passed a window. I glared at the chain the entire way. I hadn't seen any other thrall on a leash since arriving in the city. Vampires didn't need physical restraints to keep their thralls in control.

This was just the first part of my punishment.

It was probably the best part of my punishment, too. We were walking toward my fucking *trial.*

I shouldn't have expected anything less. I had tried to leave. Even if I wasn't their soulbound, I was their Mortal Bride. I had endangered more than their lives—I'd risked their covenant runespell, the backbone of the Impire. It didn't matter that I *was* the covenant.

In minutes, hundreds of judging vampire eyes would be on me. Their thralls might not be allowed to look up, but they'd be there too. Probably by order. We hadn't passed a single human or witch in the hallway. Whatever happened to us would serve as a warning.

There weren't even any courtiers roaming the hallways. The only other living beings I saw were the two male Imperial Guard walking behind me. One was dark-skinned with golden eyes, the other auburn-haired with silver. I'd seen them last night, but I still didn't know their names.

I tried not to look at them. It was my fault Estrella and Tristan weren't a step behind us.

So many people were dead because of me. They weighed on my shoulders, keeping my head ducked and my eyes lowered. If I wasn't wearing a soothing rune, the stress would have incited my pain into a wildfire.

I didn't even glance upward when dark boots with ruby-encrusted gold buckles entered my line of vision.

"Anything?" Luc asked.

"Nope," Jules said, popping the word like he wasn't mildly annoyed. "None of them have any idea who cast the bloodborne soulbond and sent us our bride."

Luc hummed, thoughtful. He didn't bother questioning Jules. Everyone broke under the Butcher's steady hands. If I hadn't yelled my every thought at him yesterday, he would've continued calmly snapping fingers one at a time until both my hands were broken.

And likely beyond that. He could just heal them immediately and start again.

There was no choice but to break. No choice but to surrender. No choice but to fail.

Jules bumped a knuckle beneath my chin. I jolted at the touch. If we weren't soulbound, I'd have fully recoiled. He tilted my head up until I met his eyes. "But they had quite a lot to scream about, like how you invited them in and deactivated their thrall runes."

The warmth of his skin pulsed into me. Every instinct screamed to close my eyes and sink into him. I forced my spine to stay rigid. "What did you expect? You broke three of my fingers."

Jules *smiled.* "I don't even consider that torture."

I glared, the words echoing Luc almost exactly. "Then why did you have to... hollow yourself out, or whatever it is you did to repress your feelings?"

Jules dropped his hand, his small grin unchanged. But something was buried underneath it, almost like guilt. "It's a weakened version of Grandpa Thaddeus's godcurse. Comes in handy at times."

"That didn't answer my question."

"I know."

Jules unclasped a gold chain bracelet dotted with rubies and pearls that started at his wrist and coiled all the way to his elbow. He unwrapped it, looping the chain around and around until...

Until it became a leash to match Luc's.

My fists clenched, nails biting into my palms. For one brief second, my anger flared hotter than despair—bright, searing, and utterly useless.

Jules latched the end of his leash to the front of my collar. "Such rage, witch. It nearly tickles."

"Fuck—"

Luc tugged. I stumbled forward, straight into Jules. My hands landed on the soft silk of his embroidered tunic. Into the strength of his chest. The chest that had glided along my back last night as he fucked me—

I gave a sharp shake of my head. But it was too late. The King of Dawn inhaled deeply. His lips twitched, his smile growing. I tensed for him to say something, to make some sort of lewd comment.

He only bopped a finger against my nose and turned away.

"Sabas rounded up the witches and got them to the throne room," Jules said to Luc. "Rox herded our favorite courtiers in a while ago. They're just waiting on us now."

Luc nodded and started forward, Jules falling into step at his side. They moved too quietly, each step a silent warning. The leash stayed taut between us as I followed, skin crawling with unease. If I fell behind or stumbled, they'd drag me the rest of the way, no question.

I didn't have to keep pace for long.

We turned a corner, and the gilded doors to the throne room came into view, Sabas and Roxiana mid-argument at their side. They both snapped their jaws shut the moment the kings appeared.

Luc's tone remained calm, but something sharpened beneath it. "Is there a problem?"

Sabas's gaze flickered to me. "Are you going to glamour her? If anyone focuses, they'll sense a flicker of her power."

"They'll find out eventually," Luc said calmly.

"And when they do, there will be challenges," Roxiana said. "Not many, but a few."

Jules snorted. "We can deal with challengers, Rox. Could be fun, actually."

Roxiana didn't rise to the bait. "Even so, the Isaurans rising against us isn't something we can brush off. Announce your new soulbond when we're sure the first threat has passed."

Jules glanced at Luc, his brows raised. The King of Dusk studied his Crown Enforcer and Crown Chancellor for a moment longer. Neither he nor Jules were concerned at the idea of a challenge, but they weighed their councilor's words all the same.

"My mother thought nothing could kill her." Roxiana's voice didn't crack, but it dipped low with quiet weight. Resentment, maybe. Her relationship with Marisol seemed as fraught as her nephew's. "Her arrogance cost us hundreds of lives, hers included."

A flicker of annoyance twisted through Luc. His jaw clenched. He didn't like being compared to the former regent. "Very well."

Jules looped his leash around his wrist, reversing the motion from moments ago. This time, I was still clipped to the end. I had no choice but to step forward, again and again, until my shoulder brushed his.

He held out his hand, palm up, and wiggled his fingers.

Nausea twisted in my gut. The last time I'd placed my hand in Jules's, he'd broken my fingers.

I couldn't get past that. I shouldn't have had to. But I would. I had to. Survival demanded it.

*Do it, Nessa.* My hand trembled as I reached for his, then forced my palm into his with a slap that echoed louder than it should have.

"Angry and aggressive." Jules held my gaze as he traced a rune over my knuckles. Shadows curled between his fingers, though thankfully they didn't turn into solid claws. "A personal favorite of mine."

I narrowed my eyes at him—and at my side, Luc arched a brow. But it was enough of a reaction for Jules, who winked at Luc over my head.

***Glamour.***

Heat tickled over my skin in a quick wave as Jules's rune activated. I didn't feel any different, but Sabas's shoulders eased slightly. Like the fear of instant mutiny upon opening the doors had passed.

Roxiana only nodded, then traced a quick symbol in the air. ***Open.*** The throne room's double doors slid open.

Two dozen vampire courtiers mingled across the wide expanse of marble floor before the daemium throne, like this was a private party instead of a trial.

Knowing vampires, it was somehow both.

Unlike the last time I was here, over twenty twisting gold sculptures lined the walls. Each one held a frozen figure of a bound witch, posed in unnatural stillness. They were twisted into all kinds of positions—dancing and leaping, some reaching out, some recoiling. Every head was tilted to the side, exposing their throats in a way that made my stomach turn.

Art and a meal, all in one.

A vampire approached one of the captive witches, their fangs extending in a flare of shadows. The witch couldn't flinch, frozen stiff as the predator approached.

The vampire fisted a hand in the witch's hair and sank their fangs into her neck. The witch jerked—and not in pleasure. As the vampire swallowed, their face contorted in pain. Their mouth opened, releasing a soundless scream.

Those witches hadn't tried to run with us. Maybe they hadn't even known what their delegation had planned. Would the kings kill them all for the acts of a few? Or was the bite of agony the only punishment they'd suffer?

I hoped so.

I feared not.

If not for the leash, I might've stopped cold. Exhaustion and fear weighed down my body, but the chain jerked tight as the kings stepped forward, hauling me into the spectacle whether I wanted it or not.

Sabas and Roxiana had let them pass first, but the Crown Chancellor stepped to the side. She didn't use a rune this time to project her voice. "Their Majesties Lucero Azaras and Julien Roche, Kings of Dusk and Dawn, Imperators of the Blood Legion, and Imperium of the Azarasians."

The courtiers scattered from the center of the room in a blink, dropping into bows with heads lowered. Along the room's edges, thralls dressed in solid black sank to their knees.

Left exposed at the center of the marble floor, just before the throne, kneeled the remaining witches from the delegation. They wore collars again, but this time, shadowy tendrils traced up their necks like veins, forming muzzles across their mouths.

Morrena's face was raised and defiant, but her delegation hadn't fared as well in the torture. Ilenia wept, scratching at her arm like she could still feel whatever the Butcher had done to her. Eral stared blankly at the floor, his eyes vacant. The other two—I still didn't know their names—seemed caught somewhere between hysterics and numbness.

I didn't have time to gape. Luc and Jules crossed the floor for their thrones, and I scurried behind them. No one looked at the kings, but more than one pair of bright eyes flicked to me.

Full of disdain.

Full of hatred.

Full of... glee?

The Azarasians expected a show. Their kings would certainly deliver.

I whipped my head forward, trying to focus. Already, my breath came faster, short and shallow. There were too many eyes gliding over my too-bare skin, judging, savoring, waiting for me to break—

I hated it here.

When we passed the kneeling witches, the kings stopped in front of me. Sabas and Roxiana continued forward, taking their places beside their soulbound before the throne.

Luc turned. No, the Conqueror turned. He stared down at me, not a flicker of emotion in his lips, his eyes, his brows. Before the soulbond, I'd have thought him cold in a moment like this, but a tangle of emotions burned in his chest. Rage, worry, and a flicker of... regret?

It couldn't be. The Conqueror didn't regret.

He stopped an inch away, a towering mass of strength and power, impossibly large and enthrallingly beautiful. An obedient thrall would've dropped to her knees at the sight. But I locked my legs, refusing, even though every bone in my body ached to sit.

Luc unhooked Jules's leash, then his own. He traced his thumbs across my lips, a mockery of tenderness. "Kneel."

Every muscle within me stiffened. My gaze flickered to Jules, but the King of Dawn remained silent for once. That smile he always wore lingered, but something darker glinted behind his *eyes. The guilt and regret Luc felt echoed through the bond, but it didn't smother the part of me that wanted her on her knees. That ached to see her yield. I wanted her to disobey almost as much as I wanted her to obey. Both made her burn with a fire I longed to let consume me—*

I shuddered back into myself. "Luc, I—"

"Your Majesty."

"What?"

"When my head, hand, or cock is between your legs, you may call me Luc. When you're on trial, I'm your king. Do not mistake the two." He stepped back and clasped his hands behind him. "Kneel, bride."

I clenched my fists, nails digging into my palms.

"Are you disobeying my direct order?"

My palms slicked with sweat at the edge in his tone. It took everything in me not to collapse, not to fold under the attention of the monster looming above me.

Well, almost everything. My nipples were hard as rocks. And I couldn't blame the soulbond, still sated inside me.

Breath ghosted the back of my neck. Jules had circled to stand behind me. "You really should kneel, lovely."

I swallowed... and ever so slowly sank to my knees. Nausea churned in my gut, angry tears prickling at my eyes. But this was only going to get worse. I couldn't stop it. I'd risked everything and lost it all. Preserving my dignity wasn't worth my defiance.

I'd need it later, for something that actually mattered.

The kings stared down at me. The itch under my skin intensified as I kneeled before them. Rising desire. Hungry. Heavy. Hot. Of course they liked this. Of course kneeling thrilled them. Especially when I loathed every second of it.

And yet, my pulse stuttered. My thighs pressed tighter together.

I wanted to scream. Instead, I glared forward, not at them, but not at the floor either.

After a long moment of silence, the kings moved as one. Luc turned on his heel and walked to their throne. When Jules passed me, he drifted a hand through my hair, almost like a caress. I resisted the shiver that prickled up my spine at the brush of his fingertips.

When they reached the daemium seat, Luc sat on the left, straight-backed and regal, while Jules lounged on the right, stretching out his legs and crossing his ankles before him. The last time I had kneeled before the kings at their throne, Éamon had died. This time, five witches kneeled at my side, and this trial would end with their deaths.

*I will not cry. I will not scream. I will not let these monsters break me.*

"Rise," Luc said into the silence of the room.

The courtiers all rose from their bows, as if holding the pose for minutes had been no strain at all. The human thralls remained on their knees beyond them. Azarasians drifted forward, lured from the statue-bound witches toward their kings and whatever it was they had to say.

Between two vampires, I caught a flash of Maire, kneeling with all the other thralls. Thank the stars they hadn't realized her involvement.

"Last night, the Isauran delegation broke into the Imperial Apartment of Dawnspear with one goal," Luc said. "To steal the covenant, our Mortal Bride, and take her to Isaura as their hostage."

Whispers broke out among the courtiers.

"In doing so"—Luc didn't glare, but the cutting edge of his tone silenced the courtiers—"they killed two of our Imperial Guard, Estrella and Tristan

Ibarra, to fuel the transportation spell that helped them escape from the castle."

It was like Luc had announced they'd killed everyone's sister and brother. Fists clenched. Voices snarled. Fangs and claws bloomed from shadow as darkening eyes fixed on the delegation. Courtiers shifted in my periphery, silks swaying and jewels flashing as a silver-eyed, brown-skinned woman in an azure gown shoved to the front of the crowd. Her dark hair flowed around her shoulder to her waist, threaded with silver and sapphires.

Luc let his gaze flicker over to her. Tension pressed through the bond, tightening my chest before it dissolved. "Speak, Alicia."

The silver-eyed vampire's throat bobbed. Her hands were clenched at her sides, trembling just slightly. "Which one, Your Majesty?"

Her voice was steady, but only barely. The devastation laced through it was raw, visible in the fine quiver of her lip as she struggled to hold her expression neutral.

"They worked together to cast the spell," Luc said.

Alicia's eyes burned. "I demand retribution."

"No."

She took a step forward. "They killed my *parents*."

My breath hitched. Parents. I hadn't known Estrella and Tristan had a daughter.

"And they will die for their crimes," Luc said, unfazed. "But they tried to steal our bride. Their lives are ours."

Alicia clenched her fist, her knuckles going stark white.

"Careful, Alicia." Jules's voice was low and almost amused, but the flippant tone rang false. "You'll find my soulbound and I have shorter tempers today. We had quite the night."

Alicia froze. Then slowly, deliberately, she opened her hand. Her gaze dropped. "Of course, Your Majesty. Forgive me."

Luc held her eyes for a beat. Then gave a single, measured nod. If he hadn't just informed her of her parents' deaths, he wouldn't be as lenient.

He turned his attention back to us, focusing on Morrena. "Do you have anything to say for yourself before we sentence you and your kin for your crimes, Morrena?"

As he spoke, her shadow muzzle faded, the darkness peeling back into two plates of daemium embedded in the collar.

Morrena's jaw clenched. Her shoulders squared as she lifted her chin, but her voice came out cold and flat. "There is nothing left to say."

The silence pressed in, fragile and unforgiving. Like the room itself was holding its breath.

She didn't say *Your Majesty*. She wasn't going to.

She would face death, but not bow to them.

Luc didn't blink. "Very well. You've committed high treason. The sentence is death."

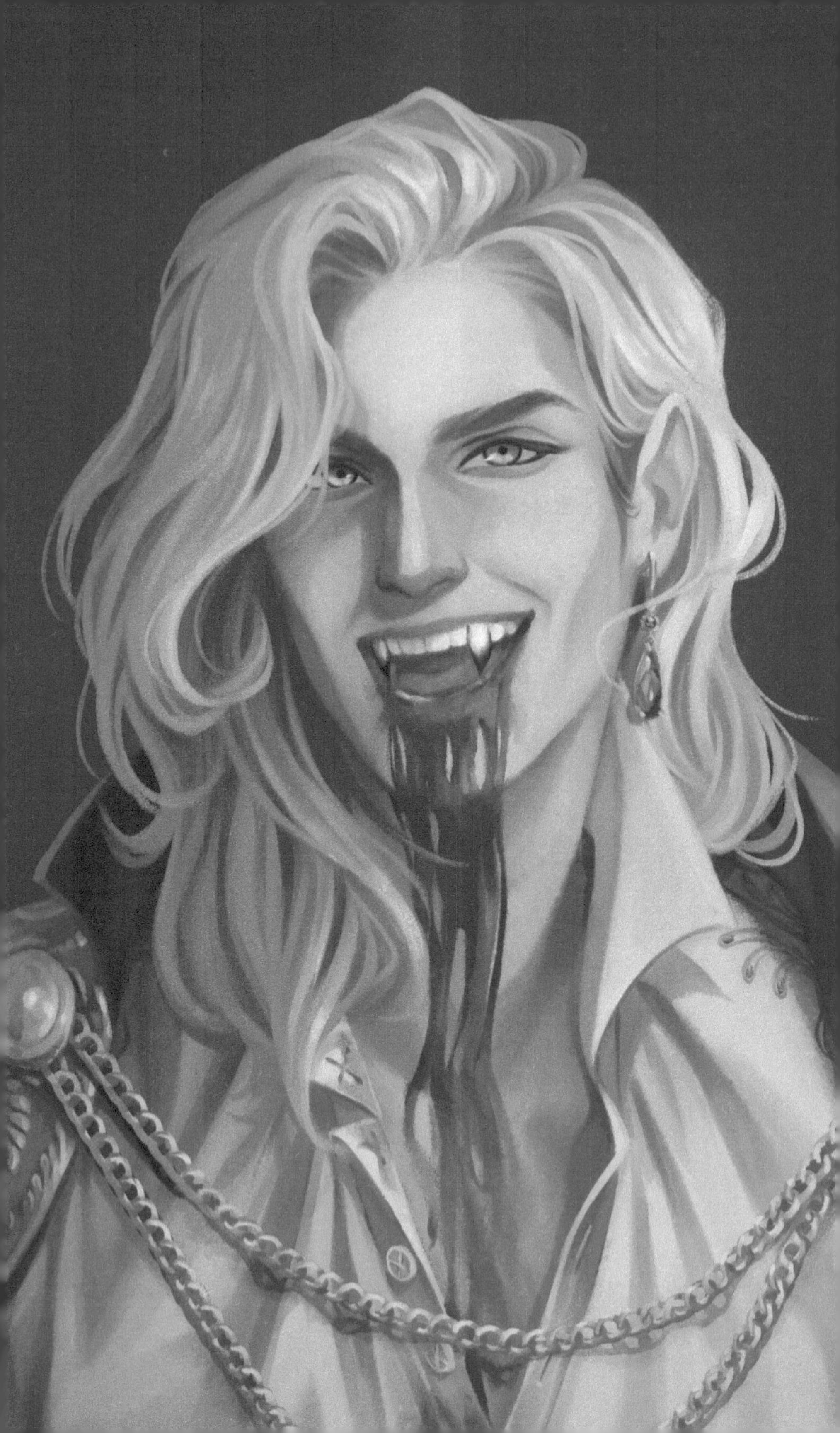

# 54

MY BREATH CAUGHT. THE sentence echoed in my ears, louder than it had any right to be. The witches didn't react, not visibly. Maybe they were too broken. Or maybe they were braver than me.

But something in me cracked.

Luc stood in one smooth motion. Jules followed a beat later, casually adjusting his tunic like he was getting ready for a dance, not an execution. His excitement flared beside Luc's steady resolve. The throne room stayed silent, the air tight as both kings stepped down from the dais together.

A small part of me screamed to stay down. Keep my head bowed. Let this happen. Let them pass.

Ilenia sobbed beside me, her whole body shaking. Eral didn't lift his head. The other two hadn't spoken since we arrived. And Morrena... Morrena didn't beg. Didn't plead. She only watched the kings descend, her expression carved from stone.

The Isaurans had betrayed me. They'd threatened my life.

But I couldn't let them die like this.

My knees trembled as I shifted my weight. A small part of me screamed to flee as the Conqueror and the Butcher approached. But I planted one foot, then the other.

And I rose—straight into the kings' path.

Everything went silent. I think. Maybe I just couldn't hear over the thundering of my heart. I had stepped in front of the *Conqueror* and the *Butcher*. Two vampire kings who ruled as mercilessly as they killed.

I couldn't hope to stand against them. I didn't have any magic. I didn't know how to use a sword or dagger, and even if I did, it wouldn't matter against their inhuman strength and speed.

I knew all that.

I did it anyway.

I couldn't stand by and let the witches die.

The kings stopped. *Stopped.* Their faces remained blank and calm, but their focus locked on me with an intensity that made me want to bolt. Luc's tension coiled like a storm held in check, dangerous and waiting. Jules's emotions spiked hotter. Surprise, amusement, and beneath it all, shameless desire.

But they didn't move forward. That was a good sign, right? They didn't have to stop. Luc walked over those in his way, and Jules cut through them with blade, claw, or fang. I was soulbound to them. They couldn't kill me without killing themselves, but they could still pick me up and move me out of their way.

Then their expressions shifted. Luc slowly arched a brow as Jules grinned with sharp menace. Every cell in my body screamed to get the fuck out of here.

Well, not every cell. A couple traitors wanted to jump them.

I raised my chin, determined not to wither under their intense gazes.

Luc's hand wrapped around my jaw a second later. "Whenever you raise your little chin like that, bride, I get unbelievably hard."

I only raised my chin higher. "That's not my problem."

His grip tightened. "Isn't it?"

A flush heated my cheeks. It was my cunt Luc would ram his unbelievably hard cock into. My body might've reacted, but I forced the rest of me still. That wasn't real. It was just the soulbond. I wasn't flustered or embarrassed. Why should I be? I was standing to save lives.

My pulse roared in my ears, but I didn't lower my gaze. I wouldn't. I couldn't. "Don't kill them."

Luc didn't hesitate. "We don't allow our enemies to live."

"I'm your enemy."

Luc's eyes narrowed, a flicker of heat behind the mask. "You're our bride."

"And if you harm our bride, I rip your face off." Jules glared at the kneeling witches. "They hurt you, didn't they?"

I flinched. The words were crude, brutal, but not wrong. The witches *had* hurt me. The blocking rune had felt like a slow death, like something vital had been stolen from me. Still, I didn't look away from Jules. I didn't let his words sway me. That pain didn't justify what the kings would do in return.

"Leave it be, Nessa," Morrena said, her voice tight. "You can't change—"

"Shut up, Morrena."

The words ripped out of me, louder than I meant, edged with all the fury, helplessness, and exhaustion curdling in my chest. She had tried to use me, caged me like I was nothing. I was done listening to her voice.

Her mouth snapped shut mid-sentence. Her jaw locked, her lips pressed tight, her eyes blown wide in shock. I blinked. Had I said it too harshly? Too loud? Morrena stared at me, unmoving. Not defiant, not angry. Stunned, like I'd slapped her.

Something in her expression shifted, cold realization crawling over her face.

I didn't stop to figure out what. I turned back to the kings. Luc had tilted his head, a glint of approval in his eyes. Jules's grin had sharpened into a smirk, like I'd just done something worth watching.

But they hadn't moved. Hadn't brushed past me. Hadn't dismissed me.

Maybe they were actually considering my words.

The Conqueror crushed that fluttering hope under his boot. "We have yet to discuss your punishment, bride. You weren't innocent in this. You assisted the witches. Without your help, two of our Imperial Guard wouldn't be dead, and you never would've stepped foot outside our apartment."

My stomach turned. He made it sound so neat. So simple.

Jules brushed a strand of hair behind my ear. "That's also high treason, if you didn't know."

I swallowed. "And what is the punishment for that?"

"Death," Luc said.

My stomach lurched. I knew they couldn't kill me—not without killing themselves—but the word still punched straight through my gut.

"But you're our Mortal Bride," Jules said, as if that explained everything. "We're limited in how we can punish you for your crimes right now."

Or ever. I narrowed my eyes slightly at him as he skirted the truth. It wasn't a lie.

"But don't fret." Jules pulled his curved blade, Thérèse, from its gilded sheath. "We can be quite creative."

I stiffened. My breath hitched. Stars, was he going to cut off a finger this time?

Jules twisted the blade in his hand until the hilt faced me, offering it like a gift. "Your punishment will be death. It just won't be yours."

Everything within me stilled.

No.

*No.*

I glanced up into golden eyes, serious behind his smile. There would be no mercy for me, just like there was none for these witches. Because we were lesser than them.

I would always be lesser than them, even as their soulbound.

I tried to repeat that in my head as my body begged me to soften and submit. As my hands twitched for the blade and my heart begged for the warmth it was so long denied.

But my feelings were only because of the bond. I had wanted to forget. I had wanted it to be real. I had wanted it so badly, I'd started hallucinating futures that would never happen. Could never happen, if this was the cost.

Jules held out his blade with the patience of an ambush predator, waiting as I struggled in the trap. Faint amusement twitched at the corners of his mouth as he waited for me to take it. Waited to see what I'd become.

Luc circled to my side and brushed the tear I hadn't realized was falling from my cheek. "If you wish to show them mercy, bride," he said softly, "you'll have to kill them yourself. We don't intend to rush."

I swatted at his hand. Stupid. The moment my skin met his, Luc's eyes darkened. They were more shadow than silver now, flaring with a heat that wasn't quite anger, wasn't quite hunger.

But I didn't back down. "Don't pretend this is a gift to me."

"I wouldn't. This is your punishment." Luc took the blade from Jules and pressed it into my hand. "This will be the first life you take, but certainly not the last."

My fingers closed around the hilt before I could stop them. It felt too natural. Too easy. A chill slid down my spine as I exhaled, shaky and uneven. "You can't make me a monster."

"We don't need to," Luc replied, his voice a low rumble. "You survived the bonding. That means we're a perfect match, pieces of a united whole."

Jules grinned. "You might be soft, lovely, but somewhere inside of you, there's a monster to match ours. We just want to meet her."

A pulse jumped in my throat. "Well, you're not going to today."

Luc swung out his arm. I flinched. He hadn't been aiming at me. I knew his target the second he moved. He didn't break eye contact as his arm lashed out to the side—

His fist slammed into Ilenia's skull.

A sickening crack echoed through the throne room. Through the bond. The jolt of impact in Luc's bones. The slick of blood on his knuckles. Crimson splattered across the marble. I gagged, and Jules flicked a settling rune at me a second later. My nausea faded.

But he drew another in his opposite hand. Shadows flared from his fingertips, etching a familiar shape into the air.

***Endure.***

Ilenia's body flopped to the floor, twitching. Twitching. Still twitching. She wouldn't fucking stop. And she never would, not with that rune crawling beneath her skin, preserving her life, stretching out the agony.

I stared, frozen. This wasn't justice. This was cruelty crafted into performance. "You're monsters."

"We know," Luc said, cleaning the blood from his knuckles with a rune.

I tightened my fist around the hellynx hilt. The edges dug into my palm, grounding me, anchoring me in the horror.

No matter what this witch did, I couldn't let her twitch for eternity, stuck on the edge of death. No one deserved that. Not even her. But knowing it was the right thing didn't make it easier.

This would be the first life I ever took. Me. My hand. My choice. There was no glory in it. Just the sick weight of inevitability settling deeper and deeper in my chest.

I had stepped into their path. I had tried to save lives. But the only way to save her now... was to end her.

Ilenia was already gone. Her body just hadn't caught up yet.

"Stop casting," I whispered.

Jules's rune didn't flicker. "I'll stop casting when you start stabbing."

I squeezed my eyes shut. Steadied my breath.

I could do this. I had to.

I didn't know the most humane way to kill her. There was no dignity left in this. No right answer. She was already dying, her skull crushed. If Jules wasn't casting the endurance rune, she'd already be dead.

This was just symbolic. Like my black gown. Like the collar. Like the leash. Luc had killed her minutes ago.

I was just here to finish the performance.

I slashed the blade across her throat. Blood spurted from the wound in a hot arc, joining the puddle already leaking from her skull. It should've been over. Quick. Clean. At the very least, final.

But Jules wasn't letting her die. Not yet.

Stars, Ilenia should've been dead twice over by now. Her skull was cracked open. Her throat had been cut. But her body still jerked, twitching with mindless spasms, muscles firing in senseless agony.

Bile rose in my throat. Tears burned at my eyes.

I plunged my blade into her chest.

Once.

Twice.

Again.

Again.

Still, she twitched. Still, her body clung to life. I stabbed and stabbed and stabbed until blood coated my arm, my chest. Until my world was blood, the body beneath me, and a keening whine that echoed in my ears, escaping my lips.

And Ilenia still wasn't fucking dead.

I spun on Jules and pointed the daemium blade at him. Soft conversation had resumed among the courtiers, but it died the instant they saw me point the Butcher's own knife at him.

The kings didn't react. Just watched, their eyes dark and hungry, drinking in every ragged breath I took. Their desire twisted low in my belly, impossible to ignore.

The fucking monsters.

I raised the blade higher, blood soaking my arms. "Stop cast—"

Someone moved behind me. I couldn't see them, but I didn't have to, not when the kings' gazes shifted over my shoulder. A hand brushed the back of my leg—

The world spun.

Bodies hit the floor behind me—no, in front of me. I was facing a different direction now, Luc at my side, his arm wrapped tight around my waist. Eral and the other two delegation witches lay dead, blood leaking from their noses and eyes. Beside them, Ilenia had finally gone still.

Jules held Morrena off the floor, one hand wrapped around her throat.

I recoiled at the sight. I knew who she was, what she had done. But she looked fifteen. Her body *was* fifteen. Morrena's toes weren't anywhere close to brushing the marble. It looked like Jules was strangling a child.

Those same hands that had just reached for me clawed at his grip. Why had she done that? What had she hoped to accomplish? It only hastened her delegation's deaths.

Had that been the point?

Her brown eyes found mine. Something passed through her gaze. A weight of things left unsaid.

If only I knew what things.

Shadows flared up Jules's hand, crackling like lightning against his knuckles. His claws solidified *into* Morrena's neck. Five long spikes pierced through her throat. Blood bubbled at her lips. Gurgled. Ran over his fingers. The warmth of it seeped across my hand like a phantom echo.

Jules jerked his hand up with a sharp, brutal motion. His claws tore through her like meat, hooking deep into her jaw.

Then he yanked.

He *ripped* Morrena's face off.

I gagged as bone cracked. Snapped. Her head collapsed into a pulp of crimson flesh and shattered bone—

I twisted around and vomited onto the floor.

Oh, stars. I'd seen so many bodies in the last two weeks. Felt so much blood spray my skin. But that had been something else entirely. Not murder, but a desecration.

I coughed hard, eyes stinging from the image burned behind my eyes. I didn't lift my head. I couldn't. If I looked at Morrena again, I'd vomit until nothing was left. The taste of bile lingered. Spit clung to my lips. My throat burned.

A flare of magic burst through the air.

My head jerked upwards. What now? Before the wave of heat grazed my skin, Jules shoved me backward, straight into Luc's chest. It should've been uncomfortable pressed between their two bodies like this, Ilenia's blood smearing between us, but it felt like home. I blinked, dazed, barely seeing over Jules's shoulder as he hovered protectively in front of me.

All I noticed were corpses.

I looked left. Right.

Every witch in the room besides me was dead.

Confusion rippled through the throne room. The courtiers looked around in silent, stunned disbelief, some taking cautious steps back, others whispering behind their hands.

The council moved first. Sabas and Cédric surged forward, passing the kings. Cédric stalked toward the bodies, gaze gleaming with eerie curiosity rather than fear. Roxiana and Isabeau flanked their Imperium, the Crown General's sword already in her hand. Roxiana's fingers glowed faintly with shadows, her expression unreadable. The four remaining Imperial Guard had entered the room in a flash, but they stayed back, waiting for their kings' orders.

"What just happened?" I whispered, my voice barely audible above the thick silence.

"Suicide runespell," Cédric murmured as he crouched beside Morrena's corpse, drawing tiny runes in the air. ***Reveal. Deconstruct.*** "The trigger was Morrena's death. Since it wasn't active, the glamour over it hid it entirely from our senses."

Luc didn't take his eyes off the bodies. "Sabas, find out if it was restricted to the witches from the last harvest or if all witches in the castle were affected."

"Yes, Your Majesty." With a nod, Sabas passed the Imperial Guard, heading into the hall.

"Morrena must have cast all of them." Cédric had shuffled over to Eral, casting the same runes. "None of the rest of the witches would have the power to hide runes from us—"

Ilenia twitched.

It was subtle—just the jerk of her limb, the shift of her shoulder—but I saw it. I blinked, sure I imagined it. She was dead. Jules had stopped casting. Her injuries had finally, *thankfully*, killed her.

Then shadows burst from her corpse.

The ribbons of black smoke shot out like spears, wrenching free of her ribs, spine, and joints. Her limbs arched into the air. The darkness drenched her, wrapping round every inch of her. It almost seemed to grow heavier, settling like a second layer of skin. Her body twisted, warped. Bones cracked as her mouth tore open into a shadowed grimace that kept stretching, stretching, stretching—

And then she screamed. The sound tore through the throne room, piercing and unholy. *Wrong*. My heart nearly stopped.

Ilenia was no longer a witch.

She was a wraith.

# 55

SHADOWS BURST FROM ERAL, from the other two delegation witches, and from the dozens of bodies slumped within the gold statues. Cédric stumbled back as the delegation—the *former* delegation—scrambled onto all fours and wailed.

I couldn't breathe. My lungs stuttered, trapped somewhere between a cry and a scream. My heart pounded so fast it felt like it might punch straight through my ribs. Heat flared on either side of me, radiating from the vampires squashing me between them. Luc's fingers moved fast, tracing two shapes across my back. Magic pulsed into my skin as he shifted and etched the same runes along Jules's shoulder. ***Shield. Protect.***

Jules's hands moved in tandem, casting different runes meant for the monsters ahead.

***Burn. Rend.***

His magic slammed into the wraith closest to Cédric, searing through its shadowed skin. The scent of burned flesh hit me like a slap as the monster only screamed louder. When the rending rune struck, its arm was torn clean off, but it didn't stop.

It just kept charging.

But Cédric had recovered from his shock. Shadows flared from his hand. ***Strike.***

The wraith flew backward into another behind it. They crashed to the floor in a snarling tangle over Morrena's corpse. She was the only witch who stayed still.

And she always would. If her death had triggered the spell that killed the others, there'd be no second chance for her.

But the others... the rest of the witches' deaths had powered the everlife runespells hidden somewhere on their skin.

All around the room, the golden statues toppled to the floor as the monsters inside them writhed and shrieked, born violently from death. The metal cracked as it hit marble. With each thrash of limbs, the wraiths broke free one by one. Cold sweat broke across my spine.

Magic heated the air. The heat of runes slammed into me from every direction. The Azarasians might wear silk and gems, but they were an impire of warriors first. Golden-eyed vampires surged forward, planting themselves between the wraiths and their silver-eyed soulbound.

This wasn't going to be like the last time wraiths invaded a court. The covenant tipped the scales.

"Isabeau, get the Dusk courtiers out." Luc's words were calm, nothing but ruthless focus beneath them. "Then guard the doors. We can't let them escape into the—"

The double doors burst open. A silver-eyed vampire attendant in navy and maroon livery stumbled into the chaos. He froze, eyes wide—

A wraith slammed into his back.

It had come *from* the hallway.

Well, fuck.

Luc growled. His arm snapped around my waist.

All around the room, wraiths leaped and charged. Ilenia—or whatever remained of her—lunged straight for us. She didn't look like herself anymore, but her shredded clothes still clung to her twisted, shadowy frame.

Jules's fingers moved fast. ***Strike***. The rune hit. The wraith stumbled back—

Another took its place.

Jules threw out his arm. The wraith crashed into him a second later. Luc spun us at the same moment, shifting so Jules hit his back instead of mine. If I'd still been between them, I'd have been crushed.

Fire tore through my forearm.

The breath wrenched from my lungs in a pained gasp. It wasn't my pain. Not really. It was Jules's, but the bond made it almost feel like mine. I peered around Luc's shoulder to see the wraith's shadowed maw buried in Jules's raised forearm. The shielding rune on his shoulder pulsed, holding the monster back from his chest, but his arm had been outside the shield's reach.

Flesh tore. Shadows writhed.

And then the pain vanished.

Gone. Numb. Jules was still there in the bond, but his sensations were sealed off, his suffering silenced.

The wraith hadn't stopped tearing at him.

The King of Dawn only grinned.

The wraith's head exploded in a burst of red. Not its blood. *Jules's.* He'd pulled his own blood from inside the wraith's throat, bent it to his will. The crimson arc spiraled upward, then snapped around the creature, slicing into its shadow-flesh.

Jules lifted his mangled arm. His fingers pressed together, shadows flaring from their tips. They fused into a single massive claw, sharp and solid as a spearhead.

He drove it clean through the wraith's chest.

Egh. My stomach flipped at the crunch of bone, the sickening squelch of organs.

I turned my chin until all I could see was Luc's chest, broad and unmoving. One of my hands clutched his doublet, while the other found its way around his back, fisting into Jules's tunic. I hadn't done it consciously, but touching them calmed the panicked thundering of my heart, even surrounded by chaos and death.

I forced my grip to loosen, but I couldn't make myself let go.

I glanced up. The King of Dusk still hadn't moved or spoken. That wasn't like him. His jaw was tight, silver eyes narrowed in sharp concentration. His other arm was raised, determination radiating off him in simmering waves.

I followed along the curve of muscle to his hand, crackling with shadowed runes.

***Imprison. Imprison. Imprison.***

Dread coiled low in my stomach as I twisted further to take in the scene.

Four wraiths had surrounded us. Three clawed at the marble, snapping and snarling, unable to break through Luc's magic. The fourth was trapped beneath Isabeau's boot, her magic funneling directly into it. Her fingers blazed with shadows. ***Annihilate.*** Roxiana stood with her back pressed to her beloved's, Isabeau's daemium sword raised as she scanned the rest of the room.

All around us, courtiers fought. The screams and spells blurred into a deafening roar. Three golden-eyed vampires surged runes into a wraith pinned at their feet, their soulbound standing behind them, watching their backs. Elsewhere, more groups formed—pairs, trios, quartets—all pushing back against the monsters with brutal precision.

The kings had felled wraiths single-handedly on the road to Montaurère, but they were far stronger than the average vampire. Even the elite, the favorites of their courts, the fiercest of the Azarasians, fought in numbers.

No wonder the kings had created their covenant runespell after the Isaurans turned the everlife runespell into a weapon.

A wraith tore free from one courtier's imprisonment rune, hitting the floor in a hard roll. But instead of leaping back into the fight, its head snapped toward us. With a snarl, it charged.

I shrank deeper between the kings with a startled yelp, the noise swallowed by the chaos. Luc gritted his teeth and added a fourth rune to his casting. ***Imprison***. The wraith halted mid-lunge, inches from my face.

My vision tunneled, stomach lurching. I didn't belong here. I couldn't fight. I didn't even know how to breathe through this.

"Why are they all coming for us?" My voice came out weak, more thought than question.

Luc didn't look at me, but he still answered, his tone tight with strain. "They want the strongest power in the room."

Oh. Fuck. All thirty-something wraiths in the room wanted to eat the kings first—and I was tucked into Luc's arm, weighing him down. I still couldn't feel anything from Jules, but his magic flared hot at my back, holding off however many more came at us from behind.

Fuck. Fuck. Fuck. I was going to die. Horribly. Painfully. I'd never finish another book. Never see the night sky again. Never know what I might've been, if I'd had more time. I'd always suspected it would end like this, but I hadn't wanted my death to hurt. So much of my life had hurt. Watching thralls die with smiles on their faces had been awful, but right now, I was suddenly jealous.

I forced myself to breathe. My panic probably pulsed strong enough through the bond that both kings felt it. I was already a liability, useless in a fight, in anything outside reading and stacking shelves. I didn't need to become a distraction, too.

Isabeau's magic flared. The wraith at her feet finally collapsed in a steaming heap. She pivoted, stepping toward the next one Luc held. Roxiana mirrored her movement, her blade gleaming.

"No, Isabeau," Luc said. "Get her out of here."

The Crown General didn't hesitate. She slashed a rune into the air. ***Strike.*** The wraith closest to us shot backward, colliding into another behind it. They crumpled in a tangle of limbs and snarls.

"Luc—" she started.

"I can handle four wraiths," he said briskly, "but not if I have to defend our Mortal Bride at the same time."

Isabeau straightened and gave a sharp nod.

Luc released me into her waiting arms. One second I was pressed against him. The next, Isabeau stood a foot away, her grip firm on mine. She didn't speak, just yanked me back as Luc raised both hands, shadows flaring at his fingertips. Jules mirrored him on the other side. His right arm was already healed, a feral smile on his lips.

Thank the stars.

I didn't want to care. They'd wanted me to kill, a punishment for running. But the bond didn't care about justice or logic. It made me ache to turn back. To rip out of Isabeau's grip and stand at the kings' side, even if I couldn't do a thing to help. Even if I'd only be in the way.

Roxiana snatched my other arm. "If you don't snap out of it, Nessa, I'm throwing you over my shoulder."

I glared at her. Roxiana was my height, but far slimmer. She could still toss me over her shoulder, and we both knew it. The idea would've been funny, if everything else wasn't awful.

The Crown General and Crown Chancellor hustled me toward the throne room doors.

Body parts littered the marble floor. Shredded wraith limbs, shadow-stained skin, blood smeared in thick streaks like paint. Morrena's corpse lay in pieces, her flesh torn open and marked with deep, ragged bite wounds. Thralls slumped in the corners, their bodies savaged. Near the door sprawled the silver-eyed attendant, his torso hollowed out, ribs cracked wide around a gaping hole.

I slapped a hand over my mouth.

*Don't puke. Don't puke. Don't puke.*

And then we were through the doors, spilling into the hall.

To the left, four Imperial Guard fought against three wraiths. To the right, Cédric hurled rune after rune at five more that charged toward him. Sabas slumped against the wall behind him, blood soaking his tunic as he scrawled weak healing runes over the gaping wound in his gut.

"Fuck." Isabeau met Roxiana's gaze, looking straight past me. The logical move was to slip past the guards, get me out, and keep moving. But that would mean abandoning Sabas and Cédric.

It didn't matter that they were vampires. It didn't matter that they upheld the system that kept millions enslaved. "You can't leave them to die."

Silver and gold eyes flickered to me.

"Luc drew shielding and protection runes on me," I said. "And I'm wearing the collar. I'll stay back. If a wraith escapes the throne room, trust me, I'll scream."

"Shit," Isabeau muttered again. Then she bolted down the hall, runes glowing at her fingertips. ***Strike. Burn.*** The spells slammed into two wraiths closing in on Cédric.

Roxiana grabbed my arm and hauled me after her. I didn't resist, but I had to half-run just to keep pace. Adrenaline fought against the leaden pull in my muscles.

***Annihilate.*** Isabeau hurled the rune with all her might at the wraith closest to Cédric.

The Crown Mage stood his ground, his focus locked on the four wraiths he was still holding at bay. I didn't know him well, but the resolve in his expression was unmistakable. He'd hold until Isabeau killed them, however long it took to save himself and his soulbound.

Sabas had finally managed to slide off the floor. He was pale but upright. His fingers traced a sluggish rune into the air. ***Imprison.*** His magic joined Cédric's, faint but steady, easing some of the strain.

Then another wraith rounded the corner.

Sabas let out a sharp, hysterical laugh. "Fuck us."

The sound was so out of place, even Cédric glanced over his shoulder. His hands never stopped moving, but his focus split for a breath too long.

Roxiana shoved Isabeau's sword into my hands. I braced for the weight, but the daemium blade was light, almost deceptively so. "Hold this. Point it at any wraith that tries to eat you."

Before I could reply, she was charging toward the fight. ***Imprison. Imprison. Imprison.*** Her magic fortified Cédric's faltering spells, holding the wraiths still for a few crucial seconds.

Isabeau slammed one final burst of power into the first wraith. The blast of heat clawed at my skin, but I didn't flinch. The wraith crumpled.

She didn't stop to celebrate. She went straight for the next.

"Psst."

I barely heard the voice over all the noise. My gaze snapped left. Behind a massive painting of a massacre, there was a narrow crack in the wall. Maire's face peered through it.

Another hidden servant's entrance.

I glanced at the four councilors still locked in combat. They were too busy trying not to get eaten to notice me. I wasn't helping them. I couldn't help the kings. I was a liability everywhere, sword shaking in my hands. My fingers ached from clutching it too tight. My legs locked, then jolted forward as another wraith shrieked nearby.

There wouldn't be any wraiths in the servant's passageways. Probably.

I darted across the hall, my slippers skidding on marble smeared with blood.

Maire pushed the entrance open wider. I squeezed through, the daemium blade angled at the floor. She slammed the panel shut behind me. The brightness of morning vanished, replaced by the dim glow of runelight. My ears rang in the sudden silence, my chest still heaving.

I turned to her, wide-eyed. Sweat soaked her skin, just like mine, but she looked otherwise untouched. "How did you escape the throne room?"

Her gaze lingered on my ruined gown, my arms streaked red with Ilenia's blood, my fingers still slick with gore. For a second, she didn't speak. Just stared like she wasn't sure what I was anymore. Then she blinked and snapped back to attention. She waved me forward, toward a narrow staircase that spiraled into darkness.

"There was a servant's entrance behind where I was kneeling," she said. "Thankfully. Otherwise, I'd be dead."

I glanced back at the entrance. The kings had handed me off to their councilors for protection. Leaving them would probably get someone in trouble, but I didn't want to stay. There was nothing I could do except press myself against a wall like an idiot, clutching a sword I didn't know how to use. "Were you watching Cédric?"

She didn't answer right away. Then, quietly, "Yes. I wanted to know... if he died, I wanted to see it."

She didn't say it with sorrow. She said it with hate. Like hope. Like the only thing worse than not losing him would be missing when he died.

I didn't know what to say to that. Maire was the mother of his son. His loyal thrall in public. A woman who hated him behind his back. My situation couldn't be the same as hers, not anymore, and she knew that now. I was the kings' soulbound. I might be their prisoner, their captive, but we were heartmates.

Even collared and shackled, a heartmate would always be treated differently than a regular thrall.

Two staircases later, Maire stopped at a section of wall and pushed. It creaked open under her hand. "We should be far enough away. They had all the Isaurans from the last harvest in the throne room. The delegation only had time to cast the everlife rune on a handful of other witches, most of whom kept to the first floor—"

"Wait." I grabbed her shoulder, sudden dread twisting in my gut. "You knew that was going to happen?"

Maire looked away. "Morrena told me before they left for the apartment last night, in case the escape failed. She bound me to secrecy with a rune. As soon as the Isaurans died, I pulled as many people as I could into the thrall passageways. But I couldn't even tell them why. Some didn't come."

We stepped into a quiet hallway. The weight of what she'd done hung heavy on her shoulders. I almost reached out. I almost comforted her. I knew what it felt like to feel responsible for others' lives. Fergus. Éamon. Edda. Riona. Estrella. Tristan.

But Maire had *known*.

I couldn't reconcile that. The kings would've killed the witches. The witches struck first. One way or another, someone was always going to die.

Which was worse?

Were they both equally terrible?

Why were all the choices always awful?

I cleared my throat. "You saved who you could—"

A snarl sliced through the hall, cutting me off.

At the far end, a wraith hunched over the gaping chest of an older woman still dressed in her thrall blacks. Its shadowed claws reached into the cavity and yanked out her heart. It squeezed the organ once, then shoved it into its mouth with a wet squelch.

I didn't hear it, not really. Not over the pounding in my ears. But my imagination filled in the sound just fine.

If it saw us, that could be my chest split open. My heart devoured like fruit.

Maybe I'd get lucky and die from fear first.

The wraith jerked. Its misshapen head snapped toward us. A shrill scream tore the air.

It charged.

Maire turned and bolted.

I followed, but I wasn't a runner. Especially not in these stupid slippers. She veered left into another corridor just as I stepped on my own skirts and hit the floor hard. The sword flew from my hand, skidding across the marble.

Snarling behind me.

I twisted.

The wraith was there. Charging. Fast.

I scrambled backward like a crab, ungraceful and wild, my heels sliding against the stone, that gaping maw of shadows nearly upon me—

The wraith went flying as a blur of black muscle and claw slammed into its side.

Titus.

The hellwolf crushed the wraith beneath his paws, bones crunching. It screeched and flailed, still trying to claw, to tear, to bite.

But Titus was born to claw and tear and bite.

He tore into the monster, ripping through shadowed flesh. His massive jaws locked around its throat and yanked. Red blood sprayed the walls. The wraith spasmed, still trying to move, even as Titus sank his teeth in again and again.

He didn't just kill it. He destroyed it. Shredded it into steaming chunks. Shadowed flesh and bone vanished between his fangs with wet snaps.

Could a wraith regenerate if eaten by a hellwolf?

I didn't know. I didn't want to know.

I slid down the nearest wall, legs collapsing beneath me. My whole body shook. Fucking stars. I had almost *died.*

The panic hit me late, a wave crashing over already-trembling limbs. My vision blurred at the edges. I pressed one hand to the cold floor to steady myself, the other to the jewels at my collar. I gripped them tight, like they were a rising star pendant.

But no godstar would've saved me.

Not from that.

Only Titus.

Maire grabbed my arm and yanked me to my feet. My blood-slick skin nearly slipped through her grip. She held Isabeau's sword now. "Run, Nessa."

Titus snarled behind us, the sound wet and unrelenting. I didn't look back. I couldn't.

We ran.

My legs were shaky. My knees buckled with every other step. I couldn't tell if I was slipping on blood or unsteady from shock, from the events of the last few days, from my illness.

Maire pointed toward a door. "This way."

We sprinted for it. Maire reached the door first and threw it open. I stumbled in after her, nearly tripping again. The sound of snapping jaws and splattering gore vanished as I slammed the door shut behind us.

I pressed my forehead to the wood paneling, gulping air. My pulse thundered in my ears. Everything ached. My legs, my chest, my tailbone. I nearly collapsed to my knees.

But we'd made it. We were safe.

With a huff, I turned to Maire. I could break down later, when all the wraiths were dead. "Should we bar the door or—"

Searing heat flared at my neck, at my back. Like every protective rune cast on me activated at once. I almost screamed at the burning sensation. It cut through the haze in my brain. I spun instinctively—

Something flared in my vision. Blood, swallowed by darkness. Bark, turning to ask. Shadows, forming a word.

***Block.***

The heat around my neck and back stopped for a mere second. But whoever cast that rune wasn't strong enough to block the kings' runes permanently.

But a second was all Maire needed.

The black blade of a daemium sword slammed into my gut.

# 56

My entire existence became pain. It tore through my nerves, raw and unrelenting. Not even the kings' soothing rune could numb an agony like this. A scream built in my chest, but only a strangled breath escaped. This wasn't just physical. It was overwhelming. It was absolute.

It was *everything.*

And yet, it was also nothing, because part of me didn't feel it. Part of me already floated outside myself, my limbs distant, my fingers tingling, looking down at the fucking *sword* in my stomach. Cutting me open. Spearing through my gut. I followed the length of the black blade to its silver hilt—

And into Maire's wide, green eyes.

She looked as shocked as I felt. At the same time, just as furious... but that fury wasn't entirely mine. It pulsed beneath my skin like a second heartbeat, hot and insistent, distant but unmistakable.

Not mine, but *theirs.*

But the sorrow in her eyes was hers alone. It belonged to someone who believed this cruelty was a kindness. Of someone who wished there had been another way.

"I'm sorry, Nessa." The words scraped from her throat, like she was actually sorry for stabbing me. "If I kill you, I kill the kings and their covenant, all in one go."

My legs buckled, useless. I sank to the floor, slow and graceless, the descent out of my control. Pain pulsed through me in jagged waves.

"If there's no covenant, thrall runespells will lose their power source impire-wide. They won't be hard to recast, but I have to believe someone will find freedom." Maire kneeled beside me like we were having some tender goodbye. Like this wasn't *murder*. "And without it, most Azarasians won't have the strength to cast the genesis spell. No other human will have to carry and nurse one of their spawn. Life for most humans might not get better, but it won't get any worse."

I just stared at her. Blankly. Numbly.

She had fucking *stabbed* me.

And now she was trying to justify it.

I laughed. Or I tried to. A wet rattle tore up my throat. Blood bubbled over my lips and slid down my chin, thick and metallic.

"If it makes you feel any better, I won't survive this," Maire said. "Even if the Kings' Council and all their favorites somehow die in the attack, the Azarasians will have me killed for daring to strike against their kind."

It didn't. I tried to tell her that, but no words came. My tongue was heavy. The edges of my vision blurred, black creeping in like smoke. Her falling star pendant glistened in the light, mocking me as I died.

Her gaze dropped to the sword. "Maybe it would be better if I killed myself. It's only fitting I die on this sword after you, isn't it?"

*Stars, shut up.* I wanted to scream it. Shout it. Rage at her. She was fantasizing about her own death like we were in this together. But I couldn't even lift my head. It took everything in me to keep my eyes open.

"I'm sorry," she whispered. "It's cruel of me, asking forgiveness while you're dying at my feet."

Maire grabbed the sword's hilt and tugged.

Oh, *fuck*. It burned just as much coming out as it had going in. I slapped a hand over the gaping wound in my stomach, but blood gushed through my fingers, merging with the drying mess Ilenia had left behind on my skin. I couldn't hold it in. I couldn't stop any of it.

This was a hopeless fight. It only ended one way.

I was so tired of fighting. I had fought for so long just to stay standing, to stay alive. I didn't want to die. I had barely even lived. But what I wanted didn't matter.

It never had.

I closed my eyes and let myself sink into the heavy dark of my mind. Away from the snarling vampires, scheming humans, and hungry wraiths roaming the halls. Away from the burning agony in my belly. Away from the regretful eyes of a woman who pretended to be my friend, holding a bloodstained sword to my heart.

Away from the two other pieces of my soul, burning with rage and panic. Trying to close the distance between us. But no matter how far they were physically, they were still here. In my mind. In me.

And I hated them.

I barely knew them.

They had made me feel alive.

In another life, I think I could've loved them.

But none of that mattered now. I leaned into the bond. I wouldn't die alone. I could never die alone, not anymore. And they yelled at me to stay. Not with words, but with something deeper, some connection beyond speech. But I couldn't hold on.

I was a powerless witch. A broken, wicked, sinful girl. I had held on for a decade.

I couldn't hold on any longer.

"I'm sorry," Maire whispered again, softer than before. I imagined her pulling her arm back. Preparing to stab, to finish it.

The blade never came.

Not to me, at least.

A tingle flared through my ribcage, almost like pain but not quite. Dull. Distant. I barely felt it beneath the agony still radiating from my wound. My brow furrowed. Had I died? Shouldn't that have hurt more?

Maire gasped. "Stars save me."

Even before I opened my eyes, I knew what I'd see. My body already knew. I slumped forward, my head thudding against a strong back. My bloodied fist clenched in soft silk. Heat radiated through me, chasing away the searing burn that still screamed through my nerves.

This was better.

Maybe dying wouldn't be so *terrible. I barely noticed the pain of the sword jutting through my ribcage, not with my soulbound gutted on the floor behind me. Jules dropped to his knees and scrambled toward our bride.*

*I wanted to turn. I wanted to take her into my arms. Take both of them into my arms. She had almost died. Was still dying. But I stayed where I was, crouched before my heartmates, my gaze leveled coldly at the trembling human who'd dared to harm what was mine—*

The heat of magic pulsed into me. It surged through my chest, rushing through blood and bone, knitting me together with threads of shadow. I gasped, eyes fluttering open.

Ruby-ringed fingers moved in front of me, tracing the same shape over and over. ***Heal. Heal. Heal.*** Jules's hand didn't shake. His casting was steady, even as blood trickled from a pour down my side, pooling on the floor between us.

Luc slowly rose to his full height before me. My cheek dragged against his lower back. My hand stayed fisted in the back of his doublet. I held on, trying to stay in my body, no matter how badly my mind wanted to float away. Before I could crumple, Jules caught me, strong arms slipping around my waist.

"I've got you, lovely girl," he murmured, his voice low and warm. "You're alright. You're safe."

I blinked slowly at him, then past him to the king now standing tall and bloodied before us. Luc glared down at Isabeau's sword sticking out of his torso. His voice was flat. "Is this my general's sword?"

Maire paled. "I—I... she—"

Luc raised a hand, silencing her. "Quiet, thrall. I wasn't speaking to you."

Maire jerked, but fell silent. I couldn't see the back of her neck, but I knew her thrall runespell had flared, activated again with Luc's order.

Jules gently swept his hands over my gown. The rune-woven fabric had already started knitting itself back together, but a small tear remained. He slipped his fingers through, brushing against my skin. ***Soothe***. Normally, I would've flinched, pulling away from someone grazing my soft, imperfect body.

But now, I only leaned into him. Fisted my other hand in his tunic. Loose strands of his hair tickled my cheek, slipping free from the knot at his nape. His presence sparked through me. It made me feel like myself again, if just for a moment. My flesh might have mended, but something in me still felt adrift, detached, not quite real.

Stars, I had almost *died*.

"Lovely," Jules said. "Luc asked you a question."

I blinked at him, trying to focus. "What?"

He stood, pulling me upright with him. "Where did you get Isabeau's sword?"

I blinked some more. What?

Jules slid one arm around my waist, steadying me, while his other hand disentangled from mine and closed around the sword's hilt. He pulled the weapon from Luc.

The King of Dusk didn't even flinch. But I did. A phantom pain lanced through my chest. Blood welled from his wound, thick and fast, spilling down his side in a dark rush, soaking through his shirt, dripping onto the stone floor.

It wasn't *healing*.

Panic knifed through my numbness, sharp and sudden. Just like my wound seconds ago, red soaked the fabric faster than the repairing runes could catch up.

Jules's grip tightened at my hip. "He's fine, lovely. Daemium wounds don't heal on their own. They need magic, that's all."

As he spoke, Luc calmly lifted a hand and sketched a rune over his chest. ***Heal***. Shadows flickered to life at his fingertips, flaring faintly as the magic sank into his body. His blood trickled from a stream to mere drops. He had enough power to repair the damage, even after dawn.

Jules handed him the sword, then added his own rune for good measure, drawing it clean and swift through the air. The rest of the wound closed over immediately.

*Isabeau's* sword. That's what Luc had asked me about. I hadn't answered. My gaze flicked to his face. His expression hadn't changed, but the bond betrayed him. The ripple of worry. The faint thread of tension.

Not for himself.

For us, his soulbound, even though we stood alive and uninjured before him.

And beneath that, a quieter thrum of concern for Sabas and Cédric. For Roxiana. For Isabeau.

Did they think I'd taken the blade from their general's corpse?

"Roxiana gave it to me," I said, my voice a whisper. "She told me to stand back while she and Isabeau helped Sabas and Cédric. They were in the hall outside the throne room. Didn't you see them?"

Luc shook his head. "We didn't use the door. It was quicker to use the throne as a runegate to this floor."

"Oh." Normally, I'd be full of questions. But the knowledge just... was. "I didn't know you could do that."

"It's daemium, too." Jules smiled, though it barely touched his eyes. "And we were desperate. I don't recommend sitting on it until we remove the runespell, unless you want to fall straight through the seat—"

"Why aren't I dead?"

Jules froze mid-sentence. His expression blanked in an instant. In perfect sync, he and Luc turned toward Maire. They hadn't looked at her since entering. She wasn't a threat, not to them. But now, the thrall raised her chin, eyes narrowed in a hard fury. Gone was the meek human she'd pretended to be.

A minute ago, she'd apologized for stabbing me. Now, it looked like she regretted not finishing the job.

The kings saw it.

And their gazes went beyond cold. They turned lethal.

If two vampires stared at me like that, I'd collapse on the spot. But Maire only met their eyes and glared back. Her fists clenched at her sides. The only sign of her fear was how tightly she held herself together, as if daring herself not to flinch.

Luc spun Isabeau's sword in his hand like it was a dagger. "Because we don't want you to be. Not yet, at least."

She glared. "Fuck you—"

"Don't speak again."

Her voice cut off instantly. She jolted, shoulders snapping tight. Luc's earlier command had only bound her to silence for a moment, but this one locked her jaw completely.

"Good idea. I don't want to hear her voice ever." Jules tilted his head. "Actually... stay still and open your mouth."

He stepped forward, taking me with him. The kings didn't exchange a glance, didn't speak. They passed me between them with the seamless coordination of instinct. I leaned into Luc. I shouldn't have. I couldn't.

But I did.

I was too weak. Too raw. Too numb to resist the pull of safety. The bond hummed with his presence, a steady pressure of attention against my mind, protective and focused.

Luc didn't move as Jules reached out. Maire didn't flinch. Couldn't flinch. Her eyes widened slightly, some silent realization blooming behind them as Jules's fingernails darkened into shadowed claws.

He shoved his thumb into her mouth—

—and ripped out her tongue.

There was no scream. Just a wet, awful sound as blood sprayed from her mouth. It splattered against the floor. Jules's chest. The collar of Luc's doublet. My chin.

I didn't scream either. I didn't cry or vomit or even blink. I should've said something. I should've felt *something*. But all I felt was Luc beside me, his body a wall of warmth, his hand steady on my back.

And yet... beneath that, buried so deep I almost missed it... was the faint pulse of disgust. Of horror. This wasn't right.

Maire reeled backward, clutching at her face with both hands. Blood streamed between her fingers. Her eyes went wide with pain, her body spasming as her mouth worked around the wound, soundless.

No rune dulled that pain. The kings didn't offer mercy.

Jules flicked his hand, flinging the severed muscle aside. "I wish I could take the time to take you apart piece by piece, Maire. But we'll have to do this quickly." Jules drew a pattern on her shoulder. ***Suspend. Endure.*** "We've a bride and castle to secure."

He stepped back, tugging her with him. Maire stumbled forward, blood still pouring from her open mouth. Her eyes were glazed with shock, but her body obeyed.

Jules took her left wrist.

Luc took her right.

Their canines elongated, shadows curling like smoke from their mouths. They didn't speak. Didn't hesitate.

They plunged their fangs into her wrists.

Maire screamed, a broken, wet sound, barely human. The agony of the bite collided with the wound in her mouth. Her spine arched, her legs buckled, but she didn't collapse.

The runes wouldn't let her.

I barely flinched. I should have. I should have tried to pull away, to scream, to cry, to move. But Luc still held me in his arms, and if he let go, I'd crumple to the floor.

So I stayed where I was, Luc's grip the only thing keeping me upright as Maire writhed in front of us. Only inches away, she twisted and jerked in their grasp. No venom. No mercy. Only hunger and vengeance.

And I just *watched*. Watched as they drained her, an echo of heat filling my body as her lifeforce became theirs. Watched as they lapped at her crimson *blood, devouring more and more. The taste of the thrall burst across my tongue, heady and rich. Not nearly as sweet as our bride, but her hatred, her terror, her pain made it intoxicating. A thrill I couldn't ignore.*

*When only drops remained, I pulled back—*

Maire's body crumpled between them, snapping me back into my own mind. Whether I'd slipped into Luc or Jules, I didn't know. Maybe both.

Her knees hit stone first, then her hip, then her cheek. A final twitch rippled through her limbs as she slumped fully to the floor, ragged breaths dragging through her mangled mouth.

The suspension and endurance runes still glowed faintly on her skin. They kept her alive. Barely. How much blood was even left in her veins? The runes didn't care. As long as the kings fed the runespell magic, they could keep her heart beating for days. Weeks. Centuries, if they wanted. Just like Jules had done to his own father.

Jules licked the blood from his lips. "What a waste. Cédric is going to be so disappointed."

Luc turned without a word, sliding his arm more firmly around my waist. I barely registered the movement. I followed, legs moving because his body willed mine forward and not because I had the strength to do it myself. Jules fell into step beside us, his boots leaving a trail from the blood-slick stone.

"I'll be back for you later, Maire." Jules waggled his fingers at the twitching thrall. "For now, lie on the floor and think about what you've done."

We passed through the doorway into the corridor. From somewhere deeper in the palace, the sounds of battle echoed—inhuman snarls and the terrible wail of someone dying. My legs buckled slightly.

Luc glanced at Jules, his voice quiet but certain. "Take her to the den. She needs—"

He didn't get the rest out.

A snarl split the air.

A wraith barreled around the far corner, its shadows writhing, claws already extended. It saw us and screamed.

An arm cinched tight around my waist. Before I could react, I was plucked off the floor and cradled against a blood-slick chest. Jules. He didn't pause. Didn't wait. He turned and strode in the opposite direction, boots slapping against stone as he carried me away from the threat.

Away from the wraith.

Away from *Luc.*

My numbness shattered, fear flooding in through the crack. I squirmed in Jules's grip, trying to turn my head. I wanted to reach for Luc. Wanted to grab the King of Dusk and drag him with us.

"Put me down."

"No."

"I thought the whole reason for the covenant runespell was so you'd have double the magic when facing a wraith?" My voice cracked, something frantic bubbling under the words.

Jules didn't answer. He didn't look back. He kept walking. Steady, purposeful. But I twisted in his arms, just enough to glimpse over his shoulder. Luc's gaze didn't waver from us as we retreated.

"Wraiths are difficult to kill for a regular vampire, little witch." He cracked his neck, the sound as sharp as bone snapping. "I'm not a regular vampire."

The wraith closed the distance. Luc didn't move.

Not at first.

Then his hands shifted, his fingers elongating into clawed shadows. But they went further than claws. His arms darkened to the elbow, black scales crawling up his skin like armor made of smoke. The Conqueror waited still until the very last second.

Then he lunged.

Jules turned the corner, cutting Luc from view.

I couldn't see him anymore. But I heard it. The sound of tearing. Screeching. And beneath it all—bone breaking, flesh ripping, the low growl of a furious vampire.

His perverse thrill thudding in my chest.

We passed into another hallway. Shouts echoed from distant rooms. Something wailed. Something else screamed. I buried my head in the crook of Jules's neck. A part of me yelled at myself to snap out of it, to not just slump in the King of Dawn's arms like a child.

But every time I tried to surface, the images flashed through my mind.

The sword in my gut.

Blood streaming through my fingers.

My vision fading until all I saw was Maire, watching me die.

Like I had watched her die.

Like I had *felt* her die.

Something shrieked, piercing through me. My body went rigid in Jules's arms. I turned my head, peeking out at the world.

Three wraiths snarled at the far end. They surged forward with that terrible inhuman wailing.

Jules didn't stop. I twisted my hands in his tunic, white-knuckled, bracing myself for the inevitable collision. But before they reached us, Jules veered suddenly, slipping through an open doorway onto a narrow balcony high above the palace grounds.

"Where—?"

"Hold on."

Without hesitation, he stepped up onto the balustrade.

And jumped.

I shrieked as wind tore through my hair. My stomach dropped. The stone walls of Dawnspear blurred past us, white and gold.

Then—

We hit the ground.

The impact echoed through my legs as his knees bent to absorb the force before he surged upright again in one fluid motion.

And kept going.

Like he hadn't just hurled himself off a fourth-floor balcony. I craned my head, breath still caught in my chest, to glimpse the narrow edge we'd fallen from.

A little giggle escaped my lips. "You're insane."

"I'm lazy," Jules said with a shrug. "This was the easier option."

The giggle didn't stop. "Only you would consider leaping off a building the easier option."

He grinned, but he couldn't hide his concern. "Most vampires would consider leaping off a building easier than facing three wraiths."

Jules approached the base of a statue of a snarling hellynx, a wide section of the pale stone embedded with carved daemium. ***Gate. Distance. Path. Arrival. Cross.*** A runegate, right there in the garden.

Without hesitation, he pressed a bloodstained palm to the stone. The gate responded at once. Shadows twisted across its surface, exploding to life with a pulse of magic. The black shimmered to reveal... darkness? I could barely see what lay beyond.

Jules stepped forward. The daemium's warmth wrapped around us like a living thing, its shadows thick and heavy.

Then we were somewhere else entirely.

Somewhere pitch black.

I blinked into the void, startled by the sudden absence of light. My heart skipped painfully.

Jules shifted his grip on me. His fingers squeezed my thigh—gentle but grounding—and I tightened mine around the silk of his shirt, curling closer to him. My face pressed to his shoulder. Slowly, my pulse settled, breath syncing with the rhythm of his steps.

One of his hands lifted, fingers slipping away from my skin to trace a quick pattern through the air.

***Light.***

Golden light sparked to life at his fingertips. Runelights carved into the rock walls burst as we passed them, casting our shadows across the cavern walls.

I gasped.

We were surrounded by stone on all sides. The ceiling arched overhead, draped with stalactites like sharp teeth. The walls glistened, veins of daemium carving through the rock. Only the floor stood in contrast—a smooth plane of polished stone, seamless and unnaturally perfect.

This wasn't a natural cavern.

Jules didn't let me linger or stare. He moved forward with quiet purpose, his steps echoing softly. The further we walked, the more daemium threaded through the walls. We must have headed toward Toreth's starcrater, the magic from the demon's Fall penetrating deep into the ground.

"Where are we?" I asked, voice thin.

"Under Dawnspear, near our den."

He said it like it was obvious. I should've flinched at the use of *our*. Should've corrected him. But I didn't. I didn't have the strength to fight the word, or what it implied.

Instead, I asked, "Why? Is the apartment not safe?"

"Thralls can access the apartment," he said. "No one else can enter the den. You can't even compare the two."

We approached a door—if it could even be called that. It towered above us, daemium-dark and rune-carved. ***Ward. Protect. Shield. Barrier. Ward. Protect. Shield. Barrier.*** The magic was so strong it pulsed in the air, a threat carved into every line, unmistakable to anyone who approached.

To try to enter the Imperium's den without permission would mean death.

Jules swiped his hand along my waist, then pressed it against the door. Pain flared in my palm. He'd chosen a sharp section, letting it puncture his flesh. The runes drank deep, greedily devouring my blood smeared on his skin, and his own leaking in a slow trail from his palm.

The door opened with a low, grinding groan.

Inside, the flicker of golden runelight greeted us. It danced across the room's rock walls, casting long, gentle shadows. Inside, the ceiling above was also perfectly smooth, as though carved from an unbroken slab. Plush maroon rugs softened the rock floor.

Jules led us through an antechamber, then into a larger room with low sofas, a wall of bookshelves, and a modest table with four chairs. There were no doors between any of the spaces, only open archways.

He passed through another. More runelights flared to life.

My gaze focused on a massive bed, draped in thick blankets the color of dried blood.

I froze.

The room looked exactly like the hallucination I'd had earlier. The one in the bathing chamber. The one I thought had come from my exhausted mind.

The one with the baby.

But I had never been here. Not until now.

My breath caught. I was losing it. I had to be.

My fingers slid limply from Jules's shirt. My senses blurred, each breath a labor. The torture. The delegation. The wraiths. The sword. Maire. All of it spun behind my eyes in a blur of blood and shadow.

My body couldn't hold the weight of it anymore. The memories, the betrayals, the things I'd witnessed. The things I'd survived.

It was too much.

The fog tried to pull me down.

This time, I let it, sinking into the blissful dark.

# INTERLUDE 6

My world was little more than screams and blood.

I stumbled through Duskfell's black hallways, limbs and organs strewn across the floor. Human parts. Witch parts. Vampire parts. The terrifying sight was familiar, like I'd seen it before. But where—

I turned the corner.

A wraith lifted its face from a corpse, strings of gore trailing from its mouth. Its dead eyes snapped straight to me.

Fuck.

The shadow-creature moved in a blink. It lunged—

No. No, no, no. I screamed and scrambled back—

The monster slammed into me.

No. *Through* me.

A scream split the air behind me. I turned in time to see the wraith sink its claws into a silver-eyed vampire. They crashed to the ground. The wraith scooped out a fistful of glistening flesh and shoved it into its mouth before burying its head in the screaming vampire's torso.

I slapped a hand over my mouth and staggered away.

This couldn't be real.

I wasn't in Duskfell. The massacre in Dawnspear was over. Before I was here, I was in Luc's head, watching him in the castle above. The halls had been cleared.

But now... I was sleeping, still in Luc's head. But this time, he was sleeping, too. If I focused, I could almost feel the kings' warmth surrounding me, Jules's arm across my stomach and Luc's breath against the back of my neck. I was in their den. Safe. Whole.

This was a nightmare. Luc's nightmare. Nothing more.

But I didn't stop running. Even if this was only his imagination run wild with recent memories, I didn't want to see anyone else torn apart.

I rounded the next corner—

And came face to face with Corinne.

My jaw dropped. Luc's Corinne. Not a painting, but a woman standing tall before me. Blood splattered her torn azure gown. A long, slender sword hung from her grip, the black blade slick with fresh gore. Her silver eyes were narrowed with the focus of a seasoned warrior. She was fierce. She was beautiful. She was regal.

Godstars, she was perfection.

She was also very, very pregnant.

My brain stopped.

Corinne was *pregnant.*

Someone walked through me. Luc. He rushed forward, axe in hand. He slammed the blade into the marble and pulled Corinne into his arms. His mouth found hers in a kiss that was desperate and possessive. I watched, stunned.

When he pulled back, his hands remained on her, one on her ass and the other splayed across her rounded belly. His silver eyes burned, bright with lust... but also with undeniable love.

Oh.

*Oh.*

I had known Luc had loved her. The Conqueror wouldn't keep a portrait on his desk and a grave in his palace garden for someone who didn't matter. But I hadn't known he loved her like this.

Just like I hadn't known Corinne had been *pregnant.*

I'd never asked Luc if he had a child. He was over five hundred years old. It wouldn't have surprised me.

But I didn't think he did.

Which meant...

"Where's Yseult?" Luc asked, reluctantly dropping his hand from her belly to grip his axe's hilt.

"She's down a floor," Corinne said with a velvet rasp. Fuck, she even sounded perfect. "Not overly panicked but..."

"But we're in a palace overrun with wraiths," Luc finished, jaw tightening. "We'll get her, and then I'm bringing you both to our den. They can't reach that deep into Duskfell."

"You can't leave, Luc."

Luc stiffened. "Corinne—"

Corinne gripped his lapels. "Marisol's dead. Our people are bleeding in the halls. You're their king. I don't care that you're three years from your hundredth birthday. If anyone has a problem with your age, they can try prying the crown from your hands. If a wraith isn't killing them right now, you will."

Luc stared at her. "Stand with me," he said. "Be my queen."

Corinne gasped, her eyes widening. "Luc, I—"

"Did you just propose in the middle of a massacre?"

All three of us turned.

Jules leaned against a wall, tossing a sword from hand to hand like it weighed nothing. His hair was pulled back, his pale cheeks streaked with blood. The crimson slicked his arms all the way to the elbows. Apparently, digging through wraith chests had always been one of the Butcher's hobbies.

Luc glared. "Did you interrupt the middle of my proposal?"

Jules grinned, entirely unrepentant. "Yes."

Corinne sighed, a fond exhale. "He's right, Luc. This isn't the time."

"As soon as the palace is secure, it will be the time—"

Luc cut off mid-sentence, his voice trailing into silence. I frowned and glanced over at him. That wasn't very... Conqueror of him. He was younger in this memory. Maybe that was it. But he was staring, completely still. Jules and Corinne had gone silent at his side.

I followed their gazes across the hall. Bodies littered the Duskfell throne room, visible through the thrown-open doors. All dead—except for a pale, dark-haired man dressed head-to-toe in black. He stood over the corpse of a dark-haired vampire, her features the same sharp elegance as Luc and Roxiana. That had to be Luc's grandmother and the former regent, Marisol Vela.

The stranger's pose held the lazy grace of a predator utterly unbothered by danger, one hand tucked in his pocket as he stared down at the dead vampire. He took in her cracked-open chest and the gaping hollow where her organs used to be with the disinterest of someone inspecting a scuffed shoe. Only half his profile was visible, veiled by a long fall of ink-dark hair, but what I could see made the breath rush from my lungs.

When his eyes flicked up, they were entirely black. Not dark. *Black.* Twisting, swirling shadow speckled with silver like a star-scattered sky.

Oh my fucking stars, that was a fucking *demon.*

He had to be. *It* had to be? Demons weren't technically male or female, but if that was who I thought it was...

I had pictured him differently.

I almost laughed. Like I could've imagined him right, no matter how many descriptions filled *The Soulborne Queen.* He made the average vampire look like a human. His beauty was bright, divine, blinding.

Almost incomprehensibly so.

Motherfucking Azaras, in the flesh.

Sort of. This was still a dream. I wasn't really here. Azaras couldn't see me any more than Luc or Jules or Corinne could, all of them a memory.

This was as close as I ever wanted to get.

How had Karra walked up to *that* with the intent to seduce and kill? I'd have passed out the second those eyes turned my way.

For a second, Azaras stared at us.

We stared back.

Down the hall, someone died a horrible death, the wet, meaty sound of it echoing in the silence.

A flicker of movement behind Azaras caught my attention. A wraith scrambled up from a blood-soaked corner of the throne room and launched itself at the demon. Craving the power pulsing from him in waves.

Azaras exploded.

One second, a man. The next, a twisting mass of darkness that tore the wraith to shreds. Heat slammed through the air, hot enough that Luc and Jules both tensed. Corinne stumbled back a step. Blood splattered everywhere. Bits of monster rained down like meat.

Eww.

The shadows didn't solidify back into a man. Azaras drifted forward in his truest form, an unnatural darkness that made my insides scream. It was getting closer, and I was standing here like an idiot—

"No."

Luc's voice cut through the panic stampeding in my brain. He stepped forward, positioning himself in front of Jules and Corinne. He looked nothing like his sire, but in that moment, I saw the resemblance in the way they stood. Unbreakable. Untouchable. Eternal.

The future Conqueror King stared down the Beast King and didn't flinch.

The shadows vanished. Between one blink and the next, the throne room was empty of fallen godstars.

All that remained was the echo of his voice, low and mocking. "As you wish, Your Majesty."

In his place sat a sharp crown of daemium, twin to the one the kings had worn during the audience.

"Well, no one can argue with that," Jules said after a heavy pause.

Luc just stared. Jules nodded toward the throne room, then tipped his chin at his soulbound. "Aren't you gonna...?" He wiggled his fingers in the direction of the crown.

Luc didn't so much as glance at it. "Azaras can keep his crown," he said, voice low. "He came to check if Marisol was dead, nothing more."

Jules straightened. "Luc—"

"No, Julien." Luc's tone sharpened as he turned toward him. "Azaras isn't giving me his kingdom. He abandoned it to rule his hell hundreds of years ago. It's not his to give."

Jules rolled his eyes and muttered, "Save some vitriol for Allegra Isaura, Lucey. She didn't even bother to hide her signature on those everlife runespells."

Luc's jaw clenched. "I don't need to save any vitriol for that witch. I have enough for both of them."

Something shifted in the dark hallway. A snarl cut through the air. A wraith burst around the corner and lunged straight for Jules's exposed back, its claws stretched.

I slapped a hand over my mouth, biting back a shout. I knew this was the past. I knew Jules survived this night and hundreds more after it. But my heart still jumped into my throat, wild with panic for the Butcher.

My captor.

My king.

My soulbound.

I didn't want him to get hurt.

And I couldn't even blame that on the bond. This surge of protectiveness wasn't self-preservation. This wasn't real. This Jules wasn't even my soulbound, technically.

The concern was *mine*.

Heat flared past me. ***Strike. Burn.*** Luc's runes ignited the air, searing a line straight toward the creature. The wraith was flung across the room, its shadows sizzling like flesh against flame.

Jules twisted toward Luc, catching his gaze. His eyes widened.

A scream tore through the air behind me, high-pitched and agonized.

Luc spun. I spun.

He had told me Corinne died during the massacre at Duskfell. I'd seen wraiths tear through too many bodies today. I thought I knew what to expect.

The truth was worse.

Three wraiths had buried their arms *inside* her. Corinne's silver eyes went wide as her skin paled. Her mouth stretched in agony as the monsters tore her open, rooting around and pulling out chunks of red.

They ate her lifeforce.

They ate her flesh.

They ate her organs.

They ate her *baby*.

I spun and gagged. Oh my fucking stars, it had its hand in her belly. I could *not* watch this. I stumbled away blindly through the carnage. Like if I walked far enough, I could walk right out of this terrible nightmare.

Corinne had died hundreds of years ago. I couldn't do anything to change it. I couldn't do anything to help.

Behind me, Luc roared. The sound wasn't human. It wasn't even vampire. It shook the ground like thunder and cracked through my bones like a godstar's fury. Power burst into the air. Raw. Unfiltered. It scorched the space behind me, blistering heat flaring across my back.

He hadn't cast a rune. He'd struck on blind instinct.

The wraiths screamed, a horrible, dying wail. Jules flew past me in a blur of motion, sprinting to his soulbound's side.

Somewhere under all the chaos, Corinne gagged.

She was choking on her own blood.

I started running.

I didn't know where. I couldn't see through the blur of tears, couldn't think past the screaming in my head. There was only blood and death and terror.

All I knew was I had to get away.

Get away, *get away, getaway*—

I slammed into something warm and familiar.

My entire body went slack. If strong arms hadn't caught me, I would've crumpled straight to the floor. But they did. They tightened around my waist, steadying me. All the tension, all the fear, drained from me. Entirely.

I slumped against a firm chest. My cheek settled against soft silk right above the slow, steady beat of a heart. I breathed in a scent I knew in my bones.

I wasn't safe in these arms, but I'd never felt safer in my life.

Lips brushed my forehead. "Wake up, Nessa."

# 57

THE FUNERAL DIRGE ECHOED through the amphitheater. Thirteen wagons rolled through the dirt, carrying the bodies of the fallen. Most bore rune-carved caskets—their occupants too mangled by the wraiths to be shown—but Estrella and Tristan lay in the open, dressed in their finest silks and bound with silver-gold thread.

I tried not to look at them. Their wagon had led the procession, following behind the kings and me along the winding road from Dawnspear to the amphitheater carved into the mountain's base. Now, their loved ones would accompany them the rest of the way, escorting their bodies to family plots.

Nine soulbound pairs and three unbound vampires. Twenty-one Azarasians. The massacre at Duskfell had apparently claimed five times as many, but the Impire hadn't experienced a single day of loss like this in nearly four centuries, not even during their sieges.

And that number didn't include the humans and witches slaughtered or transformed.

I faced the stands, rising high into the sky around the circular field. The amphitheater had enough space for two hundred thousand, nearly the entire Azarasian population. Only half that number had attended today, but every one of them stood cloaked in black, silent while the last of the wagons departed.

There wasn't a single silver, gold, or iron collar in sight.

Except mine.

I wasn't the only one who noticed. The hairs on the back of my neck rose under the weight of all those luminous stares. I'd heard someone whisper something about it when I first entered, but the sharp cut of the Conqueror's glare had silenced any further comments.

It didn't stop them from looking. From wondering. I'd tried not to fidget through the entire ceremony, but I couldn't keep my heartbeat from racing. That was as noticeable to a vampire as tapping feet or wringing hands.

All the Azarasians knew what the witches had done during the past two nights. But only a handful of the kings' favorites knew what I had done. If everyone had known...

Stars, I'd have passed out from the weight of their glares. Even a half-dozen was nearly fatal.

But at least it was over. I hated that they made me attend this—which, of course, was exactly why I was here. I might have gotten out of killing the witches, but my punishment was still death.

Just in a different form.

"Nessa?"

I tore my gaze from the stands and glanced to my right. Luc, dressed fully in black. The dirge had ended, the last of the wagons gone from the amphitheater, and the vampires in the stands had begun shuffling to the exits. Luc had his hands locked behind his back as he watched me, watched his subjects. He wore the mask of the callous Conqueror.

Underneath the mask, his emotions gathered like pressure before a storm. Anger. Unease. The faintest thread of fear. All anchored by a relentless, possessive resolve. Because I was his. I would always be, no matter *what happened between us. She could try to run a thousand times. Kill a thousand of my Imperial Guard. Stand watch over a thousand funerals. And Jules and I would still call her ours.*

*The bond demanded it.*

*And I didn't want to resist—*

I shook his thoughts away. Reading Luc was getting easier by the day as the soulbond settled between us.

I didn't say anything. I stared back at him. I couldn't fully remember the dream, but I'd never forget the way Luc had looked down at Corinne. The mother of his unborn child. The beautiful, fearless warrior. The Queen of Dusk That Never Was. I had already envied her beauty, but now I burned with jealousy.

She was everything I wasn't and everything I wanted to be. Next to her, I'd never compare.

Yet I was Luc's soulbound heartmate. The bond made him want *me.*

It was a hilarious twist of fate.

And I wished I didn't feel any of that, but I did... and Luc knew it. Both kings knew. If I could read every buried emotion behind their masks, then they could see everything behind mine. My insecurity. My confusion. My self-loathing, desperation, and hope.

What a fucking mess.

After a moment, the King of Dusk simply beckoned me forward and started toward the tunnel, where two vampire attendants held Wrath and Cala's reins.

Luc hadn't let me stray further from him or Jules than a few feet since I woke. The bed had been cold when I struggled back to consciousness, a good eighteen hours after passing out. The kings had been in the other room of the den, having slipped away in the night. After they woke from our shared bloody nightmare, my dreams had followed them as they spoke with their council.

The funeral was just the first of today's activities.

I obeyed, closing the short distance between myself and the King of Dusk. There was no point resisting. I had no power to resist. No energy, either. I might not have been injured physically or experiencing any pain thanks to a soothing rune, but the wounds from the last few days had left other, deeper scars.

Roxiana and Isabeau fell into step behind me. The Crown Chancellor and Crown General were still expected to attend to all their duties. Now those duties also included watching me. They had both dropped to their knees immediately upon entering the kings' den, begging for forgiveness for letting me out of their sight and care.

This was their penance. If they hadn't lost me while rescuing Sabas and Cédric, their punishment would have been far worse than guard duty.

Luc halted beside Wrath, the hellsteed greeting him with a firm butt of his head. He gave the beast's snout a gentle rub, the faint warmth of his affection in my chest. Softer emotions had started creeping into my senses yesterday, but I hadn't had the chance to really consider what that meant.

Despite everything, we were one small step closer to settling into heartmates.

When I reached his side, Luc didn't move, didn't look at me, but gestured to the stirrup. "Right foot first."

I resisted the urge to glare, strained upward toward the pommel, and shoved my slipped foot into place. The stretch pulled at my hamstrings. If I were any shorter, I wouldn't have managed at all.

I didn't know why Luc bothered. I could get my foot in the stirrup, sure, but I didn't have the upper body strength to haul myself onto a giant hellsteed.

His hands were on my hips a moment later. With one smooth lift, he boosted me up, and I swung my leg over the saddle. Luc settled behind me a second later, far more graceful.

I stayed stiff-backed in his arms, resisting the urge to sink into his warmth. This discomfort was different from the first time I rode with Luc, back when I thought he and Jules were lords. I still wasn't at ease with their bodies, but that discomfort felt insignificant now.

I was made to *lure* them. I was a witch. I had tried to escape. I had failed.

I had nearly died.

Every fact, every truth of the last two days, sat between us, a heavy presence in our soulbond. The kings weren't avoiding any conversation. They didn't leave things left unsaid to fester... but this was festering anyway. Our issues couldn't be reconciled with a conversation.

I wasn't sure they ever could be.

My hands fisted around the pommel. I twisted, just enough to catch a glimpse of Jules standing in one of the archways beneath the stadium's stone seating. His white-blond hair looked even paler against the black of his mourning clothes, the rubies in his ears gleaming like droplets of blood. He was speaking quietly with two other vampires, a silver-eyed woman with dark hair who looked familiar and a golden-eyed man with a shaved head.

After giving sharp nods to Jules's words, the two Azarasians turned and slipped into the shadows of the corridor, disappearing from sight.

Bright golden eyes met mine.

In a blink, Jules stood beside Wrath. "Leaving without me? How rude, darling."

Luc didn't glance over. He pulled on his hellsteed's reins, urging the beast into a steady walk. "You'll catch up."

"Sure," Jules said, entirely unbothered, already mounting Cala in one fluid motion. "But it's still not very nice."

"Are Luisa and Nico leaving today?" Luc asked, his voice cool.

"Uh-huh," Jules said with a nod. "They'll take Toreth's starcrater to Tenebra de Mar, then sail out to Surrosa. It shouldn't take them too long to hunt down Baz and André."

I turned my gaze forward, not even blinking at the names. More unfamiliar people and places. If I asked, they'd answer. But I didn't care enough to ask. If it impacted my life, I'd find out then.

"They wouldn't have to leave at all if you had Baz and André check in regularly like the other Blades."

Jules's sigh carried through the bond, tinged with an affectionate kind of annoyance. "You know Baz."

"We've been their kings for four centuries," Luc said.

Jules waved that comment away, like it was irrelevant. "I'm summoning them back, aren't I?" He paused, but Luc didn't reply. Jules released a long sigh. "They're going to fucking hate this."

I stayed quiet and let their conversation wash over me. We rode out from the amphitheater into the city streets, the rhythmic clop of hooves echoing off stone walls. Roxiana and Isabeau followed behind on their own hellsteeds, two Imperial Guard trailing after them.

My gaze wandered as we climbed the winding roads. Gilded bridges and stone paths snaked up the mountainside between buildings and estates of white stone. Every vampire we passed wore black, even those who hadn't attended the funeral. They had all at least watched the procession through the streets.

The kings turned into a wide square, heading toward a massive runegate. We may have ridden down the mountain the regular way, but there was no need to spend hours going uphill when we could get there in seconds.

Pain lanced through my palm as Luc drew blood from his hand to activate the gate. With a shudder, the dark daemium surface became a bright square before a wall of roses.

I didn't react as the runegate's warmth washed over me. Much of the city still mourned below, but a few vampires and their thralls moved through Imperium Square. A cluster of them lingered near the rose-covered wall, watching—

Everything in me went still.

Watching two vampire warriors chain a naked, bleeding *body* to the wall near the gilded Sun Gate.

Maire. Hundreds of cuts lined her pale skin, but she should've been far more bloody. She would've been, if the kings hadn't drained her nearly to death the day before. Her once-vibrant golden-blond hair was matted, tangled enough to obscure her face. Thankfully. I didn't want to see her expression.

Because she twitched.

Even from here, I could see the two runes glowing on her chest. ***Suspend. Endure.*** A pang knifed through my chest, but just beneath my revulsion came a grim satisfaction. It wasn't mine. It sank into my gut anyway, warping my horror into something uglier.

I wanted to look away, but I couldn't help but watch. "Will she hang from the wall for years, suffering for eternity like your father?"

Jules snorted. "Preserving my father's body takes more than two runes. I have to protect him from birds, maggots, the weather... I don't care enough to waste my power on that traitor."

Luc's voice rumbled behind me. "Once the crows eat enough of her, she'll die."

I swallowed hard. I didn't want to ask how long that would take. I didn't want to know. Maire had tried to *kill* me. I'd never forgive her for that.

But a day later, outside the haze of numb shock, I understood why she'd done it.

If the kings hadn't reached me in time, I'd have died—and I'd have taken them with me. Would the Impire be any safer for humans afterward? Probably not. Other vampires would take the kings' place, even if they couldn't recreate the covenant. Until humans found a way to eradicate demons and their ilk—a hopelessly impossible task—we would always be subjugated.

*They*. They would always be subjugated. I wasn't human. I wasn't a thrall.

As we passed through the gate, my stomach turned. "There's no reason to make her suffer like that."

Two heavy gazes landed on the back and side of my head. I stayed rigid in the saddle. Luc stayed quiet, his stillness edged with conviction. Jules didn't speak either, but something darker simmered beneath his calm, a hunger to see Maire suffer more. Neither of them judged the knot of guilt inside me. But they didn't share it. They couldn't. Not after what she'd done.

Luc's reply was simple, absolute. "She nearly killed us."

I gritted my teeth. There was no point arguing with them. Their minds were set. Maire had tried to kill them. The Conqueror and the Butcher would never treat murder with mercy.

As we reached the forecourt, vampire attendants bustled before the steps to Dawnspear's red door. A long row of carriages and wagons looped around the body-speared fountain, a grim monument at the center of the chaos. Azarasians moved in and out of the castle, hauling trunks and crates, loading each cart to the brim.

Because we were leaving.

The kings hadn't told me, but I had listened in on them making the decision in my dreams. The courts had just moved to Montaurère for the spring and summer seasons a couple months ago, not set to return to Tenebra de Mar until the fall. But Duskfell had been the kings' permanent home for the first century of their lives. Retreating to the familiar in times of upheaval made sense.

Especially when that familiar was built onto a starcrater that Luc could partially control, thanks to his sire. I didn't exactly know what that meant, but I was sure to find out if Allegra planned another attack.

Not that it was confirmed she had anything to do with the delegation's actions. Morrena had sworn she hadn't seen her sister and had been under the control of an obedience rune, bleeding at the end of the Butcher's blade. But the kings didn't like the timing.

But another wagon off to the side caught my eye. This one wasn't like the kings' ornate transportation wagons, but more like the plain wooden ones used to collect the harvest. The benches along either side were lined with thralls wearing silver, gold, and iron collars, each marked with glowing runes.

***Suppress. Submit. Obey.***

It was a wagon full of witches.

My frown deepened. I hadn't heard anything about that. "Are you removing all witches from the castle?"

Silence.

I twisted around. The kings didn't glance at each other, but their expressions turned eerily blank. Not that they could hide from the bond. Cold resolve radiated from both of them, threaded with the faintest edge of discomfort. It wasn't guilt. They didn't do guilt. But they knew their answer would land like a blow.

My stomach dropped.

"We're leaving Montaurère for Tenebra de Mar," Luc said, tone even. "Most of the courtiers will travel back with us, but we're sending a battalion of warriors east to Isaura. Their delegation rebelled. Their people may do the same."

"So they're taking the witches back with them?" I asked, already bracing for the answer.

"They're sacrifices for the starcrater's runegate."

I twisted so fast I nearly slipped from the hellsteed. Luc's hands caught my waist, steadying me before I could fall. I slapped them away without thinking. The King of Dusk's gaze flattened. Jules just chuckled, but it didn't hide the quiet strain in him.

Their responses only made me angrier. "You're going to sacrifice the castle's witches to the starcrater so your warriors can get to Isaura faster?"

Luc glared down at me. "And so we can get to Duskfell faster, as well."

My heartbeat stuttered. "How many lives will that cost? Holding the gate open for an army and the entire Courts of Dusk and Dawn?"

"We don't have nearly enough sacrifices for the entire Courts of Dusk and Dawn," Jules said. "Only the army, our favorites, and the palace staff will take the runegate."

"And? How many lives will that cost?"

"All of them," Luc said.

The words hit like a slap. Something inside me jolted. I felt untethered again, almost like yesterday after Maire's attack. Like Luc's voice had severed the anchor holding me in my body.

I fought through the fog clawing at the edges of my mind. Now was *not* the time to dissociate. "You're going to kill every witch thrall in Dawnspear?"

Jules dismounted Cala as a handful of attendants broke off from packing the carriages, approaching the kings and dropping into a bow. "Half of the witches in Dawnspear are dead after last night. He meant all the harvested witches in the city."

All the harvested witches in the *city*.

The words echoed in my skull, ringing louder and louder. Oh, stars. I stared at him, dread pooling in my belly.

Luc dropped to the ground a moment later, looking up at me with those molten silver eyes. Jules was uneasy at my reaction, but Luc remained resolute. "I'm not taking the risk that they weren't involved. If their everlife runespells are hidden under a glamour, we won't know until it's too late."

"You'll find out when you kill them at the starcrater!" The words burst from me, a shout through the forecourt. Eyes flickered to me, from the attendants, from the guards, from the witches. I met their gazes, the fear in them clear. And in some... resignation.

They'd known death was coming the moment they heard about the delegation's rebellion.

I hadn't.

I was a fucking fool.

Hands settled around my waist. Luc didn't bother instructing me to climb down from Wrath's back. He knew I wouldn't respond. Blood rushed through my veins, the sound pounding in my ears. My breath came in short pants. I should have surrendered to the fog. Better that than this panic, this horror.

"The starcrater will absorb their lifeforce," Luc said. "Their deaths can't fuel their transformation if they're powering our transportation runespell."

I pulled from his grip. Or, at least, I tried. "What are the chances they're all wearing everlife runespells? Maire said Morrena and the delegation only cast them after I deactivated their obedience runes."

"Slim," Luc replied, placing one hand firmly on my lower back as he guided me toward the castle. "But slim isn't zero. We aren't taking the risk."

I wanted to dig my heels into the dirt, but Luc would throw me over his shoulder. "You're talking about killing hundreds of people."

"Luc and I would kill a million mortals to keep our Impire safe," Jules said, appearing at my other side. His arm wrapped around my shoulder, caging me between them. "To keep our soulbond safe."

Tears prickled at my eyes. Fuck this life. Fuck these vampires. Fuck everyone and everything. "You're evil."

Jules only sighed. "If this makes us your villains, we'll gladly play the role."

I stopped abruptly. "No."

The kings halted, too. They didn't drag me forward. For the moment, at least. Their hands still braced me, the three of us locked shoulder to shoulder.

"No?"

I refused to cower under Luc's chilling tone, under their height and strength and power. I forced my spine straight and lifted my chin. "No."

Heat sparked in my belly. No, *theirs*. But even the barest flicker of their desire was enough to feed my own. My nipples budded. My clit throbbed. I clenched my thighs.

Why did arguing always make us want to fuck?

The corner of Luc's lip curled. "This isn't your decision, little witch."

My fists balled at my sides. I panted hard, part rage, part grief, part lust. "Please."

Jules tilted his head. "What will you offer us in return?"

Luc frowned at his soulbound. "This isn't negotiable, Jules."

"Everything is negotiable."

I glanced between them. If it could save the Isaurans, what was I willing to give? I didn't know those witches. Their delegation had betrayed me.

But hundreds didn't deserve to die for the crimes of a few. "What do you want?"

Jules pursed his lips, eyes narrowing in thought. Then he grinned, mischievous delight pulsing through him. When Luc arched his brow, Jules said, "If we can't take the starcrater, we'll have to take the road to the Capital of Dusk. And if we do, I want to fuck you against every boulder between here and Tenebra de Mar."

I stared.

Blinked.

*Oh.*

I shouldn't have been intrigued by that. I was bartering for the lives of innocents with my *captors*. But the trickle of warmth in my core became a rush I couldn't stop. Luc's nostrils flared, his pupils swallowing the silver. Jules's gaze was already pitch black.

I cleared my throat. "Every... boulder?"

"Every." Jules leaned closer. "Single." His breath brushed my lips. "One."

Fuck. I clenched my hands in front of me, before I did something stupid like grab him. "Isn't that dangerous? There are wraiths and hellbeasts."

Jules waved away my concern. "That's not a problem for us. Might be a fun distraction between boulders."

The fire burned hotter, invading my chest. "How..." I licked my lips. I couldn't believe I was considering this. "How do you define a boulder?"

There was pride behind Luc's smirk. "Good, you're learning."

"You won't like the answer, though," Jules added.

The kings met each other's eyes for a second. Then Luc said, "A boulder is any rock big enough for you to sit on."

I swallowed. "That's too many."

Jules chuckled. "I would've said every single rock, so he's being generous."

"We'd never get there if we fucked against every rock," Luc said.

"We would." Jules paused, considering. "Eventually."

"Will you both fuck me against every boulder," I asked carefully, "meaning I get fucked twice at every stop, or is it once per boulder regardless of... er, who's involved?"

I can't believe I just said that aloud.

"Even if you only have one cock inside you, we'll both be involved, lovely."

Luc considered us both. "I'd like to arrive within two weeks."

"Fine," Jules said. "Once against every rock you can sit on, with a maximum of five per day."

"Three," I countered.

"Five," Luc repeated, firm.

Fuck me. But if it saved lives, it saved lives. And it wouldn't cost me anything more than my dignity. "And in return, you won't sacrifice the witches to the starcrater?"

Jules's smile widened. There was something nearly... malicious in the grin. It was the satisfied smirk of a cat who had his mouse cornered and exactly where he wanted it. "Precisely."

I closed my eyes. I can't believe I was saying this. "Those terms are acceptable."

Jules and I looked at Luc. After a moment, the Conqueror nodded. "Very well."

He turned his forearm upward and drew a rune of shadows over his golden-brown skin. ***Bargain***. The shape shimmered the moment it was complete, pulsing once with heat before sinking into his flesh. He repeated the shape on Jules and then me. The rune warmed against my wrist, a silent reminder that the terms had been struck.

My body, traded for lives.

"Done," Luc said simply, letting go of my wrist.

"Excellent." Jules clapped before spinning on his heels. "Rox? Have them bring the witches back inside."

My shoulders went slack. Thank the stars.

A silver-ringed knuckle bumped under my chin, tipping my face upward. "We leave in an hour."

Oh. Heat rushed up my neck. I swallowed. This was going to be a long two weeks.

# 58

I SLUMPED ONTO THE mattress in Duskfell's Imperial Apartment, sinking into dark sheets. Deep voices sounded behind me, but I ignored the kings. I was exhausted down to my soul. Every inch of me buzzed with overuse, with venom, with the relentless pulse of the soulbond. My knees ached. My elbows ached. My cunt ached… and tingled, the sensation more satisfied than painful.

Stars, I hadn't thought I'd survive the trip. I had come so many fucking times. I hadn't known a body could orgasm that much.

It turned out the roads between Montaurère and Tenebra de Mar had a *lot* of boulders.

The normally ten day ride had taken thirteen to account for all our *breaks*. Nearly three days' worth of fucking. Bent over boulders. Pressed against boulders. Kneeling on boulders.

I had been *thoroughly* defiled, just like I told Deidre a month ago before the harvest.

A month. How had so much time passed, and yet so little? How had everything changed, and yet nothing at all? I was a witch, soulbound to the Kings of Dusk and Dawn. My pain was gone. The nausea had vanished. Even my exhaustion had dulled, soothed away by venom and pleasure. But my life wasn't mine. My choices weren't mine. And it seemed they never would be.

"Ah, *fuck*, I only made her come twenty-three times." Jules's complaint cut through my thoughts, pulling me back to my body. "You win, Lucey."

The King of Dawn sounded so dejected, I pushed up onto my elbow. My muscles protested the move. Without a strong soothing rune, the pain would've been far worse. "What did you win?" I asked softly, somehow both terrified and eager for the answer.

The kings didn't speak. Not a word. If not for the bond, I'd have thought they were gone. But their anticipation pulsed through me, a steady rhythm of desire and triumph. It filled every corner of my body, impossible to ignore.

A hand wrapped around my ankle.

Oh, fuc—

Luc tugged me to the end of the bed. He gripped my hips and pulled me up until I kneeled on the mattress, my feet hanging off the edge. My breath caught as my breasts brushed the cool sheets through the thin fabric of my gown. I started to press up onto my elbows.

"No." His voice was a low command, curling in my belly. He gripped the back of my neck and pressed my cheek to the mattress, my gaze facing the empty bed beside me. "You will remember this every time you sleep here in Duskfell." With his free hand, he drew a rune against my temple. "You'll remember for all of eternity."

The stroke of his finger across my skin sent a shiver down my spine. Heat flickered to life in my core, rising with each breath until my nipples tightened into aching peaks. I didn't understand how I could still want more after the last thirteen days. "Luc—"

Something warm wrapped around my wrists. Daemium shadows from the bed's towering headboard. They tugged my arms until they were stretched straight above my head. The darkness slithered between my limbs, binding me tight.

When it reached my shoulders, it curled around my throat, replacing Luc's grip at the back of my collar. They squeezed gently, a greeting and a promise. My gasp came out choked.

The mattress dipped as Jules dropped onto his back, flinging an arm over his head with a theatrical sigh. The sound was full of mock defeat, but it didn't hide the hunger rising in him. "What about me, Lucey?"

"You lost," Luc said simply, pushing my skirts around my waist. My panties slid down my legs to my knees. I bit my lip as early summer air brushed my bare ass, as soft as Luc's appreciation. "You watch."

"But—"

Luc shoved a finger into me. Brutally. Intoxicatingly. I cried out as he sank into my wet heat, until a cold silver ring bumped against me. Jules's pupils dilated, swallowing what little gold remained in his gaze. He licked his lips.

"Yes, Julien?"

"Nothing, darling." Jules reached for his trousers, his erection straining against the hardened leather. "Pretend I didn't say a thing. Pretend I'm not even here."

"No."

Jules froze, hand on his buckle. "Lucey."

"You're not coming in your hand," Luc said. "You'll come in our wife when I'm done with her."

"That's not fair," Jules said with a pout. "When I had her first, I didn't stop you."

"That was your mistake."

Jules sat up, only his hand remaining in my direct line of sight. "It was a gift."

Luc slowly pulled his finger out of me. "And what have you done to deserve a gift from me, dearest?"

Jules shuddered, the movement trailing down his arms. "What do you want me to do to deserve a gift?" he asked huskily.

"I want you to watch." Luc slid two fingers into me. I moaned. "You won't touch yourself or our bride." But this time, he didn't wait. He pumped his fingers in and out of me. "And when I'm finished, if you were a good boy, you can sink your cock into this tight,"—he slammed his fingers—"soaked cunt,"—*ohh*—"of ours."

My hands clenched in the sheets as Luc mercilessly fingered me. I couldn't hold in my whimpers. Heat flushed through my body, my face. I arched, cheek and chest sinking into the silk of the mattress.

Luc hummed. "See what you missed in your greed? Our little witch's first cries in this bedchamber."

"Shit." A second later, Jules dropped back onto the mattress, locking his hands behind his head. Those black eyes focused on me.

I clenched my fists in the sheets at the intensity of his stare. I don't know why it intimidated me. Jules had witnessed me in much more compromising positions in the month since we met. But the weight of his want made it hard to breathe.

While I knew the King of Dawn's body well now, I still didn't know *him*. We hadn't talked much beyond the superficial on our journey between cities. The kings were holding themselves back from me, ever since I tried to run.

And I'd been holding myself back from them, too.

"I can almost feel her thinking," Jules said, gaze flicking up to Luc. "Are you sure you don't need help?"

"No." Luc pulled out, then pulsed four fingers into me. Stretching me. Filling me.

My eyes rolled back as he buried his hand in me to the knuckle. "Ohh—"

My cry cut off as the shadows tightened around my throat. "Did you hear that, bride? Julien thinks I need help. You're going to beg for my cock, aren't you?"

The heat in me burned higher and higher with each pulse of his hand. After coming so many times over the past week, I recognized the climb toward the peak, staring over the edge into bliss. And Luc was forcing me there, the path inevitable.

I wouldn't need to beg at this rate.

Jules clicked his tongue. "I don't know. Our wife feels like she's going to come *soon* to me. And I don't hear any begging yet."

Luc swiveled his hand, rubbing his fingertips against my sensitive walls.

Then he pulled his hand out of me.

And didn't thrust it back in.

I tried to twist my head, but the shadows didn't let me turn far enough to glare at the King of Dusk, standing smug behind me. Stars, I needed him. The ache was unbearable now, pulsing with every heartbeat. I writhed with it, helpless in the grip of need.

Thoroughly defiled and thoroughly *addicted*. Their soothing runes, coupled with their venom, made me never want to experience anything else but this bliss again.

A snap of a buckle sounded behind me.

Luc's hands settled like iron bands around my hips. The thick head of his cock brushed through my wet center. I shuddered.

But he didn't move forward, taking me with one thrust like I knew he could. He waited, rubbing the tip of himself through me.

I swallowed and tried to shuffle back, but his hands dented my ass, holding me still.

"Obey your king, bride. Or I'll fuck that mouth of yours... and neither you nor Jules will come tonight."

"That's not fair." Jules rolled closer to me until his breath brushed my lips. "Beg him, lovely. I need to come inside you tonight. You won't deny me that, will you?"

My world became those dark eyes, edged with gold. The hands on my hips. The crown of the Conqueror's cock, sliding through my slick heat—

I yelped when he ran the head of his length over my clit. Oh, fuck. My breath came out in heavy pants. Luc wasn't joking when he said he wanted me to beg.

And I would break.

I always broke.

I wasn't strong enough to resist either of them. This was my fate, my eternal cage.

Still, I bit my lip, refusing the words.

Jules grinned.

But the bright sight was quickly overshadowed by a dark growl. The shadows around my arm started pulling me upward.

"Very well," Luc said. "It's about time I fucked that mouth of yours."

I jolted. Despite all the sex in the last week and a half, I hadn't had Luc in my mouth yet. Maybe it was because of the flash of terror that zapped through me at the very thought. I could barely take him in my cunt. How was I supposed to fit that long, thick, *pierced* length in my mouth?

"Please."

Luc stiffened behind me. The shadows stopped pulling me up. "Please what?"

"Please fuck me. Please make me come."

He hummed, unimpressed. "You can do better than that, little witch."

My cheeks burned. I didn't care. "Please fuck me, Your Majesty. Only you can make me come. Only you. Please, please, please—"

Luc growled low behind me. He grabbed my hips and yanked me backward. My word turned into a moan as the King of Dusk buried himself inside me in one brutal thrust. I stretched around him, my body expanding, welcoming him.

Jules closed the distance between our lips and kissed me. He swallowed the rest of my cry, his tongue dominating mine, taking what he wanted.

Luc slid out, then pulsed back in. His piercings rubbed against all the right places. I shuddered, screaming out, the sound swallowed by Jules.

Yes, this was right. This was perfect. All three of us, body in body in body. It didn't even matter that our thoughts, our feelings, our hearts weren't aligned, not when we were together like this.

Luc stoked the heat higher and higher in me. Jules swallowed my every yip. They claimed every inch of me until I was a mewling mess.

I tugged against the shadows holding me tight, but my arms and head didn't move. Couldn't move. All I could do was feel, tears trailing my cheeks as the Conqueror fucked me into his mattress and the Butcher devoured my cries.

Oh.

Stars.

This.

Was.

Everything.

Jules pulled back, pausing until our noses brushed. His cock strained hard at his trousers. His tension thrummed beneath my pleasure, Luc's pleasure. Their desire had grown from a tickle to a simmering heat in my senses.

"Flip her," Jules rasped.

Luc grunted, not losing his rhythm. "You don't command me, Julien."

"If you're set on torturing me, and you know that's my specialty, flip her over. Show me those beautiful, bouncing breasts and forbid me from touching them."

"Hmm."

Then my back hit the mattress. I gasped—a sound that turned into a squeal as Luc hooked his arms under my knees and plunged back into me. My arms were still bound above my head, but my entire body jerked on the bed, the movement rippling through me.

Jules groaned, eyes locked on my chest. He unlaced the top of my gown and peeled it down, exposing me for a better view. His arousal surged, the tension in my belly growing.

The Conqueror towered over me, flawless, golden-brown muscle flexing with every thrust. He watched me through lidded eyes. Those glowing shadows pierced through me in the dim runelight.

Oh, stars, I was going to come. I needed to come. Luc pounded into me, filling me to the hilt, every thrust a demand my body couldn't deny. Each ram of his hips forced a moan from my lips. He drove me painfully high, but I still wasn't crashing.

Just teetering on the edge. The bliss I craved hovered just out of reach.

Then he pressed his thumb to my clit, circling with ruthless intent. The heat in me burned from the inside out.

"Are you resisting your king, little witch?"

"No," I whimpered instantly, obediently.

Luc's thumb worked faster. "Then come for me."

"I can't." I wasn't holding back. I wasn't trying to fight it. What was the point?

But even with magic soothing my nerves, my body was broken. Always broken, forever and eternally. I squeezed my eyes shut and tried to lean into the fire, to soak in the bliss that only grew with every thrust.

"Suck her nipples," Luc grunted out.

My eyes flashed open, just in time to catch Jules's delighted grin. "You mean it?"

"Julien," Luc growled, "fucking take her into your mouth and make her scream. I want to feel her grip my cock."

Jules dropped his head to my aching breast. He sucked one pink bud between his lips, his tongue piercing grazing around my flesh. His hand found the other, rolling it gently, teasing just enough.

The slightest touch knocked me over the edge. My body clenched. My cunt seized tight around Luc's cock. I screamed, the sound torn from my throat as that thick, pierced length rubbed inside me, raw and perfect. Luc's thrusts turned erratic—

"Fuck," Luc growled as he came. I shuddered and moaned as he spilled inside me. Another torrent of pleasure washed over me. His muscles tightened, his brow furrowed, his whole body bowing with the force of his orgasm.

I shuddered helplessly beneath him, wholly his. No man but Jules would ever come this deeply within me. It was a claiming fuck, Luc marking me as his possession in his bedchamber, in his castle, in his city, in his Impire. If the Conqueror had his way—and he always did—this is where I'd remain.

His little bride, safe and warm and naked in the heart of the monsters' lair.

Luc pulled out of me with a wet pop. His cum rushed out, staining the sheets below. The King of Dusk dropped my thighs—

Jules was suddenly naked and on top of me, straddling my hips as his elbows rested near my head. "My turn!"

I yipped in surprise. Jules lunged down and caught the sound with his mouth. His hips dropped, his weight settling on me and sinking us deeper into the mattress. He hooked his fingers into my skirt and yanked it up, baring me in a second.

The shadows binding my hands dissolved when he tugged my gown off, only to wrap around my limbs again a heartbeat later, holding me tight.

He dropped his chest to mine. I gasped as his skin brushed me, my nipples rubbing against his muscles.

With a nip to my lips, Jules slid into me. My body didn't offer any resistance, not when I was slick with my desire and Luc's seed.

Jules shuddered as he sank deep, the echo rippling through Luc and me. "Fuck, *yes*—"

The shadows around my arms pulled. They dragged me out from under Jules, my sweat-slicked body sliding easily across the silk.

Jules hit the mattress. "What the fuck, Luc?"

The King of Dusk was already reclining against the headboard pillows, a glass of dark amber liquor in hand. The shadows tugged me back until I pressed against his chest, cradled between his legs.

Jules went still, crouched at the end of the bed. Wide-eyed, we both watched as the shadows spiraled down my body, coiling around my legs.

With the daemium, Luc hooked my legs over his, spreading me wide and open for Jules. Like that first night, the night they made me their Mortal Bride and the soulbond runespell activated. We'd all passed out before Jules could fuck me on top of Luc.

Luc took a calm sip of his brandy. Amusement curled beneath his control, his satisfaction dark and commanding. With his free hand, he gestured down at my body. "Continue, Julien."

The thrill that surged through Jules nearly made me gasp. He scrambled up the bed, nearly slipping in his hurry. He kissed my calf. Kissed my knee. Kissed my clit, hesitating for a moment as he circled the aching bud.

I jerked against the shadows holding my arms back and around Luc's neck. The King of Dusk hummed, a rumbling growl. His thick length hardened beneath me, pressing against my ass.

But Jules couldn't wait, couldn't tease me. Not this time. He crawled up my body, trailing kisses along my soft stomach, over my breasts, across my collarbone.

He claimed my lips as he thrust into me.

Bliss burst inside me. Inside him. Inside Luc. I cried out, but the sound came out muffled.

Luc had fucked me possessively, intensely.

Jules fucked like a savage, his movements hard, reverberating through my entire body. Through Luc's entire body. With each pulse into me, the King of Dusk's cock slid between my ass cheeks. His breath huffed in my ear, as loud as mine, as loud as Jules.

I barely heard it over the wet slap of our bodies. My fists clenched in Luc's thick curls, the only thing the bed's shadows let me touch. I held on as Jules claimed me with everything he had.

Jules broke the kiss. He twisted my nipple between his fingers and nibbled at my chin. He was too much, too everywhere. All I could do was scream.

"Stars, Nessa," Jules groaned. "I can't believe I get to fuck you for eternity."

I sobbed. "Jules!"

He slid his hand between my ribs, across my soft stomach, through my wet curls, to my aching bud. He pressed against it just right—

Luc tossed his glass of liquor aside without a care, gripped a fistful of my hair, and claimed my mouth.

Jules groaned at the sight. He circled my clit faster and faster, his thrusts never stopping.

I screamed into Luc's kiss as another orgasm tore through me, sudden and staggering. My nails sank into his scalp, anchoring me as my body convulsed. Ecstasy exploded outward from that single point of pressure, crashing over me in wave after wave. I shook, hips bucking, thighs trembling, every nerve alive and burning.

A wet gush spilled down my thighs.

I stiffened. Stars, had I just... had I...

Jules pushed off me, breath catching as startled excitement crackled through him. His cock was still rock-hard as he drank in the sight of *my* release dripping down the curve of my ass. My cheeks flamed. The heat rose all the way to my ears, but my thighs kept trembling, my body too overwhelmed to feel shame.

Luc glanced over my shoulder, his possessive gaze on my quivering cunt. A hungry growl rumbled in his chest. He released my hair and reached down between my legs, dragging a finger through the mess I'd made. I shuddered when he touched me, still overstimulated.

He pulled his finger away, glistening with my pleasure.

Stars, I had just soaked the sheets.

"Fuck, yes," Jules all but hissed, wrapping a hand around his cock. He stroked himself once—

Jules's body snapped taut, his spine bowing as he came with a strangled groan. His seed spilled across my belly in thick, hot ropes, streaking my skin. His head dropped back in bliss.

A second later, Luc followed, letting out a ragged growl as his cock jerked against my back. I felt the heat of him splash across my spine.

I was filthy, stained, sinful.

I didn't fucking care.

I couldn't.

Every part of me pulsed. The flood of their pleasure rushed through the bond, almost making me come again with them. My thighs trembled from release, my core spasming weakly around nothing. I was shaking, my limbs boneless from too many orgasms.

Jules pushed back onto his heels with a groan and raked a hand through his blond locks, turning them into a halo of wild white-gold. His lips parted in a lazy, wicked grin. "Again?"

Again? The word made no sense. It reached my ears but didn't stick, slipping through the haze of bliss blanketing my brain. My thoughts floated.

Luc sat up. I slid down his chest, my cheek grazing the sticky heat of his skin. "Again," he agreed.

I didn't have time to protest. If I even wanted to protest. Jules flipped me onto my hands and knees. My arms trembled, barely catching my weight. I blinked blearily at the King of Dusk.

"Again?" I asked, slurring the word like I was drunk on the kings.

Luc smirked and reached to steady my chin, tilting my face toward his. His dark eyes gleamed with hunger.

"Until you pass out, wife."

I FLOATED THROUGH THE gardens of Duskfell.

I let my hand drift through a bush of soft blossoms, knuckles skimming their fragile petals. The sensation danced across my skin. Everything felt too vivid, too raw. My whole body buzzed with overstimulation, every nerve humming from memory.

The steady pulse between my legs was the strongest sensation of them all. I had awoken to an empty bed, my body thrumming in every place Luc and Jules had touched. And they had touched *everywhere*, following through on their promise to fuck me into blissful unconsciousness.

Between all the boulders and consecrating the kings' bed in Duskfell, my cunt had taken a beating.

But who knew getting fucked could save lives?

I shook the thought away. It was better not to think. Because once I started thinking about the witches I'd saved, I'd start thinking about why they needed saving.

About Morrena, her face torn off, her corpse savaged by wraiths.

About Maire, blood leaking from her chin, her body left hanging on Dawnspear's walls.

About Eral and Ilenia and Estrella and Tristan and Riona and Edda and Éamon and Fergus.

I dug my fingers into my palms until I felt the crescent bite of my nails. No. It was better to not *think*. I couldn't leave. I couldn't save anyone. I couldn't do anything. So what was the point?

So I didn't think. I just felt.

I leaned into the lingering tingle in my skin, the afterglow that had been simmering since Luc pointed out the first boulder outside Montaurère. I leaned into the soulbond, sated and still within me. It would've been happier if we were with the kings. But we weren't running. We weren't resisting. We hadn't pushed them away when they touched us.

We hadn't fought the connection it tried to form.

Not entirely, anyway.

Every day that passed, every time we fucked, the elation lasted a little less.

Because the soulbond didn't just want pleasure.

We weren't companions. Karra had tried to sate her bond with Azaras through sex, but that hadn't lasted. Their emotions lingered now, a constant hum beneath my thoughts. Their physical sensations bled slowly into mine. But the bond had stalled compared to those first few days, slowed by every betrayal between us.

It wanted more.

It craved love. It craved surrender. It craved union.

Karra had started to fall for the Beast King as they slipped closer to what the Azarasians now called beloveds. And then she loved him completely when they settled as heartmates. I hadn't read Volume II, but everyone knew how their story ended.

My breathing quickened. My chest rose and fell in sharp huffs as panic crept in, seeping through me and into *them*. Their curiosity stirred across the bond before I shoved it all down.

I closed my eyes. *Breathe in. Breathe out.* That was a problem for the future. The future didn't matter.

The past didn't matter either.

All that mattered was the sun on my skin, the petals against my hand, and the low pulse between my legs.

I slowly blew out another breath, then continued through the garden. Isabeau said nothing at my back, nor did the two other Imperial Guard. Roxiana had been summoned away earlier, her Crown Chancellor duties pulling her elsewhere. Apparently not all of the courtiers were thrilled with the sudden move back to the Capital of Dusk for the summer season. If the end of spring felt like this, I couldn't blame them.

I approached the edge of the hanging garden's tier. This one belonged to the kings—their private space—but the tiers below were open to courtiers.

I leaned against the bannister and looked out over the greenery and the city beyond.

A few luminous eyes flickered up toward me… but the Azarasians quickly looked away.

The kings hadn't revealed I was their soulbound yet, but the courtiers closest to them knew something had changed. They'd seen the way the kings spoke to me at the revelry, the trial, and the funeral. How they glared and snarled at anyone who so much as looked in my direction.

Soon, they'd all know. But that didn't matter either.

"Your Majesty?"

I twisted with a frown. Neither of the kings was near. I knew that without needing to look. But Roxiana had returned. She stood beside Isabeau, her expression unreadable. "Their Majesties request your presence."

*Their* Majesties?

Ah, right. The Azarasians only used the Imperium title to refer to the rulers as a whole. If I was one-third of their soul, then we only became the Imperium when we were addressed together.

I nodded and started forward. Roxiana and Isabeau led the way back through the hanging gardens, through twisting olive trees and rows of crimson carnations, past mosaic-lined fountains and statues draped in flowering vines. The two beloveds spoke in hushed tones once or twice, but otherwise, the only sounds were the chirp of cicadas and the soft graze of ocean wind.

When we reached the palace's base, a set of black stairs led to a terrace connecting to the kings' Imperial Apartment. Roxiana and Isabeau stood aside at the bottom and gestured for me to go first.

Like I was the Queen of Dusk and Dawn.

Not just the Mortal Bride.

Not just the kings' thrall.

I didn't read into it. They weren't showing me respect. They were showing it to the parts of my soul that now belonged to Luc and Jules.

When I reached the top of the stairs, I looked out over the terrace. A circular pool of water, large enough for just a few people, rose from the stone at the far corner, three steps leading up to its rim. There were multiple seating areas—a cozy nook to my right with chairs clustered around a firepit and a shaded daybed draped in gauzy fabric at the terrace's far side. Between me and the daybed, an expansive stone table stretched beneath the open sky, surrounded by ten chairs.

Luc sat at the head of the table, with Jules beside him on the right. Across from them, two seats down, a dark-haired vampire in elaborate ruby skirts sat with her hands folded neatly on the table. Her golden eyes watched me closely. I couldn't remember her name, but I had definitely seen her before.

Luc gestured to the seat to his left. "Sit, bride."

A tiny part of me bristled at the command. But I ignored it, closed the distance between us, and settled into the chair. The bond hummed warmly in my chest at being reunited with the other two pieces of our soul. Luc watched me impassively, Jules with a small smile. They were the Conqueror and the Butcher right now. Whoever this vampire woman was, she wasn't in their inner circle.

But underneath, they burned with intrigue... and a hint of lust. Heat rose to my cheeks, tainting them with a light blush. Luc's hands on my hips as he pounded into me. Jules's mouth on my lips, my neck, my collarbone as he railed me into Luc's body. Their cocks marking me, branding me, claiming me.

The corner of Luc's lips twitched, the memories floating through my head clear enough to discern through our bond. "You didn't meet at the Red Queen revelry, but you might remember Lady Renée."

I twisted toward the vampire woman. So that was where I knew her from. She had brought Jules's gift to the courts, humans and witches bred as delicacies. My stomach turned.

It didn't matter. It didn't matter. It didn't matter.

Lady Renée's dark brows rose as I stared directly at her, but she didn't say anything. It wasn't her place to discipline the Mortal Bride.

When I didn't reply, Luc continued unbothered. "She's one of our leading geneticists. For the last century, she's been cataloging vampire and witch bloodlines."

I glanced back at Luc, at Jules. I didn't get where this was going. "And?"

"And you're a witch of unknown origins," Jules said. "If your mother won't tell us where you came from or how she crossed paths with Allegra, then we need to figure that out ourselves."

I nodded. That made sense. I should've felt something, a twist of fear or hope, but I couldn't let the question plague me. Who was I, really? It didn't matter. Not now.

I looked at Lady Renée. "Do you need my blood?"

Her rapid blinking was the only sign of her surprise that I'd spoken. "I do, yes."

A flicker of annoyance pulsed through the bond from Luc, but I ignored it. She hadn't called me by a title, but she didn't know I had one. To her, the greatest mystery was how the human Mortal Bride was actually a witch. The kings hadn't removed the glamour they'd cast on me before the trial two weeks ago, so it must've come as a shock.

I raised my hand. I didn't know if I'd like the answer, but I needed to know. My entire past was a lie. Whatever the truth was, it wouldn't stay hidden forever. I might as well face it. It wouldn't change my situation anyway.

Lady Renée reached forward.

Luc growled.

The vampire woman froze, then dropped her hand and bowed her head. "My apologies, Imperium."

In a blink, Jules stood at my side, between my chair and Luc's. He placed a hand on the King of Dusk's shoulder and gave a calming squeeze. "Forgive my soulbound, Lady Renée. He's rather protective of our bride, especially after someone tried to kill her."

"Of course, Your Majesty. I shouldn't have tried to take your Mortal Bride's blood without permission."

Jules extended his hand toward me, palm up. "Your hand, lovely?"

Fingers snapping—

My whole body twitched, but I crushed the thought before it could form. Not fast enough. Regret rippled through the bond from Jules as I placed my hand in his. He didn't feel it for anyone else, only for torturing me.

Shadows curled around his thumb, sharpening his nail into a claw. He pressed it to my skin. Blood welled to the surface from the small cut. I didn't even feel it through the soothing rune he'd reapplied just hours ago.

Jules lifted the droplets from my skin, the blood rising in a stream that floated into the air. Behind me, Lady Renée pulled a vial from within her skirts. A rune was carved into its surface. ***Preserve***. She removed the stopper, and Jules guided my blood into the bottle.

He leaned in, holding my gaze. My breath caught, unsure if I wanted to pull away or pull him closer. Then he flicked his tongue across the cut. The same way his tongue had slid over my nipples, around my aching clit, that gold piercing making *her scream. Fuck, this bond made me obsessed. I just needed Renée to take her blood and go. Then I'd be on my knees, shoving up Nessa's skirts, licking her until she came on my tongue and forgot every name but mine—*

I pulled back my healed hand, jerking out of Jules's head. The King of Dawn only winked at me.

I cleared my throat and turned back to Lady Renée. "What are you going to do with it?"

Lady Renée glanced at the kings.

Luc nodded. "Answer her."

A little shiver went through me. Luc hadn't called me his little curiosity since he discovered my connection to Allegra. I was only his little witch, his little bride. Affectionate, but distant.

I had been annoyed at the nickname before, but now, I would've given anything to hear it again. To pretend, even for a second, that I wasn't a prisoner, soulbound to monsters.

"Some of the more prominent demon bloodlines can be identified merely by taste, if you've spent as much time as I have studying," Lady Renée said. She pressed a finger to the vial's lip and let a single drop of my blood fall onto her skin. "I'll likely have to return to my lab to test it, but..."

She sucked her finger into her mouth. The moment my blood touched her tongue, her eyes widened.

Luc didn't so much as blink, but tension spiked in him. "What?"

Lady Renée poured another drop onto her finger. She rolled it over her tongue like she was tasting wine, brow furrowing. "She's a close descendant of Isaura."

Alarm crackled through the bond, but it wasn't just theirs. It was mine, too. My heartbeat stuttered. Isaura. The founder of the witch nation. Allegra and Morrena's sire.

I was related to *them*. To the woman who created me and the woman who betrayed me, who I'd watched die.

I tried to pull the numbness back over me like a veil, but it wouldn't settle. Not with that name ringing in my ears.

"How close?" Luc asked.

"Great-grandchild, perhaps?"

The kings met each other's eyes. The shift in the air was immediate. The world felt too quiet. My pulse too loud. Something silent passed between them, but I caught a flicker of it. Suspicion. Fear. Building rage.

Then Luc gave a tight nod and turned back to the vampire woman. "How quickly can you fully analyze her blood, Lady Renée?"

"I can have it done in three days, Your Majesty."

"Very well." Luc gestured to Roxiana. "Escort Lady Renée to her carriage."

Roxiana nodded. "Yes, Your Majesty."

Lady Renée rose and bowed, then followed Roxiana across the terrace, disappearing through the doors into the Imperial Apartment.

Jules crossed his arms, leaning back against the edge of Luc's chair. The bond buzzed at the back of my skull, a ringing I couldn't ignore.

Something was wrong.

Being related to Allegra was horrifying enough. But this felt like more. Like something hiding in the dark, waiting for me to see it. Something I didn't want to name.

Jules glanced down at Luc. "Are you going to say it, or should I?"

I frowned. Say what?

Luc said it.

"On behalf of Isaura and its High Council, I, Allegra, Exalted Daughter of Queen Isaura and Exalted Mother in her stead, surrender unconditionally to the Azarasian Impire. My country and our citizens are at their mercy."

I froze. What the *fuck*? Hearing her name coming from Luc's mouth made my stomach twist. Why had Luc said that—

Power crashed through me. Through them. I flinched. It struck like lightning, centering on their forearms. Exactly where Morrena's allegiance runespell had been carved. I hadn't seen the kings', but I suspected they had one there hidden by a glamour. It tied every Azarasian vampire and thrall to them.

And now... every witch.

I didn't really understand what had happened, but whatever that power was, it meant Isaura had finally surrendered. Their allegiance runespells had transferred to the Impire.

But Luc wasn't Allegra. He couldn't be. So how had the surrender worked?

A hand settled around my throat.

Luc yanked me out of the seat. Not gently. Not seductively. Painfully. The pressure sliced through the soothing rune like it wasn't even there. I choked as the air vanished. My hands clawed at his wrist. His eyes were black, so cold they burned. His rage thundered, drowning out every other sensation but fear.

I knew Lucero Azaras, the Conqueror. The King of Dusk. He'd held me. Protected me. Called me his bride. His little witch. His little curiosity, once.

And now he was choking me like I was nothing, Death in his eyes.

It was the way he stared at Exalted Morrena, a promise of pain and death.

It was the way he stared at his enemies.

Which, I guessed, I now was.

Because the only way Luc could surrender on behalf of Allegra... was if I was Allegra?

No. No, that wasn't possible. That was the air deprivation talking. That was—

That was *impossible.*

Because if I was Allegra, then I had arranged our soulbond.

Then I had sent the witches to Duskfell to become wraiths.

Then I had killed Corinne.

Then all of this was my fault.

I might have laughed if I wasn't dying.

Luc's grip tightened. My eyes bulged as I struggled for breath. My vision began to swirl, edges graying, the bond shrieking with panic.

He was fucking killing me. And he didn't care, his fury jagged and wild. He didn't care *if I killed her. Allegra Isaura. In my bed. In my soulbond. Hadn't she already taken enough from me? And now she had to take the very essence of me and merged it with her.*

*I chuckled, a dark sound.*

*Of all the people in the world, it almost made sense that Allegra Isaura was the only one who could ever match our soul.*

*Jules gripped my shoulder. "You're killing her, Luc."*

*"I know."*

*"You're killing us."*

*My expression cracked. "I know."*

*"Please, darling," Jules said softly, though there was nothing behind it. His emotions had gone quiet the moment Isaura's surrender took hold. "I know you've dreamed of it, but you can't kill her. You never can."*

*My hand didn't loosen—*

I snapped back into my body as black spots swam at the edges of my vision. My lungs burned, each second without air worse than the last.

Jules shook him, hard. "Luc!"

He released me. I crumpled into the chair, coughing violently. Each gasp scraped my throat raw. My tears spilled down my cheeks, hot and uncontrolled.

A hand fisted in my hair and pulled me back up.

I saw the glint of blackening fangs—

Luc bit me.

Agony flashes through my bloodstream. I screamed, a shrill, high-pitched sound I barely recognized. I thought I had known pain. I had lived with pain daily. I'd had my fingers broken. I'd been stabbed.

But none of that compared to this.

This was worse. Deeper. Ruinous.

I wanted to die. Instantly. If I could've willed myself out of existence to escape this, I would have. With every pull of his throat, Luc devoured something vital, ripping not just blood, but the very core of me. It felt like he was clawing through me.

It made sense now why only the height of pleasure could mask this kind of torment. Why bliss was the only thing that could compete.

Luc finally pulled back, swiping his tongue roughly over the punctures. I crumpled into the seat, sobbing, my vision blurred with tears. The kings were only shapes now, wavering outlines at the edges of my sight, but I felt them more than I saw them. They had shared that pain, but it hadn't shaken them. Luc's fury still pounded through the bond. Jules remained empty, our connection hollow and echoing.

But even their emotions couldn't drown the memory of that pain.

Luc gripped a fistful of my hair again and hauled me to my feet.

I whimpered. "Please—"

"Silence, Allegra."

Luc dragged me across the terrace into the apartment and through the sitting room, past black stone walls and low, carved shelves of dark-stained wood. We approached a runegate embedded in the far wall. The daemium shimmered faintly beneath its surface, nearly indistinguishable from the obsidian stone. Without the silver frame, it could've been invisible.

Luc sliced his finger and pressed it to the gate. ***Gate. Distance. Path. Arrival. Cross.*** The shadows of the surface shivered and wavered, revealing a dark corridor beyond.

The King of Dusk shoved me through.

I crashed to the floor of a long, dark hallway. I sucked in a breath, the air here cooler in the way only underground places could be. Stone walls closed in on both sides, smooth and unadorned except for the occasional runelight flickering weakly against the gloom. Their dim glow reflected off the polished floor, casting long, distorted shadows across the black stone.

I scrambled forward.

A boot slammed between my shoulder blades.

I screamed as pain echoed down my spine. Luc could've crushed me in half with a single stomp.

That had been him being gentle.

He scooped me up and tossed me over his shoulder like I weighed nothing.

"Fucking put me down, asshole," I sobbed, my voice breaking with every word. "I'm not Allegra. I can't fucking be Allegra."

Behind Luc, the Butcher stared at me with dead eyes. "Still pretending to be her? That scared little bride we fucked into surrender? That's pathetic, even for you, Allegra."

I flinched. His disgust cracked like a whip across the bond.

Luc started down the corridor without a word. The deeper we went, the tighter the stone pressed in, the colder the air became.

We passed through an open doorway. Steep wooden benches rose in tiers, stacked in a wide semicircle of dark varnished wood before navy upholstered seats. At the top tier in the center, a broad platform held a massive armchair. All the seats faced inward, fixed on the center of the circle.

On the wooden slab.

Seven feet long. Perfectly rectangular. Its surface was stained a deep, ugly red. Not splattered or streaked, but soaked in blood. Runes were carved into each corner. ***Anchor. Anchor. Anchor. Anchor.*** One for each limb. At the slab's base, carved into the stone floor, a draining rune glowed faintly.

My heart nearly stopped. I didn't need anyone to explain what I was seeing.

The Butcher's Block.

Where Jules tortured the Impire's prisoners. Where he turned pain into performance. Where blood was not just spilled but displayed.

Something twisted deep in my gut. My skin crawled, but I couldn't stop looking.

Was he going to torture me? Really torture me?

But we passed the block, slipping into a narrower hall lined with deep-set alcoves. Each cell was open-faced with no bars or doors. Just dark recesses cut into black stone. At first, they looked like storage alcoves, until I noticed the thin border of runes etched into the floor before each one.

***Imprison. Imprison. Imprison.***

The word repeated like a drumbeat with every step we took.

Luc dropped me at his feet.

I barely had time to suck in a breath before his magic sparked.

***Unravel. Soothe.***

Pain stabbed up through my belly, a harsh jolt. My illness surged forward, summoned by the strain in my body and mind.

"No," I sobbed. "Please—"

"You did this to yourself, Allegra." Luc's voice was cold. Distant. "Your choices were death or pain. Since I can't grant you the first, you'll suffer the second."

"What are you talking about? I didn't give myself my illness. I wouldn't choose this."

"You chose to live," he said flatly. "That's the cost of the soulshift runespell."

My breath caught. I thought of Morrena. Her cane. The spells she'd used to jump into the body of her unborn child, stretching her life beyond what any witch should've had.

What would that do to a fetus?

Damage it, apparently.

Had I done the same?

That couldn't be true. I hadn't chosen this. I hadn't chosen anything.

I was *not* Allegra.

Across the hallway, my mother curled on a stone cot in a dark corner. The openings were staggered, not directly aligned, but I could still see her out of the corner of my vision. The runelight barely reached her, just enough to catch the edge of her pale cheek.

She stirred, then pushed tiredly to her feet. Her movements were stiff, like her limbs had forgotten how to hold weight. She stepped forward into the dim glow.

The last thing I saw was her face, staring down at me with reverence.

The chamber went dark.

"I'd take a nap if I were you, Allegra," the Butcher said, his voice slithering out of the darkness. "When I return, we'll have a little chat, you and I."

I whimpered. I didn't want to. But the Butcher wasn't lying. Assuming the soulbond even worked the way they thought it did. If it did... they'd know I wasn't lying.

Wouldn't they?

But Isaura's surrender had worked. I couldn't deny that.

Footsteps retreated into the dark. The kings left me here. The bond was still there, pulsing faintly beneath my skin. But it didn't make me feel any less alone.

I didn't know it could get this dark. Sunlight had never touched this place and never would. I couldn't see my hand, even as I raised it and brushed my fingers against my nose.

I cracked.

The pressure crushed my bones, just like when the soulbond activated. But this time, it pulverized me. I had tried. Tried and tried and tried and tried. But life kept shoveling the weight onto my back, dragging me down.

My mother's harvest. My father's apathy. Deidre's harsh words. The creeping pain of my illness. My fertility score, posted for all to see. The Patriarch's skin-crawling grin. The chill of the bookshop's loft. The hunger. More pain, the days blurring.

The doom, ever rising.

And then when the day came to join the harvest, I'd thought maybe life wouldn't be so bad. Even before the bond. My family hadn't ever tried to be kind. But the kings had smiled. They'd removed my pain. My chill. My hunger.

Until they didn't.

And this time, it hurt so much worse.

"Mistress?" My mother—no, *Orlagh*—spoke from the dark.

I crawled blindly until my fingers hit the edge of a cot. I hauled myself onto the scratchy, straw-stuffed mattress. My core twisted and clawed. "Fuck off."

"But—"

"Fuck. Off." I snarled the words. I didn't care.

I couldn't do this.

I had tried. I had kept my head raised and my voice mostly steady. I had pushed through the pain and the horror. I had tried so, so hard. But the weight had kept building. And building. And building.

Mortal Bride.

Soulbound.

Heartmate.

Witch.

Failure.

Killer.

Allegra.

I couldn't hold it anymore.

So I let it crumble.

I wanted to go home. I wasn't meant for this life, for schemes and crowns and murders. So many fucking murders. I wanted drama and death in my books, not my life. I couldn't turn the page forward, skipping to the happy ending.

But this wasn't a story. There would be no happy ending. How could there be? Happy endings weren't for reality. Especially not my reality. Mine was bleak and terrible.

It always had been.

It always would be.

I don't know why I ever expected anything else.

**Nessa, Luc, and Jules will return in *Captive of Wicked Souls*.**
Follow Kate on social media at @katestevensbooks for all the latest series updates or visit katestevensbooks.com/cows (yes, the Book 2 acronym really is COWS).

**Want the exclusive spicy extras?**
Join Kate's newsletter at katestevensbooks.com/bobh-bonus for a NSFW illustration and two scorching scenes featuring boulders...

**Need character art stat?**
Keep on turning the pages to see an illustration of Nessa and the kings at the Red Queen revelry. It's *soooo* pretty!

**Psst, want all the links for this book in one place?**
Scan this QR code and get everything fast:

Did you know reviews help indie books get discovered by more readers? If you'd like to write one, you can review *Bride of Brutal Hearts* on Amazon or Goodreads.

Like sharing your favorite books with others? Join my Influencer Newsletter at katestevensbooks.com/bobh to gain access to ARCs, promo opportunities, and giveaways. Bookish accounts of any size are welcome!

Want to talk about the series with other fans? Join the Romantasy Court community at romantasycourt.com.

*Red Queen Revelry illustration by @mangomangoj*

Want more *Bloodborne Court* art? Join Kate's newsletter at katestevensbooks.com/bobh-bonus to see a NSFW illustration. View the Red Queen Revelry illustration in full color at katestevensbooks.com/gallery.

# AUTHOR'S NOTE

You made it to the end!

Woo!

First off, thank you so much, Reader, for picking up *Bride of Brutal Hearts*. When I started this book, it had been nearly two years since I'd written anything, and even longer since I wrote something I truly loved. Those two years included the second half of the pandemic, which was awful for everyone, and a diagnosis of endometriosis after dealing with pain nearly every day for months.

If you're unfamiliar, endometriosis happens when tissue similar to the uterine lining grows where it shouldn't. It can cause severe period pain, pain during sex, chronic pelvic pain, bloating, nausea, fatigue, depression, anxiety, and infertility. It affects at least 1 in 10 people with a uterus and leads to an average loss of 11 hours of productivity each week. It can affect every part of your life, from work and relationships to mental health (learn more at endometriosisnetwork.com).

Luckily, I live in reality, where things like surgery can actually help. But endometriosis is still a chronic condition, and coming to terms with that took time... and lots of therapy. Writing this book became part of that healing process (not officially, my therapist did *not* prescribe writing vampire smut). If Nessa could survive two terrifying vampire kings and endometriosis, then I could survive my 9-5 and find the will to write again.

So thank you for giving this story and my stubborn, shy, chronically ill, brave-hearted heroine a chance.

Book 2 will get darker, spicier, and eventually, more romantic. I hope you'll stick around.

XOXO,
Kate
(circa May 2025)

P.S. I know the cliffhanger was brutal. Blame the kings, not me. They're a little fucked in the head, but then again, so is Nessa. They'll get along great... eventually.

P.P.S. Want to know when Book 2 is coming? Follow me on social media (@katestevensbooks) or join my newsletter! I won't put up a preorder until the rough draft is done. If it's anything like Book 1, I'll be dragging it to the finish line kicking and screaming.

# READING LIST

Most authors end their books with a list of other things they've written.

While I've written other fantasy romances, the only works I've published are alien romances. If you're looking for something like *Bride of Brutal Hearts*, those books won't be for you.

But if you're looking for some awesome romantasies with varying degrees of darkness and spice, you should check out some of my favorites:

- *Feathers So Vicious* by Liv Zander - A very dark, very spicy MFM duology

- *The Unseelie Prince* by Kathryn Ann Kingsley - If you want a villain MMC worse than my kings, meet Valroy

- *Bewitched* by Laura Thalassa - Memnon is my husband

- *Healer to the Ash King* by Rebecca F. Kenney - A healer falls in love with a silver-haired, fire-wielding villain king during his bride tournament

- *A Crown of Tears and Treason* by Vera Raye - The most shocking cliffhanger ever (but the duology is now complete, so you don't have to wait like I did)

- *Caught in the Basilisk's Gaze* by Mallory Dunlin - Vaduin is my second husband (he'd be down for that)

- *A Kingdom of Bitter Magic* by Alaya Wells - Dragons and fae and evil kings, oh my
- *Bound to the Battle God* by Ruby Dixon - Modern girl ends up in fantasy world and tied to grumpy battle god

Want to see the reading list with links? Check out katestevensbooks.com/bobh.

# ABOUT KATE

**USA Today Bestselling Author Kate Stevens** has been devouring romance novels and absorbing every detail since she was far too young to be reading them. With a passion for sci-fi and fantasy, she loves nothing more than a captivating villain, a touch of angst, and endless groveling. She lives in Toronto, Canada, with her cute-but-demanding pets and a hoard of books.

She's the author of *Bloodborne Court*, a dark fantasy romance series. Prior to that, she published sci-fi romances including *Archlord of Exile* and the *Bride to an Alien Prince* series. Her work was featured in the *Claimed Among the Stars* anthology, which hit #42 on the USA Today Bestseller List in 2022.

# GLOSSARY

**Abyss (location)** – An underground pleasure hall beneath Montaurère

**Adé (object)** – The Butcher King's skinning dagger

**Aislin Milligan (person)** – A Maboni human and housewife; half-sister to Nessa Halloran, wife of Donal Milligan, and daughter of Deidre and Padraic Halloran

**Allegra Isaura (person)** – An Isauran witch and Exalted Mother of the Isauran High Council; daughter of the demon Isaura and sister of Morrena Isaura; has been on the run since the conquest of Isaura by the Azarasian Impire

**Alix (person)** – An Azarasian vampire, soulbound heartmate of Martien, and mother of Vérène

**Alphonse (person)** – An Azarasian vampire and former Regent of Montaurère; killed by Julien Roche

**Alvareu Republic (location)** – A seafaring vampire nation known for piracy located off the western coast of the Azarasian Impire

**Anarchists (organization)** – An unofficial rebel faction opposing the Azarasian Impire and demonblood rule

**Azaras (person)** – A demon from the Second Godsfall and former ruler of the kingdom that became the Azarasian Impire; soulbound heartmate to Karra and sire to Lucero Azaras, Titus, and Saffira; also known as the Beast King

**Azarasian (noun)** – The demonym for a person from the Azarasian Impire

**Azarasian Impire (location)** – A vampire-ruled impire on the western continent of Occida, formed after the conquest of Trost, Marsania, and Isaura by Lucero Azaras and Julien Roche

**Beans (creature)** – Nessa Halloran's cat

**Beloveds (noun)** – The intermediate type of a soulbond; allows bonded individuals to share emotions and perceive each other's physical sensations

**Birth Quota (policy)** – A reproductive mandate enforced by the Azarasian Impire in Mabon; requires all Maboni adults to bear or sire at least three children by the age of thirty or face conscription as a thrall

**Bite of Agony (noun)** – An Azarasian term for a dry vampire bite offered as a feeding option; performed without venom, resulting in sharp, unmitigated pain

**Bite of Ecstasy (noun)** – An Azarasian term for a venom-laced vampire bite offered as a feeding option; numbs pain, heightens physical sensation, and induces bloodlust

**Bloodborne (adjective)** – Refers to a rune or runespell transmitted through blood

**Blood Legion (organization)** – The military force of the Azarasian Impire

**Bloodlust (noun)** – A state of intense sexual desire triggered by vampire venom; experienced by both the vampire and the one bitten, often amplifying physical sensitivity and pleasure

**Blood Star (noun)** – The Maboni name for the red star that appears over the horizon each spring; also known as the Red Queen

**Blood Star's Guard (noun)** – The Maboni name for four dimmer stars, two silver and two gold, that surround the Blood Star

**Blood Thrall (noun)** – See Thrall

**Bond Rite (event)** – A ceremonial observance held six months after the birth of an Azarasian soulbound pair to determine the type of their bond

**Books & Bows (location)** – A bookshop owned and operated by Nessa Halloran in Corraidin; formerly also a dress shop run by Aislin Milligan until her marriage

**Border Stones (object)** – Rune-inscribed markers placed at territorial boundaries to keep out hellbeasts and wraiths

**Butcher's Blades (organization)** – The clandestine intelligence service of the Azarasian Impire; formerly known as the Blades until Julien Roche assumed command

**Capital of Dawn (location)** – See Montaurère

**Capital of Dusk (location)** – See Tenebra de Mar

**Cédric Roche (person)** – An Azarasian vampire and Crown Mage of the Kings' Council; brother of Julien and Pierre Roche, father of Rosier Roche, and soulbound companion to Sabas Borja

**Church of the Falling Stars (religion)** – A human-focused religious institution within the Azarasian Impire that venerates demons and their demonblooded descendants

**Church of the Rising Stars (religion)** – A Maboni religious institution devoted to the worship of the godstars; teaches that demons are corrupted beings and condemns their influence as evil

**Companions (noun)** – The weakest type of a soulbond; allows bonded individuals to perceive each other's emotions and subtle physical sensations

**Corraidin (location)** – A town in Mabon; childhood home of Nessa Halloran

**Court of Dawn (organization)** – One of the two imperial courts of the Azarasian Impire, presided over by the King of Dawn

**Court of Dusk (organization)** – One of the two imperial courts of the Azarasian Impire, presided over by the King of Dusk

**Covenant (runespell)** – A runespell that binds all Azarasian vampires to a shared magical system and permits the transfer of power at dusk and dawn

**Daemium (object)** – A material found in starcraters; often forged into weapons or magical objects

**Deidre Halloran (person)** – A Maboni housewife; wife of Padraic Halloran and mother of Aislin Milligan, Orrin Halloran, Saraid Halloran, Finola Halloran, and Urrick Halloran

**Delphine (person)** – An Azarasian vampire and magistrate stationed in Corraidin; soulbound heartmate of Raul

**Demon (noun)** – A fallen godstar stripped of most of their divine power and banished from the heavens for rebellion; immortal, naturally incorporeal, and capable of shapeshifting into any living creature

**Demonblood (noun)** – A general term for all creatures with demon ancestry, including demons, vampires, witches, and hellbeasts

**Demonblooded (adjective)** – Any being with demon ancestry

**Demonborn (adjective)** – Refers to a hellbeast that is a direct child or grandchild of a demon, and therefore possesses greater power

**Donal Milligan (person)** – A Maboni businessman, member of the Milligan merchant family, and husband of Aislin Milligan

**Dufresne Abattoir (location)** – An Azarasian blood facility that was destroyed in an arson attack by anarchists

**Éamon (person)** – An Azarasian human thrall of Maboni descent owned by Sabas Borja; serves as an attendant to the Mortal Bride

**Eousa (location)** – The eastern continent connected to Occida by Salathien's Bridge

**Estrella Ibarra (person)** – A member of the Imperial Guard and soulbound heartmate to Tristan Ibarra

**Everlife (runespell)** – A runespell intended to create immortality, but instead causes the bearer to rise as a wraith upon death

**Fergus Sullivan (person)** – A Maboni human

**Finola Halloran (person)** – A Maboni human and younger half-sister of Nessa Halloran

**Gadeth (person)** – A minor demon in the court of Azaras

**Genesis (runespell)**– A runespell used by demonbloods to ensure their offspring inherit their traits, even when reproducing with a different species

**Godcurse (noun)** – A divine affliction placed upon fallen godstars during the Godsfalls; unique to each demon and often tied to their nature; a weakened version may sometimes be inherited by their children or grandchildren

**Godsfall (event)** – A celestial event in which rebellious godstars were banished to the mortal realm; the First Godsfall occurred ten thousand years ago and involved a hundred exiled godstars, while the Second Godsfall occurred seven thousand years ago and involved thousands

**Godsfire (noun)** – The golden flame that trails behind falling godstars during a Godsfall

**Godstar (noun)** – An energy-based divine being of immense power; one of many in a vast celestial hierarchy

**Harvest (event)** – A ceremonial selection in Mabon during which humans are chosen through a public drawing to become thralls to the Azarasian Impire

**Heartbonding (event)** – A ceremonial union between Azarasian heartmates

**Heartmates (noun)** – The strongest type of a soulbond; allows bonded individuals to fully experience each other's emotions and physical sensations as if they were their own

**Hell (location)** – A pocket dimension created and sustained by a powerful demon

**Hellbeast (noun)** - A hybrid born of a demon and another species

**Hellsteed (noun)** – A hellbeast bred from a demon and equine lineage, used by Azarasian vampires for war and transport

**High Council (organization)** – The ruling body of the former witch nation of Isaura

**High Courts (organization)** – The Azarasian Impire's aristocracy

**Imperator (title)** – The highest-ranking officer in the Blood Legion, the Azarasian military

**Imperial Guard (organization)** – The elite military force tasked with protecting the Azarasian Impire's rulers

**Imperium (title)** – The shared title of the soulbound rulers of the Azarasian

Impire; used to refer to them collectively, not individually

**Isabeau Moreau (person)** – An Azarasian vampire and Crown General of the Kings' Council; soulbound beloved of Roxiana Vela

**Isaura (location)** – A nation on the eastern side of Occida, founded by the demon Isaura for her witch descendants; conquered by the Azarasians three hundred years ago, marking the official end of the Thousand Year War

**Isaura (person)** – A demon from the Second Godsfall and ruler of the witch nation of Isaura until her death

**Jessenia Roche (person)** – An Azarasian vampire and the soulbound heartmate to Pierre Roche

**Julien "Jules" Roche (person)** – An Azarasian vampire and ruler of the Azarasian Impire, known as the King of Dawn; soulbound companion to Lucero Azaras and brother to Cédric and Pierre Roche; also known as the Butcher King

**Karra Sorani (person)** – An Azarasian witch and the protagonist of *The Soulborne Queen*; soulbound heartmate to Azaras

**Katalina Estevez (person)** – An Azarasian vampire and the reclusive author of *The Soulborne Queen*

**Kavanagh (person)** – A Maboni human and nominal mayor of Corraidin; serves as a puppet ruler under the authority of the Azarasian magistrates

**Kings' Council (organization)** – The governing council of the Azarasian Impire; advises and executes the will of the reigning vampire kings

**Kotara (location)** – The first nation on the eastern continent of Eousa to fall to Azarasian conquest

**Lifeforce (noun)** – The vital energy inherent in all living beings and the source of magical power; can be consumed by vampires and demons to fuel their abilities

**Lucero "Luc" Azaras (person)** – An Azarasian vampire and ruler of the Azarasian Impire, known as the King of Dusk; soulbound companion to Julien Roche, biological son of Azaras, and grandson of Marisol Vela; also known as the Conqueror King

**Luisa (person)** – An Azarasian vampire who works for the Kings' Council; soulbound companion of Nico

**Mabon (location)** – An island nation of humans located northwest of the Azarasian Impire and southwest of Trost; under Azarasian control and labeled Mabon Farm on official maps

**Maboni (noun)** – The demonym for a person from Mabon

**Magic (noun)** – The active manipulation of power to produce supernatural effects, typically through runes and runespells

**Magistrate (title)** – An appointed representative of the Azarasian Impire assigned to govern a conquered city or region

**Maire (person)** – An Azarasian human thrall of Maboni descent owned by Cédric Roche; the biological mother of Rosier Roche; serves as an attendant to the Mortal Bride

**Marisol Vela (person)** – An Azarasian vampire and former Regent of Tenebra de Mar; mother of Oriana and Roxiana Vela, and grandmother of Lucero Azaras; died during the Massacre at Duskfell

**Marsania (location)** – A former vampire nation located in the southeast of Occida; conquered by the Azarasian Impire during its expansion

**Martien (person)** – An Azarasian vampire, soulbound heartmate of Alix, and father of Vérène

**Meallán Seward (person)** – A Maboni human and Patriarch of the Corraidin branch of the Church of the Rising Stars

**Montaurère (location)** – A city in the central region of the Azarasian Impire; also known as the Capital of Dawn

**Morrena Isaura (person)** – An Isauran witch and de facto leader of the Isauran High Council; daughter of the demon Isaura and sister of Allegra Isaura

**Mortal Bride (title)** – A human chosen to serve as the living conduit for the Covenant runespell

**Nessa Halloran (person)** – A Maboni human and spinster who owns and operates Books & Bows; daughter of Padraic and Orlagh Halloran, stepdaughter to Deidre Halloran, and half-sister to Aislin Milligan, Orrin Halloran, Saraid Halloran, Finola Halloran, and Urrick Halloran

**Nico (person)** – An Azarasian vampire who works for the Kings' Council; soulbound companion of Luisa

**Northern Wall (location)** – A fortified boundary marking the northern edge of the Azarasian Impire; built to defend against Tyrhar but also used as a staging point for the Impire's attempted invasion

**Occida (location)** – The western continent, conquered by the Azarasian Impire

**Odran (person)** – A Maboni human harvested as a thrall

**Orlagh Halloran (person)** – A Maboni human and former housewife; mother of Nessa Halloran and first wife of Padraic Halloran; harvested when Nessa was nine years old

**Orrin Halloran (person)** – A Maboni human and younger half-brother of Nessa Halloran

**Padraic Halloran (person)** – A Maboni businessman; father of Nessa Halloran, Aislin Milligan, Orrin Halloran, Saraid Halloran, Finola Halloran, and Urrick Halloran; husband of Deidre Halloran and ex-husband of Orlagh Halloran

**Patriarch (noun)** – A minister of the Church of the Rising Stars in Mabon

**Pierre "Perry" Roche (person)** – An Azarasian vampire; soulbound heartmate to Jessenia Roche and brother of Julien and Cédric Roche

**Power (noun)** – The capacity to store and channel lifeforce for magical use; varies by species and individual, with demons, vampires, and witches possessing differing limits

**Rafael Valcázar (person)** – An Azarasian vampire, former Crown Mage who served Azaras, and the leading expert on soulbonds

**Raul (person)** – An Azarasian vampire and magistrate stationed in Corraidin; soulbound heartmate of Delphine

**Red Queen (noun)** – The Azarasian name for the red star that appears each spring; also known as the Blood Star

**Red Queen's Court (noun)** – The Azarasian name for four dimmer stars, two silver and two gold, that surround the Red Queen

**Renée (person)** – An Azarasian vampire and highly regarded geneticist

**Riona (person)** – An Azarasian human thrall of Maboni descent owned by Roxiana Vela and Isabeau Moreau; serves as an attendant to the Mortal Bride

**Rosier Roche (person)** – An Azarasian vampire and son of Cédric Roche; soulbound to Vérène

**Roxiana Vela (person)** – An Azarasian vampire and Crown Chancellor of the Kings' Council; daughter of Marisol Vela, aunt of Lucero Azaras, and soulbound beloved of Isabeau Moreau

**Rune (noun)** – A magical symbol used as the foundation of magical casting; typically drawn or carved to channel power

**Runegate (noun)** – A fixed portal runespell used for transportation between distant locations, requiring blood or lifeforce to function

**Runespell (noun)** – A magical construct formed by combining multiple runes; used to produce a specific effect when activated

**Sabas Borja (person)** – An Azarasian vampire, Crown Enforcer of the Kings' Council, Commander of the Butcher's Blades, and soulbound companion to Cédric Roche

**Saffira (creature)** – A hellcat and child of Azaras; sibling of Lucero Azaras and Titus

**Salathien (person)** – A demon from the Second Godsfall and creator of the Salathien Hellwood

**Salathien Hellwood (location)** – A sentient, demonblooded forest sired by the demon Salathien

**Salathien's Bridge (location)** – A narrow land bridge connecting the western continent of Occida to the eastern continent of Eousa

**Saraid Halloran (person)** – A Maboni human and younger half-sister of Nessa Halloran

**Soulbond (noun)** – A runespell that binds two or more souls together; the intensity of the bond determines whether the soulbound are companions, beloveds, or heartmates

**Soulborne (adjective)** – Refers to a rune or runespell transmitted through the soul

**Soulbound (adjective)** – Describes the state of being connected to another through a soulbond

**Soulbound (noun)** – An individual bound to another through a soulbond

**Soulshift (runespell)** – A runespell that allows a soul to transfer into a new body, typically used by powerful witches to cheat death

**Starcrater (noun)** – A demon's impact site formed during a Godsfall

**Surrosa Isles (location)** – A cluster of islands off the coast of Tenebra de Mar conquered by the Azarasian Impire

**Tenebra de Mar (location)** – A coastal city in the southern region of the Azarasian Impire; also known as the Capital of Dusk

**Thaddeian Ocean (location)** – A vast body of water named after the demon Thaddeus, located to the west of the Azarasian Impire

**Thaddeus (person)** – A demon from the First Godsfall and ruler of Thaddeus's Trove; also known as the Demon in the Deep

**Thaddeus's Trove (location)** – An underwater city within the Thaddeian Ocean, ruled by the demon Thaddeus

**The Beast King (sobriquet)** – see Azaras

**The Beast's Roost (location)** – An immense daemium tower at the center of Duskfell, built atop Azaras's starcrater

**The Butcher King (sobriquet)** – see Julien Roche

**The Conqueror King (sobriquet)** – see Lucero Azaras

**Thérèse (object)** – The Butcher King's curved dagger

**The Soulborne Queen (object)** – A book chronicling the love story between Azaras and Karra, written by Katalina Estevez

**Thousand Year War (event)** – A millennium-long conflict between the nations of Azaras, Trost, Marsania, and Isaura on the continent of Occida; ended three hundred years ago with the conquest of Isaura by the Azarasian Impire

**Thrall (noun)** – An individual forcibly bound to service through a runespell, typically stripped of autonomy, rights, and legal personhood; also known as a blood thrall when used for feeding

**Titus (creature)** – A powerful hellwolf and child of Azaras; sibling of Lucero Azaras and Saffira

**Toreth (person)** – A demon from the First Godsfall who disappeared shortly afterward

**Tristan Ibarra (person)** – A member of the Imperial Guard and soulbound heartmate to Estrella Ibarra

**Trost (location)** – A former vampire nation located in the north of Occida; conquered by the Azarasian Impire during its expansion

**Turlough the Last (person)** – The only human king of Mabon, whose short-lived reign lasted twenty years while the Azarasians were occupied with wars on the mainland

**Tyrhar (location)** – An unconquered nation on Eousa beyond the Northern Wall; currently resisting Azarasian invasion through ongoing border conflict

**Una Cavey (person)** – A Maboni human and former childhood friend of Nessa Halloran

**Urrick Halloran (person)** – A Maboni human and younger half-brother of Nessa Halloran

**Vampire (noun)** – An immortal demon–human hybrid with at least 75% demon blood; capable of using magic fueled by consuming lifeforce through blood

**Venom (noun)** – A substance produced by vampires and transmitted through their bite to suppress the pain of feeding; induces bloodlust, heightens physical sensations, and increases libido over time

**Vérène (person)** – An Azarasian vampire soulbound to Rosier Roche

**Vigdis Dauthrekkr (person)** – A Tyrhari horde warlord leading assaults against the Northern Wall

**Wards (noun)** – A runespell used to shield locations, objects, or individuals from harm, detection, or entry

**Widow's Lake (location)** – A lake north of Montaurère, known for its population of hellserpents

**Willowroot Tea (object)** – An herbal infusion with restorative properties; commonly consumed by thralls to counter blood loss and increase stamina

**Witch (noun)** – A long-lived but mortal demon–human hybrid with 50–75% demon blood; capable of using magic fueled by their own lifeforce

**Wraith (noun)** – Undead beings created when a person is killed while bearing an everlife runespell; reanimated by magic, they are driven by an insatiable hunger for flesh to sustain their existence

www.ingramcontent.com/pod-product-compliance
Lightning Source LLC
Chambersburg PA
CBHW020256300726
49022CB00033B/161
* 9 7 8 1 9 9 0 5 5 1 1 3 0 *